FACES

Also by Martina Cole and available from Headline

Dangerous Lady
The Ladykiller
Goodnight Lady
The Jump
The Runaway
Two Women
Broken
Faceless
Maura's Game
The Know
The Graft
The Take
Close

FACES

MARTINA COLE

headline

'Those Others' © R. S. Thomas from *Collected Poems 1945–1990*,
published by Phoenix,
An Hachette Livre UK Company.

First published in Great Britain in 2007
by HEADLINE PUBLISHING GROUP

1

Cataloguing in Publication Data is available from the British Library

ISBN 978 0 7553 2862 8 (Hardback)
ISBN 978 0 7553 2863 5 (Trade paperback)

Typeset in Galliard by Avon DataSet Ltd,
Bidford-on-Avon, Warwickshire

Printed and bound in Great Britain by Clays Ltd, St Ives plc

HEADLINE PUBLISHING GROUP
An Hachette Livre UK Company
338 Euston Road
London NW1 3BH

www.headline.co.uk
www.hodderheadline.com

DEDICATION

For Natalia Whiteside, my first granddaughter, the heart of my heart.

I have been blessed with my children, and with my grand-children, and also with my daughter-in-law Karina.

Life, I realise, is all about what you leave behind, and the people you leave behind, when you go. God is good, and nobody knows that better than I do. My mum always said that God pays back debts without money, that what goes around comes around. I have the family I dreamed about all my life, and it's growing larger and stronger with each passing day.

I wish love, luck and happiness to all my readers, and I thank God for all the good in my life and for the happiness I encounter on a daily basis. It wasn't always like that, but I do know that the secret of real happiness is enjoying the good times while you can, and making the most of the time you spend with the people you love.

And for a special friend, Eve Pacitto. A wonderful woman.

She was always there for anyone who needed a friend, and she was a good friend to me over the years. She was kindness itself, and she always put others before herself. I'll miss her and our lovely lunches. My heart goes out to the two Peters.

For nanny Donna never to be forgotten.

It was a privilege to know you and to be your friend. Life will be so much poorer without you. God bless you and keep you, a star among stars.

And a very special mention for dear friend Diana, she really is my No. 1 fan, as I am hers. A real mate, a real character and a much-loved woman. She has a wonderful family and a wonderful personality, and I feel honoured to be your friend. Chin up, mate, and love and hugs.

And also for Delly, a sister we would all love to have.

Prologue

December 2006

Mary Cadogan was lying on her bed. She was frightened, but then she was always frightened. Frightened her husband would get nicked, and even more frightened that he wouldn't.

She didn't want to advertise the fact that she was lying here, fully dressed, on a freezing December night, waiting for the man who was more than capable of ending her life, physically as well as emotionally. Mary's breath was heavy in the room; it had the rancid smell of the habitual drinker, it was sour, it was disgusting, but no one ever mentioned that. Her drinking, like everything else about her life, was not something to be talked about openly. But everyone in her orbit was aware that no amount of breath mints or chewing gum would ever really mask it. Mary's life made them all feel inadequate, especially Mary herself.

Danny Boy Cadogan could make the most hardened criminal nervous and paranoid, especially if Danny decided he wanted to talk to them about something. Danny could make the most innocent of statements sound like a declaration of war, and the most innocuous of comments into a terrifying and threatening reality.

Mary Cadogan felt the usual tightening in her chest that always accompanied the mentioning of her husband's name. The fact that he had the same effect on everyone did little to calm her nerves. She had seen him in action, close up and personal, for years, and

1

she knew that anyone with an ounce of brain tissue would not attempt to thwart him without at least some kind of powerful weapon, even if only to turn it on themselves rather than face his wrath. Mary could see her reflection in the mirror opposite her bed. It amazed her that she always managed to look so serene, so well groomed, not a hair out of place no matter what turmoil was going on around her; no matter what was happening to her. It was a knack she had, a persona she had created over the years to make sure her husband and the father of her children did not know what she was really thinking. In fact, she had up until recently made sure that *no one* in her orbit knew what she was thinking; it was a survival tactic that had kept her from going out of her mind.

Living, as she did, in a minefield, with a man who saw any kind of disagreement as a personal affront, she had learned many years before to just agree with everything and anything he said. She *had* to agree, it was what you did with someone like Danny Cadogan. And you had to make it look like you really believed what he was saying was right, that you could suddenly see how much cleverer he was. Whether it was about a large issue, such as where they would live, or a smaller issue, such as what the kids should have for breakfast. That's how petty and childish it could get.

At first, she had believed his love for her would be enough to change him, change his domineering ways, but she had all too quickly been disabused of that notion. If anything, he had just got worse and, as the years had gone on, she had shaped a calmness and a believability that made her life if not happier, then at least bearable to the outside world.

Mary put a perfectly manicured hand up and instinctively patted her perfect hair into place. Her brother Michael had tried in his own way to make it better for her, but she suspected that he knew he had failed her, as he had failed them all, including Danny. But at least he could keep him in line, at least as much as anyone could anyway. Danny had always been a law unto himself, everyone knew that within a few seconds of meeting him. Even as a boy he had been possessed of a fighting spirit that had kept older, stronger boys away from them all and, where they grew up, that made Danny Cadogan an asset. He had been a natural-born leader and, in fairness, he had led them all in the right direction; they had all done well out of him in their own ways. But now he had put them into such a difficult position that there seemed to be no way out.

Danny's mother was downstairs with the kids, and even she was subdued, quietly listening to her godforsaken radio as always. Humming along to tunes long dead, and remembering things long past.

Michael Miles, Mary's brother, sighed loudly. 'Do you think he'll do it, really?'

'Who knows. He never lets anyone know what he has in mind. I don't think he knows what he's going to do himself, until the last fucking second.' Jonjo heard his own voice. It was, as always, neutral.

'Wait until Eli gets here, and then we'll go from there. Stop fucking acting like a child. It's all in place, now shut the fuck up.'

Jonjo knew then that this was over, even though he believed that nothing would happen tonight, or any other night. It had been for nothing. Danny would do what he wanted as always, why should that change, why did they even think they could stop him? Might as well try to stop a bullet with a tennis racquet.

Michael understood Jonjo's trepidation, had experienced it so many times over the years himself, even though he was the only person alive who Danny Boy treated with any kind of respect or decency. Danny Boy actually liked him and, against all the odds, he loved the man back. But enough was enough, for all of them. He started the car then. 'It's time.'

They drove away quickly, the realisation of what they were going to do making them both quiet.

As far as Danny Boy was concerned Mary Cadogan had no private thoughts. But she did, and she had let them get the better of her. She had actually allowed herself to believe that something good might actually happen. She'd allowed herself to dream that Danny might be taken out and for no other reason than that she couldn't take this life any more. It was like living in a vacuum: Danny controlled her every move, her every thought, he even chose her friends. And now she had shown her hand to his brother, Jonjo, had let him know the truth of their marriage, and he would always have that over her, and the same thing would happen with her poor brother Michael, and Jonjo, she knew now, was not a great one for loyalty. Tonight had proved that much.

As she lay there she wondered if it would be better for everyone concerned if she just got up, went to her car, a brand-new Mercedes, after all Danny Boy's wife had to be seen in the best, and, revving it up, whether she should just aim it at the nearest wall. Now that would put an end to it. The other scenario was to aim the car at Danny Boy himself. She smiled at the audacity of the thought. If the Serious Crime Squad didn't have the bottle when it came to Danny, what chance did she have? She would be dead within seconds if her husband survived which, knowing that bastard, he would.

Danny was always checking up on her; not directly of course, but he would make a point of going round where she had allegedly been, normally her sister-in-law's, joking around and having a laugh, then dropping the question into the conversation, as if making conversation. 'What did you two girls talk about last night, then?' Waiting to see if she had actually been where she had said. As if she would dare to thwart *him*.

She could hear him, his voice full of interest and artifice, could see his eyes watching Carole closely for any hint of subterfuge. Could see his hands clutching the coffee mug tightly, his knuckles white, his anger at her daring to go out without him making him irrational. Deciding whether Carole was telling him the truth, or whether she was covering up for her friend, and wondering what other agenda she could possibly have. If he chose to believe his own suspicious nature over his wife's friend it would cause aggravation for months. But one thing that Carole had going for her was that she was overweight. Her life was her kids and her husband, and she had no other interests in anything outside of her home and her family. Danny, Mary knew, *approved* of Carole Miles. She was one of the few people he allowed her to see on a regular basis. Carole wasn't a threat to him, he saw her as someone who would not lead his wife astray. Who didn't dress well or

4

feel the urge to go to a gym. Carole was the woman he should have married, and now she wished, with all her heart and soul, that he had done just that. She realised she was crying, a slow, quiet crying that was as controlled as everything else in her life. She had not allowed herself one normal reaction for over twenty-five years.

How had she ended up like this? How had her life, a life that most women envied her, become so bereft that she fantasised about killing herself? But she knew how it had happened, she knew that better than anyone. Tonight had been her swan song, her last chance at breaking away from him, of making a proper life for herself and her girls. But it wasn't going to happen, it would never happen, and she should have known that before she had put herself in such a stupid and pointless position. Hindsight, she decided, was a fucking wonderful thing.

'Nana, can I have another lolly?'

It was nine thirty at night and Leona Cadogan had no intention of going to bed. Her nana, Angelica Cadogan, had no intention of sending her there either. 'Sure, you can have what you want, darling. Now go and settle yourself on the sofa and I'll bring it in.'

The little girl preened happily, her long black hair and wide-spaced blue eyes so like her father's. Angelica opened her new acquisition, an American fridge, and removed another lolly with pride. Her son made sure she wanted for nothing. She gave her granddaughter her lolly and, placing a blanket over her, she kissed the top of her head.

Leona had the remote control for the TV clutched tightly in her hand, and she watched her programme without even giving her nana a second glance. Her sister Laine, known affectionately as Lainey, was already asleep on a chair. Leona was watching over her younger sister, as she was expected to do. This was a family who watched out for each other, and her nana made sure that is *exactly* what they did.

Angelica saw the child was watching *Little Britain* and shook her head slowly. Even at six years old Leona understood that humour. Her heart told her to turn it off, but at her age she couldn't be bothered with the aggravation. Unlike her own children, her grandchildren got away with murder. These two girls especially, it was as if Danny had fallen in love all over again when these two had arrived so late in the day. The other children had never been enough, but then they were not with his lawful wife. She could understand that, to an extent, Mary was a martyr to put up with him, but then he was a man any woman would be proud to call her own. If Mary had only produced sooner, after her first daughter had died, he would never have strayed. Angelica was sure of that much.

As she watched Leona open another bag of crisps she waved her hand in dismissal at nobody in particular and left the room. The sight of a man dressed as an old woman and vomiting all over the place was more than her stomach could bear. Bring back *Little and Large*, at least they were an act the whole family could watch. This new humour was way over her head. Even Jimmy Jones was preferable to this shower.

Leona was chuckling loudly, and Angelica sighed once more as she walked into the kitchen; she felt safer in there. It was, after all, her domain, the place she had spent over half her life in. It was a sight better than the kitchen she had first encountered as a bride, and just the gleam off the tiling made her happy.

As she lit a cigarette she poured herself a small whisky from the secret stash she kept under the sink, behind the detergents, where she was sure no one in the family would ever think of looking. She opened the paper and, happy that she had at least some of her family around her, she read Ian Hyland's hilarious take on the TV shows she hated, but ultimately found herself watching.

Loneliness was a terrible thing; it ate into you and, if you weren't careful, it could cause a body to become bitter. You birthed them, you brought them up, and then you stepped back. It was the way of the world, but it was a hard road for someone like her, someone who had been everything to her children, and had made sure they knew it. At least, that was how she saw it now; the truth was a different thing altogether. The past was often better viewed through rose-coloured glasses.

Now she was older and greyer, and had been forced to take a

back seat and it galled her even though a small part of her was relieved to have had the burden of them lifted from her. She had a fine house, a house that would knock the eyes out of anyone she knew, and she had a good few quid to do with as she liked as well. And, more importantly, she had a family who had all done well for themselves in one way or another. She missed the old house though, and her old friends: this place was like living in a prison camp. Everyone kept themselves to themselves, and no one thought to knock unless there was a valid reason to. No cups of tea and a quick gossip here, it was all lawns and fencing. Garages and barbeques. Radio 4 and documentaries. She was like a fish out of water, but she knew her Danny thought he had done the best for her, and she couldn't tell him otherwise, could she? Not after everything he had given her, everything he had provided for her. If he had not paid her phone bills she would have gone doolally tap, as her mother used to say, without a friendly voice now and then. For an Irish immigrant she was living like a queen but even though she missed her cronies, she couldn't bring herself to admit that to her son. So she talked to them for hours at a time, even though she knew that they were long past her and her new life, that she was different now, and it was only her son's reputation that kept them from mugging her off once and for all. She even missed that drunken bastard she had married. At least with him she could have a conversation without having to think it through thoroughly first, in case she offended him. Having a conversation with this lot around here was like a military operation, what with their 'Good Mornings', and their pleasantries.

At least the church afforded her a few friends, anyway, but even they were intimidated by her family though, in fairness, they were chatty enough when she did see them. Maybe she would go on one of the coach trips the church was always arranging for the older people, do her good to have a break from cleaning the house and waiting for the kids to come round and see her. God was good, she knew that, and God himself *knew* she had sacrificed a lot for her children. The shame was that she wasn't sure if her children realised that. Especially her only daughter.

As she sipped at the whisky she suddenly had a terrible feeling

7

of foreboding wash over her; it left her breathless with its intensity, and with a layer of sweat that left her clammy and cold. A wave of sickness came over her, and she saw the broken body of her dead husband in her mind's eye. Her son had had beaten him nearly to death, left him a cripple and had then proceeded to terrorise the rest of his life. Yet, she still loved her son, still watched over him. Even though she knew he was a bully, a vicious bully. Life had seen to that much. Life had broken them all in one way or another.

She had an awful feeling that Danny Boy was in danger, but then, he lived in a constant state of anger and danger that put him in the frame on a daily basis. The feeling was now gripping her heart, she could feel an invisible hand squeezing the life out of her. She clutched the back of her chair, unable to call out with the pain. She attempted to rise, tried to stand. Poor Mary was lying in her bed upstairs, sleeping off her day's alcohol consumption, and the girls were in the lounge watching their shite on television. She had to try and attract someone's attention, she knew that much. She was in serious trouble.

'Stop it, Danny, you'll cause more trouble than you'll prevent. Losing your temper and getting hot under the collar will gain us nothing.' Michael poured them both a generous measure of Chivas Regal Scotch before he spoke once more. 'Crystal meth is going to destroy everything we've grafted for if we don't distribute it properly and with due thought, you know that. We've already been through this, timing is key and you know it. We need to see what the demand is like before we start to supply it. For all we know, it might not take off over here. America is a different market, and they have a much larger proportion of junkies per capita than we do.'

Danny took his drink and sipped it, waiting for his friend to finish what he had to say and using the time to gather his thoughts as well as his temper.

'At the moment it's a gay drug: they always get things first. Let's pick and choose our distributors wisely because this is going to hit the streets with a fucking big bang and we have to make sure that the reverberations from that don't come back to bite us. It's not like coke and it is definitely not like grass. This is like the brown, the big H mixed in with a nuclear warhead, and it's going to make a major fucking hole in our society. We can sell it all right, we can sell anything, but even we won't be able to walk away from this if we ever get a capture.'

Michael was sitting with the man he wanted dead, and it was not something he was surprised about. In fact, he had known deep inside that it would not have come to anything because, without a break, such as a gangland murder, or a car crash, Danny Boy Cadogan was not going anywhere he didn't expressly want to go. But there was still time to make the break, time was all they had now. Michael sipped his scotch slowly, thoughtfully. He had thought this through with his usual caution. He had a bad feeling about crystal meth. He knew it was going to either take off like a Jumbo Jet on speed, or die a death overnight. The secret was to wait and see how the preliminary findings worked out before committing themselves. But Danny, as always, saw only the pound signs, and the power that a major distributor of such a product would wield.

'This has to go out through a *trusted* subsidiary company, and it can *never* lead back to us. All our tame Filth and contacts will run a fucking mile if it does. So just wait a bit, hold your hand, and let's see what develops, eh?'

Michael was speaking as quietly and as sensibly as he always did, in fact it was one of the things that Danny liked most about him. He always thought things through; Danny often joked that Michael spent a fortnight weighing up the pros and cons before he had a wank, let alone anything else. But there were a lot of people interested in this product and, at the moment, there was a growing sense of excitement in their community. Like crack before it, this was a drug that appealed to the useless, and ended up being taken by the foolish. It could be a licence to print money, and that was something that attracted them both. So Danny nodded his agreement, as Michael had known he would. It was talking Danny down that was the easy bit. As long as it was about the business, Michael knew he would be heard. If it was about grudges, however, or the slights that Danny seemed to see all over the place, then that was a different ball game. But Michael allowed for that, it let Danny get rid of some steam and it calmed him down, at least until the next time, anyway.

'Anyone in mind?'

Michael shook his head and smiled. 'Not yet, but we've plenty of time for all that. Let the drug filter through to the straights, let it hit the pavements first, see how it is welcomed, then we'll be in a much better position to make an informed decision. Until then we'll keep our options open and not rush into anything. The Russians are fucking useless at distribution and so are the other Eastern Europeans, fucking useless ponces the lot of them and, more to the point, they don't know how to work together on anything, and that will eventually be their downfall. They live big and they die young but, on the plus side, they have a large army of disposable people. We'll make a decision eventually and, when we do, it will be the right one, as always. The Colombians are still in the running, as are the fucking Blacks. Let's see who comes up with the goods first, and then wait and see how the weekend dance mob takes to it. After all, Es are so cheap now, and are easier to get than aspirin and a line of coke is cheaper than a glass of wine. Crystal meth is a *tenner* a time, and it keeps people going for fucking days; it could be the new drug of choice just because of its price, let alone its other benefits. That gives us the council estates *and* the hoorays. We need in on the beginning, for the big bucks, *but* we need to be out of the game well before it becomes the new social problem.'

Danny nodded his head sagely, as Michael knew he would. 'Yeah, you're right, Mike. As always, you've done your market research.' He grinned showing expensive and intricate bridgework. The smile was warm, it was bright, and it hid the fact that it barely touched his eyes.

Danny had no finesse, and he knew it. He spoke and people jumped. And, as far as he was concerned, that was how it should be. No one was allowed to question him except this man in front of him. His best mate, his business partner and, most important of all, the person whom he called his other half, his sensible head, in private. The only person in the world he actually trusted.

Michael had always been the voice of reason and somewhere in Danny Cadogan's brain he knew that. Mike's voice had always been the only thing that could cause him to question his own actions. Even as boys, kids together, that had been the case. They were of a size, both large men, both well made, and both had the good looks that money and prestige could only enhance. But whereas Danny had a dangerousness that had been apparent from an early age, Michael had been blessed with a reasonableness, a quietness that in its own way made just as big an impact. People listened to Michael because of Danny, then, if they had any kind of nous, they listened to him because he made a lot of sense. Women loved them, especially the kind of women Danny actively sought out. Good looking, well stacked and with a haphazard approach to romance. No questions, no demands and, certainly, no intention of refusing a request, no matter what it was, or what time of the night they happened to turn up. These women kept themselves clean, smart and well groomed, and they waited on the off-chance they might get a visit from their provider.

Both men dressed well, fucked with ambivalence, and they both liked kudos. And they saw the world as an oyster created especially for their needs. The difference between them was that although Danny had an innate shrewdness and a viciousness that had made him someone of note, it was Michael who possessed the actual acumen needed to make them as rich legally as they were from their other, less legitimate enterprises. Everything they owned they could account for if necessary, from their large houses to their diamond Rolexes. Everything they possessed had been bought on the up and up, was insured properly, and they paid their tax and VAT without a murmur. They were, to all intents and purposes, Diamond Geezers, Faces.

But to anyone in the know, they were far more than that. Theirs was an operation that was more global than the United Nations, and more local than a kebab shop. No one did any kind of business without their express permission and goodwill. Whether it was ringing a motor, or selling a snide DVD, they were involved somewhere along the line. But there was such a hierarchy involved, it would take decades of intense investigation before their names were even mentioned. Danny was far more of a threat than a twenty-year stretch could ever be and, if that was ever the case, if an accident did occur at any time and a capture came out of it, the person involved knew without a shadow of a doubt that their family would live a life of luxury and private education that most MPs could only dream about. Loyalty cost money, but it was a small price to pay when you weighed up all the other options. It was their generosity towards even their lowliest of workers that had got them this far in the first place. As Danny always argued, Tony Blair should have remembered who had put him in the hot seat in the first place, and then maybe he would still be the dog's gonads as far as the electorate were concerned. Danny had admired Blair at first, but the war had finished him as far as he and New Labour was concerned. What real leader would sacrifice his own people, his own countrymen, in a war that was not only pointless but, ultimately, unwinnable? What leader would put his own people in jeopardy because some Yank told him to? What leader would expect such loyalty without giving it back in some way? Blair had tucked them all up and, thanks to him, Danny knew that he and all his ilk would thrive. Thanks to him, the criminals were given the opportunity to expand and unite without even having to jump on a plane. Thanks to him, they could ply their trades with much more ease, because the police were far too busy hunting down terrorists.

Now Danny Boy Cadogan was the biggest Face in the United Kingdom, dealing with the rest of the criminal world on a daily basis and getting far more respect than his own prime minister. He ran an enterprise that would put the Wellcome foundation to shame, but at least he sold his drugs at a reasonable price and ensured that they were accessible to everyone who wanted them. Such was the mindset of Danny Boy Cadogan, a man who saw himself as above everything, and everyone, especially the law.

From small acorns, as his old man had always said to him. The same old man who couldn't keep a pound in his pocket if the pubs were open and his kids were starving. A man who would have applauded the new licensing laws and robbed a pensioner without a second's thought, to make sure he had enough poke to make use of them. Who would never have seen his kids if he had not been forced to by the fact that once the pubs had shut, there was nowhere else to go but home. Danny had never forgiven him for that, for the fact he would rather get pissed with his cronies than see his kids taken care of properly. It had been his father's complete disregard for anyone other than himself that had made Danny so determined to make something of his own life. He had his own father crippled and not felt a smidgeon of guilt. The bastard had asked for it and, after a while, he had got it.

They had started out small-time, him and Michael, like every big business, and now they were not only as rich as Croesus, they were also untouchable. They had money everywhere, all over the world, and they had a lifestyle that was good by anyone's standards, but not even half as good as it could be if they used their *real* money. And Danny would have done just that if it had not been for, as always, Michael's warning voice bringing him back down to earth. Danny accepted that he was still around, and still without a real nicking, and he also accepted that this was because of Michael, and Michael accepted that, without Danny, he would not have lasted five minutes in their world. He didn't have the killer instinct, the need for violence that Danny did. He was also basically straight; he was always far more interested in the economics of their deals than the deals themselves. Danny knew Michael loved the creating of the wealth far more than he enjoyed the spending of it. Michael thrived on the making of the deals, whereas Danny thrived on the excitement and the danger of their various ventures. They were a good team because of that, and they both knew it.

One day they would retire, and the world would be their playground, and then they could spend their hard-earned dosh in any way they saw fit.

Not any more though. If Michael had his way, Danny would be retiring to the big score in the sky. 'I'll meet you later in the warehouse, OK? We'll sort it all from there.'

Danny nodded absentmindedly.

Jonjo was quiet, the marks from his brother's angry attack still livid on his face. Jonjo wanted it all over, but for a very different reason than the others. Danny was his brother, and they were close all right, but not as close as everyone thought, at least not from his side anyway. This had seemed like the perfect opportunity to get Danny out of his life once and for all. Unlike Michael who, in fairness, was looking out for his sister and her children, he was looking only out for himself.

'It's make-your-mind-up time.'

Michael shrugged. The cold night air seemed to have brought them both back down to earth with a resounding thud.

Jonjo shook his head sadly. 'It's Mary I feel sorry for. We let her get involved. Then we let her down.'

'She loves him you know, Jonjo. In a strange way, we all did once. Without him, what would we be?' Michael was silent then for a few seconds before starting up the car and driving them out of the breaker's yard.

As they drove away Jonjo wondered how it had come to this, how their lives had ended up bereft of anything even resembling normality. He had been so close to his brother once, and he knew that his brother still felt a connection with him. Danny would give him the world on a plate if he could, he just never understood that not everyone was like him, not everyone *wanted* that much. As kids it had all been different, and Danny had been the only real constant in his life. Not only had Danny been his hero, his role model, but he had also been the only thing that stood between him and his father's colossal anger. Then, of course, he had *needed* his brother's strength, had welcomed it even. Little had he realised it would eventually be the thing he hated most about him. Be the thing that made him determined to bring him down.

Danny was completely out of control now, but after the night's events all Jonjo could think about was his childhood, and the fact that without his brother, he would never have survived it.

Now the man who had protected him, bullied him, and destroyed him, was finally going to die. At least he hoped that would be the case, though knowing his brother he would turn this around to his advantage and that would be the end of them all.

Either way though, tonight was the end of it, whatever the outcome. It would finally be over.

Book One

Every night and every morn
Some to misery are born.

– W. Blake, 1757–1827
'Auguries of Innocence'

Chapter One

'Am I, by any chance, keeping you up, Cadogan?'

The boy didn't answer, the fear of saying the wrong thing making him wary. He shook his head violently in denial instead.

'Oh, I'm sorry, child, did I interrupt your praying then? Only you close your eyes for two things in this life, sleeping or praying. Or am I a fecking eegit, and there's a third reason that I don't know anything about?'

'No. Of course not . . .'

The priest looked around the classroom, his arms outstretched in a gesture of complete innocence. He looked, for all the world, like a man interested in what a young fella might have to tell him.

'I mean, child, if you have something to *share* with the rest of us mere fecking mortals, if you have some kind of fecking phone line to the Almighty Himself that we don't know about, feel free to share your good fortune with those of us not deemed important enough to have the like ourselves.'

Jonjo still didn't answer him, knowing that anything he said would be misconstrued, distorted and then used against him.

'So, were you praying then, maybe to a saint, or the Blessed Virgin Mary herself. Or were you just fecking sleeping away the shagging morning? Now, I personally feel that the latter was probably the case. So, come on then, Cadogan, which is it to be?'

The priest was a short man, not much over five foot, with a

slight stoop and a drinker's gait. Grey before his time, his sparse hair was possessed of a life of its own. He always looked like he had just got out of his bed. His watery grey eyes were deep set and already had the shadows of cataracts on them. His breath was foul, all the boys who sat at the front desks complained about it. His tongue was a furry black point, and it snaked in and out of his mouth as he shouted at them. He was a fascinating chunk of human tragedy who they would remember for the rest of their lives. He was always angry inside and, as always, he vented his spleen on the nearest target he could find. His sarcasm was not only meant to demean and wound, but was also expected to be found highly amusing by the other children in his class. All the boys hated him, but they learned off by heart whatever he told them they had to, and they never forgot any of it either; he could go back to it at any time to try and catch them out.

'Were you asleep, lad? Praying to our Lord Himself, Him being such a grand friend of course, were you asking Him for a Special Intention maybe?' He looked at the sea of faces and said, with sarcasm, 'I *know* what you were doing, Cadogan, with your eyes closed and your mouth open like a gormless fecking mental retard, you were asking a favour of St Jude himself.'

He looked around the classroom, his eyebrows raised as if in wonderment, and he saw the relief in each and every pair of eyes that it wasn't them who had been singled out by him. Deep inside him the shame was overwhelming; after he demoralised a child in his care he always hated himself for his bullying. But the pettiness and discontent poured out of him as the boy he was singling out did nothing at all to defend himself from his vicious onslaught. That made him worse, made him feel they deserved everything they got. He started mimicking a little girl, a cockney girl at that, and this did manage to raise a few smiles from his class.

'Oh, Saint Jude, Patron Saint of *no* 'Ope, could you help me find me brain at all?' He sniggered then, enjoying his own wit, enjoying the boy's embarrassment more.

'Well, was that why you had your eyes closed tight while I was attempting to instil a modicum of education into that thick head of yours?'

'No, Sir, I mean, Father . . .'

Jonjo's voice was shaking with fright, but that didn't make him seem any less in front of his school friends, they would all have been the same had they been the one on the receiving end. Father Patrick was a hard case and they knew that. He was capable of bodily dragging a lad from his seat and thrashing him with fists and feet, for no reason other than he felt they were looking at him cross-eyed. That was a favourite expression of Father Patrick's, looking at him cross-eyed and, as most of the boys in the class were from Irish stock they knew exactly what that meant; it meant they had looked at him without respect, without giving him what he saw as his due. What it really meant though was that he was half pissed and looking for someone to take his anger out on.

The boys knew they had to accept his punishment, none of their parents would take a child's word over a priest's. None of the children there would have expected their parents to do that anyway, after all he *was* a priest. Christ's emissary on earth. He had his own creds as far as they were concerned. The fact that he had given up his chance to have a family, indulge in the sex act, and had dedicated his life to the betterment of others was enough for them. Who wouldn't get the arse now and again after that kind of promise? So they took what he had to give with a stoic calm that actually enraged him even more.

'Sleep was it then, you *were* having a fecking nap! A quick bit of shut-eye! Do your parents not make you go to bed at all? Are you up half the shagging night to be so tired during the day?'

He had already dragged the boy from his seat and, feeling the solid weight of him, the priest knew that soon he would be too big for this kind of treatment. He was a lump, like his brother before him, another fecking thicko who had driven him to distraction on more than one occasion, and he set about Jonjo with a renewed vigour, knowing this was probably the last time he would get the opportunity to do so. Once they could look him in the eye he left them alone and Jonjo was big for his age. Thank God he was still so in awe of the church that he wouldn't even consider fighting back.

These children were the bane of his life, they were the scum of the earth. He knew that what he did to them was wrong, but he couldn't help himself. In fact, the more they let him, the worse it seemed to make him. As he saw them watching him with a mixture of terror and acceptance, the more he wanted to beat the living crap out of them. They were a class of criminals in the making, none of them would ever amount to feck all. He was teaching them for nothing, filling in their time and his, until they hit the factories and he was finally put out to grass, and that galled him. These boys were able to get one of the best educations in the world for free, and none of them understood the importance of that. No wonder he took a drink. These children, poor as they were, had the opportunity to better themselves, and it cost neither them nor their families nothing, and they still didn't want to take advantage of it. Didn't understand how lucky they were to have that handed to them on a plate. To have the choice, a choice that was not offered to most of the world's population. And *he* was stuck here, teaching this shower of shite, because he was not deemed good enough to be put somewhere his learning would actually be of some practical use. If they were the bottom of the scrap heap then where did that leave him? And then they wondered why he took a nip to get him through the day.

Jonjo took his beating with quiet resignation and the priest, his anger now spent, his bony hand aching, went unsteadily back to his seat. 'Open your bibles, go to the Revelations of Saint John the Divine, and make sure you all know it inside out and back to front by the morrow, because I'm going to question you on every fecking word he wrote down and woe betide anyone who doesn't know the answers to my questions.'

The boys did as asked, confident in the knowledge that they knew it far better than he did. Revelations was his usual request and they obliged without any fuss.

Jonjo was dying to rub his aching shoulders, but he knew better than to do anything like that. Father Patrick would see him, and that would just start the whole bloody thing off again. He gritted his teeth and prayed to the Holy Virgin, asking her with every ounce of sincerity he possessed, to please stop him from wishing the priest dead at every available opportunity.

Father Patrick saw the boy's face and said angrily, 'You, you little fecker, can serve at the Mass for a week. The early one.'

'Yes, Sir. I mean, Father.'

The six o'clock Mass was a bastard, he would have to be up and out by five thirty but, on the plus side, his mother had always attended, so at least he would have a bit of company on the journey anyway. Something he knew she enjoyed as well. Plus, if he took communion he was guaranteed a decent breakfast; fried egg and fried bread at least. His mother rewarded them richly for their sacrifice, she dreamed of them all accompanying her to early Mass. It was only really to make the other women there feel inadequate because their children weren't beside them. His mother put a lot of store on what other people thought, especially when it involved religion and the church itself. It was just a shame that they only accompanied her when they were in trouble. Not that she let a little thing like that spoil her enjoyment, of course. To see them serve at Mass was enough for her, and she had so few good things in her life that, like his brother, Jonjo was happy to do it, just to see her pleasure and then to bask in her goodwill.

He was brought back to reality by the priest turning his vitriol on to a small Italian boy with huge dark eyes and an asthmatic's cough.

'Is this whole fecking class suffering from a plague of galloping narcolepsy? Is a sleeping sickness taking over from the usual bore-dom and ennui that I encounter every single day, or is it that, once more, the deadliest scourge of all has reared its ugly head, that old enemy of mine, hereditary stupidity? An English kind of complaint, not something I ever encountered in all my years in Ireland.' Father Patrick was on familiar ground now, this was something they listened to on a daily basis and it was also something that Father Patrick didn't ever expect an answer to. He was talking for effect, happy just to hear his own voice.

Jonjo relaxed, rubbed his shoulders surreptitiously, and wondered if his sister was all right as this was her first day at school and her first day alone in the world without either of her brothers to look out for her. Even at eight years old he understood the ties of family and about taking care of his sister: his mother had made sure of that much.

*

'I want my money, Mrs Reardon.'

Mrs Reardon looked at the tiny woman standing on her front step and she smiled with an ease that belied her usual demeanour. All innocent now, she said quietly, 'And what money would that be, Mrs Cadogan?' She sounded genuinely interested in whatever answer she might be given, her heavy arms were crossed over her ample chest, and her feet were planted slightly apart, giving her the stance of a street fighter. She was not a woman to cross, and she knew that, had made sure of it, in fact. And this little thing with her thick black hair and pink-cheeked anger was about to find that out the hard way.

If push came to shove she would give her the battering of a lifetime before sending her on her way with a flea in her ear and the threat of the police. The Irish were renowned for their temperament, idle wasters, who wanted a day's pay for doing fuck all.

'You know full well what money I am referring to, and I'm warning you now, I'll get me due and you'll rue the day you tried to spite me.'

Elsie Reardon was impressed, despite herself. She often tendered work out and then collected the money owed, keeping it for herself. These women were ten a penny; as she watched one walk away another fifty were willing to take their place. Cleaning was hardly rocket science, and even the scruffiest of them were able to scrub a floor or a window. She had found that the first few weeks were when they worked their hardest, showed the most willing. So the householder would be thrilled at the job done, and she would be guaranteed a regular stint. The high turnover of staff was rarely noticed by the people who were employing them, so she was able to keep most of the money earned for herself.

'Look, love, I gave you a chance and you didn't make the grade. The lady of the house requested that I send someone else in your place.' She smiled again, her meaty arms lifting her pendulous breasts up as if to emphasise her point.

Angelica Cadogan was angry but, like her elder son, it wasn't evident to anyone around her. She had a slow burning anger that she could unleash at will and, when she did let it go, the results were spectacular.

'You're a fecking liar and you know it. Mrs Brown has asked me to stay on permanent like, and I've said I will. So give me *my* money.'

Elsie Reardon was aware that most of her neighbours were watching the performance on her doorstep with anticipation. A fight was always a crowd pleaser. 'Do yourself a favour and fuck off.'

Angelica looked at the large unkempt women before her, she took in the grubby clothes, the hair still in its rollers from the day before, and the bright-red lipstick that was applied without any kind of finesse. Putting her large shopping bag carefully down on to the pavement, she squared up to the woman and said quietly, 'This is your last chance to pay me what you owe. I need that money, I earned it, and I won't leave until I have it safely in my purse.'

Elsie Reardon laughed then, really laughed. It was a nice laugh, in fact, in any other circumstance it would have made Angelica join in, share the joke. Instead, she drew back her fist and, smashing it into her antagonist's face with more force than expected, she quickly grabbed at the head full of rollers and, using them as a lever, dragged the protesting woman onto the pavement. The fight was over quickly, and with the minimum of fuss. Angelica could fight, could *really* have a row if she needed to, but that was the difference between the two women. Elsie Reardon could talk a good fight, but she couldn't actually have one; she depended on her bulk and her mouth to win the day for her.

Angelica, however, was a natural fighter. She took a child's sock from her coat pocket, a long white school sock she had filled with stones from her garden, then she set about battering the woman with gusto. Angelica knew that she would get her money, and she also knew that she was a fool to have trusted this woman in the first place. But this had been easier than she had believed possible. Reardon had had a fearsome reputation and she had taken that from her.

She'd had no choice. Her old man was once more on the

missing list, and she hadn't even enough money to buy a loaf of bread. So, either way, she had to call in the debt owed her. She had tried asking politely and it had been futile, the hammering had been the decider. Finally, the money was paid over and she thanked the woman and walked back home with her head held high. In Bethnal Green market she bought a few bits and pieces for the kids' dinner, and worried once again how the hell she was going to pay the mountain of bills she had indoors. Big Danny, as her husband was known, had been gone for three days and now she knew she had no hope in heaven of getting any money out of him. It was Monday and she had last clapped eyes on him on Friday morning as he had left for work. She knew she had more chance of getting the Pope's inside leg measurement than getting any money out of the man she had married.

But what really hurt was the fact that she had been reduced to brawling in the street for a paltry fifteen bob, and that was something she would never forget and, as her husband would find out soon enough, she would never forgive, either.

Big Dan Cadogan was a seriously worried man. He was in a pub in north London drinking a pint bought with his last few bob. He had been on the missing list for three days and he was not only skint, he was now the proud possessor of a very large gambling debt.

He could vaguely remember getting into a card game with some heavy-duty players, and that was about all he could remember for certain. That he had been had over was a given; when under the influence of the toxic shandy he was an easy mark. But the worst thing was that he knew he had been the orchestrator of his own downfall – as usual. When drunk he was convinced he was the poker king of east London. He had more than likely bluffed away the six hundred quid he now owed on a pair of twos or an ace high. Cards were his downfall; one game was never enough and, coupled with the drink, he was a real liability. He had no recollection of any of the hands he had held, or the people he had played with. All he knew for certain was that he owed the Murray brothers six large and, like many a man before him, he was not stupid enough to argue the toss over the finer points of his predicament. Not only was he unable to recall actually losing the money in the first place, he also knew that they would have witnesses to all that or, worse, that they would not even give him any kind of real timescale in which to pay them. They had already told him that he had one week to bring them their money before they would come looking for him. On their first call he would lose a finger or experience a broken bone or two, after that it would be open season.

But knowing that didn't make him feel any better. In fact, it made him feel worse because he knew that whoever he had played with had taken a major advantage. The bottom line though was that a gambling debt was still a gambling debt, so it had to be paid – even if that meant that his family went without. You could owe fortunes to a tallyman, even a debt collector, but a bet was a different ball game. It was a matter of honour to see that it was paid in full. The threat of violence aside, he would rather chop his own fingers off than be seen as a welsher. What he needed was a plan, something that would get him enough money to honour the debt and save his reputation.

Ange, as he called his wife, was going to cut off his balls and serve them up in a casserole when she heard about this, and he knew that he would be honour-bound to let her do just that to keep the peace. As hard as he could be with her, as handy as he was with his fists when the fancy took him and her fucking big trap was open, which, they both knew, was more often than not her downfall, he also knew that this time he had gone too far. His usual blarney and aggressiveness would not be enough to shut her up this time, she was in the right, and a woman with right on her side and three hungry kids was a woman capable of murder. Ange had a temper and, unlike him, she didn't need alcohol to fuel it.

He owed a fortune and he had no way of paying it off. For the first time in his life he was genuinely frightened. For the first time in his life he knew he was going to have to run.

Danny Cadogan was nearly fourteen, but he looked much older. He was already touching six foot and his body was filling out nicely; his mother was already despairing of ever keeping him in a pair of shoes that actually fit his enormous feet. Today he was in agony because even his father's old boots were tighter than a vicar on a pub crawl. He was a big lad and that was a plus most of the time, especially when it came to getting a bit of work. His main bugbear was that he seemed to be growing bigger by the day. This would have been a welcome development if he had been born into a family with a regular wage, especially if that wage had gone into the household instead of over a bar or across a card table. But that was not something he could do anything about; his father was a law unto himself. Danny Junior had always put himself about, earned a few bob in whatever way he could so that when his mother was at panic stations over his father's absence, as she was now, he could allay her fears a bit by putting some food on the table.

As Danny shifted the scrap metal for a local merchant, he saw that the man was watching him again. Louie Stein was always on the look out for good earners, and this kid was a grafter if ever he had seen one. He worked without a break, his young arms straining against the weight of the lead as he piled it neatly against the far wall. It was out of sight if Filth came around, and yet it was near enough to the front gates for a quick removal if that was required.

Louie walked over to Danny Cadogan and smiled, his gold teeth glinting in the weak sunshine, reminding Danny of a shark he had once seen in a picture book.

'Why aren't you at school?'

Danny shrugged and carried on working.

'Answer me, boy. If someone asks you a question you should at least attempt an answer, even if it's just a fabrication. A lie.'

Louie's words were clipped and Danny knew he had annoyed him. So he stopped what he was doing and, looking into the small man's wrinkled face, he said seriously, 'I need the money. What other reason would there be for doing this all day?'

He said it respectfully, but Louie knew he was also trying to be sarcastic. He understood that, liked the boy for his spirit. He weighed him up; he was very young but he acted like a boy much older than his years. He had the arrogance that extreme youth seemed to command, still sure in the knowledge that he had many years ahead of him in which to live his life and achieve a few of his dreams, his goals.

'Why do you need the money so badly?'

Danny looked at the older man with a mixture of pity at his obvious stupidity and a natural cunning that made him want to see how the conversation progressed in case he could use it to his advantage. 'Me mum needs a few quid in her bin, she's skint.'

Louie nodded, as if expecting the answer he had received. 'You're Big Dan Cadogan's boy, aren't you?'

'Why ask me when you already know the answer? It's not a secret.'

Louie grinned once more. 'A little bird told me that he is into a couple of hard cases for six large.'

Danny forced his face to remain neutral, and he shrugged theatrically, as if this news was nothing to get wound up about. 'He'll pay them, what are you fucking telling me for?'

Louie shrugged back, his shrunken body lost in the folds of his gabardine suit. Then, laughing, he wiped his nose on a dazzling white handkerchief he pulled from his trouser pocket with a flourish. It was like a magician's movement, exaggerated and over the top, and Danny knew he was paying him back for his overstated shrug.

'Forewarned is forearmed, my boy. Remember that, it will hold you in good stead all your life. Now, shift that lead, Filth will be scrabbling around soon; they know it's here but they don't like it if it's on display. I pay them to look the other way and they take the money, as long as they don't feel I am extracting the urine, if you get my drift.' He laughed once more, his bony shoulders shaking with his idea of mirth.

'Out of sight, out of mind. Another great saying to add to your collection.'

Danny rolled his eyes in annoyance. 'I'll bring a pen and paper next time, shall I? Write everything down in case I forget it.'

Louie walked away, his laugh louder than ever, and Danny watched him with anger and shame in his heart. Six large, that was a lot of money. The few quid for his day's collar seemed like nothing now. He shook his head at the shock of the man's words, at the realisation of what they actually meant to him and his family. Six large. It was enough to buy a house, and his old man had gambled it away when they couldn't even pay the rent on the roof over their heads, let alone buy it. And he was reduced to wearing a pair of boots so dilapidated that even his father had abandoned them. His mother was dressed like someone from the good old days, and his brother and sister were both far too young to understand about the intricacies of money and what you actually needed it for. And yet, despite that, his father, his fucking *useless waster* of a father, had lost a small fortune on the turn of a card.

Louie watched the lad as what he had told him sank in. He saw how he picked up the heavy lead and swung it as if it weighed nothing. He knew he would work out his anger before going on his way. He knew the boy was upset and he was sorry for that, but Louie knew that if it had been him, he would have wanted to know about it sooner rather than later.

He had five daughters himself, five lovely girls with great personalities and no real looks. Danny would have been a blessing for someone like him, someone to leave his business to, someone to carry his name on. Life was unfair, but then you played the hand you had been dealt, as his father had always said. But, if you were really unlucky then you found yourself playing the hand the Murrays dealt you. Fucking gamblers, losers every last one of them. And this boy and his family would be branded as losers along with their old man; a debt like that was owed by everyone even remotely related to the debtee.

Young Danny Cadogan could feel old man Stein watching him, and the shame of his situation made his face burn. The six large was still in the forefront of his mind and he knew that what Louie had told him was the truth. The old boy was trying to soften the blow, better it came from him than hearing it from a hairy-arsed debt collector one Saturday morning. He wondered if his mother knew, and whether he should be the one to tell her. Life was hard, and this growing-up lark was not all it was cracked up to be either. He went back to stacking the lead, hoping the physical work would help take his mind off his troubles.

*

Annuncia Cadogan, known as Annie, was in her element; for the first time in her life she was alone. No mammy watching her every move, and no brothers making sure that she didn't do anything to make their mammy angry. She sat in the small classroom and beamed a wide and pretty smile at all who looked in her direction. It was the smell she had noticed first, a mixture of floor polish and fresh paint. Now though, added to that was the musky scent of thirty small children, some bathed for the first time in weeks. Most of the children were wearing their older siblings hand-me-downs, and a few others, like herself, were in painfully new uniforms that caused them to stand out even more than the Asian kids, who were still new to the area and spoke English with an accent.

Like many of the children around her, Annie had a working knowledge of the Bible, and of the church itself. A lot of the children were from parents who educated their offspring in the Catholic religion, even though they weren't beating a path to the church door themselves. They just didn't have the time or the inclination after a hard week's work. Work took precedence over a lot of things in England and, unlike Ireland, where most of their parents hailed from, the church, though still a big part of their lives, didn't dictate their every waking hour.

Carole Rourke was sitting next to her and Annie held her hand tightly as she listened to the story of St Francis of Assisi. She loved hearing about him because she prayed to him nightly that she might be allowed a pet of some kind. Her mother had refused her requests for a dog or a cat, but she was sure a rabbit or a hamster might be within the realms of possibility.

As her first day at school passed she felt the weight of her home life being lifted off her shoulders, and she hoped that this feeling of excitement would not leave her. By home time she had decided that this place was not going to be the bane of *her* life as her brothers seemed to believe it was theirs, and she was looking forward to coming back the next day – much more than she was looking forward to her father's eventual return to the family home, even though she knew she was his favourite.

Trouble was brewing there and she knew it would come sooner rather than later. Her father was a man who was either terrorising the life out of them all, or making them laugh their heads off. There was never a happy medium where he was concerned. But this new school lark would guarantee that she was out from under her mother's watchful gaze for a few hours at least.

'Oh, Jesus fecking cross of Christ, six hundred pounds! Are you sure, Dan? Surely even that fool I married wouldn't be that stupid?' But even as she spoke she knew it was the truth.

'I'm sorry, Mum. Louie Stein told me about it today; I think he was trying to be helpful. I know he's a front wheel, but he's always been straight with me. He's offered me some more work this week and all.'

Angelica wasn't listening to him now, she was reeling with the news her son had just imparted. The consequences would be dire; that much she knew. There was no way they would be able to raise that kind of cash. If they had been able to get their hands on six hundred pounds they would have been living the life of Riley and eating like a gladiator on his day off. Her husband had pulled some stunts over the years, but this was a blinder – even by his standards.

Danny watched his mother as she digested the information, and he knew that she had not even noticed the two pound notes he had placed on the table. His father's debt had made his contribution to the household look paltry by comparison. He was working when he should be in school, he was dressed like a tramp when how he looked was all important to him, he had few friends because he couldn't afford to take part in any of their teenage high jinks; even the Saturday morning pictures was out of his league. He was an outcast among people who were classed as the poorest of the poor. He was trying to make a difference for his brother and sister, ease his mother's burden, the same mother he knew, who was not even aware of the sacrifices he made to try and lighten her load. Turning from her he went into the bedroom he shared with his younger siblings and, lying on the bed he shared with Jonjo, he forced back the tears, because he knew they were a luxury he couldn't afford.

Chapter Two

Danny was quieter than usual, but no one noticed. He was living on his nerves, waiting for his father to come home and, at the same time, hoping that he didn't turn up. His younger brother and sister were both feeling the tension in the household and he was past putting their minds at rest. His mother, however, gravitated from cursing her husband over hill and dale, to crying because she was convinced he was dead somewhere. Stabbed or beaten to death over six hundred quid. Then the reminder of the amount he had foolishly gambled away would set her off on a tirade of cursing once more.

Everyone knew about it now, so, on top of everything else, they were a talking point for the whole estate. Something his mother, always a proud woman, found very difficult to cope with. It was as if their whole life was now under scrutiny, and they didn't know how to react to it. His father was becoming smaller and smaller in his mind, his absence making Danny resent him, even though he knew that, until his father could pay his debt off, it would be madness to come anywhere near this estate, let alone his family.

As Danny made a pot of tea, he heard a hammering on the front door and, turning down the gas underneath the boiling kettle, he walked out into the small hallway. Pushing his mother into the bedroom with his younger siblings he shut the door firmly on them all. The terror was already enveloping him, this was the knock he had been waiting for and, now that it had finally arrived, he knew his courage was deserting him.

31

'Open the fucking door, we know you're in there.' The voice was full of hate and the knowledge that whoever was listening to it was already frightened. It was a debt collector's voice, the voice of someone who had said those same words over and over again, and yet meant them more each time.

Danny stood in the small hallway gritting his teeth as he willed the shaking that had suddenly attacked his body like an ague to stop. Then, swallowing down his fear, he opened the front door, just as the hammering started up once again. 'Relax, what do you want?' His deep voice and irritated demeanour was not lost on the visitors.

Danny was looking at two men; one tall and thin, the other short and fat. He saw a facial similarity and assumed, rightly, that these were the Murray brothers of local legend. They were both blond, with thin straggly hair and small brown eyes. They had the same flat bone structure and rounded, Slavic-looking features that they had inherited from their mother. They looked like a pair of simpletons, an act they had perfected over the years to make people think they were harmless. An act that they dropped when they had achieved their objective, which was either entering someone's home or playing the police for fools if they were called out.

'Is your dad in, son?' The smaller one spoke in a friendly and amiable fashion.

Danny shook his head. ' 'Course he ain't. He's hardly going to come back here knowing you are after him, is he?'

Walter Murray, the elder of the two brothers, and also the taller, nodded in agreement at Danny's answer. He seemed thrilled at the response, as if the words had been exactly what he had wanted to hear. 'Fair enough, son. So now, you understand we have to enquire as to whether you know where he might be.'

Danny shook his head once more. 'He can fuck off as far as I'm concerned and, if you see him before I do, you can tell him that from me.'

Danny knew that his conversation with the Murrays was being overheard by most of the neighbours. That was the downside to these flats; nothing could ever be kept private, no matter how personal. Even the neighbours' sex lives were a topic of conversation, they could be heard copulating by everyone who shared a wall, floor or ceiling with them. You got used to it, as you did hearing their toilets flushing or their baths running. Now that the gossip was about them he understood why people got so angry about it.

Walter Murray looked at the large young man before him, took in his wild-eyed fear and boxer's stance. He was game, the kid, if nothing else.

'Look, son, if we don't locate him in the next few days and collect the dosh owing, then we will remove everything from this flat; beds, chairs, the lot. Then we'll come back again and take whatever else we can find.' The threat was evident and open.

Danny looked into his eyes with genuine bewilderment. 'Why do you want to hurt us? My old man is the one who owes you the money, and you've more chance of being paid in Bulgarian luncheon vouchers than getting six large off him.'

Wilfred Murray, the shorter of the two brothers grinned, and it was a calculated and deliberate movement of his face. There was nothing there to make an onlooker think he was actually enjoying himself. 'Are you a bit thick, mate?'

Danny swallowed down his anger and, forcing his face into a mask of innocence he said quietly, 'Well, I must be. As far as I'm concerned you have done us lot the favour of our lives; the old man disappearing was a bonus for us, mate. But I warn you now, you come near my family again and you'd better come mob-handed, because if I survive your next visit I'll make it me life's work to hunt you two down and obliterate you.' It was said without anger, and with a quiet dignity that made the large young man in front of them seem almost menacing.

'Hark at him! Fucking Harry Dash! Are you having a tin bath, son?' Wilfred's laughter was loud and laced with sarcasm.

Danny didn't make any kind of movement, he just stared at them. He saw that he was much bigger physically than the pair of them put together. He was a big lad, he knew, and he also knew that, thanks to his father, he was having to act the hard man and face down two notorious thugs. But he knew that if they threatened his family he would have to do what he had threatened.

He put his hand up then, an instinctive movement, and pointed a warning finger at the two men.

'I mean it. If you come near my family I will not be responsible. If it takes me the rest of my life I'll find you and I'll kill you. See, my father is the one you have the fucking argument with, not us. And, while you're at it, ask yourself what kind of person really believes that someone who lives here could have six large sitting in his back pocket. You've got more chance of getting a wank off the queen than recouping that money, and you know it.'

Walter knew the boy spoke the truth but they had collected debts from poorer people than this over the years. It was amazing what people were capable of when under pressure. Walter's fist shot out and connected with Danny's face, sending the boy flying backwards. As Danny hit the brown-tiled floor he saw his mother fly out from the bedroom with a small axe that she had raised above her head and, before he could stop her, she had brought it down, with all her might, onto the smaller man on her doorstep. Danny saw him drop like a stone, and then he saw his mother wrench the axe from the man's chest and aim it at Wilfred's head. It connected with his shoulder and his scream was heard all over the estate.

'You fecking touch my kids and I'll fecking destroy the pair of you.' She was hacking at the two men now, and they were both bleeding profusely from their wounds. As she hit them, and screamed her anger into their faces, Danny pulled himself to his feet, grabbed his mother around the waist, and pushed her into the kitchen. Seeing the kettle, and hearing the two men coming into the flat, their shock now giving way to anger, Danny picked the kettle up and slung the contents into both their faces. Their screams were loud and long, but his mother's shrieking seemed to drown them out.

As Danny looked at them, the scalded skin on their faces, the open wounds from his mother's attack, he wondered if he had wandered into a nightmare. His father had a lot to answer for and, when he finally showed up, he would make sure he knew exactly what he had caused.

He shoved the two men out of the flat. As he grabbed hold of Wilfred his hand took off a layer of skin and he knew that had to hurt like fuck. Then he slammed the front door and, leaning against it, he waited until he could breathe properly once more and the urge to vomit had passed. Then he went to his mother; she was still in the kitchen, clutching the axe in her arms as if holding a baby.

'What have we done, son?' She was shaking her head, and he noticed just how tiny she actually was.

The noise outside had died down, and he assumed the Murrays had taken themselves off to the local hospital for treatment.

He could hear his sister Annie crying, and after he had pushed a wardrobe against the front door, he calmed his mother down and hugged his sister to sleep. Then, taking the bloodied axe from his mother, he sat on the floor and waited for the next instalment of the drama that was suddenly his life. Jonjo came and sat beside him, the fear in his eyes almost tangible and Danny knew that if his father was to come home now, when he had finished with him, the Murrays' wounds would look like they had been on a day trip with the WI. Six hundred lousy quid. Their lives had been destroyed over a poxy six large, and the man who had caused all this upset was, as always, nowhere to be seen. He had been left alone to protect his family while his father was on the trot, and he was terrified that he wasn't strong enough to do the job. His mother was white-faced with fear and shock, and he knew that she would never get over the day's events and, in all honesty, neither would he. His fourteenth birthday was only five days away and he wondered if he would live long enough to see it.

The Murrays' reception at the Cadogans' spread like wildfire. Louie Stein shook his head in sadness and made a point of being seen going to the boy's flat on a regular basis. He knew that his presence would be duly noted and passed onto the people involved. He had a certain kudos in as much as he was good friends with a lot of the Faces around and about. In fact he made a point of telling everyone he spoke to about the young man who worked for him having to take on the Murrays to protect his little sister and brother. The mother, he laughed, was a Face in her own right. Angelica the Axe Woman, as he called her, was soon part of urban legend. But the Murrays would eventually want some kind of revenge; that was only human nature. That they had not called in the police was not remarked on. After all, if they had, they would never have been able to hold their heads up again. It was tantamount to grassing, and the fact that the police had not come to investigate, even though the facts were common knowledge to all and sundry, spoke volumes as well.

Even the Cadogans' parish priest, Father Donovan, a huge surly man who saw his flock's daily fight for survival as a personal affront, had made a point of visiting two or three times a day. His presence had been appreciated by Danny as well as his mother. It had given them the seal of approval, said they were the injured party and that brought a lot of people round to their way of thinking, seeing as the Murrays were Irish Catholics as well.

But Danny was unable to relax, wondering constantly when the Murrays were going to arrive and exact some kind of revenge. He wouldn't leave his mother and the kids alone, and when he was at work he made sure they were safe and surrounded by people. That was the easy bit. The hard bit was the waiting and, after two months, he knew that the time was near for a visit, and he accepted the inevitable.

His father was still on the missing list, and Danny found his hatred and distaste for the man growing by the day. He was a big lad, but since working for Louie he had developed muscles that had not been there before. He was broadening by the day, his shoulders and chest had become more pronounced, and his hands were rough and calloused. He knew he looked much older than his years, and he made a point of dressing up. While his peers were wearing cheesecloth shirts and baggy flares, he dressed in shirts and tailored trousers. He was already looking like a gangster, and he knew it was a style that suited him. His build and his natural swagger were suddenly a familiar sight in Bethnal Green, and the eyes that never seemed to show any emotion made the girls swoon at his approach. He was a local hero, and he milked it for what it was worth. He knew that when the Murrays finally surfaced he would need all the help he could get, and he made a point of cultivating anyone he thought might be an ally. His natural cunning was all he had going for him, and he was lucky enough to have it in abundance.

*

Angelica was still trying to locate her husband, and so far it had been a fruitless and frustrating two months. No one seemed to have seen or heard anything about him. To all intents and purposes he had dropped off the face of the earth. But she knew him better than anyone, and she was convinced he was shacked up with one of his birds, waiting it out, letting his family take the heat for him. Angelica had always known he was not the most trustworthy of men, but this latest stunt was out of order – even for him.

She knew her daughter had been badly affected by that night. Annie had always been excitable, but the Murrays' visit had unleashed a nervousness that was apparent to anyone within five minutes of being in her company. She was unable to sit still, and her chatter was constant and without any kind of structure. She could have three conversations at once, and her nervous laugh was enough to bring tears to her mother's eyes. A daddy's girl, she was the only person in his orbit he actually seemed to genuinely care about, and she believed her father was the greatest thing since the ascension into heaven of our Lord himself. It was painful to watch Annuncia pine for her father, and even harder for Angelica to stop herself giving the child the facts of life before she was ready to hear them. One day, Angelica knew, she would work him out all by herself; she didn't need it spelled out for her – no matter how tempting her mother found it. The Murrays were enough for her young daughter to worry about, and worry about them she did.

And what kind of men were the Murrays? Who in their right minds terrorised women and children? And anyway, what would their revenge be now, seeing they had come off the worst in their initial encounter with the Cadogans? It was Danny she was really afraid for, she knew he was likely to be the one targeted. She also knew that was exactly what he hoped would happen. He had taken to dressing like a thug, suited and booted now, he was earning a few quid, though determined not to pay his father's debts for him, and assuming the role of head male in the household. A role Angelica was happy for him to fulfil, even though she knew it was wrong; that he was a child when all was said and done. But he was also the only thing keeping them from penury and the pavement.

He had even paid off the back rent, and obtained items of furniture she had only dreamed of possessing. He was a good lad, a kind brother and son, and now she knew he was also a very *capable* boy. Big Dan Cadogan had left a void in their lives, and this youngster was trying to fill it, trying to take the onus off her and his siblings. Christ himself knew it was a hard road for him, and a harder road for her, his mother, because she was witness to it all, and she took whatever he managed to give her.

Her Danny Boy, her first-born son, the love of her life, had skipped adolescence and commenced straight to adulthood. He had taken to walking home through the back roads, knowing that he would be an easy mark for anyone who wished to pick him up in a car, or savage him on the quiet. He wanted the reprisal over and done with so they could get on with their lives.

The violence of her own part in the Murrays' attack had shocked her. A fighter all her life, she had never before used a weapon; she had never had to. Her children's safety had brought that part of her fighting spirit to the fore. She knew in her heart though that the Murrays would not, indeed *could* not, come back at her over it. That would not be tolerated, in fact, if she ever even got mugged, the finger of blame would be pointed firmly in their direction. They knew that as well as she did. Even their own mother, a heavy-set Yugoslavian woman with pink cheeks and a wrinkled neck, had voiced her displeasure over her sons' actions. Mothers were out of bounds, as were kids, and it had taken her family's trials and tribulations to get that point across to the Murrays. But, like her son, she would be relieved when the Murrays finally made a move; at least then they could get on with their lives.

Danny was taking his tea break with Louie and, as they sat side by side on an old crate, they were both aware of the easy camaraderie that had developed between them. Danny was grateful to his employer for standing beside him, for making him feel there was at least a glimmer of light at the end of the tunnel. He knew Louie was watching his back and, since no one had ever done that for him in his short life, the gratitude he felt was pitiful.

The breakers yard now had a tidiness that was only apparent to those who actually worked there. Over the last two months Danny had systematically sorted through pile after pile of scrap metal, separating the copper, lead and iron into piles of their own. The cars, their main source of income, were everywhere, and the crushed remains of them were piled up like a huge metal wall. Once the carcasses were stripped of parts they were useless, and therefore disposed of quickly and cleanly in the huge crushing machine that Danny could now operate in his sleep.

When the totters came in these days their scrap was easily disposed of and placed on to the appropriate pile, and anyone who wanted car parts was now able to go straight to whatever they wanted without half a day's search. Louie was thrilled with what the boy had achieved. Even though the yard was really a blind for his other businesses, he was pleased at how much more efficient the place was now, thanks to this young lad's hard graft. He had also taught the boy how to barter the totters for their scrap, and Danny had turned out to be a real natural. He had a feel for the place, knew instinctively what was worthless and what would make a few quid. He was not only as strong as an ox, but he was also shrewder than people realised. He was able to do a good deal while letting the other party think they had got the best of the bargain. In his game that was an important part of the job.

Danny had even started to ferret out and salvage a lot of the stuff for himself. Louie paid him a finder's fee, of course, and he saw the thrill that Danny got from making a few quid on the side. It was a necessity in their world, that need to make a good deal, make a few quid over the odds, even when you were rolling in it. The cars were a separate business altogether, but Danny was like most young fellows and loved anything with four wheels, he was even able to distinguish which make of car a part was from. Passing trade was often young men looking for an exhaust pipe or new gearbox for their car and, before Danny, Louie would have had to stand there and watch them while they searched, to make sure they didn't half inch anything else while they were there. Now though, Danny would accompany them, chat to them about their needs and wants and, nine times out of ten, lay his large hands on the item in question within minutes.

All in all, it was a much easier life for Louie, and the company was also welcome. He liked the boy, admired his work ethic, and the fact that he was keeping his family fed and housed without making a song and dance about it. In fact he never mentioned it, just got on with the job in hand, took his wedge, and turned up the next morning. He was all that any man could wish for in a son, and yet his father had left him without a word, even though he had to have heard what had gone down with the Murrays. After all, it had become the talk of the Smoke, even the Faces from north London had mentioned it to him.

Still, he had done his bit for the lad, made his case with anyone and everyone he dealt with, and he was sure that the Murray boys wouldn't want a repeat of their last outing with actual grown men. They were renowned for their scamming of people and, as long as they stuck to conning the likes of Big Dan Cadogan, they were safe enough. In the real world, however, the serious criminal world, they would be hard-pushed to get past Go, let alone collect two hundred or, in this case, six hundred. It was all relative anyway. Five quid was a lot of money if you didn't have it.

The fucking pair of shitters had asked for it and, for once, someone had given it to them. The fact that it was a young lad and his mother must gall them, but then such is life. A low profile and a rethink of their business practices would have been sufficient for most people after a debacle of that magnitude.

Danny was the one people were siding with, because he was an innocent, just defending his family, and he hadn't run away, he was still waiting for a meet of some sort to try and resolve the situation once and for all. The boy was a fucking dream, any man other than Big Dan would have been tempted out of hiding by the intimidation of his family. Danny's old man was still AWOL though, and that was something no one would ever forgive, or forget. Especially not the young man sitting beside him.

Svetlana Murray was as worried as her Irish counterpart. She knew that if everything went pear-shaped again, she could easily find *herself* on the receiving end of a similar attack. It was like the law; once a precedent had been set and accepted into common usage, it could easily become the norm. Women and children were off-limits where violence or debt collection was concerned, and her sons had transgressed that particular unwritten law and made to pay the consequences of their actions. They were being cold-shouldered, and they knew they were. Even so-called friends were suddenly blanking them. It seemed that the boys had gone too far this time and public opinion was that they had crossed the line. Well, they had paid a terrible price for that, they were scarred for life. Her younger son had taken the brunt of the boiling water and she was sure it was only his hate that was keeping him on his feet. Walter, she knew, was willing to swallow his knob and let it go. It was Wilfred who seemed unable to let the matter drop. Like a lot of short men, his father included, he was forever trying to prove himself, and her warnings about the public sympathy the Cadogans were receiving seemed to be falling on deaf ears.

It was the Irish in him, she could only use that as an explanation for her younger son's absolute denial of any wrongdoing where the Cadogans were concerned. Walter had always been the peace-maker, even as a boy, whereas Wilfred had been the one to bear a grudge. Even as kids she had seen that trait in him; if they argued about something Wilfred would bide his time and, when he was ready and no one was expecting it, he would pay his brother back, more often than not with interest. Now though, his natural gift for holding an grudge could easily become the whole family's downfall, and she was not about to let that happen. She loved her boys but, like most people in their orbit, she didn't actually like them.

Michael Miles waited outside the scrapyard until it was dark. He was smoking the last of his Dunhills and he wished he had brought another pack out from their hiding place. As he stamped out the glowing butt, he heard his friend calling out his goodbyes and, fixing a smile on his face, he prepared himself for what he had decided to do.

Danny saw him immediately and stopped in his tracks. Michael could see the anger in his friend's face and tried to diffuse it by saying gaily, 'What? Have we fell out and I don't know about it?'

Danny sighed heavily. 'Do me a favour, Mike. Get on your fucking bike and leave me be.'

It was an expression that they had used all their lives, get on your bike, or drive home will you. It should have been amusing, not a serious criticism. The nearest they had ever got to any kind of conveyance was if they nicked one for the afternoon. Even then they put it back rather than sell it on or dismantle it. Both were agreed that thieving someone's wheels was not a kosher nick. In fact they had agreed that if they had been lucky enough to have been furnished with bikes they would have both understood someone borrowing it for a few hours. But actually to be in possession of the said vehicle, and then to lose it, would have been too much for them to bear.

The two boys looked at each other, neither of them willing to back down and neither of them able to make this situation right. Since the Murrays had turned up at Danny's home he had studiously ignored Michael, believing it to be for the best. It had hurt.

'You're me best mate, Danny. Your problems are my problems.' Michael saw his best friend close his eyes tightly in anger but carried on talking anyway, 'I just want you to know you ain't on your own, you'd do the same for me, surely?'

It was a question that they both knew needed an answer.

'I wouldn't need to do this for you. This just wouldn't happen to you, Mike. When this all comes on top, and it will, you'll be sorrier than shit if you are dragged into it. Use your fucking loaf.' He looked at his best friend. Like him, Michael Miles was dark-haired; he had an easy way about him and a knack for ferreting out anything he wanted to know. Unlike Danny, he wasn't a natural fighter, he wasn't a natural antagonist. Together, they were a team.

Then Michael smiled, and it changed his whole face. His smile was his best asset, though he wouldn't be aware of that fact for a good few years.

'That's as may be, Dan, but we've been mates since Infants. If you blank me again I'm going to get a complex.'

Danny laughed despite himself. 'Look, Mike, you know the score.'

Danny held his arms out in a gesture of supplication.

Michael grinned again, knowing he was halfway home. 'Fucking Murrays. They're only half-Irish anyway, so what's to worry about?'

They laughed together, both pleased their friendship was back on, and both worried at what might befall them because of that.

Chapter Three

'Do you think maybe he's dead?'

Danny sighed heavily and stopped himself from answering his mother's question honestly. Personally, he hoped the old bastard *was* dead. At least if he died the debt died with him and all this shit would be over. It was the waiting that was doing his head in, the apprehension; he was at a stage where he would almost welcome the Murray boys and their retribution, just to get it over with once and for all. But he didn't say that, of course. Instead he answered her with quiet anger, his voice higher than usual and laced with the general feeling of annoyance and irritation that her questions seemed to generate in him. ''Course not, Mum. He's keeping a low profile, that's all. You know me dad, once it's safe he'll sneak back in here like nothing ever happened, and you'll make sure no one ever talks about it to him in case he gets offended or, God forbid, has to explain why all this shit happened in the first place.'

The disgust in her son's voice was not lost on Angelica Cadogan, and it was only her son's new status as head of the family that stopped her from boxing his ears for him. Without him they would have sunk without trace, she was more than aware of that, but his hard work made her feel so guilty and useless that she actively disliked him at times. It was unnatural having to kowtow to such a young boy, a boy she had birthed and brought up, a young boy who was suddenly the scourge of the household. In the months since her husband's disappearance, Danny had not only paid off all their debts and put them on to a decent footing, but he had also, somewhere along the line, become a bully. He now queried every aspect of her domain, from the cleanliness of her home and children, to her squandering of the money he now provided on a regular basis. He was so young, and his youth was why he couldn't give to them all without expecting something in return. His new role as head of the household was all an act. And a frightening act at that, because he was portraying what he thought a father should be and, as he had never experienced a real one in his life, it was causing no end of problems. He was like a caricature of what a parent should be, and there was not a lot she could do because she needed the money he was providing for them all.

In all honesty, she had never been so well off in her life. The fact that she had a good idea of what she would receive as her house-keeping each week had changed everything, but her son's insistence on knowing what she had done with every penny was starting to wear thin. He made her feel inadequate, made her feel nervous around him. He made her private little purchases seem wrong, shameful. Who wouldn't need a small nip now and then when they were as plagued by troubles as she was? Who wouldn't need a stiff drink to face the lonely nights without a man to warm her, and that man her legal husband, the father of her children? She conveniently forgot that Big Dan was useless, had never once taken on the mantle of fatherhood except to beat the boys or her, depending on how drunk he was.

Sighing, Danny forced a kind and gentle note into his voice before saying reasonably, and with as much truthfulness as he could manage, 'If he was dead, Mum, we'd have heard by now. Think about it, Old Bill would have informed us, wouldn't they? It ain't like he wasn't *known* to them, was it? Fuck me, Mum, he was always on the nick, they knew him better then we did. They certainly saw more of him than we did, anyway.'

She didn't answer him, the truth of his words penetrating even her pig-headedness. She sat down at the kitchen table and said sadly, plaintively, making her son feel even worse than he already did, 'I worry about him, Danny. He's still my husband, your father.'

Her son stared at her for long moments and she knew he was disappointed because she wanted her husband back with her, even though he was the reason for their current predicament. If only Danny was wise enough to understand how marriage and commitment worked for her generation.

Danny Cadogan smiled sadly. 'Well, if he does come back, he'd better toe the line this time, Mother, because I won't fucking stand for any more of his nonsense.' Finally he vented his pent-up anger. 'This is your last chance to put your kids first and, if you don't, then I swear to God, I'll walk out that door and leave you all to it. If, and that's a big if, your old man does come back, he will have to come through me first and, believe me, I won't be making it easy for him. He's a liar and a ponce and an easy mark and I won't forget what he's caused, even if you choose to. To be truthful, if I knew where he was I'd serve him up to the Murrays meself, without a second's thought, just to get them off our backs. People only do to you what you let them, that's what you've drummed in my head all of my life. Well, watching you and him, I'd already learned that much at an early age.'

Ange didn't answer him, she didn't know what to say.

Louie Stein was pouring himself an early morning snifter, the large brandy he swallowed after his morning coffee, which he referred to as his eye-opener. His wife saw what he was doing and rolled her large brown eyes at the ceiling but she didn't make any kind of comment. He could feel her annoyance though, and that just made him pour an even larger measure than usual, reasoning that if his actions were going to annoy her, then why not give her something to be annoyed about?

She placed his usual breakfast on the table, a small poached egg and a slice of bread and butter. He then did what he always did, pushed it away and lit a cigarette. He loved his wife, she was a good woman, but he also understood that they were at a point in their marriage where the only excitement either of them felt was when they were at loggerheads. He understood that, welcomed it even. Their youthful silences had taken its toll on them both; a decent row, they had found, cleared the air for a while and gave them both a good laugh afterwards. After all these years all they had in common were their grievances, real and imagined.

'Are you going to tell the lad?'

He shrugged nonchalantly, flicking his ash onto the poached egg, something that was normally guaranteed to cause ructions. This morning though, Sylvia Stein ignored it, knowing her husband was trying to steer the conversation onto something else entirely. Well, she was not about to let that happen, she was genuinely interested in how he would react to what she had told him. She refilled his coffee cup, and then, for the first time ever, she refilled his brandy glass. Sitting back down she put her elbows on to the table, then she placed her head onto her hands and, raising her eyebrows comically, said loudly, 'My God, Louie, would you put me out of my misery?'

His laughter was genuine, and she knew he would sound her out, see what she thought he should do with the knowledge he now possessed. Knowledge she had imparted because her sister Irene heard everything and, unfortunately, repeated it all.

Walter Murray was on the mend, he knew that because for the first time in months he had woken naturally and not because he was in pain. He studied his reflection in the mirror on his dressing table and admitted that he didn't look much worse than he had before. Unlike Wilfred, he understood the economics of their shared situation and, like his mother, he knew that all that was left for them was damage limitation.

The boy, Cadogan's son, had only been protecting his own, and the fact that he was only a kid had tempered his anger, whilst that same fact had inflamed his brother. Wilfred wanted to annihilate him. He saw the boy and his demise as their only saving grace, couldn't see that any kind of retaliation would only make their lives even harder than they already were.

Their reputation had preceded them. All the time they had scrounged a living off no-hopers and the dispossessed, they had been tolerated. Now, thanks to that boy, and his fucking bum chum Louie Stein, they were suddenly public enemy number one. So, other than tracking down the father, and that would happen sooner rather than later, ponces always shat in their own nests eventually, they could only try and make amends. This was a concept his brother was having serious difficulty in taking on board.

Walter stared at his reflection, marvelling at the livid red marks that would always be a reminder of that fateful morning, not only to him, but to anyone who happened to gaze upon them, and he swallowed down the urge to cry. They had been brought down by a fucking kid, a teenager who was being talked of as the new Face in town, who people discussed as a serious contender for future skulduggery. The boy's stand had placed him in the path of greatness and, worse than that, had put him into the psyche of every Face in the Smoke.

The boy had a fucking career before he could even shave, a serious rep was his reward for standing up for his family. The eyes of everyone would be on him; he was a lump, he had an attitude, and he was respectful to those in the know. Now Wilfred needed to understand that before this all got completely out of hand.

Big Dan was not feeling such a big man these days. His decision to go on the trot had not worked out quite as he had envisaged. Even though he had known it was wrong to welsh, he had seen himself leaving all his woes behind, his wife and kids included. He had seen himself as a single man, going out into the world without the ties and the problems of a married man. Saw a gorgeous flat for himself, a few quid in his bin, and a new lady to take care of him. But, like everything else in his life, nothing that he yearned for had come to pass. He couldn't bring himself to stop the gambling, he couldn't bring himself to settle in Liverpool, and he still couldn't find it in his heart to walk past a public house without blessing himself.

Now he was back in the Smoke, and his amour of several years' duration was finding out, like many a mistress before her, that the fantasy of someone else's husband was far better than the reality, when the said husband finally landed on their doorstep. And, to top it all off, it seemed that his son, the useless bastard, had taken on the Murrays and, through that one act of bravado, was now some kind of fucking local hero. It would be laughable. If he had a laugh in him, of course.

Louie Stein watched Danny as he operated the crushing machine. His old friend and employee Cedric Campbell had trained the boy up and passed over the reins with a willingness that made him realise just how old the man had become. Really he was paying him a wage out of habit, and Cedric, he knew, turned up for work every day for that exact same reason. But what could he do? Age had a habit of creeping up on you. One day you were part of the in-crowd, the next thing you knew, the in-crowd were planted or in homes. It was brutal but it was a fact of life.

Now he had word, on very good authority, that this boy's father was skulking in a flat in Hoxton, waiting for the opportunity to launch himself once more into polite society. That time being, of course, when he would feel at his safest, and when his son had smoothed the way for him. The skulduggery and disloyalty of family would never cease to amaze him. How the people closest to you could tuck you up without a second's thought, and with a smile that would make Orphan Annie look like a wide boy, had been proved to him over and over again.

That Danny's father was once more back on the scene, and it was only a matter of time before he made a personal appearance, was hard for Louie to understand. He didn't know what to do for the best, tell the boy, forewarned and all that, or keep schtum and wait to see what happened. Maybe, just maybe, Big Dan Cadogan would go on the trot once more and a major calamity might be averted.

He sighed and, winking at Cedric, he waved to Danny, indicating that he wanted him in the office. Danny shut down the crusher quickly and made his way over to the dilapidated shed that served as their sanctuary from Old Bill, errant totters and, more often than not, the outside world in general.

Scrap metal was not a business that encouraged friendliness with rivals in the same game, or had any kind of glamour that might attract the opposite sex. Scrap was an earner, but only to people who knew how to offload it, respected it, and were willing to put in the time and the effort that would then warrant some kind of trust. A scrapyard had to be up and running for a good few years before it was designated a walking trust fund for the criminally minded. It had to be around long enough for people to see and accept it as an established business. A scrapyard owner needed the knack of being able to talk to all walks of society and, more importantly, Lily Law, without arousing suspicions from anyone they might be involved with. It was a fine line that needed to be drawn, and it was also a difficult position for someone who, for whatever reason, was not a people person.

Scrap was serious bunce, scrap was a serious earner, and scrap was a cash business that left a lot of room for creative accounting and afforded the time and effort that was often needed to ensure a long and happy partnership with a variety of different businessmen. In short, scrap was a fucking earner, but that earning potential could only be fully utilised by someone with the brains and the acumen to know a good deal within a nanosecond, and who would offer a decent scotch a nanosecond after that. Young Danny was a natural, he looked at home in the yard, and could spot a good deal a mile away. And, most important of all, he wanted the wedge.

Now Louie had to decide whether to keep his trap shut, or steer the boy onto a course that was even more crooked than the man, and he used that term lightly, who had sired him. It was a melon scratcher all right, and Louie wasn't sure what the best course of action might be.

Angelica Campbell was sitting at her kitchen table, the *new* table, provided by her son, who took great pains to remind her of that fact at every given opportunity. She wished her daughter was still at home, wasn't at that school where all she seemed to be learning was rudeness, and a knack for annoying the life out of everyone she came into contact with. Angelica was fingering her rosary, she often asked for a small Intention during the course of the day, convinced that a minor request would not be ignored. She had never trusted the power of prayer enough to ask for her husband's return or, before that, his fidelity. She knew that a miracle of those proportions would be about as likely as a win on the pools. But she was unsettled in herself, couldn't seem to relax at all. It was a feeling like no other in her life to date. As if she was waiting for something, but she didn't know what that something might be.

The knock on the front door was almost welcome, it gave her something to do, and she launched herself out of the chair and into the tiny hallway within seconds. Opening the door she was struck dumb at the realisation of who was standing there. Wilfred Murray grinned at her, displaying his large, yellowing teeth, and an almost indecent amount of gum. The health service in this country was free, and that included dentists, and yet she had never seen so many sets of harrowing choppers in her life until she had got off the boat at Fishguard.

Wilfred was inside the flat before she had time to wish him a good day, a feck off, or to even scratch her arse.

Michael Miles came into the scrapyard at just after three twenty, early even for him. Louie Stein waved nonchalantly at the boy. Knowing he was a good friend of Danny's he was now used to seeing him around the place. Michael was a nice lad, he had an analytical brain that would always earn him a living if he had the sense to turn his thoughts to such a thing. He was a natural robber, but a book robber rather than a bank robber, a difference that quickly became apparent to anyone who dealt with him. The boy could add up in his head faster than a calculator, and he liked the mathematics of everyday life, a bonus for anyone out to earn a wedge without the benefit of tax and insurance. Between them, he knew Danny and Michael would one day make a winning team. He hoped that, if and when that day arrived, the team they played for would be his. Danny, he knew, had the front needed to get on in their kind of business. Michael, on the other hand, had the acumen that should take him into an office but, because of his personality, would definitely bring him into the criminal fraternity at some point in his lifetime. He had the nous but not the staying power needed for the big wages. His idea of a pension fund would be an off-shore account and a flat that even his wife didn't know about.

These two young men were Louie's lifeline to the real world;

watching them grow up and helping them to mature was the only thing that stopped him eating one of the guns he rented out on a daily basis, or leaping into his own crusher. He was a natural depressive, and he knew that. But a man in his position needed a son to make his later years worthwhile. He was now looking at leaving his life's work to one of his daughters' husbands, while praying for a grandson in his spare time. To have a son and waste the opportunity was a crying shame, was criminal as far as he was concerned. He saw the serious look that passed over Danny's face as Michael talked to him and decided that the matter of the boy's father's emergence once more into the world of the hoi polloi had been taken out of his hands. He was liking young Michael more every time he saw him.

Wilfred was unsure what to do now he was confronted with only the mother of his prime antagonist. In fact, thanks to his own mother's words of warning, this woman and her nervous coughing was making him feel, for the first time in years, that he might actually be in the wrong.

His mother had pointed out that the attack with the axe was no more than she would have done herself for her own children. That a mother would protect her young because, with good fathers being few and far between, the only person a child could really count on was the woman who had grown them, birthed them and nurtured them. Now, here he was, confronting someone who, at any other time, he would feel honour-bound to help carry her shopping home.

Angelica was terrified but casting around for a weapon of some kind. This man was not getting near her children without going through her first. She cursed her husband and his gambling once more; his weakness for the cards would always be his downfall. It was almost like praying, she had cursed him so often she could now do it while thinking of something completely different. This revelation disturbed her almost as much as it pleased her.

Wilfred however, was nonplussed. Now he was here, he wasn't so sure that he could settle the score this way without retribution being heaped on his own family.

Angelica sensed his indecision and said softly, 'Go home, son, my husband isn't worth all this trouble.'

Wilfred was still standing in front of her, and she knew he was debating what course of action he should take now. Thanks to her husband and son, his world had been blown apart, a nuclear bomb couldn't have done more damage.

'Would you like a cup of tea, son?'

'You sure me old man's hit the pavement, Mike? Only I can't see him coming back this way meself.'

Mike nodded, his eyes flashing in annoyance. 'Me mum told me, and you know her, Dan, she should work for MI5, nosy old bag she is. He's been seen about Hoxton, at his bird's drum. I think he will surface now because you've sorted out the aggravation. Let's face it, there ain't no way anyone will let the Murrays get away with their usual fucking bluster now, is there?'

Danny wasn't so sure about that. His old man had made a few enemies over the years and a debt was a debt when all was said and done. They might not relish the Murrays' approach to collecting what they saw as owed monies, not when it involved a woman and children, but if they wanted to take it out on his old man then that would be a different ball game. In fact, if this was true, he would deliver him to the Murrays in person. At the end of the day, it would diffuse the situation and make his old man finally accept the consequences of his actions.

'I'd better warn me mum, and then we'll see what occurs. For all we know this is all a load of old fanny.'

They left the yard together, Louie watching them with relief. It would be sorted out one way or another now.

Danny and Michael walked into the flat slowly, both tense and both trying their hardest to be nonchalant. They were expecting Big Dan Cadogan, as he liked to be called, to be sitting in a chair, comfortable and at ease with himself and his surroundings, as always. Instead, they came face-to-face with the smaller, and the meaner of the Murray boys and Danny said loudly, 'Is this a social visit, or do we need a weapon?'

Wilfred Murray shrugged, seeing the extreme youth of the boys as if for the first time. Saw their bulky, muscular young bodies and knew that one day Danny, at least, would be someone of note, someone who would command respect. Unlike him and his brother, Danny Boy Cadogan had a presence even now and a few years down the line it would become more pronounced; he was going to leave a mark on everyone he came into contact with. The irony of that thought didn't escape Wilfred, he felt the tightness of the scalded skin on his face and the memory of the pain inflicted on him was still recent enough to make him feel queasy.

Wilfred wasn't sure why he had been so determined to come here, it was a small flat overfilled with people and, like his own childhood, was overshadowed by a bully who would rather put his money over a bar than into his home. He had noticed the difference in the place since his last visit. It felt different, it was spotless, it even smelled different. In fact it reminded him of his own home when his father had been banged up and his brother and himself had finally felt able to relax.

He smiled. 'I came for your old man, I hear he's been seen out and about.'

Danny took his mother's elbow and steered her none too gently from the kitchen. Wilfred and Michael could hear her protesting as her son roughly pushed her into the front room.

'Stay there, Mum. Just for once do what I ask you, eh?' The shutting of the door was loud in the quiet of the apartment.

Once he was back inside the kitchen Danny grinned. 'If I find out where the old cunt is hiding, will you go after him and leave us alone?'

Wilfred nodded sagely. This was going even better than he hoped.

'Mike will tell you where he is, but first I want you to promise me something, Wilfred.'

Wilfred laughed. 'What? Ask me anything, you're a fucking little star.'

Danny grinned. 'When you see him, promise me you'll hammer the fuck out of him, cripple him.'

Wilfred laughed again, louder this time. 'That is a promise, mate.'

Danny stopped laughing. 'I ain't joking, I want you to *hurt* him, batter the fuck out of him, because if you don't, I will.'

Wilfred and Michael looked at each other then, both unsure of how to react to such blatant hatred.

'And you tell him it was me who grassed him, won't you? Make sure he knows it was me who served him up.'

Wilfred nodded again, not sure what answer he was supposed to give.

Danny Boy was in a good mood and, taking his little sister's hand, he walked her to the local Wimpy bar. Jonjo followed sullenly. Like his brother he was big for his age, and he had the thick dark hair that was the Cadogan trademark. Inside at last, Danny settled his siblings into their chairs and, motioning for the waiters, he said loudly, 'Are you all on fucking holiday or what? I've had boils lanced quicker than I've been served in here.'

People laughed at his jovial tone. Danny was already known for his quick wit. A young Turkish boy went to the table immediately. 'What can I get you?'

Annuncia heard the respect in the waiter's voice, saw the way her brother was being treated, and decided to use the advantage while she had it. 'Get me a burger and a milkshake.'

Danny looked at his little sister and marvelled at her knack for reading a situation in seconds and then using the knowledge to her advantage. Jonjo was, as always, quiet and Danny ordered for him, getting the same meal for them both.

'You all right, Jonjo?' His brother shrugged and Danny noticed that while his sister had a new uniform on, Jonjo was wearing hand-me-downs. Hand-me-downs that had been handed down to Danny many years before. He was suddenly sorry that his brother was having to dress like the other poor kids. Sorry that they were cursed with a father who didn't give a toss about them one way or the other. Even more sorry that he hadn't noticed his brother's predicament. Danny was fourteen years old and already he understood that clothes *did* make the man, no matter what anyone else might think. If you dressed well, spread a few quid about, and looked the dog's knob, people automatically treated you better. He had realised that, since working for Louie Stein and finally being in a position to buy himself decent clothes, ensuring that the bills were paid at home, and even managing to save a few quid, made all the difference to how you perceived yourself at the end of the day.

Now, with his brother and sister beside him, feeding and watering them, all the while knowing their father was getting the shit kicked out of him, life was suddenly about opportunities and bettering himself. It was the first time in years he had felt this good about anything. His father had brought him into the real world and, for that, he would always be grateful. But his father had also ruined his life and his brother and sister's lives without a second's thought. Now though, if everything went to plan, he would see his father crippled and damaged; what a wonderful outcome from such a terrible situation. He hated his father with a vengeance, hated his selfishness and his disregard for his children. Hated the way he treated their mother, who still loved him, even though he didn't want her, even though a slag from Hoxton with badly dyed hair and a definite squint was his preferred company these days. The hate was building up inside Danny, and he welcomed it, relished it, because all the time he was hating he was feeling something at least. His little brother was watching him and, winking jauntily, he said loudly, 'Hey, Jonjo, no school tomorrow, we're going shopping. You look like a fucking tramp, mate.'

Jonjo grinned, displaying the even white teeth that were the only decent thing their father had passed on to them. 'Thanks, Danny. I really appreciate that. Father Patrick rides me all the time—'

Danny's face darkened. 'Does he? Why, who the fuck does he think he is?'

Jonjo felt the first stirring of fear then. 'Oh, Dan, he doesn't mean the half of it.'

Annie watched her brothers in wonderment, knowing before Jonjo that Father Patrick would rue the day he picked on a Cadogan.

Chapter Four

Louie Stein was waiting for Danny Boy when he arrived at work. Danny had been half expecting something like that; he knew that Louie would want to mark the day for him. Louie understood where he was coming from, understood the absolute disgust he felt for his father and his father's antics. As Danny walked into the office he grinned. 'What you heard then?'

Louie smiled in return, a bitter twisted smile that said more about him than he realised. 'You slippery little fucker, you served your old man up, didn't you?'

Danny didn't answer him, he knew he wasn't expected to anyway. This was the way of the world, people told you things and you let them tell you. As long as you didn't answer either way, everyone was happy.

'What a stroke you pulled there, my son, a masterpiece of public relations and justifiable retribution. Everyone's a winner.'

Danny still didn't say a word.

'He was taken into the Old London late last night, in case you're wondering. The Murrays paid him out severely but I am sure he expected something along those lines. Now he's back in the fold, so to speak, older, wiser and definitely in mortal agony.' He laughed once more. 'Fucking *fourteen*, and you sorted that lot out. I'm glad I ain't on your bad side. Now, get your arse in gear and shift that scrap. I'll make you a cup of tea and a cheese roll and, if you're very good, I'll give you an early shoot.'

Danny smiled his thanks and, walking away from his mentor, he

59

smiled to himself. The Murrays had better have dealt out a serious punishment; he was depending on it. If his mother wanted that skank back so much, then he would make sure he had been neutered first. Like an errant tom cat he would have to stay close to home in future.

Big Dan was breathing with difficulty, and his wife was praying over his prostrate form with vigour. He was desperately ill, of that there was no doubt, but that he would recover, she knew was a certainty. He was battered and bruised, broken in body and, please God, in his mind too. She wanted him back for appearances' sake, and to thwart the whores he had seen fit to mix with throughout their married life. He was *her* husband by rights, and if this hammering gave him a renewed outlook on his life then she was all for it. She wasn't a fool, she knew her son was behind it and she also knew that her son had done it as much for her peace of mind as for his own. A man incapable of movement was a man who would stay at home. If not by choice, then by circumstance.

Danny would never forgive his father for the trouble he had brought to their door and, in fairness, she didn't blame him for that. He had looked out for them, as he should; after all, he was the oldest child. It was his job to make sure that they were all taken care of and, God love him, he had done that all right.

And now her husband was lying here, dying, especially if you listened to his version of events, and unable to move without screeching like a banshee. Well, God was good and he had a strange way of sorting things out. As she took yet another cup of tea from the young nurse, Ange smiled happily to herself.

Jonjo was cringing once more. As usual Father Patrick was making fun of him because it was easy. Father Patrick had a deep voice that belied his small stature, on the odd occasion he said a Mass it was a very uplifting experience for the listener; his voice detailed the Last Supper with a deep and resonant belief that was as honest as it was unbelievable, for anyone looking at this priest would never have credited him with such depth of emotion.

'Ah, I see that, as usual, we are expected to let this criminal skulk in a corner to hide the shame of his family. Would you look me in the eye, boy? Is that too much to ask of a Cadogan? A fine Irish name that's wasted on the likes of you, I might add.'

As Jonjo prayed for deliverance from the man who rode his back at every available opportunity, the door to the classroom opened and the boys who had been giggling, most of them against their better judgement, suddenly went deathly quiet. Father Patrick was dumbstruck for a few seconds.

Then he said loudly, in a voice dripping with sarcasm, 'Well, well, well, if it's not *another* Cadogan. Like we haven't got enough to contend with already. Have you maybe forgotten where you live? Or do you think you might come back and actually learn something this time? Only, if I remember rightly, you made this one here look like fecking Einstein in comparison.'

Father Patrick felt safe enough in his robes, knew that there were few boys of the Catholic faith stupid enough to try and outdo a priest. So when the punch landed it was as unexpected as it was painful. He dropped quickly and cleanly, a white flash of pain was all he remembered. Without a word to anyone Danny Cadogan left the classroom, shutting the door quietly behind him. The boys were round-eyed and open-mouthed with astonishment at what had occurred and as Father Patrick pulled himself off the floor with the aid of his desk, Jonjo Cadogan knew that the baiting he received on a daily basis was finally over. In fact, Father Patrick never once spoke directly to him ever again.

Svetlana Murray opened her front door and gasped in horror at the person she saw standing on her grubby doorstep.

Wilfred, however, called the boy into the house with gusto, and she went back to the kitchen quietly, but with her ears pricked for the first hint of trouble. Walter watched the boy warily, he knew he was an unknown quantity and, even though they had taken his old man with impunity, he was still worried Danny Boy Cadogan might come down with a serious dose of guilt.

'All right?'

The two men nodded.

'You?' This was said quietly, with an emphasis that was not lost on the younger man.

'Never better.'

'Make a pot of tea, Mum, and close the door, eh?'

The three men looked at each other and the tension went from the room. Danny took in his surroundings, marvelling at the luxury they seemed to live in though, in his opinion, the place was still a shambles. Nothing matched, nothing had been bought with any kind of plan in mind. It was like a jumble sale or a second-hand shop. Danny sat down respectfully, and the brothers followed suit, noting his demeanour. He had a mission in mind, had thought through what he wanted to achieve and how best to ask for it.

'The old man will live, but he'll be a raspberry, left with a permanent limp and a face like a boiled shite, as me mother would say. But that is over and done with now, ain't it?'

The two brothers nodded, still quiet, still waiting to hear what he had to say for himself.

'I actually popped by because I heard you had a few pharmaceuticals coming in in the near future and I think I can offload some them for you.'

'Oh do you? And where will you do that then, up the park?'

Wilfred's voice was heavy with sarcasm, and the redness of his face reminded Danny of what had occurred between them not so long ago. So, with that in mind, he bit back the retort that sprang to his lips and, smiling at them both in as friendly a manner as possible, he said quietly, 'Nah, actually I was thinking more of dealing them out. I have a few mates who could shift them in pubs, discos, that kind of thing. I want a few thousand Dexedrine to knock out, sale or return. If I nause it up, I guarantee you will not be out of pocket. If I do, well, we're all quid's in.'

'What 'bout if you get a tug? Would you be able to keep your trap shut and handle the situation?'

Danny grinned then. 'What do you think?'

The deal was already done and they all knew it.

Danny watched his father through the doorway that led into the ward. The glass was grimy and as he watched the interaction between his father and mother, he noticed his reflection and saw that his face was drawn, that he looked older than his years. This, he decided, was a good thing. Considering the last few months, it was a wonder he didn't look like Methuselah.

His mother was fussing around his old man as usual, straightening the bed and wiping his face for him. He could already see the annoyance in his father's stiff demeanour. In his striped pyjamas, and with his unshaved face, he looked vulnerable. Danny could see the likeness to himself: the dark hair, the blue eyes. He could see the build he had inherited from a long line of ditch-diggers, or such like. It was odds on that no one in his family had ever made anything of themselves; if they had, his father would have rammed that fact down his throat. Danny hated him with a passion that surprised him, even seeing him battered and bruised didn't affect him. What did touch a nerve though, was his mother's reaction to it all. She was happy he was once more in the frame, the woman who his father had no more thought for than a rabid dog. His father knew that would change now, that he would depend on her to make sure he had a bed in his own house. The house that was now his in name only, the bills finally being paid on a regular basis and the cupboards stocked. Danny knew he would enjoy the hold he had over this man now, would enjoy being in charge of them all.

He was going to relish taking away the one thing his father had always had to fall back on; being the big I am, the fucking bully who beat them to vent his frustration at himself. Terrorising his wife and kids because that gave him a feeling of superiority, especially when he had been found out in some way by the people he broke his neck to mix with, drink with, gamble or whore with.

This had been a long time coming, and he would make it his life's work to pay the old bastard back for every punch, every kick, and every thrashing he had received from him. It had been easy to hurt people, a knack he assumed he had also inherited from his father, too easy really. People talked a good fight but very few could actually have one. Most people were cowards like Big Dan Cadogan, his so-called father.

Well, this Cadogan was going to make that name mean something other than drunk, other than waster; he was going to make it a name that garnered respect. And he knew that letting the old man come home would give him a good standing. After all, family was everything, no matter what they did, you were supposed to forgive them. Well, he didn't have that kind of forgiveness in him, he knew that much.

His mother came out then and, holding his arm gently, said, 'Come in and talk to him, Danny Boy. He's always asking after you.' The plea was in her eyes and her voice. Danny knew she was worried about what was going to happen to them all, how the dynamics of the household would change. He knew his new-found confidence and his total disregard for his father was something she wasn't sure how to deal with. He understood that better than she did.

So he smiled at her, his handsome young face making her heart hammer in her chest. 'I've come to take you home, Mum. Don't worry, he'll see enough of me to last him a lifetime when he comes home.'

Michael Miles loved London, and he especially loved east London on Saturday nights. It was full of women and girls, all on a mission to enjoy themselves. And he was in a position these days to make sure that happened for them. Thanks to Danny, in the last six months they had been able to spread their little pill-pushers all over the place. It was a good earn, and never in his life had Michael had so much money. It was amazing the effect a few quid could have on a body.

The house was noisy, the TV blaring as usual, and the smell of fried food was overpowering in the small space. As he combed his hair back, he could see his father watching him from the hallway. He knew his father had been in the pub for most of the day and was probably waiting for the bathroom so he could evacuate, in a noisy and deliberate fashion, the beer and jellied eels he had consumed that afternoon. He could smell the stink off him from here, but he didn't begrudge him. He worked all week in a foundry, sweating his cods off to feed them all; as far as he was concerned he was entitled to his Saturday piss-up.

Later on, he would go down the working men's club with his

wife, as usual. And start the whole process all over again. Sometimes though, with a drink in him, he could get erratic, especially since *he* had been making a name for himself with Danny. His father was happy enough with the benefits of his largesse, but now and again a paternal half hour came over him, and he would warn Michael, graphically and loudly, about the pitfalls that were almost certainly waiting to befall him. It was all a load of old pony and trap, but he would listen quietly until his father ran out of steam, and then he carried on as normal.

His old man wasn't a bad bloke, he was just caught in a trap of his own making. He was thirty-three years old and he looked more like fifty. He had a wife and three kids before he had even driven a car. He was his father, and that knowledge pained Michael more than he cared to admit. But he had stuck it out and, where they lived, that alone was a result. In his own way his father cared about them all, even his wife who was so big these days she was out of breath just walking up the two flights of stairs to their flat.

Now, his mother he was ashamed of. He loved her, adored her, but he would not be seen with her for anything. She had once been a beauty but now she wore shapeless clothes and sturdy black patent shoes that were slit down the sides to allow her bunions free rein. She had always been a happy woman, except when she'd had a drink or two, or three, with a ready smile, a constant stream of trivial conversation and a dedication to church. If Michael murdered the whole street she would stand by him. But walking with her now, being seen with her particularly when she was on the rag, was something he couldn't abide any more. And she was getting worse. It was his secret shame because everyone liked her when she was sober and no one said a word out loud about her but he knew, deep inside him, he knew that they were thinking things. Because he thought those things himself at times.

'Do you want to get in here, Dad?' His voice was respectful, as always, and he smiled at his father in the mirror to let him know he could see him.

'You're all right, son.'

His father moved out of his line of vision and he heard him go into the kitchen, his bare feet slapping on the brown-tiled floor.

Michael closed his eyes tightly. When he had a place of his own it would be somewhere he enjoyed going home to, not just a place to lay his head and keep the rain out. Like Danny said, they wouldn't end up like their parents, they were going to live their lives to the full. Or die in the fucking process.

'They're fifty pound a thousand, that's a fiver for a hundred, at three for a pound on the open market it's a nice little earner.'

The man nodded sagely. Danny didn't like him. He had a wonky eye so you weren't sure if he was looking at you or waiting for the bus to come round the corner. But he didn't care about that.

'Where'd you get them?'

Danny stared at him in mock incredulity. 'Who are you, me fucking dad?'

The man sighed heavily; he was obviously under the mistaken impression that he was a force to be reckoned with. 'Are they kosher?'

Danny looked into the face of a junkie, the dark circles and sunken cheeks were bad enough, but he also had the added bonus of dilated pupils and scummy flecks of creamy mucus at the corners of his mouth.

'Look, mate, do you want the fucking things or not?' It was dark, and the night air was damp. Danny wasn't about to get into a full-scale conversation with someone who was hard-pushed to remember his own name most of the time.

Jethro Marks nodded. 'I ain't got much choice, have I? You've removed Brendan, haven't you?'

'What you on about? I ain't done nothing to no one. He moved on and I moved in, simple as that. Now, show me your wedge and we'll do the deal.'

Jethro pulled a wad of money from his back pocket and, snatching it impatiently, Danny counted it quickly. He knew it wouldn't be light, but you could never be sure with speed freaks. Especially if they fancied themselves as dealers. He passed over the bag of pills, which *were* on the light side, a hundred and twenty out in fact. But junkies never noticed things like that. Counting the bag of goodies would be beyond him, even if he could have got his head together enough to attempt it.

Danny slipped the money into his overcoat pocket and watched as the man hurried away. Danny gave it a few seconds and then he walked out of the dark alleyway. As he stepped into the brightness of the street lamps he scanned the road for anything he might consider suspect. Bethnal Green high street was busy. Considering it was ten thirty at night there were a lot of people about. Mainly youngsters, around his age and younger. He nodded to the people he knew, and stared out the ones he didn't. It was noisy, even in the cold, motorbikes were revving and music was blaring out of eight-tracks. Everything from Elvis to The Who and the Stones.

In his suit and overcoat Danny looked far more adult than his contemporaries, most of whom were dressed in cheap winkle-pickers and bum-freezer jackets. It made Danny feel a little stab of sorrow for them, because he knew that they had no idea about life, their own or anybody else's. The girls looked all right though. At least most of them did: if a girl had a bust and a good head of hair she was already sought after by the time she was twelve. Girls, he had noticed, also had a better eye for fashion than lads. They had their mothers' make-up and perfume, hairspray and stockings. Girls were also often willing to make their own clothes, and the majority did this well.

As Danny walked up the road towards the train station he clocked each and every girl surreptitiously, checking out their faces and figures, and he was aware that many of them were looking back at him. A couple of brazen ones winked at him and smiled with their heavily painted mouths, their cigarettes held elegantly away from them, like the women they admired in the films and tried so desperately to emulate. Their back-combed hair was glossy under the street lamps, and their eyes were alert for the first sign of male interest that might come their way. It was their stomping ground; too young for the pub and too old for the park so they hung around in groups learning the intricacies of the mating ritual and enjoying their first steps in adulthood.

Danny knew that he was well known these days and considered quite a catch because of his burgeoning reputation, and that a sneaky smile would bring some of the girls over to him. So, winking at a blonde with heavy breasts and a skirt that was tighter than a nun's crack, he beckoned her to follow him.

Five minutes later she was leaning uncomfortably against a stall in the station toilets as he thrust himself inside her roughly. Afterwards he was annoyed to realise that she hadn't even bothered to put her fag out.

'Hello, son. Your mother must have stuck you in a pile of horse shit when you were a baby, you've grown bigger every time I see you.'

Timmy Wallace was a big man, with a robustness that made lesser men feel envious of him. He was an ex-bare-knuckle boxer who now ran a small drinking club in Whitechapel for the Murray brothers. They had taken it in lieu of a debt and, against all odds, had made a success of it. Although this was due more to Timmy's endearing personality and refusal to let anyone take a liberty than anything else. Every few days Danny called in there and, over the months, he had built himself a rapport with most of the clientele.

The place was small, dimly lit, and no one was going to lose any sleep if a fag was put out on the floor, or a drink was spilled on a table. It smelled of dusty wallpaper, cigarette smoke and Bitter. The clientele were Faces who either wanted a quiet drink with no juke box, to make a deal of some kind, or play cards in peace and quiet. Women were not encouraged and, on the rare occasions they did cross the threshold, they were tolerated for only a short while. Danny Boy loved it there, felt comfortable in this world of men, real men. As he slipped through the bar to the rooms out back he always felt a buzz.

'He is a fucking lump all right.' This came from a regular called Frankie Daggart, a bank robber with stunning good looks, and a fearsome reputation as a ballroom dancer. He grinned at the cheek of this kid, and enjoyed seeing him getting more and more confident as the time went on. 'Want a drink, son?'

Danny shook his head and grinned. 'Nah, thanks anyway, Frank. I still have a few calls to make before I can relax.' The men all smiled at his level-headedness: he looked twenty if he was a day. His old man must be kicking himself at the trouble he had lain on this lad's young shoulders. All the men agreed that if they had been blessed with a son like him they would have thanked God for him every day of their lives. He was a Brahma, a diamond, a fucker in the making.

As he slipped through to the back Danny could feel the goodwill emanating from all the men cluttered around the bar and it was a feeling that he cherished. Frankie Daggart was waiting outside for him when he left, a little over an hour later.

Jonjo loved his little sister but she got on his nerves. She was crying again. If she actually cried it would be different, but she didn't, she just whined. Now, at almost eleven thirty, she was getting a second wind and as he went to go into the bedroom he was almost knocked flat on his back by his mother.

She slammed into the room and shouted angrily, 'What the feck is wrong with you now?'

Annie screamed as her mother's rough hand came into contact with whatever piece of skin she could get to. After a few minutes she stopped the beating and, straightening up, she pointed a finger at the terrified child and said loudly, 'If I hear your fecking voice once more, I'll brain you, do you hear me? Your poor father is trying to rest in there, and all you can do is aggravate the shagging life out of everyone.'

She roughly pulled the covers over her daughter's shoulders and left the room. Her whole body was bristling with anger and frustration, her tired face showing the strain of her day-to-day existence. Living in this house was a constant battle of wits and her nerves were shot. Her husband was now able to move about with the aid of a stick, and her elder son made him feel he had to be grateful for every bite that went into his mouth.

Her husband was a shadow of the man she had married: the life had been drained out of him. He was quiet, even taking communion once a week when the priest popped in for a natter. As she went back into the bedroom she nailed a smile on her face and, pouring two glasses of scotch, she handed one to her husband, trying to ignore the fact that he only livened up when offered alcohol. Even that had to be done on the quiet; if Danny Boy knew, he'd go ape shit. Part of his daily enjoyment was seeing to it that his father was dry, and stayed dry. He used his father's own frail health as a weapon against him, knowing that the man couldn't do anything to stop him. Wouldn't even try.

'She needs a firm hand that one, I should have put me foot down when she was born.'

He didn't answer her, but then Ange knew he wouldn't. One-sided conversations were now the mainstay of her life.

Michael was waiting by the scrapyard, and he was freezing. As he drew deeply on his Dunhill cigarette, he kept his eyes skinned for any movement in the shadows beyond. He hated this bit of the night, he never knew what time Danny would get there, and he felt vulnerable with the wedge of money he had to carry around. His fear was finding someone lying in wait for him, determined to relieve him of his dough and give him a hammering into the bargain. The darkness was unfriendly here, the shapes of the piled-up scrap looked intimidating in the blackness. The smell was smoky, thick with dust and rust; it made him think of death for some reason. The two German Shepherds who ran loose in the yard of a night to discourage thieves were used to him now. They were oblivious to him, but he was wary of them, knowing that they were kept half-starved to make sure that they were irritable and vicious enough to scare off any errant looters. Danny could walk in there and they'd run at him like long-lost relatives after a pools win, all rolling tongues and wagging tails. Danny always had a treat for them, made a fuss of them; even their owner was impressed despite himself, they didn't even really seem to like him. They were handy though. If anyone did happen to walk by, they went berserk, throwing themselves at the fences and guaranteeing that the person soon went on their merry way.

Michael was numb with the cold now. His ears were aching and his teeth were on the verge of some hefty chattering.

'All right?'

Danny was behind him, and the loudness of his voice made Michael nearly jump out of his new shoes. 'Fucking hell, you nearly gave me a heart attack.'

70

Danny was laughing loudly, a deep resounding laugh that echoed around the place, making the dogs run to the fence barking ferociously.

'Shut up, you noisy pair of fucking gits.'

Danny was still laughing heartily and the dogs started to whine. Danny rattled the fence to annoy them, and Michael suddenly wished he had not got involved in any of it. His dad was right about Danny; he was a looney tune, and it was at these times he was reminded of that fact. The dogs were almost tearing at each other now because they couldn't get to them and Danny was winding them up by barking at them and rattling the gate chains. Michael watched him for long moments, waiting until he tired of his game. If he said anything he knew Danny would prolong it just to be awkward, to irritate him.

Michael lit another cigarette and offered it to his friend, and Danny took it from him eagerly, bored now by his baiting of the dogs and annoyed he had not provoked a reaction from his friend. Danny smoked in silence, petting the dogs now, his hand rubbing their ears, the animals pleased at the attention.

'Fucking horrible things, how you can stand to touch them, I don't know.'

Danny turned to face Michael and, frowning, he said seriously, 'Don't let them know you're scared, they can smell it off you. Dominate them and they'll do whatever you tell them without a second's thought.'

Michael had a feeling he wasn't talking about the dogs, but was warning him that he had sussed him out.

Then, sighing, he said amiably, 'It's fucking taters ain't it, mate? By the way, I picked up a bit of work from Frankie Daggart tonight. He wants me to sort out a lad who has been hassling his sister's boy.'

Michael didn't answer him, he didn't know what to say.

'Thought I'd show willing, like, see what occurs. You in or what?'

Michael nodded his agreement, as Danny had known he would.

'Got me poke then? I want to get home, it's fucking freezing out here.'

Chapter Five

'Where's me blue shirt, Mum?'

It was said with the voice Danny Boy used when in the presence of his father, a deep, slow drawl that dripped with deliberate insolence.

'Hanging in your wardrobe, son. I washed and pressed it this morning.'

Danny walked from the kitchen slowly, his huge bulk making the small space feel even more claustrophobic. His father watched him go with tired eyes. The boy was out of control and there was nothing he could do about it. To think that a child of his, a child of his blood could turn out so vicious was something he pondered on a daily basis. He was a size, and he was confident enough to know that his bulk was his greatest asset. Like many a man before him, he would earn a living off his wits and his muscles. Even the priest gave him his due, which alone told him more of his son's rise in the world than anything else.

As Big Dan sipped his tea he looked down at himself, at the wasted leg that dragged behind him, and the knuckles that were scarred from trying to stop the crowbars as they had rained down onto his prostrate form. He looked around the kitchen, saw the dramatic difference that was echoed through the flat and wondered at a boy who was so single-minded he could achieve all this just to prove a point.

His wife Ange was a bundle of nerves. She sat at the small table and sipped at her tea, her usually open face grey with worry. But he had no sympathy for her, the boy had been ruined by her from the moment he had entered the world. Aching all over, and lighting a cigarette, he smoked and drank the last dregs of his cold tea. The noise grated on his wife's nerves as it had since her first visit to his mother's house and the realisation that he had no manners at all, and had been brought up in a filthy hole by a woman who could barely string a sentence together.

Big Danny had always remembered that look on her face, could still feel the flush of shame as he looked around him, and the first stirrings of his colossal anger. An anger this little woman could inflame with a look or a word.

Now he was dependent on her, but he was getting better all the time. Eventually he would be more mobile, the doctor had assured him of that. It was what he was living for, then this scum would be out of his life once and for all.

Danny Boy walked back into the kitchen and, studiously ignoring his father, buttoned up his shirt, slowly. Every movement was calculated to irritate the man who had sired him. Then, tucking it into his trousers, he stretched languidly. Taking a wad of money from his back pocket he peeled off ten five-pound notes and threw them into his mother's lap, hushing her protestations that she had plenty by giving her a hug and a kiss. 'If you need anything else, you let me know, there's plenty more where that came from.'

His father was staring at the floor so Danny forced his head up and, looking into his eyes, said quietly, 'By the way, the Murrays send their regards.'

Jonjo was watching the little play from the doorway, his sister quiet for once as she drank in the drama of it all. Annuncia thrived on any kind of excitement, and now her eyes were bright as she surveyed her father's humiliation.

'Get yourself off now, son.' His mother would have pushed him out of the front door if she could have got away with it, and they all knew it. When Danny finally left, the whole family breathed a collective silent sigh of relief.

*

Frankie Daggart was sitting in his car outside Upney Station, listening to the radio and watching the girls as they walked by. The young men today didn't know how lucky they were, the birds were all half-naked and up for a bit of a lark. In his day you had to know where to go to bag a sort, and even then it wasn't a guarantee you'd get your leg over. That was only guaranteed with certain paper money or coins of the realm, plus copious amounts of alcohol. But he'd prided himself on never, ever paying for it outright, no matter what the occasion.

As he pictured a series of pornographic scenarios with various young girls, he was broken out of his reverie by Danny Boy Cadogan opening the passenger door and bringing a blast of arctic air inside with him.

'All right, son?'

'Yeah, you?'

Frankie was disconcerted by being caught with his metaphorical pants round his ankles and, starting up the car, he drove them to the nearby Railway Tavern.

Once inside the doorway Danny watched in awe as Frankie was greeted by each and every person, offered drinks on the house, and finally seated nearest the fire. A place where they could talk in peace, where no one could overhear their conversation, and where they were seen as *Faces*.

The place was buzzing with people and they all automatically shook hands with him, Danny Cadogan, because he was with a local hero. It was heady stuff and Danny basked in the reflected glory, wanting this for himself one day. He knew Daggart was a Face, but this reception was like nothing he had ever experienced before in his life.

'Sorry about that, son.'

Frankie could see the admiration and naked ambition in the boy's eyes and laughed to himself. If he was correct in his assumptions, this little fucker was going to make a mark that would reverberate for generations. Either that or he'd get an early life sentence for murder and his investment would be wasted. It was a chance he was willing to take anyway.

'Now, about this ponce who's earholing my sister's kid.'

Danny listened with barely concealed excitement as Frankie explained the whole sorry situation, and then described, graphically, what he saw as the only remedy.

Danny Boy couldn't wait to sort out this little problem. It was his in, it was his guarantee of approbation. It would earn him more than a few quid, it would earn him the kudos he needed, wanted. Depended on for his new livelihood.

Louie Stein was happy for once, spring had finally sprung and the days were getting longer. The yard was working at full capacity and his other business dealings were on the up. Even the totters were in a good mood, they suffered in the winter, out in all weathers, trying to grab a pound; they weren't known as hardy perennials for nothing. He was in the Portakabin watching young Danny working outside. The boy's strength was phenomenal, all the heavy lifting had broadened him, he really was a lump now. As Louie saw him making a rude gesture at a passing policeman he laughed out loud. He was a case and, from what he was hearing, he was getting his name known in the right quarters. He was a young one, but he had no fucking care for anyone else and, in their world, that was a bonus.

Louie called the boy inside a little while later and placed a large mug of tea in front of him. Danny took it gratefully and, settling himself comfortably in the filthy old armchair that was now his designated seat, he blew on it vigorously, before taking a large gulp. All the time he had been working for Louie he had never once asked for or made a beverage off his own bat, he waited till he was either given one, or told to make one. He had good manners. It was another of the things Louie liked about him.

'You got some fucking muscles there, mate, I was watching you throwing the steel about like it was polystyrene tiles!'

Danny smiled, accepting the compliment as his due.

'How are things going with the Murrays?' It was said in conversation, but there was an underlying interest that stemmed more from personal experience: something it seemed that they were both aware of.

Danny shrugged his massive shoulders. 'OK. I'm earning, they're earning.'

Louie nodded. 'Good. Remember what I told you.' He lit them both a cigarette and, passing one to the boy, said harshly, 'That pair would tuck each other up without a second's thought, so outsiders are deemed fair game. Now, I've heard a rumour that they are about to get a tug, so you keep a low profile for a while, OK. Use any reason you want, but don't score off them for the next few weeks.'

Danny listened to his friend and mentor and then he said quietly, 'Thanks for the heads up, Lou.'

But this knowledge disturbed him. How come Louie was warning him, but not warning the Murrays? After all, he was just a kid. And how did he even know it all in the first place and, more importantly, what was he personally supposed to do with this knowledge, now that he was in possession of it? It was a melon scratcher all right, and it certainly merited serious consideration before he could make any kind of decision. He wanted to weigh this all up and decide what course of action would be best for him in the long run. This was going to be a crucial decision in his life, and therefore not one to be taken lightly.

In fact, Louie giving him advice like this made him paranoid. He was just a kid, and the Murrays were a force to be reckoned with. He only had to look at his father to be reminded of that. He had to think long and hard about his next step.

'Come on, Dan, finish your food.' Ange was panicking now, her voice trembling with fear. She wanted him out of the way and was hurrying him up in case golden boy came in early. Well, his son and heir, golden boy, could go fuck himself; he wasn't in the mood for him at the moment.

'Please, Dan. Don't upset him . . .'

She was frightened of a teenage boy and, what was even worse was that so was he. Big Dan clenched his fists until the pain was too much, then he exploded. 'Will you *shut* the fuck up, Ange.'

Jonjo and Annuncia were both wide-eyed at the turn of events; their father almost sounded like his old bullying self.

'You're like a fucking scratched record, repeating yourself over and over again. Well, I've had it. Now, piss off, woman.'

Jonjo, at nine, was already a big lad and, seeing the hurt and shame in his mother's face, slammed his knife and fork onto the table and bellowed, 'Don't talk to my mum like that. You useless old bastard . . .' He was close to tears, and his dark-blue eyes were glistening in the light.

Angelica suddenly saw the similarity between her younger boy and Danny; both the living image of the man they despised and, gently sitting back down, she put her hand over her mouth, as if she was going to be sick, and held it there tightly, near to tears herself.

Dan looked at his younger son. He had never really taken any notice of him, of any of them really except for his daughter; when she set out to get his attention it was difficult to resist her. Now, as he watched the lad reach over and pick up his plate of food and throw it angrily into the kitchen sink, he saw that they were all more like him than they realised. They were all deeply flawed, just like their old man, and that legacy would hound them for the rest of their days.

He grinned nastily. 'Thanks, son, you saved me a job.'

'Fuck off.'

His mother's hand made contact with the side of his head and the pain was immediate.

'Jonjo, don't you dare speak to your father like that.'

Jonjo was holding his injured ear as he cried, 'And you can fuck off and all . . .'

His father's stick hit him on the back before he could move out of his reach and the blow knocked him flying. He hit the sink head first with a sickening thud, and the blood was pouring from the gash within seconds.

As Jonjo felt his mother picking him up he tried to escape her grasp, but the feel of her arms around him was too seductive; it had been years since she had held him for any reason. Annie was now at hysteria level, her terror for once genuine as she saw her mother trying to stem her brother's bleeding with a tea towel.

Her father looked on, white-faced and silent, as he surveyed the damage he had caused. All the time his ears strained for the sound of the front door opening and his son coming home to all this carnage. Don't go looking for trouble, his old mum used to say, it'll find you soon enough. If only he had bothered to listen to her now and again, so much trouble in his life could have been avoided.

Colin Baker walked down the road with his usual jaunty air. He was tall for his age, and at seventeen he had the poise of a much older boy. He wore his hair long and greasy, and his skin was a purple mass of acne. He had a slight stoop already, and he favoured rocker-style clothes and music. His big regret in his short life was that he had no motorbike, but that was something he was working on. He was a natural-born bully, and he made a point of using this ability at every available opportunity.

Unknown to him, the small lad with the gentle ways and thick brown hair, who he tormented on an almost daily basis, had finally cracked and reported him to his mother. Had Colin been aware he was the nephew of a known bank robber he would have tempered his anger. However, oblivious to the boy's heritage as yet, he enjoyed making his life miserable for no other reason than that he could.

As he got to his road he was surprised to see a young fellow in an expensive overcoat leaning on his front gate. He went straight into his hard-nut role: legs akimbo and hands on hips.

'What the fuck do you think you're doing?'

Danny looked him up and down as if unsure whether he was animal, vegetable or mineral. 'I was about to ask you the same thing. Colin, ain't it?'

Colin nodded slowly, unsure of himself now, wondering if this chap might turn out to be good news. He doubted that, but he was ever the optimist.

'I have a message for you from a mutual friend, *Colin*.'

Colin knew that the exchange was being watched by half the street and he opened his arms wide as if inviting a confidence.

'Do you want it now, mate? The message, I mean,' Danny said.

Colin nodded again, his natural antagonism coming to the fore. 'Well, don't stand there all night, if you got something to say, fucking say it.'

Danny's fist crunched his nose, and with that first punch the fight was well and truly over. Colin crumpled and concentrated on covering his head and face with his arms to minimise the damage. The beating was swift, brutal and very public; all the requisites needed for a warning in their world. When he was finished, Danny had hardly broken a sweat.

'That's from Frankie Daggart on behalf of his nephew, Bruce. Fucking leave the kid alone. You hear me, cunt?'

Frankie had watched everything from the comfort of his navy blue Jaguar. He couldn't have clumped the boy, he was too old, and it would have been seen as necessary but well over the top. Having Danny Cadogan, a younger lad, doing it for him, would be seen as a stroke of genius. But this young boy had a definite edge; he fought like an old hand. He had a calm and calculated precision that was instinctive. He could row all right, there was no doubt about that. But he did it with aplomb. He did it with a genuine disregard for the victim, and that was practically unheard of in this day and age. Weapons were the new order; a good fucking hammering, man to man, was not often observed any more. The boy had done good, and he would pay him well.

As they drove back to the yard Danny was shocked when Frankie said jovially, 'Poor old Bruce, bless his heart, he's as queer as a ten-bob clock. But he's a game little fucker for all that.'

Danny didn't answer him, he didn't know what to say. He wasn't sure he would have taken the job had he known that. Queers frightened him: they were an unknown quantity. But he kept that to himself, he wanted Frankie's goodwill. Nothing more and nothing less.

Annuncia was asleep; for once in her life she had done as asked without any arguing or scenes. The fright had kicked in and sleep was the only remedy. Once his head had stopped bleeding, Jonjo understood that it was not as serious as he had believed. Head wounds always bled profusely and, once it had stopped, he was disappointed to see it was little more than a small gash. His mother cleaned the kitchen up, and then made them a cup of hot sweet tea.

Then she tried to salvage the situation with her middle child. Jonjo was like his elder brother in many ways, but she was thankful for the fact he didn't have Danny's knack of turning even the most innocent of remarks into a declaration of war. She loved her children, she did. And she knew her husband's treatment of them had been disgraceful over the years, but he was *still* her husband, their father, and nothing could ever change that fact. Married in a church, they were tied for life; that was what Catholicism was all about. Especially when it suited her.

Tucked up safe and warm in bed, Jonjo listened as his mother tried to explain to him why he must never tell his brother what had happened. Her voice was soothing and quiet, and he knew that was only so his brother, should he creep into the house, wouldn't overhear what was being discussed.

'It would cause murders, child, you realise that, don't you? Now, surely you wouldn't want to think of your mammy having to referee those two again?' She was attempting to make light of the situation while, at the same time, reinforcing the seriousness of his actions if he decided to grass.

'What about Annuncia though, she'll tell him.'

Angelica closed her eyes in relief. That question said he was going to keep quiet. 'You leave that little madam to me.'

He smiled wanly. 'Why does he do it, Mum? Why don't Dad take care of us?'

She kissed his forehead gently then, stroking his hair, she sighed heavily, 'If I knew the answer to that the Dalai Lama would be out of a job!'

This son of hers was caught up in the middle, as usual. It was the bane of the middle child's life. Caught between the first-born and the last-born, they were often left to their own devices. 'He doesn't mean the half of it. Your father is a very unhappy man, you know. He's ashamed of what he did, ashamed of the fact that his gambling nearly brought disaster on us. Ashamed that his son has had to take over the reins of this household. Had to put bread on the table and a roof over our heads.'

Jonjo started to laugh then, his dry sense of humour coming to the fore. 'Mum, he never did any of that anyway.'

They laughed together, conspirators for a few moments. 'But he *wanted* to. That was once his dream, but sometimes, son, life makes it very difficult to do the right thing. Life can grind you down, especially if you never get the breaks, the chances that other people seem to get in abundance. But he's still your father, Jonjo, still your flesh and blood, no matter what he's done.'

She smiled down at this handsome boy of hers, whose life was blighted because the man she had married had more interest in women and horses than his own family. Poverty had a way of making people lose their reality; drink, drugs, gambling and whoring were symptoms, not the actual cause of people's unhappiness. That was the thing they spent their lives trying to blot out, trying to get away from, even if only for a few hours. It crept inside them, numbed them, changed them, it was like a cancer.

Big Dan Cadogan listened to his wife's voice and, for the first time in years, he felt the urge to cry. After all he had done to her, after everything that had happened between them, she could still find it in her heart to defend him to the children, the same kids he often conveniently forgot about for weeks, even months at a time, in the same way as he did her. She was just another reminder of his failure, another reminder of his complete uselessness.

Danny Boy would scalp him for this latest debacle he knew and, in a way, he welcomed that happening. It was going to happen, so it was best to get it over with once and for all. If nothing else, the Murrays had taught him that much.

Michael was listening intently to what Danny was telling him. They were sitting in a café off the Mile End Road nursing milky coffees and chain-smoking cigarettes. Neither of them liked smoking, it was just something they did to make them feel grown up. The café was far too warm, the windows were steamed up, and the smell of grease was heavy in the air.

The café owner, Denis, was a heavy-set Cypriot with a thick head of dyed-black hair, a gleaming smile, and a wandering eye. He also provided the best hash this side of Marrakesh market. Because of this he had a bustling clientele and an easygoing manner, due mainly to the fact that he smoked a large percentage of his stash himself. All the young people loved him. During the day the place was packed out with the general populace; the olds, the workers, and the displaced. But once the evening arrived, it was jukebox heaven, and a place for the teens to sit and chat over a coffee, all the while practising being a grown-up. Leaving school at fourteen was a rite of passage for these kids, and whatever their parents allowed them to keep from their wages they would spend wisely but quickly over the weekend. The weeknights were therefore mainly used by the up-and-coming young Faces. These were either classed as the new generation of prison fodder, or the new local businessmen, depending on how they conducted themselves and earned their living. Every once in a while though, a real Face would emerge, someone who would be a real name. Someone who would one day not only be feared but also respected.

Denis came over to the table and placed another two coffees in front of them; pulling out a chair noisily he sat down. It was gone midnight and there was a lull in customers. Leaning on the table he said easily, 'Hey, Danny, I hear you can shift stuff.'

Danny shrugged nonchalantly. 'So?'

'I am going to Cyprus for one month. My Cypriot wife is having a baby and I must go there. May she have a boy this time, please God. Marianna will run this place for me with her sister, but I need someone to keep my regular customers supplied. You know what I mean, yeah?' He winked at the two boys.

Danny knew what he meant, all right, his smile said it all.

'It's only for a short while, and you'd be well paid for it. So, what do you say?'

Michael watched as Danny processed the information, then he said quietly, 'How much will we get?'

'A oner, payable when I get back.'

Michael frowned then, and Danny smiled as he heard the outrage in his friend's voice. 'How many people you talking about us supplying for you, Denis? How much do they want, how often do they want it and how much running about does this all involve?'

Danny shrugged then, his eyes hard. 'Well, answer him then, Denis. He ain't called the human abacus for nothing, is he?'

Denis was surprised at all the questions, but brought out a small, dog-eared notebook from his trouser pocket and threw it onto the table. Michael picked it up and quickly scanned the pages, working out the economics of the deal.

'What is he doing, Danny?'

Denis was now nervous: Michael had not been a part of the equation. He had heard nothing about him at all.

Danny sighed heavily. 'He's working it all out, mate, that's what he does, see? It's what's called his forte. Look and learn, because if you ain't earning to your full potential, or you're trying to rip us off, this little fucker will know.'

Denis didn't answer and Danny went silent while his friend worked out the possible returns they could expect from their new friend's business. Finally, after fifteen minutes, he politely handed the notebook back to Denis.

'So. What do you think, Mike?' Danny sounded bored, without an interest in any of it.

Michael shook his head slowly. 'Not worth the aggro really, Dan. A oner a *week* each, then maybe . . . We'd have to do drops all over the Smoke and, as we don't drive, and as we're not car thieves, it will mean a lot of public transport. Given the time this would take, then combine that with the risk factor and we couldn't do it for any less than a oner each a week for the duration. That will be four hundred a month, times two.'

Denis was laughing his head off at these two young men; he knew Danny was sound as a pound, he had asked around for a while and it was this boy's name that kept cropping up. But, watching them like this, working out the pros and cons was as ludicrous as it was hilarious. Marianne's brother would do it much cheaper, but he would serve every one of his customers up light, causing them to look elsewhere. He was also looking to keep it out of his English wife's family's hands. This boy, this Danny Cadogan, was already working for the Murrays, among others.

'We also want a cut off each person we weigh out. You are on the trot, we will look out for your end. We won't offer anyone an in, or shout your rout about: you have my word on that.'

Denis knew this would cost, but he also knew he wouldn't lose anyone. Once he returned they would fade back into the woodwork. It was a win-win situation, and he knew it. 'You've got a deal.'

'Half the money upfront, and the rest on completion.'

Michael was serious as he said that and laughing uncontrollably at his front, Denis held out a meaty paw and the boys shook hands with him.

'You two are fucking funny. Come in tomorrow night and I'll walk you through it all OK? Anything you want, boys, it's on the house . . .'

He was laughing as he left them, but he also guessed that one day they would be his superiors. Danny, anyway. He was on the road to perdition, the road to riches, the road to his own personal hell. Denis could see that this was a boy who would need careful handling in the years to come, and woe betide anyone who didn't have the sense to work that one out.

Danny and Michael looked at each other for a few moments before Danny said, 'Well done, Mike. You have a gift for working out fractions, don't you? Well, for that, you can skank a third of the action, fair enough?'

Michael nodded happily, it was a third more than he had expected. He would have done it for nothing. He knew that the weekly wage he had astutely commanded for himself from the Greek would be taken over and a percentage given back to him.

But Danny knew that Michael would be worth his weight in gold when any future deals were going down. He was a fucking diamond, and he had his best interests at heart. Danny would gather the work in and Michael could work the earn out. They were a good team, had been best mates since they were little kids, and Danny knew he could trust him. And, in this new, grown-up world they were entering, that was more important to him than anything else.

Big Dan was in the kitchen, an empty mug in front of him, the radio playing Del Shannon gently in the background. He was waiting for his son to come home. He was stiff and aching, the tiredness that was now his constant companion was threatening to overtake him. He would never fully recover from what had happened to him, physically or mentally, but he was feeling stronger as each day passed. But the urge to gamble, have a little flutter, was overpowering sometimes. It made him edgy as he imagined the time being wasted, sitting in this fucking flat, when he could be out playing cards with his cronies, or smoothing out his frayed edges with a few stiff drinks and a close encounter with a bit of strange.

His wife had driven him mad over the years; the harder their lives had got, the easier it had become to find reasons for not going home. And seeing Ange out working that first time had just proved to him that they could get by without him. The feeling of suffocation his wife and children brought to him at times made his drunken absences almost necessary. He knew that he had been kidding himself for years and that his son's hatred of him was justified. He could even understand his elder boy's actions over the six hundred pounds owed. When he thought of that amount now, sober as a judge and with a clear-headedness that he had last experienced over fifteen years before, he could see what he had become.

But, even knowing that, and accepting his part in the whole sorry saga, he couldn't stay in this house a moment longer if his son didn't make the atmosphere easier. For Ange and his younger brother and sister and, ultimately, for him.

Sober and contrite, he had seen the disarray he had caused in his family's life; he had seen it with a clarity that had brought back memories of his own childhood and his own father's neglect. He had bullied his father at the end, sensing his weakness and going in for the kill, much as his own son was doing to him now. Now he knew that, without a doubt, the sins of the fathers were visited on the children even unto the third and fourth generations.

God help the poor bitch who landed his elder son. He would end up torturing her, but all the while he would really be torturing himself. It was as if his own father had been reincarnated as his namesake. He had hated him all his life, and then, somehow, he had turned into him. Now his son hated him in the same way he had hated his own father. His old man, another Danny Cadogan, would have loved this. His mother though, had not had even a shred of loyalty in her bones. She walked away from them all without a backward glance. Gone for weeks or months on one of her benders when life got too much for her. Whereas his poor old Ange, God love her, had far too much loyalty for her own good. Especially where he was concerned.

*

Danny was staring down at the twisted body of his once proud father. His mother was beside him, her eyes frightened, as they always were when she looked at him these days. 'Leave him, let him sleep, son. You get away to your bed and leave me to deal with him.'

Danny watched his father wake up and slowly take in his surroundings. He looked old, old and haggard, and he wondered why this didn't bother him at all. But then, considering the beatings he had taken off him over the years, coupled with the scams, the lies and the mental abuse, he supposed that was just natural. He would never forgive his father for the sheer hatred that he had engendered in his young body. For the humiliation he had heaped on them all because he had gambled their daily bread without a second's thought for the consequences. His father was, without doubt, a worthless cunt, a useless wanker. And he loathed him.

His mother had become a bundle of nerves though, and this irritated him as much as it upset him. She was always trying to keep the peace lately, trying to make them get on. She'd start off wanting them to hate him, which they did, then wanting them to forgive him, which they couldn't. Standing there in her old nightie and her overlarge dressing gown, she looked much older than her years. But then she always had done, and it was all down to this man: her husband.

'Go to bed, Mum, will you.'

Ange heard the flat tone her son used when he was near his father, knew it was meant as an insult to him, and knew it was taken as one.

She opened her mouth to speak once more. She was unsure how to deal with the situation, knowing her husband was at the end of his tether.

'Go to bed, Mum, for fuck's sake. And stay there.' Danny grabbed her by the elbow then, and escorted her none too gently from the confines of her kitchen, and she didn't try to stop him. There was something in his voice, in his demeanour, that put paid to any kind of reaction on her part.

As he opened her bedroom door to push her inside he whispered, 'Do me a favour, Mum, just for once keep out of it.' He closed the door behind her, firmly, and with a finality that communicated itself to everyone in the house.

His father watched him warily as he came back into the room, the flat was too small to keep anything a secret. He had come to see that all the arguments and fights over the years had been heard by not just his own family, but by everyone else in the near vicinity. Being sober and sensible was a harsh judgement on a man.

Danny looked down on his father, the big man who was suddenly nothing more than a crumpled wreck. Any fear that he had felt was long gone, all that remained was hate.

Big Dan was once more in charge of his emotions, remembered that he had a mission of sorts. 'This can't go on, Danny Boy. It's not doing anyone any good.'

He saw his son smile, and he looked so like himself it was uncanny. He could see himself at the same age, strong in mind and body. Saw what *should* have been, *could* have been. And was reminded of the life he had wasted, until finally, after years of being so drunk, so fucking out of it, that he had finally arrived at this moment, this awful, awkward, fucking terrible, embarrassing moment and he had not even seen it coming.

'What, and you think that I ain't sussed that out for meself?' Danny Boy grinned, his strong white teeth reminding his father once more of what he had lost over the years, not just physically but mentally. He was a shadow of his former self, a caricature of the man who had fathered three children and who didn't even know them or anything about them.

Until now, that had not bothered him one iota. 'Seriously, son. We have to—'

'Shut the fuck up!' Danny shook his head slowly. His eyes were without emotion, something people didn't notice until too late; his smile was usually enough for most people. Like all good-looking mortals he got away with murder. He interrupted his father with a force that shocked them both. 'I *ain't* your fucking *son*, me mother's son *maybe*, but you are *fuck all* to me.'

'I'm your father no matter what *you* might wish and, believe me, *son*, that ain't something I'd broadcast to the world. But, this ain't about us, son, it's about them.' He pointed towards the hallway with a gnarled, smoke-stained finger and his righteousness and bitterness amazed them both.

'You've got some fucking front.'

'More front than Brighton, me son, something you seem to have inherited, whether you like it or not. But this stops *now*, you lairy little fucker. I'll go, leave, if that's what you want, but I'll go because I choose to, and not because you drove me out.'

Danny Boy looked down on the man who had fathered him and said, seriously now, 'That was for me mother's benefit, I assume.'

Big Dan Cadogan smirked and, hunching his shoulders up while holding out his arms in a gesture of friendliness, he said seriously, 'I'll walk, son. I'll go.'

Danny Boy aped him, hunching his own shoulders and opening his own arms out wide, he bellowed, 'Oh! Hark at you, the big I am or, as we prefer to think of you, Dad, the big fucking I ain't. Because you're nothing, mate, a big zero, the only thing keeping you under this roof is me mother and, like you, she's fucked herself.'

'You love the bones of that woman, and you know it.'

'Do I? I wonder about that lately. Now, sit back down and shut up while I give you some advice. Advice I would take on board if I was you, because you are finished as far as I am concerned. This is my gaff now and you'd better remember that.'

Chapter Six

Big Danny wasn't sure how to react to his son any more. He looked at the boy who had grown up under the guidance of his haphazard parenting. The boy who he knew had every right to hate him, the boy he was sorry he hadn't bothered to get to know because he seemed like someone who would make his mark. The same boy who had seen fit to cripple his own father without a speck of remorse, and he knew that it was too late to do anything about it, to lessen this boy's hatred and anger. He shook his head slowly.

'I don't expect anything from you, no more than you would from me. But listen, son, I fucking well ain't sitting around letting *you* dictate to me. I would rather sleep in the gutter.' It was said with real meaning, emotion. It was also said far too late, and they both knew that.

Danny sat down opposite his father and lit himself a cigarette. Meanwhile, Big Dan's courage was deserting him by the second, and he was overwhelmed with guilt at the realisation of what he had inadvertently created and unleashed onto the world. He knew now that this boy of his was devoid of any real human emotion. He was a cold and callous young lad who cared for no one, and talking to him was pointless. He reminded him of himself.

'The gutter is somewhere I think you are far more acquainted with than I am, Dad.'

It was an honest statement and it hurt. Big Dan saw himself, and the picture was terrifying; he was too far gone in life to be able to answer for his mistakes. But, that aside, his son bothered him enough to make him listen to his advice.

'Do you see yourself now, Danny Boy?' He was going to try to make this boy listen to him and understand what he could teach him. What he could help him with, in their world, their dangerous world. 'Well, sonny, I've got news for you. You *are* me, mate, you are like the spit out of my mouth and, do you know what scares me most? I'm a pisshead, a gambler, a fucking nonsense, but what's your excuse, eh?'

He laughed then, and it was a deep, full belly-laugh. 'Oh I'm going, son. I'll get out of your fucking way, don't worry. You can have them, the whole fucking tribe. But remember this: one day this will be *you* sitting here. I'm your future and, like me, you'll be hated by the people who should love you the most. I hoped you might listen to what I had to say, but you'll never listen to anyone, will you? Mr Know-it-all. You're a *cunt*, like I am, and my father was before me. I just want you to do me one favour, right?'

He sighed then, heavily, as if it was all too much for him, which it was. 'Look out for this lot, will you? Because I won't. I've naused it up, just like you will. But try, like I tried, to make it all right. It's harder than it looks.'

Danny saw his father then, saw him as he always had, taking the easy way out. Passing the buck, forwarding his responsibilities onto the nearest mark. He smiled himself then, his father's double, forcing himself to keep calm, to stop himself from ripping the man to pieces. He needed him at this time, he needed his knowledge and his acumen. 'Shut the fuck up, you ponce, and listen. Before you walk away from us once more, answer me this one question.'

'What fucking question is that then? Why should I fucking do anything for you, eh?' And he laughed again, a spiteful, nasty laugh.

'Because if you don't, *Dad*, I'll fucking *kill* you. And that is not an idle threat. I'm just waiting for you to give me an excuse to take you out of the game once and for all. You have to prove to me that you have something I *need*, something I *want*. If you can't do that much . . .' He left the sentence unfinished, knowing his father was more than aware of what he was really trying to say. He was offering him an out; now it was about whether or not he chose to take it. The atmosphere was heavy with suppressed violence, both knew that one wrong word was all that was needed to herald a bloodbath of Olympian standards. Danny Boy was just looking for an excuse to lose it big time.

Big Dan Cadogan looked at his son, and knew that he must be in dire need to request his expert opinion. It was a chance to redeem himself, and he was happy to take it.

'What do you want to know then?'

'Can I, or can I not, trust Louie Stein?'

Big Dan sighed. His shock at the question threw him, making him wonder what had brought it about in the first place. The question had actually *piqued* his interest. Something that had never happened before. Suddenly Big Dan wanted to know what was going on; he missed being on the front line, knowing what the buzz on the pavement was. 'Trust the Jew over who?'

Danny Boy smiled lazily. He knew his father had finally sussed out his quandary and now wanted to know who else might be in the frame. 'Who do you fucking think?'

Big Dan sat back in his chair, knowing that his answer had to be as truthful and as honest as possible if he wanted to help this son of his. Which, despite the boy's arrogance, he suddenly found that he did want to help him. Really wanted to help him, for no other reason than that he cared. This shocked him even more than it would have done his son, if he had known.

'Well, the Murrays are carrion, fucking parasites, I should know that better than anyone, as I'm sure you understand. Louie Stein is like the Virgin Mary in comparison. But why are you asking me all this now?'

Danny Boy ignored him. He had no intention of getting into any kind of conversation with this man. 'Has Louie Stein *ever* been suspected of grassing anyone?'

His father shrugged and shook his head slowly. 'Not that I know of but, remember this, son, Louie has been around for the duration, whereas the Murray boys rely on the likes of me, and that includes *you*, son. I ain't excusing what I did, what happened, but I honestly don't remember *any* of it, and the Murrays took us for six large. Us, mate, because once I owed them, *you* all owed them, young as you were. Oh, I know you'll go your own road, but I hope you have better luck than me where that pair are concerned. Bollocks to you and your fucking dreams of the big time. The Murrays will destroy you and laugh while they do it.' He pulled himself to his feet slowly, his body felt like it was on fire with pain. The stiffness was in every joint, and the popping of his bones was loud in the room. 'You served me up to them, son, and I accept that, you did what you had to for your brother and sister. I mugged us all off, so I know what you did better than anyone. But don't you ever think for one moment the Murrays will *respect* you for it. Because they won't. They use everyone and anyone. Louie is the dog's knob in comparison. You could trust him with anything.

'Louie has a few Filth on his pay, of course he does. He'd have to in his game, wouldn't he? I'd hazard a guess he's had a whisper and he's just putting the hard word on you, warning you to be careful.'

Danny Boy nodded in agreement. It was the answer he expected, he had trusted Louie but, as a young man, he needed his first impressions to be accurate. He had to learn the hard way how their world worked. He was fourteen going on ninety, and he had to be seen to back the winning team. He was sensible enough to know that he did not have the experience to do that yet. Though his instinct had been proved right, that Louie wasn't a grass, it still didn't mean he was on a winning streak.

'Do you realise that this is the longest conversation we've ever had in our lives, *Dad*? Don't you find that sad? I do.'

Big Dan looked down into his son's eyes; it was like looking in a mirror. Oh, hindsight was a wonderful thing. For he had lost them all, just as he had finally understood how wonderful they really were, how blessed he was that they were his flesh and blood. Now it was too late to make amends, to tell them how lucky he was to have them in his life. He could cry with the realisation of how great his kids actually were, and how he had never bothered to find any of that out because he was too busy gambling and whoring, too busy forgetting that they actually existed in case he had to do something about it.

Danny Boy watched his father as he battled to keep his emotions under control, and he sighed once more. This man was everything he hated, everything he was determined not to be, no matter what happened to him in this life. But now that this moment had come, he knew he couldn't let him go, let him leave them again. After all, people admired him because he let this old ponce live under his roof, even after what he had done to them all. Family, after all, was family. The East End code, the biggest fucking lie of all. The lie to end all lies really.

And if he let him go, who knew what he would say once he was back on the drink, back on the game circuit, back on the pavement, back losing and, subsequently, back needing money for his bets or his alcohol. He was a liability, there was no doubt about that. But he was also a fountain of wisdom where the Faces were concerned. For that alone, he would humour him, use him.

'I appreciate what you're telling me, *Dad*, and because of that you can stay. You *are* staying, I take it?'

Closing his eyes Big Danny accepted his fate. Unlike him, his son had a shrewd head on his shoulders and, though he was only a boy, he looked every bit the man and, more to the point, he was being treated like one by most of the people in his orbit. All the years Big Dan had bullied and controlled his family, ignored them, or conveniently forgot about them, were now coming back to bite him on his arse and there was nothing he could do about it. He had created this monster and it was evident that he was not going anywhere until this boy had decreed that he could.

As his son stood up to leave the room he pulled a half-bottle of Black & White whisky from his pocket. Placing it gently on the table he said sadly, 'You drew first blood, Dad, remember that in the future, won't you?'

'You all right, son?'

Louie's voice was low, but Danny could detect the nervousness that was there lately. Stein's voice had developed a slight quivering quality that wasn't evident to anyone except those closest to him. Danny didn't know how to react, wasn't experienced enough to suss out the situation properly, and this galled him. He shrugged his enormous shoulders and smiled gently. 'I'm all right, Lou, give me a break.'

Louie didn't say anything for a while, instead he poured them both a cup of tea. Danny looked round the office and, as always, his eyes skimmed over the pictures of semi-naked women Sellotaped to the door. They were there for no other reason than they were expected. Danny Boy knew that Lou had no real interest in the fairer sex; his wife and kids were enough for him. And with five daughters Louie Stein was uncomfortable with pictures that depicted girls younger than them. Danny Boy also knew though, that the majority of the men they dealt with spent their lives either eyeing up, reminiscing about, or talking about strange. And therefore it was part of the image, that was all. Strange was on *his* mind, but he was a kid; these pictures were a statement against old age. He could get a hard-on if he stood too near a spin-dryer. This lot would be hard-pushed to get an erection unless their wives won the accumulator on the bingo. They were all talk, all they had was their imaginations, and Danny Boy was sorry for them because of that. No woman would ever dictate his life, his leisure time or, indeed, his fucking wages. He was far too shrewd to get involved in that kind of game. He was keeping his family because of shite like that. Because his father saw his own world as far more important than his kids' world, with their wants and needs.

As Danny glanced at the dark-haired girl in the picture, her legs splayed apart and her heavy eye make-up only serving to highlight her extreme youth, he wondered at the world of men. Men like his father, men like the Murrays, men who cared for no one but themselves. This girl was a wank, a toss, something to be used over and over again, even when she was a pensioner; the pictures would be around till the next millennium. Tits and arse, after all, were tits and arse. But at least she had a reason for flashing her clout; her kids more than likely. Women did things for their kids that were deemed awful by the majority of the community they happened to live in. Men, though, seemed to be forgiven for the most heinous of crimes.

Pictures were all right, but nothing like the real thing. He loved the world he had discovered; hot, wet girls and buckled knees. The breathlessness before and after the event, even the feeling of disgust as the girl tried to make conversation with him as she tidied herself up. Especially as, by then, all he wanted to do was leave as soon as possible.

Louie watched him and grinned. He could remember the constant hard-on years. When life was still for living and summers seemed far too long and humid. 'You might not believe this now, son, but one day the world *won't* be your fucking oyster any more, one day those girls on the wall will cease to be a possibility in your mind; they'll be a fucking fantasy you hate yourself for instead. One day, *you'll* wake up and thirty or forty years will have flown by. One day, if you ain't careful, you'll be *me*.'

Danny Boy smiled gently, his even teeth and square jaw reminding Louie how young he actually was, and how he would give anything to swap places with him if it was at all possible. 'Could be worse, mate, I could end up like me father.'

Louie didn't laugh at that as was expected, instead he shook his head and said abruptly, 'Listen, that will never happen to you, not if I have anything to do with it anyway.'

Louie's complete dismissal of anything like that ever happening to him pleased the boy; it was his biggest fear and they both knew it.

Louie lit himself a cigar, pulling on it loudly, concentrating on it for long moments, savouring the bitterness of its taste, and the smoothness of the smoke when he eventually blew it out. He sat down then, opposite the boy, and stared at him rudely, his eyes taking him in from his shoes to his eyebrows; it was the long look, the once-over. It was a deliberate act, and Danny watched and waited for the man's final remarks.

'Did you heed my advice about the Murrays?'

Louie knew the boy was still a raving virgin where their world was concerned, and he also knew that this state of affairs wouldn't, and couldn't, last long. He blew a long, slow line of blue smoke into Danny's face, knowing then he wouldn't get an answer from him. Knowing the boy was worried about the advice he had been offered, and also knowing the boy had good reason to feel like that. Why he felt the need to justify himself, Louie Stein wasn't entirely sure. He had more or less convinced himself it was because he *liked* the boy, but he knew it was about more than that. 'Look, Danny, I am telling you this as a learning curve, right? I had a dabble recently with a few Faces from the Elephant and Castle. They told me to watch my back where the Murrays were concerned. I passed that gem of wisdom onto you; they own most of the Filth in their domain, and their opinions are sought after by the majority of people I work with or drink with, do you get my drift? So, if you are determined to pursue the criminal footpath, my advice would be to learn the difference between a spinner and player. Keep your head down, your mouth shut, and your arse up, that way you'll never go wrong.' He puffed on the cigar once more, the smoke so dense that Danny had to wave his hands in front of his face to disperse it.

'One last thing, son, never bite the hand that's good enough to feed you either.'

It was a threat, a friendly warning, and Danny knew it was meant well, that Louie was offended and that he had every right to feel that way; he had been good to him, and it was only Danny's youth that had made him so suspicious. It was a learning curve all right, that Louie would be in the know should have been evident to him, something he knew instinctively. He was aware he had been chastised and he was grateful for that. It meant he was still in with a chance, still on the payroll.

Danny sipped his tea, digesting everything with his usual calm, and Stein admired his stoic demeanour. He knew the boy had accepted this reprimand with equanimity.

'You're a good kid, Danny, *kid* being the operative word here, of course. But don't fucking push it, you're new on the pavement, and you're a funny little fucker. People like you, but all that can change in a heartbeat; you ask the Murrays if you don't believe me.'

Louie puffed on his expensive cigar, it was making his eyes water, but he loved it. Churchill had smoked these very cigars, though he had probably got them for free. He, however, purchased them cut-price from a little Greek fella with a temper that was worthy of a much larger man. He knew everyone who was anyone, and he had made it his life's work to keep them all on-side. He kept out of personal feuds if it was at all possible, and he never discussed anything he overheard. In his line of business that had to be a guarantee. The boy's obvious uneasiness over his friendly advice had angered him; he had stuck his neck out to help him in more ways than one. Although a part of him understood the boy's reticence, knew he was a brand-newey and still wondering what end was up, another part of him was aching to slap him down.

Danny stood up and shook the hand that was feeding him and his family firmly, the smile on his face displaying what he regarded as the required expression of remorse he felt was needed. But the damage was already done; they both knew that.

Mary Miles was walking home from school with Jonjo Cadogan, and as they passed her block of flats they giggled. She was supposed to be at Mass, and he was supposed to be playing football, they had told the lies so often they came naturally to them. As they walked towards the waste-ground that doubled as a park, they heard her brother Gordon approach on his bike.

'Look at that bleeding thing, ain't you embarrassed to be seen on it?' Jonjo's voice was heavy with malice; he resented the intrusion into their little world. Even though he didn't think Mary harboured any of the feelings that he did, he still resented any kind of intrusion, even from her brother, her flesh and blood. His love for her frightened him at times; it was so intense. Just to be near her was enough for him most of the time, but when someone else entered the equation he couldn't control his feelings. Gordon, however, rarely brought out the jealousy inside him, he was her brother after all, but he spent so much time with her that Jonjo saw him as a nuisance, as a necessary evil.

Gordon grinned knowingly. He had the same golden hair as his sister and the same crooked smile. They were a handsome family, and they knew it. Mary was already blossoming and that was why her older brother watched her like a hawk. At nine she already knew too much for her own good, and she understood how easy it was to get the males in her life to do whatever she wanted.

Gordon skidded to a halt beside them, his heavy body

cumbersome and making him seem even more gauche than usual. The bike was a mongrel. It was an embarrassment really, made up from bits of scrap he had salvaged from friends and neighbours; functional but ugly. He was slaughtered because of it, yet he knew that it was a means to an end. He had wheels, which was more than a lot of his contemporaries could say.

He had learned many years before that front was the main ingredient needed to survive on the streets, and he possessed it in fucking glorious abundance. Now he grinned once more, only his sister knowing that he was seconds away from clumping his friend and neighbour over his derogatory remark. 'I ain't embarrassed, Jonjo, it's one bike more than *you've* got, whatever it looks like.'

Jonjo knew when he was being put in his place and he accepted the reprimand with good grace. After all, any bike was indeed better than no bike at all. 'I was joking, can't you take a fucking joke?'

Gordon shook his head sadly. 'No, actually I can't, not from the likes of you anyway.'

He looked at his antagonist with real hatred as he said loudly, 'You coming home, Mary? Mum was looking for you.'

Mary Miles sighed heavily; if her mum was on the prowl that meant she was pissed as the proverbial newt. It meant pain, physical as well as mental, it meant hours of drama and recriminations, and it also meant she would be expected to sort it out with the Filth when they arrived; and they would arrive, her mother would make sure of that. It was her new party piece, and she enjoyed the drama of it all.

The police were used to Mary's intervention when her mother was on the rag; they relied on her, in fact, to talk her mother down, and to settle any disputes that were on her current agenda. Her mother had started to have arguments with the neighbouring households without a second's thought; vicious, violent rows that were always her fault, and always ended in a physical fight. A punch-up was now her mother's release valve, it was how she coped with her everyday life. She had become the local joke and it made her kids' lives unbearable. They had to live with her personal vendettas, her increasingly frequent drunken ramblings and, worse that, they had to face their classmates, all more than aware of the situation or, more often than not, whose parents were on the receiving end of the shouting and swearing.

Parents were a pain, but she didn't care about any of that. Not until she had to anyway. All she cared about was the here and now, the future was a foreign country. Now though, thanks to her brother, Mary Miles had to go home and investigate her mother's latest escapade, find out who she had fought with, then try to smoothe it all over. It was so unfair; all she wanted was a regular life, no more and no less.

'Is she indoors, Gordon?'

He grinned then, displaying his perfect teeth.

'She is now. She's *indoors* with Lily Law; they've nicked her for assault and battery, threats to kill and discharging a firearm.'

Jonjo started to laugh then, the charges didn't really surprise any of them. Mrs Miles was a case; she was a one-woman arrest record. She was the loveliest lady in the world when sober, but give her a drink and she was a fucking nightmare. She was already on a suspended sentence for her last foray, that included shooting out the optics in the pub, and then somehow arguing it was mistaken identity. She was also still on bail for breech of the peace and lewd behaviour, this was caused by her insisting on stripping off in the local working men's club while threatening the real stripper with death on pain of torture and destruction. Her sin being that she had accepted a drink off Mr Miles while his wife was within their vicinity.

Jonjo was sorry for his friend, but she had become used to this kind of thing happening. Her mother was the stuff of nightmares, a drunk who saw insults and aggro where there wasn't anything remotely troublesome going on. She could make a simple 'Good Morning' sound like a declaration of war. She also had access to an air gun that no one, even her own family, could ever lay their hands on. She could be drunk as a skunk, but she always managed to hide the bastard thing before she was finally tracked down. When she had slept it all off though, no one was sorrier than she was. In their world though, a woman who drank was vilified far more than a man. Women were still held up as paragons of virtue, even if their old men were robbing, thieving, lying shitbags. The women were held accountable for their actions, the men weren't.

'Discharging a firearm? How did she get hold of the gun this time?'

Gordon shook his head, the smile gone from his eyes now. 'I don't know, Mary, I think it was the old man's. He was probably going out on the rob again.' It was said simply, without any emotion or excitement.

'I better get home, Jonjo . . . See you tomorrow, eh?'

Jonjo nodded, wondering at her calmness, knowing that if her mother was found guilty she would be looking at a lump and a half.

'Good luck, mate.'

Mary laughed sadly. 'Good luck? What's that when it's at home?'

Chapter Seven

'My life is shit, son, and you know it. You've made sure of that. Me own husband afraid in his own home, I never thought I'd live to see the day.'

Angelica Cadogan sounded for all the world like a woman hard-done-by, as if her husband was innocent of any charges that might be brought against him. Danny couldn't believe his ears.

'You fucked your own life up, Mum, then you fucked up ours.'

'I gave my life to you children . . .'

'Pull the other one, Mum, it plays "A Hard Day's Night". You never gave us *fuck all*, and you know it.'

Danny Boy turned from his mother, refusing to listen to her ranting.

'Don't you dare turn your back on me, boy.'

He sighed in annoyance, wanting to hurt her as she had hurt him, had hurt them all. 'You'd serve us all up in a heartbeat if it got you an audience with your old man, and we all know it, Mum. We have lived with that knowledge for years. You only care about us when you're alone in the world, when the old man goes on the trot. Once he's back, you blank us again.'

The truth hurt and Angelica knew that better than anyone. It was why she was getting so angry with this boy before her. Her first-born son, the lad who had kept it all together and made sure they were taken care of. Her guilt and shame made her lash out then, 'You vicious little bastard . . .'

Danny Boy held up his hand and said sadly, 'Don't do this,

Mum. Please. He's fucking scum, he always has been, and you know that better than I do. Don't try and justify his behaviour, or your treatment of us because of it. Look, Mum, I'm fucking warning you, please don't start me off on one. Not tonight.' He was pointing his finger in her face, his anger was there for anyone to see, and she knew it was taking all the strength he possessed to pretend that he didn't know what she wanted from him. It was a game they had played many times in the past. Only this time he wasn't going to let her get away with it. They both knew he wasn't going to play her game any more.

She shook her head sadly, her eyes dark with pain and her tears now genuine. 'Please, son, do this for me, eh? He's my husband, your father . . .'

She was almost begging once more, and they both knew it. For Danny it was enough to break him down, but only if he had been foolish enough to let her empty words have an effect. Instead, he had hardened himself to her pleas. He hated her for the fact that she saw this drama as even necessary, that she thought he was that soft she could still talk him round, even after all that had happened.

'I've said he can stay. But I still hate him, Mum. Don't make me start to hate you as well. He cares nothing for this family, stop trying to make him into something he ain't. Something he can never be. Never was, for that matter.'

His mother's face was screwed up in temper, her voice loaded with malice. 'He is a cripple, thanks to you. He has nothing any more. We're all he's got now, boy.'

Danny Boy shook his head in consternation. That she was trying to garner some kind of sympathy for his father was too much, was going too far.

'He might be a raspberry ripple, Mother, but no one cares about that, do they? If he had been left to his own devices the same thing could have befallen any one of us. He beat us all, you included and, if we'd been left a raspberry, he would not have given a flying fuck. But then you know that, don't you, deep down in your fucking so-called heart. He could have crippled you or me in his hey-day. Kicking and punching us, shouting the odds. He put his fag out on your face, I saw him do it. So bollocks to him, and bollocks to you and all.'

He stepped towards her then and, for the first time, she felt in fear of him; he could almost smell it off of her. It didn't make him feel bad, it just reaffirmed his belief that without him this family would have sunk without trace. This woman, his own mother, aggravated him nowadays: she just made him more aware of how base and how untrustworthy most women could be. She thought he was a live one, a fucking Greebo. Thought he was cunt enough to swallow her old crap and let that leech back into all their lives as if nothing untoward had happened. He, Danny Boy Cadogan, had taken on the mantle of man of the house, had taken over the bills, everything. He had been forced to. That they had never been so well-off in their lives was a bonus, yet she would still rather be at the mercy of that ponce, his so-called father, than be with her own kids. Be content with her children, her real family. She wanted the man who had destroyed them all in one way or another. It was a real eye-opener for him.

And it hurt him to know his mother still felt the need of the man who had almost brought about the family's downfall.

All this aggro for a bunk-up, for a shag, because that was all that this could be about. His father had given them nothing all their lives except a harsh word or a good hiding. His mother, on the other hand, had spent her life trying to avoid all of that, had tried to protect everyone, herself included, from his drunken assaults. Now she was acting like they were a fucking perfect match, a love job. He had sacrificed his childhood for her, for his family, and she was asking him to forget the past, act like it had never happened. She was asking him to pretend they were all hunky-dory; it was a fucking diabolical liberty on her part.

She was obviously missing him in some way. But how? She couldn't be missing his silver tongue, that was for sure. Nor his fucking humungous wallet. They had only seen him when he was borassic lint, when he had spent his wages, had one bet too many. Pissed up and itching for a fight was when they finally got him. Then he would come home to them like the avenging angel of Christ. All fists and terror, bad-mouthing her, beating her up, then taking her to his bed with a threat and a punch, his kids left to listen to it all as they huddled under the covers waiting for him to start on them.

This latest thing though was all about her, her needs. Was about her getting her fucking end away. Gnawing the bone. It was a disgrace as far as he was concerned. For the first time ever she had enough money, she didn't have to scrub anyone's house, didn't have to kneel on anyone's floor, and it still wasn't enough for her. He couldn't provide the main ingredient she needed. Heating, light, food, drink, a bit of bingo when she fancied it, was second rate, all she seemed to want was her old man back in her bed, no matter what he had done to her kids, or to her, for that matter. Women, he now realised, were not to be trusted. All his life his mother had run his father down to him, all his life he had heard nothing except how fucking useless he was and how he should never be like him.

And he had listened to his mother for years; she was the fountain of all knowledge, especially where his father was concerned. Plus he had seen it with his own eyes. Seen what a useless cunt for a father he had been lumbered with. Consequently, none of them had any time for him, except their little sister, but she didn't count. No one begrudged his love for her, that was expected, that was the only decent thing he had going for him as far as they were concerned.

Now though, it seemed, if you listened to their mother, this father of his was on a par with the Second Coming. He was now more sinned against than sinned, a poor man who had been trying to fight the odds all his life. What fucking drainhole did she think her sons had climbed out of?

He paid all the bills, something his father had been loath to do all his life. Ergo, as far as he could see, that meant that *he* now ran the whole fucking shebang. Just because his mother was once more a wife, it didn't mean they had to jump on the bandwagon with her.

A raspberry ripple, a fucking cripple, and that was all thanks to him. She only had her husband home with her because he *couldn't* go anywhere else, even if he wanted to. But that didn't mean they had to fucking kowtow to him. They had long memories; even if she chose to rewrite history, it didn't mean they had to. He would use the old coot, but if she thought they were going to start playing happy families she could think again. He had to make that plain to her, make her see that she was getting the old man back, but it didn't mean that he was once more the dog's gonads. 'I've said he can stay, Mum, for you. But don't you *ever* fucking try this old fanny with me again. The kids are my responsibility now, as you are. You and him made sure of that much between you. I ain't got nothing on my fucking conscience where you're concerned. I wish you could say the same about us kids. He means nothing to us, fuck all. We know him too well, Mum, and there ain't nothing you can say that will make us care for him now. It's too fucking late.'

His mother's white face was not affecting him any more; his anger was overpowering in its intensity. He was sick of her, sick of her turnaround, of her trying to make out her husband was someone he wasn't. 'Don't push me too far, Mother, because you can't look out for your kids, so I have had to do that for you. You forget all about that part of it, don't you?'

Ange was looking at this son of hers, wondering where this anger came from, yet all the time knowing it was to be expected. In her heart of hearts she knew, as always, that she was letting them all down, that her kids knew she was putting her husband over them once more, putting her marriage over their well-being. She knew they were right, but it didn't change how she felt.

'I'm warning you, Mum, don't ever make me choose, and don't ever make me angry like this again. Unlike you, I have what is known as loyalty. Something that you and that ponce who calls himself my father would know nothing about.'

She nodded sadly. 'But he can stay?'

He nodded, his clenched fists apparent and his utter disgust at her actions telling her this was final. There was no more talk left for them. This was the end of it. It was only when she turned away from him that he saw she was pregnant again, and the realisation of her utter betrayal was such that it nearly sent him over the edge.

*

Louie knew something was bothering the boy but no amount of careful questioning could make him confide what it might be. He had wondered if it was a girl: he knew the boy was active in that department and he knew the girls liked him, they walked past the yard in their finery, smiling at the boy and, more often than not, getting no response whatsoever. He was a treat-them-mean, keep-them-keen type of lover. At least that was the impression he gave. As Louie watched him talking to a totter, and doing a deal for some scrap copper piping, he knew that whatever ailed him was colouring his whole life. He looked older, as if he had the weight of the world on his young shoulders. And Louie knew that this state of affairs couldn't go on for much longer. The last few weeks had seen a great change come over the boy and it wasn't for the good either; that much was apparent to anyone who knew him.

And he knew Danny Boy better than anyone by now. For all his bravado and his fighting nature, he knew that underneath he was still a kid, a kid who was keeping his whole family from penury, and making sure that his siblings had a better chance at life than he had. And, if the gossip was true, another child was on the way, and the father was masquerading as a cripple so the chance of him ever doing an honest day's work was about as likely as the Pope giving lessons in contraception. As Louie waved the boy over, he wondered how he was going to ask him what was going on, what his reaction would be to his queries, and whether or not he had any real right to interfere in the boy's private business.

Michael was working out how much they were earning from their new businesses; in the last few weeks they had been handed a lot of smaller debts that were seen as far too cheap to be called in with serious violence. Danny Boy was seen as a new up-and-coming young Face and the men who were owed the money knew that any business they passed over to him would also be seen as a gesture of kindness. After all, the boy needed a few quid for his family's welfare, so it looked as if they were just giving him a heads-up. In reality, people were collecting money they would normally write off until serious damage was called for. That would generally involve the borrower asking for more dosh at some point, and then the rest would be history. All in all, it was an earner for everyone involved.

And Michael knew that if you looked after the small amounts, the pennies, then the pounds, seemed to multiply at an alarming rate, especially when, like them, the pounds were still important.

They were the new rude boys, the answer to everyone's prayers. Danny Boy Cadogan would hammer the fuck out of someone for a score; in everyone's eyes that made him a winner. He got to keep the poke, and the person owed the money was suddenly unwilling to let the debt ride the usual course.

It was a win-win situation once again and Michael, like Danny Boy, was all for making the most of it. Exploiting a situation was their mantra, and it seemed to be catching on. They were also being asked to supply puff to a new clientele and that pleased them. They were being talked about, were sought after, they were like the new kids on the block and they were loving every second of it. Every Face in the Smoke was aware of them, liked them, admired them. They were kids, no threat to anyone yet, but useful if a small job came their way. This was what they had talked about, prayed for. Little acorns.

It was dark, the night air was cold, and the distant sound of a police siren broke the silence. Danny was seriously drunk and the cold night air cut through his lungs every time he took a breath.

He had left the scrapyard hours before; guessing that Louie was going to give him one of his fatherly talks, he had gone on the trot. As much as he liked the man, there was no way he was going to discuss this situation with him. The shame was too much to bear; it was bad enough that everyone knew his father had more or less dumped them all, leaving them up shit creek without the proverbial paddle.

As he walked towards Shepherd's Market he felt the anger building up inside him all over again. He was fifteen and he had the weight of the world on his shoulders. But he would use his father to better himself, make himself look the big man. The generous son. He was, after all, his flesh and blood. Then, when the time was right, he would take great pleasure in aiming him out the front door once and for all.

Tonight he had had a meet with a Face from Silvertown, Derek Block, and he had agreed to collect a few debts for him in the coming weeks. Then, after they had concluded their bit of business he had gone on the piss big-time. Derek Block had found his drunkenness highly amusing and had actively encouraged it. Danny Boy decided he liked Derek Block more than he had thought possible. Considering the man was a fucking cretin of the first water, he had been pleasantly surprised at how much he had enjoyed getting pissed with him. Now he was once more alone and, though full of alcohol, he still managed to walk a straight line and look relatively sober.

Danny Boy was dressed smartly as always, a nice dark suit and heavy overcoat making him look older than his years. His mother and her pregnancy, her disgusting betrayal of them all, was at the forefront of his mind as he strolled through Shepherd's Market.

It was late, so he eyed up the last few working girls surreptitiously, they were the dregs of their tight-knit society and that caused his anger to boil to the surface once more. He took deep breaths, determined to get his anger and his temper under control. He liked the brasses, they were easy pickings. He knew where he was with them, and he didn't have to be nice if he didn't want to. They were nothing more than a commodity to him; they scratched his itch without him having to pretend he liked them. His sexual appetite was enormous and he knew that it was far bigger than all his contemporaries' put together. Most of them wouldn't know a shag if it fell out of a tree and hit them on the head. They had to be content with talking about it, all the time making sure their right hands were in perfect working order. But he needed to release his pent-up aggression regularly, and the sex act did that for him.

The market was nearly empty and he walked on briskly now, wishing he had not left it so late. Then he saw a young girl in the shadows; she was obviously new to the pavement, her skin was still clear and her eyes didn't have the feral glint that came with experience and the overuse of her body for monetary gain.

She smiled at him sheepishly, and he motioned with his head for her to follow him. He could hear the clacking of her shoes on the pavement as she struggled to keep up with him, and he grinned to himself. He was leading her away from her comfort zone and it was late; she was obviously in dire need of money. She was wearing a short satin skirt, a tie-dyed shirt and an Afghan coat that had seen better days. Her long, slim legs were bare, and the high-heeled shoes she wore only served to hinder her progress. He stopped in a doorway and watched her as she teetered towards him. Her heavily made-up face showed her nervousness, and her clothes made her look ridiculous. He smiled as she sidled up beside him.

In the dim light he saw she was actually really pretty, no more than seventeen years old, and seriously stacked. Her smile revealed small white teeth, and a trust that was completely wasted on him.

Danny Boy stared down at her for long moments. She had thick blond hair, wide-spaced blue eyes and a tiny, heart-shaped face. Her creamy skin was still smooth, without the tell-tale lines that street walkers seemed to acquire at an early age. Her garish make-up made her look even younger than she was and her wide smile was genuine. And she was devoid of the usual banter and chat that heralded the request for money in exchange for sexual services. She was a brand-newey all right.

'How much?'

She shrugged, her slim shoulders making her look even more vulnerable. 'I don't know. What do you normally pay?'

She had a quiet voice, and her breath was evident because of the cold. He didn't answer her. Instead, he pulled her towards him and, grabbing her, he began to feel her all over. As he squeezed her breasts roughly she closed her eyes tightly, and he forced her legs open with his knee. Pushing her backwards against the shop door, he kissed her. Forcing his tongue into her mouth, he explored it as if she was a real girlfriend. She tasted of Wrigley's chewing gum and cigarettes. Danny never kissed brasses; this was a one-off for him. As he fingered her she sighed, then he kissed her so violently she couldn't breathe. She tried to pull away, but he held her there by grabbing a handful of her hair, pulling her head back until she thought her neck would snap. Then, panicking, she realised that he was determined to hurt her. He bit down hard on her bottom lip and she cried out in pain. Danny tasted her blood and it only served to make him more excited. He had released her breasts from her top and he lowered his head and sucked and bit at them until she was crying with the pain and humiliation. Picking her up in his arms he positioned her so he could thrust himself inside her and as he felt the tightness of her, he knew that this was what he had been missing out on: that she was relatively unused so her body was still firm and exciting. The fact she was dry, sore and in agony didn't enter his mind, he was lost in the feelings she had created in him and, pulling her legs around his waist, he pummelled her until he felt himself coming.

'You fucking slag, you fucking whore.'

He repeated those two sentences over and over again, and she realised he had no idea he was even saying anything.

As he groaned loudly and came back to reality, he heard her voice telling him to stop. She was fighting him now, her pain and hurt making her stronger. Grabbing her wrists he slammed her hard against the wooden door. The force knocked the wind out of her and her little face screwed up in pain and bewilderment. She looked at him and knew then that he was really dangerous, knew his good looks hid a demon. She stopped trying to fight him, and waited for him to finish, knowing then that any kind of resistance was useless. When it was finally all over he held her close, his breathing loud and ragged in her ears.

The burning inside her was real, and she knew he had hurt her, really hurt her. Her legs had been pushed so far apart that she felt as if her hips were about to break, and her back was raw from being slammed into the brass handle of the shop door.

Danny looked down at her once more, he had never felt like that before. Her youth and inexperience had excited him in a way he had never believed possible.

The pain was unbearable and, as he placed her gently onto the ground, she winced. She couldn't stand up, and she grabbed at him then. Her legs buckled and she dropped onto her knees. The pain was overwhelming: she knew she was bleeding, that the warm wetness between her legs was not just from him.

Danny watched the girl's face and, as his head cleared, he knew he had fucked up, knew that he had really hurt her. She was doubled over, and he hastily rearranged himself until he was decent once more. Then he looked around him, checked in case someone was in the vicinity, had been witness to his actions. The road was empty, and the girl was now attempting to stand up. She was clutching at his overcoat, trying to drag herself upright. Her pretty face was screwed up in pain, and he could see the terror in her eyes at what had befallen her. He could smell her now. It was a bitter, sweaty smell and it made his stomach heave. He saw her legs, blue and mottled from the cold night air, and the dirt that was ingrained around her ankles. Her thick hair was greasy and, as her fingers clawed at his coat, he was aware of chipped nail varnish, and nicotine-stained fingers. Now he had sated his appetite the reality of what she was hit him. She was filthy, her eyes sunken, a junkie's eyes. She was a runaway, the scum of the earth and he was ashamed to admit he had shagged her.

'Please . . . I can't get up . . .'

Her mouth was a dark cavern now, and he had kissed her, with her custard teeth and smudged lipstick. He felt the bile rise inside him and swallowed down the urge to vomit. His fist was loud when it connected with her forehead and, as she collapsed onto the dirty floor, he kicked her. The blow was so powerful it lifted her off the ground and Danny felt her ribs crumple as they came into contact with his well-polished brogues. He stepped back and looked down at her as she writhed in agony on the cold pavement, her cries high-pitched and her eyes screwed up with pain. He kicked her again, this time in the back of her head. The force of the blow sent the girl sprawling across the pavement and Danny watched her as she attempted to crawl away from him.

She was quiet now, unable to scream or talk, her instincts telling her she couldn't defend herself, all she could do was try and get away from the person who was hurting her. As she tried to absent herself from the terrible situation she had found herself in, she knew in her heart that it was futile.

Danny looked around him. The street was still empty, and most of the lamp posts had broken bulbs, the older women on the game saw to that; the darker the night the more likely they were to earn. He stared coldly at the girl again, her suffering was evident, and yet it didn't affect him one iota. He watched her as if he was outside, looking in on the whole situation, as if it had nothing to do with him at all. He walked to where she was lying and, kneeling down, he looked at her closely. She was bleeding profusely, something he had not noticed until now. She was lying on her back, her mouth opening and closing as she tried to beg him to leave her be. But nothing was coming out of her mouth except blood.

Danny wondered briefly why he didn't care about her, didn't feel anything about her obvious suffering, then he wondered if anyone could place them together. It was like watching a scabby dog dying. And he was sure that she was actually dying. No one could survive the blows he had inflicted on her. But, as he tidied himself up, brushed down his overcoat and ran his fingers through his hair, he wondered at a girl who was so base she would give herself to anyone with the cash needed. Fuck her, and fuck all women like her.

The alcohol he had imbibed liberally earlier on was wearing off now, the shock of his anger and the consequent outburst was sobering him up. As the girl slipped into unconsciousness he stamped on her head repeatedly, making sure she wouldn't see the light of the new day that was rapidly approaching.

Afterwards, as he walked home he saw the first rays of light, and marvelled at how beautiful the world could be, even though it was peopled with women like his mother and the nameless girl he had encountered that night.

He knew that by letting his father stay he would get more than a few Brownie points and he would concede that much to further his burgeoning career. That his mother was prepared to defend the man who had almost destroyed her family he found hard to digest. That she wanted him more than her children was a real eye-opener, a real learning curve. Even though he was still half-cut, the hurt he felt inside was still raw enough to bring tears of self pity to his eyes. He had worked his arse off to put food on the table and clothes on their backs, minimise the damage his father had caused, and his mother didn't care about any of it. She was more interested in the ponce she had married than the kids she had birthed.

As he walked home, Janet Gardner, a sixteen-year-old runaway from Basingstoke, died all alone on the pavement, the imprint of

Danny Boy's shoe on her face as her boyfriend-come-pimp was wondering where the fuck she had got to with his money.

Ange was still up when her son finally came home. Her biggest fear was that he would leave them to get on with it; she knew that would mean her once more working all the hours the good Lord sent, even though she was full of baby. As he walked into the flat she was standing in the kitchen doorway, her tubby body and thick greying hair showing her age.

They looked at each other then and, smiling gently, she went to this son of hers, this man who had emerged suddenly from out of nowhere, and she hugged him. 'Where have you been? I was worried about you.'

Danny Boy shrugged gently. 'I had a bit of business, Mum. Don't worry, I am over the worst.'

'Can I do you a bit of breakfast, son?'

He shook his head sadly. 'Nah. I need a few hours of sooty and sweep, get me head together for the day ahead.'

'There's blood on your coat, take it off and give it to me, son. I'll sort it for you.'

Danny looked down and saw that the girl's blood had been sprayed all over the front of his overcoat. It was still fresh, deep-red in colour, and he felt the urge to vomit once more. He could smell her again, the rancid odour of an unwashed body that was never evident before he slept with them, but always seemed to linger afterwards.

He slipped his overcoat off and she gently folded it over her arm.

'Try and see it from my point of view, eh?'

He didn't bother to answer her, his brother had got up and was watching them closely.

'Had your look?'

'Fuck off.'

Danny was still laughing at Jonjo's front as he went to his bed, all the while listening to his mother berating his little brother for swearing.

Chapter Eight

'She's got a heart that's harder than a whore's handbag and, let's face it, I should know.' Big Dan gave his usual shrug as if to imply his wife was the Devil Incarnate and then, craftily, knowing that what he was saying was tantamount to blasphemy because of his son's reputation, and also knowing that the men around him admired his courage in saying it all in the first place, said, 'But keep that under your hat, boys. Remember the war, careless talk cost lives.'

Big Dan listened with satisfaction at the scandalised laughter all around him. He knew it was really more a case of sycophantic laughter. Knew that in the real world, their world, he was only tolerated these days because of his son. But he milked it for all it was worth anyway. That his son had no real interest in him wasn't something he was inclined to dwell on, but the fact that his boy relied on his intimate knowledge of the local Faces and local folklore was what was really important. It was because of that that he still had a role in life of sorts. He was tolerated by Danny Boy all the time he was useful to him. So he made a point of gathering as much information as he could, in the hope that it would eventually be of interest to his son. This was what he craved though, the company of other men, the warmth of the pub, and the centre stage. He was still classed as a raspberry ripple, Danny Boy had seen to that, but on the upside he would never have to work again. He couldn't, even if he'd wanted to, which, in all honesty, wasn't an issue as far as he was concerned. He was not capable of any kind of manual labour any more, and that was all he had been fit for, even at his best. In fact, sitting in his local with the resident no-necks was as good as it was going to get for him, and he was sensible enough to know that. He earned his keep though, not only did he keep his eyes and ears open for any titbits that might be of interest to his son, he made sure that anything he heard was factual before repeating it. But he also helped enhance the boy's reputation with skilful innuendoes and half truths. Over the last year, since Ange had lost the baby, he had made himself as indispensable as was humanly possible. It had been hard graft, but he had persevered and liked to think he had accomplished at least a mutual tolerance, if not respect.

There was no love lost between the two of them, but there was a truce of sorts, except for the occasional bout of unfriendly fire. Namely when his son came home drunk and took the first opportunity available to cunt him into the ground. He never rose to the bait though, he just sat back and waited for the boy to run out of steam. He knew that he was deserving of most of it anyway, and at least Danny didn't bring it out of their flat and into the public domain. In front of people they were civil to each other, and he knew Danny Boy was respected for his treatment of a man who had, in effect, destroyed and abandoned his family. That Danny had gimped him good and proper was common knowledge, that Danny Boy had then welcomed him back into the fold had now become part of the local folklore.

It made him look big, look magnanimous when, in fact, he was just another vicious little fucker masquerading as a nice guy. He should know, the boy took after him. Big Dan knew his boy was going to be a Face, he was halfway there already: hence the welcome wagon wherever he went. No one wanted to antagonise the boy, and if *he* could find it in his heart to forgive his old man, then most people were willing to follow suit. After all, whatever Danny might have done to him in the heat of anger and retribution, it didn't mean he would stand back and let anyone else get away with it. After all, he was still his father, and that counted for something in their world, no matter how useless the person in question might be.

He was earning as well, the boy was earning serious money these days, and he was on speaking terms with everyone who was anyone. No mean feat considering his tender years. He was a prince-in-waiting all right. A vicious, hateful, and devious prince who had the knack of making people like him. It was his open face; he looked for all the world like an angel, as if butter wouldn't melt.

Well, they would learn and, when they did, it would be too late. That much his father knew, even if they didn't. They would rue the day they gave this son of his permission to hunt on their territory, because hunt he would. It was second nature to him. He would take everything they had acquired away from them, one by one, piece by piece, that smug smile of his still on his face. He was a natural-born scavenger, fucking carrion.

If anyone needed a job doing these days, then Danny Boy was always available, and his sheer size, coupled with his quiet and respectful demeanour, had endeared him to everyone in the criminal community. He could handle himself, that much was evident. Even he couldn't dispute that, and the fact that he had the knack of controlling his violence and, when it was deemed necessary, could even prolong it, was an added bonus. His youthful exuberance was part of his overall charm.

Danny Boy was becoming known for his drug dealing and also for his ability to sort out problems discreetly. He could collect a debt, arrange a firearm, or deliver a message when necessary. He could also charm anyone with an ounce of brainpower, while making sure they never forgot him. He knew instinctively how to manipulate any situation for his own benefit, and he was sensible enough to make it look like everything he did was for the good of whoever was paying his wages at the time.

This boy he had bred made Big Danny realise just how useless he had been for the best part of his life, and it made his current situation all the more apparent because he was now reduced to poncing drinks by trading on his association with his own flesh and blood. Forced into acting all the time, as if what had happened to him was of no importance, was insignificant in the great scheme of things. As if being crippled by his own flesh and blood didn't affect him one iota.

As his elder son walked into the pub Big Dan felt the usual sickness in the pit of his stomach, felt the breathlessness as his heart started beating rapidly. He feared him more than most people; he had far more reason to.

Danny Boy walked into the warmth of the public house with his shoulders back and his head held high, as if he owned the place. He strode across the dirty floor of the bar, his youth and expensive clothing immediately marking him out as different. He had the polished appearance of someone twice his age, and he also had a presence that was reminiscent of the old-style villains. He looked what he was, a serious handful.

People made a point of acknowledging him, and he acknowledged them back; depending on their ranking in the world of criminality, he either nodded, shook hands or slapped backs. He knew the game, and he could already play it like a veteran. His handsome face, as always, belied his real emotions. He looked pleased to see everyone, made them feel as if they were important, had a smile and a wink for any females in his line of vision. The women loved him, he had the animal attraction that all seriously violent men possess. Certain women were attracted to it, loved the idea of being with someone so dangerous, even though it was normally the end of their lives as they knew it. It was once the men had been bagged that the real trouble started. Getting them was one thing, keeping them was another thing entirely. But the kudos of having them as their beau was enough to keep them interested, make them work overtime so they could reap the benefits of such an association. And the benefits were huge for a young girl with nothing more going for her than a good figure and a keen sense of fashion. Such an association was a passport to a life of ease and, in most cases, luxury, especially if the man married them. A few kids were the equivalent to money in the bank, providing the man in question didn't get his collar felt of course. As most of the girls in the pub were still technically schoolies Danny Boy was in his element. He stood at the bar, all bravado and brooding good looks, and waited for the girls to approach him. As he ordered a drink he turned to where his father was sitting perched on a stool and said pleasantly, 'Another one?'

Danny smiled as his father nodded nervously. He loved the stir he created wherever he went, loved the fact he was a someone now, a fucking handful, that he had a rep. The fact he was treated with respect by his elders was like a balm to his tortured soul. He needed it, and the more he experienced it, the more he craved it. He also loved the fact that it drove his father to distraction, he knew just how hard it was for him to keep up the pretence and live with the knowledge that he was only a part of their world because he, Danny Boy, allowed him to be. One word from him and the old bugger would be outed without a second's thought. But seeing the respect his father got because he *was* his father was like a salve to Danny Boy. It was further proof of his own importance, and the old man was handy at times: he had a nose for the pavement that was spot on, so they both benefited from their public truce. He looked at his father with mocking eyes and then proceeded to ignore him: he could feel the atmosphere he had created with his presence and enjoyed it. He saw the way people glanced his way surreptitiously, afraid to catch his eye yet, at the same time, hoping he would single them out and, by doing so, enhance their own reputations. It was a powerful feeling, and he thrived on it.

Lawrence Mangan was a man of few words. He was a quiet and seemingly inoffensive man who was friendly to the point of embarrassment, generous to a fault, and as mad as the proverbial hatter. He was tall, well-built, and had deep-blue eyes that were always smiling, and always on the lookout for a mark. He was a man who was known all over the Smoke, and who was respected by everyone and anyone. Even the Old Bill had a grudging respect for him because he was always in on everything that went down, yet they had never *once* been able to prove anything against him. He had never even had a caution, or a fine.

Lawrence Mangan, Lawrie to his friends, had a loyal workforce who knew better than anyone how dangerous he could be. The few people who had been stupid enough to upset him had a habit of disappearing off the face of the earth. Never to be seen again.

Lawrence Mangan knew how to keep himself out of trouble, and he also knew that his only chance of survival was to recruit the best of the best. He made a point of only dealing with people he trusted implicitly, people he then made sure earned a good wedge and who were intelligent enough to understand that he was not a man to trifle with. He had dispatched people without a second's thought many times in the past, knowing that the only way to be really safe was to do his own dirty work. He was hardly going to grass himself up, was he? People, Filth included, could think what they liked about him, about his lifestyle, it was proving it that was the hard part.

Now though, he was faced with a quandary. One of his oldest associates, a good friend, had been unfortunate enough to have got his collar felt. Not something that would normally bother him too much. What was bothering him was the fact that the man in question had been given bail. What's more, the bastard was sitting right here in the same bar, looking for all the world as if nothing had happened.

Jeremy Dawkins had been captured fair and square by the plod with a boot full of guns and enough ammunition to take on the British army, or at least give them a run for their money. In fact, a few of the guns had once been owned by said army.

Now, to anyone in their world and, given his previous form, he should have had more chance of getting a wank off Doris Day than making bail. Hence Lawrence's suspicious thoughts on the matter in hand. Jeremy was one of only a handful of people who were capable of doing him any real harm, and that meant he had to make sure Jeremy didn't get that chance. If Jeremy was about to serve him up, and there was a good chance he was seriously considering that because another capture would guarantee him such a hefty sentence that he wouldn't come back home till his great-grandchildren were in their dotage. That fact meant he had to make sure that Jeremy didn't get the opportunity. If he had already talked the big talk with plod, and that was a given as far as he was concerned, then they would be on the watch. So he had to make sure that if anything did happen to Jeremy he couldn't be implicated in any way. He knew he had to assume that Jeremy had already given them enough information to whet their interest in him personally. The man wouldn't give them anything really important until he had brokered himself a decent deal. He had enough sense to know that when dealing with the Filth you never gave them anything too edifying until you had your guarantees in place. They were not known for being fair-minded when dealing with known and habitual criminals.

There was a chance that Jeremy had indeed had a touch, and that he was telling the truth when he said his brief was a miracle worker, however, that wasn't a chance Lawrence was willing to take. Jeremy was living on borrowed time, even though he wasn't aware of that fact yet.

As he sipped his glass of port, Lawrence decided he was more than likely living on borrowed time as well, thanks to this treacherous bastard. Though he couldn't prove anything, he had found through experience that it was always better to be safe rather than sorry. Smiling happily at Jeremy he raised his glass in a toast, and watched as the treacherous bastard smiled happily back at him while returning the gesture. He needed to box-clever with Jeremy, he was an old hand and would be on the lookout for anything remotely suspicious; that ruled out using anyone in their immediate circle to solve this problem once and for all. Not that he would feel comfortable with that scenario either.

Jeremy was far too shrewd to let anyone he knew near him, he would have to be taken out by someone he wouldn't suspect. Like now; Jeremy didn't suspect that *he* had sussed him right out, knew that there was no way he would get bail, get a cab home from the Filth's local hangout. He had done too much bird, had too much form: his only get-out-of-jail-free card was to put someone else in there instead. Well, that someone wasn't going to be him.

He needed a new Face, a young buck, someone looking for a chance to make the transition from a good living to a fuck-off way of life. Someone who would be sensible enough to keep their trap shut, yet who was also strong enough to take Jeremy on without too much thought. In fact, he had to find himself a brand-new Jeremy to replace the old one. The thought made him smile and, as he listened to the banter and talk around him, he was quietly planning his old friend's demise. This was a job that needed to be done sooner rather than later. As his old Granny always said,

123

either shit, or get off the pot. He knew just the bloke to solve this problem for him, and he decided to sort it sooner rather than later.

As Danny watched his father giving it the big one at the bar, he wondered why he didn't feel anything for him any more, not even anger. Didn't feel anything for anyone, in fact. His mother he loved, on one level, but she had disappointed him too much: he looked after them all for no other reason than how it looked to the outside world. He was seen as the good guy and he wanted it to stay that way. People admired his loyalty, even though he didn't really have any. Didn't suffer from his conscience, didn't have trouble sleeping at night. His life now consisted of making money and proving to the world he was a somebody. In fact, how he was perceived was of paramount importance.

The smell of cigarettes and stale beer was assailing his nostrils: it reminded him of his father. The pub was overheated, exacerbating the stench of cheap perfume and even cheaper clothes. He wanted better than this for himself, much better.

He saw Louie walk through the bar then, a welcome breath of cool air heralding his arrival, and he knew that tonight was going to be a watershed in his life. He swallowed his drink and went into the back room of the public house quietly, unobtrusively, all the time knowing that he was being watched by everyone in the place. Especially by the girls who frequented this shithole of an establishment. As he slipped through the door he felt the power of having all eyes turned on him.

'You're a fucking poser, do you know that?'

Danny laughed at the accusation.

The room was small, it had peeling wallpaper, a threadbare carpet and the universal stench of hopelessness that seemed to permeate even the nicer boozers in east London. There was money to be made, but it was not wise to advertise that fact.

'You look well, Lou, what's all this about?'

Louie could see the difference in the boy and part of him was sorry at the change in him. He was a man now and, after tonight, if he took on the mantle being offered to him, he could never walk away from this life. If he did as requested, he would become a fixture, a permanent part of their society. In short he was going to offer him the credibility he knew this young man craved. For him it was a win-win situation: for young Danny Boy it would seal his fate once and for all. Be careful what you ask for, eh, you just might get it.

Ange Cadogan was sipping her tea, and listening to *Mystery Voice* on the radio when her son came into the kitchen. As always, he brought in the smell of the pavement. It was peculiar to him and, even with his aftershave and his expensive clothes, she still associated it with him. He was opening the drawers and removing things, his movements precise and, as always, quiet.

'What you after, son?'

He looked over his shoulder at her and grinned. 'If anyone asks, right, I was home in bed by eleven.'

She didn't even bother to answer such a ridiculous statement. 'What do you want that lot for?' She saw her boning knife, bread knife and apple corer being wrapped in a clean tea towel.

Danny didn't answer her. Instead, he said, 'When the old man gets in, tell him you saw me go to bed, right?'

He placed the package inside his coat, and turned towards her fully. 'He's still in the pub, pissed out of his head. Don't you dare let on about any of this, right?'

Ange nodded at him, her eyes heavy with accusation.

'There's money in the top drawer of my dresser, take a oner and do whatever you have to, take the kids out, and stay well away from here until I tell you otherwise. OK? Just keep them away from here and keep your trap shut.'

She didn't say anything, and that annoyed him.

As he left the flat a few minutes later, she sighed heavily, wondering what new trouble he had landed himself in now. She didn't move from her seat: the truce was still in place, but these days she gladly overlooked her son's behaviour, preferring to pretend that everything was hunky-dory. She was actually more interested in when her husband would finally arrive home, and what condition he would be in when he arrived. It was the only way she could cope with it all. If she didn't dwell on it all too much and concentrated on the other kids, she found that her life was at least bearable.

Michael knew that what he was about to do would catapult him into the real world; so far he had been the brains of the outfit. Now though, he was being asked to actually take part in Danny Boy's quest to conquer their world. He knew that if he had refused, he would be finished. And that Danny was depending on him to make this night's work go smoothly, without a hitch of any kind. He also knew that Danny was drawing him in, making sure he couldn't back out of their partnership because, after tonight, he would finally be a fully fledged member of the criminal fraternity. This was serious business; this would ultimately make or break them. But, in his heart, he understood that nothing would go wrong, because Danny Boy Cadogan wouldn't let that happen. And that there would be no going back after this. But he was not geared up for this kind of scam, in fact, he had made a point of stepping back from the actual day-to-day running of their little firm, even though said firm was only successful because of Danny Boy's reputation. He was seen as no more than the partner, the mate. It was Danny Boy who had the real rep, and he had earned it. And, in fairness, he had made a point of enhancing it at every available opportunity. Michael knew how to work out the financial side, but it was Danny who made sure the money was available to them in the first place. Michael's family depended on him now, as did Danny's: he had made a deal with the Devil and that ponce demanded his pound of flesh.

That was why he was sitting in a damp cellar off the Bow Road, waiting for Danny Boy to deal with his latest victim. Only this time, the victim was not going to be allowed to leave with a broken limb and a stern warning: this time they were being paid to make someone disappear.

It was a daunting task, and only his fear of Danny's anger, and his need to take care of his family, was keeping Michael from running as far away as possible.

'He's still out for the count.'

Danny sounded relieved, even though Michael knew he was not going to renege on his promise to Lawrence. There was no way this could be stopped now, it had gone too far. The man lying on the floor would never let them get away with this, it was now a case of do or die. And he, for one, was terrified of what they were going to *do*: knew that if it all went pear-shaped it was the end for them.

Danny Boy looked down at Jeremy as he lay on the cement floor. His hands were tied behind his back and his face was already a swollen wreck. He knew that once he came to, the pain in his shoulders and neck would be unbearable agony. He was also bleeding from his eyes and ears. None of these things bothered Danny; he had no sentiment any more, for anyone. If anything, he was intrigued by it, by the human spirit. And anyway, Louie had provided this safe haven for them; all the screaming in the world would not bring anyone knocking on this door. So, unlike Michael, Danny Boy didn't fear the arrival of the Old Bill. Lily Law was the least of their problems. His fear comprised of not being able to execute the job he had been given properly, not displaying the correct amount of finesse. This was the decider as far as he was concerned.

He lit a cigarette and pulled on it deeply. 'You all right, Mike?'

It was a genuine enquiry and Michael answered him with equal seriousness. 'Not really, but I'll survive as always.'

His answer made Danny laugh.

'Fuck him.' He knelt down then and stubbed the cigarette out on Jeremy's face. The burn brought the man back to consciousness and he groaned loudly.

'Awake, are we?' Danny spoke as if he was addressing a small child in his care; his voice was friendly, his open face devoid of any kind of emotion. Picking up the apple corer from the floor, he held it over the man's right eye.

'This is your last chance. Have you to talked to Old Bill about our mutual friend?'

The man looked at the handsome young man leaning over him and, pulling his lips back over his teeth, he said angrily, 'Fuck you.'

Jeremy knew he was a dead man and he was determined to go with as much dignity as he could muster. He knew all of this would be discussed at length with everyone he had ever dealt with in his life and at least he wanted the satisfaction of knowing he went out with a bit of aplomb. A bit of respect.

Danny sighed again and, looking at the man's terrified face, he said sadly, 'I am going to take out your eye in a minute, and then, if you still insist on being a hero, I'll take out your other eye. I'll dismantle your boat-race inch by inch until you tell me what I want to know. So don't be a fucking mug, you're a dead man anyway.' Then, before Jeremy could answer him, he slammed the apple corer into his eye socket, wrenching out the eyeball, and a large percentage of his cheekbone. The scraping of metal against bone was sickening. The screaming seemed to go on for an age, and the blood was everywhere. Michael watched in horrified fascination then, feeling the vomit rising up into his mouth, he emptied his stomach over the floor.

Danny stood up and, lighting himself another cigarette, he ignored his friend's dilemma. Instead, he went to the small table by the door and poured himself a large whisky. He placed the apple corer onto the table, with Jeremy's eyeball still stuck inside it and, picking it up once more he poked it out with his index finger, watching as it dropped on to the dirty floor. He stamped on it, grinding it into the dirt.

Picking up his drink, he downed it quickly then, pouring another one, he took the glass over to Michael, who was still heaving. 'Drink this, you fucking tart.'

Jeremy was quieter now, the excruciating pain, and the realisation of what was actually going to happen had finally hit him. He was squirming in his own blood, and aware that he really was in trouble. He knew now that Danny Boy Cadogan was that rare breed of man, a sadist who actually enjoyed this kind of job. A man who enjoyed inflicting pain on people and was willing to do whatever was necessary to make sure that he had answers to any questions he deemed important.

Michael swallowed the whisky in two gulps. The sweat was pouring off him, Danny could smell it, even though the stink of blood was heavy in the air. He could also smell victory, knew that Jeremy was going to tell him whatever he wanted to know.

He walked Michael to an old typist's chair and made him sit down, fussing over him tenderly. Michael was staring at the remains of a perfectly good eyeball and feeling the nausea once more.

'You all right, mate?'

Michael nodded eventually, his belly still determined to empty itself of its contents.

'You're so chicken-hearted, the bloke's a fucking grass for fuck's sake.' Winking gaily, he went back to where Jeremy was groaning in agony and knelt beside him once more.

Jeremy was babbling incoherently, trying to release himself from his bonds. He was delirious with pain and nearly insane with the knowledge that this boy wasn't going to talk of his death with respect, he would joke about it, enjoy his final moments by making him beg for an end to the torture. He was beaten, and he knew it.

Listening intently, Danny finally learned what he wanted to know. 'See, you know it makes sense.'

Then, smiling happily, he proceeded to torture Jeremy anyway, watching the way his body writhed in agony, studying the terror in his face, listening intently to the guttural groans he forced out when actual speech became impossible. Danny Boy was fascinated by this death. He knew he was going to see, up close and personal, someone leave this earth, leave not only all they knew, but also everyone they knew, behind them. He felt the power of his position, of knowing this man's life was his to give back or to take away. Eventually he became bored with his games, and fed up with Michael's pleas for him to stop what he was doing, and he finished the man off once and for all.

It was a learning curve all right, but the recipient of the lesson wasn't the dead man on the filthy floor, it was Michael. He knew this was the first of many such nights, and he also knew that Danny could never let him walk away now. He was as much a part of this event as Danny was, because he had allowed it to happen in the first place. As he emptied his stomach once more, Danny's laughter at his friend's obvious weakness rang in his ears.

'Get a fucking grip, Mike, the cunt was a grass, he had this fucking coming.'

Danny Boy lit a cigarette and poured himself another drink. His hands were thick with dried blood and, toking deeply on his Embassy, he said gaily, 'Did you see Caroline Benson's tits tonight? She is definitely on my to-do list.'

Michael didn't answer him, he didn't know what to say.

'No one will ever find him, Mr Mangan.'

Lawrence nodded almost imperceptibly, pleased with the boy's respectful demeanour and the aura of someone who knew they had done a blinding job.

'Well done, son. Now I know what the treacherous cunt told the Filth, I can get it sorted.'

Danny didn't say any more. He knew when to keep his trap shut.

Mangan had seen the body before they had disposed of it, and he appreciated the fact that Danny Boy had washed and scrubbed himself up before making an appearance before him to get his well-earned lump of wedge. He didn't insult the boy by reiterating how important it was that what he had done was not to be talked about, *ever*. He knew that wouldn't be an issue. Once he was on the firm, people would put two and two together anyway. But wondering and knowing about something were two completely different things.

Filth would be placated as usual, with money, and the opportunity to pander to whatever vices they might favour, whether that was gambling or women. It was a pointless exercise for them now; without Jeremy and his testimony they were fucked. It was now a damage limitation exercise all round. But Mangan would never be mentioned personally, no matter what.

Lawrence threw a large brown envelope across the desk and Danny Boy Cadogan marvelled at the thickness of it, and knew that one day this would be him. He was determined that Lawrence would be his equal, not his employer.

'There's twenty grand in there: ten for your wages, and ten as a retainer. You work for me now, son. But you keep that to yourself for a while. I will pay you every six weeks, and when I need you again I'll be in touch, all right?'

Danny nodded and picked up the envelope. He placed it inside his overcoat without opening it. 'Thank you, Mr Mangan. Sir.' He spoke with the respect he knew the man's reputation demanded.

Lawrence watched him leave, saw the strength of him, the solidity of his young muscles and the viciousness of his personality. Danny Boy Cadogan would be an asset all right. He had the ability to do what was requested without the urge to discuss it at length. This kid had, after all, taken on the Murrays and crippled his own father. He knew how to play the game all right.

Hearing him leave the premises, Lawrence Mangan walked casually through to his other office. Then he looked at his old friend and said happily, 'You put me wise there, Lou, the boy's a card all right. A hard little fucker.'

Louie shrugged nonchalantly. 'He's a good kid, but take my advice and keep him in check. You saw the condition of Jeremy when he'd finished with him. If I know Danny Boy he enjoyed every second of it. He's like a vicious dog; keep him fed and watered and he'll be all right. Starve him or aggravate him, and you'll have trouble on your hands.' Louie was sad as he spoke, remembering the young lad who had first come to work for him at the scrapyard. That lad was gone now, and he would never come back. That was the downside of the world they lived in, and Danny Boy Cadogan, thanks to the man who had sired him, now fit into that world perfectly.

Chapter Nine

Michael opened his eyes to the bright daylight and, feeling the burn, he closed them again. He felt the afternoon all around him; knew, without looking at the clock ticking loudly beside him, that it was at least four or five. The day was already gone.

The girl stirred, and it alerted him to the fact that he was not alone. Squinting, he opened his eyes once more and sought her out, saw that she was curled up in a ball, her tight body touching his. He was relieved to find that he didn't know her from Adam. She had long blond hair and a baby face: from what he could see she had slim shoulders and good legs. He racked his brains trying to remember something, anything, about her. He couldn't.

He slipped from the bed quietly and unobtrusively and consoled himself with the fact that he wasn't in his own home so he could maybe fuck off before the usual talking started. Birds amazed him at times. They fucked you, a complete stranger, then expected you to treat them like visiting royalty. He loathed them all.

As he pulled on his clothes he glanced at her again. She was a nice-looking little thing, a bit flat-chested for his liking, but definitely not a barker, and he had woken up with more than a few of them. Right sights some of them: dogs in fact. Then, to add insult to injury, they had been under the mistaken apprehension that, because he had fucked them, they had some kind of rights over him. It was embarrassing, sometimes they even approached him in public, all chewing gum and mascara, their over-familiarity making them the enemy before they had even opened their traps.

This had to stop, it was becoming a fucking joke. As he slipped his feet into his loafers he noticed, with a sinking heart, that she was now wide awake and watching him.

'You going, then?'

It was a question, no more, no less. He nodded, determined not to get into any kind of discussion with her unless absolutely necessary.

'OK, will I see you later on?'

She was cute in a young girl-next-door turned slag kind of way: her whole body now tensed up with regret. He realised that she was as much in the dark as he was about the previous night's events.

'I'll ring you later.'

She laughed. Then, sitting up, she stretched languidly, her taut young body on full display, suddenly making him sorry to be leaving her so soon, before saying innocently, 'I ain't got a phone, mate, but leave *your* number and we'll see, eh?'

He nodded, all the while wondering where he was, and how he had got here in the first place. It smelled like south London, why that was, he didn't know, but it was the impression he got from the surroundings.

He was halfway down the narrow stairs before he realised that he was in some kind of squat, and nearly at the front door before he noticed Danny Boy leaning against the door jamb that led into the front room of the house, his usual grin on his face.

'You all right, Mike? I was worried she had fucked you to death.'

He still looked tidy, he still looked fresh. Michael envied him his ability to snort amphetamines all night before drinking himself sober, all the while looking as if butter wouldn't melt in his mouth.

'I feel like shit, Dan.'

Danny grinned then, 'Don't take this the wrong way, Mike, but I sort of worked that one out for meself.'

He motioned for him to follow him through to the kitchen, and Michael knew he had no choice but to do as requested. The front room was empty except for a dark-haired girl who was asleep on the floor. She was still wasted, but her long black hair struck a chord in his mind. He stepped over her prostrate form, and walked

134

into the tiny kitchenette. The stench of rubbish and unwashed bodies assailed his nostrils and he placed a hand over his mouth to stop himself throwing up. 'What a shithole.'

Danny was still grinning as he opened the back door and walked out onto the scrap of concrete that masqueraded as a garden. There was an old sofa out there that had seen far better days, but it was available and looked comfortable enough, so they sat on it together. The sounds and smells of a usual Sunday afternoon were all around them. Radios blared and the aroma of roast meats filled the heavy afternoon air with promise. Suddenly they were both ravenous.

'You were out of your nut last night, do you remember anything?'

Michael shook his head slowly. 'Not really, no. Is the car outside?'

'It better be, there's thirty grand in the boot.'

Danny was laughing once more and Michael closed his eyes as the memory of the night before's events filtered into his consciousness. Placing his head in his hands, Michael groaned loudly. 'We didn't, did we? Oh fuck, Dan, tell me we didn't!'

Danny was roaring with laughter now, and his laughter was infectious, making Michael laugh with him. 'Lawrence is going to kill us, Dan.'

'No he ain't, he asked us to do something and we did it. The money is in the car, the debt has been settled and we have bunced ourselves in the process. Everyone's a winner.'

'But thirty grand . . .'

Danny was deadly serious now, his laughing demeanour gone. 'We earned that money, fair and square, and no one will deny us a bit of spare cash. It was there and we took it. End of.'

Michael knew that his friend was talking the truth. They had collected a gambling debt for Lawrence, a usual occurrence these days, and the man they had been sent to shake down had been fortunate enough to have finally experienced a big win that afternoon. In fact, he had more than enough to pay what he owed, and set him up for future losses. They had taken Lawrence's money first, as was to be expected. Then they had decided to remove the rest of the man's winnings as an example. At least, that's what they had told each other anyway. High as kites, they had robbed him really; they had even used a gun. But they had seen his stash and decided that they were entitled to a percentage of it to compensate them for all the trouble they had gone to chasing the slippery fucker all over the Smoke.

The man, Jimmy Powell, who had a rep as someone who did not make friends easily, had made the hiding they were to have delivered for his tardiness somehow turn into a vicious beating, not only because they had decided that they wanted his money, but because he had laughed at them and fucked them off. He had made the fatal mistake of not taking them seriously as now he had the poke to pay them off, he had thought he was home and dry. More fool him.

It had been a robbery all right, but it was also an easy earner. They felt that they had only exploited an opportunity that had presented itself to them, now where was the harm in that? They weren't the first, and they certainly wouldn't be the last men to take advantage of a chance to line their pockets and settle a score at the same time. And the man in question wasn't really in a position to complain, was he? After all, he was the reason they were there in the first place. The fact that he had a few quid extra on his big day was his bad luck. Fifteen grand was not to be sneezed at, and the man was a lying piece of shit who had happily given them the run around for weeks. They felt they had earned the extra bunce for their dedication to their job; and the simple fact he had tried to mug them off. But they both knew that this went much deeper than that, that this was really about Danny Boy letting Lawrence know they were not happy with the situation any more. He was using them as gofers, and making it a point to remind them of that fact at every available opportunity. He made the mistake of thinking that a few quid in their bins would guarantee their loyalty.

They were testing him, *they* knew that and, more to the point, they knew that *he* knew that. In the last few years he had used them for many a dirty job and they had obliged, willingly. But, at twenty, they were real men and they wanted more than he was offering. Money was easily obtained, it was something they both had the knack of gathering. Danny was champing at the bit though, wanted free rein to do what he wanted, when he wanted. Michael had a feeling he would get that and, as usual, he would be dragged along for the ride. This wasn't the first time they had stepped over the unwritten line, and it would not be the last. It was, though, the first time they had taken a large amount of cash on the side; this was serious money, gangster money.

All that was left now was seeing how their latest escapade would pan out. It was a melon scratcher; they had taken a chance, a fucking big one, and now they had to wait and see how it played out.

Michael, like Danny Boy, had a feeling they would either be trounced when they least expected it, or they would finally get the approbation Danny so desperately craved. Either way, they would know before the day was over.

Mary Miles was fifteen and she already attracted attention wherever she went. It was the wrong attention and she knew that because, somehow, her mother made her feel guilty about it. She acted as if Mary could personally stop it at any time, if she *really* wanted to. Men looked at her, young and old, and she felt their interest in her as if it was a tangible thing. Even though she did nothing to encourage them.

By the time Mary was twelve, she had developed a huge bust, almost overnight; it was the envy of all her school friends. But her mother made her feel as if it was just another thing she had done to disappoint her. The lovelier she became, the more she felt responsible for her mother's obvious upset, and the less she felt any kind of self-respect. She thought her body was grotesque, and she listened to her mother's warnings about how she would end up going to the bad with serious disbelief. While drunk and vicious her mother destroyed her at every available opportunity. She had became a by-word where they lived; her capacity for alcohol was legendary, but she was still cute enough to make sure her daughter never got the chance to wander the streets with her mates. Michael, who Mary adored, was a worse jailer than her mother in many respects, but at least he had her best interests at heart.

As she knelt in the church she could feel the eyes of her mother boring into her back. She was praying hard, as usual, and she was praying for the same thing she always prayed for: freedom. Not just from her mother, but from the environment she lived in. Freedom from the drink, the squalor, and the constant vigilance needed to survive in their world. Mary hated the way she was coerced into doing what was expected of her, yet she knew she allowed it to happen because it was easier that way. Her mother had a knack of making her feel a despondency that would have taken other girls, so-called more experienced girls, years to comprehend. Mary knew why men looked at her, she even enjoyed the feeling it created sometimes, after all it was the only real power she had in her life. Plus, it annoyed her mother, which was a bonus as far as she was concerned.

Mary looked like her mother. Beauties, both of them, but whereas Mary wanted the chance to embrace hers and enjoy it, her mother was determined to make sure she didn't go the same way as she had. Determined to make sure she didn't waste it on some-one who would never see beyond it. Religion had been her solace, and she had embraced it with a fervour that had aggravated her parish priest and given her a certain cachet in her circle of friends. No matter how pissed she was, she always went to early Mass; it was how she justified her behaviour. No matter what she was accused of, and as she remembered little of her drunken escapades, accuse was a word she knew was used often, she attended Mass religiously. The pun always made her laugh, but the hypocrisy of her life was lost on her.

She was going to watch this one like a hawk though, and personally make sure that she didn't throw herself away on a useless ponce at the first available opportunity. If she used her loaf Mary could make a good match for herself, but only if she was watched over closely and counselled wisely. The sap was already rising in her; men were already interested, and she them, and Mrs Miles was determined to personally make sure that her daughter went to someone who could give her more than children and heartbreak. Someone who would look after her and who would bring her, not just a few quid, but respect on her family. She wanted her to realise that once the so-called love wore off there was nothing left for most women except existing. Once the looks went and the body grew fat and sagged, there was nothing left for them except trying to get by; only, by then, you had a handful of kids hanging on your breasts and suddenly existing was all you could focus on for any length of time.

She should know, she had been existing for years and now she depended on her son for her daily bread. Michael was a good boy, but without Cadogan he would have sunk without trace a long time ago. Like his father before him, he lacked balls and, if he fucked up, then this girl, this beautiful child, was going to be her golden goose. With Michael making a name for himself she should make a good match; she would be honoured because of her brother. Without him she was fodder for the first good-looking boy with nice teeth and a way with words.

Love and lust, two completely different things, only you didn't realise that until you grew up and had a few kids under your belt. By then, of course, it was too late to rectify your mistakes; you were saddled with a man who you had not only lost respect for, but who you still needed, albeit for all the wrong reasons. Money, being the main one; fear of poverty and making the rent was suddenly the driving force in your life. Well, that was not going to happen to her Mary if she had anything to do with it. She was keeping her in reserve, and daily Mass was part of her master plan. Well-stacked and virginal, she was already making waves and, though Mary wouldn't thank her just yet, she would one day in the future. After all, life was hard enough as it was without throwing herself away on someone who would only let her down.

As the Mass commenced she lowered her head and prayed for the guidance she so sorely needed. God was good, and so was her daughter, and she was going to make sure she stayed that way. Her life was not going to be repeated by this girl of hers; she was going to have all the things a good man could provide, and she was going to make sure that she also benefited from her daughter's good fortune. She had earned that much, whatever anyone else might think.

*

Ange had dressed the kids in their finery and taken them to the cinema; her son had asked her politely to take them out for the day. It was a rare treat for them, even though she was never short of money any more. In fact, she had found that she didn't really want to take them anywhere now she finally had the wherewithal to do so. Promising them things had been one thing, doing them another.

That her son made sure they were all right for money suited her right down to the ground, that her husband was constantly vilified and abused in his own home distressed her. But she had swallowed because the thought of going back to the old days terrified her, yet now the rumour was that Danny Boy had blotted his copybook with Mangan, so once more her thoughts turned to revenge.

Danny was a force, a serious force, and she was ashamed to admit that she was frightened of her own flesh and blood. But, if she was honest, even she didn't know what he was truly capable of. That he was now a name and that that name had given her the prestige she had always craved was forgotten. It was amazing how easy it was to forget what her husband had really been like in his heyday. How simple it was to totally rewrite history in her own mind and make him out to be a saint, convince herself he was nothing more than a misguided man who was widely misunderstood. Since his run-in with his son, he had become the husband she had wanted him to be. He was no good to anyone really, not any more. Not in the true sense of the word anyway. In fact, he was incapable of anything even resembling lovemaking, and she told herself she was glad about that. He said he was impotent, but she knew that was because he didn't want her any more. Not since she had miscarried the last child, and Danny Boy had made his feelings clear about the situation. Since then their physical relationship had gradually dwindled until, now, there was nothing between them. She consoled herself with the fact that there was nothing going on with anyone else, either. Not only was her husband crippled, his fear of Danny made him keep himself to himself. And who would want him, anyway? Now they talked, had the relationship she had dreamed of all those years, and it wasn't what it was cracked up to be. His philandering had often been the cause of the fights between them, fights where she had never been the victor, but where the making up had been impressive. Now she wanted that back again, only it wasn't going to happen, and she was left with a son who tolerated his father and, if she was honest, frightened his own mother. He had changed so much, and not for the better.

As she looked at her younger children she wondered at a life that had promised so much and delivered so little.

Michael Miles was tired out, and as he sat in Ange's spotlessly clean kitchen he yawned loudly. Danny Boy was already on the way. He was striding around, his pent-up anger visible to anyone who knew him. He was bristling with annoyance because he knew that Mangan was going to give him a tug. He saw it as a personal affront, and was already seething with anger because he was convinced people would know what was going down. You could do a lot of things to Danny Boy Cadogan but showing him up publicly was a definite no-no. It was the one thing that anyone who really knew him would be sure to avoid.

But Mangan didn't really know him, so Michael was certain that today was going to be another memory that he would have to file away for future reference. Danny was a star in so many respects, he was a good mate, a generous friend and he would kill for him, he was sure of that much. Unfortunately, he had found out to his dismay over the last few years that Danny was capable of killing on a whim. He enjoyed his notoriety, and was determined to make the most of it. He was also unable to cope with criticism of any kind, even from someone like Lawrence Mangan, who not only provided him with his daily bread, but was also known to put the fear of Christ up most people of his acquaintance.

'Keeping you up, am I?'

Michael grinned, but his heart wasn't in it. ' 'Course not, but I am fucking cream crackered.'

Danny Boy nodded, and began his pacing again. His tread was heavy on the linoleum and his hands were clenched into fists. He was ready for whatever calamity might befall him.

'Relax, will you? Mangan ain't a cunt, Dan, he'll understand the economics of the situation when we tell him what happened. But promise me you won't cause any unnecessary aggravation, start shouting your mouth off? Remember, we need him more than he needs us. For the time being anyway.'

Only Michael could say that to him, and they both knew it. Anyone else saying it would have been demolished on the spot. It was part of Danny's charm as far as the older men were concerned. He lived by the old codes, naturally, and that was always going to stand him in good stead. He had the arrogance of the old-time villains, the need to be appreciated for what they were, and the determination to be treated how they felt they should be treated, not only by the general public, but also by their contemporaries. He was, in a lot of respects, a thug who expected even straight people to live by the criminal code. It was a tribal thing that Michael believed went back to the Dark Ages. Respect was all some people had and it was important to them, more important in fact than anything else. It stroked their egos, and their egos were, more often than not, all they had to keep them above the common herd.

'I'll be OK, as long as he don't fuck me about. But we are entitled to an earn and he knows that, at least he should know that by now.' It was said with his usual certainty. Danny was old school and, as it never occurred to him that not everyone lived by the same code as he did, when he found out different, it always disappointed him and caused him and everyone around him untold grief.

Michael was saved from answering by the quiet knocking on the front door. Mangan had arrived at last and he answered the door with a sick feeling in his guts. Danny was capable of taking offence at a moment's notice, and Mangan was of a similar disposition. Michael's nerves were shattered already, but he swallowed deeply and plastered a friendly smile on his face; it was the least he could do.

Lawrence Mangan looked at the two young men who he knew were going to be a problem to him sooner rather than later if they didn't get what they saw as their due. He smiled that easy smile of his. He could feel Danny Cadogan's animosity and, in a strange way, admired the boy for his front. Admired him for his complete belief in himself and his actions, no matter how over the top they might seem to others.

Danny was arrogant and Lawrence knew that he was being talked about by everyone who mattered. That was actually Danny's main weapon at this moment in time. He was being courted by more than one Face who saw the opportunity to utilise his natural antagonism. The boy also knew exactly what he was capable of, and he revelled in that knowledge. It was in his stance, his demeanour. It occurred to Lawrence that Louie's prediction was spot on; the boy would eventually make the grade and, when he did, woe betide anyone who had tried to stand in his way. He would have to make sure he felt more appreciated in the future, let him off lightly for this latest escapade. Watch his back and, when the time was right, he would know instinctively what to do about him. The boy was an anomaly and he would make good use of him until such time as he made a decision on how to proceed.

He had underestimated this kid and, as he stood in the boy's home, he understood why his need to be noticed was so great. It was a shithole, a very clean shithole admittedly, but a shithole all the same. Danny Boy Cadogan had seen off his own father, so any-one else wouldn't seem too much of a problem in his mind. He wanted to be a Face, a serious Face, and he was determined to make that happen, no matter who he had to destroy to achieve that end.

The silence was heavy, thick with menace until finally it was broken by Michael, who said quietly and respectfully, 'Can I get you a drink, Mr Mangan?'

It broke the atmosphere, and the tension evaporated as Lawrence smiled again and nodded his head in agreement. Then he said jovially, 'You lairy little fuckers! Jimmy Powell is in a right two and eight.'

Danny knew then that he had got away with his latest piss-take and that felt good. He liked to push the boundaries and Lawrence Mangan was the first in a long line of people whose boundaries he would make a point of obliterating. He had stepped over the line and got away with it; he was amassing money at every turn and he would now be used to his full potential. Mangan had no other options left open to him. Danny would work hard and wait patiently for the next opportunity to present itself. Money was crucial to his plans, and he was determined to amass enough money in his lifetime to cure any ills that might come his way. That included this man standing before them. When the time was right he would take him out and take what he had from him. He would do it with the minimum of fuss and the maximum of aggravation. He would use this ponce as the springboard for his career in villainy but, until that time came around, he would do as he was asked, and he would fulfil his obligations with a smile and a respectful demeanour.

Life was going to give him everything he had ever wanted or craved, that much he was determined on.

Big Danny Cadogan knew all about his son's latest escapade, and the knowledge annoyed him. In fact, it was the main topic of conversation wherever he went and that disturbed him more than he'd like to admit. The boy was a legend in his own lunchtime and the jealousy was eating at him like a cancer.

As he drank his tea and scanned the *Racing Post*, he surreptitiously watched his younger son as he hung on to his elder brother's every word while, at the same time, asking him for a favour, as if he was the real man of the house which, of course, to all intents and purposes he was.

'What you telling me all this for, Jonjo?' Danny Boy's voice was low, full of friendliness and brotherly affection. Jonjo was close to him, at least as close as anyone could be anyway.

'Please, Danny, everyone's getting one this Christmas.'

Jonjo was staring at Danny, open-faced and convinced that if he asked enough times for what he wanted, eventually he would get it.

That was the usual scenario, especially if he asked for whatever he wanted in front of their father. Jonjo knew that Danny Boy liked to show off his largesse in front of him. Liked to show him that he could more than provide for the family. It gave Danny immense satisfaction to see his father belittled by his younger son's demands. This was what made Danny Boy feel good, at least for a short while, anyway.

'I reckon you might be in with a good chance of getting what you want this Christmas, Jonjo, but only if you help Mum around the house, and look out for your little sister. We have to take care of each other in this family, we're all we've got, mate.'

Jonjo breathed a sigh of relief, a heavy, heartfelt sigh that told him and everyone around him that his new racing bike was more or less in the bag, subject to him making sure he made no major fuck-ups, of course.

'But I do look out for them, Danny, I always try to do my bit.' This was a smart dig at his father and, as he knew it would, it made Danny Boy grin.

Ange listened to the conversation with a heavy heart. While she was pleased that her life wasn't the hard round of grafting it had once been, she was sorry her husband had lost out on the love and respect of his children. Even if it was for no other reason than he was a lazy bastard. But he was her lazy bastard and that was the main thing as far as she was concerned.

Danny Boy was getting a bit too above himself, and she didn't know how to curtail his behaviour any more. Since the loss of the last child he had been distinctly offish with her, and she knew she would have to fight hard to regain any kind of relationship with him before she fought once more for her husband's place in the household. Life was hard, and getting harder by the day. The wheels of God grind slow, as her mother always said, and she was getting tired of waiting for the outcome.

Her daughter waltzed into the kitchen all shiny hair and perfect teeth and she saw Danny Boy's face light up. This girl was the highlight of his days, and she knew it, and she made sure her parents knew it too. She was a little madam who needed taking down a few pegs and Ange would wait until that time was upon them, then God help the little mare. She would enjoy smacking the smug look off of her lovely face.

As Annuncia looked at her mother with her usual irritating haughtiness, Ange had to stop herself from lashing out there and then. Instead, she waited till the girl was seated and then she placed a plate of bacon and eggs before her, the tension between them almost palpable.

Danny Boy was observing the usual morning ritual between mother and daughter and, leaning forward in his seat, he barked out loudly, 'Where's the thank-you for your mother, then?'

It was said with such anger that both mother and daughter literally jumped with fright.

'She just cooked you a breakfast, and you waltz in here like the Princess Royal without a word to throw to a dog.'

'I'm sorry Danny . . . Thanks, Mum . . .' She was looking at her mother now, her eyes huge with fear and her voice trembling with emotion. She didn't look in her father's direction as she was more than aware that he wouldn't be sticking in his two pence to defend her.

Ange tried to diffuse the situation, her sorrow for this daughter of hers making her earlier annoyance forgotten. 'She's only a child, Danny, sure she's grateful enough, aren't you, girl?'

Jonjo pushed his empty plate away and sat back in his seat, hoping this latest upset didn't nause up his chance of getting a racing bike. Trust his sister to fuck up as usual. Danny Boy had once more turned on a coin, reminding everyone sitting round the breakfast table that he was not someone to be taken for granted.

Even Danny Boy was sorry now, sorry for upsetting his little sister, but if there was one thing he couldn't abide, it was disrespect. And his mother, whatever he might think in the privacy of his own thoughts, was still *his* mother and, as such, she should be treated with respect if only for no other reason than that.

Book Two

Hate takes a long time
To grow in, and mine
Has increased from birth;
Not for the brute earth . . .
. . . I find
This hate's for my own kind.

– R. S. Thomas, 1913–2000
'Those Others'

Chapter Ten

1980

The casino was not too busy and Danny Boy scanned the few remaining customers with a practised eye. He smiled and nodded at some of the clientele and deliberately disregarded the others with his usual disdain. He knew who to keep on-side and who to studiously ignore, this had become a part of his daily demeanour. People expected this behaviour from him. He had created a persona; he was friendly to anyone with a name or connections, but not overly obsequious. He treated them all the same, and was quick to reprimand if he thought they had stepped over his imaginary line. Anyone else was below his radar and therefore not worthy of consideration.

At twenty-five he was a big man with huge shoulders that looked good in his expensive suits. His hair was kept short in a college-boy cut, and he held himself well. He had the stance of a boxer, of a much lighter man. He still had his boyish good looks, only now they were marred by the frown lines that had developed over the years. He looked hard, even when he was laughing and joking with people. There was something about him, a dangerous side to him that was evident to most people he came into contact with. When he exploded, which was often in his world, he was a sight to see; his huge muscles rippled with the pent-up anger inside him. He looked what he was; a handful, a looney tunes and, most of all, he looked like someone who was going places.

Provided he didn't get his collar felt, a capture, he was on the road to riches.

As Danny made his way through to the foyer he had his eyes everywhere and, confident that no one was going to get out of order, he slipped through to the small office at the back for a rest.

It was the early hours of Sunday morning and he had a few things to sort out before he finished his day. He went into the small toilet cubicle that was hidden by a thick velvet curtain and, slipping off his jacket, he put the tap on full. As the water got steadily colder he rolled up his shirt sleeves and sluiced his face and neck. The icy cold of the water made him shiver and he dried himself on a rough piece of towel, rubbing hard to warm up his skin. This was something he did regularly: he was often tired out as he worked such long hours at his different jobs. But it suited him; he liked to be busy and he liked to be *seen* to be busy. It was another string to his already cluttered bow. He heard Michael come into the office and went out to greet him.

Danny had his usual smile on his face and Michael was, as always, amazed at how well he looked, considering.

'Did you get it?'

Michael nodded, and poured them both a drink while Danny Boy tidied himself up. As he shrugged on his jacket again he said quietly, 'How's your mum?'

Michael took a package from the inside of his overcoat and placed it on the desk. 'She's still alive, I think even the fucking doctors can't believe it. But she won't last long. I put the other eighteen blocks in the usual place.'

Michael gulped on his whisky deeply. Even though she had been a nightmare of a woman, she was still his mother when all was said and done. It was the shame he hated having to deal with, knowing that everyone was aware she was lying in hospital. The DTs had taken over at last, and she screamed and swore about all and sundry while her body finally packed up from the years of boozing. 'She's bright yellow, like a fucking daffodil, Dan, and still demanding a drink.'

Danny was quiet for a few moments. He wasn't sure how to deal with this latest drama in his friend's life. 'How's Mary taking it?'

Michael shrugged. 'I'm not sure, she turned up just before I left. Kenny dropped her off but didn't hang around.'

The suppressed anger was in his voice, anger that his sister was sleeping with Kenny Douglas didn't sit well with him. The man was twenty-five years her senior and he wasn't what could be called reliable. In fact he was a thug, a vicious, womanising thug. He made his poke by intimidation and using young men looking for a bit of kudos. It was no surprise that he had never seen the inside of a police station; he ran his operation with nothing more than threats and intimidation and his young workforce were more than happy to go down for him if it all came out on top. They wanted to be known as part of his gang; it guaranteed them a measure of respect. Kenny also made sure their families were taken care of, so he came out of it like big benevolent Harry, when in fact he was nothing but a user. He was now using his sister and it irked him. But because Kenny was still a Face to be reckoned with, with extensive criminal contacts, not least Lawrence Mangan being an old school chum, he had to give him the respect due to him because of that.

'The man's a cunt.'

Danny didn't answer. Instead he opened the package and, holding the block of amphetamine in his hands, he ripped off the plastic coating and nibbled on a corner. Within seconds his lips were going numb and he relaxed a little. This was good gear and they would out it in no time. This was the game now; recreational drugs, clubs and gambling. That little sideline had already amassed them enough money to open this place and purchase a couple of boozers. They were keeping a low profile in many respects, but those in the know were watching them with interest, as he had expected. Already they were being approached to do things without Lawrence, and it was all because of this white powder that was suddenly in abundance. He had the contacts, and he had the strength to go it alone. No one could sell it without his express permission, and he made sure that people knew that. Anyone with dreams of being a dealer were soon disabused of that notion with a pick-axe handle and a bicycle chain. Retribution was quick and bloody, as befitted the type of people they were forced to deal with.

Now they had it more or less sewn up and it was a serious earner all right. This stuff would make his fortune for him, he was determined on that. Only a few more weeks and they would come out into the open and, when they did, it would be violent and bloody, and it would also catapult them into the stratosphere of criminal enterprise. He couldn't wait to get started.

Mary looked down at the wreck that had once been her mother and swallowed down her impatience. She just wished the woman would die and leave them all alone. Instead she was babbling away to herself, the ravaged body that had once held so much promise and vitality was now almost skeletal, the skin literally hanging from the bones. She looked so frail, even her hair looked defeated, and that long, thick hair had always been her crowning glory. It was thin now, broken at the roots and stripped of any discernible colour. Drink was a terrible thing when it got into people's souls. Her mother had drunk herself into this caricature of a woman, and it had not been a pretty sight. She had been the cause of so much hurt in her life and now she was dying and, like everything else she did, she was making it as hard as she could for her children.

Mary saw Michael outside the doorway and smiled sadly. He looked awful; she knew their mother's death would hit him hard. Despite everything, he still loved her, and so did she in her own way. But now she wanted her gone so they could pick up the pieces and get on with their lives. She saw her reflection in the window, she looked good and she knew it. Knowing her mother had once looked just like her was unbelievable; seeing her now it was hard to believe she was even human. All her life she had been told by this woman that all she had going for her was her looks and she knew now that her mother had been right to caution her. She was older now, had seen what could happen to a girl without the nous to take care of herself. She was with Kenny because he gave her the lifestyle she craved, and in a funny way she was sorry her mother wouldn't live to benefit from it any more.

She left the room and went to her brother's side. 'You all right?'

He nodded. 'How's Gordon?'

She sighed. 'You know him, Mike, he came in for a few minutes and then shot off. He can't cope with it.'

Michael wiped a trembling hand across his face. He was sweating again, the pressure was getting to him and, like his sister and brother, he wished his mother would give up the ghost and let them get on with their lives. It was so depressing watching her getting weaker and weaker by the day, all the while knowing that there was nothing anyone could do to help her or ease her suffering.

'You go and get a coffee, I'll sit with her, OK?'

Mary watched him go into the room and, walking to the lift, took her cigarettes and lighter from her handbag. She was going to sit outside in the freezing cold and have a smoke. Anything was preferable to watching her brother's suffering.

Inside the room Michael looked at his mother and, sitting by her bedside, he held onto her hand. She opened her eyes and grinned at him, the rancid smell of her breath was overpowering in the room. She was lucid, her eyes had lost the child-like vacancy of the previous day. She was alert, her usual cold-eyed calculating self once more.

'Mikey, Mikey, son, please get me a drink, will you? Just a drop to keep the cold out, eh?' She was pleading with him, as she had so many times before. She was such a manipulator, such a force and, even in the throes of death, she could still exploit her considerable talent for using guilt to its full advantage. Lying on the pillows in almost a sitting position because of her chest problems, she looked old, and she looked defeated. It was only her eyes that had any kind of life in them now. And they were imploring him to let her have the only thing she had ever really wanted in her life.

'I can't do this on me own, I need a sip to get me through it. Please, mate, just one last drop and I'll go with a happy heart.'

She was pulling herself off the pillows in her earnestness, trying to sit up properly to emphasise her point. She had been begging him for days to give her a last bottle of the hard and now he did as she requested. Slipping a small bottle of Black & White whisky from his pocket he held it up so she could see what he was going to do for her. As he poured the rich yellow liquid into the plastic beaker she was crying, 'You're a good boy, Michael, a good son, I knew you wouldn't let me down, not now, not at the end . . .'

As he placed the plastic spout between her lips he heard someone coming into the room. It was their parish priest, Father Galvin, a huge bear of a man who had a legendary capacity for alcohol himself.

'Ah, Jesus, are you giving her the Holy Water? It's the act of a Christian, son, and it will send her on her way with a lighter heart.'

He was going to give her the last rites, and Michael watched as he unpacked his small valise, smelled the herbs and the oils that would herald the end of his mother's life, mixed with the heavy scent of whisky, and decided this was a fitting end to her suffering. Like the priest said, it was what she wanted now, all he could really he do for her: a final act of kindness. Mary came back into the room and smiled as she saw him refilling the beaker with whisky. Her mother was sucking at the grey-tinged plastic spout like a new-born baby at the breast, the sound loud in the quietness of the room.

Two hours later she dropped into a deep sleep and her children thought she would never wake up again.

Then she opened her eyes and said sadly, 'Don't waste your lives like I did, and watch out for one another.'

Then she was gone.

Both Michael and Mary were unprepared for the torrent of grief her passing actually caused them when they finally realised that she really had passed away.

The priest blessed her one last time and, pouring the last of the scotch into a grimy glass tumbler, he said robustly, 'The end of an era.' Then, holding up the glass in a toast to her, he said sadly, 'To a good woman who couldn't slay her demons, no matter how hard she tried. She's in the arms of her saviour tonight.'

It was too much for Mary and she broke down then and cried the tears she had held back for a lifetime. Whatever kind of a mother she had been, she was still the only mother they had, the only mother they had known, and now she was gone and none of them knew how to react to that because they had wished her dead for the best part of their lives. The nurses came in and, with their usual tact, they ignored the empty bottle of whisky, even though they must have been aware that it had hurried her passing, and busied themselves instead with laying her out, exclaiming all the while at the way the lines had suddenly been smoothed from her skin, and at how much her daughter looked like her.

Louie was sitting with Lawrence Mangan, enjoying one of his large cigars. The heavy blue smoke wrapped itself around his head and he breathed in its pleasing aroma. These were real Cuban cigars, not for resale in this country, but a welcome addition to their black market trading.

As they sipped their brandies Louie waited patiently for Lawrence to say what was so obviously on his mind. He knew it would concern young Danny and Michael, and he also knew it was a subject his friend had been returning to with annoying frequency over the last few months. Until now he had not made any kind of remark, detrimental or otherwise, he had just listened and let the man get it off his chest. But he had watched and listened to everyone around them and knew exactly what all this pissing and moaning was leading to. He was disappointed in this man, but not overly surprised. After all, you didn't get where Mangan was without a few moments of skulduggery that you would rather keep quiet about but, by the same token, he was complaining about his best earners. Only now they were also earning for themselves outside his family, and he didn't like it. But they were young bloods and they needed to make their own mark. It was the way of their world, what most of his contemporaries expected. As long as they got a drink they were happy enough, and they kept a good earner on their payroll.

Lawrence however, wasn't like that. He had a kink in his nature that was the result of a deep and abiding jealousy of anyone who he felt was doing better than him. Jealous of anyone who might just be on the right side of a good idea, an earner that he saw as something he should be on the receiving end of. Envy was not a deadly sin for nothing; it caused more wars in their world than anything else.

'Lairy little fucker didn't even come at the appointed time, mugged me right off. I tell you, Louie, they either work for me or they work for themselves. There ain't no middle ground here.'

Louie shrugged, as if young people were nothing more than that, young and restless, it was to be expected. The gesture annoyed Mangan and he threw back his drink quickly, his cigar was smaller and far less conspicuous than Louie's and he dropped it into the ashtray with an angry sigh.

'I had fucking Boris the pimp on the blower the other day asking me to give them a message! *Me*, take messages for my fucking staff? I mean, what am I, a cunt or what?'

Louie sighed, his lovely cigar was being wasted because of all this tension and trouble, he liked to relax with it, give himself over to the sheer pleasure the fucking thing brought him. Now he placed it carefully in the ashtray before saying quietly, 'What is wrong with taking a message for someone? In the grand scheme of things it's hardly a fucking mission, is it? I take messages for people all the time, you included. It's called being a mate, being a fucking normal person. We organise our whole lives through messages, coded or otherwise, we use them to set up deals or to make meets with other like-minded individuals in the hope that the Filth won't cotton onto anything. So a message, my friend, is just that, a fucking message. Now get over it.'

Never, in all his years, had Lawrence Mangan been spoken to like that by Louie. In fact, it was such a shock he was dumbstruck for a few moments as the enormity of what Louie had said sunk in.

It seemed his radar had been on the right course, the boys were planning something and even Louie had been forced to take sides. It seemed he was going to take theirs. Louie watched the different expressions on his friend's face and sighed; he knew exactly what was going on in his mind and it grieved him. Lawrence had never learned the art of sharing, it was his biggest failing. And everyone knew he had outed people on the sly; you didn't see your partners getting nicked without your collar being felt. But no one had ever been able to prove it, and so he had been given the benefit of the doubt on more than one occasion. Now though, he was being talked about as a grass, and not as a Face. Louie had the feeling this was the doing of Danny Boy Cadogan and he knew he was doing it to justify whatever little drama he had in mind for this man in the near future. Danny Boy was like a fucking police dog, he could sniff out skulduggery like they sniffed out cannabis, with a cheery demeanour and the least amount of aggro. But once he found it, all hell broke out.

He could smell treachery, and he loathed it. Danny was still a young one, but he was also schooled in the old ways, the old codes and, as such, he would go far in their world. It was time for him to make his mark, why couldn't this man let him, and be happy for him? It was a fucking disgrace the way he was sounding off and that kid was earning him a serious wedge on a regular basis.

But he would try and save the day if he could, even though he knew it was a waste of time. Lawrence was well past his sell-by date, and everyone knew it but him. There's no way Boris would have left a message, treated him like an errand boy, if that wasn't the case. In fact there had been a few rumours lately about Lawrence's attitude and his greediness. He never really let anyone else have an earn off him if he could help it.

Lawrence was still looking at him with undisguised shock. 'Louie, what the fuck you on about?' He was genuinely grieved and it came across in his voice, which had somehow risen a few octaves.

Michael was sitting in Danny's mum's, listening to Elvis Costello through the thin walls of the kitchen. He was singing about watching the detectives, and the neighbour obviously liked it because it had been turned up to full volume. The neighbour was obviously on a death wish of some sort, because there was no way Danny was going to swallow that racket when he finally turned up.

As Michael looked around the neat and tidy room he couldn't help but compare it to the filthy dump he had been brought up in. The sheets were rarely changed on the beds, and the kitchen was never cleared of clutter. They had grown up with the stench of unwashed bodies and continual dramas, their mother's drink problem had affected them all, especially Mary and Gordon. Over the last few years he had seen to it that someone came in and cleaned, and his mother had been thrilled about that. Then, after she treated them like shit, he had been forced to replace them on a regular basis. Seeing Mrs Cadogan's scrubbed table and shiny sink he felt the lump once more in his throat for what should have been. He had done his best, but it wasn't the same as having someone around who knew how to be a proper parent.

The whole house was in bed, except for Danny's father, who was watching TV in the small lounge. He was once more drinking himself into oblivion and Michael wondered again at the dependence on alcohol in their immediate circle. It was like a cancer, eating away at the root of everything and everyone it touched.

As he sipped his coffee, he heard Danny Boy's footsteps on the cement stairwell and, lighting a cigarette, he waited for the balloon to go up. He wasn't disappointed.

Jamie Barker was a slightly built lad with a penchant for cannabis and a permanent grin, courtesy of a fight he had in Borstal when a knife had been slashed across his mouth. The resulting scar made him look either overfriendly or frightening, depending on the time of day or night. He was now living with his maternal aunt, Jackie Bendix, in the flat next to the Cadogans'. Alone, he had smoked himself senseless and, unfortunately for him, decided to turn up the radio for his own personal amusement.

The hammering on the front door had spooked him and, leaping from his seat, he threw the grass he had purchased that evening out of the front-room window, believing the caller was probably Old Bill. As he opened the front door he took the full force of Danny Cadogan's large fist in his face and, curling himself up into a ball, he took the kicking being delivered, with a quiet grace that actually impressed his assailant.

Dragging the boy up by his long, straggly hair Danny bellowed, 'You ever take a fucking liberty with my personal space again, I'll fucking kill you stone dead.'

Then, going into the flat, he removed the offending radio from its usual place on the windowsill in the kitchen and aimed it over the balcony onto the concrete pavement below. An elderly woman came out and, smiling happily at Danny Boy, said gratefully, 'I wondered what time you'd be home, son, that noise was getting on my bleeding nerves.'

Danny Boy grinned at her, all friendliness and respectful kindness.

'You're welcome, Mrs Dickson. What a fucking liberty, eh, assuming we want to listen to his fucking racket. Now, get yourself back inside, it's cold out here.'

Like all the women in the flats she loved him, there was none of the usual noise and squalor they had once been used to. Danny Boy Cadogan made sure of that, and for that reason alone, he was worshipped. Coupled with his respectfulness for older people and his insistence on living in a noise-free environment he was treated with almost reverence by most of the neighbours. Thanks to him they all lived in a crime-free capsule that made this block of flats a haven for everyone who lived there. Unlike the rest of the estate they didn't have anyone urinating in the halls, no youngsters hanging around, no burglaries and no unexplained fires either. It was wonderful.

As she closed her front door Danny looked at the young man groaning on the dirty floor and, aware that he was being watched from behind most of the net-curtained flats around and about, he lifted the boy up carefully and took him back inside the flat. Dropping him none too gently onto the couch, he surveyed the boy's bleeding face and decided he'd live, so he left him there. But once more, he had caused a small commotion, and that would once more mean that he would be talked about with friendliness by his grateful neighbours, thus enriching the reputation he had already garnered for himself. When he went inside his own home he saw Michael sitting at the kitchen table and remembered his friend had just lost his mother. Going to him, he hugged him tightly and, as Michael started crying, he whispered over and over again, 'I'm so sorry, mate.'

Big Danny Cadogan listened to his son's gentle voice and was as ever amazed at how mercurial this son's temperament could be. From a beating administered for what he saw as an infraction of his personal space, he was now the good friend, the decent bloke, and Big Dan knew, in his heart of hearts, that it was all an act. Everything his son did was an act of some sort. Unfortunately, most people in their world didn't pick up on that fact until it was too late.

*

Mary Miles was lying in bed, staring up at the ceiling as her boy-friend of two years pumped away at her body. It was the last thing she wanted at this moment in time, but Kenny's clumsy attempt at comforting her had turned into a sexual act, as he had intended it to. Everything came down to a sexual act where Kenny Douglas was concerned and, even though he gave her all the things she needed these days to survive – money, prestige and a wardrobe of clothes envied by her peer group – she was still unhappy with her lot, and this grieved her. Her mother's death had hit her hard, harder than she had expected. In fact, the knowledge that she wouldn't be there any more was frightening. Even though the woman had been a nightmare for the best part of her life, Mary had finally, after all these years, begun to understand her mother, understand why she had taken her solace in drink. Mary had more than a few mates who were already cooking children, or were even on their second, and learning about how hard it was to exist without the cushion of money, or a decent bloke to see them through the week. Well, as she had promised her mother, that wasn't going to be her and, even though this man might not set her heart on fire, he was good to her in his own way and she was grateful to be under his protection.

Michael was making his way in the world and, between them, they would look out for Gordon as best they could. The tears were once more threatening, and she blinked them away. Crying wasn't going to solve anything, and Kenny might not take kindly to his sexual gymnastics being curtailed until he had sated himself. She could smell the acrid aroma that seemed to cling to his pudgy body. Even after a bath he still had the stench of the gutter on him. She supposed she did as well. But at least her perfume and make-up masked it long enough for her to forget where it had come from. Poor Kenny, for all his big talk and his big cars, he still looked what he was: a wide boy. A Face. It was evident in the gold he wore, and the clothes that he purchased; no amount of money could hide the fact that he had literally no taste and that his new-found wealth sat uneasily on him. He still felt more at ease in a speiler or a corner pub than in a nice restaurant or decent drinking club. As her old mum always said, you could take a boy out of the East End . . .

As Kenny came inside her and she felt the shuddering that heralded the end of his bodily assault, she hugged him closely. She pulled him into her young arms and feigned the love she knew he craved. No man in his right mind could believe that without a good few quid and a decent standard of living he would have had the bird of his dreams anyway. It was one of the reasons men tried to be successful; a good-looking woman on their arm was all they eventually needed to prove to the world they had made it.

It was a fair trade though: in return he gave her more or less anything she asked for. And Mary Miles asked for a lot.

'You all right, babe?' His voice was thick with phlegm and she felt the bile rise inside her. When he coughed deeply to clear his throat, hawking loudly, she felt the urge to physically attack him, so disgusted did he make her feel. But, as always, she forced a smile onto her lovely face and nodded her assent. He never questioned her too closely for fear she would answer him truthfully and break the tenuous link that kept her beside him in his bed.

'Feel better?'

She nodded once more as she marvelled at a man who could reach the age he had, yet still remain in blissful ignorance as to whether or not the woman lying underneath him had actually achieved anything even approaching an orgasm. Sitting up, she took the glass of brandy and Babycham from the bedside table and gulped at it greedily. She was praying it would help her sleep, help her find a measure of peace, not realising that her poor mother had done exactly the same thing many years before, and for exactly the same reasons.

'Thanks, Louie, we really appreciate this.'

Louie shrugged, and Danny noticed that he was getting old, shrinking somehow. And he was getting frailer. It was sad to see that, and Danny was amazed at how the realisation made him feel very protective of the old bugger. He would never forget that this was the man who had given him his first opportunity at earning when his father had fucked up so badly, who had taken him under his wing, and who had then looked out for him in one way or another ever since.

'I thought I would give you two a heads-up but, listen to me, boys. I knew you were plotting against him and, to be honest, I don't blame you. I hear everything, as I told you many years ago. Now, I'll offer you another piece of advice: when you take him on, make sure you let the powers that be know, as an actual fact, that he was a grass. It will not only put the brakes on any comebacks you might incur because of his age and position in the world, but it will also guarantee you a lot of goodwill from the right people. You might have to deal with the usual ice creams out to cause a fuss, but they are nothing to worry about in the great scheme of things: you need the goodwill and the blessing of a lot of people if you want to take your drug business into the big world.'

Michael grinned. He liked old Louie, he spoke sense, and he didn't preach to them.

'I have fallen out with him bigtime over defending you two, so don't fucking let me down.'

'We won't, Louie.'

'I'm sorry about your mother, she was an extraordinary woman.'

Michael and Danny both grinned at his attempt to find something good to say about her.

'That's one way of describing her, I suppose.'

For some reason the two young men found it hilarious and they started to laugh. Louie finished his drink; it was good to get grief out of your system and, if laughter was the tool the boy needed, then let him laugh. It had been a strange few days all round.

As he watched them roaring with laughter, Louie saw the menace in them, and the youthfulness that made them believe they were untouchable, indestructible. He didn't have the heart to tell them that Mangan had been just like them once. A young blood with the whole world waiting for him, and the certainty that it would always give him the best that life had to offer. He sensed that this wasn't the time or the place.

Chapter Eleven

Gordon Miles was standing outside his block of flats with his good friend and sometimes co-conspirator, Jonjo Cadogan. He couldn't believe he was going to bury his mother in the next few hours. It felt surreal. That she would not make old bones had been a given; he had always guessed the drink would do for her quicker than life itself. But he was still shocked, she had been such a big part of their lives even though, like his brother and sister, he had secretly wished her dead many times. Now she had finally gone, it felt wrong. He felt guilty for his thoughts, even though they were perfectly normal.

He was a big lad for his age and, like his friend, he was a watered-down version of his older brother. The day was icy cold and, dressed in his new black suit and cashmere overcoat, he looked much older than his seventeen years. He watched silently as a crowd gathered: he knew they were coming to pay their respects to a woman who had been, for the most of them, a thorn in their side. He had wondered, as his sister had, if people would turn up just to make sure she was *really* dead. That would make more sense. So many people would be glad to wave her off this day and, as guilty as the thought made him, deep down, he knew he was one of them.

The day was heavy with rain, the damp was everywhere, flattening the women's hair and seeping through the thin jackets of the men standing around smoking and chatting in small groups. This was a scene they had witnessed many times over the years, a funeral was like everything else in their mundane lives, a bit of excitement, light relief, a topic of conversation. A funeral like this would be talked about for months. The casket alone was rumoured to have cost the national debt, and this for a woman who could drink most of the men under the table, and who, in her last years, didn't have a kind word to throw to a dog, who had treated her children like dirt. She had left them alone, forgot about them for days on end, had relied on them to take care of themselves. She had become a by-word for bad parenting, and the perils of drink for women.

It was also being talked about because of the fact the older Miles boy, Michael, was now a Face around the town, and he was in league with the new local lunatic, Danny Boy Cadogan. A young man who had not only crippled his own father, something even the most generous-minded of individuals found hard to comprehend, but who had also single-handedly stopped a lot of the gang crime on the estate just by his presence. For that alone people liked him. He had achieved with a few heavy blows from a wheel brace and a few choice words what the police had been trying to achieve since the place had been built just after the war. He was a local hero in many respects, and his shine had rubbed off on everyone around him. There was a frisson of excitement in the air as a black limousine pulled up and three large men with solemn faces and expensive suits got out. It was Kenny Douglas and it had been a long time since he had been seen in this neck of the woods. He was more of a Bethnal Green boy, a Valance Road cowboy as the locals referred to them. He was already lighting a cigarette as he carefully surveyed the faces around him, always on the lookout for anyone who might wish him harm. There were a lot of people like that in his world due to his bad attitude, and his habit of falling out with his contemporaries for the most childish of reasons. He was high maintenance was Kenny, and everyone knew that about him. Not the most handsome of men, he had the air of someone who did not have a lot of time for the niceties in life. Anyone outside the game would feel the menace emitting from him and instinctively give him a wide berth. In his world, this same menace had become his passport to riches. Now, as he looked at the drab people observing him as if he was some kind of exotic bird, he felt the futility that poverty seemed to spread like a blanket wherever it decided to settle. This was too close to home for him, a reminder of his past; he was better than this now.

As a kid he had buried his father in very similar circumstances, but without the money to give the old cunt a decent send-off. His father had gone out of the world in a pauper's grave, buried with a crowd of other no-hopers. They couldn't even put up a headstone for him, all they could afford was a vase for flowers, flowers that no one was going to bring for him. He had achieved little in his life, other than the hatred of his children, and the dislike of everyone else he had ever came into contact with. The shame was still there for Kenny, though. The shame of being the offspring of a drunk.

Anyway, today he was only here for Mary, no other reason than that, and he was determined to make that point to her brother and his sidekick. A young man, it seemed, who was just as determined to make his mark in their world as he had been. The boy was doing all right, no one disputed that, and he had a few Faces in his corner, but he was also a lairy little fucker who would one day rub the wrong person up the wrong way. The boy bothered him lately, as did Michael Miles; they were a good team and they had a fine little crew. That actually worried him more than he cared to admit. Truth be told, the boy frightened him; he had a look in his eye that anyone with an iota of brain cells could see concealed a seriously deranged personality. Well, the ponce was about to find out that Louie fucking Stein wasn't enough to take on any of the established Faces in the surrounding areas, and today was as good a day as any to make that point. Twenty-five and brash, Danny Cadogan was nothing more than a caricature of his own daydreams. He was dealing drugs, collecting debts, and had just dipped his toes into the world of anabolic steroids. He was no more than a prison sentence waiting to happen.

Danny Boy might have crippled his old man, and rubbed out a debt, but that counted for nothing where the likes of him were concerned. It just showed him up for the treacherous cunt he really was. Everyone thought he was such a fucking good boy: that his father had deserved all he had got. But, at the end of the day, he had crippled his own flesh and blood, had taken out his own father, piece of shit though he might be. It was out of order, a fucking liberty. The boy was being fêted for something so heinous there was no precedent in their world to justify it.

So today was going to be the day Danny Boy found out that his reputation wasn't enough to take on the *really* big boys, not by a long shot. Kenny felt his stomach rumble and wished he had eaten breakfast, but he was taking communion today because his mother was going to be there, and he knew it would please her. Plus, he hadn't been to Mass for a few weeks and this was as good an excuse as any.

Mary was sitting in her old bedroom listening to her cousin Immelda as she chattered on about what food had been prepared at the pub and how much it had all cost. Immelda was a big girl with beautiful eyes, heavyset legs and the beginnings of a seriously thick moustache. She had a very kind personality and had moved into the flat recently to keep everything going, and now she was trying her hardest to guarantee her place in this household rather than have to go home, where she was used as an unpaid skivvy. If Mary said she could stay there, no one would dispute it. Mary was a Face in her own right through Kenny Douglas, and she was hoping her cousin would use her new-found power to keep her where she was. She couldn't go home now, she was enjoying this little bit of freedom, loving her life for the first time ever.

Mary stood up, she understood exactly where her cousin was coming from, and said sadly, 'Immelda, stop worrying, this is your gaff for as long as you want it to be. OK?'

Immelda held out her chubby arms and Mary walked into them. As she hugged her, she said with real emotion, 'You fucking star, cuz. I can't go back to that lot now, they'd drive me up the bleeding wall.'

Mary laughed softly, a laugh she would have laid good money on wasn't inside her. But it was, and the two of them laughed together, both feeling relief, and for similar reasons. The unloading of a parent, a parent who had no real place in their world, but who they had to put up with anyway.

Mary, though, had the edge, she was burying her mother and,

as sad as that was, she couldn't wait for the day to be over and done with so she could put it behind her once and for all.

They were still hugging when Michael walked in and motioned to her that the funeral cars had arrived.

'There's a good turn out, anyway.' He said it with relief. If no one had bothered to come and see what had been spent, their mother would have clawed her way out of the grave and demanded they did the whole thing over again. She loved a bit of show, and adored drama of any kind, catapulting herself into the centre of any that she might come across during her daily wanderings. Michael was only sorry that she couldn't have been there this day, she would have loved it. She was where she had always wanted to be, in the centre of it all, the focal point of everyone's life.

Mary didn't answer him. She looked very sophisticated in a fitted black Ozzie Clarke suit with a tight pencil skirt and huge jet buttons that only emphasised her slim figure. Her blond hair was styled perfectly, hanging down her back in a thick curly mass, and she had never looked lovelier. Her wide-spaced eyes were made up expertly and gave her an innocence that was long gone. Michael was proud of her and how she looked, proud she had risen above the local opinion of their family, and proud she was strong enough to cope with what life threw at her. God knew they'd all had to develop thick skins over the years to combat their mother's antics when in her cups.

It was poor Gordon he worried about, the boy had been closest to his mother, he had been her baby. He was going to talk to Danny Boy about setting him up with a proper little earner until such time as they could suss out whether or not he would be an asset to them or a drain on their resources.

As they walked downstairs Mary could feel Danny Cadogan's eyes on her and she glanced at him with her usual disdain, even though he made her heart race and her legs feel weak. She had been secretly in love with him since she was a schoolgirl, and she had hidden it well. She had always known that if he had even guessed, he would have found it amusing, and she couldn't have borne it if he had laughed at her, ridiculed her.

He was looking at her with genuine sadness and she dropped

her usual guard for a few moments and smiled at him. The smile transformed her face, and Danny saw the hunger for him in her eyes and wondered what she would be like in the kip. He had a feeling she would be a handful: he was convinced that Kenny couldn't ring her bells, not in that department anyway. He was far too old for her, and far too jaded for their relationship to be any kind of a real love job. Not on her side anyway. Kenny was a means to an end, and even he must have been aware of that much. If he wasn't, then he was a mug. He could take her off him with a wink and a smile, and one day soon he would. When the time was right; when it would do the most damage. Danny Boy was quite looking forward to it.

Today though, he was sensible enough to know that this wasn't the time or place to settle any scores, no matter how pressing they might seem. Today was Michael's day, and he was going to ensure it went off without a hitch. After all, Michael was not only his best friend, he was also the real brains of their outfit and Danny needed him far more than he let on.

'Come on, mare, I'll walk you out.'

As his arm circled her shoulders she started to cry, and he cradled her head with his free hand as he pulled her into his arms. She buried her face in his chest in the way many a grieving woman had before her and, Danny being Danny, he used the excuse of comforting her to cop a quick and sneaky feel. She felt every bit as good as he had expected her to.

The pub was packed out, and the heat, combined with the alcohol that was not only free but was also being provided in huge amounts, had given the wake a real party atmosphere. This was not unusual in the Irish Catholic community. People tutted their heads and acted as if it was a disgrace, but to them a funeral was a celebration of death: it heralded the deceased person's journey into heaven, into a much better place. Especially someone as troubled as Mrs Miles. As the music got louder and the voices more raucous, Danny Boy stood with his parents and surveyed what was quickly becoming his own little kingdom. People came up to him and shook his hand, even the fathers of his old school friends gave him his due, and this was noticed by all the people around them.

Kenny Douglas was a little worse for wear and Mary, Danny could see, was not impressed with that. He was supposed to be by her side, making sure she was comforted on this day, the day her mother was buried. Kenny was acting as if it was any other day, he was on the piss and out for a row. She knew, like everyone else there, that he should have greeted Danny Boy and her brother at the graveside, but he had not bothered to do so and it had annoyed her. It had also annoyed her brother and his partner-in-crime. Michael felt slighted because he *was*, after all, Mary's older brother. Danny Boy felt slighted because he felt he was now in a position that should have guaranteed him the respect of his fellow Faces. A lot of people had used this funeral to show their solidarity with the two young men who were making such a stir in their world. They greeted and offered condolences, all the while wondering what these lads could be used for in the future. Wondering what they might have to offer when they became permanent fixtures in their own right. They were on the cusp of the big one, they were grafters: it was more a case of *when* they would come into their own, subsequently most people were ready to give them their due. Louie Stein was also watching the situation with his usual canny expression, looking for all the world as if he noticed nothing, when in fact he noticed everything. This, he surmised, was a recipe for disaster all right. Kenny was mugging them off, and that would not be forgotten in a hurry. This would need to be addressed as both parties would demand closure at some point, and Louie had a feeling he knew who the victor would be when it all went off, and off it was going to go sooner, rather than later, by the looks of it. He watched and he waited, and marvelled at how pride could always guarantee a fall at some point. Kenny Douglas was about to fall from a great height and, like Danny Boy's father, he wasn't going to recover from it any time in the near future.

Raising his glass to Danny Boy, Louie saw Kenny looking at him with obvious disgust and he laughed loudly before raising the same glass to him and his cronies.

Lawrence Mangan was also watching the proceedings and, as far as Louie was concerned, this was, in a lot of respects, a bloody good platform for Cadogan to finally make his mark. It was going to happen, it had been on the cards for a long time; someone was going to find out just what the little fucker was capable of.

Funerals, he had always found, reminded people of their own immortality, as well as reminding them that everyone died at some point: it was a given, especially in their world, where lives were often cut short for no other reason than they had picked a fight with the wrong person. To make old bones and still be out of stir was a difficult feat, and one that was only achieved by the best in class.

Today, Louie was sure, would prove that fact once more, would remind everyone that a new generation was coming up through the ranks with a heavy hand and a cheery smile. It wasn't rocket science, it happened in every walk of life. Famous actors had to stand back and watch younger, fitter men take over from them. It was the law of the pavement; youth would always win the game of chance. They had the edge because they had nothing to lose but everything to gain; it was success that held most people back, the fear of losing what they had gathered over the years. It made them soft, gave them a false sense of security. It made them make mistakes, and people like Danny Boy Cadogan could smell a mistake like a lion could smell a wounded gazelle. It was instinctive, it was what made the world go round, and it was fascinating to watch. As Danny winked at him Louie knew he had backed the winning horse; the boy was itching for a real fight, and now he was finally going to get one.

Mary was in the toilet repairing her make-up when Kenny stumbled in. He was drunker than either of them realised and he was out for an argument.

Mary had been avoiding him all day, preferring to stand with that fat cousin of hers, and the same women she denigrated on a daily basis for their blind devotion to men who she felt gave them nothing of any importance except children and grief. She really pissed him off at times, and this was one those times.

Mary knew the signs and she sighed, ready for the argument she knew would be forthcoming sooner rather than later. 'What do you want, Kenny?'

Her whole attitude was one of disrespect and open hostility, she was also drunker than she thought, but at least she had an excuse: she had just buried her mother.

'You what?' He was in the mood for a row, he was always in that mood when he had been drinking, only today she didn't care. She wasn't interested in *him* or his fucking histrionics.

'Oh, piss off, Kenny, I ain't in the mood.' Her voice was low, bored-sounding, and he knew that was how she felt about him twenty four-seven, if she was honest. He knew she had never really wanted him, not how she would have if they had both been of an age. He was older than her in more ways than one and it was beginning to come between them. Like all men with younger women he was aware that he was only wanted as long as he had something to offer her. Now, though, he knew she didn't want anything he had to give. The novelty had worn off, and he knew it.

That situation had been fine in the beginning; she was young, tight, and had a pair of tits to die for. She had been arm candy, like many women before her, but now he honestly loved her, every bit of her, and his pride was not going to let her go without a fight. He sensed she was on the out, wanted shot of him, and he also knew that her mother was the real reason she had been with him in the first place. She was now in a position to leave him without her mother's poison dripping into her ears, reminding her of how hard life could be without a man to take care of her. He knew she wanted Danny Boy Cadogan, he had seen the way she looked at him: it wouldn't take a blind dog long to sniff that much out. Now, as she stood there, looking at him with undisguised loathing, Kenny felt the urge to kill her. He wanted to wipe the smug smile off her face and pay her back for every time she had let him fuck her when, in reality, she had not wanted him anywhere near her. He had played along with that charade from the off, and now, if she thought he was going to meekly walk away, his tail between his legs while his cock was replaced by Danny Boy Cadogan's, she could fucking well think again. He owned her, he had paid for her, and she wasn't going nowhere until he told her she could go.

'Who're you fucking talking to, eh? Who the fuck do you think you are?' He was gritting his teeth, and the anger was dripping from him like sweat. Mary looked at him again, a part of her sorry for what she was going to do, but nevertheless determined to extricate herself from him once and for all. She felt like a young girl for once, felt like other girls her age, and she knew that she had the looks and the brains to get any man she set her mind on. But she also knew that she couldn't take any more of Kenny Douglas with his dry humping, his mean-mindedness and his cow-eyes. It was over, and they both knew it.

'Look, Kenny. I don't want to argue, not today of all days. I just buried me mother . . .'

Kenny grinned nastily, the fury he normally kept buried deep inside himself now on the surface. He was making her nervous, making her scared, and as he saw the fright on her face he felt the power flowing back into his bones. She was not leaving him, especially not for Cadogan, showing him up in front of all his mates as if he was a cunt. She would go when he *told* her she could go, and not before.

'Please, Kenny, don't do this, eh? You could have any girl you wanted . . .'

He was still grinning at her. 'But I want you, mare, and you, my little love, are going nowhere. If you think I'm going to let you make a fucking show of me, you better think again, girl. I'll see you dead first.'

Mary knew he meant every word he said and the fear settled once more on her heart. She knew he had to have put one of his men on the door of the toilet, otherwise someone else would have been in there by now. This knowledge told her that he was not in here for any other reason than to lay the law down, whether she wanted him to or not. He was telling her that she was trapped, and she knew that was very probably the case. He was proving a point at her mother's burial, proclaiming his power over her. Reminding her, and everyone else, of his right to ownership. He had bought her, and he knew it. It was because of that that they could never really be happy together. Trust was not something a relationship like theirs could ever be based on. They were both in it for all the wrong reasons. And she couldn't do this any more. Her mother was gone; she didn't have to think about anyone but herself now, and the drink was talking for her.

'Up yours, Kenny. You can't *force* me to want you. I ain't your fucking wife.'

'Don't you dare bring her into this. Don't you fucking dare start your antics with me tonight . . .'

She turned away from him, and looked at herself in the mirror. She could see him staring at her, could see the desperation in his eyes and felt a moment's sympathy for his predicament. It was all about other people with Kenny, what they might be thinking, what they might be doing, what they could give to him, or what he could take from them. She was no more than another possession as far as he was concerned. No more and no less. He had invested time and money in her and, because of that, he felt he could do what he liked with her, to her. She was going to unload him though, no matter what he did to her. It was now or never, and they both knew that. If she capitulated now, she was finished. He was attracted to her because she was so independent, once that changed she might as well dig herself a grave next to her mother because this man would take great pleasure in burying her.

She tidied her hair, flicking it back over her slim shoulders. She could see the want in him, and she said cattily, 'Do what you like, Kenny, but this finishes tonight.'

As he launched himself at her, she instinctively covered her head with her arms, knowing he would go for her face. Knowing he would be out to destroy her looks as well as her spirit.

He was punching her now, and she felt the savageness of his blows on her frail shoulders. But she wouldn't beg him to stop; if she did, he would be the victor in this war, and she'd never get shot of him. She would take whatever he dished out, at least then he would probably leave her in relative peace. But she had to let him vent his spleen, let him hurt her; it was the only way she would ever get truly shot of him.

As he yanked her towards him, she could feel him pushing her legs apart and, when he ripped away the scrap of silk that passed for underwear and forced his fat fingers inside her, she finally screamed. She was scratching at his face and eyes with her long, red nails, and she fought him with every ounce of strength she could muster.

She could feel the blood dripping from her mouth; it was warm, salty, and the pain that wracked her body was excruciating. Kenny was like a man demented, and she knew she had caused it all, caused this to happen because she should never have let it go so far in the first place. She had deliberately misled him, used him, had taken what he had to give, and now she was paying the price for that. Her mother's death had made her realise what was really important, what she was missing.

Then, suddenly, Michael and Danny were there, and Kenny was being dragged off her. She watched in silence as they kicked him over and over again. Danny Boy was enjoying it, was using the man's head like a football. She could see the pleasure on his face as he let rip, knew he was thrilled to have a good reason for his violent outburst. Her mother's funeral was no place to lay down the law: Kenny had let the drink overcome his usual good sense. He knew that, and she knew that.

She listened as Kenny begged for his life and she closed her eyes when Danny Boy Cadogan took out of his pocket a brand-new Stanley knife and used it to slash at the man she had led on for so long. As Kenny's blood sprayed over the dingy grey walls she felt the bile rise inside her, but she swallowed it down. She forced herself to remain calm, because this was suddenly far more serious than it should have been.

Michael, wide-eyed with anger, pulled her into his arms, while screaming at Danny to kill Kenny, to hurt him, and she knew then that what she had caused this night would have reverberations for years to come. Not just for her but for the three of them.

Lawrence Mangan listened to the debacle with everyone else and, like everyone else, he did nothing to stop it. But he knew then that these boys were out for the big one, were willing to take on the world to get what they saw as their right. He realised then, like Kenny, that he was not prepared for this new breed of villain. These young boys who were willing to kill on a whim. For no other reason than they felt like it. Who used a venue like this to make a point, and make that same point seem righteous? Kenny and Danny Boy were due a straightener and, in the real world, it should have come about in private and without the added bonus of a young girl's virtue being in doubt.

When they finally walked out of the ladies' toilet, Michael and Danny were both covered in blood and confident in the knowledge that no one there would speak against them. Even Kenny's henchmen were willing to swallow their knobs and let it go. If anyone had thought they were out of order it would never have happened in the first place, they would have steamed in and defended their boss. Instead, they had been left to do what they wanted. It was an eye-opener all right. Not just for the people observing, but for Danny Boy and Michael as well. They had been given the green light by the powers that be, and they were loving it. Michael had hated the treatment of his sister by Kenny and now, at last, he felt he could hold his head up. His mother was dead, and her conviction that Mary should sleep her way to the top was gone, buried with her. He felt like a man now, and he was acting like one.

The funeral was talked about for months, and the death of Kenny was quickly forgotten about by the police who had not cared that much about it anyway. They had a good idea who had taken him out, but they were of the same mind as everyone else. It had been on the cards for years: his demise had just been a matter of time.

Danny was sitting with his mother. They were easy together at the moment because she wanted something from him. She always wanted something from him, and his natural reaction was to give it to her if he could. She wanted him to pay for his sister to go on a secretarial course, and he was more than willing to do that. Annuncia was desperate to be a secretary in a big firm. It was her dream and Danny Boy was all for granting his family their dreams if it was within his power.

'Mum, you know I'll bankroll anything that will help her get on in the world. She's shrewd enough, and if this is what she wants then this is what she can have.'

'You're a good man, Danny Boy.'

His mother was huge now; her only real pleasure was eating since they had all grown up and away from her. She still cooked her gargantuan meals, only now she seemed to be the only one eating them. His father was still well able to tuck in, but even he had trouble demolishing the portions she had taken to dishing up.

Since the debacle with Kenny Douglas his mother had taken to treating Danny Boy with a new respect. Their reaction to Kenny's outrageous behaviour at the funeral was seen as him and Michael being decent, upstanding young men who had taken umbrage at the treatment doled out to a sister. None of the men attending that day, and no one who had heard about it afterwards, could fault them for their prompt action. Kenny Douglas had been out of order, and the fact that he was now dead as a doornail, was seen as nothing more than divine retribution.

Even the police had not bothered to pursue the matter for long, choosing to believe he had been set about by a person, or persons unknown. That was the common excuse they used when they knew what had gone down, but had no intention of doing anything about it. It would have gained them nothing to charge two young men who, to all intents and purposes, had done no more than any man in that situation.

That Danny Cadogan was now courting Mary Miles only added to the romance of the situation. It had been a nine-day wonder, and it had given them all a kudos that was worth its weight in gold bars.

Danny and Michael were greeted like visiting royalty wherever they went, and they were also being offered more work than they could cope with. The casino was now a hangout for the criminally minded, and their wages had escalated so much they were unable to keep track of it all.

They were set up for life, and now what they had to do was take out Lawrence Mangan. Mangan wasn't as enamoured of them as everyone else, and he was very vocal about that. In fact, his opinions weren't making him any new friends, and that alone should have made him button his mutton. Instead, it just made him even more determined to prove his point. He was not going to bow down to a couple of kids he had employed, and who had the audacity to take down someone of such stature he was regarded as one of the main players in their world. What the fuck was that all about?

So Danny and Michael enjoyed their new-found popularity, and were waiting patiently for their chance to remove Mangan permanently. Danny was in his element, and his mother's adoring glances were more than enough payment as far as he was concerned. As she told anyone who would listen, she was proud of him.

His main grumble was she wouldn't move away from the flats now that he was in a position to buy her a house, she had refused time and time again. She liked it where she was and, as she told him, she would be like a fish out of water anywhere else, and he had to swallow that for the time being.

He was now ensconced in a large apartment on the King's Road, and he loved the freedom it afforded him. But he still did the majority of his work in this little flat; the opportunity to get his washing done while rubbing his old man's nose in it at the same time was too good to pass up. Life was good, and he was prepared to make sure it stayed that way, no matter what he might be called on to do to guarantee that.

Old Bill had given Danny Boy and Michael the equivalent of a hunting licence and, knowing they were protected from most things, gave them a feeling of complete confidence. It was costing them, of course, Filth didn't come cheap, but they were worth every penny because without them they couldn't have plied their nefarious trades with such openness and security. Danny was finally where he wanted to be. The sad part was that it still wasn't enough for him.

Louie was watching and waiting, as per usual, before he made any kind of judgement. Over the years he had made a point of keeping a low profile and his opinions to himself until he knew the whole story. One thing he had learned was that people edited their bad deeds even more than they would embroider their good ones. He had always covered his own arse by waiting patiently until he knew exactly what direction the wind had decided to blow.

Michael looked older somehow; he seemed to have ripened overnight. Whereas Danny Boy had always had the look of the man about him, Michael had been blessed with what old ladies called boyish good looks. Now though, it was as if someone had wiped the innocence from his face, and replaced it with suspicion and hostility. He trusted no one, and this was evident by the way he questioned even the most innocent of statements.

As Louie saw them grow into their new roles in the world, he decided that the time had come to put them wise about what was expected of them by the powers that be. He was sorry he had to do this, in many respects, because they were still under the illusion they were working for themselves. If only life was that easy.

In their world, you were only allowed to work if you showed willing, and were prepared to make a generous donation now and again to whoever was *allowing* you to work in the first place. Up until now, they had not really understood the economics of the world they had decided to conquer. It was his job to explain the pecking order to them and, at the same time, make sure they understood that this was a non-negotiable situation. They had been allowed to run riot for a long time; now they were to be reined in and used, just like everyone else.

But they were shrewd enough; they should have sussed this all out for themselves. He was aware that Danny Boy would be the problem child of this comedy duo, but he was also confident that Danny Boy would swallow his knob and do what was expected of him, namely accept his fate and wait his turn, like they had all had to. They were finally accepted, were finally in the world they had courted so earnestly, now they had to prove themselves worthy of it, once and for all, and that was always the most difficult bit.

But he had confidence in them, well Danny Boy anyway; he had seen greatness in him even as a young kid, the man, he was sure, would become a phenomenon. He hoped so, because he had been working for them behind the scenes for years. Not that they would appreciate that, of course, like all youngsters, they thought it was their right. They thought they had earned it. Well, did he have news for them.

Chapter Twelve

Jamie Carlton was laughing, and he had what was generally agreed to be a seriously funny laugh. It was deep, it came from the heart and it was infectious. He was the only person, Danny Boy joked, who actually guffawed. Jamie himself was tall, thin and, at twenty-four, he still didn't need to shave. He was smooth-skinned and so fair he couldn't go out in the sun without going bright red and looking like a Belisha beacon. His father was Donald Carlton, an old Face with a crooked smile, a vicious state of mind, and a genuine belief that Jamie was not his son but, because he was still legally married to the boy's mother, he had to show willing where the boy was concerned or lose face. So he treated him as a son, gave him an earner, while his suspicions grew all the time.

Jamie, as luck would have it, had a knack for bookmaking. He could lay off a bet in his sleep, and he made his staff in the betting shops so nervous that tills were never more than a penny out, and he hoped against hope that his father's suspicions were unfounded. However, he could understand why his father felt as he did. His mother, a lovely woman, was not exactly what you could call the faithful type. Indeed, she had been seen with more men than Danny La Rue. It was a terrible situation really, because Jamie knew he was accepted as a Carlton, but he also knew that his position was tenuous, to say the least. In fact, if his father decided to give vent to his suspicions, he would become an outcast in minutes. And he was determined to make sure that didn't happen. If his father was to die, however, there was no way anyone would or could question

179

his paternity, and he could get on with his life without that shadow of doubt hanging over him. As his father was short, dark-skinned, overweight and bald, Jamie could understand better than anyone why he was so preoccupied with his only child's parentage. Even as he understood this, after all, he had been taller than his father since he was twelve, he was still prepared to take his old man out to ensure he got what he saw as his due. Whatever the rights and wrongs of the situation, it wasn't his fault. He'd had no control over any of it whatsoever. He was, to all intents and purposes, Jamie Carlton, and his father had put his name on the birth certificate, so he was legally his old man.

Now though, his father's suspicions were getting beyond a joke. Especially since his old man was now shagging a twenty year old with firm tits and an active womb; Jamie therefore felt that this had now become a pressing problem. A new baby on the firm would cause untold aggravation, especially if the said child was unlucky enough to look like the ugly ponce who had sired it.

Basically, he wanted to ensure he got what was coming to him, and he also desired the exact same thing for his so-called father. He loved the man but, at the end of the day, he had to cover his own arse. Hence his new-found friendship with Danny Boy Cadogan, a man who, like himself, had experienced problems with the man who had sired him. Like Danny, he was finally at the end of his patience, after all, you could only invest so much in relatives; eventually they proved they weren't worth the time or the effort needed to keep them close by. Relatives were all right, provided they lived in another country.

As they sat together, he was aware of Danny Boy's dangerous air. Like most real Faces, Danny had the knack of making everyone around him wary. It was a useful tool in their world, and Danny was already making a name for himself because of it. Even the Filth were giving him a wide berth, accepting his new status, and more than willing to overlook his obvious mental defects; mainly that he had no conscience and had an unhealthy belief in his own righteousness.

Danny Boy Cadogan was what was commonly called a looney tunes, a radio rental; in short, a nut-box. He was also a very clever negotiator who acted as normal as the next person until someone aggravated him. These two had been dancing around each other for a few weeks, and this meet, Jamie was sure, would cement their relationship.

People like Danny Boy Cadogan were imperative to the criminal cause. In fact, without them, they were all fucked. Because the Dannys took the heat off everyone else, the run-of-the-mill Faces who did their business behind closed doors. As his father Donald had always told him, the *real* Faces were the ones you *never* heard about. The ones who kept a low profile, who were willing to let the more flamboyant Faces make their mark in the public psyche, leaving them alone to earn a crust in peace and quiet.

That was proving to be more true by the day. It was the eighties, the old-timers were banged up, and the new generation were more than willing to take on the mantle of the old boys. Only now they had the added benefit of newspaper exposure, along with the goodwill of the general public. Punk rock had laid the foundations for the new breed of anti-hero; people were so heavily taxed now that they admired anyone with the front to tip the authorities' bollocks. A bank robber was seen as someone who had the nerve to take back what the government was stealing off the average man on the street. People weren't so judgemental about how a living was earned, and nearly everyone benefited from the black market; the clothes and other sundries that should have been out of their reach were there for the taking, were being sold in most pubs, working men's clubs or local market stalls around the Smoke. It was a big earner, and everyone was a winner. For the person who supplied the goods, it was a win-win situation.

Now though, Jamie wanted Danny Boy to take out his old man, therefore leaving the door open for the youngsters like themselves to finally come into their own. It was the law of the pavement, weakness was something that was watched out for, and violence was also something that was celebrated in the right quarters if it got them what they wanted. In fact, it was the only thing that guaranteed new blood, new Faces on the firms and, ultimately, a new order. Once he had done the deed with Danny Boy, Jamie's father would be just another crime statistic whose previous and abundant criminal acts would guarantee the Old Bill's utter disinterest in the matter. That, coupled with serious amounts of wedge of course; after all, everyone had bills to pay, holidays to book, and gambling debts to erase.

Jamie had a good feeling that this young man's acquiescence was a foregone conclusion. Because, like himself, Danny Boy Cadogan was looking for an edge, was patiently waiting for the chance to push himself to the forefront of their new world order. Drugs and clubbing were the path to riches, and they knew that better than anyone. They also knew how to make sure their new businesses were accepted and overlooked by the powers that be. All in all, it was as good a reason as any to take the old fucker out.

Danny Cadogan knew exactly why he was there, he wasn't a fool, but Jamie also knew he would have the sense to play the game with the required panache, act shocked at the sheer audacity of the favour requested of him, pretend a reticence he didn't feel, and then, eventually, after much soul searching, do the deal that would in effect end his father's life while starting off his own. It was sad; he had been a good dad in his own way but he had to watch his own arse and he couldn't be expected to watch anyone else's. Anyway he would give the old boy a good send-off; horse and cart, a decent coffin, and a piss-up that would be talked about for generations. After all, it was the least he could do.

Danny Cadogan could have written the script for him, and they both knew that, so the meeting was beneficial for them both in more ways than one. Together they were a powerful force, and they knew that; in fact they were so in tune that the bullshit was kept to the minimum on either sides. Respect was the order of the day, and Michael, observing them, was once more amazed at how easily Danny seemed to find the right connections, and how easily he fooled everyone into thinking they could control him. Well, Donald was going to be used as an excuse to take out Lawrence Mangan as well; Danny Boy wanted to kill two birds with one powerful stone and, as Lawrence Mangan and Donald Carlton were both known associates to the Filth and the criminal fraternity in general, it would be seen as a fair hit. Everyone would know the truth though; that Mangan was getting on everyone's nerves with his constant mug-bunnying about Danny Boy and his so-called bad attitude since his shocking removal of Kenny. If they could pull this off, they would leap into the stratosphere of their chosen fields. Pull it off they would. Danny had been waiting for something like this his whole life, and he wasn't about to fuck it up. These two young men had both known they would reach this moment; now all they had to do was make sure that what they had planned didn't backfire.

Ange was worried. She had heard rumour after rumour of her son's involvement in a lot of not only dodgy, but dangerous, enterprises. That in itself didn't bother her as such; it was the world they lived in, and it was these dealings that afforded her the standard of living she was enjoying so much. What was worrying her though was the fact that her son was disregarding not only her advice about it, but his father's nod as well. Donald Carlton wasn't a fool. Like every-one else he knew the score, knew what was happening around him. He would hear the whisper on the pavement about Jamie's treachery at some point, after all, she knew about it, so the chances were he did as well. Her own son, in fairness, was a slippery little fucker when the fancy took him so she had kept her own counsel and hadn't mentioned any of it outside the house. It was her husband who was the real worry; she knew for a fact that he was not pleased about his son's latest scheme. In a way she could understand that, he found it hard to forgive and forget what had been done to him over the years but, as he had been the orches-trator of his own downfall she couldn't really feel that sorry for him. She understood that it was hard for him to see his son making such a success of his life, especially since he had fucked his own up so spectacularly, never having managed to get past first base. She felt that Danny and Michael discussed too much of their business in front of him. She knew it was a calculated act as far as Danny Boy was concerned, knew he enjoyed rubbing his success in his father's face while disregarding the fact that he had punished the man enough for what had happened in the past. But her main fear was that her husband might use the information he had garnered to teach his son a lesson. That he could use his knowledge to guarantee his revenge on the child who had, in effect, usurped him, not only in his own home, but also in the community he had lived in all his life. People gave him the time of day, but only because his son still gave him a modicum of respect in public. If Danny decided to blank him, then so would everyone else. He was *tolerated*, no more and no less, and he knew that as well as his son and everybody else did. Big Dan Cadogan had been living on his nerves and on borrowed time for far too long. It was human nature for him to see his son's demise as the only way he could ever be truly secure. It was also the only way he could hold his head up once again. Donald Carlton would appreciate a heads-up and that would guarantee her husband an easy ride for the next few years. Even though it would involve his own son's death, Ange could understand that, at this moment in time, that would actually be the reason for him grassing in the first place.

Carlton was a hard bastard, and his son's paternity had been a topic of conversation for many years. It was now an urban legend and, even though the boy looked like his paternal grandmother in drag, it was still something that Donald was troubled by. As all women knew, men liked to think that the kids who carried their name were actually *their* kids. Men pointed out their son's likeness to themselves and others around them with a gusto that was brought on by their natural suspiciousness. A cuckoo in the nest was never an ideal situation and, as there was only the one child, Donald Carlton had good reason to believe the boy was more than likely an impostor. None of his birds had ever reproduced either, unlike the wife, but even she had been barren for many years before the much trumpeted arrival of young James. Donald Carlton was now with a young girl and, if the gossip was anything to go by, he was covering her at every available opportunity in the hope of a new sprog, and a chance to redeem himself.

It was a tragedy all right, but it was also a dangerous situation for her elder son. She was caught between a rock and a hard place; she had to either tip Danny Boy the wink, all the while keeping his father's name out of the frame, or she let nature take its course and bury either her husband or her eldest child.

So she sat alone, she drank her tea, and she plotted. If push ever came to shove, Ange knew in her heart, without question, which of the men in her life she would protect. Life was a bastard at times, and her life was overshadowed by bastardy on a daily basis. It wasn't fair, her having to choose, but then, what was fair in their world?

Mary was watching her brother as he made himself a sandwich. Gordon had been a bundle of nerves since the funeral and Kenny's untimely outburst; she had noticed that Gordon was suffering from what was generally referred to as his nerves. He spent most of his time with Jonjo Cadogan; that didn't bother her but what did bother her was her younger brother's reliance on drugs. If he wasn't popping Drinamyl, the new name for purple hearts, he was dropping Mogadons, and sleeping the days away. Moggies as they were known, were sleeping pills that were readily available and used by junkies to settle them before or after a fix, depending.

As Gordon spread salad cream on a slice of bread she said gaily, 'Not going out, Gordon?'

It was Friday night, and any teenager worth their salt would be out tonight. Gordon shook his head and she marvelled at the likeness to his older brother. Michael was like his twin. It was uncanny.

'Jonjo's coming round and we're going to chill out, listen to a bit of music, and relax.'

She nodded and he gazed at her distantly. 'You all right, mare?'

She smiled then, a real smile at his obvious concern for her, and said sadly, ''Course I am. I worry about you, that's all.'

He grinned, his handsome face open and honest. 'Well don't, OK?'

Mary nodded, but she also knew that her little brother was not handling the events of the last few months very well and she was determined to try and do something about that. Like their mother he tended to obliterate the days instead of living them. Like their mother he couldn't handle the real world when it crept up on him. With him it was the drugs; they were his way out, and she knew that she had to talk to Michael and Danny Boy about him before it was too late. Where they lived, getting wasted was seen as a natural progression; there was not a lot of incentive to make something of yourself or get gainful employment. In fact, like a lot of his generation, he couldn't see the point in it all. Jobs, real jobs, were few and far between; unless you had family in Fords at Dagenham, or in the print, you didn't really have much choice in life. Both those jobs were still being worked by the third generation of the same families. It was a guaranteed in and, once in, it was a job for life; the unions had seen to that.

Michael could have given him an earn, but he hadn't bothered because Gordon wasn't exactly the energetic type. He wasn't a boy who had put himself about for a few quid, a paper round, whatever. He was more of the taking type. Coupled with the fact that his IQ was lower than his shoe size, and that he wasn't mature enough to be trusted with anything that might involve discretion, he was pretty much left to his own aimless devices. This, she knew, had to stop. He had to start taking responsibility for himself; Michael was making it far too easy for him.

'What are you on, Gordon?'

He smirked at her, and she suppressed the urge to smack him one around the face, 'Who are you, mare, the police?'

She grinned, her short laugh full of sarcasm as she said nastily, 'I could be, Gordon, if you ain't careful. And if you bring the Filth to this door you'll bring on the wrath of not only Michael but also Danny Boy Cadogan as well.'

She let the words sink in before adding, 'Now, for the last time, what the fuck are you on, and where did you get it from?'

Michael was sipping his drink and watching as Danny Boy homed in on Pakash Patel. The man was heavyset, with a handsome face, and a reputation as a real player; a serious gambler who was known to pay his debts promptly. He was also renowned for his gargantuan appetite for gambling, whisky and leggy blondes. He was also now into drugs. Not the usual drugs of choice, but anabolic steroids.

The craze for body-building that had suddenly caught on in the seventies had finally given way to gyms and sports clubs springing up all over the place. Men now craved a body like Arnie and they didn't want to work too hard for it. A few injections could guarantee them the biceps of a gladiator and, unfortunately, the temperament of a scalded rhino. Pakash Patel had the contacts Danny Boy needed to take the steroid market into the twentieth century. Patel had family in the medical profession; most of his relatives were doctors or pharmacists, the fact that they were also involved in the distribution side of the drug industry was an added bonus as far as Danny Boy was concerned. As the law stood, it was perfectly legal to possess steroids; it was only illegal to sell them on in large quantities. These were a drug that could therefore be sold freely in any sporting establishment on the quiet, with the minimum of fuss and the maximum of profit. Anyone found in possession of it just had to say it was for their own personal use and that was that. Danny Boy saw the niche in the market and was seriously determined to exploit it to the fullest extent. Any drug was an earner, everyone knew that, but something like these, that were so easy to get hold of, and so easy to pass on it was laughable; it was amazing really that no one else saw the potential.

As Danny Boy laughed and joked with Pakash, he was working out how much he could nick from him without the man feeling insulted. He had already invested in three gyms, as a partner so silent that the taxman would still be trying to work out who he was when they picked up their retirement cheques. It was a doddle. He was also negotiating all his deals with a renewed vigour in light of the fact that he would soon be one of the main players on the stage of villainy. These were exciting times.

Pakash was grinning, his expensive smile showing the bridgework that his older brother, a dentist, was famous for, and the suit he was wearing telling the world that despite the money he had it couldn't buy him good taste. He looked cheap, and Danny would always hold that fact against him, even though he knew it would work in Patel's favour.

Now though, as he walked him through the casino to his little office, he was amazed to see just how sure of himself he was. Pakash was into him for a small fortune, and it was this that was to be the catalyst for a good working partnership that Danny Boy would ensure was far more beneficial to him than to Pakash. But then, Pakash would expect that, he was, after all, a cockney boy who understood the situation. He would be on an earner, but he would also have the protection of Danny Boy for the foreseeable future, something that was worth far more than cash on the hip. It was something he could use to gather more money with less aggro.

In fact, Danny Boy was so sure of his premier position that he was caught off guard when Pakash Patel asked him about a whisper he had heard on the pavement concerning him and James Carlton.

Michael observed that it was the only time in his life that he had ever seen Danny Boy Cadogan lost for words.

Donald Carlton was sitting in his girlfriend's flat nursing a large scotch. The flat was small in comparison to the house he lived in with his wife. The same wife he had stood by for nearly thirty-two years. The woman had slept her way around London, but still thought he was mug enough to believe her when she swore she had been faithful to him. He was a man of the world; he knew that he should have outed her years before, it would have made his life much easier. She was a whore. A woman who had the morals of an alley cat and the face of an angel. She had been the only thing in his whole life that had never made any sense. She had the knack of making him believe what he wanted to believe. Now, though, he just couldn't do it any more.

Men he trusted, loved even, who had worked for him since day one felt his total humiliation as if they had lived through it themselves. They had not said a word against her, and had not questioned his reasoning when he had taken her back after yet another of her escapades. But it was over now. He had no feelings left for the woman who had produced a child, who had led him to believe that the child was his, and who had hinted, when thwarted, that any number of men could have been the sperm donor.

He had met his latest girlfriend at a nightclub in Ilford; he had walked into the Lacy Lady to pick up a few quid owed to him by a local Face. He had seen Deirdre Anderson standing at the bar, and it was as if they had both been pole-axed. She was stunning; a tiny blonde with huge eyes and a tidy body. He knew by the way she dressed and the way she talked, that she had been around the track a few times, but he also knew, without a doubt, that she was as smitten with him as he was of her. For the first time in his life he was content, an emotion he felt wasn't appreciated as much as it should be.

In this little apartment of hers he could relax, really relax. Young Deirdre might only be twenty years old but he knew, without a shadow of a doubt, that she loved him. Knew that she was faithful to him, and that she was in for the long haul, age difference aside. They were kindred spirits.

She had decorated the place with the finesse of a drunken hedgehog, but even the garish wallpaper and mismatched furniture just made him feel even more at home. This was a place that was lived in, really lived in, and a place where the people inside its walls were more important than the price of the fixtures and fittings. It was a place where time stood still and he could just enjoy being a man, without the constant reminder of his wife's infidelity.

As Donald heard Deirdre letting in his guest he sighed and swallowed his drink down with one gulp. Pouring himself another large drink, he sat on the Dralon sofa that was far too big for the room it resided in, and wondered at what he was going to be asked. He forced a neutral expression onto his face and made himself smile as Big Danny Cadogan walked into the room. His broken body made him clumsy, and the Murrays' violent handiwork reminded everyone who saw him of what could happen to people who didn't think their actions through properly.

'What's the big deal then, Dan?'

Big Danny Cadogan lowered himself painfully into an armchair and answered him with the same forced jollity, 'Get me a drink, and I'll tell you.'

The atmosphere was ripe with mutual distrust and unspoken innuendo. Both had suffered at their son's hands, and both had learned to live with it, but for all that it still didn't make what had happened to them any easier to bear.

Deirdre sat in her kitchen sipping a coffee and enjoying the fact that her beau saw her flat as homely enough to do business in. She was happy enough to wait for Donald to conclude his meeting before going in to him. She was a good-natured girl who had been delivered of a child at seventeen that had died shortly after birth, and she was of the opinion that, after such a traumatic experience, life was too short to waste. It was all about making the most of everything positive around you, and not dwelling too much on the negative.

'Pakash was only repeating what he had heard on the street, Danny.'

Louie Stein had listened to everything that had been said with his usual interest. He nodded at Michael's words and said sadly, 'He's right, Danny Boy. And you have made a right fuck-up, end of.'

He spoke the words with a crushing finality that he knew was destined to cause the boy before him untold aggravation. He had been caught out, had been well sussed, and now he needed to get it sorted sooner rather than later.

Danny Boy looked at Louie for his advice now, something he had not done for a long time. But, as he had been in the past, he was once more willing to hear what the old boy had to say on the matter. 'Am I on the out over this, Louie, tell me the truth.'

Louie smiled faintly, his age making his skull look like a death's head, and it occurred to Danny and Michael that he was an old man now. That he was now actually one of the people they were determined to push out of the frame, while at the same time taking from them what they had worked for all their lives.

Unlike the others in the equation though, Louie knew he was needed by these two young bucks, and would be for a long time to come. His opinion was still being sought, and his advice was accepted by them as valid. He knew that one day, if he wasn't careful, he could be in the same boat as Kenny, Mangan and Carlton. He also relied on the fact that Danny Boy was loyal to his friends, and that he also expected that same loyalty back. Louie believed he had backed the winning horse all those years ago but, as with all bets, only time would tell if he had been correct in that assumption.

Louie took a deep drag on his cigar and, blowing the smoke out slowly, he watched it curl around his head. Then he forced himself up straight in his seat, his eyes focused on Danny Boy as he explained the situation they had found themselves in, and offered them a solution that he felt would do the least damage to them all. Poking a finger at him he said earnestly, 'I fucking despair of you two at times. Jamie Carlton couldn't keep his trap shut if his life depended on it. He suffers from verbal diarrhoea, brought on by a mistaken belief that everyone around him enjoys hearing his fucking voice as much as he does. He has one thing going for him at this moment in time, and that is the man whose name he happens to share, the same man, mind, who he is so desperate to eliminate. You are now in the frame for anything that might befall Donald Carlton, even by accident. If he gets run over, if he slips in the bath and drowns, or hangs himself with his shoelaces, someone, somewhere, along the line will take great pleasure in linking you to it. Our world thrives on *gossip* but, as hard men, we don't call it that, we refer to it as gathering information. Well, it's gathering all this information that gives us the edge over the rest of the population. Now, you have been seen consorting with young Jamie on more than one occasion, and that has been observed by the powers that be, which has made it the cause of much discussion. The only advice I can give you now is this: you had better shit, or get off the pot, boy. Either way you need to show everyone what your intentions are, and what you expect to gain from your actions. And, after tonight, I would suggest that anything you do decide to undertake had better border on the extreme. Donald is well liked, unlike Mangan. He had the sense to make friends of people who were, in reality, his natural predators. He did this by making sure they all got an earn off him, and that, my boy, is the secret of success in our world.'

Danny and Michael listened to him with their usual quiet respect; not only did Louie talk sense, there was no doubt about that, but he also knew the lay of the land, being, as he was, a natural gossip. Louie collected information; he had learned that, no matter how trivial the chat might be, how outrageous the story, nine times out of ten it would contain an element of truth. People had died, painfully, over gossip; people had disappeared off the face of the earth over gossip. This was because, in their precarious world, idle gossip could be the cause of a hefty prison sentence, or the reason why your once-thriving business was wiped out overnight.

For the first time ever, Danny was unsure what to do next. Louie could feel his indecision and his heart went out to the boy. Unlike Michael, who was a natural-born accountant, Danny Boy would always be the one whose reputation would be their passport to any riches they might acquire. It was Danny Boy Cadogan, whose reputation for quick and violent retribution, would ensure they were not challenged by any of the other young hopefuls. It was Danny Boy Cadogan who he continued to believe would see him into his old age, who would make sure he wasn't ever fucked over by the likes of himself. He had already left the boy a large portion of his assets, and he trusted the boy to take care of things for him, and see his wife and daughters all right when he finally popped his clogs. Danny was a young blood, but he had the old-style morals that would stand him in good stead for many years to come.

Danny had listened intently to everything his old friend had said, and the words 'border' and 'extreme' were the only ones that seemed to have sunk into his psyche. If his meetings with Jamie had caused this much talk, then he had to sort out the problem sooner rather than later and, as he had always advocated, there was no time like the present.

Chapter Thirteen

Deirdre was lying on her side, quietly snoring, her slim body covered with a fine sheen of sweat and her long blond hair lying over her shoulders like a blanket. She had kicked off the duvet, and Donald sat in a chair watching her as she slept, marvelling at the knowledge that she was totally his.

Since meeting her, he knew he had become soft in his old age. Unlike the way he had felt about his wife all those years, she didn't make him feel like he had to prove himself to everyone, didn't feel that he had to watch her like a hawk. It was a liberating feeling, this love he had for her. It had shown him what a real relationship should consist of, made him aware that his marriage, his relationship with his wife, had been unhealthy. It had made him realise that he had wasted what should have been the best and the most productive years of his life on someone who had no real care for him, no respect for him, or even the position he held in his world, the world that she needed to keep her in one piece.

And now his son. Rather, the boy he had brought up; he had known, deep down, from the beginning, that the boy was nothing more than a cuckoo in the nest. And a very expensive nest it had been at that. That same boy, it seemed, who was out to get him and who had enlisted other young blood to help him in his quest for greatness.

Jamie was out to take what he thought was his by rights, and he was also prepared to see his so-called father buried in the process.

It hurt; he had been good to the boy, he had *never* allowed his own anger or frustration at his situation to spill over into the boy's life. He had seen the boy as, well, as much a victim as he was. Had seen him as the innocent party in the abortion that was his marriage. Now Donald was paying the ultimate price for his easy-going nature; the boy was of an age where he wanted to secure his inheritance even though he had to know by now that he couldn't father a child without divine intervention. He wondered if Jamie knew who the culprit was; if his mother had told him the truth. He doubted it. In all honesty, he didn't think even *she* was aware of that fact herself. She had fucked so many men the boy's paternity could basically be traced to anyone within a ten-mile radius.

What he did know, though, was that his relationship with this young woman had been the cause of his son's deep insecurity. He knew that his son's biggest fear was another child arriving, a child that would be his in every way. Donald knew that would never happen; with all the women he had fucked over the years, if he had been firing live ammunition there would have been proof of it long before. The truth was, and he couldn't tell Jamie this now, of course, was that he had long ago resigned himself to having his name live on through him. Through Jamie, through the same treacherous little fucker that he had given that name to so proudly all those years before. After all, he had lived the lie so long, it was stupid not to keep it up after he was dead. Now it seemed he would be dead long before his allotted time if his surrogate son had anything to do with it.

He heard a faint noise in the hallway and, assuming it was Deirdre's cat coming through the flap in the front door, he lay back in the chair and feasted his eyes once more on the true love of his life.

It was only when the door burst open, and he saw Danny Boy and Michael bearing down on him like avenging angels, that he realised he had left it too long to do anything about any of it now. Danny Boy smiled that wide smile of his, the same smile that made him look for all the world like a normal healthy young man. Which just proved that looks could be deceiving all right.

Deirdre was now awake, and her frightened eyes were wide open, making her look like a demented smurf.

Donald realised then that he had been expecting this, which was why he had not been able to sleep, and he knew then that he had accepted his fate, welcomed it even in some ways. 'So, what's brought you here, Danny Boy? Your father has already been in and asked me to spare you if it all goes off. Begged for your life, he did, unlike my namesake who wants me taken out. I assume you haven't spoken to your old man yet.'

Danny looked at the terrified girl and motioned for her to stay put. Then he dragged Donald Carlton out into the hallway by his clothes, the sheer force of his strength making the man's feet leave deep drag-lines in the shag-pile carpet. And, with the smell of pine disinfectant in his nostrils, and the hysterical weeping of Deirdre in his ears, Danny Boy shot Donald Carlton in the face at point-blank range. The noise was not as loud as he had expected it to be, yet the blood was far more than he had anticipated. It was only when he realised that the man was still bleeding profusely because his heart was still beating, that he shot him once more, this time through the back of his head. Brains and bone were scattered everywhere, especially on Danny Boy's trousers but, shrugging nonchalantly, he looked at the ashen-faced Michael and grinned happily. Then, licking his finger, he chalked an imaginary 'one' in the air before saying happily, 'One down, and one to go.'

Michael pulled himself together and, going back into the bedroom, he looked at the weeping girl on the bed but, before he could say anything, Danny Boy was beside him and, dragging her by the hair out into the hallway, threw her onto the lifeless body of her lover and said loudly, 'Go to your mum's, or a mate's, just fucking go. You ever open your fucking trap about tonight and I'll hunt you down like a dog.'

He knew he wouldn't have to repeat the words, there was no way she was ever going to open her mouth about the night's events. And, even if she did, she wouldn't live long enough to testify. He had given her a fucking result and, if she had any brains, she would realise that and act accordingly. She was local, she knew the score: trap shut, and she would be left in peace, a few quid would wing its way to her when the heat died down. She would learn to live with the situation. She wasn't the first woman to be caught up in a personal vendetta and she certainly wouldn't be the last. She was gone in minutes.

Michael and Danny Boy left the flat then, and Danny made a point of locking the front door behind them. Let Old Bill break in if they had to, he was certainly not going to make it easy for them. Now he had decided what he was going to do, he just wanted it all over. The adrenaline was coursing through his veins and he felt alive; extreme violence always gave him a rush, and he knew he enjoyed it far more than he should have done.

As he walked out of the flats with Michael he saw a group of youths not much younger than them. They were scrutinising him and he looked back at them as if seeing them for the first time. They were scruffy, they were obviously on drugs and, to him, they were the lowest of the low. The fact that any one of them could have been him had he not had the strength of mind to make his mark on the world bothered him. It was a reminder of where he had come from, of what he was fighting against on a daily basis. His early start in life had pretty much guaranteed him a useless existence. He knew that better than anyone. His father had tried to make sure he had not had a chance of making anything of himself. Had made it plain that his life and his younger siblings' lives were not worth anything to the man who had been the reason they were there in the first place. He had been conceived, like the others, without a thought for the consequences of the sexual act, and without any love whatsoever. He knew that these young men, with their skinheads, their Levis, and their officer boots had been conceived in exactly the same way. It was as if they had been born knowing they were worthless, that their lives were not precious to anybody, least of all themselves. That the futility of their existence was just further proof that they were nothing more than a celestial joke, only they were the recipients of that joke, having never meant to be in a position where they belonged anywhere.

Michael, who had already unlocked their car and was still reeling from the gun shots and Danny Boy's complete easiness with death, swallowed down his fear of the person he loved more than anyone else in the world. He knew this night would make them or break them and, even though he didn't really want any part of it, would have preferred to have stepped back and dissolved quietly once more into the obscurity he craved, he also knew he couldn't do that. He had to see this thing through to the end, even though he wanted no part of any of it.

Danny Boy snarled at the boys, knowing they knew exactly who he was, and hating them for knowing who he was, for wanting to be like him, as if that was an option. They were the cannon fodder he would use when the need arose. But he forced his anger away, they had heard the shots and were streetwise enough to guess what had gone down, so he walked over to them and said in a friendly manner, 'All right, boys, any chance of a fag?'

Michael watched as the young thugs searched through their pockets for cigarettes, all praying for the opportunity to be able to say that Danny Boy Cadogan had spent time in their company. Guaranteeing their loyalty and their silence.

If it hadn't been so sad to see, it would have been laughable.

Ange was unable to sleep; her husband had gone out hours earlier and had not been near or by since. Usually this didn't bother her, but as she suspected he had gone to see Donald Carlton she felt she had a genuine reason to worry for a change. Big Dan had gone to try and limit the damage that he might have caused with his careless chatter. It was her husband's big trap that had seen to it that her son's private dealings had somehow become common knowledge. Even though he had sworn to her that he had not talked to anyone of import, he had still not been able to resist talking about his son's private and personals with people Danny Boy would have crossed the road to avoid. It was Danny Boy's own fault; he had talked too much in front of his father, a man she had never once told anything of any import because he had what was known locally as a loose lip. Danny Boy, however, had not been able to resist rubbing in his new-found status, had enjoyed letting his father know how well he was doing, and how much he was earning. It was something she could understand to an extent; Danny Boy was still only a boy really and, as such, he was programmed to act like one. But, for someone who had carved such a unique niche in the world, she had been annoyed that he was willing to spoil it all just to make a point to a man he had already cowed years before.

She slipped from the bed and pulled on her dressing gown; it had a pretty floral design that made her look fatter than ever. Not that she was bothered about that fact, what she looked like was something she had stopped worrying about many years before. As she went to the kitchen she heard whispering. And, walking into her daughter's bedroom she was stunned to see her daughter, her beautiful but ignorant daughter, sitting on her bed kissing a young man with a ponytail and a degenerate look in his eye. His leather jacket was thrown casually across the wicker chair she had painted white so lovingly many moons ago. And his trainers, as they called them now, were unlaced and lying on the pale pink carpet she had hoovered only that morning. Annie was half dressed, her shirt was open, and her jeans were lying in a crumpled heap on the bedspread beside her. It took Ange a few moments to understand fully what they had actually been doing when she had walked in on them, then it was the realisation of what was so obviously going on between them that sent her over the edge. Like she didn't have enough on her plate with a murderer for a son, she now had to deal with a whore. Turning on the light, she looked at the daughter she had adored and, seeing her as she was at that moment, her mouth smeared with pink lipstick and her heavy breasts rising and falling from her earlier exertions, Ange lost any hope of curtailing the temper that she knew was legendary to most people in the world she inhabited. As she launched herself at her daughter the young man was already off the bed and pulling on his shoes. He was not a local boy; if he had been the knowledge that she was Danny Boy Cadogan's little sister would have guaranteed his refusal to step inside her home, no matter what she might have offered him. The boy was watching the mother and daughter as they rolled around the bed, all hair and teeth, their language shocking even to him. As Ange punched her daughter as she would have punched a man, the boy practically ran from the room, leaving his new amour to sort it all out by herself.

Annie was already crying and the mascara she had layered on so thickly was burning her eyes out. She stopped fighting her mother then, she knew she was out of order, but she also knew this was something that was going to happen again and again. She hated the way she was kept locked up like an animal. Hated having to account for every second away from the bosom of her family. Loathed her mother who, she was sure, only curtailed her because she was jealous of her youth and her popularity. Ian Peck might not have been the answer to a maiden's prayers, but he had made her feel like any other teenage girl with his kisses and his false promises.

'Fuck off, Mum, and leave me alone.'

She was attempting to disengage her mother's hands from her hair. She knew that a lot of it had been ripped out in the mêlée. She was also aware that her lip was bleeding and, as she tried to sit herself up, she was surprised at her mother's sudden retreat. Standing in the doorway Ange turned and looked at her daughter and it seemed to her that, for the first time ever, she could see the girl for what she really was.

'You whore . . . Is that what you go to the night classes for, is it? To learn whoring. You even talk like one now as well.' She was almost spitting out the words in her anger. Her heart was hammering so hard inside her chest she really thought she was going to have a heart attack.

'You fucking bitch of hell, that you'd bring that scum into my home, the home I clean and polish so you'll have a nice place to live, the home I try and keep *safe* for you, so you'll never know the power of fear. And what do you do, eh, you sully everything with your fucking whoring . . .'

She once more launched herself at her daughter, the blows flying fast, and with all the strength she could muster behind each one. She concentrated on her daughter's face and shoulders, determined to leave her mark on her. Make sure the girl remembered this night as vividly as she knew she always would.

As Ange felt her fists sinking into her daughter's soft flesh she was aware of a hatred that was so intense she could almost taste it. Seeing her girl, her baby, with her jeans off and her top wide open displaying her breasts, while that little bastard took what he wanted, his cock hanging out of his trousers and her daughter's hand caressing it, would never leave her. She would be reminded of it every time she looked at her daughter, no matter if Annie took to wearing a yashmak. That terrible image was now burned onto her memory and it had removed every other picture she possessed of her young daughter's life. It was not only the fact she had brought a boy into her home, into her bedroom, it was more that she knew now that her daughter, her baby, was not a good girl; she knew instinctively that her daughter had done this before. She knew, as sure as anything, that this girl was happy to be touched and used by the likes of that young man. A greasy-haired stranger who had seen her precious daughter as nothing more than a filthy interlude in his quest for sexual favours and easy gratification. Her daughter's complete ease with her state of undress told her mother that she had done this kind of thing many times in the past. It took a long time before young women felt confident about showing off their bodies and, as far as she was concerned, only whores were comfortable stripping off for complete strangers. Ange finally felt her anger wane and stopped the brutal attack that had left her daughter bloody and bruised. She stared at Annie as if she had never seen her before in her life then, shaking her head slowly, she hawked deep in her throat and gobbed into the face of the daughter she had once revered and adored.

Lying on the bed, the spittle running down her cheekbone and the blood seeping into the cotton sheets, Annie cried like she had not cried in years. Unmoved by her daughter's sobs, Ange left the room quietly, shutting the door gently behind her. It was a symbolic act: she had shut her daughter out of her life already; never again would she look at her without seeing that grubby boy's erect penis, and her daughter's overflowing brassiere. She would always see the cheapness of the child she had tried desperately to keep innocent, keep pure. Had tried so hard to keep her away from the hurt of men like her father, and the knowledge of what they were capable of.

Ange was heaving now, the urge to be sick was overwhelming, and she rushed into the toilet. She knew her daughter could hear her as she heaved, and she was glad about that. It was only when

Jonjo brought her in a cold flannel and wiped her face with it, that she finally let go of her tears.

Lawrence Mangan was lying in his bed, a smile on his face, and a fag in his hand, as he watched the woman sucking at his cock as if her life depended on it. The woman was a stunner, her good looks almost obliterated by the deliberate overuse of the war paint that only expensive whores managed to get away with. He assumed it was because they knew they were worth more than the average bird. They were well-versed in their trade, and their heavy make-up made up for the sexlessness of the actual encounter. They looked like women from magazines; they weren't real and they weren't there for any other reason than the money.

This one though, for all her clever machinations, had no chance of getting him up again; he was ready for a hasty goodbye and a kip. He never let the working girls stay over, he believed that they were thieves, that the nature of their job made them amoral, until eventually, they looked at everyone in their orbit as a mark. They would lift a pair of cufflinks, a bottle of deodorant, it didn't matter, but they would lift *something*. He had experienced it before, and punished the girl severely. She had been on her way out the door with his watch, a plain gold Bulova but, as far as he was concerned, it could have been a jewel-encrusted Fabergé egg. The point was she had been on the nick, and he would not let something like that go without at least a mention. He had blinded her. His anger at her audacity had caused him to go over the top, and a bottle had somehow been smashed into her face. As far as he was concerned, she had asked for it. He then had had her removed by two of his best minders, and they had taken her away in complete silence, never referring to that evening ever again. So, once bitten twice shy. He pulled the girl's head up roughly and, pushing her away from him, he waved her away as if she was a troublesome fly.

Linda Crock had been here before with punters; once they had what they wanted, they took their shame and guilt out on the girl they had used. Well, fuck him, she had got her money beforehand; Mangan's reputation was of a useless lay, a man who would attempt to get his fun for free by intimidation and by using his reputation as a so-called Face. Well, she had been dealing with pimps since she was fourteen years old and it took a bit more than this bloke to rattle her cage. She had the money safe and sound, so she didn't have to pretend an enthusiasm she didn't feel any more. She also knew that men like him got their just desserts in the end anyway. As she dressed she replaced her usual sexy look with a haughtiness that told him he had just been had, and that she was an actress worthy of the West End stage.

Her demeanour unsettled Lawrence, and he was quiet as she sorted herself out. She didn't even say goodbye; he had assumed she had gone to the bathroom, and it had taken him a while before he had realised she had actually left. He knew he had been mugged off, and it annoyed him. That it was by a woman who sold herself to anyone with the correct amount of money regardless of age, weight or personal hygiene, hit a nerve somewhere. It made him see himself in a less than flattering light. Most of the working girls he came across knew of his past indiscretion and so played the game until they were at least safe and sound outside his front door.

He was still seething at her arrogance when he heard the tap on the front door and, grinning, he got up to open it, wondering what the fucking loser had left behind and determined to make her sweat for it, whatever it was. She needed a reprimand; most women did in his experience. As he opened the front door, his expression one of inconvenience mixed with loathing, he realised too late that his worst nightmare had just come true.

'You all right, girl?' Jonjo's voice was low, and his cannabis-loaded voice told Annie he was stoned out of his tree. He crept in and sat on the edge of the bed. In the light of the bare bulb from the landing he could see his sister was battered to a pulp. He didn't feel an iota of sorrow for her though, she had let herself down badly and, when he had finally cottoned onto what was happening, he had been as disgusted as his mother at her behaviour. He still wanted to check she was OK though, his mother could really go to town when the fancy took her. She was a real brawler, as short as she was.

He looked at his sister's ravaged face and sighed, 'I've talked her out of telling Dad or Danny Boy. All right?'

Annie nodded, the tears spurting hot and salty from her eyes now, his sympathy making her more upset than she actually was. Feeling sorry for herself she began to sob, placing her right arm gingerly across her eyes and her left arm over her chest, as if to hide herself from him.

'Who was he?'

She was unable to answer him, her crying was so severe.

He smiled sadly and, taking her hand from over her eyes, he looked down at her in earnest and said, truthfully, 'If you don't tell me, Annie, I will recount this night's events to not only our dad, but to Danny Boy as well. So, make up your mind who you want to tell your sordid little story to.'

She was bleeding still, her lips were swollen up and she could taste the blood that had dried on them, could feel the stinging from the bald patches she knew were now all over her head. Clumps of her thick hair were everywhere; she could see them lying all around her, and the sigh made the tears come hot and heavy once more.

'I ain't fucking about, Annie, who the fuck was he?'

She was shaking her head, and he saw the extent of her beating. Even her ear was bleeding, one of her earrings had obviously been ripped out at some point during the fight and now she had a sliced lobe that, he guessed, wasn't going to heal up in a hurry. His mother had really done a number on her, and so she should.

'Come on, before I get impatient . . .'

Annie sobbed and, holding her hand tightly across her mouth, she whispered brokenly, 'I don't know, Jonjo, I swear, I met him outside the café in Bethnal Green.'

Jonjo sat back from her then, his back arched with shock and temper, and his sister noticed how much he had grown into himself the last few months. He wasn't as big as Danny Boy, but he was still a fair old lump, and, when he pushed his face down into hers, she was reminded of just how violent this family of hers could be when any of them felt their world was being threatened.

'You better be fucking kidding me. You mean to tell me that you brought a fucking stranger into your home, and you let him strip you off and almost fuck you?'

She was aware that he was on the verge of killing her and she tried to calm him down, all the while wishing that her night had not ended in such a violent and frightening way. What had possessed her to bring the boy home with her, why had she not done what she usually did and let him take her to Vicky Park, or up an alleyway? Why was she doing this in the first place? But she knew why, she was rebelling against the regime that kept her locked up like a fucking nun and, because of the name she carried, the name that made sure no one ever came near or by her. She didn't answer him, instead she buried her face in the pillows and cried as if her heart would break.

Jonjo looked at his sister, who he loved, but any sympathy he might have harboured for her disappeared. Grabbing her arm he dragged her around to face him and said, once more, 'This is your last chance, cunt, give me a fucking name or I'll give you what the old woman give you, only I won't stop until you're dead.'

Annie knew he meant every word, he was already bringing back his fist to carry out his threat and, before she knew what had happened, she said quietly, 'He's from Romford, his name's Ian Peck.'

Jonjo lowered his fist slowly and, after looking her over once more, as if she was an overflowing sewer, he got up to leave. At the door he turned and said viciously, 'Fucking Romford, you're having a laugh, ain't you?'

She was crying once more as he closed her bedroom door none too quietly behind him. She was repeating the same words over and over again in her head, 'I must get away, I must get away.' But she knew that would be impossible, she would only go out of this flat feet-first in a box or on the arm of a husband. At this moment in time, the former was without doubt her preference.

Lawrence Mangan knew that he had been smartly out-boxed, and he also knew he was not going out without a fight. That these two youngsters could come to his home, his fucking *home*, and act like they were the dog's knob was practically beyond his belief. As he looked past them, he saw two of his workforce, his so-called minders, watching the proceedings with vacant eyes and knew that they were in on it. Knew that the men he paid a wage to, who he had been so convinced were his loyal minions, were waiting to see what was going to happen to him. In that moment the fight left his body, and he realised that, for all his money, and his connections, no one was going to come to his aid, even if he could ask them to. As he saw the grinning face of Danny Boy Cadogan, he knew that he would be the only witness of his own demise. When Danny Boy pushed him back into his bedroom, he saw Michael Miles holding a carrier bag full of tools and Danny Boy empty them out onto the bed, and it finally dawned on him that his demise was not going to be quick or, indeed, painless. Danny Boy wanted pay back for every slight he had ever experienced from him, real or imagined. He was going to use him as a warning, as a theatrical occurrence; his death would herald the boy's entrance into the world of the real grown-ups.

As the seriousness of his situation was sinking in, Danny Boy sliced Mangan quickly and cleanly across both eyes with a box-cutter, the action effectively blinding him in his own blood. As he sank down onto his knees, his hands instinctively covering his face, he could hear himself begging for mercy with all the humility he could manage, with all the self-pity he possessed, and he hated himself for it. He pleaded with the boy to finish him off quickly, to let him go like a man, not to torture him as he had tortured others, because he was, after all, a Face, and that should count for something. Eventually though, he could only weep and plead until, finally, he was simply groaning, accepting his fate and praying that it would be over quickly. But he knew that was impossible; Danny Boy Cadogan was out to set a precedent, was out to make his mark in a spectacular manner. He was guaranteeing his acceptance into the world he wanted so badly to be a part of, to ensure that he was seen as a future main player.

Then, his natural antagonism coming to the fore, he screamed out blindly, 'Look at me, Danny Boy, look at me long and hard, because one day this will be you.'

Danny Boy laughed at him and then said chirpily, 'Your eyes look like boiled eggs covered in ketchup. I bet that hurts, don't it?' He slapped him none too gently across the face.

Lawrence's blindness now made him even more frightened than he was before.

'Remember that old saying, Lawrence? What goes round fucking comes round. How true is that, eh?'

Lawrence could picture young Danny Boy then, from his strong jawline to the powerful shoulders that he never made any attempt to show off, and he knew his eyes would be blank, but his excitement at the thought of a kill would be overwhelming. He had heard all about Danny Boy's overly casual attitude to violence, even by their standards, but he had never dreamed that it would one day be turned on him. Now he knew that his own viciousness and hatred was coming back to bite him.

Danny Boy was a thug. He had underestimated him and what he was capable of. He also knew that this would bring Danny Boy Cadogan to the forefront of everyone's minds. A Danny Boy Cadogan was needed, Lawrence understood that now. There hadn't been anyone even remotely like him for a long time. He was that maverick villain, that mad bastard known to the police as a psychopath and, to his friends and neighbours, as a nice bloke who was afflicted with a terrible temper that, unfortunately, he couldn't control.

His eyes were screaming with pain, and his body was already going into shock, the tremors so acute he was having difficulty breathing. He could hear Michael moving around as he searched the premises for anything that could be used by them in the future to further their own ends. He knew that his life's work was going to finally be spent by a couple of fucking thugs without thought or reason, and that he would only be remembered because of his gruesome death. Danny Boy knew what he was doing, and even now he had a sneaking admiration for him, even as he hated him with every bone in his pain-wracked body.

When he heard Danny putting the tools in some kind of order, Lawrence went quiet and he prayed for death as he knew it was inevitable.

Danny Boy whispered in his ear, 'We're going to have such fun, Lawrence, and I am determined to make sure you don't miss out on any of it. I want you around for the grand finale.'

*

The condition of Lawrence Mangan's tortured body hit every daily paper, and caused an uproar for a few weeks over its severity and the fact that organised crime was once more safe and well in the capital of this great country. It was eventually knocked off the front pages by a randy vicar whose wife was nearly as amoral as he was.

The events of that dreadful night had worked in Danny Boy's favour though; he was now not only respected, but also feared as part of the new breed of criminal that was gradually pushing out the older men. The sheer violence they used to gain what they wanted was now becoming commonplace and, amid all these rising stars, was Danny Boy Cadogan with his unique brand of villainy. The Yardies, the Greeks, the Turks and the Chinese all saw him as a force to be reckoned with, as did the majority of the home-grown criminals he consorted with. What no one was saying out loud, however, was that the demise of two men, both classed as social dinosaurs, or agitators, had opened the door to all sorts of new earners. These young men were bringing in new money-making schemes, and were then spreading the wages around with an almost childlike abandon. They were still willing to take the chances and still too young to have succumbed to the fear of being caught, of being found out, and then having to accept the consequences. Ergo, a hefty prison sentence. They were young enough to believe that a twelve would see them come out in their late thirties with enough time on the clock to make their mark all over again.

Between them they had brought in a new lease of life to the older, bomb-damaged generation, and were also giving out work to the younger, more virile members of the community and helping to swell its numbers with much-needed new blood. All in all, the murderous and greedy intentions of these two young men had worked in their favour, even better than they could have predicted. But, like the men they had removed, it could just as easily work against them.

Chapter Fourteen

'Come on, mare, give us a quick flash and a bacon sandwich.'

Mary laughed lewdly at Danny Boy and he hugged her to him tightly. They were on the beach at Brighton, and she was enjoying their easy camaraderie and grateful that he was happy to wait until she felt ready to take the relationship further. It wasn't that she was a wilting violet; she had enjoyed her fair share of men, and boys, come to that. But she sensed that this was what Danny wanted from her and she was desperate to please him. He was everything to her now; when he had taken out Kenny it was as if a weight had been removed from around her shoulders. There was no need to lie about bruises or bumps any more. There was no need to try and talk her way out of trouble just because Kenny had decided to be awkward and make her sweat with fright. No more being dragged from the bed by her hair at three in the morning. With Danny Boy she felt safe and secure, actually felt wanted and needed and loved. She didn't listen to the things that some people were saying about him, the things he was accused of doing, the torture, gun-running, drug-dealing and loan sharking.

She knew that people thought that she was the only person who could bring out the kind and generous side to him; the man who was talked about in hushed tones since the tragic deaths of Donald Carlton and Lawrence Mangan. Rumour was that Lawrence's kidneys, liver and spleen had turned up in the freezer of an abandoned caravan that had been found dumped in Brighton after weeks of being parked up in Louie Stein's yard. It had been a five-day wonder at the time, and it had also ensured that Danny Boy Cadogan went down in local folklore as the baddest of the bad. He was revered by the people he had on his payroll and the people he was good enough to earn money for.

Even her brother Michael was now a part of the new generation of Faces, the new order who were rich and successful and not ashamed to show it. Who, thanks to Danny Boy, were able to make a generous living and, because of that, pledged their allegiance to him. Danny understood that to get people on-side, you had to offer them an incentive, make sure that no one else could tempt them away. He did this by giving them a good living, and then encouraging them to invest in his legal businesses. Michael was the one who found the opportunities for legitimising the money they earned; Danny was how they earned it in the first place. And it was a good partnership because of that. Her brother, she knew, didn't have the killer instinct; that was Danny Boy's department. And, even though she knew, better than anyone, that the rumours about him were true, it didn't turn her away from him, if anything, it just added to his attraction. She liked the danger of him, the feeling that, for all his violent reputation, he was soft-hearted where she was concerned. She felt she had tamed him and that, coupled with his new-found status, was more than enough for her. She knew that Michael was not really happy with the situation, but she understood his concerns and brushed them aside. She knew exactly what she was doing and, for the first time in her life, she was really in love.

'Let's get married, eh?'

Mary was astonished at his proposal and he laughed at the look of incredulity on her lovely face.

'Really, Danny?'

He shrugged then, and the power of him was obvious to her. She knew that other women would always be a problem where he was concerned, and she accepted that fact. She knew she had to if she wanted to make a life with him. Men like Danny Boy Cadogan were always going to be around the kind of women who would be willing to be used by him, even if it was just briefly, and feel honoured by that. A few might manage to keep his interest for a longer while, she was a realist, and she accepted that as well. Strange would be laid out on a plate for him all his life; he was a Face and, as such, young girls would always be up for it. Mary accepted that, to be his wife, the mother of his children, she would have to overlook his sexual infidelities. Would have to learn to deal with them, because she also knew that a church wedding would guarantee his loyalty and his respect. Once married, there would be no going back on either side.

Mary knew that a priest marrying them would be her passport to having him constantly by her side. He still attended Mass, and he took communion; like her he felt the shadow of the Catholic church in all his daily actions, and she knew that his belief in the sanctity, the sacrament of marriage would always colour his every act, would also bring him back to her, and their children, no matter what. That was important to her now, Kenny had made her realise that what she wanted was love, real love; on her side as well as the man's. Her mother's influence was still in place though, Mary wouldn't have married Danny Boy if he had not been able to provide for her and keep her in the manner she had become accustomed to. She had wanted him since her school days and now she had him. Her feelings for him were a bonus.

As they planned their life together it never occurred to Mary that he might not be the man she believed him to be; she saw him as a romantic hero who had saved her from a man who had hurt her, a man who had known deep inside that she was only with him for what he could give her. Who had known, like Danny Boy knew, that she had slept with more men than was good for any of them. Like many a women before her, she was seeing Danny Boy as she wanted him to be, and not as the man that he really was. But she loved him, and made plans for their future together, completely unaware that her past would always be between them.

As she hugged him to her, and whispered her words of love, she felt the happiest she had ever felt in her whole entire life. For the first time ever, she was completely secure, totally happy, and his strong arms holding her tightly eased the gaping void that her mother's death had left in her life. As he slipped his tongue into her mouth she was aroused, as always, and she wished with all her heart that he could have been her first. She had wasted the most precious thing she possessed, her virginity, without realising just how important it was in the great scheme of things. Had never realised that it was the one thing most men prized over everything, and that most women didn't have the sense to see that it was a one-time only offer. That, once it was gone, it could never be replaced, and she wished that someone, at some point in her young life, could have explained its importance to her. Its emotional importance to the girl in question; for her self-worth and her self-belief.

Mary had seen her virginity as nothing more than a means to an end, something to get rid of, something that was a stigma some-how, when in reality it should have been a means to a *beginning*, not an end. As a gift to be presented to someone who would appreciate its value and her sacrifice, and treasure the experience with her. She had wasted it, and now she was living with the consequences of her frivolous attitude. Too much, too young, that was her problem, and she regretted her hard-headed approach to life. She would spend her life making up for it, she knew, because Danny Boy would always know that some other man, in fact, many other men, had been there first. And she wished to Christ that was not the case.

But, like many a woman before her, she had to live with her foolish actions and try to make the best of what she had. He had killed for her, how many women could claim that kind of devotion? And what more could he do to prove his loyalty?

Louie was smiling at Danny Boy and Michael as they walked towards his scruffy old offices; he was rich as Croesus but he still had the same tatty old Portakabin he had always had in his yard. He possessed plant worth in excess of half a million pounds. His car crusher alone was worth more than most politicians' houses. But he was old school, and didn't believe in bringing attention onto himself by looking like he was in possession of a few quid. By being what he termed ostentatious. Unlike these two, with their Jaguars and their hand-made suits. Even though they were making good coin with their clubs and their other legit businesses, mainly the casinos, to him they were still flaunting their wealth and asking to be investigated. Filth didn't mind a tickle, and didn't mind a few bob for extras such as school fees or exotic holidays but, at the end of the day, if they were told to scrump someone's wages, they would. It was the nature of the beast, and they would go scrumping without a second's thought, because they were first and foremost Old Bill, and they had to be seen to be doing their jobs. They couldn't put themselves in the frame, could they? It stood to reason that they would have to have a spring clean at some point, that was why they were often referred to as Filth. But, as always these days, he kept his own counsel; he had voiced his opinions about all this on many occasions and seen the polite smiles and barely suppressed irritation his words had caused. His advancing age had suddenly made him a muppet, and he was sorry that his knowledge and advice, gained over many years in the game, were not seen as the jewels of wisdom he believed them to be. But, being a man of sensitivity and crafty intelligence, he had wiped his mouth and kept his thoughts to himself. These were young men without any kind of fear where Old Bill or illegal enterprises were concerned, and that was their prerogative. Personally, he had never sailed too close to the wind, but then a wife and five daughters could do that to you.

What he did know though, was that Danny Boy was the reason he was suddenly getting so much work offered to him; his instincts all those years ago had paid off, plus, unlike everyone else, he genuinely liked the boy. Michael Miles though, was a different kettle of fish; the jury was still out on him as far as he was concerned, though Louie knew that Danny would always keep him in his place. Danny Boy was the thug in their equation, he was the brawn, not the brains. Danny didn't have the staying power; once he started something he was already looking for the next thing to add to his agenda. The day-to-day running of it was not for him; he was the grafter, the hunter. He wasn't the accountant. That was the domain of Michael; he was the money man, a natural-born accountant, and he had proved himself a serious contender as far as that was concerned anyway. They were now worth a small fortune legitimately, and could explain away anything they owned or possessed with the minimum of aggro; Michael had seen to that.

But the point was, they were still drawing too much attention to themselves, and that was never a good thing in their game. This was still a country that attempted to uphold its laws and, with the advent of the serious crime squad and the IRA causing murders, literally, it was also a country looking for people to blame. Those blamed were generally from the normal criminal fraternity, only now their nefarious earnings, from anything from the bets to knocked-off clothes or electrical goods, were said by the Government to be in some way financing the Irish cause. It was shite, and everyone in the know was well aware of that; the Irish had their own fucking network, they didn't need anyone else. They had money coming in from America, from all over. But it was a good enough reason to bring the public on-side, and it had worked, and that was why their world was now a dangerous place, especially if you were not sensible enough to keep a low profile. Still, Danny Boy had the back-up of enough people to make sure he was protected.

As Louie grinned at them both inanely, he opened his office door wide and, motioning with his head to the young lad who was now fulfilling Danny Boy's old job to leave them alone, he sat back behind his desk. Opening the bottom drawer he took out a bottle of Bell's whisky and had poured them a drink by the time they had removed their expensive overcoats and sat themselves down.

His drink was the largest, and he gulped at it before saying merrily, 'So, what brings you here?'

As if he didn't know.

Annie was watching her future sister-in-law as she examined her wedding dress with the same exactness as a bomb-disposal expert would a defused explosive. She was even checking over the hand-stitching on the seams, and Annie felt the usual annoyance building up inside her. That Mary was beautiful didn't bother her; she knew she was as beautiful in her own way. It was the fact that Mary, through the simple act of being her brother's intended, now generated the interest and friendship of just about everyone she came into contact with. Annie understood that to an extent; she generated a similar reaction, but it still galled her. She had expected to be asked to be a bridesmaid, as was usual, but the offer had not been extended. She knew that Mary was uneasy about it and, as she couldn't take it out on her brothers or her mother, she was quite happy to take her ire out on her sister-in-law to be. It was bad enough that she had been punished by her family for what they saw as her lapse in morals; knowing that Mary had lapsed far more times than she had was something she found hard to digest. Her mother had not really given her the time of day since the debacle with Ian Peck, neither had Jonjo; in fact he had made a point of ignoring her at every available opportunity. Only her father had bothered to treat her with anything even resembling kindness, but then she had always been his favourite. Danny Boy however, had not really been any different towards her, so she could only assume he didn't know the whole story. If he had, surely she would have heard about it by now? So she was pleased she had not had to face his wrath along with her mother's. She had been severely battered, and she knew Danny Boy would have accepted her mother's explanation for her bruises by saying that she had mouthed off, or stayed out too late. A hammering was not out of the question where she was concerned, even one as vicious as she had experienced at her mother's hands.

As Ange lifted the white tulle dress over Mary's head and then carefully placed it on a hanger, all the time chatting away about the forthcoming wedding preparations, Annie bit down hard on her bottom lip to stop the words she was aching to say from spilling out. Instead, she walked from the front room carefully and, once in the kitchen, forced herself to relax.

In the three months since her mother had given her a hiding, she had realised that her place in this household was very precarious. On the one hand she was Danny Boy's sister, so that made sure she was treated with respect outside the home, but that also made sure that no one would ever have the nerve to approach her for a date. She was not allowed any real freedom any more, so her days of going out to places where she could be whoever she wanted to be were over, and the loneliness and hurt were overwhelming. But the worst thing was that her mother couldn't look her in the eye any more; the situation that had caused such a rift was always there between them, and she was drowning in her own guilt and stupidity at letting it happen in the first place.

'Cheer up, Annie love, it might never happen.'

She turned to her father then, saw him as she had seen him for years, a crippled excuse for a father, and as the poster boy for her brother's wrath, and she hissed, 'As you know better than anyone, Dad, it already fucking has happened!'

Big Dan didn't argue with her; he knew it was pointless to say anything to any of them. They all lived in the shadow of Danny Boy, and he couldn't see that changing in the foreseeable future. Like him, she couldn't leave, couldn't walk away, couldn't choose anything for herself; like him she was trapped.

As Ange bustled into the kitchen he knew that she felt the atmosphere acutely, that the situation was breaking her heart too, her daughter's fall from grace had all but broken her, he knew that, but, as always, she acted as if there was nothing untoward going on. It was as if she was waiting for her cue from Danny Boy to see what the next step was to see how she should react, just like everyone else did; himself included.

'Jamie will be the one to suffer, Louie, if it falls out of bed. All I want from you is a few guarantees, a few names of people you think might want to invest in this business venture.'

Louie was nervous, but not so nervous he didn't feel the cold hand of anger as it gripped his heart. Danny Boy should have respected him enough to take his initial 'no' as verbatim, not try and argue his case and talk him round. He was at panic stations, but he swallowed down his dread. He knew he had to force his point across or he would be caught up in the madness that was Danny Boy Cadogan. He was too old for this, too old for the worry of establishing a new enterprise; especially one that would be pounced on by the Filth if they ever got wind of it. For the money Danny and Michael were laying out, it would never be enough if the Filth in question ever got their expensive new collars felt. They always rolled over if they got a capture; there wasn't enough money in the world for them if they had the threat of prison hanging over them. Bent Filth had a much harder time than anyone in stir, they were even more vilified and hated than their honest counterparts; a nicking off a bent Filth was seen as an abomination, a fair cop was one thing, an occupational hazard, but a nicking off someone who was classed as a grass was another thing entirely. They had not only let down their own from the moment they had taken a back-hander but, once captured, they had then rolled over and turned on the hand that had been feeding them. It was outrageous and beyond anything most people could comprehend.

Bent Filth always reverted to type and the fear of being placed in the general prison population with men they had stalked and cautioned in the past, always assured their complete cooperation. As far as Louie was concerned, there wasn't enough poke in the world to keep any Old Bill on-side for the duration if it all went pear-shaped.

'You cheeky little fucker, I said "no", how many more times . . .'

Louie was angry, so angry he was now without any fear whatso- ever. This wasn't about declining a deal any more, it was about respect. About the fact that he had always looked out for this boy from when he was a kid. It was about not allowing himself to be intimidated by the boy's self-assurance and his obvious expectation of agreement.

Michael was amazed at Louie's front, he was also surprised at his absolute negation of what Danny Boy had requested. He saw that Danny Boy felt the same way, and was pleased that he was not going to force the issue.

Danny stood up, he was so upset that he was physically agitated, so disconcerted by Louie's words he was nearly in tears. The obvious distress he was feeling made Louie feel awful. He realised then that Danny Boy had actually thought he was offering him a prize, an in, an earner, for no other reason than he wanted to reward him for his years of friendship. It was an eye-opener.

Danny Boy hastened to make amends. He was unwilling to throw away years of friendship on such a small misunderstanding, but at the same time unable to control that famous temper of his. He needed to vent his spleen, even though he knew it was out of order.

'Louie, calm down, mate, I just wanted to put you in the frame, that's all. You could make a few quid, a good few quid, and you know I would guarantee that you wouldn't ever be mentioned, not even in passing . . . So why are you fucking mugging me off? Am I some kind of fucking Greebo that you think you can dismiss me like a fucking ice cream?'

Louie was standing in front of him now, trying to calm him down. He was trying to hold onto his hands, bring him back down to earth, not let Danny's temper get the better of him. He knew Danny was on the verge of losing it completely, and he was sorry to the heart that he had misjudged the situation so badly.

Michael, although not as big as Danny, was still a fair old lump and, jumping from his seat, he pushed Louie out of the way. Grabbing Danny Boy's shoulders he held him at arms' length, using all his strength to keep him still, to stop him from becoming too agitated and therefore having to burn his anger off by wrecking the place. He was looking into Danny's eyes, trying to force him to calm down.

'Oi, come on, Danny, you know he didn't mean anything cuntish . . . He's an old man and he's set in his ways . . . Now, stop this. Stop it. Louie is one of your oldest friends. Remember? He is your main man. Relax, come on, calm down, mate.'

Louie watched in sheer terror as Danny Boy gradually calmed himself, as he forcibly brought his emotions under control, and he finally understood that this wasn't the same boy he had mentored. This was the boy who had a reputation these days as a calm and cold-blooded adversary. But he also knew that this was a hot-headed man who was completely unable to keep a lid on his temper if he felt in any way challenged or thought that his plans were being thwarted. He knew then, at that moment, that Danny Boy Cadogan was that rarest of breeds; a real and bona fide lunatic who could only get worse. There had been a few of them over the years, but never one as shrewd as this mad bastard in front of him. Danny Boy was bereft of any kind of reasoning, was unable to see further than his own wants and desires, and that was always going to make for a dangerous and untrustworthy man.

As Louie watched the whole scene unfolding in front of his eyes, saw the way Michael talked him down carefully and calmly, and saw the way Danny Boy finally responded to him, he knew then that eventually no one, no matter who they were, would ever be able to rein Danny Boy Cadogan in. The damage was already done; he knew better than anybody how this boy had been forced to take on the mantle of protector at a very young age, had needed to, in effect, save his family from the Murray boys and also to pay them back for their audacity. Louie knew how he had been forced to stand up to them and make sure he was the victor. Something he had only been able to do because of his championship, because of the fact that he, Louie, had put the hard word on everyone and taken this boy under his wing. Now he was seeing a side of him he had always known existed, but had believed would only ever be used against his enemies. Never against his friends.

As Danny Boy turned to him once more, his eyes now focused and his face open and full of the pain he felt for his outburst, he grabbed Louie into his embrace, into his enormous arms and hugged him so tightly he thought he might pass out with the pain. 'Dear God, help me.' He could hear him repeating it over and over again.

Michael watched them, his dark-blue eyes screwed up in pain, and his whole countenance one of somebody who knew that they had just tamed a wild beast, and knowing that they wouldn't be able to do that for much longer.

Walking unsteadily from the Portakabin, Danny Boy went to his car, a navy blue Jaguar and, leaning with his back against the bonnet, he closed his eyes tightly and prayed softly for the strength to regain his self-control once more.

Michael sighed heavily, the deep quiet that had now descended on the confines of the Portakabin was almost eerie. Even the usual noise of the traffic seemed to have stopped; it felt as if they were both suspended in time.

The sudden ringing of the telephone was so loud it made both men jump. Louie let it ring, and when it finally stopped, both of their nerves were shattered.

'He don't mean it, Louie, he loves the bones of you . . .'

Louie didn't answer him, and Michael watched Danny Boy outside as he lit a cigarette and took a deep drag on it. He sighed once more then, this time with relief. Once Danny lit up, it usually meant he was over the worst of it.

'How often does he get like this, Michael?'

Michael shrugged, and Louie admired his loyalty even as he felt the urge to slap him soundly across his face. Michael's handsome face was troubled; away from Danny he looked far more virile and handsome. Next to Danny Boy he seemed to be watered-down somehow; seemed weaker and less masculine. Yet Michael could have a row if the fancy took him; he was just not as inclined to fighting as Danny Boy was. He was submerged in Danny Boy's shadow and that was a shame because that shadow was now huge, thanks to his latest skulduggery.

'Answer me, boy. How often does he lose it completely like that?'

Michael shrugged; his natural reaction to any kind of questioning about his partner and best friend was to keep quiet. It was how they lived, but he also respected Louie and knew he deserved some kind of explanation, so he thought for long moments before answering, 'It depends, he's just got a lot on his mind. What with the wedding, the businesses, you know what he's like. He don't mean the half of it.'

Louie picked up his cigar from the ashtray, his hands shaking noticeably and, lighting it, he said with renewed force, 'For the last fucking time, *boy*, how often does he go off like that?'

Michael wiped a hand across his face. The film of sweat that was now plainly evident was caused by a nervous reaction to the questions being asked, and they both knew that.

'About once a month, but he can handle it, and I can handle him if needs be, so there's no need to discuss this with anyone else, is there?'

Louie was appalled at Michael's open-handed threat, but he was also impressed with the boy's loyalty, even though he felt that he was crying out for a fucking slap. They both were. Danny Boy especially.

'And you are quite happy for him to marry your sister, are you?'

Michael didn't answer him. Instead he motioned for him to be quiet as Danny Boy came back into the office, his face now settled into a smile.

Looking sheepish and ashamed he said to them both, 'What can I say, eh, guys, never poke a gypsy in the eye with a sharp stick; it will only end in tears.'

They laughed then, but they all knew it would never be the same between them again. Danny Boy had stepped over the unwritten line, and Louie would always have that in the forefront of his mind; the trust was gone now. Danny Boy, on the other hand, would have to live with the fact that he had, with a few choice sentences, alienated the man who had provided him with every opportunity he had ever been offered.

Danny Boy couldn't help his anger; he expected people to do as he requested, and he expected them to do it quickly and without question. If he felt he wasn't getting the right reaction, he tended to lose sight of the big picture, the main goal and, when he was also under the influence of amphetamines, as he was today, his usual anger, which he could more or less keep under some kind of control in normal circumstances, tended to escalate out of all proportion.

'I love you, Louie, you know that, mate.'

He was already cutting himself a line on the dirty desktop; six lines of speed were lying there, big, fat white lines that should have been for six individuals instead of just Danny Boy and then, with a rolled-up fiver in his hand, he snorted them, one after the other. He lifted his head up and holding a thumb against his left nostril sniffed so hard it forced his head back on his shoulders and left him looking up at the grubby old ceiling. His earlier antics were forgotten now, and he was all good-humoured bonhomie.

It finally dawned on Louie Stein that Danny Boy Cadogan's colossal anger would only get worse as the years went on. That he was so unstable he was a danger not only to everyone around him, but most of all to himself. It also occurred to him that there was nothing he could do about any of it without landing himself right in it on all sides. Danny Boy had also always had the edge; now he knew it was because he was five-pence short of the full shilling. He was a nut job, his father had seen to that, and the knowledge broke his heart.

*

Mary and her cousins were laughing and joking as they made sandwiches and tea. Ange was thrilled with the girls being round her house so much, and was surprised at how much she enjoyed their company. To have the house once more ringing with laughter and happiness was like a salve on the canker that was her life. Even Danny Boy seemed happier in himself, though you could never be sure where he was concerned. He was so strange at times, but she knew that he was only trying to earn a living for them, so she allowed for his moods and the hurtful remarks that he directed at anyone he felt was even remotely trying to sneak out from under his jurisdiction. The only person who seemed able to do as they pleased was his father, and that was, in itself, a personal slap in the face. His complete disregard for the man spoke volumes.

Now, as she watched the girls chatting and laughing, she knew that Mary was only there because her own mother wasn't around any more to give the poor child advice, not that she would have given her any advice worth taking, of course.

Ange felt the weight of the responsibility she had been given, and she prayed that this marriage would stop her elder son from coming round to her home so much. She was relying on Mary Miles to take over the burden of her son, his black moods, and his colossal anger.

She sat in the small lounge and Mary brought her in a cup of tea. As she took the cup and saucer from her, she looked at the girl sadly, and said quietly, before she could stop herself. 'Don't do it, Mary, he's a hard man to live with and, God forgive me, I should know. Think about what you're doing, child. You've not long buried your mother . . .'

Mary was scandalised at her future mother-in-law's words and she frowned deeply; her pretty face showing her contempt for what the woman was implying, and believing it to be nothing more than a jealous mother's rambling. A last-ditch attempt at keeping her favourite son at home with her. Mary saw the sadness in Ange's eyes and was sorry for her, wondered if she would feel the same when her own son was about to leave his mother's home. In fairness to Ange, Danny Boy had been the breadwinner for a long time and, with her new generous spirit, she almost understood that

222

she could resent another woman taking her place in her son's affections.

Mary put her slim arms around her dumpy future mother-in-law's neck and kissed her gently saying, 'Don't worry, Ange, I'll never take him away from you completely. He loves you and I love him for that, for the way he's looked out for everyone.'

Ange didn't answer her, instead she put her head on the girl's ample bosom and cried like a baby. That's how they were, arms entwined, and their faces wet with tears, when Danny Boy and Michael walked into the room.

It was a scene that stuck in his mind and left him with a feeling of deep unease. Michael was, as always, thrilled at anything that he saw as emotional, loving, and Danny Boy copied his friend's reaction, as he had copied his reactions many times in the past. It was Michael who he emulated, who showed him how to respond to situations, because he never knew how to. He actually had no real feelings except jealousy and anger. He was sensible enough to know that the feelings he lacked were the feelings most people felt on a daily basis. But he had long ago stopped feeling anything really, especially fear, empathy, sorrow, happiness, or love. As he saw his mother and Mary hugging he felt nothing but annoyance. He smiled though, as he knew he was expected to.

When they had stopped hugging and crying, he smiled and winked at his mother and future wife as they walked happily from the room, both easier now that they had finally got onto each other's wavelength. Danny decided the closeness that was suddenly springing between the two women was unhealthy, it made him feel left out of it all. He would have laid money on his mother not being as happy about the forthcoming event as she had seemed to be. In fact, Mary and his mother together like that made him feel not only uneasy, but their obvious affection was something he had not anticipated so had not allowed for it. He didn't want them to be allies, he wanted them as separate entities, both at his beck and call, each in their own little boxes.

Michael, who he cared about more than he had ever cared for anyone, was thrilled at the new-found relationship. He felt his sister needed a mother figure and said so, and Danny Boy acted as if he felt the same way. But he believed in divide and conquer, and he would divide them and conquer his wife if it was the last thing he did on this earth.

As they both sat down at the dining table Danny Boy said quietly, 'By the way Michael, I want Louie out of the game.'

Michael looked at him for long moments before saying, 'Fuck off, Danny, you can't mean that, he's been like a father to you.'

Danny Boy grinned. His handsome face, as always, making him look a lot nicer than he actually was. He had a smile that could melt even the hardest of hearts, even though it rarely reached his eyes.

'I ain't had much luck with the father I was lumbered with, have I? Once the wedding's over, I am going to have a fucking serious sort out, and you had better be prepared.'

Michael had suspected that something like this was on the cards, and he had guessed that Danny Boy, being Danny Boy, wouldn't wait for an opportune moment. He was prepared to steam in and fuck the consequences.

As he watched him chatting and laughing with his sister, Mary, and acting like he didn't have a care in the world, Michael wondered why he was so loyal to him. He knew Danny Boy was not someone to cross, yet he also knew that he was probably the only person, other than his sister Mary and his poor mother Ange, who could actually make Danny Boy Cadogan change his mind when and as it was needed.

And he was determined to make him see that Louie was the best thing they had going for them, and remind him of how much he had helped them out in the past. Danny Boy had not been right for a while, but Michael knew he had gone through these deep depressions before, even as a kid, so he was willing to wait until he felt better again and then talk him round. Danny Boy was capable of changing his mind in an instant, so he would work on that basis. Even as he was planning what he would say to him, a little voice was telling him that Danny Boy was getting further and further away from reality, and his sister was going to have her hands full once the marriage was in place. But he knew that Danny Boy was the glue that held them all together, and he also knew that anyone who had experienced what he had at such a young age was bound to be plagued by suspicion and paranoia.

Michael Miles still justified his friend's outlandish behaviour, and he still couldn't admit to himself that he was actually in dire need of psychiatric help. In their game, Danny's personality was considered a bonus, and Michael was already in too deep to walk away, even if he had wanted to.

Chapter Fifteen

Danny Boy was watching the priest, who was already half-cut; his breath was heavy on the air, the distinctive tang of cheap whisky making most of the people within a six-feet radius of him turn their faces away in disgust. Danny Boy was pleased to see him finally slipping a couple of extra strong mints into his mouth and start sucking on them furiously. He had obviously done this before.

He was a big old boy, with the look of a typical Irish priest; a natural-born brawler who had eventually succumbed to the lure of the Catholic church. Danny Boy liked him and was pleased that he had gone to confession the night before. He had done his confession happily, as always. He enjoyed unloading his sins, lifting the burden of guilt they could create, and saying his acts of contrition with a seriousness and deep belief that would amaze anyone who knew him intimately. Danny Boy was a chancer, a waster, but he was also in the thrall of a much greater power. He admired his God, admired the fact he had created a church from fuck all, and loved being a part of that church, even if it was only a quiet acceptance, a quiet belief. A private matter.

After his confession he always enjoyed sitting in the quiet of the church, alone, taking in the stations of the cross, and praying for his plans to reach a good and plentiful fruition. It was a lovely old church, and he had lit a couple of candles for the people he had personally helped to shake off their mortal coil. It was important to him that he remembered them in his prayers. It appealed to his sense of the ridiculous. He was known as a devout Catholic, a regular attendee of the church, and he knew it made his street credibility more interesting.

For all his bastardy though, he genuinely respected the church and its beliefs. Like Jesus, he saw himself as someone who was trying to make the world a better place, but who was being crucified for that left, right and fucking centre. The Filth was bad enough, but the old boys he was dealing with lately were reminiscent of the old moustachioed petes from the twenties and thirties. It was unbelievable the way they acted up over anything new and innovative. He wondered how the fuck they had got to where they were in the first place, without someone fucking aiming them out of it. How could you stay at the top of your game if you didn't have the sense to diversify? Drugs, especially steroids and other prescription medicines, were a huge earner for the right people. Appetite suppressants, slimming pills, as they were more commonly called, sleeping pills and other medication such as Valium or Mandrax, coupled with amphetamines, were a must-have for the new generation of youngsters who wanted to go out and then *stay* out for as long as was humanly possible. The amphetamine culture was here to stay and, although cocaine was the drug of choice for people with a few quid, as it had been since the late 1890s, when Coca Cola had been advertised for its magical power to relieve fatigue, with over five grams of cocaine in each bottle sold, it was no wonder people didn't feel the need to sleep. Speed was now a requirement of the new giro generation. It was cheaper and easier to get hold of than coke, and it was guaranteed to make the night last longer. Skag, on the other hand, was like LSD, only really an earner on the right estates, with the right dealers and the right clientele. This consisted mainly of people who owned at least one Pink Floyd album, and didn't feel the urge to leave their home for what they saw as a good night out. Most heroin addicts tried dealing at some point, and that was a waste of fucking time and energy, they always junked more than they sold. But, with the right dealer, there was a fortune to be made in them there veins.

Danny was having to argue these basic facts with the very people who he felt should have already *known* what was the new must-have designer drug. They were supposed to be at the top of their game, have their eyes on the ball. Well, after today, he was going to be a married man with a wife and the prospect of a family. He knew that he would be seen by the powers that be as *settled*; they were still unsure of loners, men who were not in a settled relationship and were therefore deemed incapable of rational thought. A family man, they believed, was more inclined to think things through, and less likely to put himself in any position of danger that might very well see him on the receiving end of a big sentence. It was sound economics really, and the fact he was marrying the woman whose beau he had taken out was seen as quite romantic. Well, the day had finally arrived and he was to be married at last. He wished the day was over already so he could get on with the night's affairs. But time passed eventually, even a lifer saw the light at the end of the tunnel one day. Time passed, fast or slow, it passed in the end; any graveyard held the proof of that much.

Danny Boy was dressed in a grey morning suit and top hat; he felt a slight unease, but was still confident as he knew that his build carried the outfit off perfectly. Mary had set her heart on a traditional white wedding and Mary, as he had told her so often, could have what the fuck she wanted. He had wanted to possess her for a long time, and the thought of taking her this night was overwhelming. He had ironed out Kenny, the so-called love of her life, and taken the prize. To know that Kenny was dead appealed to him, appealed to his sense of what was right and fitting. He knew he needed a wife, and he wanted a family for no other reason than it was what people did, it was what most people strived for. Marrying Mary wasn't going to curtail his nocturnal activities, he would carry on as always. Only now Mary would move into his new house with him and take care of him and his needs and he would give her children and she would be fucking grateful that he had picked her up out of the gutter she had sunk into by fucking someone as low as old Kenny boy.

Having a wife would be a laugh, he was looking forward to saying, *my* wife, *my* kids. It was something he knew would give him an air of normality and respectability that he knew was lacking in his life.

He saw Louie and his wife standing nearby; they were a lovely couple and his wife was a really nice lady, a woman who had obviously never had any carnal thoughts in her life, not even about her poor husband. She was a real Brahma, a real lady. He felt a sudden sorrow at his bad behaviour towards his friend; like Michael said, the man had helped him more than anyone else in his life and how had he repaid that kindness? He had lost it, threatened him, felt the urge to obliterate him. He knew he had to get his temper under control, most of the time he could do it, but every now and then it got the better of him and he just exploded. The scary thing was that there was often no reason for his outbursts, and he couldn't care less about the consequences when they hit him. He just had to let the anger out, and anyone within his eyeline was fair game. He winked at his old friend and smiled, acknowledging him with an ostentatious wave that was seen and then filed away by everyone in the church. It showed that Louie was a valued friend, almost family, and Michael smiled happily at the gesture.

Michael was standing beside him, his top hat and tails were not as smart as they should have been, but then Danny had made sure of that. While everyone else had rented their suits, Danny had gone to a Savile Row tailor and had his made-to-measure. It was the real deal, and he knew it made him stand out from the other men around him. He looked like a few quid, and that was exactly the kind of impression he had set out to create.

As Michael chatted, Danny affected his usual amiable demeanour of nodding and smiling that made Michael believe he was listening to what he was saying. He was, in fact, looking around the church, impressed at the amount of Faces who had deemed him worthy enough to tempt them into attending his wedding. No one, as far as he could see, had refused his invitation. In fact, he had a full attendance record for the first time in his life. He saw every major crime family of every nationality, and every outside gang was present, meaning the people who resided north of the Watford Gap; all had either come in person, or they had sent a representative of high-standing. Jamie Carlton was there, in the thick of it, which put paid to a few of the more choice rumours about him. That knowledge pleased him. It was a public declaration of his new status and he wanted to use it to put pressure on the people he felt should be investing money in his new businesses. Once they put in a few quid he could stop worrying about them trying to take it over, or muscling in for a percentage. If they harboured delusions of grandeur, for example, dreaming about trying to elbow him out and then attempting to claim the main prize for themselves, he would be far too entrenched for them to get even a fucking toehold. He just wanted their poke and their undying goodwill, anything else was just bunce.

As he pictured the money he was going to collar, he heard the first few bars of Mendelssohn and, plastering a big smile on to his face, he turned and watched his soon-to-be wife as she floated down the aisle on a cloud of white lace and very expensive perfume. She looked fantastic, there was no doubt she was a good-looking girl, but she was also soiled goods and that meant he would have to watch her like a hawk. She had been a girl, as everyone there knew. A lively lass, a bit of a laugh, a good lay. She had a rep that was as outstanding as it was annoying. But she was radiant now as she walked down the rose-petal strewn aisle to her new husband's side, amid gasps of admiration from the women, and grunts of lechery from the men. Danny Boy knew they were grading her from one to ten, and not finding her lacking. She looked absolutely stunning, and so she should, the dress had cost the national debt, and everyone remarked on that fact. She was like a movie star, and that was *exactly* the impression she had set out to create for herself.

Like her beau she had seen this wedding as the social event of the year and had made sure she was dressed accordingly. They had taken over a local nightclub for the reception, and the food was being prepared by a top London chef. The music was going to be spectacular, and the late-night buffet was costing them as much as the sit-down meal. The Rolls Royces were booked for the whole day, and would take them to Heathrow later on that night to begin their three-week honeymoon in Mauritius. All in all, this was going to be the wedding of the decade, and she was already, without a doubt, the best-looking bride they had seen for many a year. Fuckable, yet virginal, and that was something she had not been since her school days.

*

Ange looked at her sons as they waited for the bride to arrive. She was happy enough, and her husband was standing beside her, his tails a bit too big on his bony frame, but still looking good on him. He had been a handsome man in his day, and still was if he bothered to get himself dressed up. She saw her daughter's petulant face, and she understood her hurt at not being a bridesmaid. She knew Mary had wanted her for the job, but it was Danny Boy who had put the kibosh on it; he was not impressed with her at the moment. She could sympathise with him though because she felt the same way towards her herself. The girl was a fecking whore in the making and this might just be the nudge she needed to set her straight.

As Ange scanned the church she was also seriously impressed by the people who had turned out to see her boy married. She knew the guest list was making her husband green with envy and she didn't care. She was making the most of her moment of glory, what else could she do? She had learned, a long time ago, to make the most of whatever came her way. Life, more often than not, had a habit of disappointing her so why not enjoy the good times while she could?

'So the tenth of May will be your wedding anniversary then?'

Mary nodded happily and her brother Gordon who she had thought looked so handsome in his tails, said loudly and drunkenly, 'A white dress, sis?'

She was already feeling the shame of his glare. He was not afraid to say his piece, afraid to offend. He was a bastard when he was drunk. Like their mother he couldn't just have a few drinks, he drank seriously.

'Stop it, Gordon, not now. Danny Boy won't swallow your jokes.' She was attempting to warn him, but it was a friendly warning that she knew he could not help take on board.

He grinned at her then, and she realised he was past talking to, and she wanted to physically harm him. He always had to cause a scene, always felt the need to hurt everyone around him. Any other time she felt a deep sorrow for him, but today she hated him for it, today she had hoped he would not act up. But she could see the hate in his face, the flushed redness from the drink he had already imbibed, the recklessness of someone who had not yet come across Danny Boy with the hump.

'That's a bit like putting the cart before the horse ain't it, sis, considering your past form? You've had more cocks than a hen house. I heard you was so popular in the pub that they named a toilet stall after you.'

He was looking at her with his usual drunken amiability, this was a stance he took so that he could act contrite the next day. He would say that he was only joking. Mary felt the smile freeze on her face. Gordon was always the first to cause trouble, and she was sick of it. She had been fool enough to believe he would behave himself today. She should have known better; at his age, he thought he was the dog's gonads, and she had never bothered to disabuse him of that notion. She had spent her life sticking up for him, and now she was sorry that she had not done what everyone else had, given him a wide berth and left him to get on with it. Once he had a few drinks he was a nightmare, he was his mother's son all right. Alcohol made him angry and vicious, made him into an evil mirror image of his usual self.

As she looked into his eyes she saw the calculated and wicked glint still there, and knew he was too far gone to be reasoned with. She glanced round her; the club they had taken over was decorated with lilies and white roses, the whole colour scheme creams and golds. It looked stunning, and her little brother, as always, had to put a vicious barb in where nice, friendly chat would have sufficed. He was so eaten up with jealousy and hatred when he had taken a few drinks that he often got a smack across the earhole from his unsuspecting victim. And always people he thought cared about him, people he didn't think would be hurt, offended or humiliated by his words of wisdom. His excuse was always the same, he had only spoken the truth, as if that fact alone would wipe out the pain and the trouble he had caused. Knowing that the truth, in their world, was the last thing most people were interested in. The truth was, more often than not, an expensive and much over-hyped emotion that was, in actuality, a destructive and dangerous force.

The truth was not for the likes of them, and this brother of hers knew that better than anyone. He was a bastard, and he was not about to give her any kind of leeway; he was determined to break her heart. He was not bothered about his words, or the effect they might have, he was lost in the moment, already unable to distinguish between her pain and his obvious cruelty. And he had promised her he would behave, promised her he would not drink until the evening. She now had to accept that, young as he was, he was an alcoholic as well as a drug addict. A complete pisshead who cared nothing for her or her new husband's feelings.

This *day* had been all she had thought about for weeks, all she had cared about, and all she had talked about. Gordon, like Michael, had known how much this wedding had meant to her, how much she depended upon its success so her marriage could start off on the right foot. Gordon, more than any of them, knew how much she had depended on her family's cooperation, to not only ensure the day went off without a hitch, but also to guarantee that there would not be any embarrassing moments. Now he was the instigator of his sister's humiliation and it wasn't fair.

She had planned this day down to the last detail and, now that it was finally here, now that she was legally married and her life more or less sewn up, it was on the point of imploding because of a few choice words uttered by her little brother with a drunken arrogance and fatal finality that she knew was going to make her fall from grace all the more spectacular. That her little brother was the one who was showing her up in front of her friends, at least her new husband's friends, was harder to bear than anything he was saying about her. That he was so obviously enjoying his ruination of her big day was hard for her to comprehend. She couldn't ever imagine herself doing something so heinous, so hateful to her own family. But why would she hurt him, after all, *she* loved him.

She felt the sting of tears at the enormity of his betrayal, and blinked them away angrily. Then she whispered in his ear brokenly, 'Shut your fucking mouth, Gordon. Who do you think you are?'

She looked into the face so like her own and marvelled once more at how he could hurt her like this, could enjoy the spiteful words, as if she was his worst enemy. How could he enjoy making her feel so bad about her lousy family on the biggest, most important day of her life. He always made a point of targeting her, making her feel like nothing. She knew it was because he *could*, because he knew he would always be a *nothing*, a no one, and that was why he felt such joy when he hurt her like this. He borrowed money from her, and used her when he needed anything, and he resented her for that, for her generosity. Instead of feeling thankful that he had a sister who loved him and was more than willing to help him out he resented her for her generosity and hated himself because, without it, he couldn't exist. She finally knew what he had known all along. Gordon was a ponce, a twenty-four carat drunken ponce, devoid of conscience and unable to grasp the rudiments of daily life. He was ruining her wedding without a second's thought for her or her husband. That knowledge would plague her for the rest of her life. Anyone else and she could have stood it, but her little brother's betrayal was too much for her to take.

'You rotten bastard. Stop this, Gordon, and I mean it.'

Gordon laughed. Away from Michael's side he was quite a good looker, but, next to Michael and this sister of his, he looked what he was; a cheaper, much rougher version of his siblings. He knew that, and it was one of the reasons he always had to cause upset whenever they were together like this. He opened his blue eyes wide, acting innocent, then, placing a grubby hand across his mouth, he said loudly and sarcastically through his nicotine-stained fingers, 'Oh, sorry, sis, what's the official story then? That you're a born-again virgin? Surely Danny Boy hasn't forgotten Kenny, he had a bit of a problem with him didn't he? *You* must remember Kenny, sis, surely, I know I do.'

He had finally stepped over the line, and somewhere in his drink- and drug-addled brain even he knew that. Knew he was out of order, was going to pay for his treachery, knew his sister was never going to forgive him.

None of the small crowd nearby were official friends of either her or Danny Boy really, they were what she termed as the alternative guest list. People Danny felt had to be invited, as opposed to people they wanted to invite. So her brother's antics were all the more outrageous because they were not used to him like her friends were, they were not in a position to shout him down, to tell him to stop his lunacy before Danny Boy heard him. These were people who were actually on the lookout for a bit of gossip about the night, who were not there to wish them well, but were there just to show their face, show a bit of goodwill and give a decent present to show how far on they had come in life. For them to witness her little brother's tirade was more than she could bear, especially as she knew every word would be repeated and picked over by half the London underworld for years to come. Her lovely day was ruined, the day she had sweated blood over planning was going to be a terrible memory like so many other bad memories in her life, especially where her family were concerned. But, knowing that everything was now ruined anyway, and that all she could do really was effect some kind of damage limitation, she smiled as best she could and said through her gritted teeth, 'Danny Boy will kill you for this, Gordon, he won't swallow your fucking antics like we do. You are making a mockery of a man who, as you rightly pointed out, is capable of killing to get what he wants. He is also capable of killing people he thinks aren't giving him the respect he feels is his due.'

The last few words were as much for the benefit of the people listening in, a tacit reminder that Danny Boy Cadogan was capable of extreme and excessive violence when pushed over the edge. She was suddenly worried now at Danny's reaction to her little brother's actions. As much as he could irritate her, she still didn't want to see him hurt. Leaning forward, she whispered in his ear, 'You've ruined me day for me, I hope you're happy now.'

He leaned back, his boyish body cumbersome in his grey tailored suit and shouted happily, 'I'm over the moon, sis. Couldn't have happened to a nicer girl.'

Then, looking around the beautiful room, he said even louder, 'Mum would have loved this. She'd have felt like me, Mary, that you're acting like you're better than everyone else, and trying to pretend you are happy. Well, you don't fool me, girl . . . You're a fucking mug . . .'

Mary was really crying now, because he was so far off the mark it was laughable; he believed she was doing what her mother had expected of her, marrying Danny Boy for what he could offer her as opposed to what she might want. Her mother would have pushed her into the marriage and then slaughtered her because of it. Her brother's usual drugged and drunken ramblings were generally ignored by family members, but this was public, tantamount to mutiny, and she wasn't about to let him get away with it any more.

As she stood there in her long white dress, her veil touching her slim shoulders and her high-heeled shoes crippling her, she felt a terrible sense of foreboding, as if this was a warning to her about how her life was going to be from now on. It was so real she felt as if she was going to pass out, and she wanted that to happen, just so she could get away from this feeling, and from her brother's vitriolic ramblings.

Jonjo Cadogan was in shock, he had always known that his friend was a bit of a headbanger, but to hear him talking to his own sister with such disrespect was unbelievable, and on her wedding day as well, the day she had married *his* brother and taken *his* family name. Jonjo felt the anger erupting inside him then, and suddenly he understood his brother's need for their family's name to be honoured. For the first time ever, he felt the urge to defend his family name. Danny Boy had always seemed over the top to him, his hatred of their father and his determination to make their name mean something had always seemed stupid, unnecessary. Now though, it seemed perfectly reasonable. Danny always said, all you had at the end of the day was your name, and that made it the more important because it was something you either respected or you were ashamed of. Your name was all you had, the only thing that you couldn't ever deny. Now, listening to Gordon, he saw for the first time what Danny Boy had meant by that. Your name was all you had. You had to give it away one day, to your bride, or your children, and then you had to live up to it, or you had to live it down. Your name was the only thing you ever really owned, for good or for bad; that choice was yours. Danny Boy was trying to reclaim their name, make it mean something once more. He had given it to Mary Miles, and her brother had stamped on it without a second's thought. She was a Cadogan now, and her shame was now his.

Jonjo lost his usual good-natured camaraderie and he hissed at his old friend, 'You cunt, you fucking bastard. You think you are going to get away with that, do you?' He brought his fist back and planted it firmly into the centre of his friend's face, knocking him flying. As he went to carry through his attack Mary grabbed his arm.

'Please, Jonjo, get him out of here, please get him away from me.'

She was white with fear and her humiliation was obvious to anyone who was watching her, and that was now most of the guests. Ilford Palais was packed out and she could feel the eyes of everyone burning into her.

'Don't worry, Mary, I'll fucking sort him out. I don't know why he does it but he won't be capable of saying anything else once I finish with him.'

He was so sorry for her, she was almost burning with humiliation. 'No one listens to him anyway, mare, everyone know he talks bollocks.'

He was trying his best to make her feel better but they both knew it was not working. As she began to speak, she saw Michael and Danny Boy walking purposefully in their direction and her older brother linked Gordon's arm in a friendly way, while dragging him up from the floor roughly. Then he started to walk him out of the club as if nothing untoward had happened, Jonjo following them.

Mary leaned against her new husband's chest and cried, really cried, her day was ruined. She was overwrought and the drink had lowered her defences. But, instead of holding her as she had expected, Danny Boy grabbed her arms roughly and pushed her away from him, his handsome face marred by the spitefulness of his words.

'Happy now, are you? Everyone chattering about what a dog you are. Even your own brother is disgusted with you. What a fucking day, eh, me wife is unmasked as a slag by her own fucking brother.'

Mary couldn't believe what he was saying to her, couldn't for the life of her comprehend his anger and his disloyalty. How could he condone her brother's words on their wedding day? How could he let other people think that what Gordon said was true, even if it was? Their whole life was about front, about believing what you wanted to believe, about making your life up as you went along. If Old Bill was to come to her house and ask where her husband was at any given time, she would not hesitate to say he was with her, whether he had been with her or not. Her husband's words could only exacerbate her brother's; Danny Boy's anger could only make Gordon's diatribe seem even more believable. She was now almost begging him to take her side, something she knew she should never have had to ask of him. He should be making her feel better, be making her feel safe and secure. 'No, Danny Boy . . . Come on, you know he talks rubbish . . .'

Danny Boy looked down at his new little wife and enjoyed the humiliation she was feeling. He didn't so much want a wife as a scapegoat, someone he saw as nothing more than a means to an end. Now, thanks to Gordon, he saw a perfect opportunity to start off his married life with a wife who was already wrong footed, already unsure of her power.

Mary was a good-looking girl, a babe, and also a fucking know-all if she was allowed to give vent to her feelings. Priding himself on always seeing any opportunity when it presented itself, he knew that this was one he couldn't miss. If he played his cards right he could cow her for the rest of her days, and he used the moment without any qualms whatsoever.

'You are a right fucking prize ain't you, your brother mug-bunnying about you in front of everyone.' He shook his head with a calculated and theatrical disgust.

Then, pushing her away from him, he walked out of the club without a backward glance, leaving her alone and distraught, and without a shred of self respect.

It was the talk of London the next day because he didn't bother to come back again and the new bride eventually went to her new home alone. It was awful for her and no one knew what to say.

Everyone went home, but before they went they tried their hardest to find something nice to say to her before they left. But it was too late, her day was ruined, and her brand-new husband had gone AWOL.

The honeymoon was cancelled, and the reception was wrecked, but she still sat there, full of hope, in their brand-new detached house, the house that they had so lovingly decorated and furnished, and she prayed for him to return to her on this night of all nights.

She finally passed out blind drunk at six in the morning; she was still in her wedding dress, and she was still cherishing the belief that he would come back to her at some point, it was their wedding night. She believed that he couldn't really have been so cruel to her, that he couldn't really have humiliated her in front of basically everyone that they knew. But she knew she was wrong, as she had been wrong about so many things where her new husband was concerned.

Danny was drunk as a lord, and the girl he had picked up at some point during the night's revelry was now snoring her head off beside him in a strange hotel room. She had not looked so heavy last night, or so hairy; she had a much more luxuriant moustache than most of the men he knocked around with. But, in fairness, she had been game and, from what he remembered, she had given him a good few hours. Her thick black hair was heavy as a rope, and it was fanned out around her head making her look much more exotic than she actually was. He was looking at her with genuine interest, amazed at what beer goggles were capable of doing to a man's brains. In the usual run of things he would not have given this bird a second's thought. Now he had spent his wedding night with her, and that knowledge made him smile. She turned over in her sleep and he saw how flabby her belly was. He knew then that she had kids somewhere, and his dislike of her was now ten-fold. Who the fuck was taking care of them while she was out whoring? He hated it when he woke up with mothers, somehow it made everything seem even more seedy than it really was. The babies they had birthed at least had the right to a mother who wasn't a fucking trollop; at the end of the day it wasn't that much to ask was it?

He poured himself out a stiff drink and, as he did so the girl stirred momentarily in her sleep; he now believed she had heard the splash of alcohol in her subconscious and, once more, wondered at a woman who could lower herself so much she would be quite happy to wake up next to a stranger without any kind of shame. That he had slept with her didn't enter into it. He was a man, and he was built to chase strange. It was in a man's nature to fuck indiscriminately, whereas women were expected to have a modicum of decorum. He knew God had provided women like this one expressly for men like him.

He wondered what his wife was doing now, was she awake and wondering what had happened to her lovely day? The very day that she had gone on about so much he had felt the urge to scream. He wondered what her cunt of a brother was doing, considering he had caused the fucking rift in the first place. She was a lovely girl, but he would have dumped her anyway at some point in the day, she had needed knocking down a peg or two, flash prat she was, and her brother had inadvertently provided the excuse he had needed to do just that.

Now Michael was also on board with his tantrum, because it was his little brother who had caused the rift that Danny Boy had wanted so badly. All in all, it had worked out well. He knew the importance of being discussed, and how a spectacular scandal could catapult someone into the psyche of everyone around you. His wedding would guarantee his name going down in the annals of the local folklore. He would be respected for his open-heartedness when he took his wife back. It had been the same with his father, his public treatment of his father had garnered him many a friendly pat on the back. He had crippled him because of his gambling and his wicked abandonment of his family, and leaving them in enormous debt. And yet he was liked because he still saw the old boy all right. It was good PR. He was the main talking point of the Smoke today, and he knew it. That he had walked out of his own wedding, and a fuck-off expensive wedding at that, would cause ripples that would reverberate for many years. He would live it down, there was no shame on him, but Mary never would, and that was what he had wanted. To make her see what she was getting herself into. Gordon had played right into his hands and, for that, he would be forever grateful. She was all he had ever wanted in a woman, but she was also all that a lot of other men had wanted in a woman. He hadn't fucked her before the big day because he couldn't really bring himself to go where Kenny and the others had gone before. Yet he still wanted her to be his wife, and he had deep feelings for her. The fact that those feelings were often on the verge of hatred was something he had accepted long ago.

As he remembered the feeling of his flaccid cock inside this sleeping girl a few hours earlier, the stickiness of his come inside her, remembered the thick wetness as it had dripped down on to her thighs as he pulled out of her, then the sickly stench of her when he had finally awoken, he thought of his new wife and wondered how many times this same situation had happened to her. She had put it about, and now he had to make something good come of this marriage. He had wanted her, but he couldn't get past this; the fact that she had been seen like this by so many other men, had been used like this. He had made his point, and now she would spend the rest of her life regretting her colourful sex life, he would make sure of that. He remembered his mother's swollen belly after his father had all but destroyed the family he had created and then abandoned as and when the fancy took him. That she could have welcomed him back into her bed was, to him, the ultimate betrayal considering what he had caused them. When she had miscarried that child he had felt the last vestige of love leave his body and he had celebrated that fact. She had wanted his father and she had got him, and he had made damn sure that they paid the price for their treachery. He took on the mantle of man of the house as a young kid, and yet his mother had been willing to let his father come back and carry on as usual, even though it would mean her children could once more go without. Women were fucking carrion, they lived off whatever they could get from the man who was fucking them. He knew the truth of that better than anyone. He had put his life on the line, fought the Murrays and made a life for himself because of his father's fucking gambling and his mother's fucking selfishness. Six hundred quid had been the cause of his life being so fucked up. Six hundred quid, that was now what he classed as spending money, as fuck all, as nothing. Well, as his father used to joke, marry a whore, she can't ever get any lower. So he had done just that. Now he had to face the music and he couldn't wait.

Michael was sipping coffee and smoking a Turkish cigarette in the small office of the casino he owned with Danny Boy. He was still in shock at what had occurred the day before and he had almost convinced himself at one point that it had never happened. That he had dreamed it. But he knew it was true, and that knowledge plagued him. His sister was in bits, and her big day, the day she had been looking forward to with so much excitement had been ruined. Gordon was now sober and contrite, his sorrow so genuine it was heartbreaking to witness. Not that it had stopped him from giving him the hiding of his life though. That his own brother could have been the cause of such distress was what had made him depressed. Mary had looked beautiful, and Danny Boy, his best friend and partner, had been so looking forward to the big day, that when it had finally arrived they had all sighed with relief. That Danny Boy had not been able to take what Gordon had said about his new wife was a given. Danny Boy, he knew, was far too proud to have swallowed that kind of a show up. That he had left the reception was, to his way of thinking, probably a good thing, that he had not murdered Gordon was a result in itself. As he had tried to explain to Mary, Danny had only left the party so he didn't do anything foolish, didn't let that famous temper of his get the better of him.

Not that Mary could see that yet, and he understood her hurt over his absence and her bewilderment that her little brother could have been the cause of it in the first place. She had sworn never to speak to him again. Ever. Well, Gordon would think twice before he let the drink get the better of him in future; he was now in absolute terror of Danny Boy coming back to take his retribution for the destruction of her wedding day. If Danny did decide to take umbrage he would have to wipe his mouth; at the end of the day

Danny would be well within his rights. To talk about her like that, at her own wedding. Her wedding to a man who could kill without a second's thought. Who could torture someone for hours on end and actually enjoy their screams of terror. What the fuck was the boy thinking of? It was an abortion, it was the most outrageous thing he had ever experienced in his life, and he still didn't know what the upshot of it all was going to be.

Mary Cadogan, as she was now known, awoke to see her husband of one day stripping off to get into the shower. When she opened her eyes and saw him standing there she felt her heart almost lift itself inside her chest. She pulled herself upright with difficulty, the drink from the night before giving her a raging thirst and a thumping headache. As she watched him walk naked towards the bathroom she was amazed that he had not spoken a word. It was as if they were all right, as if they had not had the drama of the day before. He called over his shoulder lightly, 'Make us a cup of tea, love, and take that fucking dress off, will you? I thought I'd come home to Miss Havisham.'

He was acting as if there was nothing out of the ordinary going on. She was disorientated, still half pissed, and she looked around the bedroom she had decorated with such happiness and saw her reflection in the mirror on the dressing table. She looked awful, her eyes were rimmed with black make-up and her tears had stained the skin on her face and neck; she looked old. As she observed herself she remembered the day's events and swallowed down the tears once more. Her mouth was dry, and she could smell herself. As she stood up she felt herself sway and hoped that she might pass out and die so she didn't have to face the rest of her life, but she didn't. Instead, she pulled off her wedding dress. It was ruined, and she left it in a heap on the bedroom floor and dragged on the silk dressing gown she had bought with her new husband in mind. She started to take off her make-up, wiping her face gently, all the time her ears were straining to hear the sound of the shower being turned off. She was expecting a fight, and she knew that there was nothing she could do to avoid it. How on earth would Danny Boy ever find it in his heart to forgive them all for the travesty that was their big day. She sat on the end of the bed, the bed she had believed would be the place where they would lie together, love together, and talk together. Now it was messed up from where she had lain and cried her heart out. It was the shame that was now bearing down on her, the sheer disgrace that was overwhelming her.

Danny Boy had asked her to make a cup of tea as if this was a normal day, as if everything was OK. She knew his reputation as someone with a short fuse, a quick temper, but she had never believed in a million years that it would be turned on her. So she sat there, and she waited for him to finish what he was doing, and decided to accept whatever punishment he decided to dole out.

When he walked back into the bedroom, his body glistening with the water from his shower, she almost flinched. It was only now, seeing him naked, that she realised just what a big man he was. He was solid, all muscle and soft skin. She felt the tears come once more as she saw what she was going to have to give up. He stood before her, and she looked up into his handsome face. The face she had dreamed about for so long, and saw that he was smiling at her. The lazy, relaxed smile that fooled everyone into thinking he was one of the good guys.

He was looking at her, his dark blue eyes devoid of anger, instead they were soft and caring and Mary couldn't believe that he was not berating her for the destruction of their wedding day. 'Are you all right, mare?'

He sounded concerned, so kind and gentle that she wondered if she was dreaming.

She shook her head sadly. 'I am really sorry for what happened, Danny Boy, I am so very sorry. Gordon doesn't know what he's saying half the time . . . He drinks, he's always on drugs . . .'

She was trying to justify her brother's behaviour and she didn't know why; he didn't deserve her loyalty, he had never shown any towards her.

Danny knelt down in front of her and said quietly, 'He was only telling the truth, mare. Tell the truth and shame the Devil, remember. You were a fucking whore, and I have to live with that, don't I?'

He grinned then, his even teeth pristine and his breath all cool and minty from the toothpaste he used. He was still smiling, and his words finally broke her spirit. He stood up and said gently, 'Now, make the fucking tea, will you, and don't ever make me have to repeat myself again.'

Chapter Sixteen

Mary was waiting for her husband to come home, but her nerves were so bad she was shaking like the proverbial leaf. She was sick inside, the cold sweat covering her body making her skin tighten, making her teeth chatter amongst themselves. She could feel the fear inside her, and knew that she had expected something like this since her first date, the danger that was Danny Boy was the attraction. The knowledge that he was an unknown quantity had attracted her, even though she had not admitted any of this to herself until now.

She looked in the bathroom mirror and saw that she was immaculate, as always. Despite what had occurred at their wedding she still made a conscious effort to look her best, look as if nothing could, or would, faze her, a trick she had learned from her years with Kenny. People only knew what you told them, only saw what you wanted them to see. Her mother had hammered that into her head since she was a child, a child with huge breasts and the knowledge of a woman three times her age.

You're sitting on a goldmine, you play your cards right and you'll never want for anything. Her mother's words were still crystal clear, except for the fact that she had actually fallen for Danny Boy many years before. He had been her childhood crush, her first love. Now she wasn't sure what he was, or even what *she* was any more. All she knew now was that she was in danger, grave danger. He had shown his hand, his true feelings for her, and that had badly frightened her. She knew her humiliation was complete because he had known she would have him back in a heartbeat.

Her make-up was perfect, her skin was clear, and her thick, dark hair was salon fresh. Even at the worst time of her life, she was inordinately aware of how she looked, how her outward demeanour would guarantee her coming through this with at least a modicum of self-respect. She took a deep breath and willed herself to calm down. Danny Boy had never really appreciated her natural nervousness, in fact, it angered him, and yet his anger only served to make her nervousness even worse.

She never knew whether he was going to come home to her; he was a law unto himself in that respect. But, if he did come home, she wanted to be ready for him as she had always been. She had spent the best part of the day making herself look beautiful for a man who she knew despised her, but who, she also knew, would never let her go. She was his now, and there was nothing she could do about that. It was too late. Danny Boy had destroyed her in a few short words, and her own brother had happily given him the ammunition he had taken great pleasure in firing right back at her. Gordon was unaware that he had been the conduit for the reason that her brand-new husband would use as an excuse for bad behaviour. Danny Boy was not a man to let things pass him by, not someone who would turn the other cheek. He was a man who looked at every opportunity and then worked out how best to turn it to his own advantage. In short, he was not unlike herself, they were both users, and they were both willing to use whatever means they could to further their own ends; unfortunately she had believed that they could have worked together on that in the future. Not use it against each other.

Danny Boy had the knack of making her feel like absolute shit, and she was on the brink of believing him. She looked at herself once more in the mirror and wondered at how this had happened to her. She remembered Kenny and what she now saw as his easy-going ways, remembered Danny Boy when he had been so determined to get her. How he had made sure she had felt wanted, and how he had made Kenny seem lacking to her. All her confidence had now left her, had disappeared almost overnight, and she knew that was precisely what Danny had wanted to happen, had ordained. She knew that he had not slept with her before the marriage because he had known that would throw her off the scent. He had been determined to destroy his arch-enemy and that somehow included her. He had finally taken her, one week after the wedding fiasco; he had taken her roughly, viciously, and she had been unable to walk for days after. His use of her, which was no better than his use of a common prostitute, was the final nail in the coffin of their so-called love. He had not only hurt her physically but, more to the point, mentally. He had deliberately, and with serious amounts of malice, taken her like a dog would take a bitch in heat, without any kind of care, or love, or real want. It had been nothing more than an act of destruction, an act of hatred. The final betrayal of their love and the final nail in the coffin of their real lives. He had wanted to make a point, wanted to make her realise just how little he really thought of her, wanted her to feel like she was less than nothing.

And it had worked. He had done his homework, and he knew she was too proud to admit her mistake out loud, and she was now far too frightened to do anything about her situation. Her fear of her husband was overwhelming. She knew without a second's doubt just what he was capable of where she was concerned.

She had finally accepted her fate, accepted his complete ownership of her. She had known then, as she knew now, that leaving him would *never* be an option; he would kill her first, and he was an old hand at that. She also knew that their marriage was, for some reason, very important to him. It was something that he cherished, something he saw as not only important but, even more frighteningly, as something decent and good. Even after everything he had done to her.

The public humiliation, the loss of face and, worst of all, the guarantee that no one would ever see her as anything more than his wife, the wife he had married even though it was now assumed she wasn't worthy of him. He was a clever man, a vicious man, but he was also a man of means, a man who was looked on as someone to respect, admire. He was her husband, and that was the most terrifying thing. She was tied to him, and the tie was not something *she* could break, that would only happen if *he* decided it had run its course, if *he* wanted out of the marriage.

Their actual life together would be, she knew, fraught with danger; he saw her as some kind of trophy, she saw him as some kind of maniac. He thought nothing of dragging her out of the bed by her hair at three in the morning, a favourite trick of Kenny's, accusing her of all sorts. Accusing her of conducting affairs with his friends, even though he knew his so-called friends would never have had the guts to bed her, even if they had wanted to. She was aware that he knew his accusations had no basis in fact but, like everyone else around him, she didn't try to argue with him about it. You didn't argue with the Danny Boys of this world, you did whatever it took to keep the peace. You swallowed whatever he doled out and hoped against hope that things would get better. Even though you knew that they never would.

Mary knew that Danny needed her to vent his spleen on, and needed her to be acquiescent, needed her to allow him his rage. She was already becoming immune to it, was already able to shut herself off and let him take out his enormous anger on her without even a groan of pain. She was pleased that this, at least, pleased him, that her complete subservience was enough to keep him relatively happy anyway.

The home they shared was spotless, as he expected it to be; she was even afraid to sit on the furniture in case she made it look used, dented the cushions, or stained it somehow. The house was huge and, like a show home, it was perfect, but it had no soul. There was nothing real around her, not even a photograph, to make this place feel like a home. Danny Boy hadn't even allowed her to *see* their wedding photos, much less let her display any of them. But she had gone behind his back on that at least; she had asked Michael to purchase a small album of their day on the quiet, she had wanted it for their children's sakes. She knew that one day those photos would be important to the people they might have created. She wanted something to prove to them her validity in their world.

She knew Danny was desperate for a child, a son. And she had a child inside her, *his* child, and she was excited about that, hoped that this baby would bring them together again, would cancel out the wedding fiasco. Deep inside she understood that her hopes would be dashed, but she still prayed that her pregnancy would stop his angry assaults upon her body for a while, and stop the viciousness of his words. He spoke to her with a calm hatred that was as disgusting at it was regular. She wondered just when this had suddenly begun to seem like perfectly normal behaviour, and when she had actively stopped trying to make him like her again. She wondered when she had started to actually believe that a child would stop the nightmare that was her marriage.

She saw that she had gnawed off the lipstick she had applied so carefully throughout the day, and as she reapplied it, she held back the tears, the tears she knew were not only useless, but also guaranteed to wreck the perfection of her face. Danny Boy could arrive home at five in the morning, and she knew that he still expected her to be sitting there with full make-up on, waiting on him with a smile on her perfect face and the promise of complete submission from her body, and he always got exactly what he wanted. Even though she might have to wait for hours and hours, it was worth it to keep the peace. She waited and she waited for his arrival home, and she calmed her nerves with a few drinks as she sat alone and watched the clock, sometimes for days on end.

She hated him now, with all her heart and soul.

Danny Boy and Michael were arranging to pick up a few parcels of aspirin, which was how they referred to the anabolic steroids they were already distributing in large amounts throughout the south east. The parcels were innocuous; wrapped in plain brown paper they looked like a birthday present, but they actually contained more drugs than anyone would ever believe. Danny Boy had been spot on with this money-maker, the drugs were not only necessary to the people who acquired them, they were also semi-legal. No one could actually prove that the drugs, when seized, were not for personal consumption, which was why they were picking them up for themselves. No one cared enough about the body-building population to make sure they were safe. Danny Boy was aware of their dangers and, like anyone else involved in any kind of business, he knew all there was to know about his product. He knew that the drugs caused violent episodes, that the men taking them on a daily basis were kidding themselves because, without them, they couldn't hope to achieve the body mass they so desperately desired. He knew that the drugs were bought and injected without any medical knowledge whatsoever, and that they were usually only half the strength of legitimate drugs anyway. He also knew that the people he supplied them to were flakes, wankers, who were not prepared to put in the hours that were needed to guarantee the body they desired, and that once they took the drugs in question they would come back time and time again for more because they were unable to function properly without them.

It was a win-win situation. It was also a market that was growing by the hour. Danny had picked up this load for one reason only. To spread them out and about into his world, and to get the general consensus on their veracity. He had been assured that they were good, that they were worth their weight in gold. If this was proved to be true, Danny Boy was set to pick up the equivalent of a lorryload once a week. They would be dropped at the scrapyard, and Louie would get himself a good drink for turning a blind eye.

Michael was, as always, quiet, they both knew that their new venture was a money-spinner, and they also knew that, since the wedding, they were somehow unable to get back to their original friendship.

Mary was Michael's heart, at least that was what he had believed, still believed. Since the marriage, however, she was rarely seen out and about. She was also rarely seen in the marital home; if anyone went there she was either in bed or out shopping. He knew she was there though, just not showing her face, and Michael didn't know how to broach this subject with Danny Boy. After all, Mary was now his wife and, as such, she wasn't really under Michael's jurisdiction any more. This bothered him, it was like a lot of things in his life, he knew he should do something about it, but he also knew there was nothing he could do. Unless Mary came to him directly and asked for his intervention, he could only stand back and wait until he knew the score. In his heart though, he was not looking forward to her arriving on his doorstep, Danny Boy was not a man you could reason with. And, if truth be told, personally he would rather not have to. The abortion that had constituted the wedding that had been to blame for his sister's retirement from public life had been such a public embarrassment, such an awful situation. If he had been on the receiving end of it, he wasn't sure he would have coped as well as Danny Boy had. That was the bugbear, he knew his friend had been mugged off and the fact he had still allowed Mary access to his home was to his credit in many respects. Any other man would have fucked her off big-time. At least, that was the general consensus anyway, though most of their older contemporaries were already onto a second or third wife of dubious character, and even more dubious morals. Youth being the only real requirement, the brains being used up by the first wife, the main wife. The woman who had stood by them through thick and thin, whose only sin had been to get old, and get old just as the dosh started rolling in. A young bird was a requisite these days, it gave the men in question the illusion of youth, made them feel powerful once more. It was only when they actually left the marital home that they seemed to realise the foolishness of their actions. By then they were well and truly lumbered. Young girls on a regular basis were a pain in the arse. Once the fuck was complete, what was there to keep a man enamoured?

Gordon was still on his shitlist, and the fact that Danny Boy had not attempted to give the boy a reprimand was worrying him enormously. Danny had not asked him about Gordon's where-abouts, or enquired about his well-earned injuries. He had known deep inside that Danny Boy could not let the boy get away with his actions, knew that he would have to make some kind of stand, not just for his sister, but for them all. For the family and for their reputation, but he had not done a thing. This was what had made Michael so uneasy, and it was this same uneasiness that he sensed that made Danny Boy want to guffaw his head off. The fucker seemed to be enjoying it all, and he knew that Danny was watching him closely to gauge his reactions. Testing their friendship, a friendship that had spanned years, and that they both knew had always been one-sided. He needed Danny Boy much more than

Danny Boy needed him. At least that was what he believed anyway. Danny was watching him now, surreptitiously, with a quiet dignity that was as annoying as it was false. Danny Boy knew how to press the buttons required for whatever emotion he was determined to generate in his antagonist. Danny was a fucking looney tune in many respects. He enjoyed other people's discomfort. He was also the only person that Michael actually cared about, admired. He didn't want to fall out with him over his own sister or brother. He knew first-hand what a treacherous cunt Gordon could be when the fancy was upon him. And he didn't want to actually have to *do* anything about his sister's situation, unless he absolutely had to. It would have to be a last resort.

Danny Boy was more than aware of his friend's worry, his friend's nervousness and shame at what had occurred on his sister's wedding day.

He knew he was going to have to box clever, Michael and Mary were very close and he appreciated that. However, she was a Cadogan now and the sooner Michael Miles accepted that fact, the better off he would be.

Michael was a cowed man, he was unable to work out the situation, was unsure what role he should actually be playing in this petty drama. All Michael knew was that Danny Boy seemed to be in the right, but he actually *felt* that his sister had made the biggest mistake of her life. Danny Boy was a bully, and like all professional bullies he knew how to make it seem that everyone else was in the wrong, and that he was in the right. For the first time ever, Michael questioned his best friend's actions, and questioned his own part in his family's downfall. For the first time ever, Danny's anger was turned on him and his, and he knew, deep inside, that he didn't have the guts to do anything about it. He wasn't able to take Danny on, no one was, he was a law unto himself. His own cowardice was more than he could bear and, like his sister, it was gnawing away at him like a cancer.

Louie was worried; he had arranged for the pick-up as requested, and he had also paid off his youngest daughter's boyfriend, who had been good enough to arrange the drop. He was a good kid in a lot of respects, determined to make the best of himself, ensure himself a future of sorts, with his help. The boy was a good-looking young man, and he had arranged with the boy's father for the boy to meet up with his daughter and fall in love. A love that had personally cost him the national debt. The boy was sensible enough to know a good deal when he saw one, and he had grabbed at it with both hands. But he was a nice lad, and he was willing to marry up if that was what it took to get himself a good job and a good life. He felt guilty about that, and he hoped his daughter would never be any the wiser about it all; it was hard for a girl, a good Jewish girl anyway, to meet an appropriate boy these days. That his youngest daughter had met up with, by herself, a fucking bubble and squeak, a *Greek*, of all things, while at the technical college was bad enough. That the said bubble and squeak had then had the audacity to actually knock on the front door of his home and request her by name, while dressed like a fucking tourist and displaying a set of cheap caps was, in all honesty, a fucking piss-take of Olympian standards in his book. Hence the new young man in her life, and the poor Greek boy's unlucky accident that entailed not only a car crash but also, thanks to Danny Boy Cadogan, the serious fear that the threat of the loss of his penis could entail. He had backed off then, faster than a bent Filth on a drugs raid, leaving the floor open for a new toss-pot, a new Jewish toss-pot of Louie's own choosing.

His youngest daughter was the prettiest of them all, and that wasn't saying much, he knew. So the knowledge of his recent purchase, one that entailed a suitable young man for his baby, would not be celebrated by the daughter that he loved more than the others put together, especially if that fact was to become common knowledge. He was ashamed that the only good looker in his set of puppies, the only one who *could* have found a man for herself, had to be manipulated like all the others. He had purchased husbands for each of them, and, God knew, the others had needed his help. All he hoped for now, God willing, were some grandchildren, grandchildren he prayed would look like their fathers.

'You making a cup of tea or what? I have a little bird waiting for me.'

255

Danny Boy's voice was harsh as always, and his grin told Louie that he was after something from him. A regular occurrence.

Louie grinned. Like Michael, he was not sure of Danny Boy any more, especially after his latest actions, this blatant womanising for starters, and he didn't want to know too much about it either. The wedding had made people wary of talking to him too deeply. No one knew what to say to him, or how to react to it. Danny Boy seemed to be oblivious to other people's uneasiness about what had occurred. In fact, if he didn't know better Louie would say that the boy was actually enjoying the notoriety of it.

Men like Danny Boy were a one-off anyway, they fucked indiscriminately and they loved in the same way. He was newly married and that was usually enough to guarantee a man's fidelity. For the first year anyway, but then, after the wedding night, who could say what was right and what was wrong? Some women, as he knew from personal experience, weren't the most accommodating of people when they had finally acquired a wedding ring. In fact, they often became born-again virgins and that could irk. It made the man in question feel he was being used, and that was generally the case. The marital bed became a battleground and, without realising it, the wives gave their new husbands the green light to hunt out strange. As his mother had always said, if the man doesn't get it in his own home, he'll get it in someone else's. It was the nature of the beast.

So, like everyone else, Louie didn't say anything at all, that was the easiest option and it guaranteed he didn't have to hear more than was deemed necessary. Once someone opened their heart to you, it was then expected that you would give an honest opinion on their woes. Some kind of advice, and that was not something he wanted to get involved in. Danny Boy was not someone you advised in matters of the heart. In any matter come to that, he was not stable enough to confide your true thoughts to anyway, he was someone you told nothing more than what you *thought* they might want to hear. Louie knew that whatever might happen in the future, his opinion of Danny Boy and his new kith and kin would not be something he discussed out loud. He prayed that the boy was not here for advice, yet a little voice was saying quietly in his shell-like that Danny Boy would *never* lower himself to ask anyone for advice anyway, it just wasn't in his make-up. And he would never admit to having made a mistake, he was too proud, too arrogant.

As Danny sat on the ancient leather sofa, and looked at his friend's haunted countenance, he felt a feeling of peace wash over him. He was pleased to be reminded of his old haunts, of his first real earners. It was Louie who had set him on the path to riches all those years ago, and he knew that he was a lucky man because of that. He would never have set him wrong, in fact, he had always made sure that he was well taken care of; Louie was the reason that he was where he was today. He was thankful for his kindness and his trust. It had been his salvation in many respects. He understood that Louie deserved his respect, and he knew inside himself that he was also one of the only people he genuinely cared about. Who he would trust implicitly, no matter what the situation.

'You all right, Louie?'

Louie grinned, but Danny Boy noticed his lack of vigour, his lack of interest in his surroundings, and wondered what had happened to make his old mate so depressed. So he said, in as friendly a manner as he was capable of, 'Once again, mate. You all right, Louie?'

He was genuinely interested, his voice full of tenderness and an achingly honest interest, which worried Louie more than anything else.

'Yeah, mate, 'course, and you?' Louie sounded a lot more relaxed than he actually was.

Danny Boy grinned once more, and he said with a laugh, 'I'm on top of the fucking world, mate.'

'You sure about that, son?'

The words were out before either of them could do anything about it. They hung there, between them, the sheer weight of them making both men regret them immediately. Danny finally nodded, after what seemed to Louie like an age, and then, sighing heavily, he changed the subject with what was obviously a deliberate sneer, an insult of sorts, 'So, you have another fucking wedding, do you? Handsome girl, your youngest one. Fucking stunning in

257

comparison to the others. So, where is the dirty deed to be done this time, eh?'

Danny Boy seemed genuinely interested as always, even though Louie knew he was more than aware of the situation. Of his trawling for unmarried men in their world so he could place his daughters on to the fields of matrimony and, hopefully, find them fitting mates, young men who he could trust. Men he could give a decent living to, who he could control.

'I know how much you love them, Lou. I'd do the same, mate, if it was me.'

From anger and sarcasm, he had once more become the loyal friend. It had taken mere seconds. With one of his lightning changes of mood he had salvaged the day, salvaged their friendship and, at the same time, reminded Louie of just how dangerous this young man could be. And there was no two ways about it, he was capable of anything to realise his own ends.

Louie knew that this young man, who he had tried to look after like a son, who he had watched grow up and who he had employed all those years ago, was now a dangerous fuck who even he was wary of. And yet he knew that Danny Boy could be all sweetness and light too, but only because it suited him to be. He was being the big magnanimous mate now, the old friend, and it was just another one of his many personas. Another one of his strange moods. Louie regretted his kindness to this man all those years ago, he knew now that the boy's own father, Big Danny Cadogan, had blanked him for good reason. But that was in the past, it belonged to a bygone age. So Louie smiled, his ageing skin grey and dry. His faded blue eyes were not able to hide his real feelings and emotions about this young man before him. Danny Boy, he knew, could see his fear and his disgust at how he had eventually turned out. Danny Boy, he knew, relished the fact that he had managed to infiltrate the powers that be through him, and his contacts, and that none of them had understood his strength until it was far too late, himself included.

'It will be in the usual place for Jewish weddings, Danny. The synagogue . . .'

They both laughed then, Danny Boy knowing that it was

Louie's wife who would insist on that much. Louie was past caring about anything like that where his girls were concerned and everyone knew it. He had weighed out ten grand on each wedding, a precedent his wife had set and which had become the expectation of each of his daughters. Each was determined to outdo the others, not only on the expense of the wedding, but also on what they saw as style. But none of them had any style whatsoever; they were like council house girls on pools winner's money. It was laughable really, except they were not inclined to find the humour of the situation like everybody else was.

'Good man, I like the synagogue, it has class, like the Catholic church and, let's face it, once married there it's for life, and that's all the women in your family are interested in, ain't it?'

Louie nodded his agreement at the truthfulness of his words, wondering if this meeting might turn out better than he had originally anticipated.

Then, sitting forward in his seat, his huge chest straining against the material of his expensive suit Danny Boy said happily, 'But changing the subject, mate, how much for this yard?'

The question was so unexpected, so unbelievable, that Louie was not sure he had heard him correctly. His old face was stretched in wonderment, showing his shock and his disgust at the question asked of him. 'I beg your pardon?'

Danny Boy shook his head in mock despair at his old friend. He acted as if this had all been discussed earlier, that he was just waiting on the final decision. That it was a foregone conclusion. His sarcasm was evident now as he said slowly, deliberately.

'I said, *Louie*, how much for this lot.'

He opened his arms to encompass his surroundings, as if it was the most natural thing in the world to ask for one of your closest friend's livelihoods.

He didn't really ask, Louie realised, in case of a refusal, instead he just demanded what he wanted. There was no room for negotiation, no second chance. No way he would accept a resounding no. He was asking the price, not requesting a negotiation of any sort. He wanted this yard, and he wasn't about to let that go. Louie knew he was already living on borrowed time. What Danny Boy wanted, Danny Boy got, and he didn't care who he destroyed in the process.

This was the young man who Louie had taken under his wing all those years ago, who he had been forced to defend many times over the years. And who he now knew had nothing even approaching loyalty in his physical make-up. Who was devoid of anything even remotely resembling deep feelings for another human being, who had, in effect, once been his right-hand man, who he had made sure had been given an in into their world, and who he also knew, had at one point recently, been quite willing to wipe him out permanently. Suddenly, Louie had to accept the fact that this boy was not worth his time or his effort. Like his daughters, he had been a let-down, only this boy had let him down in a much more spectacular fashion, because he was now determined to take what was Louie's, what he had spent his whole life building up into a viable business, had spent years accruing, not only the goodwill of his many rivals, but their respect as well. Danny Boy was taking his livelihood, without a thought for where it would leave him, or how it would affect his family. The worst thing of all was that he had brought this viper into his life, he had nurtured him, helped him, and stood by him. For what? So he could walk in here and take what was his without a backward glance? He would take it without a second's thought as to what he had done for him over the years. He had created a monster, and this monster had taken great pleasure in biting him on the arse. This, he knew, without doubt, was the truth of the matter.

Louie knew he had been a hair's breadth away from the grave through this young man. He had already felt the full force of his displeasure. He knew, first-hand, how fickle he could be in his pursuit of his own ends. He had even forgiven him that, had tried to justify the boy's actions. He'd made excuses for him, and he had been wrong. Danny Boy was willing to take whatever he felt he needed to further his career, and he would take it without a backward glance, even from someone who had taken care of him and loved him like a son. Danny Boy, it seemed to him, was, to all intents and purposes, a fucking sociopath, and now, on top of everything else he had acquired over the years, it seemed he now wanted *his* yard. Wanted it as a child would want a sweetie or a toy from another child. He wasn't even asking him for it, he was telling him he *wanted* it, there was a big difference and they both knew that. Danny Boy was a law unto himself all right. He was also flavour of the month with all the big earners, and Louie knew that he would never have the bottle to challenge him over this. He was old, was aware of how fragile he had become over the last few years. He just didn't have the nerve to go against him; even the friendship that went back to this boy's childhood wouldn't cut any ice, he was sure. Danny was not in the market for refusals of any kind, for anyone going against his wishes, standing in the way of what he wanted. Danny Boy expected people to go along with him and, because of his reputation as a fucking mad bastard, people tended to do just that. It was easier for everyone that way. And the men he now dealt with were willing to turn a blind eye where he was concerned because he could guarantee them results. Guarantee them regular money. Serious amounts of money, and that was the bottom line. Danny Boy was now basically a law unto himself, could demand what he wanted and get it without too much fuss. For Louie though, the worst thing was that he knew that Danny Boy was taking his yard off him for no other reason than that he *could*. Danny, he had noticed many moons before, was a gatherer. He was willing to take what he wanted indiscriminately from anyone and everyone in his immediate orbit.

Especially from the very people who had helped him on his way.

Ange was worried about her daughter-in-law, the girl was a bundle of nerves. Mary had always been a confident girl, even as a kid. Now, as she sipped at her tea, Ange was amazed at the difference in her. Mary was, as always, immaculately turned out, and she was also on the verge of a nervous breakdown. Ange knew how hard her brother's outburst had affected her, knew that her son had also felt the backlash from it. Normally she would have felt an affinity with Gordon, would have felt that what he had said would need addressing at some point, because she had believed then, like many a mother before her, that no one would ever be good enough for her son and she knew this girl's reputation around the streets.

But all that had changed now. She had watched the gradual destruction of her son's wife, and that bothered her. Mary had been the victim of not only her own menfolk, but also the victim of the man she had married, the man who should have been the first one defending her, no matter what the truth was of the accusations. The girl was wasting away in front of her eyes, and her huge eyes had the hunted look of a cornered animal. She watched the clock constantly, her fear tangible to anyone unlucky enough to be in her company. She was white-faced and drawn-looking, like someone who had been handed down a death sentence even though they were innocent. And, knowing how her elder son had tortured his own father, and even herself, when he had deemed it suitable, she knew it wouldn't be too hard for her to believe that he was once more enjoying someone else's downfall.

That she was Michael's sister would be part of the game as far as Danny Boy was concerned, her son needed to control everyone around him. He needed to be the one who orchestrated their every move, good or bad, even though the people involved might not realise that for a very long time. When they finally did understand, it was always too late to do anything about it. He was a demon when the fancy took him, and he was all the worse because he actually enjoyed the chaos he caused. He was unnatural like that, but that was also what made him so desirable to the men he courted for work, and also the women who threw themselves at him. She was aware that they all thought they could control him, but nobody could. Her Danny Boy would gradually wipe them out, take what was theirs and step into their shoes, all the time smiling and making the next person up in the chain of command believe he was only out for *their* best interests. He was clever, he was slippery, and he was one dangerous fuck. He was gradually taking over everything and everyone around him, and he was doing it with a smile, with his natural charm that blinded people to his real nature. He was successful because he dealt with people who were as greedy as he was, and he used that weakness to his own advantage. This little girl, however, was a shadow of her former self; her eyes were constantly on the go, watching the door, watching the clock. She was terrified of her husband not coming home, and yet she knew she would be even more terrified when he did turn up.

'Are you sure you're all right, Mary?' It was a gentle query, spoken with a softness that belied her real agenda.

'I'm great, it's just I worry about Danny, you know.'

Ange nodded sympathetically, as if this was perfectly normal behaviour from a new wife. The girl was trying hard to relax and it was painful to watch. She was gritting her teeth so hard her whole jawline was jutting out, making her look terribly vulnerable when, in reality, it should have made her look strong, made her look dependable. She had the same determination as her mother, and the same good looks that even years of chronic alcoholism hadn't completely destroyed. Yet, in a few short months she had somehow gone from an independent woman to this travesty of a new wife, a nervous wreck who pretended that her life was wonderful when it was obvious to anyone with even half a brain that her life was untenable. That she dreaded her husband's presence almost as much as she craved it. And Ange could understand that better than anyone.

'Why do you worry about him, Mary? He can take care of himself. I'm more worried about you, girl. You seem preoccupied and distracted a lot of the time. You can talk to me, you know. Is everything all right between you? Are you happy?'

She was looking into the face of her daughter-in-law, all the time knowing that the girl would never utter a word against her husband, was worried that she had been sent by her husband to try and catch her out, to see if she was capable of being disloyal.

Mary smiled then, a beautiful smile that Ange knew had taken all of her considerable willpower to produce. She looked perfectly normal then, beautiful, like a real young wife; that is if you didn't know the score. She even managed to look pleasantly surprised at the question asked of her, and if you weren't aware of the underlying terror inside her breast, you might be conned into thinking that your probing questions were out of order. Were rude even.

'Oh, Ange, you are a strange one. Most mother-in-laws try and find fault with their sons' wives. Danny wouldn't like you asking me all these things about him . . . He's like me, close-mouthed and happier for it.'

It was a veiled threat and they both knew it. Ange knew then that this girl would never open up to her or anyone else. Her son had made sure that she was far too scared ever to openly disobey him or talk against him. He had what he wanted, a walking, talking, living doll, and she knew that there was nothing she could ever do to change that. She couldn't change this poor girl's life, make her feel easier inside herself, give her someone to confide in, trust. Because this girl was now a prisoner in the huge, expensive house that she had once bragged about to anyone who would listen to her. She was a prisoner of her own beauty and her own arrogance. Once this girl had looked down on her mother-in-law, treated her like the hired help, had seen her as nothing more than an old woman, a standing joke. Had never imagined that her own life could have ever emulated hers in any way, shape or form. Somehow though, this knowledge didn't make her mother-in-law feel any better.

Chapter Seventeen

Michael was eating his meal quietly. It was early evening and he liked this time of day; he had picked up the bulk of the money that they demanded regularly from the smaller businesses in their orbit and, unlike the majority of their peers who thought it was only pennies and half-pennies, he knew that it weighed out into a serious wedge over the course of a year. Look after the pennies and the pounds *always* looked after themselves. So many people in their game chased only the big dollars these days, but it had been proven over and over again that it was the little amounts that added up over time. They were also overlooked by Old Bill, in fact they were overlooked by everyone. A few quid was seen as a touch, a drink. A bank robbery, on the other hand, was seen as a piss-take, the forcible removal of a huge amount of money and therefore worthy of Filth's notice. Unless they were forewarned, of course and, thanks to Danny Boy and Michael, they were warned well in advance. But the rents, as they referred to the smaller amounts, went unnoticed by the powers that be, so there was no need to give anyone a drink or ask for them to turn a blind eye to the transactions. Coupled with the rest of their London earnings, the rents were actually worth enough to keep them in the style they were now accustomed to, without any of their other business deals. They used youngsters as the fall guys, new Faces, and all they gave them was what amounted to pocket money, but the boys they employed would be happy to do it for nothing. As long as they could brag that they worked for Danny Boy Cadogan, were on his firm, they were happy. The perks from that kind of liaison were legion and these days the lower down the ladder, the more chance of loyalty if a capture was ever to occur. It was the so-called Faces with a few quid and a certain lifestyle who were more likely to grass. It stood to reason, they had so much more to lose. Consequently, the youngsters were courted and sounded out for the top jobs later on in life.

Michael admired that about Danny Boy, his acumen was spot on, he knew that no one else would bother with what they saw as a few quid here and there, they saw it as too much aggravation these days. That few quid though, when multiplied, was a lot of fucking dosh, and yet without Michael to sort out the finer details of it all, nothing would ever have come of it, like a lot of their businesses. Danny had the ideas, he just didn't have the dedication that was needed for the day-to-day running of it all. Danny Boy wasn't capable of keeping his eye on any particular ball, because once he had set that ball in motion it was basically forgotten about. It was then left to him, Michael, to see that the little details, such as the collecting of the monies or the distribution of largesse, was sorted out with the minimum of fuss but with the maximum of profit. Michael could do it in his sleep. It came naturally to him, what didn't come naturally, however, was the actual finding of these earners. Whereas Danny Boy could see them as plain as day. He would then pass them over to his friend and forget about them for the most part, until suddenly, out of the blue, he would question him closely about how well they were doing and whether he thought they could expand on them in any way now or in the future. Michael always had the answer to his questions the moment that he asked them. He could tell him down to the last penny what that particular business was worth or how much it had earned them overall. Michael knew that this was his strength, and that it was also Danny Boy's weakness. He also knew that Danny Boy was quite capable of bringing in someone else to fill his shoes at any given time. He didn't think he would, though, because he knew that he was the only person Danny Boy had ever really trusted. He had known the original Danny Boy Cadogan, known him before the Murrays had fucked with his head, and before their outrageous demands had sent him on to the road he was now on. He knew exactly how his father's betrayal had affected him, and all his family come to that. He knew how important it was for him to be respected, to be revered, to be treated like royalty. Danny Boy Cadogan had made sure that he would never again hear his name said without respect, never again hear it shouted out with a demand for the payment of debts, or in any derogatory way at all. Danny Boy had made sure of that much, not just for himself, but for his family as well.

Yet Michael still sometimes resented the fact that he was expected to remember everything that they were involved in, while Danny Boy didn't even bother to concern himself with the day-to-day running of it all. He knew he should be grateful that Danny left him to it and trusted him a hundred per cent. He knew that without it he would not be where he was today. It galled him sometimes though, that he was the real brains of the outfit, the money-man, the real money-gatherer, and he was still treated by some of the people they dealt with as the hired help. It was Danny Boy that people wanted to see these days, even though it was him who sorted out the nitty gritty, the day-to-day running of it all. Yet he knew that was a natural occurrence, Danny Boy had a presence; he possessed a powerful magnetism that people in their world were attracted to. He had that certain something that made him different from all the other up-and-coming Faces on the pavements. Danny Boy had the edge because he was, without shadow of a doubt, a fucking headcase and, the scariest thing of all was, he didn't pretend he was a nutter, like a lot of the so-called headcases it was evident to anyone who came within fifteen feet of him that he was the real McCoy. A bona fide looney tunes who was capable of turning on a sixpence. Who had no idea just how fucking unpredictable he could be. No idea that his behaviour was seen by the people they dealt with as beyond the norm, he even frightened hardened criminals, but they used him even as they secretly despised him.

He had got the Murrays to cripple his own father, an act that had set him on to the road of villainy in the first place, and he had made his name by removing *anyone* foolish enough to stand in his way – permanently. He had more than a few scalps under his belt, and they were not the scalps of nobodies, ice creams. Danny Boy had taken on the best like Jamie Carlton, and won. And he had tagged behind him as he always had, and did what was required of him without question.

They were like a rock band in many respects. Danny Boy was the front man, the singer, whereas Michael was the backroom boy, the person no one really noticed but who made sure that everything went smoothly. If Danny had not married his sister then his allegiance to his friend would never have been called into question. But, no matter what she had done, what she was, she was still his sister, and Danny Boy should have remembered that fact and respected it. She was his wife and Danny Boy had chosen to keep it that way, and he wanted her to be happy again. Michael couldn't bear the sadness in her eyes, all the while knowing that his best friend was the reason for it.

Michael was sitting back now, forcibly relaxing himself into the comfort of the leather chair, attempting to control his breathing. He was in a small Indian restaurant on the Mile End Road. He liked it here, they provided good food and a congenial atmosphere. Now, thanks to him, they were also willing to accept parcels on a regular basis. These parcels could contain anything from guns to drugs, and they were paid accordingly, pleased to be a part of the new breed, and confident that this would guarantee them the monopoly in their area for a few years at least. Any restaurants that might now open in their vicinity would be owned only by their relatives, so no harm would be done to them personally. It was how the world was now working, and they knew that to survive in it they had to take a more active role, and their children too, especially those who had been born in the locality and were streetwise enough to see the logic in these new business deals.

Michael was pleased with his negotiations, and he knew that one day they would be useful in other ways. The people involved would be loyal to them and, like Danny Boy always said, you never knew when someone might come in handy. This from a man who, when he deemed someone to be of no further use, was capable of cutting them off like a cancerous tumour without a second's thought.

The secret with Danny Boy, Michael knew, was to always make sure you were useful to him in some way. Even his own father had sussed that much out. Michael closed his eyes once more, and tried to stop the hateful thoughts from overtaking his mind. If he wasn't careful, the anger he felt inside him, that was simmering away on a daily basis, would boil and overflow, and he knew from experience that anger, without an outlet of some kind, could be a very destructive force.

Then he saw his brother Gordon walking into the restaurant, as large as life. He saw his brother's open face, so like his own, and the confident stride that told him that Gordon now believed that enough time had passed, that what had happened at his sister's wedding had been forgotten, and he was due not only his forgiveness but, knowing his little brother, everyone else's as well. Michael watched warily as Gordon made his way towards his table. He was dressed like a reject from Spandau Ballet, his leather jacket and boot-leg jeans were accentuated by the blond streaks in his thick, dark hair. His roots were already well grown-out, and that made him look cheap, like a dole-queue boy. He was a scruffbag, as his mother would have called him, and Michael was ashamed of him. How anyone could walk about like him was beyond his understanding. Jonjo was of an age and he always looked tidy, smart, but then he had to deal with Danny Boy who, like him, abhorred the men who were slaves to fashion. Despised the nonces who wanted to look like a particular pop star. They were laughable, an embarrassment. You needed to look serious to be taken seriously by the people you dealt with.

'What do you fucking want, Gordon?' Michael was curt, embarrassed to be seen with him. Up close the boy was even scruffier than he had first thought.

'I was sent to get you by Jonjo. Mary is in the hospital, she's lost the baby.'

Mary was alone in the small room reserved for the women whose babies were no longer inside them. At least that is how she thought of this place in her own mind. It was quiet here, but she could hear the muffled cries of the women in labour not two minutes' walk away from where she lay. Through the window in the door she could see the patients as they wandered past, some going for a crafty cigarette, others going to the day room to watch their favourite programmes. These were women with big lumps in front of them, women who were, without doubt, pregnant. She was jealous of them all, of their huge pendulous breasts, overblown hips, even their stretch marks.

Her baby had slid out of her without a murmur, a three-month-old foetus that she had hastily rescued from the toilet bowl. Had wrapped gently in toilet paper and clutched in her hand tightly to show it to the doctor in the hope that he could do something to prevent this ever happening to her again. She couldn't even cry now. She was devoid of tears. In fact, she felt numb, as if the baby had taken everything she had ever she felt with it when it had decided to leave her. Even her own baby had not wanted to stay with her, even her own child had abandoned her, and who could blame it for that? She was a pariah, she was unfit to be a mother.

But she had wanted that baby so badly, had desperately believed that it would bring her and Danny Boy together, would have been the reason for them starting their life anew. He had not come to see her, had not bothered to even send her a message. He had left her alone, left her to grieve for their baby all by herself.

She was to go down to theatre in the morning to have a D & C, make sure that the baby was all gone. Scrape out the last little bits of her child, the last remnants of her baby. Apparently. According to one of the nurses, lots of women lost the first baby, and she had then said that she shouldn't worry too much about it. Easier said than done, unfortunately.

She couldn't help worrying, Danny hardly ever came near her any more and, now that this had happened, she wondered what his reaction would be when she finally went back to their home. Finally faced him.

This poor little child had been her last hope, had been the thing she had pinned her dreams on. No matter what happened to her and Danny, she would always have had this child, would have had someone to lavish all her pent-up love and affection on. Now that was gone, and she was once more a failure. She had failed in even this, the most basic of female requirements. She knew of women who produced regularly without a day's illness, dirty, rotten bitches with a brood of kids trailing behind them, the mothers unable to care for them properly, letting them play out till all hours of the night. Not realising how lucky they were to have them, what a privilege it was to be blessed with them. And here she was, unable to produce even one.

The tears finally came then, hot and salty, and she didn't even try to stem them in any way. She was sobbing, and the release felt good. She knew now that Danny Boy was not coming, so she could cry with impunity, really let rip. She cried for the baby she had lost, for her marriage, but mostly for the mother that she missed so desperately because, no matter what happened in life, there was always a bed for you at your mother's home. All the time she was alive her children had somewhere to go. Somewhere to run to, and somewhere to call home.

She now knew that all her mother had said to her over the years had been the truth, she should have married someone who would have taken care of her, someone who loved her, who could have given her a good life. She also realised, too late, that she should have loved her mother properly, while she had still had her, as bad as she was, as much as she had annoyed her with her drunken antics because, once your mother was gone, they were gone, and no one could ever replace them.

Michael and Danny were in the yard: Louie had been given what Michael thought was a fair price, and they were now going through the books he had kept. There were two sets, one for his perusal, and one for the taxman. That was the beauty of a cash business, no one ever knew what you had really earned, and no one was ever liable to find out either. Not unless you were stupid enough to tell them, anyway.

They were both interested in the scrap business, it was a good front as well as a good earner. Lorries and cars pulling up at all hours wouldn't look out of place, so it was ideal for them, and they were determined to make it turn a decent profit, not that Louie had done too badly with it. But, like a lot of the older men, he had missed out on a lot of opportunities because he had been nervous of trying anything new. Danny wondered if they would be like that one day, and dismissed the thought immediately. He would always have his eye on the new, on the main chance. He couldn't even imagine himself old, not as old as Louie anyway. That seemed so far away, so long into the future. He smiled at the thought of it.

'You all right, Danny Boy?'

Michael's voice broke into his thoughts and he was perplexed at the question, then he almost laughed out loud as he remembered what had happened. What had prompted the question in the first place. Michael was sorry for Danny Boy and Mary: the loss of the baby had been a big blow to them both, he was sure of that.

'I'm all right, mate.'

It was a dismissal and Michael knew it. But he understood that Danny didn't want to discuss it. He also knew that he had not been to the hospital either. In a strange way he understood that as well. Men didn't cope as well as women with that kind of thing. He had explained that to Mary, tried to get her to understand that Danny was grieving in his own way. He didn't really believe it any more than she did. But what could he do? He was caught between a rock and a hard place, and Mary was even getting on his nerves lately. She was like the prophet of doom, and he was pleased to leave her in the hands of the women for the time being.

Ange had been a star, as had Annie. Annie was the last person he had imagined being such a staunch friend. It just showed you how wrong you could be about somebody. Carole Rourke, an old school friend, had also been a regular visitor and, for some reason, that pleased him. Mary had been in hospital for ten days now: she had not seemed able to get over what had happened to her. Michael knew she was not as ill as she made out, that she was delaying going home. He knew that she was devastated about the loss of the baby, and he also knew that she was dreading going back to that huge, empty house. But he believed that the sooner she went home the better it would be for them all. Danny had lost a child as well, but no one seemed to think about that.

'I am going to put Jonjo in here, let him run it for a while, see how he goes.'

Michael nodded. He had expected as much. Plus Jonjo was a good worker, and reliable, even if he was not the sharpest knife in the drawer.

'We can concentrate on the outside business then, and use this place as a base. The casinos are getting too well known now, and the people who frequent them are also bringing down a lot of heat with them. But that is what earns us the dough, so this place is ideal really. It's tucked away, yet on a busy road, and it's difficult to nose about in here without giving us a fair warning. Old Bill would be hard-pushed to raid this place with the dogs running loose.'

They both laughed. They had acquired a young lad from their estate who had three large Dobermans. He was paid to sit on his arse all day and watch his animals as they roamed free. If anyone wanted to come in, they were rounded up and locked in the night hut until the business was completed. They were lovely dogs, but they were not the most social animals on the planet. They were worth their weight in gold though, the half-inching of car parts had literally stopped overnight. In fact, they had not realised just how much could be nicked in broad daylight until now. Though Michael wondered privately if the fact that now Danny owned the yard might also be a contributing factor. Louie had always assumed that the people he dealt with on a daily basis were kosher: now it seemed that they were not as trustworthy as he had thought. Danny was not impressed with this knowledge as he had run this place for Louie as a kid and even his eagle eyes had missed a lot of the scrumping that had taken place.

So, on the bright side, they knew that they were already quids in where the parts were concerned, and already quids in on their drops. The drops could be done here on a more regular basis and without them having to weigh out to Louie for the privilege. As they made their plans, they were both aware that the money they were now making was really serious. It was the kind of money people dreamed about, and they were also aware that serious money had to be made to work for you, otherwise it was pointless having it in the first place. Money, as they both knew, came back to money.

*

Mary and Carole Rourke were in her kitchen, Carole was looking around her in awe. She had never seen anything like this place except on television. The fitted kitchen was real wood, the work-tops were granite and the appliances were state of the art. She was gawking in open wonderment at what Mary now saw as her usual surroundings. She was used to it here, and she didn't have the heart to tell Carole that she was frightened to make a mess in her own home, frightened to use most of the appliances that were still in pristine condition. That she felt more of a guest in her own home than Carole did, that, other than the cleaning and washing and, of course, cooking, most of the house was alien to her. Danny acted like she was the lodger, and treated her as though she was nothing more than the hired help. But she still carried on the charade that everything was all right, that her marriage was perfect. She had too much pride to do otherwise. As she sat there now, and looked at the kitchen through Carole's eyes, she saw just how other people really saw her and saw her perfect life. If only they knew.

Carole smiled, she was thrilled at her old friend's good fortune. Even though she had lost her baby, she was pleased that she had such a beautiful home to recover in. To her, this was the equivalent to winning the pools, and she was happy that her friend had been blessed with such a wonderful husband, someone who could provide for her and the children she was sure would arrive in the future.

She was so glad she had decided to make the trip to the hospital when she had heard about Mary's miscarriage. She had only wanted to let her know she was thinking of her, and cared about her. She'd only intended to pop in for a few minutes, see if she needed anything, or if she wanted her to do a few errands. But Mary had been so pleased to see her, had been so touched that she had thought of her, that they had bonded all over again, as they had years before, when they had been little kids.

Carole had been even more thrilled to see Michael Miles, her old neighbour and school friend and her girlhood idol. Carole was a big girl, heavy-hipped, with lush breasts that were the object of many a man's desire. She was very pretty, but in a quiet way, not like Mary who knew how to make herself noticeable. Carole had wonderful bone structure, with high cheekbones and deep-set blue eyes that were framed by long, dark eyelashes. She had honey-blond hair that was as natural as the rest of her. It was long and it curled slightly at the edges giving her the look of an old-time movie star. She wore little in the way of make-up, but she didn't really need any. Her kindness shone out of her like a beacon. In reality, the two women were like chalk and cheese, but they were already as close as they had been as children and Carole had guessed, though she would never say it out loud, that Mary wasn't as happy as she should be. She put it down to the loss of the baby, but in her heart she knew it went much deeper than that. As they sipped at their tea, she saw Mary stiffen in fright at the sound of the front door opening, a few seconds later the huge frame of Danny Boy Cadogan filled the kitchen. He looked at Carole and his face split into a wide grin.

'Fuck me! Look who it is! Hello, Carole, love.'

He was genuinely pleased to see her, and Mary watched as Carole stood up and he hugged her close to him. His huge arms dwarfed the girl who was now chattering away to him in a way that she couldn't even imagine any more.

'What a lovely place you've got here, it's out of this world, Danny Boy.'

Mary saw him swell with pride at the words, knew that he, like her, didn't really see it any more, didn't value it like he should, but still appreciated the way Carole was so impressed by it. She reminded him of just how well he was doing, how far he had come.

Danny Boy let Carole go reluctantly; she felt good, her voluptuous figure was pleasing to him, felt good in his embrace. He stared down at her, seeing the plump cheeks that were smooth and devoid of any foundation, her full lips always ready to smile. He saw the soulful eyes that had captivated him as a boy. A boy who had not felt good enough for a nice girl like her. A boy who had never had the opportunity to even play at courting like his contemporaries. He'd been too busy sorting out his father's fuck-ups and his siblings' lives. Looking at Carole now, he realised just what he had missed and also, thanks to her honesty and excitement at his home, how far he had actually come since those days. It was amazing really, Carole Rourke was the only person to make him feel happy inside himself for a long time. Her open face and her thick blond hair, untouched by any kind of dye, was refreshing. As he looked at his wife, at her carefully applied make-up and her thin frame, he was reminded of the travesty his marriage had turned into, the sham of a life that they lived through on a daily basis.

Carole smelled of Vosene shampoo and Knights Castile soap. She was real, she felt real, and he suddenly wished that he was coming home to her, coming home to her with her truthfulness and her honesty. She smelled of the things a good woman should smell of; even her perfume, Topaz, was from an Avon catalogue, an aroma his wife would not be caught wearing if her life depended on it was, to him, perfection. She was bright, she was natural, and she was a virgin: he would stake his life on that much. Beside her, poor Mary was like an also-ran and he was aware that she knew that as well as he did.

'You sit down, Danny, I'll make the tea, mate.'

And he did just that, happy to be in his own home for the first time since he had purchased it.

'He is a bastard, Ange, and you know it.'

As she laid the table for their tea, Ange was silently praying. Her husband was determined to make the loss of the child Danny Boy's fault and she wasn't about to join in. She knew that poor Mary had suffered an unfortunate event, as her own mother would have described it. And she also knew there was plenty of time for them to produce a child. Her husband though, wouldn't let it rest, and this from a man who had beaten his own children from her body without a backward glance.

'The vicious ponce. I wish I was in me full health because, I swear to you, I'd swing for that bastard . . .'

Jonjo was listening to his parents' conversation as he had many times over the years. The flat was so small that it was impossible not to hear what was being said. In fact, like his sister, he had made a point of *not* listening to it all over the years. Of turning up the radio, or the TV, putting on a record, so that whatever was being said was kept private. Now though, he was actively on the listen.

Now he worked for his big bruv, earned a decent wedge at last, and had, at the same time, discovered the power that respect could bring to a body, he felt the loyalty for Danny Boy welling up inside him. Stepping into the kitchen he said maliciously, 'Who the fuck are you to talk about our Danny Boy like that, eh?'

Ange was mortified, as was her husband, and she recovered the power of speech first. 'You shut your trap, and sit down. I'll not have you talking to your father like that . . .'

Jonjo, a big lad now, and a lad who had a long memory of his father's fists and feet, said abruptly, 'Keep out of this, Mum, and remember who you're talking about. We'd have been hard-pushed for a fucking bit of scram if it had been left to this cunt to provide for us. He dumped us with a regularity that even *you* must have noticed.'

Big Dan Cadogan knew the boy wanted to fight him, knew it had been on the cards for many a long year, and he also knew that he didn't want any part of it any more. Once he would have welcomed his younger son's words, would have taken great pleasure in beating them out of him. Now though, he knew he wasn't capable of doing that, wasn't even inclined towards it. Instead he kept his own counsel and didn't answer the young lad who was a menacing force, who was now dangerous to him.

'I am on the earn thanks to Danny Boy, and I pay me fucking way. Don't ever badmouth him in front of me, right. You don't even whisper his name in my presence, you old bastard. You fucking useless old ponce.'

Jonjo watched his mother and father as they exchanged glances, glances that told him they were working together against him. That they thought he was still a kid who could be silenced with a harsh word or a cross look. Whose own mother was willing to overlook his humiliation, would encourage it even. She would back her husband up, even though she knew he was in the wrong. Jonjo was not going to let that happen ever again, and he wanted this confrontation, needed it.

'Sit down, son, and stop all this nonsense.'

It was his father's voice that did it, the way he tried to act as if they were bosom buddies, as if they had some kind of rapport.

As his sister watched from the hallway he launched himself at his father and, as he felt his fists pummelling the ancient flesh, he felt, for the first time in his life, as if he was in control of his own destiny. Felt the pent-up anger and hatred spewing out of him even as his mother tried desperately to stop the beating. Knowing that she was still sticking up for the man who had terrorised them all at some time or another made his anger grow stronger and he pushed her away roughly. He knocked her into the table, saw her try to keep her balance, and knew he should care about what he had done to her. That he should try and make amends, somehow. But he couldn't.

He was aware of the kitchen, of the new cooker, the decorating that had been done at his brother's expense. But he was seeing it as it had looked when he was a child, scratched and scuffed, nothing in the fridge, and the Christmases without even a bit of grub, let alone presents. The birthdays that were bleak reminders of this man's selfishness and his determination to drink and gamble away any money that came his way. His determination to forget the family who had depended on him, had expected him to look after them, look out for them, like other men did for their families, for the children they had brought into the world. The children who he had conveniently forgotten about. It was as if all this hatred was overpowering him, making this moment, this event, so important he daren't let it go.

When his mother finally dragged him away from his father's prostrate form, Jonjo stood in the middle of the kitchen, his knuckles bruised and bleeding, the sweat pouring off him and he saw Annie white-faced and crying, and he knew then that it had all gone too far. That, like Danny Boy, he had left it too late, that the man he hated wasn't a man any more, not in the true sense of the word anyway. Seeing his father bloodied and bruised didn't give him the peace he craved, it just exacerbated his own loneliness. The knowledge that the man who had sired him had no real time for him, and never would have, just amplified the hatred he felt for himself.

He saw his mother helping her husband up from the floor, saw her seat him tenderly on a chair and knew that her actions were wrong: that it was him, her child, she should have been looking out for. But then, she had always put their father over them, over all of them. No matter what stroke he pulled, or what danger he placed them in. She had always sacrificed them for him, for the man who had treated her like shit. She only really wanted them when he had gone from her, was absent without leave, had abandoned them all, his mother included. Well, he was a man now, and he was not going to let anyone make him feel less than he was, ever again. Danny Boy had given him a role to play, had provided him with a niche, with a life that he was actually enjoying. Overnight, thanks to Danny Boy, he had the kudos and the respect he had always craved. His new job had given him the pride in himself he had always dreamed of.

He even stood differently, his shoulders were back and his head held high. For the first time ever, Jonjo *liked* himself and, if it had been left to the man who had sired him, that would never have happened; he would have made sure of that.

But he had made his point, had showed his hand. He had won the day, had shamefully beaten up a cripple, a man who was incapable of really defending himself. Now, hopefully, he could let it go.

Chapter Eighteen

Mary looked beautiful, and she knew it. Even though she was troubled, she knew that she was still a beautiful woman. A head-turner. It wasn't vanity, it was just common sense. She saw herself in the mirror and she knew that, even when her life was impossible, when her heart was heavy, and her husband's hatefulness was weighing on her mind, somehow or another she still looked lovely. She knew it annoyed Danny Boy; even when she had hardly slept a wink, she still looked good. Now though, as she watched her brother courting Carole Rourke, she felt the first stirrings of envy inside her breast.

Michael was enamoured of Carole, of that there was no doubt, as was her own husband. Danny Boy loved her, she was one of the only people he had any real time for. It was magnificent to watch; she couldn't believe that it was her husband, her Danny Boy. He chatted to Carole with an ease that was as effortless as it was astonishing. She loved her friend, but she couldn't help but envy the way she managed to calm Danny Boy down with a few choice words. She could talk to him about anything, and he actually listened to what she was saying, he even laughed with her. A real laugh, not his usual sarcastic or premeditated laughter. He actually seemed relaxed with her, and enjoyed himself. Once Michael married her, and she knew he would, she would have her friend on tap everyday. She was glad in one way, but terrified in another. This Danny Boy could be more scary than she realised.

Danny was observing his wife and Carole Rourke as they sat

together. They were like chalk and cheese. Carole was the antithesis of Mary, she wasn't plastered in make-up, necking drinks like there was no tomorrow. He knew Michael was onto a winner with her, and he was pleased for him, even as he envied him his good fortune. Carole wasn't going to need watching, Carole was a good girl in all ways. It came naturally to her, she was a nice person with a good heart and she would be a wonderful mother. Unlike the women around them, she didn't feel it necessary to flash her thrupenny bits to all and sundry; she was what years before was called a decent girl.

The pub was getting packed now, and Danny was also eyeing up the local talent on the quiet. He knew Mary was aware of his roving eye and he was glad about that. She was pregnant again. He hoped she managed to hang onto this one but he wasn't getting his hopes up. Once she produced a child he would celebrate, until then, he had no interest in any of it.

His eye strayed to the bar area, three men were there, all Faces, all waiting patiently for him to approach them. He loved that, loved the fear he created in everyone around him, especially the older criminals. The men who had once ruled their little empires and who were now sensible enough to know they were outclassed. The people he needed the most were the ones who had once held his position in the world, seeing them defeated was a buzz he knew he couldn't do without. He was at the top of his game and he knew it; he was also determined to stay there. He wasn't going to get complacent, sit on his arse and wait for a young gun like him to come along and scrump his apples. He was going to make sure that he kept his position in the world. He would only relinquish it on his death, and not before. He would do whatever it took to stay where he was and keep his crown firmly on his loaf of bread. These men had made the mistake of believing they were invincible, and now they had to swallow their knobs in his company, and tug their forelocks to keep on the earn. He loved it.

A young girl with long, black, heavily gelled hair and scrawny legs was smiling at him saucily. He knew the look and he winked back at her, his handsome face softened by the girl's promise.

Standing up, he walked over to the bar; everyone was aware of him and he knew that, made sure of that, in fact. He was big, but then so were a lot of men. But he had the menace and the presence to carry it off. He smiled at the three men who had travelled from south London to meet with him. They were all nervous and that fact pleased him. The main player was a man called Frank Cotton, he was a big man, but age had softened his physique and he was running to fat. At forty-nine he was established enough to create a stir wherever he went, but he was also guilty of loosening his grip on the reins. He had his poke and the thought of doing any real stir kept him from making any rash decisions. He had greying blond hair, deep-blue eyes, and his wrinkles were all laughter lines. He fancied himself as a bit of a card, and loved a good joke. He was capable of great friendships and he was also capable of murder. Like Danny Boy, he had been accused of it many times, but no one had ever accused him to his face, Old Bill included. What they guessed, and what they could prove, were two very different things. Frank was pleased that Danny Boy had finally deigned to approach them; he had worried they were being mugged off by him. His two compatriots, Lenny Dunn and Douglas Fairfax, were getting restless. It always amazed him that the lower down the food chain people were, the quicker they seemed to take offence at any so-called slights. He understood the nature of patience, and the sense in waiting to see what occurred before taking the appropriate action necessary. Considering that, in their line of work, that could entail a gun and a stern lecture, it was the only sensible course of action for anyone with even a modicum of intelligence.

Lenny and Dougie were both stocky, balding and devoid of anything even remotely resembling a sense of humour. They were earners though, and that was all Frank really cared about. He also knew it was what Danny Boy Cadogan cared about as well. Danny Boy Cadogan wanted to share his new-found bounty with them, and Frank was shrewd enough to know that he would want something back in return. He was happy enough to do business with him; the boy was more than able by all accounts and he was more than willing, what more could he ask for? Well, that remained to be seen, didn't it? Danny was smiling at them, and Frank and his two partners were treated to the full force of his very unpredictable personality. It was this that finally made Frank extremely wary. He knew from experience that the Danny Boys of his world were dangerous because they were basically thugs, and thugs were not geared up to run things; they didn't have the staying power or the temperament. Danny Boy, so he had heard, could rustle up a scam with the best of them, and knew an earner from a hundred paces. He was already a player in their world, and a big one at that. Frank was only approaching them now because they were among the few people in the Smoke who weren't already involved with him in some capacity. He had avoided this day for as long as he could, but now he wanted an in; he needed the boy's criminal contacts, as well as his tame Filth, to expand his drugs' business. By all accounts, no one around him could handle anything over three kilos without his express permission. The boy could also get his grubby little hands on anything, from steroids to blue ones. From a bit of Jamaican grass to a Nepalese temple ball, Danny Cadogan had it sewn up, and that suited Frank no end, he just wanted to distribute it; he wasn't arsed about the importing side of it all, because that's where the big sentences were handed out. Distribution meant he could take a back seat and let everyone else worry about a capture. He made sure he was always three people away from any kind of police investigation.

As they shook hands and ordered drinks Frank was reluctantly impressed with Cadogan's laid-back demeanour. He was a dangerous fuck, there was no doubt about that, but he was also capable of being a charming bastard when the fancy took him.

As Michael Miles joined them, he relaxed a little bit more, he was the one with the head for figures; he was the one who, word on the pavement said, could turn a fiver into a ton overnight. He looked like a brain-box and he seemed much more approachable than his partner-in-crime. But, as he knew to his detriment, in their world you *never* judged a book by its cover.

'He's a cunt.'

Michael sighed once more. He wasn't in the mood for this tonight, he was meeting Carole for a meal in Ilford and he was already ten minutes late as it was. Not that Danny Boy would care about that.

'Look, Danny, Frank's all right, and he will bring in a good wedge. You said as much yourself. He's shrewd, he knows the score, and he is upping his investment every time we see him. So, leave this tonight, eh? I'm meeting Carole and I'm already late as it is. I'm going to ask her to marry me . . .'

Michael's handsome features were now rearranged into a wide smile. He was amazed at Danny Boy's quietness at his announcement. He looked stunned by the news and, for a few seconds, Michael wondered if his friend was actually worried about his choice of woman, even though he knew Danny thought the world of her. Then Danny Boy seemed to collect himself and, grabbing him into a bear hug, he said happily, 'Oh, Mike, that's the best news ever, mate.'

Michael could feel the strength of him, knew that this was one time when he could really relax around Danny Boy, because he loved Carole and it showed. He thought she was the dog's gonads and he told Michael that at every available opportunity. His first reaction, stunned shock, had thrown him for a few seconds, and he had wondered, briefly, if Danny Boy's friendliness towards Carole had been false. But no one could fake Danny's affection for Carole, or hers for him. But that was all it was, affection.

'What a fucking Brahma you got yourself there, mate.' Danny was over the moon for his friend and, pushing him away, he said loudly, 'Go on, get your arse in gear, business can wait till the morning. Frank can go on the back burner until I decide what to do with him . . .'

Michael's happiness was marred by the words and he grinned sadly, his long arms outstretched as he said, 'You can't kill anyone else, Danny Boy and, anyway, Frank has done nothing to you. Plus he's a fucking good earner . . .'

Danny was straight-faced now, the happiness of seconds ago gone completely, and his scowl, which could strike terror into the hardest of hearts, was evident. 'He's a lairy cunt and he needs taking down a few notches . . .'

Michael knew that his meal with Carole was not going to

happen. So he rang the restaurant and made his apologies. Carole being Carole, was good-natured about it; she understood the business he was in and she was intelligent enough to know that things happened. It was one of the things he loved about her; his sister Mary, on the other hand, would have gone mental. In her heyday she would have forced the issue, made Danny go to her, created murders over one broken date. But Carole didn't bat an eyelid, she was laughing as always, and told him she'd see him later that night.

Danny Boy was grinning as he came off the phone. 'She didn't give you one bit of grief, did she?'

Michael shook his head. 'Nah, she knows the score, Dan.'

'I still think you should go to Carole, we can sort this out in the morning. I bet she's even good about that, eh, you sneaking off like the fucking lodger at daybreak.'

Michael laughed then, at the image Danny Boy had created, 'Look, Dan, I'll let you into a secret, but you have to keep it close, all right. She's still a fucking virgin. I'll have to marry her just to get me leg over.'

Danny was astonished, even though he had guessed as much. That Michael had won such a prize pleased him tremendously, but a little voice was goading him at the same time. That could have been him; he had wanted Mary because someone else had her. And again he wanted what someone else had, as always. No, he was fucking lumbered.

He forced the thoughts from his mind, ashamed at his thoughts about his best friend and poor Carole.

'Fucking hell, I could have told you that. She's a good girl, old Carole, a decent girl. I am so pleased for you, mate.'

And he meant it, every word. He didn't want Carole in real life because he knew his lechery would have broken her heart. He loved her enough to not want to hurt her in any way, shape or form. She was his best mate's bird, and he was glad she was finally off the market. She wasn't a beauty, in the traditional sense of the word, but she was a woman to aspire to. She was someone who the man who finally bagged her would treasure. She was a real lady, and he would always love her from afar. Now that Michael was going to marry her, he actually felt relief. As his best friend's wife she would be off-limits to him and, therefore, he couldn't hurt her. His reasoning made perfect sense to him, because whatever he wanted, he made sure that he got. It never occurred to him that Carole might not have wanted him; that, as far as he was concerned, was a given.

'Look Danny Boy, leave Frank alone. Promise me, we are earning fortunes from him. Fucking megabucks, and if anything happens to him, we would make a lot of enemies. He's got his creds with everyone in the know and, anyway, he's a nice bloke.'

Danny smiled again. His white teeth were like a movie star's, and his face crinkled-up in all the right places. He was a severely handsome man and Michael wondered, once again, how such good looks could mask such a vicious personality.

'But he's a cunt. He thinks he's the fucking dog's bollocks and he ain't. I am weighing him out on a regular basis and he is on the earn. Everyone is on the fucking earn, thanks to us two. But he is extracting the urine, and I know he is, and no one takes the fucking piss out of me.'

Michael sat down on the old sofa that Louie had been kind enough to leave for them. He sighed, and the sound was loud in the confines of the small room. Michael was frightened now, he knew that Frank was not someone to be lightly missed. He was a nice bloke, he was a good earner, and he was a fucking Face. A *real* Face, and he knew that was what annoyed Danny Boy so much. But he was frightened of Danny's reaction, he was quite capable of going round Frank's house and shooting him without any real reason whatsoever. Just because Danny Boy Cadogan felt threatened by Frank's busy social life. He was liked, he was respected, and Danny was fucked off because he felt he had waited too long before he had approached them for the earn. Frank was courteous and friendly, and Danny saw that as a piss-take because he wanted to. He wanted a reason to destroy him, wipe him out. Michael felt the steel band of a headache encircle his forehead, and the pain was electric. He knew it was tension, knew it was brought on by worry. Knew that it wasn't going to go anywhere in the near future. In fact, he was already adept at living with it.

'Look, Danny Boy, he ain't taking the piss out of you, all right, he fucking *likes* you. He *admires* you. But you know as well as I do, he is a man who has a good reputation around town, and if you start a fucking war with him, or take him out, we'll lose a lot of goodwill and a lot of fucking money into the bargain. He's married to Barry Clarke's sister, for fuck's sake, and Barry is a mate. So let it go, will you, at least for the time being anyway.'

Danny was looking out of the window, he was watching the dogs as they patrolled the grounds. He knew Michael was talking sense but that didn't really bother him too much. It was the mention of Barry Clarke that got him going. That brought a curious thought into his head. He suddenly knew how to kill two birds with one dirty, great big stone. The thought made him smile again. 'Go on, Michael, get yourself off to Carole. I promise I won't do anything to anyone, OK? Scout's honour, dib dib dib and all that.' He was laughing again, and pretending to salute him, like a little kid would.

Michael noticed that Danny was totally relaxed once more, the tension had seeped from his body in seconds, leaving him looking like an overgrown schoolboy.

'Get home to Mary tonight, Danny Boy, she needs you . . .'

Danny Boy nodded sadly, and they both avoided any more conversation after that.

Mary was lying in the bath, her rounded belly was in evidence above the water and she was trying to ignore it. She had a large glass of wine and, as she gulped at it, she was listening out for her husband's car. He wouldn't be home, she was sure; it was a Wednesday night and he rarely came home on a Wednesday. But she never knew anything for sure where he was concerned; he could come rolling in at any moment and she knew that her drinking alcohol would cause ructions. But it was the only way she could relax, her nerves were shot and, like her mother before her, she needed a drink to take the edge off the day. She lay back in the warm water and sighed loudly. The bathroom was huge, like everywhere else in this empty house, and the bottle of wine she had opened was calling to her. She finished the glass off in two gulps, the acidic taste of the Liebfraumilch in her pregnant belly making her burn inside. The indigestion was unbearable, but she knew that was preferable to sobriety.

As she poured herself out another large glass, she started laughing to herself. Catching her reflection in the mirrored tiles on the walls all around her, she was amazed as always at how good she looked. Her hair was piled on top of her head, and her skin was smooth and soft. Her make-up was flawless, and yet she was pissed out of her head. She decided it must be a knack she had, a genetic thing she had inherited from her mother and father, both renowned piss-artists in their day. She saw the swelling of her breasts, they were fuller now, not that Danny Boy cared. He still took her as he would an animal. No niceties at all, just a fuck and a grunt, and she was ashamed to admit that she welcomed even that much from him. She knew he had a young girl, another one, a seventeen year old with the brains of a parrot and the body of a goddess. She had seen her, she was a natural blonde with huge blue eyes and the blank expression of a fucking retard. She wondered what his regular bird made of her, probably jealous of her lifestyle and her wedding ring.

She instinctively laid a hand on her belly. She was five months gone, but bigger than she had ever been. This was the baby that would sort out all her problems, she was sure about that. She was singing softly to herself, the wine glass balanced on her tummy and a cigarette dangling from her perfectly manicured fingers when she realised that someone was watching her from the doorway.

'You fucking whore. You drunken fucking whore . . .'

She was frozen with terror at the sight of him. She dropped the cigarette into the bath water, her fear so acute it was hanging on the steamy air, her face was stretched in dismay, her mouth a perfect 'O'.

He walked slowly towards her, and his huge body, stiff with his anger, reminded her of how strong he was, how hard he could hit. He snatched the crystal wine glass from her shaking hand and, throwing it at the wall above her head with all his considerable strength, he shattered the mirror tiles, along with the glass itself. She felt the shards as they rained down on top of her. He was almost exploding with suppressed hatred, she could feel the heat of his anger burning into her.

'You'd drink with my baby cooking inside you, after all that's happened. You're your mother's daughter, all right, you fucking drunken cunt . . .'

She was still unable to move, all she could do was look at him in absolute shock and horror as he loomed over her. His face was twisted in anger, his huge body rigid with fury. As he grabbed at her she flinched, bringing her arms up to protect herself, thinking he was going to slap her face, or pull her out of the bath by her hair. So she was unprepared for what he actually did to her. Grabbing her ankles, he dragged her legs up towards him, forcing her head and upper body back into the bath. She was totally submerged, unable to breathe, and she tried to fight him off, tried to free herself from his grip, the water going everywhere, she was panicking, trying to lift herself out of the water, desperate to take a breath of air. She could feel the burning inside her nose as she started to breathe in the bath water . . . Unable to hold her breath for any longer, she was gradually losing her energy, felt the darkness that heralded her losing this battle for air when suddenly he dragged her head up from out of the water, and she was gasping for breath, her lungs bursting. But within seconds he was forcing her back into the water once more. All the time he was swearing and shouting at her, and as she felt herself finally losing consciousness she prayed that this was final, that she would not wake up ever again.

Ange was worried, and she did what she always did when anything bothered her; she cooked and cleaned. She used to laugh years before, when the kids were babies, that her problems were the reason why she had the cleanest house in the street. But those days were gone; she had not known what a real problem was, she knew that much now anyway. Her husband had been a trial, but those days seemed almost worthy of nostalgia lately. He was a different man.

She was worried about the boys and about that whore of a daughter she'd spawned, but she worried mostly about her husband. Since Jonjo had attacked him, he had seemed to have lost the will to do anything. He didn't even go to the pub any more. In fact, all he did was sit around and smoke; she provided those. And she also made sure he had a drink to soften the edges of his life. But she knew he had already given up on himself. It was in his eyes, in his stance. He didn't even eat anything unless she kept on at him, cajoled him, she had even forced him at times. He was wasting away in front of her eyes, and she didn't know what to do.

The doctor said he was depressed, said the pain was probably a contributing factor, but he was talking out of his arse; the man was destroyed, had been demolished by his sons, and there was nothing she could do to change that. Jonjo didn't care about his father at all, he saw him in the same way Danny Boy saw him. As a useless appendage, less than human. In one way she understood their feelings toward him, he had used them and abused them all over the years. But he was still their father. Still her husband and that should have meant something to them. Instead, they thought he was a joke, the man who had sired them, and she was left with two sons who were completely out of control. Danny Boy was a holy terror, whose only saving grace was that he still attended Mass on a regular basis, and her younger son was following in his footsteps. On top of that, she had a daughter who was already well on the road to whoredom, and was under the mistaken belief that she was somehow immune to any kind of parental control. It was an awful way for a mother to have to live her life. Especially as she was unable and unwilling to admit anything was out of the ordinary where her family was concerned. Especially in public; it went against the grain, it was anathema to her to ever criticise anyone in her close family no matter what they might have done. Her instinct was to protect them, care for them. No matter what, and that even meant looking out for the skank that passed as her daughter these days.

Her husband was staring blankly into space as usual, and his voice made her jump as he said quietly and with a determined anger, 'We managed to breed animals, Ange, get over it. Stop letting it bother you.'

He turned to her and looked into her eyes and, for the first time in years, she knew he was actually talking to her, not simply answering her or pretending an interest in what she had to say; he was trying to tell her something important. She surmised that this sudden lucidity on her husband's part was because he was suddenly afflicted with the urge to communicate his feelings towards her for the first time in his life.

'They aren't animals, Danny, they are our children, they are our flesh and blood.'

He shook his head sadly, his beaten face slack again, making him look like the cheap bastard he had always been.

He didn't answer her, and she knew that he should have been very vocal on the subject, and she knew she had been expecting this for a long time, and wondered why, now that it was here she was so surprised. She tried to make him change his mind, change the outcome of their union, even though she had known for many years that it was inevitable.

'Don't leave me, Danny. Don't bail out on us.'

He smiled then, the deep creases that amounted to his life etched into his skin and his voice as he said with a short laugh, 'He's a fucking vicious bully, your son, and you know it better than anybody. He even tortured you for years though you'll never admit to that. He has that poor girl living on her nerves, and you still won't admit that he's a fucking headcase. He's finished me, I can't live like this any more. He ain't my flesh and blood, Ange, he's nothing to me. If he died tomorrow I'd put the fucking flags out. As for the others, they're like him. You brought up a litter of pups who haven't got one decent bone in their bodies between them. You made them like you; they pretend that they live perfect lives, pretend that they're perfectly happy, when none of them knows the meaning of the word.'

The words hit her hard, as he knew they would. He wanted to hurt her, make her see that whatever he had lacked as a father, it was her mothering that had done the most damage. She knew that, like the children he was so quick to denigrate, he couldn't take the blame for anything they might be accused of.

'They are our children, you're the one who encouraged them to be like they are. Even your daughter, the only one of them you ever gave a toss for, has inherited your bloody traits. She's a whore in the making, sleeping with anyone who'll have her, even though she knows her brother would be capable of murder if he knew the score. I gave you the best years of my life, and I've tried to keep this family together, even after all you've put me through. So don't you dare to try and place any blame on me for the moral bankruptcy that you passed on to your offspring. It was *you* who left us out to dry, *you* who caused your eldest son to become the man he has, *you* and your selfishness that has brought us to where we are this day. Danny Boy took over from you, and he did what you should have done for us. So stop trying to pass the buck, and just once in your life, take responsibility for your actions. Or, in this case, your complete lack of action where the care of your family was concerned.' The anger had finally surfaced, as he had known it would.

'You're an angry woman, Ange, and you've passed that anger onto all your children. None of them has anything even remotely resembling compassion or affection for you, me, each other, or anyone else in the world for that matter.'

'And who do you think made me angry, eh? Why do you think you are in the state you are? Are you honestly trying to blame it on me? I was the one who tried to make this all better, I was the one who always welcomed you back with open arms. No matter what you've done to me or the kids, I've never stopped loving you, ever. I stood by you no matter what. Even now, I'm still trying to make you realise what you have got. Make you understand how much we need you. So don't try and make me feel that your leaving us will make me think I was the cause of our suffering because that crap don't work with me any more. You are the one who made your kids into thugs, not me. If I was guilty of anything, it was going out on the graft, making enough money to feed and clothe them all. I didn't gamble my money away, or drink it with my cronies in the dingiest pubs I could find. I never weighed out my wages on the nearest old whore I could find. That, my darling, I left to *you*. Let's face it, Danny, it was the only thing you were ever good at.'

Her tirade was as unexpected as it was true, but Big Danny Cadogan still didn't think she deserved to get the last word in. He was making up for every slight, every cross word and, more to the point, he was determined to leave her with the knowledge that he was bowing out without any kind of guilt whatsoever.

'Oh, Ange. You finally got what you wanted, your blue-eyed boy all to yourself. The kids all saw you as the saviour of the family, and I let them think it. I let you be the victim you insisted to them you were. You might blame me for how your life turned out, but you had a big part in it all. You could have dumped me years ago, and given them a fucking fighting chance, yourself included. But you didn't, and I can tell you now, I wish you had. Because it would have made everyone's lives that much easier.'

She was saved from answering him by a loud knocking on the front door. She walked slowly and painfully through the immaculate home she had created and wondered what new trouble could be waiting for her on the other side of the freshly painted front door. She knew from experience that no one knocked here any more unless there was a specific reason for it. That reason was always because something bad had happened again, and so she opened the door with the resigned expression she had cultivated over the years, the one that told whoever was brave enough to approach her that she was ready and able for anything they might be inclined to divulge. This time though, there were tears in her eyes and a catch in her throat and, for once, she didn't try to disguise them.

Like her husband, she had finally had enough herself.

Chapter Nineteen

Outside her home, Annie Cadogan extracted herself from Arnold Landers' arms with difficulty. He was a big man, and his heavily muscled body was a constant reminder of just how physically powerful he actually was. It was a big part of his attraction, that and the fact he was a well-known Jamaican drug dealer who was also renowned as a womaniser and a hard-case. He was a Rasta man with a penchant for youthful white girls and heavy gold jewellery. He was also a nice bloke who was liked by most of the people he dealt with. He had a friendly demeanour and was known as a man's man. Someone to be looked up to and respected. Annie though, was unlucky enough to be the only girl who he actually felt a deep affection for. Her tight body, coupled with the fact that she had a healthy disregard for him, was very attractive to him. She was the first female ever to make him work to guarantee her affections. Her brother's reputation was something he was aware of, but something he didn't really let bother him too much. In fact, he was pleased she was so well connected; he had every intention of taking this relationship to the max. He was a plastic Rasta, a Catholic by birth, thanks to his fiery red-headed mother. Like Bob Marley before him, he had felt inclined to embrace the dominant colour of his skin because it was the most obvious sign of his parentage. However, until now, he had not really thought too deeply about the ramifications of his religion or his lifestyle. Annie had caused him to have a complete rethink on his way of life. She was like a drug to him; he knew in one way that she was dangerous, but he also knew that his life before her and, more to the point without her, was no life at all.

She had crept under his skin, and she resided there with his permission and with his deep regard. Without her, he knew he would be broken-hearted. This was all new to him, and he hoped she felt as strongly for him as he did for her. As she smiled at him, her even white teeth and huge blue eyes making him feel the usual lurch in his breast, he grinned back happily. Her long, dyed-blond hair was silky smooth and he pushed a huge hand through it gently. Loving the feel of it, enjoying the power he knew she wielded over him.

He wasn't a fool, he knew she had been around the turf a few too many times for his liking; in fact he knew she had far too much mileage on her than would be good for either of them in the long run. But he didn't dwell on that now, because he also knew that she was capable of generating deep feelings in him that were as confusing as they were exciting.

'I wish you would stay with me tonight, Annie. I am getting pissed off with this creeping around, you know. We have a good thing going, as Maxi Priest would say. Why can't we just be together?'

Annie shrugged uneasily, knowing that her feelings for him were not what they should be, and suddenly aware that she might just have bitten off more than she could comfortably chew. He was sexy and exciting, but he was also a man who would do to her what her brother was doing to his wife. Would control her every move; like Danny Boy, he was a man who expected his partner's complete and utter obedience. He would be a worse candidate than her father in the marriage stakes, and that was saying something. She also knew that, like the men in her family, he wouldn't go away without a fight. She was desperate to get away from him now, desperate to try and make some kind of sense of this new problem she had brought on herself.

'I'm too young to make any kind of big decision about my life, I keep telling you that. Now I have to get inside, my dad will be worried about me.'

She sounded so young when she spoke, and she looked so innocent he forgot for a few moments just how experienced she actually was. That she could suck a cock like a pro, rolling a joint at the same time.

Arnold watched her as she turned away and put her key in the lock, and smiled gently to himself at the way she tried to manipulate him. He started walking away.

As Annie let herself into the quiet darkness of her home, she was still wondering about her relationship with her latest beau; it was only when she walked into the kitchen that the reason for her initial unease became apparent. Her screams brought Arnold to her side within minutes and opened up a can of worms that guaranteed her life would never be the same again.

Her father had blown his brains out in the kitchen, and bone and skin, along with blood, seemed to have permeated everything around him. The scene was so horrific that even Arnold, who prided himself on his strong stomach, was hard-pushed to keep his dinner from joining the carnage all around him. It was so unexpected, and the sight so appalling, that he didn't know what to do for a few minutes. He knew that the girl he loved was looking at what remained of her father's face, and he pulled her out of the room quickly. He pushed her face into his chest as if that would wipe out the images she had witnessed.

Annie was still holding onto him tightly when Jonjo arrived home a few minutes later. It didn't occur to any of them to phone for the police or an ambulance. They both knew on a subliminal level that Danny Boy would need to be told what had happened before anything could be done about this latest catastrophe.

Jonjo was rooted to the spot and, like his sister, the shock set in quickly, and that told Arnold that he would have to take charge for the time being at least. He did take over and, without realising, it he made his journey into the bosom of the Cadogan family much easier than it would have been otherwise.

The first thing he did was remove brother and sister from the scene of the crime, and then he set about tracking down Danny Boy Cadogan with the least amount of fuss possible. But, before he did that, he quietly and unobtrusively removed the note he had seen among the human debris that was now covering the kitchen table.

297

*

Mary was white-faced and drawn, but even the young doctor at the hospital was uncomfortably aware of how lovely she still was. The loss of her child was bad enough, but the news that her father-in-law had committed suicide seemed to have hit her harder than he thought possible. It seemed to outweigh the loss of her baby, and he noticed that she seemed even more terrified after she had been delivered of the news. He wondered at her state of mind, even as he understood her husband's need to be with his mother and siblings at this tragic time. He was sorry for her though; another miscarriage, and such a late one too, was not something he felt she needed to experience alone. As he offered all the usual platitudes, he could not help noticing the lifelessness behind her eyes. It was almost as if she was already dead inside herself, and her body was existing as a separate entity, devoid of any kind of feeling or emotion.

He left her with her brother and his girlfriend, glad to hand her over to someone else, and unable to account for the feelings she engendered inside him. He knew that there was something radically wrong with her, yet was unable to pinpoint exactly what that might be. He heard her crying softly and was pleased that she was finally letting some of her emotions out. She was wound up tighter than a watch spring, and he knew she was going to unravel spectacularly in the near future. He had seen it time and time again.

'Are you all right, Mary?' Carole's voice was low, and dripping with concern.

Mary looked at her friend, at her open face and her easy-going kindness; envied her the way she could breeze through life without any real problems. This was exacerbated by the fact that she could never tell her about the real circumstances of her own life. Could never let on about the abortion that passed for her everyday existence. She was still comforted though, felt easier just knowing her friend was there and cared about her. It had to be enough, she knew the truth of her life would not welcomed by any of the people important to her.

She was tired out and she was also desperate for a drink, a real drink, not the watered-down orange juice she was sipping out of habit. She smiled at her friend and sighed before saying quietly, 'How's Danny taken his father's death?'

Now that her brother had left the pair of them alone she felt brave enough to enquire as to her husband's frame of mind.

'Not good, mare, in fact, he seems to be a bit too calm and collected to me. But then I think a suicide is something that no one knows how to react to, do they? It was such a brutal death as well. He put the gun into his mouth and shot his brains out.'

Carole shut up then, unsure if she should have been so honest considering that poor Mary was already in bits, but she was also worried about poor Danny Boy as well. After all, he had received a double blow, his father's death, and the loss of his child. She knew Michael was unsure of what to do for the best where his sister and her husband were concerned, and she was hoping that she could take some of the burden from him. He was expected to keep things going until everything settled down once more, however long that might take.

'How have Ange and the others taken it?'

Mary was asking because she knew it was expected of her, not because she had any real interest at all. In fact, she was glad he was gone, it was one less thing to worry about where her husband was concerned.

'Annie found him, and it's hit her hard. As for Ange, well, she is devastated obviously, as is Jonjo. Though I think Jonjo is mainly feeling guilt. He had no time for him really, did he?'

Mary shook her head sadly and both women were quiet for a few moments. Then, grasping her friend's hand firmly in both of her own, and hugging it to her chest tightly, she said, sorrowfully, 'Look, Mary, I can't help being worried about you. They said you had passed out in the bath. Are you all right? Do they know what caused it?'

Mary extricated herself as gently as she could from her friend's embrace without causing offence and, shrugging lightly, she held out her hands in a gesture of supplication.

'No, Carole, they say it's just another one of those things. No real reason for it and, with my previous miscarriage, I don't think they even really look for a reason. And, let's face it, there's far too much going on to dwell on the loss of another baby. If I think about it too much it will break my heart all over again.'

Carole nodded almost imperceptibly before whispering, 'Will you be all right Mary?'

The question was loaded and they both knew it; this was the first time Carole had ever hinted at her problem. Mary saw her chance and took it, grabbed at it with both hands. Relying on Carole's innate sense of fair play. 'Could you do me a favour, Carole? Bring me in a bottle of vodka? I need something to take the edge off all that's happened. They keep trying to make me take antidepressants, but I don't want to get hooked on pills. I just need to sleep, that's all, and a few drinks might be the answer.'

Carole felt that her friend drank far too much as it was, but she was also aware of the extreme circumstances that caused her to. Not being a drinker herself, she saw no harm in agreeing to do as she was asked. She was only trying to help.

'Thanks, Carole. I appreciate it.'

Thrilled with how easy it had been to get her friend on board Mary forced her face into a tragic mask before saying. 'Keep this quiet though, Carole. I don't want anyone knowing how depressed I am. Danny Boy has enough on his plate as it is, without worrying about me.'

Carole nodded, but she wasn't entirely sure she was doing the right thing by agreeing to this. She knew that Mary drank far too much as it was. But then she also knew she had a lot on her plate. Danny Boy's father had left a mess behind him that went deeper than the blood that seemed to be everywhere and the stunned shock of his family at his actions. Who was she to refuse her friend the solace that a few drinks might bring her? She was so unhappy these days and, even though she didn't say too much about it, she guessed Danny Boy and Mary were experiencing some marital problems. Michael hinted as much, and she knew he was worried about her as well.

But Michael was overwhelmed with work and she didn't want to worry him with anything else at the moment. He was already close to crumbling under all the pressure, and she knew he was worried about Danny Boy's reaction to all that had happened. Danny was under a lot of strain, saw his father's suicide as a personal affront to him. Michael was taking on the brunt of the businesses and looked tired and strained. She wished there was something she could do to help him in some way.

As she left the hospital, she was surprised to see Danny Boy's mother, in full church clothes, entering the hospital. She was on her way to see her daughter-in-law and Carole was secretly pleased that she hadn't noticed her. She really didn't know what to say to her about what had happened; a natural death was one thing, but for a practising Catholic, a suicide was the worst sin a person could commit. There was no way to console someone because the person concerned had left themselves without any hope.

She hurried home, wondering what exactly she was getting involved with. As much as she loved Michael, she wondered at times if his business interests were a lot more than she could cope with. Once they married she knew that her part in their union would entail her knowing a lot more than would be good for her. She was like Mary, though; she knew she wasn't marrying an angel and she accepted that, as she also knew her life would be lived with the knowledge that she could lose the man she loved to the criminal courts. She felt a shiver of apprehension at what her life could become. But then she forced the thoughts from her mind, and told herself that being with him was all she was interested in.

Michael poured himself a stiff drink and swallowed it, enjoying the burn as it went down into his belly. He needed a livener, and the brandy was hitting the spot. He leaned back in the chair, and surveyed the office around him. The dingy hole that they spent so much time in was looking even shabbier than usual. He knew Danny Boy stayed there sometimes, and that he brought company with him. He wondered how a man with so much money and so much success could still feel more comfortable in these kind of surroundings. He knew Danny cheated on his wife, his sister, but he knew too that was the nature of that particular beast. He knew his sister had known his rep when she married him, in many ways she had gone into the marriage with her eyes open much wider than Danny Boy's. She was her mother's daughter, and Michael knew she had married Danny for what he could provide her with, as much as anything else.

And Danny had provided for her, she lived like a queen. She had everything a woman could possibly want. Now she was finding out what it was like to not get everything handed to her on a plate; she couldn't produce a child for Danny and he knew that was burning him up inside. He saw himself as a man's man, and he had already fathered a baby by one of his amours. At least, that was the rumour going round anyway. Michael could smell the stale cigarette smoke everywhere, and the sourness of a room used for thirty years without the benefit of a cleaner. He could hear the low growling of the dogs as they roamed the yard and he knew they were the best protection in the world, no one in their right mind would attempt to enter these premises; if anyone even walked near the fence they went into overdrive. He poured himself another drink and, lighting a cigarette, he pulled on it slowly, listening to the sounds of the night outside. The traffic was just a low drone, the rush hour was over and the road would become quieter by the hour. It was amazing really, every time he sat like this it reminded him of just how far they had come over the years. Now he was a rich man, and a respectable man in his own way. He was known as the moneyman of the outfit, and he liked that. Michael enjoyed the way he lived and was determined to make sure he stayed living it large. He was worried about Danny Boy though, he was getting more and more difficult to handle by the day. He took umbrage with everyone he had contact with, found fault, saw slights where there weren't any. Michael was known as the only person who could talk Danny Boy down; in fact he had been approached a couple of times to act as an intermediary for some of their clients. But this business with Frank was a real worry. Danny hated him; he had taken a dislike that was as outrageous as it was without any kind of foundation. The real problem was that Frank was not someone who could be treated with anything other than the friendliest of smiles and the ultimate of respect. He had a lot of friends in all the right places. Although Danny was, in effect, the Alpha male where the business was concerned, he had sewn up the drugs alone, and no one worked anything of any real note without in some way answering to them. He and Danny Boy were the only Faces who could guarantee people a regular and hefty return on any money they invested. They also paid off most of the Filth in the Smoke, guaranteeing that their merchandise was almost untouchable, earning them the nickname the untouchables. They had two high-ranking Met officers and one who worked closely with the new branch of the Flying Squad, who predominantly dealt with the new breed of men known as supergrasses. Since the seventies this had become an increasingly large problem in the criminal community, causing unrest and distrust among many of the men who had previously been tight. These new grasses were usually small-time Faces who had been captured, fair and square and, thanks to the heavy sentences being doled out by the courts, were more than willing to open their traps up about all and sundry to save their own sorry arses. One sniff of the Old Bailey and they couldn't open their big mouths quick enough. They were not prepared to go down and do their bird like a man, these people were willing to serve up anyone for a reduced sentence and the chance of parole. It was an abomination as far as everyone was concerned. In fact, Danny Boy's new-found status was based on the fact that there was no one willing to grass on him; his rep was so entrenched in local folklore that no one was brave enough to ever put his name in the frame for anything. Danny joked that he could shoot the pub up in broad daylight and no one would make a statement against him, such was the fear he instilled in everyone who came into contact with him. His father's crippling and subsequent suicide just made Danny Boy's reputation stronger. He had wiped out anyone who stood in his way, and he was still without a stain on his character as far as the law of the land was concerned.

But Michael, as much as he welcomed his friend's fierce and completely warranted rep, knew, instinctively, that Danny Boy could not get away with this behaviour for ever. Eventually, even he would cross the wrong person, and that was something that Michael was determined to ensure never happened. It was why he was so worried about Danny Boy's dislike for Frank. Lifelong enemies were made for less in their community, and Frank had the goodwill that Danny Boy should have been courting, not spurning. A good partnership guaranteed each side a little extra protection in their daily war against getting captured, but any bad feeling was a good reason to forget the criminal code: who would go away for someone they didn't even like? It stood to reason.

When people kept their traps shut, stuck their heads down and did their time, they ensured that their family was more than taken care of. Once they opened their mouths though, they brought a lot of trouble on themselves; hence the need to take as many people out of the game as quickly as possible. The fewer people still left out on the pavement, the less chance of being permanently taken out of the game one dark night by a stranger with a shotgun or a machete. Michael was amazed that Danny Boy didn't understand just how dangerous his position could be if he made too many enemies. He was still a Face, and he was a Face of repute and good-standing, but that could change in a heartbeat if he didn't learn to control his anger.

Michael saw the lights of Danny Boy's car as they shone across the office walls, heard the barking of the dogs and the loud creaking as the gates were opened. He poured himself another drink and braced himself for the coming meeting with his best friend. Danny wasn't a fool, and he knew that he only had their best interests at heart. But it still wasn't a conversation he was looking forward to though.

'You look better than I thought you would.'

Ange was attempting to smile as she spoke, but the effect was awful. She looked what she was; a woman on the edge. That she had loved the man who had left her alone yet again, this time for good, was never in doubt. It was just that, unlike her, no one else understood why. Ange had seen something in her husband that seemed to have eluded everyone else he had ever come into contact with. His own children included.

Mary watched her warily, unsure now of this woman who, it seemed to her, had spawned a man even she was frightened of. But the visit was welcome because Mary knew she had to get as many people on-side as possible. She hoped Ange was here as a friend and not an enemy.

'I always look good, Ange, that's the problem.' She said it sadly, without the gentle slurring that made her sound even sexier than usual. Her voice was low, deep; she always sounded as if she was on the verge of taking her clothes off. It was another thing her husband hated about her. She made porn queens look like amateurs, and it was all without any effort on her part whatsoever.

Ange was drawn, her wrinkled face seemed to have aged drastic-ally overnight. She was looking at her daughter-in-law sceptically, as if she had never met her before, as if she was weighing her up.

Both women were quiet for a while, Mary because she didn't feel comfortable with her mother-in-law. For the first time, she felt as if she was judging her, and it was not something she had ever experienced before. At least, not from Ange, anyway. Ange was generally someone she spoke to, but didn't really bother with. Her own son had no real respect for her and who could blame him? She had taken his father back even after he had destroyed the family she professed to love so much. Taking him back had been like a kick in the teeth to her elder son after everything he had done to keep them together, keep them fed and clothed. He had kept a roof over their heads that was paid for and was, for once in their lives, a certainty. A definite. He had made sure his mother wasn't out scrubbing floors and washing other people's clothes and had become the husband she had always craved; the man she had dreamed about. Danny Boy had taken on the mantle of the father, and they had all been the better for that. He had knocked his pound out in the pursuit of his family's happiness, and he felt proud at what he had accomplished for them all.

Ange Cadogan had been set like a jelly and, despite that, she had still chosen to take back the man who had caused them so much grief and heartache in the first place, who had caused his elder son to become a robber and a burgeoning young Face just so that he could take proper care of his family. A family that had never had it so good, and who had finally accepted that their lives were so much better without the father they secretly despised; the father who had no care or interest in any of them, their mother included.

305

Ange had set in motion a chain of events that had reverberated down the years and caused untold misery for everyone involved. Now, the woman Mary had ignored, had acknowledged as and when it suited her, who she had no real connection with, was suddenly important because she had Danny Boy's affection.

'Did they say what it was, what caused it this time?'

Ange's voice was low, full of compassion, and Mary responded to that. She almost cried with relief at her kind words. 'No, Ange, they said it was just one of those things.'

Ange nodded sadly, and sighed gently. Her heavy coat and carefully applied lipstick made her look like a mannequin. There was an unreality about the situation that Mary couldn't put her finger on.

'You're shaking, Mary, you're trembling like an Eskimo playing strip poker. Look at your hands.'

Mary looked down at the covers and Ange saw the beauty that she knew her son despised, even as he loved it. She knew what Danny Boy was like, he was far more like the father he had destroyed than he realised. Than any of them realised, in actual fact.

'I know you drink, and I know you drink on the quiet and, if I was married to my son, I would probably do the same, girl. He's a fucking vicious, vindictive bastard. But he still deserves a child, and you'd better get your act together, lady, and produce one, or he'll kick your arse out the door so fast you'll hit the pavement running. Now, I want you up and about for the funeral, and I want you there by my side as if we're all really sorry he's gone. I want to give him that if nothing else.'

Mary nodded, unsure of this woman now. Unsure of the power she seemed to have garnered for herself almost overnight.

'I'm sorry about Big Danny . . .'

Ange flapped her hand in impatience, and said wearily, 'Don't say it if you don't mean it. He's gone, and we're all still here. Focus on that. But I don't want any sympathy that isn't genuine. Not from me own anyway. You'll stand there with me and your husband and you'll stay sober. Your poor mother, the lights of heaven to her, had the curse of the drink and all. It's a haven for the destroyed, for the unloved, and for the weak.'

Ange wiped a hand across her mouth then, as if wiping away the words she had just said, even as she knew the truth of them. In her heart she knew her son tortured this girl, knew that he was capable of great wickedness and his wife would always bear the brunt of it; she wondered if he had a hand in the loss of the babies. She hated that she even thought he might be responsible, because to even suspect him was like admitting it was true. So she pushed the thoughts away, as she always had, and said, 'You're like a thorn in his side; he's eaten up with you, wanted you so much he could kill for you and, like everything else, once he gets what he wants he sets out to destroy it without a second's thought for how his actions might reverberate on those around him. Now, I am here to offer you my support, but you have to do your bit. That means cutting down on the drink and taking care of yourself. Once a child arrives, a child born in wedlock, he'll come round. He's a lot more like his father than he realises, and he'll never leave you if you have his children. His personality is such that another man would never get the chance to have what he's had, even if he doesn't want it any-more. So, listen to me now; get a child and you'll have a bargaining tool with him. Because you need something to hold over his head, make sure he sees you as an asset of some kind in the future; make him take care of you. If you don't listen to me now, Mary, you're on your own. But you get to the funeral and you make sure my Danny Boy behaves himself. Take control of your life, girl, you might be surprised at his reaction. All the time you let him walk over you, he will.'

Mary Cadogan had never heard her mother-in-law talk so much. It was as if the death of her husband had opened her up to the world around her. As if his absence had finally destroyed the shackles that had kept her so close to him, no matter what he might have done to her. And he had pulled some stunts in his time.

'Don't let that boy drag you into the dirt, and don't let him control the rest of your life. I know him better than he knows himself. He is not kind to you, I guessed that a long time ago. Listen to me when I say this, *don't* give him a reason to hurt you, he doesn't need one. If you provide him with one, he'll use it to justify his behaviour. Now, I'm off; I've said my piece and the rest is up to you.'

She stood up and Mary saw a woman who had finally grown into her own skin, a woman who had lost the only thing she had ever really cared about in her life, and who was actually relieved about it. Now her husband was gone, and she could relax because, like the son she had produced, she was pleased that, at least with her husband's death, no one else could have him now. He couldn't leave her; he was finally and irrevocably hers. His death had enabled her to finally let go and, for the first time in years, she was doing just that.

At the door Ange looked back at the girl lying in the starkness of the hospital room and her features softened for a few moments. Then she said quietly, 'He'll never let you go, and you will never understand him. What you can do now is make the best of what you've got. Like we all did, your mother included.'

Her words hung on the air long after she had gone, and Mary was still sobbing as if her heart would break when the nurses finally organised an injection so she could get some much-needed sleep.

Chapter Twenty

Danny Boy looked around the packed church and, being contrary of nature as always, he decided he was pleased at the turnout his father's funeral had generated. His ego was thrilled that they were all actually there just for him, for his benefit, not for the useless ponce who had created him, and who he had ultimately seen fit to annihilate. His father's death affected him not one iota; he had lost any kind of affection many years before, and he had never tried to regain it in any way, shape or form. His father had been a pain in the proverbial arse as far as he was concerned, and his demise had been nothing more than a cowardly act; something he had expected, even welcomed. Why should he have to grieve for someone who had been dead to him for a long time? But the fact that so many people had bothered today assuaged his ego, made him happy because it showed the esteem people held him in. If he hadn't been the man he was, this ponce would be planted without a fucking bunch of daffodils from the nearest garage. There had been enough flower arrangements delivered that morning to cover twenty graves; Danny's only consolation being that the sheer weight of them might keep the old fucker down if he had any notions of going out on the haunt. He wouldn't put that past the old cunt either; he'd probably still go out on the rob in the afterlife. Thieving wanker that he was. His thoughts made him smile and he bowed his head quickly so no one would see the smirk on his lips.

He had a sudden flash of memory, when the Murrays were at his front door all those years ago. He felt the fear envelop him once more, and the anger at their threats and intimidation. They had expected him to roll over and let them bully him and his family at their leisure. He had dug deep down inside himself to fend them off, and discovered that day that there was a vicious, more violent bully lying dormant inside him, and the Murray brothers had unleashed it. It suddenly occurred to him that he had a lot to thank his father for. If he had not been such a useless cunt he might never have realised his full potential. Without his father's gambling debt he could have ended his days working like any other fucking Joey, trying to make ends meet and looking forward to voting every five years. He could have ended up a bar-stool philosopher like his old man. He saw then that he had actually had a near-miss, that he had dodged the bullet of mediocrity and embraced his destiny. Without his father's marathon fuck-ups he could have ended up like any other bloke he had grown up with; a grafter, someone who washed off the sweat that other men, cleverer men, made their fortune from. What an existence that would have been.

He was responding to the Mass without thinking of the words. He just wanted his communion; lately, he needed it, for some reason. He had even been seen at the six o'clock Mass on a regular basis. He liked the early Mass, liked the quiet of the church; even welcomed the old men and women who frequented it with their disappointed faces and the stench of second-hand shops hanging around them. They were like a lesson to him on what not to be, they reiterated his belief in himself and his perception of the world he inhabited. He would never be them.

Danny bowed his head and prayed; he meant every word he said and he knew that God understood that, understood him. Like Christ, he had experienced the trials and tribulations of all the great men. Jesus had been tortured, he had been mocked, and he had risen above his humble beginnings and made his mark on the world. People might not still be talking about Danny Boy in two thousand years, but he was confident he wouldn't be planted and then forgotten about, like so many of his peer group would. He was already a legend, he had iconic status. Christ had been served up by his old man, and he had experienced the same fate himself, except Danny's father had been protecting his own carcass and had no interest in the fate of his family.

Danny felt sorry for God at times because, like him, He was lumbered with cunts the majority of the time. He had to sort out their problems and make sense of their stupid lives for them. Had to try and give them something to believe in, to hold on to. For the majority of them, all that meant was making a few quid and being given the opportunity to make something of their stupid and pathetic existences.

The priest was speaking louder now; his voice always rose when he said the Gospel. Well, there might be many mansions in *His* father's house, but he had a feeling the Holy Father wasn't about to let his old man in to sully the place up. Myra Hindley and Adolph Hitler would be further up the line than his old man. He watched his wife as she held on to his mother's hand; they had been acting like best mates lately. He could see the shadow of Mary's eyelashes on her cheekbones, she had great bone structure, reminiscent of the old-style movie stars. She was immaculately dressed, as always, her dark clothes were seriously expensive and her hair had been washed and blow-dried to a glossy sheen. She was a stunner all right, the whore. He felt the anger once more, the hate that seemed to overwhelm him at regular intervals. His wife always looked so fucking calm and so fucking collected. She was like a doll, a parody of a real woman. She seemed the picture of health and vitality, except that he knew that everyone around her was taking bets on how long before her liver gave out. She was drinking like the fish she stunk of. No amount of perfume could disguise the stench of treachery that emanated from her. She was like a fucking leech, an albatross hanging round his neck. He tore his eyes away from her before he felled her to the floor with one almighty punch, even the sound of her shallow breathing was enough to antagonise him into a murderous rage. He should never have married her, he should have done what everyone else had, fucked her and left her.

Danny was gritting his teeth and he consciously relaxed his facial muscles, aware that he was being observed by the majority of people around him. He would not show any emotion at all to these toss-pots; his reputation would be in tatters if he did something that stupid.

He looked over at his little sister, she was a looker and all, and she was dressed, for once, with a little bit of decorum. Unlike Jonjo, she wasn't easy to take care of. Jonjo had accepted that Danny knew best from an early age, knew that he had his best interests at heart. He was a good kid but his sister was a fucking nuisance. She was like the old man, thought she was above everyone else. Was under the mistaken apprehension that she was special somehow. Well, she had a fucking shock coming her way in the near future.

Danny was feeling the heat of his anger again, and he took a few deep breaths to steady himself. In fact, he was aware that his anger was actually at the point of boiling over. His hand went instinctively to the envelope that was concealed inside his overcoat pocket. He knew it was still there, but he was unable to stop himself feeling for it every few minutes. The contents were enough to cause him to actually lose his breath, so great was the betrayal he felt inside him. That the man who had written the words had killed himself shortly afterwards was not something he would ever dwell on. After all, he knew the old bastard had never suffered from any kind of loyalty so, in a way, he was surprised at how great his sense of betrayal actually was at his father's final actions. Although he didn't know why he felt the betrayal so acutely; it wasn't as if he had cared for him in any way.

That his father could have grassed up his own son though, could have written down the words that could have been the cause of his own flesh and blood being locked away until the next millennium and beyond, was absolutely outrageous. In their world that was worse than murdering your own kith and kin. It was a disgrace, but it was also something that left a stain on the family concerned. It was assumed grassing was genetic; it cast a pall over the remaining relatives and left them all as suspect. Untrustworthy.

That his father had topped himself rather than stick around to witness the result of his disloyalty was typical of the man who had sired him. If he, himself, had not been so well connected, this statement could have been his swan song. It had names and dates, it was almost like an anthology of his criminal pastimes. The old bastard had tried to take him down and, thank fuck, he had not succeeded. His old man was such a coward that even his death had been cowardly. He had probably been lying there planning his own son's downfall, and even that hadn't given him the guts to hang around long enough to see the carnage he could have caused. He had topped himself in case his scheming had backfired on him, which it had of course. Spectacularly.

He hoped the old fucker was watching these proceedings, seeing his life being played out and knowing that his son had weighed out a fortune to ensure he was buried in hallowed ground. That was for his mother's benefit, not his. She was like the old shawlies from his childhood, the old Irish women who prayed for everyone else, and who spent their miserable lives whispering their purgatorial prayers, who still believed that all souls would be sent there, no matter what they had or had not done, and that it would take hundreds or thousands of masses for them to finally be released and deemed worthy of entrance into the Kingdom of Heaven. The Pope might have outlawed this practice but old habits died hard. It was still a deep-felt belief for a lot of the Catholics in the world. Purgatory was a given, and a lot of people spent a great deal of time praying for loved ones; determined to see them out of the fires that were a forerunner to hell. Personally, he prayed the old bastard burned for eternity and beyond. Like Christ he had been betrayed by those close to him, unlike Christ he had not had to endure prison or a loaded court case. His Pontius Pilate was still out there somewhere, he was convinced of that. He had dodged the bullet this time, and this was never going to happen to him again. He would make sure of that. He believed in the essence of his religion, after all, he had been there when it had been beaten into him by the priests and the nuns. He knew that his life was already mapped out, and that his eventual destiny was just a foregone conclusion. He had been singled out for greatness and his father's weakness, his gambling, had been the spur he had needed to realise that. His father's addiction had actually made his destiny. God was good, and God was also adept at making sure you understood the benefits of a good and decent life. He pointed you in the right direction, if you only had the sense to listen out for His voice. His father, Danny Boy accepted, had been the catalyst for him to emerge from obscurity and rise rapidly to the heights. He only wished that decency wasn't such a big part of his lifestyle; if it was left to him he would have let the fucker rot in the street. This funeral was his last act of contrition as it were; he had paid in many ways for what he had done to his own father. He had quickly gauged the general consensus about his actions, and he had known that it was in his own interests to bring him back into the fold. It had worked, he had become a hero overnight. The generous and forgiving son.

Now he was burying the man with all the pomp and ceremony his ill-gotten gains could provide, a man who, the rumour mill had it, felt so guilty over his previous actions that he couldn't live with himself any more. What a crock of shit, but he was willing to give credence to the lie. It suited him, and it made him look magnanimous and civilised.

The priest had been given proof that the old man was suffering from a depressive illness and two doctors had put their signature to letters stating his father was not in his right mind so they could now plant him with clear consciences. The hypocrisy was not lost on any of them.

Danny beat his chest gently as the first bell tolled, losing himself in the imagery of his religion. He walked slowly and deliberately up to the altar rail and knelt down humbly; he accepted his communion wafer with a silent passion. This was the buzz that he loved, this was the real reason for living. As the wafer dissolved on his tongue he felt cleansed once more, could feel the power of truth coursing through his body. He could feel the rush of the people who had come to pay court to him this day. He knew without doubt that he was a real *Face* now; this funeral had brought that fact home to him.

He was untouchable, and he knew that now.

Mary was sitting with Annie, and the younger girl was observing the people around her with her usual arrogance. That her father's death had affected her was obvious, that she was now looking for the angle that could best accommodate her was also noticeable. She was milking this for all it as worth.

Annie knew that she needed some Brownie points with her brother and she knew that she needed them sooner rather than later. He spoke to her, and he acknowledged her; that much was evident to anyone watching them together. But she felt his indifference, and the coldness that told her she had been relegated to the bottom of his list of priorities. She had slept around once too often. She had mouthed him off and pushed him to the extreme, but she had never believed that he would do this to her. He was, to all intents and purposes, blanking her, and that must never happen. Like her father before her, she had a natural antipathy to a day's collar. In fact, the thought of working for a living was the worst thing she could think of doing. It really was not an option for her. She was the baby of the family and he should be looking out for her as his little sister; she knew that he gave a good performance in public, he had to, it was expected. But she also knew that she wasn't worth anything to him, she brought nothing to the table and, in their family, that was of paramount importance. She had to find an angle; somehow change her position in this family. Danny Boy was capable of disowning her, and she knew her rep wouldn't stand up to scrutiny, so she had to make sure that never happened.

She could see Arnold Landers chatting with her brother, and the sight of the two men so close together depressed her, she knew that the only thing keeping her in Danny Boy's eyeline at this moment was her burgeoning relationship with Arnold Landers. Without him on-side Danny would push her away without a second's thought. She knew her mother was now at her elder son's mercy, once and for all, and that his wife was terrified of him into the bargain. She saw the way Danny Boy was approached by everyone, watched as Michael batted off the lesser of their minions and allowed access to only those he deemed worthy enough of Danny's time and energy. And even they were treated with a quiet disdain: men who had made their reputations while Danny Boy was still no more than a drunken twinkle in his father's eye now vied with each other for his attention, for a few brief words with him, the chance to publicly be seen with him, to be accepted by him as one of his own. Such was Danny Boy Cadogan's power over them. She hated him. She hated the power he wielded, even as *she* craved his interest in her and in her life. She loathed him for making her feel like this.

If keeping Arnold Landers on board was what would guarantee her brother's respect then that is what she would have to do. Her father's death had left them out on a limb in one way or another; they were all dependent on Danny Boy, they had been for years. Now he had buried the last link to his past, to his family's humiliation, and it had given him the strength he needed to finally show his hand. He was acting like the main man, was looking around him with glee. He was finally where he wanted to be and no one could, or would take it away from him. Danny Boy was pleased at Landers being part of this venture; he had the means at his disposal to sew up the south London connection. He was a real Brixton boy, and he was more than willing to distribute *and* contribute to his community. For a reasonable stipend, of course.

Annie smiled gently at Arnold Landers and he smiled back; he knew that he was on the road to untold riches, thanks to a little bird with a big family and even bigger tits.

Arnold knew a serious money-box when he encountered one, and Danny Boy Cadogan was his passport to riches beyond his wildest dreams. He was also trumping said money-box's sister, so it was double bubble as far as he was concerned. He wasn't a mug, he knew this the only chance he would ever get of playing with the really big boys. It was the only in he was going to get and he was going to take advantage of it, snatch the fucker's hand off. He wanted the best that life could offer, and he was standing here, in broad daylight, with Danny Boy Cadogan, being introduced to people he had only previously heard of and, in extreme cases, glimpsed from a distance.

This might be the eighties, and the government might pretend this was an equal society, but everyone on the streets knew that was a crock of shit. Even the drugs trade was controlled by a few choice people, and they were predominantly white. Arnold saw this as his chance to even the score. Bring it home. Make his mark and, along the way, settle a few scores of his own. So he nodded, he smiled, and he acted as if he was thrilled to be there which, of course, he was.

The wake was in full swing and the Irish songs were threatening to drown out the conversation. The Shandon Club in Ilford had not seen the like for many a year; it was packed to the rafters and the drinks were free and copious. Jonjo watched his family partake of the alcoholic beverages with a gusto that amazed even him. His father was well and truly planted and he felt nothing, not even a smidgeon of regret. Slipping into the toilets he entered the cubicle and locked the door behind him then, sitting down, he removed his equipment from his suit pocket. He kept it in an old bicycle repair kit tin that he opened with a flourish. He took out a needle, a syringe, and a quantity of heroin. It was just a today thing, he needed something to take the edge off; at least that's what he told himself, anyway. He was quite happy to use his father's death as an excuse to get out of his brains, even though the day meant nothing to him. His father had ceased to mean anything to him a long time ago; it was Danny Boy he was worried about these days. As he burned the brown on a small spoon he felt the excitement begin to build up inside him. Pulling the liquid into the syringe he held his breath, contemplating the shit-coloured liquid that would be his passport to oblivion and a few moments' respite, respite from the life he hated so much that just living in it for a few hours was too much for him to bear. Tying a length of leather around his forearm, he tightened it with his teeth, teeth that were now going green, were crumbling inside his mouth from the constant gritting, and that made eating anything even remotely crunchy impossible.

Jonjo finally slipped the needle under his skin and forced the heroin into his body; he watched closely as he washed it back into the syringe, enjoyed seeing his own blood, red and thick, filling the vial and then, holding his breath again, pushed it all back once more, into his bloodstream and his brain. The rush was quicker than usual, and his euphoria was short-lived. But, after a few minutes, he felt able to function once more; he had allowed himself enough to get high, not enough to get wasted. There was a difference. As he sat there and felt the calmness envelop him, he sighed loudly. Uncaring, for a few minutes, who might be nearby, who might realise what he was doing, he was nodding, was relishing the feeling that was overwhelming him; was finally without thought or care for anyone else in the world around him. The brown had taken over, he was at one with the universe.

Within minutes he had forgotten that he was at his father's funeral, all he heard was the music and the deafening sounds of glasses being picked up and emptied by people he didn't care about. The world was suddenly a reality of his own making and he felt the force of this reality with a vengeance. As Jonjo walked carefully out of the men's room he heard the familiar words of Danny Boy, and they were far more poignant than they should have been. Especially as the real live Danny Boy had been looking for him for the last ten minutes . . .

Ange sat with her daughter-in-law and her daughter and felt the heartbreak that her family had forced on her. Big Danny dying like he had was bad enough, but to see his funeral used as a platform for her elder son to further his career was not something she cared to dwell on. Her daughter was a whore in the making, but she was also as terrified of Danny as his own wife seemed to be. Ange knew her son was a bully, she also knew that she had never bothered with any of her kids really, not like she had her first-born. She had played at being the mother she felt was expected of her, what other people thought of her parenting skills had been important to her, as it had most of her generation. But, if she was honest, the only child to ever really get any of her attention and love was her Danny Boy. The others had never really stood a chance.

Now, Danny Boy was standing there, a violent and vicious man, and she was the cause of his transformation from a kind, nice boy to the man he had become; devoid of any kind of empathy or care for anyone around him, herself included. She loved the approbation and the respect she garnered because she had birthed him, loved the way people who had once treated her with contempt now went out of their way to acknowledge her, give her the time of day, whether they wanted to or not. Until today, as much as her son's

318

influence had made her life easier, he had still known that her real allegiance was with his father, the man he saw as ruining all their lives. Now Big Dan was dead by his own hand, and she felt the guilt in every breath she took, and with every beat of her heart. Her mother had always told her that no woman could have their cake and eat it too, and that was a truth she had ignored to her peril. Her son provided the cake and they had eaten it, her husband included. Now it was time to pay for her folly, and pay for it she would. She knew that better than anybody.

Ange felt the atmosphere around her acutely and knew that her son had seen this day as a triumph, had seen it as a means to an end. She also knew that the fight had left her, she was bowed down under the weight of what the man she had loved so much had left behind him. He had died as he had lived, without a care for her or any of his children, and that knowledge hurt.

The room was crowded with the elite of their world, and her son was the main attraction, even she knew that there was no going back after today. It was as if this was the end of her life as she knew it, but it was also the beginning of the life her son would now force her to live. Her son, her golden boy, scared her out of her wits. She realised that his father's death meant nothing more than as a social event, was just a reason for him and his business partners to meet, drink and talk among themselves. But she had lost the love of her life and, no matter what anyone said about him, he had been her husband. Someone there should have the decency to point that much out to this son of hers. He acted as if she was the enemy, even though he was giving her husband the funeral that most women dreamed of. No one attending could even pretend that this was all for his father's benefit, or indeed hers, for that matter; the attitude seemed to be that this event was more a mockery of his father's life than a celebration of it.

The Irish songs were all part and parcel of the occasion, the drink was copious and of industrial strength, but the underlying sentiment was not one of sorrow at her husband's death, it was more like a festival in honour of her elder son's achievements. And Ange's heart was heavy because, no matter what he had done, he was still her boy, and she would have to stand beside him and fight for him with the last breath inside her body, if needs be. That was expected of her, and that was all she could do to guarantee at least some kind of say in her other two children's futures.

Frank Cotton was walking towards him and Danny Boy plastered a smile onto his face. Frank moved with the grace of a man who knew he had a niche in the world, a man who had the confidence of his reputation to keep him safe, keep his head held high. Danny Boy shook his hand firmly, felt the coolness of the man's skin, the smoothness of his hand; it was the touch of someone who had never known a day's real collar in their life. Danny was catapulted back to his youth, to afternoons spent lifting scrap from one place to another, to the throbbing ache of his muscles screaming with pain in the bitterness of the winter cold. And his dislike of Frank Cotton came once more to the forefront of his psyche. He looked smug to him, far too sure of himself, he felt as if Frank was laughing at him, that he saw him as an object of ridicule, as someone he could mug off in public, mug off at his *own* father's funeral.

Michael was watching the pair of them warily and he saw the change in Danny Boy's countenance; it was, as always, a lightning change, and he closed his eyes for a few moments in distress before he stepped in and swiftly took over the conversation. It was done well, with the minimum of fuss and, to the untrained eye, it would have looked natural, normal. It was anything but.

He knew that Frank Cotton himself was aware of his intervention and he admired the way he acted as if nothing was amiss. Michael appreciated that, warmed to him for making his life so much easier. In fact, he wished for a few moments that he was in league with him; he knew life would be much easier if that was the case. He also knew Cotton would be aware when he had been blanked, and he had just been royally blanked by Danny Boy Cadogan; that much would be evident to anyone with even a microbe of nous about them within a five-mile radius.

As Michael watched his sister neck another large drink, at the same time as watching his friend of a lifetime intentionally turn his back on Frank Cotton, he wished he could disappear, just evaporate into the atmosphere once and for all. But he couldn't, and what he had to do now was ensure that this public and deliberate insult didn't encroach on their business dealings in any way. Danny was striding away from them all quickly, with the stiff shoulders and hard face of a man who saw himself as deeply wronged. He was acting the part as always, setting up his next move with his usual military precision. Sighing heavily, he followed him outside, hoping against hope that he could talk some sense into him.

Frank Cotton was angry, and that was not an emotion he had felt very often in his life. In fact, he prided himself on his calm exterior and his composure where people like Danny Boy were concerned. He saw them as beneath him, a necessary evil to be endured, but never encouraged in any kind of way. That he was at the mercy of this thug was bad enough, that said thug was determined to call him to account for supposed war crimes was blatantly obvious to anyone within farting distance. Cadogan had the monopoly on the street and he accepted that, even admired him for it. But he wasn't about to bow down before him like a complete mug. This was not the usual youthful arrogance, something he could shrug off as high spirits. This was a deliberate and calculated insult and he knew that he had no choice but to front Danny Boy up and retrieve what was left of his character before it was too late.

Danny Boy's father's death was one thing, but he had only attended this funeral under duress in the first place; for no other reason than a financial motive. A good enough reason in their world. He was here showing his respect, nothing more, and certainly nothing less. Now though, his limited patience had run out and he wanted a serious showdown, and he wanted it sooner rather than later. His friends also knew that this was not something they should or could interfere with. The occasion itself, Big Danny Cadogan's funeral, didn't have enough kudos to rule out any kind of definite tear-up. In fact, the general consensus was now that this was a funeral that was, in actual fact, *crying* out for a tear-up. Frankie Cotton was suddenly the odds-on favourite to make this sad occasion into a memorable incident. A lot of the people there would enjoy Danny Boy's fall from grace if Frankie Cotton actually managed to muller him. On the other hand, if Danny Boy was to get the upper hand instead, then none of those observing would be any the worse off. So, for the majority of the onlookers, this was a win-win situation and although most wanted Frankie to win this bout, no one would admit that out loud until after the event and, of course, only then with the sure knowledge that Frankie Cotton had actually trounced the young pretender once and for all. A death certificate would suffice, after all, they had to earn a living.

Frankie walked from the club with a frown on his handsome face and murder in his heart. He knew this was make-or-break time, and he also knew he was a fool to have let it get this far in the first place. But it was too late to back away now, he had to teach this young pup a lesson and, truth be told, he was looking forward to it.

Outside, in the cold night air, he felt the rush of adrenaline that was the forerunner to a real fight, and he wanted a fight, wanted to teach this fucker a lesson he wouldn't forget in a hurry. He had tried to make some sort of working relationship with Danny Boy, but he knew now that it was never going to happen. Any kind of connection was out of the question, the boy wasn't intelligent enough to put aside his personal feelings. Everyone worked the streets with people they didn't like, often people whom they didn't even trust. But they built a mutual and beneficial relation-ship for the sake of the wages that had to be paid out to their workforce. It was sound economics, but the boy had no real understanding of the real world and that was his main problem. Well, he might have the roids and the monopoly on all the other drugs, but that didn't give him a fucking get-out-of-jail-free card. The boy needed a lesson, and he was going to get one, whether he liked it or not.

As Frank walked over to where Danny was standing, he was already tensing his body up for a fight. His heavy-set build was intimidating to anyone who knew who he was and what he had been capable of over the years. He could hear the quiet chattering of the audience that had now gathered outside the club, waiting patiently in the freezing night air for the fight to begin. Danny Boy smiled broadly as Frankie approached; it was a big, beaming smile, as if he was greeting a long-lost friend. Frankie's face was almost comical in its confusion. He saw Michael Miles shake his head slowly before stepping backwards into the shadows.

Frankie was nonplussed for a few moments; he knew he looked like the aggressor and he also knew that, if he had any sense, he would have come out on to this pavement with a weapon of some description in his hands. The boy was a big one, and he was handy, that much was known by everyone. In fairness, Danny Boy Cadogan could have a row. But then, so could he; in his day he had been this fucking muppet. Unlike Danny Boy though, he had always given respect where it was due. He supposed this was a generational thing, the new generation thought the older Faces were all ice creams. Mugs, fucking wombats. Well, he had just about taken all he could take.

As he opened his mouth to speak, he barely saw the glint of the claw hammer that was suddenly winging its way towards his face; the first blow took out his right eye and collapsed the socket itself, along with the main part of his cheekbone. Dropping to his knees he was thankfully unaware of the other thirty blows that followed in quick succession and that guaranteed his entrance into East London Cemetery.

Danny was still hammering Frank long after he was unconscious. He was too far gone to even remember that he was being watched by what now amounted to a jury of his peers, and he was far too involved with what he was doing to realise that no one was saying a word. The silence was deafening, and the animosity he had caused almost tangible.

Michael watched sadly as Danny Boy destroyed, once and for all, any goodwill they might have enjoyed. He had reduced his own father's funeral to a fatal tear-up, and that was something Michael knew he would never live down.

Frank's friends and colleagues watched with quiet intensity as he was practically obliterated in front of their eyes, and not one of them lifted a finger to help him. That didn't mean that they didn't care about what had happened to him though.

When Michael finally pulled Danny Boy away he saw, with a sinking heart, three of the most influential Faces in the Smoke motion to their minders to remove Frankie and take him to the nearest hospital. They looked at each other and Michael knew that Danny Boy was all but finished. Then he removed an envelope from his overcoat pocket and, waving it in front of everyone's faces, he said sadly, 'He asked for that. This is a statement he made to the Filth accusing me of all sorts.' He then pulled the statement from the envelope and ripped it up into little pieces before throwing it on to the filthy ground. Walking back into the club, Michael and Danny could hear the police sirens in the distance. They knew that others would follow suit.

In the toilet Michael watched as Danny Boy washed his face and hands fastidiously before combing his hair and straightening his clothes.

'Supposing someone decides to pick that paper up, Danny?'

Danny Boy smiled his crooked smile and said, innocently, 'So what if they do? *His* signature's on it, not me old man's, you don't think I'd fucking be stupid enough to do something like that do you?'

Michael didn't bother to answer him. Danny stared into his eyes through the grubby mirror above the wash basins and said happily, 'I told you I didn't like him, didn't I?'

Michael sighed heavily then and, taking all his courage into his hands, he whispered, 'You couldn't let it go, could you? You couldn't just try and get on with him. You had to cause fucking murders . . . You don't need me, Danny Boy. For a start, you don't listen to a fucking word I say, do you? Thanks to you we've just lost our biggest asset. You've not only accused him of being a grass but you've also compounded that lie with a false witness statement. You're out of fucking order, Danny Boy, you're out of the frigging loop.' He was shouting now, his anger had finally surfaced, and he was beyond caring any more about how Danny Boy would react to his criticism.

Danny Boy laughed, still watching himself in the mirror. He was acting for all the world as if this was a normal day, and they were having a normal conversation. It was almost surreal. 'Shut up, you tart! I have spent ages laying the groundwork for today's little fracas, and you better back me up on it, boy. There is no way in this world that cunt was seeing another birthday, at least not while I

324

have a fucking breath in my body to prevent that happening. And you had better remember that I don't suffer fucking fools or cunts gladly, Micky boy, ask your fucking sister. Now, calm yourself down and let's get back to me dad's funeral, shall we?'

'Don't talk about Mary like that, Danny . . .'

Danny grinned the handsome grin that caused grown women to consider adultery and young girls to consider losing their virtue. He was like a devil in disguise.

'What are you going to do about it, Michael? I am carrying the fucking lot of you and you had better keep that in mind for the future; you'd better remember who pays your family's fucking bills and who you fucking owe loyalty to. I saw you slope away, you fucking snake, you slippery cunt. Well, after today, I am free of any restrictions and I am going to go all out to achieve my goals. So, stick that one up your pipe and smoke it, you fucking treacherous cunt.' He carried on combing his hair carefully, all the while singing a quiet rendition of 'Forty Shades of Green'.

Michael Miles understood then that Danny Boy had finally burned his boats, and, unfortunately, he also understood that Danny Boy had burned *his* boats as well. He had always known that without Danny Boy Cadogan he was nothing; now it seemed that, even with him, he was actually even less.

Book Three

Charity and beating begins at home.

– John Fletcher, 1579–1625
Wit Without Money

Chapter Twenty-One

'Jonjo, would you ever get up out of that fucking bed? Danny Boy will be here soon.' Ange's voice was almost at crescendo level and her panic was finally communicating itself to her younger son.

Jonjo was rocking, still half-stoned from the night before, and also feeling the complete and utter fatigue that heroin seemed to wrap him in. It was a deep tiredness, it made his bones feel almost fluid, and he had begun to enjoy the luxurious sensation. The only thing that could normally tempt him away from this, tempt him out of his bed, was when he had to score again. Once the brown was gone, used up, he seemed to get a new lease of life; he was up, dressed, and round the dealer's in a matter of minutes. Once he had purchased his drug of choice and returned home, the energy left him once more and he hated the intrusion the real world insisted on forcing on him again. Danny Boy was always ranting about it; that junkies were just lazy fucks who used the smack as an excuse not to join the real world. Danny argued that they were quick enough to score, so why was it that they were not as quick to earn a crust; they would rather mug an old lady for her pension or live off the green, a giro, and anyone who saw that as a viable alternative to a wage was classed as scum in his mind. No one in their right mind signed on the dole; why would you let anyone know where you lived? Skank off the government? Off people who were mug enough to pay taxes? The dole was for old people and hospitals, not for the able-bodied. It was a joke; there was a realm of opportunities out there without succumbing to government hand-outs. Danny wouldn't even let his workforce sign on. He felt it brought too much attention to them and Danny Boy also knew that they were more liable to be grassed or watched if they were claiming the green. Also, he saw the pittance offered as a piss-take, and only worthy of people who were unlucky enough to be straight. In their game the dole amounted to beer money, fag money; it wasn't worth the ag. In fact, it brought unwanted attention, as did a wife on the social security. Danny Boy saw anyone who signed on as a scrounger; he saw them as taking the bread from pensioners' mouths. If more people signed off, the more money for old people and kids in hospital. For the real one-parent families and the people with disabled children.

Danny Boy Cadogan had strong views on people he saw as scroungers and his younger brother knew that better than anyone. Danny provided for his mother; she had no chance of living meal-to-meal any more, or dreaming of winning the pools. She was set like the proverbial jelly. If Danny knew he was claiming the Jam Role there would be murders but, like all junkies, he saw any money as drug money, no matter how small that amount might be. So he signed on and claimed benefits on the snide. He was terrible with money and he knew that. He was also shitting it in case Danny Boy found out what he was doing. He was getting a good wedge from him but, like everything else, it disappeared before he knew where he was. In fact, he was weighing out so much on drugs that he actually owed money all over the Smoke. The brown was bad enough, but he also had to buy the jellies, the Librium capsules that he combined with the heroin to mellow him out. They relaxed him, helped stave off the shakes and the trembling that seemed to be with him constantly these days. He also spent fortunes on amphetamine sulphate, which he needed to wake him up and give him the boost he required to get out of the house when Danny Boy demanded to see him. He wondered if Danny knew about his habit, and decided once more that he didn't. If Danny Boy knew he was on the brown he would go ballistic. Jonjo also knew that no one was going to inform his brother either; no one would want to be held responsible for serving him up. He had already scratched a couple of local bully boys and they were not exactly champing at the bit to reclaim the debt. He knew he had a result because no one was about to threaten him or chase him for a debt that they knew was socially unacceptable in his circles.

In fact, Jonjo knew they only let him have it on credit because he was Danny Boy's brother, and he was quite happy to use that to achieve his ends. He also knew that he was fast running out of people he could scratch up. He would be forced to go to the Turks soon, and they were mad bastards who were capable of ignoring his family connection and breaking his legs anyway. He was getting agitated once more and, like all junkies, he had the annoying habit of constantly checking his stash, as if, without his regular monitoring, it would dissolve into thin air. He was feeling under the mattress as a matter of habit as his mother's voice was once more hammering through his bedroom door and, jumping from the bed, he screamed out on to the landing, 'All right! I heard you the tenth time for fuck's sake, you silly old bitch!'

As he walked back into the bedroom he heard his sister running up the stairs and he braced himself for the onslaught he knew was coming. She was getting on his nerves lately; she was determined to be Danny Boy's blue-eyed girl, and he had a sneaky feeling she was going to achieve her goal. She had sussed out his little habit many moons ago, but he was confident she would keep it under her hat. He had enough on her to blow her out of the water and, as luck would have it, she knew that as well as he did.

Annie might have the love of her big black man, but she also had the love of a big white one as well. In fact, since the old man's demise, she had the love of anyone who was kind enough to buy her a vodka and blackcurrant or, in extreme circumstances, and times of crisis, a lemonade. She was a fucking slag-bag and, as she stormed into his bedroom he yelled, 'Fuck off and leave me alone, Annie.'

She was so angry, her breathing was loud and heavy. She could smell the sweetness of his sweat; it was heavy in the room and it had the heavy addict's tang to it that caught in the throat of the unsuspecting. She kept her eyes on her brother, saw the emaciated body that was normally hidden by his baggy clothes and said nastily, 'You'd better shut your fucking trap, if Danny Boy knew what you got up to he'd annihilate you, and he's just pulling up outside . . .'

Jonjo was white-faced in seconds, and she laughed loudly as he started to get dressed quickly. Everything was forgotten now as the panic set in.

'Joke!'

Annie was laughing her head off at the terror she had caused, and he closed his eyes for a few moments before allowing his body to relax once more, then he chased his sister down the stairs to get his revenge. He saw his mother standing in the kitchen, and he stopped in the doorway to look at her. She looked so small, so dejected, her grey hair thinner than ever, and her eyes were sunken; she looked old, old and frail and the image scared him. He walked in and, opening his arms, he pulled her into them. Instead, she pushed him away roughly, saying, 'I know what you're doing and I'm ashamed of you. My son a fucking junkie. Well, if you don't stop what you're doing then I'll tell Danny Boy meself, and he'll kill you.'

He dropped his arms listlessly and, shaking his head, he said loudly, 'Oh, Mum, don't make me laugh, does it really matter what kills me?'

Annie was saddened by his words and, putting her arm around his shoulders, she forgot their usual antagonism as she snapped at their mother, 'Leave him alone, we all need something where that mad bastard is concerned.'

'Whatever he might be, at least he ain't on fucking drugs.'

Annie shook her head slowly, her beautiful heart-shaped face was screwed up in consternation at her mother's words, at her righteousness. 'I wouldn't be too sure about that, Mum, he's had his moments. But then, you would score them for him if he asked you to, wouldn't you? Well, he's worse than drugs, he's worse than war, he is a one-man fucking demolition unit. He is human cancer. He destroys everyone around him, and that includes me dad, your husband. So, bear that in mind when you're vilifying us, eh, you two-faced old cow.'

Ange was already pulling herself up to her full height which, compared to her children, was not much. And she looked her daughter over slowly, as if her eyes were disgusted by the sight she saw. 'One of these days, you miserable whore, you will get your comeuppance, and that big mouth of yours will be shut up once and for all.'

Annie pulled her brother from the kitchen, shouting over her shoulder loudly, 'Oh *piss off*, you old bag, *you* can't hurt us, no one can any more. We're immune to it now. You made sure of that when you let your blue-eyed boy take the fucking whole house over, when you let him torture me dad, and ruin all our lives. I hope you're pleased with yourself, hope you're proud of your family. A junkie and a whore, oh, and a murderer, we don't want to leave anyone out, do we?'

Ange was fuming at the girl's words, at the truth of them. She was trying her best to keep this family together, to keep them on a even keel. Why didn't this pair understand that she had no say over Danny Boy, not any more. She was only trying to look out for them, stop Danny Boy from finding fault, from taking his annoyance out on them. Why did these two always see her as the bad person? She was only looking out for them, she was only trying to help. Why were they so angry with her; she had tried her whole life to make things easier for them, to protect them. They were the ones who caused all the grief, they knew what Danny Boy was like; they knew how he viewed the world. They knew she couldn't control him. All she wanted was to see them safe and secure. All she wanted was to see them settled, see them happy. But even as she told all these things to herself, she knew that what she wished for was an impossibility, Danny Boy would see to that. Danny Boy saw to everything.

'Oh, Michael, stop being a fucking tart.'

Danny was striding around the office of the casino, his huge body encased in an expensive suit and his immaculate hair shining in the morning sunshine. Detective Inspector David Grey was watching him closely, and he was not impressed with the way he had taken the news he just imparted. Namely, that he was in the frame for the murder of Frank Cotton, among others. That he and his colleagues were having to use all their contacts and trust funds to keep a lid on this man's fucking activities.

'Excuse me, Danny Boy, but you are on the road to ruin. You can't go around killing people and expecting to get away with it. You've got to sort this out, and you've got to sort it sooner rather than later.'

Danny Boy looked at the man as if seeing him for the first time. He took in the thinning hair, the shiny fabric of his off-the-peg suit, and the ragged nails that made him look like a door-to-door salesman. He was beneath his notice in the real world, in his world. That this muppet felt he actually possessed enough power to question him and his actions was unbelievable. In fact, Danny Boy was now wondering what the fuck he was even doing letting this piece of Filth into his place of work in the first place.

Recognising the signs, Michael tried to calm the situation down. He was terrified that the next person to go on the missing list would be an Old Bill. A bent Old Bill admittedly, but a Filth all the same. If Danny lost it with this prick, and he was a prick, his words and his attitude proved that much, they would then be in a position that all the money in the world couldn't buy them out of.

'Hey, come on, Dave, let's get this in perspective . . .'

Grey stood up; he was a big man, and he had a big personality. That was how he had ended up on the take in the first place. Gambling and women were his forte. He liked to be on the fringes of the criminal underworld; he got the best seats at the boxing and he got the money he required to live a little when the fancy took him. He was in possession of a nice big semi, a luxury car, and was in the process of buying a place on the Costa. But even he knew that Danny Boy could never be immune to having his collar felt unless he lowered his profile a bit.

'You can't go around fucking attacking people at will, no one has that kind of power any more. And I can't fucking guarantee you won't be nicked if someone ever puts your boat-race in the frame. I can only do *so* much, you have to keep your temper in check and do any fucking future sorting out in the privacy and comfort of your own home, or warehouse, or fucking concrete bunker. Anywhere, in fact, where no one can see or hear you. Do you get my drift?'

Danny Boy stared at the man for long moments and Michael knew that this was either going to be the worst day of his life, or the last day of Grey's life. He knew Danny Boy better than anybody; he had always suspected that his brain was wired differently to the rest of the world's. He had no real care for anyone or anything, he did what he felt was expected of him, what he felt the world around him would expect him to do.

Danny Boy saw himself as a maverick, as a thinker, an intellectual. He believed his views on everything were the only views worth pursuing. He was a fucking nut-bag and David Grey should know that better than anyone. He was paid to clear up their shit, to neutralise Danny Boy's temper tantrums and sanitise him for the local judiciary; most of whom were in his debt in one way or another. He knew that Danny Boy was not someone you could talk down to, or reason with in any way. His behaviour was not up for discussion at any time. Danny Boy expected people to do as they were told, jump when he demanded them to; especially when he was the one paying their wages.

David Grey was like most bent Filth, he thought he had the edge in the relationship he earned the majority of his poke from when, in reality, the moment he took a bung, he was relegated to lower than the shit on their shoes. A fair cop was one thing, no one really minded that; it wasn't an ideal situation, but it was understandable. A bent Filth, on the other hand, especially one expressing an opinion that he had not been paid for, was something else entirely. It was tantamount to a mutiny, he was paid to ensure this didn't happen, not lecture them on the laws of the land. Grey didn't have the brains he was born with if he thought he could get away with this.

Danny Boy was already pouring himself a large drink; even at this early hour alcohol didn't seem to affect him like it did other people. He could drink a bottle of brandy and still drive his car, talk sense, and negotiate a deal with stunning precision. It was another one of his foibles, that, and the coke and amphetamines he snorted with impunity. Throwing the drink back in two gulps he turned to where Grey was sitting and threw the heavy cut-glass tumbler at him with all the force he could manage. It smashed into the side of the man's head, and the force knocked him to the ground. As he lay there stunned, the blood seeping from a large gash behind his right ear, Danny loomed over him and said quietly, as if talking to a small child. 'What part of "I *own* you" don't you understand?'

Michael was on his feet, and waiting to see what Danny Boy was going to do next. Grey was lying there, curled up in the foetal position, his arms covering his head, expecting another assault at any moment. He was realising for the first time ever exactly what he was actually dealing with. He was getting a taste of the Danny treatment and he was now fully aware of what his role was in the drama that was young Cadogan's life. He was no more than a foot soldier, a means to an end. His dreams of using Danny Boy until he had achieved his financial goals receded into the sunset, along with any thoughts he might have had about leaving this operation of his own free will. He was, he knew without a second's doubt, finished. Even if he was lucky enough to leave this room alive, which was debatable, his life as he knew it was over.

Mary felt sick, but it wasn't the morning sickness she craved, it was the sourness of her hangover that was causing it. She stood up unsteadily and crept towards the coffee percolator. As she poured out a cup of the thick strong brew she inhaled the aroma and swallowed down the sickness once more. The kitchen was filled with bright autumn sunshine and, spooning sugar in her cup, she went back to the huge scrubbed, wood table and gingerly sat back down. In the three months since her father-in-law's funeral her life had escalated out of control. She daydreamed about her husband's death. It was with her constantly. As she washed up, made beds, or watched TV, the thoughts were always there.

Mary's favourite daydream, usually after her first drink of the day, was of getting a knock on the door in the middle of the night; it was the police, telling her that her husband had been shot through the heart and brain repeatedly. She liked to know from the off in these fantasies that there was no way her old man could survive, even in her dreams she wasn't wholly confident he wouldn't come back to life just to spite her. Her pretend sorrow, and her inner jubilation were there in abundance. These thoughts kept her going, stopped her from going over the edge completely.

As she poured a shot of vodka into the coffee she felt the tension seeping out of her body, and the vision of her husband's body lying in the mortuary was once more foremost in her mind. His face was gone, his lovely teeth, and the sensuous mouth that hid the cruelty behind his smile was shattered and broken. She sighed with contentment at the picture in her mind's eye, enjoyed the momentary feeling of freedom these thoughts brought her.

She was feeling nauseous once more and, swallowing the bile down, she rubbed at her throat. Her long, slender fingers were heavy with jewelled rings that befitted the wife of Danny Boy Cadogan and her nails were painted a pretty pink, manicured into perfect ovals. Her slim wrist was adored with a diamond-encrusted watch, and around her long slender throat was a heavy gold crucifix which she played with unconsciously. With her heavy hair falling around her shoulders and her porcelain skin Mary looked, for all the world, like a woman without a care in the world.

All her life her mother had urged her to get by on her looks, to get herself a Face, someone who could provide for her. Once you landed him, and produced a couple of ankle-biters, you would be settled for life. Money, a nice drum, and the respect that went with any name. Mary had managed the first one; she had married a Face, a fucking serious Face who was classed as the most dangerous man in the country. She had not, however, managed the second part of the plan. The children were either frightened out of her by her husband or beaten from her by him. Don't end up like me, girl, had been her mother's mantra and she too had been determined that her mother's drunken lifestyle would never be hers. Well, she raised her coffee cup to her mother in a silent toast, 'I am you, Mum, I'm you with money.'

Her laughter rang out loudly in the empty house and she bent over as if in physical pain, and eventually cried like a baby for the woman who had destroyed her daughter's life before it had even really begun.

*

Michael and Danny were still arguing about how best to take care of Grey as they pulled up outside a small council house on the Caledonian road. It was a fine day. Bright but cold, both wore heavy overcoats and leather gloves. Their breath was hanging on the air and Danny Boy was laughing quietly. As they pulled up in their BMW they were greeted by everyone who was going about their daily business. Danny Boy, for all his reputation as a bad bastard, was also seen by the majority as a fair man, as a generous man.

'Grey is lucky I didn't fucking rip his nuts off and shove them down his fucking treacherous, deceitful throat. You can't let Filth get a foot in the door, Michael, especially bent Filth. He will get a serious fucking clump off me at some time in the future, but at the moment he sees you as his saviour. So naturally he'll come to *you* in the future. Well, use him up and wear him out, as the song goes. Now, shut the fuck up and let me sort this lot out, eh?'

As they approached the front door it was opened by a tiny woman with a walking stick and a large smile. The obvious affection she felt for Danny Boy was in her eyes and, as he hugged her tightly on her tiny door step, she was chattering away, her voice harsh and husky from a lifetime of cigarettes and hardship.

'Come in, my darling, I've got a bit of grub on. I know what you two are like for feeding your bleeding faces.'

Inside the house the warmth was overwhelming. It was a cloying heat from the new central heating system Danny Boy had installed for her a few weeks earlier. The tiny house was spotless, the decorating new but very dated, and the smell of bacon and eggs drew them both into the kitchen. They left their coats on the sofa in the front room and, rubbing his hands together, Danny Boy said childishly, 'Don't let on to me mother how much I love your scran, she'd brain me.'

Nancy Wilson was almost on the point of exploding with pride at his words, as he knew she would be. Her son, Marcus, was eighteen months into a twelve-year stretch in Parkhurst and he was sitting it out without a murmur. He was a good bloke, a decent bloke and Danny repaid that by making sure all was well with his kith and his kin. His mother had never had it so good and she knew it.

Marcus had a son, Joseph, who was nearly eighteen now, and his wife, Joseph's mother, a beautiful girl from a good family, had died of cancer when the boy was nine. Nancy had brought him up while her only son had earned a bit of wedge. He had been caught on the rob and Danny Boy had been behind his endeavours. Consequently, he was now Danny Boy's responsibility, as was his immediate family. Hence his regular visits to this house. Danny Boy always made a point of showing his face at times like this; he knew it was noted, commented on, and added to his prestige. The personal touch was his calling card, it gave him kudos and respect, especially from the older generation. He also felt obliged, he knew that Wilson could have sold him up the river and done a deal, these hefty sentences the courts were handing out didn't augur well where loyalty was concerned. He had a twelve, that meant do two thirds and get out for good behaviour; which put him away for at least eight of those years. Danny Boy actually felt a deep gratitude for that kind of loyalty.

'You're looking good, Mrs Wilson, as always. How's things?'

Nancy placed two mugs of tea on the table and went back to her stove before replying happily, 'I'm all right, son. Marcus sends his best and wanted me to thank you once more for all your help—'

Michael cut her off mid-sentence, as was expected of him, 'You tell Marcus we think he is a blinder, Danny Boy was just saying how much we all miss him.'

Nancy Wilson was made-up with those few words, as he knew she would be. Never in her life had she been treated with such respect, had so many people looking out for her and asking after her. She went to Crisp Street market and everybody made a fuss of her; she knew it was because of these two men sitting in her kitchen.

She loved them for it, and her devotion to them, especially to Danny Boy, was guaranteed. Her son heard how well she was taken care of and it took a load off his mind. He was also in possession of a single cell because of his contacts, and he had the added bonus of a good few quid when he came home, and the knowledge that he was safer than a chief fucking fireman at a bonfire party. In reality, he had never had it so good either.

As the two men tucked into their bacon and eggs, Nancy replenished their mugs of tea and buttered thick wedges of toast, happy that she had company, and such prestigious company at that. She even had an account at the local cab rank, paid for, of course, by these two men in her kitchen. She didn't have to do the usual bus trip to visit *her* son, go up the social security and beg them for the fares needed. Didn't have to sit for hours, waiting to give some young girl her train or bus tickets and get treated like shit as she waited for them to be reimbursed. She went by taxi, and the driver stopped for lunch and kept her company on the ferry ride over to the Isle of Wight. She was also put to the head of the line, no queuing up for her, and no one minded that either. It was heady stuff to a woman who had been trodden on all her life. She told her son how well she was treated and she knew it put his mind at rest.

'How's young Joseph doing?'

It was the question Nancy had been waiting for and she pulled up a chair before answering.

Her old wrinkled face was a picture of tragedy as she answered, 'Danny Boy, I'm almost demented with worry about him.'

Danny Cadogan placed his knife and fork neatly on his plate as he gave her his full attention. 'Why? What's he been up to then?'

He was all concern as he gave her the full force of his personality.

Nancy Wilson lit a Benson & Hedges cigarette before answering him, she knew the power of a dramatic pause; she had learned that from her husband. He should have been on the stage, him. Useless ponce he was.

'He's on the half a crown, ain't he? I thought you knew . . .'

Danny and Michael were both stunned for a few seconds. 'Fuck off! Not young Joe, what on earth would make him go on the brown? He's not stupid, he's on the ball.'

Nancy took a deep breath before saying sadly, 'Jonjo, Danny Boy, he got him on it, I thought you knew. That's why I wanted to mention it to you today. Jonjo is always round here on the want. Pair of wasters the two of them but, Danny Boy, your brother is the ringleader here, him being older and all, and that's not me being an overprotective grandmother. I had a word last week about them stashing it in my house. In my fucking *home*. I found it in the bottom of Joe's wardrobe when I was cleaning. You've got to talk to them. I don't want Lily Law round here with a warrant, and I don't want my only grandchild to be found brown bread either. I ain't mentioned it to his dad because I didn't want to worry him. Banged up in there, well, you know the score yourself. Least said, soonest mended when you're going through a big lump. After all, why worry him, it ain't like he can do anything about it, is it?'

Danny was astounded at her words and, for a few moments, he digested the information, unsure for a few seconds if he was actually hearing her right. Then he picked up his knife and fork and resumed eating.

'I'm sorry, Danny Boy, but I had to tell you, son. I'm at me wits' end, and the way he talks to me! Fuck off this, and fuck you that, and that Jonjo is as bad. I mentioned it to your mother at bingo the other week and, do you know, she cuts me dead now. Not a sodding word from her. I was only trying to warn her, you know. A word to the wise and all that.'

Danny Boy grinned at her as if he was totally calm and collected, but Michael could see the way his knuckles had whitened and how his eyes were now filled with malice.

'Don't you give it another thought, Mrs Wilson, I'll have a word, get it sorted. Now, have you got any of your famous bread pudding on the go?'

Nancy smiled happily. She was convinced her problems were finally over, now that Danny Boy was taking control of them. She had every faith that he would have them sorted in no time; he owed them and she knew that and, more to the point, Danny Boy knew that.

''Course I have, I makes it special for you two, don't I.'

Michael had suddenly lost his appetite. Carole was right, he was living on his nerves, and his nerves were tighter than a virgin's arse and getting tighter by the day. He was living a life fraught with the dangers of Danny Boy's precarious personality, and the worst of it all was, he actually cared for the man. Much more than Danny Boy Cadogan actually warranted.

*

Jonjo was aggravated, and it showed. He was still waiting to be picked up and taken to his designated place of work. It was made all the more annoying by the fact that he knew this so-called work could have been done by anyone with the brain capacity of a retarded hedgehog. In fact, that would make them over-qualified in many respects, at least a hedgehog would have had the sense to keep out of the fucking freezing cold. With his habit, the approaching winter was not a welcome addition to his life. In fact, he was living a lie of Olympian standards. It was a lie so big, he was already trying to think up excuses for living it in the first place. Danny Boy treated him like the muppet he knew he was. That still hurt though because, like his older brother, he was afflicted with an overabundance of pride. Unlike his older brother, however, he didn't let that stand in his way if a few quid could be earned with the least amount of collar. That he was a ponce in every sense of the word was a given, that deep inside he resented his idleness, was something he had to come to terms with. But the lure of the brown was so seductive, the annihilation of anything even resembling normality was too good an opportunity to pass up. He liked this life, at least he accepted it, which was a different thing altogether.

He was his father's son, and that was not something he would ever admit out loud; that Danny Boy was watching over him was not something he dwelled on either. He hated being such a fucking crawler and he hated that everyone around him knew the truth of that. He hated that he was spoken to for no other reason than his last name was Cadogan, and that Danny Boy saw fit to see that he had some kind of employment. That he was a glorified gofer was not something he dwelled on. He did what was requested, and then forgot about it. He knew that was exactly why he was not asked to do anything of importance, was not treated as a vital and important part of the Cadogan empire. He hated that, even while he was secretly pleased about it. If Danny Boy gave him responsibility he couldn't fuck off and leave it to whoever had been assigned to watch over him on that particular day.

When he finally heard Danny Boy's key in the door he was truly pleased to finally know what he was likely to be doing that day.

Danny filled the doorway, his huge body was, as always, its

usual, intimidating self. 'Sorry, mate, I had a few things to do. You all right?'

He pushed past his little brother abruptly and, going to his mother, he kissed her gently on the cheek before saying sadly, 'Me dad's stone arrived from Italy yesterday. I want you to go with Michael and make sure you're happy with it, all right. I think it's the nuts but, at the end of the day, I might be weighing out for it but you know what you want it to say.'

Ange was over the moon at his words, as he knew she would be. He knew her big fear had been that the grave would be left unmarked. He was sorry she didn't know her elder son well enough to know he would never let that happen.

'It's black Italian marble, Mum, cost the national debt and, without trying to make you feel bad, there's room enough for your details when the time comes. I hope you're pleased with it.'

Ange was already pulling on her coat, and Danny Boy helped her into it with a gentleness that belied the colossal anger he was holding inside himself.

As she left the house a short while later, he shut the front door behind her gently. Then, turning to his younger brother he stared at him for long moments before saying jovially, 'You *useless* little cunt. I *want* your kit, I *want* your brown and I *want* your fucking arse, in that order.'

Annie heard the commotion, but was sensible enough to turn up the radio in her bedroom; there was no way she was going to interfere in this latest of dramas. Not even when she heard Jonjo's voice begging for mercy, and the muted thumps that accompanied his terrible pleading. Danny Boy was doing what he saw fit to solve the problem of her brother's life and, for once, she was in total agreement with his actions and his deeds. Jonjo needed a short, sharp shock, and now he was getting one, courtesy of the man who, once word hit the streets that he knew of his brother's unfortunate habit, would then sanction Jonjo's retirement from the drug-addicted community. As much as Annie hated Danny Boy at times, she knew his reputation as a Face gave them all a lot of freedom in their community.

Chapter Twenty-Two

Carole looked beautiful. Even though she was not the usual size ten, the dress she had chosen for her wedding was spectacular. She knew she had Mary to thank for that. The dress emphasised her good points and hid what were jokily referred to as her child-bearing hips. And she wanted children, she wanted them desperately. Like Michael, she felt the need to procreate, to build a family network that consisted of her own flesh and blood. Carole looked over at Mary, she looked so lovely that Mary wondered why she wasn't jealous of her in any way, jealous of her good looks. Her voluptuous figure and tight, taut limbs.

Mary had helped arrange everything. As matron of honour Mary was far more beautiful than the bride, but Carole had consoled herself that as she was her husband's sister, that didn't matter. She was grateful for her friend's input, knowing that she would not have made the right choices if she had been left to her own devices. Carole was not like the usual Faces wives, women and girls schooled into the world they inhabited, and who were conversant with their husbands' nefarious interests. Like the men they craved, they were almost all amoral, and saw pound signs where other women saw love. They rated a man on his reputation and earning potential, a real Face was their ultimate dream. They were generally familiar with the prison system at a young age, and had no real qualms about a man who was vicious or vindictive. In their world those attributes guaranteed them a good earn. A middle-aged man with a pot belly and acne scars was actually seen as a catch if he had enough zeros in his accounts, the most unusual-looking men could become the object of jealousy and envy. These women went into their romantic relationships in the same way that their men went into business deals, with their eyes wide open and their main interest in what the alliance could bring to the table for them and, ultimately, their families.

Carole though, was genuinely in love with Michael Miles, as he was with her. She also knew that Danny Boy held her in high esteem, and she was thankful for that much. He was someone she was in awe of, but who she also actually liked. He was always kind and respectful towards her, and she had accepted that he had his own way of going about things.

As she stood outside the church she wondered if Michael's stag night might cause him to be late, but she knew she didn't have to worry about that too much. Michael would never do anything intentionally to hurt her. But when her husband-to-be's brother told her that he was already inside the church and waiting impatiently for her arrival, she relaxed immediately.

Annie grinned at her. She was a lovely looking girl, and Carole wondered at how someone blessed with so much beauty could allow herself to be used like she did. In fact, she didn't understand the girl, period. She slept with anyone and everyone, she suspected even Michael had been tempted by her. Annie used her body as a weapon and it was a very dangerous weapon at that. Her brother's lifestyle and obvious respect made her into an asset for a lot of them around here. Not that bedding her would be a hardship, of course. Her own rep, however, made her damaged goods no matter what her last name was. Annie was like an accident that had already happened and, instead of waiting around for the ambulance, she just got herself up, brushed herself down, and then waited for the next accident to arrive. She was a deeply unhappy girl and her self-destructive antics were like a lot of her contemporaries'. Women in their world were judged by their sexuality from an early age; schoolgirls were regularly checked out by men who could have fathered them. They were all desperate to be grown-up, to be seen as adult. A child was seen as an identity; they were not teenagers any more, they were *mothers*. A title they felt made them into adults overnight.

Carole had been brought up as a good Catholic girl and, unlike a lot of her friends, she had taken that role seriously. Not that she had been pursued like the others, she had not advertised her wares or dressed provocatively. If she had done, she wouldn't be marrying this kind man today.

Like Michael, Carole saw these women as they really were, and not as they wanted to be seen. That what people thought of them and the lives they were purported to live, meant more to them than their actual day-to-day living was incredible to Carole's way of thinking. She wouldn't change places with any of them for all the money in the world. Their lives were such shams, and that they knew that as well as she did, and yet did nothing to make their lives better irritated her. Even as she understood them. A Face was a catch; look at her with Michael; he was a Face. To the majority of the women here, she had won the fucking pools two weeks in a row.

But Carole felt a connection with him, especially since they had become an item. And people treated her with the utmost respect, something she had never experienced before, even the people who had seen her as beneath their radar before now went out of their way to claim a friendship, make a claim to any kind of tenuous link to her family that they could manage. It was laughable really, except the people concerned were so earnest that she didn't like to let them down. She was automatically nice back. It was her nature, she was a good person, and she knew it was beyond her to be nasty, or rude to anybody deliberately. Michael had told her to let it go over her head, a giraffe's fart, he called it. But she was not comfortable with it at all.

Still, after today she could choose who she continued to be friends with and who she didn't. Not that she would be horrible to anyone, of course, but her new status would afford her the luxury of not having to acknowledge anyone specifically unless she chose to. She could be a nice and friendly acquaintance to the women in her world, and then just concentrate on her new husband.

Carole had such a great reputation locally, everyone knew her as being kind, friendly, and the first person to offer any help if anything should occur within their community. Her marriage to

Michael, Danny Boy's right-hand man, had actually cemented her standing in the community, though she did not immediately realise that. She only hoped that her life with Michael would be everything she hoped it would be.

Mary was pregnant once more, and this time she seemed to believe she would hold onto the child full-term. Carole knew from Michael that Danny Boy had not been home for weeks, and this made her think that could be the reason Mary's pregnancy had not evaporated like all the others. Danny Boy was the picture of kindness to her and, as much as she liked him, and she did like him, she guessed he was not the best husband in the world. She also believed it wasn't any fault of Mary's. Danny Boy would have been the same, whoever he married.

Arnold Landers looked very handsome in his morning suit and Carole saw his sprightly gait as he walked over to them. He was a very handsome man, and she knew that Michael, like Danny Boy, rated him highly. He had the south London operations all sewn up, and that was not an easy task, by anyone's standards. She only hoped that Annie saw the good in him before it was too late. In fact, she hoped he was the man who would lead her young friend back onto the straight and narrow. Arnold was not the type of bloke who would swallow his girlfriend's antics without a fight. But then again, he had to find out about them first. Although, having said that, the way that Annie was carrying on, that could prove to be much sooner than anyone expected.

Carole steadied her breathing and as she heard the first strains of her chosen music, the theme tune to *Gone With the Wind*, she walked slowly down the aisle on her father's arm. Her head was held high, and her heart was open and waiting for her new husband to fill it with the love she knew he had in abundance.

Everywhere she looked, people were genuinely pleased for her, the wedding guests were all looking at her expectantly, as if her marriage would change everything about her new husband's life. He was Danny Boy's partner, although she knew that was a loose term for Michael's actual place in the firm. He was the real brains of the outfit, but she understood how people saw Danny Boy as the main man in the relationship, and she also understood why it suited

Michael for people to think that. He was the only person who could talk Danny Boy down.

It also meant that when Michael went in for the kill, no one would ever expect it. Though his wife-to-be wasn't aware of that fact yet.

Carole saw Danny Boy watching her intently as she walked down the aisle towards her new husband and she made a point of not making eye contact.

She was radiant, as brides were supposed to be, and she was also beautiful, really beautiful, for once in her life, and she felt it then and there for those few minutes, she knew how it felt to be Mary. All eyes drawn to you because of how you looked, and conscious of that.

Michael was waiting for her with a deep and abiding love that seemed to radiate from his open face. It caused many a tear to fall from the eyes of the women in the church, and many a snide comment from the males attending the occasion.

Ange cried, she saw Michael as the son she wished she had been lucky enough to have been blessed with. She now saw Danny Boy as the Devil who, she knew, would annihilate anyone on a whim. But she put aside her anger and fear because this was one wedding she knew she would enjoy.

The smoke was like a grey cloud in the bar of the hotel, the women and children were in the ballroom, the disco was loud, and the lighting was dark enough to make even the older women look mellowed out. The buffet was spectacular and plentiful; two young men in chefs' whites made sure it was replenished at regular inter-vals and everyone was more than impressed. After the five-course meal that afternoon, this was totally over the top. But it was, as everything in their world was, expected. This was a show of power as much as anything else, from the doves outside the church to the piper who had piped them into the Park Lane Hotel. It was class, as more than one person had remarked that day; this was all put down to Carole, of course. The latest Queen of the Underworld.

The men were laughing and joking, Michael had done his duty, danced the first dance, and, after cutting the six-tier cake, he had circled the room talking to everyone with his brand-new wife by his side. Now, he was relaxing with the boys, as was expected of him. As he sat by Danny Boy in the plush surroundings of the bar he marvelled at just how far they had come in the last ten years. They were the top of their game, and there was no one who could come even close to taking their crowns from them. The only way things could fuck up was if Danny Boy let his legendary temper get the better of him. Michael had already smoothed over too many acts of violence and he knew that Danny himself was more than aware of that fact. Danny Boy was not a fool, he knew no one was completely safe from harm, and he was trying to keep himself in check these days. His rep was enough to get what he wanted from people, he didn't have to prove anything to anyone. Even the Faces outside the Smoke kowtowed to him these days. He was the business, the main man, and he was living it large.

Danny was also banging a new little bird who, it seemed, might be on the way to taming him. She was a tiny little thing, with a neat figure and huge blue eyes. She was a civilian as well, she worked as a secretary in an office in the City, and he was besotted with her, despite his other bit of strange, who had also had his kid.

Michael thought she was as thick as two short planks, but she seemed amiable enough, had a pleasant way with her. And, what was classed as a bonus as far as he was concerned, she didn't want to be a part of this world. She was happy enough with a meal and a few good nights out.

As they chatted Michael saw a tall man with a balding head and large yellow teeth come into the bar; he was obviously drunk and, as he wasn't one of his guests, he ignored him. They were sitting in the centre of the room, about fifteen of them, huddled around two tables. There was champagne and brandy laid out for their use and, as they all chatted together and told hilarious stories, the man, a resident in the hotel, bought a drink and, passing by their table, he accidentally bumped into Danny Boy and spilled his drink, a large whisky, onto Danny Boy's jacket.

Danny Boy stared at the offending stain as everyone at the table went quiet. The man was mortified and, as he began to apologise profusely, everyone braced themselves for Danny Boy's reaction.

Just then Carole popped her head inside the bar to see what condition her husband was in, and her eyes locked with Danny Boy's. She smiled at him, blissfully unaware of the situation, and called out happily, 'I'm depending on you to make sure my husband doesn't get too drunk.'

Michael smiled at her as she went out again and, turning back to the situation in hand, he was amazed when Danny Boy grinned that boyish grin of his and said jovially, 'No harm done, mate. We've all done it, overindulged on the Gold Watch.'

Signalling to the barman, who had picked up on the tension, he shouted, 'Oi, John, get this geezer a fresh drink, stick it on my tab.'

Everyone relaxed then as Danny Boy waved the bloke off and sat back down without any kind of reaction.

Michael looked at his old friend and felt the urge to cry and, when Danny winked at him, he knew that this man, for all people said about him, real and imagined, was a good friend to him. He had restrained himself from correcting the stranger's lack of manners and, even though for most people that wasn't really an issue, where Danny Boy was concerned, it was something he would normally feel honour-bound to do. Even at the expense of ruining a wedding reception; with Danny Boy, his reactions to certain situations was instinctive, not the result of drunken bravado like most of the men at these tables. Danny Boy actually believed, deep inside, that a lack of manners was worse than killing someone. It showed a poverty of respect, not just for the person concerned, but for themselves as well. Michael knew that the men with them were as aware of this as he was, and he also knew that this story would be told many times in the future. It was an action of deep loyalty and friendship and Michael knew that better than any of them. Not just towards him, but towards his new wife as well.

Jonjo was laughing, and Annie was pleased to hear the sound. As she stood with him and listened to the jokes that were spewing from their old neighbour, Siddy Blue, she was also feeling the effects of the wedding party. It was late now, and the day was almost over. Kids were stretched out on chairs, coats covering them as they slept the sleep of the innocent. The DJ was playing the slower songs, the dance floor was spotted with couples dancing together, some in the throes of new passion, the majority sick of the sight of each other.

Siddy was a scream, and he had a repertoire of jokes that seemed to be endless. He was in his forties, with a thin frame and a thick head of hair. Even Danny Boy was laughing his head off. Siddy told his jokes fast, he hammered them out one after the other, he was a regular at any social gathering.

'How about this one, Danny Boy, Old Bill knock on a door at Wanstead flats and a kid of about twelve answers, he's got a glass of scotch in his hand, a prostitute on his arm, and a fucking dirty great big joint in his gob. Filth says, is your dad in, son? Kid says, does it fucking look like it, you cunt?'

Everyone creased up again, then Danny Boy looked at his little brother and said loudly, 'It was him, Siddy, fucking Jonjo here. He liked the old Persian rugs.'

He ruffled his brother's hair as he spoke, and Annie relaxed, it was the first time Danny Boy had addressed him directly in months. Since the day he had found about his habit and then proceeded to hospitalise him, he had never once spoken to him directly. He completely ignored him, only spoke to him through a third party.

Jonjo was so pleased at his brother's notice that he laughed delightedly. Danny Boy was finally over his pique, and that meant he was once more in the bosom of his family. That Danny had also joked about the reason for his initial anger spoke volumes, it meant he was over it, could finally forget about it. He was willing to give him another chance. The relief that Jonjo felt was overwhelming.

Michael walked over to the table then and said happily, 'I'm taking my new wife off to the honeymoon suite.'

Danny stood up and embraced him, really held him close, and it was seen and remarked on by everyone who had witnessed it. As the two men hugged, Danny, his voice weighed down with emotion, said brokenly, 'You got a fucking good one there, my son, a fucking Brahma.'

Michael looked at his old friend and said happily, 'I know that, Danny Boy, this is the happiest day of me life.'

Siddy, listening to the two men talk, said loudly, 'Make the fucking most of it, Mike, ten years from now she'll look like her fucking mother and who wants to fuck her when they're at home?'

He laughed at his own quip, and it was only when Danny Boy upended the table and dragged him from his chair that he realised he had gone too far. His remark was a staple at weddings, it was just something the men said amongst themselves; it was proof that they were men together. It was usually followed with ribald comments about the dangers of married life from the experts among them. No one really meant what they said, it was just a bit of fun. However, the words were listened to by Danny Boy Cadogan, who was now coked out of his nut and unable to calm himself down. To whom, suddenly reminded of his own wedding and his own married life, the comment was like a red rag to the proverbial bull. He wanted a Carole, he wanted this, and he knew somewhere inside him that it was impossible. He destroyed everyone and everything he came into contact with, and that knowledge stoked the fire of his anger. He had never had a chance, his father had made sure he would never be the person he wanted to be; his father had sold them down the river, and he had never got over that. All he had inside was a great big ball of hatred and despair that caused him to be immune to the usual feelings and emotions that kept everyone around him from turning into an animal on a whim. The coldness of his own life was not something he dwelled on until, like now, when it was so patently obvious even he had to admit to it.

As Danny Boy attacked his old friend and neighbour, the scene was watched by everyone in the place with a mixture of astonishment and adrenaline-induced excitement. When Michael and Arnold dragged Danny Boy off the prostrate man, the blood was everywhere, although his wounds were mainly superficial. It was Danny Boy's screaming that was the real shocker, 'You cunt, you fucking animal, talk about that girl like that . . .'

Danny Boy was still attempting to kick the prone man as Arnold and Michael pulled him from the ballroom. The table was broken and glass and alcohol was everywhere. Women were gathering up their children, and men were collecting jackets and wraps, ready to leave the scene of the crime. No one was willing to get involved in it. Danny Boy was not someone you interfered with when he went on a mental.

Mary watched as her husband was taken from the room, and she knew she ought to go and try and sort him out. Try and get him to see reason, calm him down. But she knew it was a fruitless exercise, so she didn't bother. She only stood up when Carole came running towards her, her wedding dress splattered with blood, and the tears pouring down her face. She was shouting hysterically. 'They've put him a car and driven off with him. He was like a lunatic, Mary, threatening everyone and trying to get back inside. The manager's called the police and an ambulance for poor Siddy, Michael's driven him away somewhere. They've all gone, Mary. What am I going to do? He's ruined everything, he's ruined it all.'

Mary sighed and, remembering her own wedding, she said sadly, 'Welcome to my world, Carole.'

Denise Parker was asleep when she heard the hammering on her front door. Dragging on her dressing gown she went out into her tiny hallway and shouted though the front door, 'Who is it?'

Michael called out calmly, 'Open the door will you, Denise?'

She opened the door with her usual scowl and stepped aside as Danny Boy walked in, flanked by Michael and Arnold. He could barely walk, and she raised one perfectly plucked eyebrow as she said flatly, 'What's all this about?'

Michael shrugged as they walked past her; it didn't occur to her not to allow them entry into her home. She could hear her baby crying and she shut the door and went into his room to quieten him. The flat was beautifully decorated, and she took a deep pride in it. Her son's room was magnificent, with expensive wallpaper and a cot that had been delivered from Harrods, along with matching furniture. She settled the boy down quickly, and then she went back into the front room where Danny Boy was lying on the sofa, obviously out of his nut. Michael placed a couple of wraps on the coffee table and said quietly, 'He's done a bottle of Courvoissier and enough speed to knock out the Cambodian army. He asked us to bring him here.'

Denise nodded as if this was the most natural thing in the world.

Arnold was not so blasé about this sorry state of affairs, but he kept his own counsel. He just wanted shot of the whole situation, Danny Boy especially.

'Leave him here, Michael, I'll sort him out.' Denise was already settling herself down beside him, and Danny Boy was grinning at her as if they were both in on some kind of big elaborate joke.

Outside, Arnold looked at Michael and felt the man's despair at the turn of events. 'You should get back to your wife, man.'

Michael nodded tiredly. The dawn was breaking and he was desperate for his bed. Desperate for the feel of his wife's body, of her warmth.

'You did me and Danny Boy a right favour tonight and we won't forget it.' Arnold got into the car but didn't reply.

As they drove away Michael said sadly, 'He don't mean the half of it really. Danny Boy has a lot to contend with in his own way.'

Arnold didn't answer him, he was just bowled over by the loyalty and generosity of the man sitting beside him, and he knew he wouldn't have been so good about the turn of events if the same thing had happened to him.

Calming down Danny Boy Cadogan for two hours in a freezing cold Portakabin while rabid-looking dogs patrolled the scrapyard they owned was not his idea of a fucking wedding night. They had poured the drink down his throat and listened to his angry opinions on everything from unemployment to the state of the prison system. They had been reduced to nothing more than by-standers until Danny Boy Cadogan had eventually allowed himself to be medicated with alcohol and a shitload of illegal narcotics. It was a real eye-opener all right, and it had convinced Arnold, once and for all, that Danny Boy Cadogan really was a bona fide fucking madman. A twenty-four carat nut-job. But he kept his opinions to himself; he had a feeling that was the best policy where these two were concerned. He knew one thing though, the relationship between Danny Boy Cadogan and Michael Miles was far more complicated than any marriage could ever be.

'Who was she then?'

Michael shrugged. 'No one.'

They drove the rest of the way in silence.

*

Denise looked down at Danny Boy and grinned. His coming to her flat like this was almost a romantic gesture as far as she was concerned. That he used her was not something she let bother her for any length of time. She loved the fact he was here, with her, that he would be seen leaving her flat the next morning; she believed that he somehow needed her.

Denise actually loved this man, and she knew it. She loved his strength, his viciousness, and his name. That her friends and neighbours would see him jumping into a cab home from her place was like a balm to her. She had his fucking son and he acted like that meant nothing to him, but he knew where to come when things were going pear-shaped. That he came to her when he was out of his head, she saw as a compliment. She actually believed he cared for her but his wife was standing between them and their destiny. Well, she had given him something that bitch had never managed. A son. Danny Boy Junior. He was like him as well, big and heavy-boned with the deep-blue eyes and thick Irish hair that made complete strangers remark about how good-looking he was. Danny Boy had ignored her for months, she knew about his latest little escapade, the little secretary. Well, she still lived with her mum and dad so he knew he wouldn't be welcome around there. This was his haven, his safe place.

As she kissed him she could taste the bitterness of his tongue, could taste the yellow coating that the brandy and drugs had put there. She pushed her tongue into his mouth urgently, flicking it around, pushing it in and out the way he liked. She could hear him groaning, and felt a moment's euphoria at the knowledge he wanted her.

'I missed you, Danny Boy.'

She was confident in herself now, thought she had the upper hand. He opened his eyes and looked around the room, the room he had paid for; he had given this girl a lot of his time and money. Through his jumbled mind he knew he had been out of order, knew that the demon he lived with on a daily basis had reared its ugly head again, but the feel of her hand inside his trousers as she rubbed his cock was good so he closed his eyes again and tried to enjoy it. But he was feeling so drunk and stoned that he was numb and, pushing her away roughly, he sat up and, realising where he was, he started to laugh. 'Make me a drink, girl, I'll cut us a few lines, eh?'

Denise grinned at him then, pleased he was finally coming round; happy he was livening up a bit. She went to the kitchen and got him a can of Tennent's from the fridge. Denise, like a lot of girls in her position, always looked good. Even when going to the shops she made sure she had full make-up on, and that she was dressed as if going on the date of a lifetime. She went to bed with her hair perfect and her sexiest underwear on. She knew that this bastard could turn up at any time, and when he did, she wanted to look her best. As she poured the lager into a glass she glanced at herself in the mirror she had propped up on the kitchen windowsill. She thought she looked pretty good considering the lateness of the hour. She was a pretty girl, and she had burned her boats for the man who had given her a child and then promptly forgotten about them both. Like many a girl before her, she had mistaken sex and lust for love, and now her son was the reason she was starved of both. There were not many men who would venture into territory that Danny Boy Cadogan had conquered. In many respects, her life was over the day she had decided not to abort his baby. If she had been older and wiser, and knew what she knew now, she might have flushed the poor little fucker down the toilet. However, she had not done that, and he was with her, as was his father, though how long he would be there was anyone's guess. But every time he did this to her, turned up out of the blue, he made her believe all over again that she might be in with a chance with him. That he might one day come and stay for good.

As she snorted a large, white fluffy line, she knew he was watching her, and she liked the attention he gave her at times like this. He fucked her rigid, and she knew she was wrong to let him use her like he did. But he was so seductive when he was vulnerable. She knew he was a looney tunes, knew he was a fucking cruel bastard when the fancy took him, but for her that was the attraction he held. She liked that she could tame him, not all the time, but sometimes, like now. When he would fuck the arse off her and then tell her how much he loved her, how she could fulfil his appetite for sex and companionship. He didn't put it into those words of course; she read into whatever he said to her what she wanted. She was adept at conning herself that he wanted her as much as she wanted him, that it was his wife, his legal wife, who was the stumbling block where they were concerned.

She sat at his knee, and he ran his hand through her long blond hair, and the feeling was overpowering. The gentle touch was enough for her then. She had him now, she was his. He pulled her round until she was kneeling before him, the soft leather of the sofa creaking as he shifted his weight while he pulled his trousers down to his ankles. She watched him avidly, everything about him was electric now. He sat back in his seat and splayed his legs, his trousers and underpants around his ankles. His cock was huge, bulging with blood and she caught the smell of his sweat and his semen as he forced her head down hard onto it, pushed it into her mouth without any preamble whatsoever. And, as always, she sucked on him as if her life depended on it; she made such a meal of it he was entranced. But what he saw wasn't Denise, he saw his mother, pregnant and penniless, but still allowing his father back into the house, even though he had sold them all down the fucking Thames. He saw Mary, another fucking slag-bag, another one who had had more cocks than Liz Taylor. He saw Michael's new bride and, as he came, he forced his cock right down the girl's throat, her choking sounds only making his enjoyment last longer. She was almost retching when he finally finished and, breathing heavily, feeling the pounding of his heart, the crashing sound in his ears that always reminded him that he was alive, he watched as Denise took a large swig of his lager to wash away the taste of him, sanitise her mouth, cleanse it of his cum.

Stretching, he suddenly felt tired, and as he watched Denise cutting up another few lines he said nastily, 'You *fucking mongrel*, you're like a fucking Electrolux, hoovering up the white and sucking off anyone with a wrap in their pocket.'

He saw the hurt in her eyes, saw the hatred there that always made him feel as if he had achieved his goal where women were concerned. They were all the same, they used you, they always had a hidden agenda. The more you treated them with kindness and respect, the more they fucking believed you were a mug. He was a mug; his mother had never had it so good and yet she had still blanked him for a man who had given her nothing except kids and grief. He hated it when he was like this, when he let things bother him. He hated that he had been cunted off by his own flesh and blood, that nothing he had ever done had been deemed good enough. Even his father had tried, with his last breath, to take him down with him. He knew that the majority of people in this world were takers, were users, and he liked the fact that the Denises and the Marys of this fucking dump were too thick to see that.

'Don't you fucking talk to me like that, Danny Boy, I ain't fucking having it. No one talks to me like that.'

She stood up, a smudge of white crusted around one nostril, and she drew herself up to her full height, ready to fight with him to regain her self-respect.

He loved her then, knew she was a fit mother for his son, loved her anger, loved that she *would* fight him, and he grinned at her, his whole demeanour changing in seconds.

'Where's this son of mine, eh? Let me see this boy I pay through the nose for.'

She rolled over then, as he knew she would. As she always did if he showed the least bit of interest in their son.

In reality, he felt nothing, not for her, nor for anything she might have produced from her body. But she didn't know that, and he was not about to inform her of it. She had served her purpose, and all he wanted now was a few hours' kip and a cooked breakfast. Not a lot to ask in the grand scheme of things.

Chapter Twenty-Three

Danny Boy looked down at his daughter and smiled. Mary had finally delivered a child, a full-term and lusty child. A child that was strong of limb and ridiculously healthy. After the other babies, this one seemed almost too perfect. He never thought she would manage it, would produce a living being. It had taken her long enough. That he had been the cause of each miscarriage Mary had experienced was conveniently forgotten about, he now saw himself as the wronged party in the play that constituted their married life, as the man bereft of children because his wife couldn't manage even that much until now. Until this tiny scrap of perfection had been created by Him especially to make up for all the disappointments in the past. It was as if she had been especially ordained, somehow, to survive when the others had not. In his heart he knew a son would not be welcome, not really. Not for the first child anyway. This daughter had been just what he needed; a girl. He loved girls, females. He could control them.

As he looked down into the deep-blue eyes that he knew would become just like his own, he felt, for the first time in years, a twinge of genuine emotion. Real affection and love. This tiny bundle was all his; he almost could feel their kinship, as if it was a living thing, as if their bond was tangible. Her tiny body and perfect limbs were like some kind of amazing miracle that he had never known about until this moment. The feel of her was like nothing he had ever experienced before. Her little hands had him almost mesmerised as he gazed at them with genuine incredulity. So tiny, so perfect.

Already grasping, she was grabbing at the air, he liked that about her. And he felt that, one day, there would be a lot for her to grab hold of. She was the only female he had ever felt any kind of respect for, the only female he knew would take precedence over his own life. It was a real eye-opener, and it frightened him; loving someone more than he loved himself was a novelty.

Her tiny mouth opened in a mewling cry that seemed to tug at the very heart of him, the noise creating inside his chest an almost primeval urge to protect her, and a feeling of ownership that was as powerful as it was frightening. He saw this child as he had never ever seen anything before in his life, as a perfect thing, a warm and innocent human being, a person that *he* had created, and who depended on *him* for everything. Unlike his outside children, this child, this baby born in the blanket of his marriage, he felt a real and a deep affinity for. Even Mary, lying there, devoid of make-up, tired out and exhausted from the difficult birth, yet still somehow looking better than most women in their prime, suddenly seemed to create an affection inside his chest that he had never felt for anyone before.

Mary smiled at him tentatively, and her nervousness made him feel bad momentarily, for the first time in years he really wanted to make her feel loved. Cared for. Make her feel *better*. But he honestly didn't know how to do that, he had got out of the habit of being nice to her somehow. She was a good old bird, and he knew that, in her own way, she was an asset to him. But, unlike this daughter here, who already cried out for his attention and demanded his consideration, she had folded much too soon. Buckled under him without him even having to try very hard. So he looked back at his daughter and, as he hugged her tightly to him, he knew his life would never be the same again. This was real, this was something he knew he could do right, properly. This girl would never want for anything, he would make sure of that; she was the biggest thing in his world. He knew that he had finally found his Achilles heel, and it had turned out to be this tiny scrap of humanity, this noisy, demanding little person. From this day forward he knew that he had a weakness at last, and that weakness was this child and the need he felt to protect her from harm.

He had built a wall up inside him, he had been neutered many moons ago by his father's hate and indifference, but this child made him realise that kids were more than just an appendage. More than just a drain on your finances. He would not be his father's son, he knew he would move heaven and earth for his kids, and for Mary; as the mother of his children she was now above reproach. This baby was the best thing in his life. Children, he realised, were all you had at the end of the day.

They were authentic, they were the only thing you could ever really call your own in this shithole that passed as a life. He had prayed for some kind of sign, something to prove to him that this existence was worthwhile, and he had been rewarded, given the answer all right. It was his little girl, with her blue eyes and her hypnotic stare.

His smile was wide and genuine as he felt the strength of her, this daughter of his, even though inside, he was terrified at the power this child held over him. That she had arrived at such a crucial time in his life was not coincidental, he was at the pinnacle of his success and this baby was the icing on the cake, as far as he was concerned. Grabbing Mary roughly, he hugged the two of them to his chest and, for the first time in years, felt utterly at peace with himself.

When Mary placed the child to her breast he felt a passion for her that he had not even known existed.

Mary Cadogan had wanted this man's love, and now she had it, she had it in abundance. It was so powerful, and she was so grateful for it, that the consequences of her husband's new-found adoration for her didn't even cross her mind.

Arnold and Michael were both listening intently to Danny Boy as he sounded off about their new business partners in Spain. He was overexcited about this new venture; it would make them a lot of money. But, really, that was neither here nor there, what excited him was that this new deal would finally place them at the top of the tree in criminal terms. To be the person who controlled Marbella was on a par with running the country; he was like a prime minister, he would decide who got what and, more importantly, who got fuck all. He would head the company that decided on every aspect of the Spanish dream, from how much the expats paid for their cars, to how much they would weigh out on their villas. Villas that could not even be built without his express say-so. He would determine what went up their noses and what food they would purchase from the local supermarkets. Anything that they bought or sold would, in some way, be controlled by him and Michael. His arm would be so long it would stretch across the Med to Morocco and beyond. From drugs and guns to the produce on sale in the local markets, he would be the person who would be responsible for all of it. Fuck Sainsbury's, he was better than Harrods; if you wanted it, needed it, or desired it, he would make sure you got it.

Danny enjoyed the power he held over everyone in his immediate orbit and beyond. No one could earn so much as a fucking peso without giving a percentage of it to him, it was the equivalent to having a licence to print money. It was real bunce, and the casino he owned out there was bringing in more poke in a week than all the London scams together. Michael had really surpassed himself this time and, with his acumen and Danny Boy's natural animosity, the deal had been done with the minimum of aggravation on all sides. The removal of a few obstacles, namely the people who had previously been in control, was already forgotten about by the majority of the people living out there.

Danny Boy was determined not to make the same mistakes as they had, namely creaming off too much money from the legitimate workers. No one could survive if the actual grafters, the people who did the day-to-day fucking shite, the mundane and boring, the actual daily toil, were not happy with their end, their earnings. That much stood to reason, and Danny Boy was aware that goodwill was the staple diet of all dictators. Without it, they were completely fucked.

He was not going to make the same mistake as the Connors; they had let their power go to their heads, and made the fatal mistake of letting him get a foothold, it had started with the drugs trade. From that vantage point, he had watched and waited until, eventually, he had forced them out. Without the drugs and the gun trade, the Connors had ended up as nothing more than muppets. The equivalent to local bully boys. Without the backing of their Arab counterparts they were reduced to flying into Gibraltar like tourists, because no private carriers would entertain them any more. That meant, of course, that the Old Bill could easily track their movements. Especially as Danny Boy had leaked their names to the relevant parties beforehand anyway. He had learned, many years before, that grassing could be lucrative. The Connors, who had somehow not been nicked or charged, had somehow disappeared, never to be heard of again. And, as no bodies had turned up, it had to be assumed they were on the run from the authorities. Minus their wives and children of course.

Spain was such a big market, and it was so lucrative that whoever was running it was accepted as the elite of the European underworld. Even the Krauts had not managed to get a toehold in Marbella, and it wasn't for lack of trying either. The Spanish didn't like them any more than the Brits did, and it wasn't just over a couple of world wars and a few football games; the Germans just didn't have the presence of mind that was required for this sort of venture.

The Spanish themselves had not been quick enough, had not predicted the British need for a safe haven and winter sun. In fact, other than the Arabs, no one had really understood its full potential. Even the Connors had never really expanded as they should have done, relying on too many other people to do the job for them. That was like giving a bank robber the keys to their local Barclays; eventually they were going to let themselves in and take whatever they could. Stood to reason really.

So, anyone going in with the money and the right connections was guaranteed to be welcomed with open arms. Danny Boy and Michael had done just that. Now it was sit back and enjoy the sunshine.

His new baby daughter had given him a new lease of life, he was on the want again, and he had not been on the want like this for many a long year. His daughter would have the world on a plate, and the plate would be worth more than most people's fucking houses. Such was Danny Boy's new credo. He grinned at his two friends and said nonchalantly, 'Oh, by the way, we need to have a word with young Norman Bishop. I think he needs a bit of friendly advice.'

Arnold stood up quickly. Always the first to do a good turn, he said happily, 'Do you want me to get him for you, or are you going to the casino?'

Danny Boy grinned. 'You bring him to me, that would be lovely, bring him to the scrapyard, would you? I'd hate to be over-heard, what I have to say to him is private.'

Michael was annoyed, the day-to-day running of things was his domain, always had been, because Danny Boy never bothered with anything once it was up and running. Even this new Spain project would be forgotten about once it was the norm; that was his strength in their partnership. He prided himself on being the one who kept on top of things. He resented Danny Boy coming in like this and not consulting him.

'Why do you want to see him? What's going on? He's one of our best workers.'

Danny Boy just shrugged and said, 'What's your problem? I just want a word, that's all.'

'What about, Danny? Why do you want to talk to him?'

Michael was really angry and it showed. He was one of the only people on the planet who could express that emotion in front of Danny Boy and get away with it. Everyone knew that, especially Arnold Landers. He had watched these two at close quarters and he felt he knew the score even better than they did.

Danny Boy grinned, that handsome grin that he kept in reserve for when he wanted to keep his real feelings to himself. 'Who are you, Michael, the fucking police? Now you're fucking making me be a cunt. I can't tell you now, can I? You'll have to wait and see, won't you?'

Arnold smiled, the thought of his earn once the Spanish end started to make money was all he could think about. He was thrilled, but he was also aware, on some level, that Norman and his minions were well below Danny Boy's notice in the general scheme of things. He smelled trouble, but he wouldn't lay money it. He kept his own counsel, after all, he was only on the edge of this world, the world he so desired. Once he made his mark he would ensure that his name was synonymous with fair play and hard retribution. That was his dream. His goal in life.

And, without this big mad bastard it would never come to fruition, and he knew that better than anyone. As much as he rated Michael Miles, he knew Danny Boy was the real deal, and he knew that if he wanted to make his mark, then it was Danny Boy Cadogan who would ensure he did it with the minimum of fuss and the maximum of monetary advantages. Danny knew that a good earn bought people, brought them on-side, even when they didn't want anything to do with you. Danny Boy Cadogan knew, as *he* knew, that money didn't only talk to most people in their world, it fucking sang them their favourite song. He felt Michael's annoyance and, making a point of avoiding his gaze, he went to pick up young Norman with a heavy heart.

Ange was watching her daughter-in-law as she settled the child. She was a lovely looking baby, and why wouldn't she be, the parents were both very handsome. As Annie also watched the little tableau she was smiling unconsciously, her lovely face almost feral with the need inside her to produce a child herself, this little baby with her huge eyes and her innocence had created a need that Annie had not even known existed. She determined then and there that she would produce one herself; that she would be the one to give Arnold a little boy or girl. She knew her antics were well out of order and, seeing how Danny Boy was with him, she knew that it was in her best interests to see this relationship through to the bitter end. And she knew that where she was concerned, bitter end would be exactly where it would all end up, if she wasn't careful.

Carole had left earlier, and Ange and Annie were both getting ready to leave. Mary looked fantastic. She was almost beaming, and her eyes were bright with hope and happiness. Danny Boy was finally succumbing to her charms and from baiting her, from his usual viciousness, he had suddenly become her soulmate once more. She actually started to feel as if she had a chance with him, she now saw this new baby as the means to her very worrying end.

Once Mary was alone, she placed the baby into the cot beside her bed then, opening the large bag she had packed for just such an occasion, she took out a bottle of vodka and poured a large measure into her water glass. She gulped it down quickly, terrified her husband would come in the door at any moment. She was drunk, already out of it, and she lay back on the pillows knowing that she was not capable of anything much.

This child, she knew, was the most important thing in Danny Boy's life, and that meant she was now under even more pressure to make good. The child she had prayed would make them closer, might drive them even further apart because she would now be under the microscope that was his notice. A quick drink to soften the edges would now be out of bounds, her whole life would be pulled apart and inspected for this little baby's benefit. She knew she had signed her own death warrant.

Mary felt the uselessness of her own tears, heard the plaintive cry of the child she loved, and who could be the cause of her mother's demise. It hit her then, with stunning clarity, that this child would be her watershed, would inadvertently be the end of her life as she knew it.

Later, as she watched her new daughter sleeping, watched her little chest rise and fall with each breath she took, Mary understood the real role of a mother. What the big secret of motherhood was about. You looked after your child, no matter who had fathered it, and no matter how much you might hate them deep down inside. A child was there for the duration of your life and, if you were really lucky, they buried you, and not vice versa. A mother would give her own heart to ensure the child she had created would live on, would be happy to do so. Would be loved. Even if they were unlucky enough to have Danny Boy Cadogan in their corner, claiming his kinship at every opportunity.

As Mary looked at her baby, all she could focus on was the fact that she had lumbered this beautiful child with a father who was as volatile in his affections as he was in his working life. A man who was as dangerous in his loving kindness as he was in his anger and hatred. She had, in effect, given this child nothing more than a bully who would use her for his own ends, and use those very ends to torture her for the rest of her life. Mary was crying again when the nurses popped their heads through the doors, and nothing anyone said could console her this time. Her fuck-up was glaringly obvious to her, even if it wasn't to them yet.

The happiness she had dared to embrace was now weighing her down, and making her question her judgement; how on earth could she have ever believed this child was going to make everything all right? Nothing could ever be all right in her world now, no matter how many fucking babies *he* allowed her to produce.

Norman looked decidedly uneasy; Arnold felt that he was being overly jovial, overly friendly towards him. Arnold wasn't a fool, he knew that the Normans of this world loved Bob Marley but didn't actually have a black friend. They talked a good liberal, but it was a different ball game when they were faced with a real, honest-to-goodness black man; suddenly they were nervous and unsure of a percentage of the population they had never actually met up with, or mixed with in any capacity. God bless the Catholic school system; it guaranteed a multi-racial environment for their pupils, and also guaranteed that the Danny Boy Cadogans of this world had something the majority of the country didn't have access to; the opportunity to meet and make friends with other outcasts in British society. It was hilarious in many respects but, like everything else, it was also sad, sad and irritating. Arnold felt more English than most people; he was black, but he had been born and bred in the country he loved. Like Danny Boy and Michael, he was the product of immigrants, Irish immigrants at that. He knew that, like his counterparts all over the British Isles, he was coming into his own at long last, and he resented the Normans of the world for making him feel that he was different. That he was somehow not as fucking good.

That feeling was what had made him forcibly shove the man into his car, and caused what could only be described as a bad atmosphere between them.

Norman was fucking shitting himself, and Arnold couldn't understand why that was. He had not threatened him in any way, shape or form, even though he had felt like it. So he blanked him, ignored him. When they finally pulled into the scrapyard he had lost interest in the ponce; Norman, who he had quite liked, was now nothing to him. He had finally revealed his true feelings and it hurt. They were all fucking on the scrump, so what made Norman think his scrumping was more important than anyone else's?

As they pulled up outside the office, the guard dogs were snarling and barking with an intensity that would frighten a lesser mortal. It was dark, and Arnold knew there was something not right about this meet, but he also knew it was in his favour not to remark or react to that. He waited patiently for the dogs to be rounded up and housed, and then he opened the car door with a flourish that told Norman he had made an enemy for life.

Inside the office the atmosphere was charged and all four men were more than aware of that fact. Smiling in a friendly way, Danny Boy invited them both inside.

Norman knew he was in trouble, but he tried to front it out. What else could he do? He walked into the warmth and quiet with a swagger that told everyone there he was acting, he was trying to front something out. But what?

Michael watched as Danny embraced Norman, watched as he poured him a drink and sat him down as if he was a valued member of their community. Which he was, as far as anybody knew. But Danny Boy never did anything without a reason, and now all they could do was find out what that reason was.

Arnold sat beside Michael, interested now to see what this was all about, knowing that somehow he had led this stupid boy into his worst nightmare. He had already picked up on Michael's uneasiness, and Norman was not exactly what anyone would call relaxed. But Arnold felt though, that anything that might go down on this night was not really his problem. Anyone who thought they could fuck Danny Boy off was entitled to everything they got, and more. If Norman was on the blag, then he had asked for anything that might be doled out to him in the next few hours.

Arnold sat down quietly, without any fuss. He had learned at a very young age how to blend into the woodwork.

'All right, Norm?' Danny was grinning once more, looking for all the world like a genuinely happy and contented man.

Norman smiled stiffly. He had heard about this yard, but he had never actually visited it before. It surpassed his expectations, everyone knew an invitation here was like a declaration of war. People who had visited this yard were never seen again. That was urban legend; it was also believable. A lot of people had disappeared over the years, and Danny Boy had been blamed for their disappearance. Not out loud, no one would actually go that far. But it was accepted that, if you crossed him, or if he thought you had crossed him, Danny Boy tended to delete people from his businesses and his life.

'You all right, Danny Boy?' Norman was nervous.

Danny grinned again, his handsome face open and trusting. ' 'Course I'm all right, why wouldn't I be? I go to Mass, I have a new baby, a lovely wife. What a lucky fuck I am.'

Norman nodded in agreement. He was young for the job; he had what was known in their world as good connections, family members who had stood up for him. People who had guaranteed his undying loyalty and who had never, in a million years, thought he was capable of having over Danny Boy Cadogan; it was inconceivable to them. Who would be that stupid?

'Everyone's been telling me what a fucking asset you are, Norm. I am over the fucking moon, you've really put yourself out, you know. Really done me and Michael a favour, I mean, we're busy boys, ain't we, we can't watch everything as closely as we'd like. So we depend on people like you to do that for us, don't we, Michael?'

Danny snapped his head round to face his old friend, and Michael knew then that Norman was not leaving this room while still conscious. Michael knew that Danny Boy had the edge, and he was interested to know where that edge had come from.

Norman was already in the past, and everyone in that small, confined space knew that. Danny was chatting to him in that low, interested voice he had. He asked him a question with such guile, Norman thought for a split second that he might be serious. But he looked at Michael and Arnold and knew he was being humiliated.

'Do you go to Mass, Norman? I do, and so does Michael here; we go because we see God as our role model, He is what we aspire to be.'

Norman didn't say a word, he knew he was fucked and he was trying to find a way out of this dilemma. Then, 'Come on, Danny Boy, what have I done, eh? I know you've got the arse with me, but why? I earn you a fucking good wedge . . .'

Norman was depending on his familial connections to get him off the hook, so he decided to confront Danny Boy before Danny Boy could confront *him*. He was under the impression that attack was the best form of defence. He also believed that his family connections would guarantee his safety. The Bishops were an old south London family, they had their creds, and they also had a foothold in the drugs trade. Without them, Danny Boy and Michael would not have garnered their own foothold so quickly. Unfortunately, without Danny Boy and Michael, they would not have had such a huge demand. So Norman, fool that he was, believed he might actually be in the driving seat.

Michael and Arnold waited for Danny Boy to do what he always did, which was to destroy, with malice aforethought, whoever he believed might be mugging him off. But they also knew he was cruel enough to play with his victim first.

'Do I look like a cunt to you, Norman?' Danny was standing now, his arms outstretched. 'Come on, you know you've been fucking having me over, so let's get straight to the point, shall we?'

Michael was watching the two men with a deep and heartfelt anxiety; he knew that Danny was doing this for his benefit, was teaching him a lesson somehow.

Norman didn't say a word. He sensed what was coming and he didn't know, for the life of him, how to stop it. It occurred to him that it didn't matter who his family might be, no one was going to front up to this man before him. He had been well and truly sussed out, and the knowledge was enough for him to accept his fate.

'Imagine I am your priest right, Norm, not Michael, who you normally deal with, but me, Danny Boy. I would say to you, forgive me Father, for I have *skimmed*. And *you* have, you've skimmed a fucking fortune off the bets, ain't you? Well, I have been looking over the fucking books and, unlike my friend here, I don't trust you as far as I can fucking throw you. And I have decided that your penance will be three Hail Marys, two Our Fathers, and a broken neck. By the way, I have already squared this with your family. Who, incidentally, think you are as big a cunt as I do. So don't imagine the cavalry will be rushing in to save you at any point. Because they won't. You've earmarked one per cent of my earnings on top of the wage we give you, a fucking good wage at that, and that is not acceptable. That is such a piss-take, it's like saying you believe I am a fucking cretin, ain't it? You have also cunted off my best mate, my wife's brother, who, unlike me, trusted you. So, how do you think I feel about that?'

Michael knew then, as did Arnold Landers, that Danny Boy was making a point, that this young man, with his bad haircut and his adverse head for figures, was being slaughtered so Danny Boy could prove a point. The point being that, even though Danny might trust Michael as the money man in their partnership, he was, in his own way, more than capable of keeping his eye on the ball. That he still looked over their nefarious businesses, and had a handle on their finances that was now proven to be a lot closer than anyone thought.

Danny looked over at Michael, who was embarrassed at this revelation, who knew his trust in this boy had not only been misplaced, but had also been used to prove a point. Who was going to suffer so Danny Boy could remind him that he might not be, as he often put it, the sharpest knife in the drawer but who, it now seemed, was sharp enough when he needed to be.

Michael wondered briefly who could have grassed Norman up from the casino. It made more sense that he had been found out and the information had then been passed onto Danny. He had trusted the boy; he had not had any reason not to. After all, he came well recommended. He felt a fool, but he knew that Danny Boy would use this as a leveller, make him feel he was the shrewder of the two. Especially after the Spanish deal; Danny was sending out a message all right, not just to him, but to everyone who worked for them.

Arnold watched the scene before him with interest, wincing slightly as Danny Boy took a claw-hammer out of the desk drawer. Danny then began to undress slowly, chatting, taking off his jacket and shirt, worried about blood spattering on his new clothes. And, all the time, he eyeballed the terrified young man, berated him for his foolishness, shaking his head as if in abject disbelief at his actions. Danny looked calm, he looked friendly, and he looked strong. When he brought the hammer down onto terrified Norman's kneecap he was actually smiling. Arnold knew then that Norman Bishop was going to regret his fucking tea-leafing big-time. The dogs' excited barking drowned out Norman's shrieks of pain. Though they didn't last that long; it was the low moaning sounds he made much later on, coupled with the stench of his blood, that really set the animals off.

Chapter Twenty-Four

'Are you sure you're OK, love?'

Mary nodded, the baby was at her breast and her husband's kind words frightened her. He had never been the compassionate type. Not in private anyway. He had fooled everyone into believing he still cared for his father, even though he had hated him with a vengeance. So his sudden interest in her now was unnerving.

As Danny Boy walked across the bedroom towards her, she flinched visibly. She drew her head into her shoulders and put up her right hand before her face, as if it could ward him off, stop him hurting her. The action annoyed him, caused him to grit his teeth in anger. She was a drama queen, always trying to cause a fucking international incident. But he was not about to let her get away with that. Smiling down at his little daughter's face, he looked at his wife once more, feeding off her fear. He was enjoying her trepidation, knowing that the uncertainty of his mood was all she thought about when she was with him and, more to the point, when she was without him. He sighed loudly with irritation. Settling himself down on the love seat inside the bay window of their bedroom, something he had always seen as an ironic addition to their boudoir, he lit a Portofino cigar and watched her silently as she fed the child, her lovely face tight with fear, her nerves so taut he knew he could have played a tune on them if the fancy took him or he had been musically minded.

Danny observed his wife as he would the monkeys in the zoo. At this moment in time he loved her, really loved her again. As he had, years before, when he had made it his mission in life to take her from the man he felt was beneath her. Beneath him for that matter. But it was *she* who had been beneath *him*, she was a dog, and that was always in the forefront of his mind. He knew, without a doubt, that she would fuck anyone who could provide for her, and he also knew that that knowledge was no basis for a marriage of any kind. Especially to someone like him. He knew he was not the average Joe, but then that's why they lived as they did, and he provided for them all so well so he could instil fear where none had been before. He had no respect for her, why would he? He knew, and she knew, that she could have been anyone. Anyone at all, she had just happened to belong to someone he had been determined to thwart.

But, at this moment in time, she was all he had ever wanted, with her breasts heavy with milk and her skin luminescent, with not a mark on her after the birth. Still taut, soft, and still without a blemish. She was like a Valkyrie: she was a strong and wonderful mother and wife. He knew he could trust her and that was important to him. No matter what, he knew she would never turn on him. It wasn't in her nature, she was loyal, and that was the most important thing as far as their relationship, what was left of it anyway, was concerned.

She could still arouse him on the odd occasion. Even though, like most men, the same dinner every night had become a chore; fucking the same woman was an abomination as far as he was concerned. God liked to punish, he knew that from first-hand experience. The adultery commandment was a piss-take really, coming from a man whose only son had been banged up in nick, beaten mercilessly, and then crucified for the sins of the world. Danny Boy felt that adultery, like stealing, was only really there for the weak. For the people who had no fucking respect for themselves, who would sin with impunity anyway. God knew the fucking skulduggery that the average man was more than capable of, otherwise he wouldn't have countenanced business deals, except lending money from church premises, of course. He was right to have the ache about that, but the majority of His commandments were not relevant in this day and age. But it didn't mean they weren't there for a good reason. They had been put in place for the ice creams of the world, not for the leaders of men. For people with a bit of nous.

And, let's face it, there was a get-out clause, providing he believed, which he did, and providing he was genuinely sorry for any sins he might commit along the way, which he was, he was safe as houses. Best religion in the world was Catholicism, as his old man would preach when drunk as a skunk: you could smoke, drink, gamble and fuck. Providing you were sorry you could commit murder, encourage mayhem, and covet what the fuck you liked. Well, he coveted his neighbours' wives, he coveted a bit of strange on a regular basis, and he coveted it with as much gusto as he could manage.

Women were built differently, thanks to God, they all felt different, and there were too many of them for any real man to ever really be faithful. Every few years a new crop was there for the taking, suddenly allowed in pubs and clubs they were young and new and they were so tempting to any man with a few quid and a good chat-up line. They were there for the use and for the enjoyment of the male of the species. Men were genetically geared-up to spread their seed. A quarter of the population were bringing up cuckoos in their nests. Children that they believed were theirs, when in fact they were no relation whatsoever. He knew better than anyone the complete and utter disloyalty that women were capable of. His own mother had proved that to him many years before: he wouldn't trust any of them as far as he could throw them. None of them warranted it. They were fucking liars and schemers. He had sussed out that all you could really do to protect yourself was make sure your wife was too scared to go on the cock, was far too terrified of being found out, and therefore was not likely to try her hand at adulterous skulduggery of any description.

He did try though, to keep himself faithful, as a good Catholic, and he was a good fucking Catholic; he loved his God with a vengeance. Like everything in his life, he didn't treat it lightly, but it was hard at times. Especially when the wife of your choice was such a fucking cunt. Such a fucking let-down.

He also knew, and he was sure of this, that God had a sneaking

Martina Cole

admiration for him. He knew that as well as he knew his own name: God watched over him, He understood him, and appreciated him. That meant a lot because his God was the only other male in his life he would ever allow to be above him. Who he felt was on a par with him.

As Danny felt the sudden rush of excitement the sight of his little daughter generated inside his chest, he knew without a doubt that there was a God. Only a God could have created something so perfect, so wonderful. He could hear the sound of her lips as they sucked noisily on her mother's breast and knew in his heart that she would be bottle-feeding the poor little mare by the time he came back from Spain.

'I hope you ain't fucking still drinking, mare.'

Mary shook her head slightly, her arms wrapped protectively around her daughter's fragile body. Her husband's words dripped ice and she knew he was capable of attacking her on a whim.

'Don't start that again, Danny Boy, please. Not tonight.'

She was begging him, her voice heavy with her nervousness, with trepidation. He wondered at how she had the front to talk to him like that. That she could actually believe he gave a fuck what she thought, or might want in her life. He didn't answer her, just sat there, biting on his bottom lip, his eyes full of laughter and mirth, as if she had said something hilarious.

The cigar was glowing menacingly in the darkness of the room, and Mary felt the panic rising inside her. He was quite capable of putting the cigar out on her face, on her breasts or on her back. It would not be the first time he had done it, though he usually only hurt her where it wouldn't show. He beat her on her arms and legs, her stomach and back. Places where she could hide the marks, and he knew that she would hide them. She could never admit that she allowed him to hurt her, it was like admitting defeat. She was also worried about how Michael would react; what he guessed, and what he knew, were two different things. As much as she loved Michael, she would never intentionally put him up against Danny Boy. No one could win the wars he started on a daily basis. Danny Boy was a lunatic, and a righteous lunatic at that. He did not see anything wrong with his actions, or his thoughts on how people should live, or react to their environments. There was one way of living, and it was his way.

Danny sat back on the seat, his body was too big really for it: he was balanced on the edge as usual. The room was beautiful, all creams and golds, it screamed out money and expense. It should have made him happy, but it didn't. In fact, he hated it. He hated that he needed to justify his wealth, that he had actually been much happier living at his mother's house, letting her take care of him. She might have been a miserable old bag at times, and guilty of loyalty beyond the scope of most people he knew, but she certainly knew how to look after her elder son. She had taken good care of him, and he had lived in that little place and been happy. Until she had decided, out of the blue, to take the old man back. That's when it had all gone pear-shaped. When he had finally understood the role he actually had in her life. Provider, shoulder to cry on, surrogate father for the kids she had produced for a man who used her like he would have used a Kleenex tissue.

His brother's addiction had been the direct result of their father's fucking antics. Although he had seen it as nothing more than a weakness, the same weakness his father had suffered from: instead of drink and gambling though, it was the brown. Skagheads were weak, they were cowards. Everyone knew that. Smack was like the tranquillisers a lot of so-called women took to ease the pain of their boring fucking lives, mother's little helpers. Narcotics were the new alcohol, and who could blame people? Those were the same individuals who watched *Dallas* and listened to *Top of the Pops*; as far as he was concerned, in many respects, heroin was the lesser of those two evils. But his brother's drug use he had taken personally, had seen as an insult to him and everything he believed in. And as he also knew that the little fucker had not been near it since the capture, he saw his brother's rehabilitation as a personal triumph. Danny felt that his brother's immediate cessation of any kind of illegal medication proved that addicts *could* stop if they really wanted to. He had no respect for Jonjo now though. Anyone who could lose themselves like that, could lose control without any kind of responsibility for their own life, and *pay* for the fucking privilege, was a knob, a prick. A fucking no-neck, a useless wanker.

Now, if Jonjo had maybe felt the urge to stimulate himself, snort a bit of coke, a bit of speed, even inject a few steroids, that he could have understood. But the brown, no fucking way. That was a piss-take, an affront to everything he had tried to avoid.

Jonjo was a has-been before he had even begun his life, in Danny's eyes anyway. He could never trust him now, how could he? Once a skag-head, always a skag-head. That was a given in their world. In fact, when he read the Sunday papers and saw all those rich kids, Blandford and the likes, throwing their lives away, lives that were fucking well worth the living given their circumstances, he felt the futility their parents must feel. The money they had, and all it did was enable their kids to embrace laziness, allowed them to become nothings. All that poke, hundreds of years of grafting to make a fortune, and for what? A generation who embraced socialism, who pretended money meant nothing to them, and who could only afford that attitude because the money would always be fucking there. Their ancestors must be turning in their graves at the utter fucking disgrace of it.

Danny hated the world, hated what it had become, what it stood for now. Even the Falklands had been nothing more than a reason to make the electorate forget the high unemployment. At least, that was what he felt about it all. Like most robbers though, he loved Thatcher: she had inadvertently made it easy for people like him to launder their money. They could buy a property for cash, mortgage it, and then invest in businesses, no matter how fucking unstable they were. As long as they had somewhere in the title, they were all as safe as houses. They could be closed down in the morning and reopened in the afternoon, no one owned anything, all the plant needed was on lease-hire so no one cared about the plant involved; no one actually owned it. They just changed the name on the forms and laughed all the way to the bank. It was that simple.

Thatcher allowed the man on the street the opportunities that had previously only been open to the upper classes. She had given the masses not only the opportunity to purchase their council houses but the chance, through that very act, to become middle class. She had created a whole new set of Tories because a mortgage had a funny way of stopping people from striking. Mortgage companies wouldn't let you pay your arrears off at a pound a week like the councils did if you owed them rent, the mortgage companies didn't give a flying fuck about you. Out on the pavement without a by your leave. They also had the added advantage that they owned more of your property than you did.

Cads and fucking bounders, the lot of them. Well, those epithets were now fair game to anyone with a few quid and a warehouse somewhere. He had seen how the land was lying, knew that it was only a matter of time before the Common Market would hold them all to ransom. He knew that the time was close when Spain and its islands would finally come into their own. At the moment, they still wouldn't extradite, but that wouldn't last. Eventually they would have to, eventually they would *want* to. Even they would want shot of the very people they were now courting so desperately.

Now Danny had the Spanish conquest in his bin, and he knew it was a fucking good scam, a lucrative and long-running scam. He knew this would take him into the future and beyond, he knew that as well as he knew the woman who had delivered his only legitimate child was not, and never could be, a natural blonde. He had made a good move getting in there so quick, tendering out the lesser jobs, making sure they were given to people he liked and felt he could trust. He had made a few enemies over the years; his kind of personality guaranteed that would happen, but he also knew the power that a good earn could create in a workforce. And he always guaranteed a good wedge and, on top of that, a damn good back-up if it all fell out of bed.

Love him or loathe him, Danny knew that the men he employed appreciated that, knew that if they got a capture from Lily Law all they had to do was keep their heads down and their arses up. If they did that, their families would live better than they had ever lived before. Danny Boy and Michael were very good in that respect. People were queuing up to be a part of this family, and that was a good thing, a good advert for them. It meant they didn't have to poach anyone, they just sat back and waited for people to come to them.

Danny wondered once more at how he could have a wife of such beauty and she didn't interest him at all. In fact, if she had not given birth at last to a fucking living child, a child that, luckily enough for her, looked like him, he would not even be here now. He would have been in Spain weeks ago. But this child fascinated him, she drew him to her like no one else before. She made him almost happy, almost contented. She made his heart soften for a few moments.

'Do you remember when we were courting, mare? Remember how we used to laugh all the time?'

Mary nodded sadly. Her thick hair was tied back from her face and her eyes suddenly looked with interest at the man who tortured her at every available opportunity. She was like a dog who, no matter how much it had been treated badly by its master, still came back for more. Her loyalty was the one thing that had never, ever, been in question.

'I love you, girl, and you know that. I love this baby, but I have a lot on me mind, mare, and you need to understand that for the future. I am the main breadwinner, you know. I have to go out and earn for us.'

Mary nodded again, knowing that this new-found affability could disappear at any moment. Knowing that this friendliness could turn to hatred in seconds. He was talking for his own benefit, not hers. As she looked down on the head of her new daughter she wished him dead, wished him away from her so she could feed the bloody child from a bottle like normal women. Instead, she kept a neutral expression on her face and waited for him to make the next move. She had learned many moons ago that fighting him was pointless, arguing with him was fruitless, and making eye contact with him when he was like this could be fatal.

'Will you be all right while I'm away, you and the baby? You won't get pissed and forget about her will you, mare? Leave her to her own devices. Expect her to make her own feeds, and change her own arse? Only, I still ain't sure I can trust you on your own.'

Danny watched as the tears rolled down her face at his words, knew that her biggest fear was this child's demise. He knew that he had ruined any kind of bonding process between Mary and her child because she would be too worried about fucking up. Would be too worried about him and his return, to concentrate on anything else.

'I'll be all right, Danny Boy. How long will you be in Spain anyway?'

He knew she wanted his answer to be months, knew she was praying for him to stay away for as long as possible. But, instead of being wound up, as he would usually be, he felt a rush of affection for her. He knew he treated her badly at times, but he had the knack of forgetting about that when it suited him. Sometimes though, on rare occasions such as now, he felt the burden of this and guilt at his treatment of her. He knew that what he did to her was wrong, not just in his eyes, but in God's. He cared about his immortal soul, he cared that he bullied her at times, but he couldn't stop himself. She was her own worst enemy where he was concerned. She acted like she was better than everyone, and she wasn't.

'You don't need to know how long I'll be away, Mary. Who do you think you fucking are, questioning me, eh? The police? I'll be back when I get back, and not before. Why are you questioning me about it? You got a fucking fancy man then?'

Danny knew that what he was saying was rubbish but, as always, as soon as he said it out loud he felt it was probably a viable argument. Felt that he was more than likely in the right. She was beneath him, and that knowledge pleased him; without him she was *nothing*. Without him she would fucking starve. He walked over to her and knelt on the bed. The baby was asleep, her gorgeous little body happily snuggled into her mother's for once. Danny kissed her little head, breathing in the aroma of his daughter, admiring her perfection. Then, as Mary pushed him gently away from her, he watched as she placed her carefully into her cot, the cot that had been delivered by Harrods with all the pomp and ceremony Mary felt befitted her and her offspring. Then Mary got back in their bed, her lovely face nervously awaiting his next move. Danny pulled off his clothes quickly, dropping them on to the floor. She watched him without a word, in complete silence. Danny knew he had a good body, knew that it was a powerful tool;

that he looked good to most people, male and female. He also knew that his wife avoided him like the plague.

He lay beside her, he could feel her dismay at his touch and, as he kissed her deeply, pushing his tongue into her mouth, feeling the warm texture of her tongue, he squeezed her breasts painfully. He felt the power she always engendered in him as he forced her legs apart and, even as she whispered to him about the pain she was in, as she begged him to wait a few weeks longer, until the doctor told her that sex was safe, as she cried bitterly because she was still full of stitches from the birth of their child, he pushed himself inside her roughly and rode her like a roller coaster. He knew that what he was doing to her was wrong, yet he enjoyed it all the more because of that. He was determined to make sure she knew who was her boss before he went to Spain. Determined to make sure she remembered him and what he meant to her and her child.

When he finally finished with her, felt himself coming inside her, she was crying silently and, as he looked at her lovely face, then saw the blood all over the sheets, he knew that he had been right about her. Without this baby she had finally produced for him, she would have been kicked to the fucking kerb sooner rather than later. Her main attraction these days was that her brother was his best friend and partner. But Spain had worried him, because he would need to commute for a while, and this wife of his was far too pleased about that for his liking. She had needed to be reminded of what he was capable of when pissed off. Needed to be reminded of his wrath. She was lying there now, curled up on her side of the bed, crying softly, looking vulnerable, her lovely hair spread around her like a halo, and then he loved her again. For a few minutes he saw her as the mother of his only child. His only legal child anyway, a child who would be baptised, loved, and taken care of as if she had been born into royalty. Which, in many ways, of course, she had. He was criminal royalty and, as such, his children already had the edge over most of their contemporaries. But for him, now, Mary was still in some ways an unfortunate mistake, and he wished he had waited a while before he had lumbered himself with her for all eternity.

But what was done was done, she was his wife, there was no divorce now, and that was that in their world. He could do what he wanted to do, with anyone he wanted to do it with, whereas she had no choice but to do whatever he decided she *could* do. And, if he dumped her, that was her lookout. No man would touch her with a barge-pole now.

Mary knew he wouldn't do that to her though, she knew he would still be hovering over her when she was in a coffin. He felt that, as her husband, he owned her and, to all intents and purposes, he did. She was desperate for him to abandon her and his baby, even as she knew that he would not leave her with this child. She would leave without her, leave this house alone. And she also knew that, without him, she would not last five minutes. He was not a man who suffered fools gladly; he was also not a man who would suffer anything he didn't want to. She knew that his goodwill was more important that anything else in the world to her and to her child. He was also capable, she was convinced, of dumping her and this child if the fancy took him. She didn't feel confident that even the birth of this little girl could guarantee this man's undying affection or loyalty to either of them. Her or his daughter. He was capable of walking away from them both, dumping them at a whim, as if they didn't exist, without any consequences whatsoever. Who, in their right mind, would dare to question his motives? Certainly not her brothers, she knew the truth of that better than anybody. She knew that if that did ever happen, no one would ever come to her aid. Without him, without Danny Boy, her husband, she was finished, and that knowledge hurt her more than anything else. This child's birth had proved to her once more just how much power he had over her life. And now her children's lives. He would make a point of running their lives as he did hers and everyone around him.

This meeting with her husband had shown Mary just how much of a coward she really was, how desperate she was to stop any kind of confrontation. She knew it was a pointless exercise anyway. Danny Boy would wipe her off the face of the earth and laugh while he was doing it. He saw her as nothing more than the shit beneath his shoes, as the sister of his best friend. A friend he cared for more than he did any one else, even his own family. The knowledge hurt her because she still cared for him, and she guessed that he knew that, and that was why he made her feel even lower down the food chain that she really was. After all, as Danny Boy's wife, she was literally guaranteed deference and respect from everyone who came into contact with her. If he didn't give it to her in private, he made sure she was afforded it in public.

Life was so hard for her and the birth of her little daughter, a daughter she was too frightened to name without her husband's express permission, had just exacerbated her fear of him, this child had tied her completely to a man she knew hated her, as he hated all women. But he was the Face of Faces now. He was the ultimate Face, the main man.

Danny's name was whispered in certain circles, and his reputation talked about with awe by the people who dreamed of being him, even as they knew it was not an option, could never happen. They knew, as she knew, that they didn't have the nerve to be a Face. A real, honest-to-goodness Face. It took a lot more energy and a lot more time than most people were willing to give. It was something that was ongoing, that was there twenty-four-seven. They knew that was only available to a few men; those men willing to do whatever was necessary to keep their reputations intact.

The Danny Boys of this world were few and far between; they were one-offs. Scary fuckers who thought only of themselves, thought only of how others might perceive their actions and who were for the most part dangerous bastards with huge egos and a natural dislike for their fellow man. Men they would wipe out without any kind of remorse. Because, as far as they were concerned, they had asked for everything they had got. It was that simple, that easy for them.

Mary was in agony, her stitches were broken, and the stinging sensation, the burning she felt was almost too much to bear. Blood was everywhere, and the knowledge that all she wanted was a drink depressed her even more than what had just happened to her. Danny Boy had achieved what he had wanted all these years. She was finally broken, physically and mentally. And they both knew that.

*

Danny Boy was standing on the balcony of his suite. The hotel was not only upmarket but also very discreet. It was luxury such as he had never experienced before in his life. He was looking out at the sun-drenched beach, marvelling at the crystal blue waters of the Mediterranean. He could see a family sitting together, watching their children as they ran in and out of the gentle waves, and saw a life that he had never even guessed existed. He saw how a family could enjoy the sunshine, enjoy each other's company for real. He felt happy watching them, felt that he was finally at peace with himself.

Danny saw this new venture as something he could embrace with a zealousness that would shock his contemporaries. He knew, without a doubt, that this was the way to go. Knew that Spain and all it could offer would become a big part of the London scene. He knew, instinctively, that this was a scrumpers' paradise.

And he owned it; this was all his. From the timeshares to the bars and clubs making their mark from Marbella to Benidorm, Danny Boy was the main benefactor for the majority of people now hiding out here, people who needed a safe haven from the UK authorities. He was in his element, and he was treated like visiting royalty.

Danny Boy liked the fact that, thanks to the new world they inhabited, Europe was waiting to be conquered. The screaming Ab Dabs and the Bubble and Squeaks were lining up to sell their wares to an unsuspecting public. From Morocco to Athens, thanks to British Telecom and British Airways, the drugs trade was thriving. In fact, it was reaching out to the rest of the world. South America had a lot to offer. Especially the Colombians, who had already conquered the American market, and were now ready to supply the rest of the Western world. Cocaine had become the designer drug of choice, snorted by movie stars and rock singers. It was seen as a stimulant that had no real downside. It had once been the domain of the very rich; now though, thanks to the miracle of modern shipping and air travel, it was readily available to anyone with the money to pay for it. The eighties were the era of big hair and big borrowing. Even the wannabe dealers borrowed with a recklessness that left the Danny Boys and the Michaels amazed at their stupidity. They were willing to borrow out the money of course, it was good business. Unfortunately, unlike Barclays or Lloyds, they foreclosed on those loans quicker and with much more violence than was necessary.

It was a great time for everyone involved, and it was also a time for reflection. Money was made overnight by people who had not got the brain capacity to deal with their new-found wealth. They tended to arm themselves up to the teeth and had the annoying habit of snorting their own product. This enabled Danny Boy to gradually get back his initial outlay, reap the benefits of his own personal lending rate then, when the fancy took him, take out the same people who were now, inadvertently, and through no fault of their own, his competitors. He loved it.

His natural antagonism made this new venture an agreeable and very lucrative earner for him. He gave the people concerned the wherewithal, both the money and the access to the drugs needed, to ply their trade, and then he foreclosed on them when they least expected it, taking back not only his initial investment, but the future earnings they had coming to them. He liked Spain, but he didn't like having to depend on other people for the product. But even he knew that he had no choice but to broker it, like everyone else in their game did. But it galled him nonetheless. He hated that he couldn't produce the product himself. That he had to depend on others to do it for him. But he was determined to change that. As the end of the eighties approached, Danny decided that he would get a foothold into the suppliers if it killed him. He was determined to make a name for himself in as much as he would be the first outsider to finance his own crops. He would not only chase the fucking dragon, he would slay the bastard while he was at it. Never content with being on the periphery of life and, against all the advice he had sought so earnestly, he felt that he was within his rights to demand a percentage of the actual crop itself. He had done it with the Jamaicans for their grass and he had done it with the Turks and the skag. It was a buyers' market now, the world. And it was so small that anywhere could be accessed in what amounted to hours. Danny Boy was not prepared to sit back and be a minor player any more. He was now prepared to invest so much money that he would be *the* main player in Europe.

Against Michael's advice he set the chain in motion, still believing, as always, that he had an inbuilt knack for seeing an earner when it reared its ugly head. As 1990 loomed, Danny Boy Cadogan was unaware of the animosity his actions had caused. He was the top dog, the Face of Faces. Unfortunately for him, he had not allowed for how his actions might be misconstrued by not only his workforce, but also by the very people he dealt with on a daily basis. Danny Boy thought he was invincible and, in many ways, he was, but he had the knack of making enemies where there should have been friends. He also had a knack of destroying people he felt were even remotely dangerous to him and his pursuit of happiness. His complete indifference to their plight did not make him any friends. In fact, it only gathered him enemies. Enemies who smiled at him, all the while waiting for him to put the final foot wrong. Danny Boy was more of a danger than he had ever been, and that was the opinion of everyone in his orbit.

The Old Bill included. He knew that better than anyone, but he wasn't about to let on. He heard a gentle knocking on the door of his suite, and he turned and walked back through the sitting room to open it. He was amazed to see Carole standing there and, when she walked inside without a word, he knew something terrible had happened.

'What's going on, what are you doing here?'

She sighed heavily and said quickly, 'Sit down, Danny Boy, there's been a terrible accident.'

Carole was holding his hand, and pushing him towards the plush sofa he had been admiring earlier. As he sat down he looked into her kind face, and was once more overwhelmed with affection for her. Which was precisely why she had been sent to tell him the bad news. Of all the people in the world, she was probably the only one who could impart it without fear of retribution.

'What's happened? Is it me mum?' He assumed that was what had brought her over to Spain.

She shook her head slowly.

'It's the baby, Danny. The baby passed away in her sleep. Sudden Infant Death Syndrome. SIDS. Or cot death, as it used to be called. It was no one's fault, mate. I'm so sorry, Danny Boy.'

Carole saw the look of horror that crossed his features, saw the terrible pain that was etched onto his handsome face, and wished there was some way she could make this all better for him. But she couldn't. To finally have a child, and then lose it had to be the hardest thing in the world. Especially for poor Mary, who was inconsolable.

Carole was as devastated as Danny Boy was, and he knew that, could see it, knew that she cared as much as he did. Knew why she had come to tell him the news. Knew that he would take it from her and from no one else.

'You need to come home, mate, need to sort it all out. Mary is in bits. She haemorrhaged and is back in hospital.'

He nodded almost imperceptibly.

But the damage was done, and nothing could repair it. He felt appalling guilt, he had not even allowed Mary to name the child; he was going to do it when he got back. He had thought it was funny, seeing his wife squirm as she tried to refer to her baby without actually calling it anything. All because she was too frightened to ask him what she was to be known as, what he would decide to call her. Now, his little daughter had died without a name, and that bothered him. It bothered him a lot. He felt such a deep feeling of loss then, and the depth of the feeling surprised him. That he had done his daughter, a poor little child, a grave injustice was foremost in his mind. And, for the first time in years, he cried.

Book Four

Be a sinner and sin strongly,
but more strongly have faith
and rejoice in Christ.

– Martin Luther, 1483–1546

Chapter Twenty-Five

Jonjo was angry, really angry, and it showed. He was spitting as he talked, a sure sign of his terrible temper. Nowadays he had a reputation for his short temper and for his even shorter attention span. If he didn't hear what he wanted to hear within a certain amount of time, he lashed out, and he lashed out royally.

Jonjo was not the boy he had been all those years ago, and he was definitely not the same person who had depended on the needle for fulfilment. He was now a big, heavy-set man with an attitude that had already been remarked on by more than one judge. In fact, it was only his connections that had stopped him being put away for a seriously long time. He was a force to be reckoned with, and his past misdemeanours were forgotten about, much to his delight. He was ashamed of his past, ashamed of his weakness. But he now felt that he had vindicated himself. He had pulled himself together and left his junkie past behind him. That he was now, he believed, seen as his elder brother's right-hand man was evident. And that he relished this position was patently obvious. Jonjo had grown up and, thanks to his brother, he had grown up quickly and with a kink to his nature that made him as unstable and as dangerous to all around him as his brother. He had no feelings whatsoever any more, it seemed they had died out overnight. He was now classed as his brother's clone, as Danny Boy's stand-in, as his stunt man, particularly when he had had a drink.

What had once been Jonjo's Achilles heel: his caring nature, his need to hide from the real world, had been replaced by a man who felt absolutely nothing for the people he was sent to threaten and collect money from. He was a bully and he embraced this new-found freedom. Embraced it and used it for his own ends. Jonjo had finally succumbed to his brother's way of life and had been surprised to find out how much he actually enjoyed it. He not only enjoyed Danny Boy's approbation, he also enjoyed the benefits of his brother's way of life. He was proud of his reputation as a head-fuck, he loved that he was capable of instilling fear into everyone around him. Jonjo had accepted that this was the only way he would ever get on in the life he lived in. The money was great, and the kudos was something he knew he would never again be able to live without.

Jonjo grinned at the two men in front of him; they were minor dealers in many respects, but they had made a major mistake and overordered and he knew from experience that they had placed it out with their friends, expecting to coin it in. They'd served it up to people who they had believed, in their rank stupidity, were as sound as a pound. That they would bring them back the profit they were now depending on. It would be laughable if it wasn't so tragic. He was sorry for them because he knew they had been tucked up. But that wasn't his concern, let alone his problem. They had entered into an agreement and, even if the Filth had raided them and taken their stash, they would still be honour-bound to pay what they owed. How many of his friends had invested large amounts of cash in the belief that a shipment of grass would be forthcoming, only for that same grass to be captured by the Filth? They'd lost their investment, large or small, with a shrug of the shoulders and the relaxed acceptance that the deal could have gone either way. It was the nature of the beast. It was the world they had chosen to live in.

Next time, these two would ensure that they only dealt out to people who they knew they could really trust. They would see past their greed, past their profit and, basically, they would finally understand what their financial commitment meant to the people involved. In effect, if they had any brains at all, the next time they dabbled in the drugs trade, they would have the sense to save him a journey, and themselves a lot of pain and aggravation by making sure that they had the money that they owed beforehand, to be paid bang on time, thereby avoiding a seriously dangerous occurrence, brought on mainly by Jonjo's failure to listen to any excuses. He couldn't listen to them anyway, even if he had wanted to. His brother didn't want to hear them, so that meant neither did he. It was pretty basic really; if people had the sense to think about these things before they went into them feet first and all guns blazing, they wouldn't get themselves into so much trouble to begin with. Greed had a lot to answer for. And the drug trade seemed to generate greed in everyone it touched, whether it was the dealers or the users. Seeing the fear behind these two eejits' eyes, Jonjo was once again reminded of the folly that seemed to go hand in hand with get-rich-quick schemes. They were never thought through properly, never given any real consideration, except that they just might make the difference that most people needed to get on in life. To make people feel they were finally on a winning streak. These two, for example, were worse than usual; they had not even had the sense to find out whether the people they had dealt to had the means to repay them, whatever might have happened. Serious dealers only dealt with people they knew could pay their debt, even in times of trouble. It was the same with bookies and gamblers. Unless they could cover their bets themselves, it was a mug's game because, win or lose, you still owed the poke. And though a bookie might take your money, they rarely had a bet themselves. That was because they knew the odds were stacked against the punter. This pair of fucking drongos had handed their life savings over to people who had seen them as the equivalent of winning the pools. Who had never had any intention of paying them back. They had this coming to them, it was a foregone conclusion. But, that aside, whatever might have happened, right or wrong, they still owed a lot of money to the wrong people. Money that still had to be repaid, and repaid in full. This was a learning curve for them, and it would hopefully send out a message to others of their ilk. To pay up and shut up. As Jonjo went to work on them, he was thinking about his mother, and the promise of a roast dinner that night. He found that concentrating on the minutiae of life, the mundane, made his job so much easier. At that moment in time, the thought of his roast dinner had far more meaning to him personally than the fate of these two chancers.

As he arranged to remove their cars, along with anything else that could be sold off quickly, Jonjo was reminded once more that this would have been him had he not been tugged by his older brother, and shown the error of his ways. He was a lucky man all right, unlike this pair, who were already crying their eyes out. And he hadn't even got to stage two yet.

Carole was tired out, but she was happy. The kids were in bed and she was happily awaiting the return of her husband at any moment. Michael had been away in Marbella for the last few days; she knew he was only there because Danny Boy didn't like going anywhere alone any more. He was funny like that these days. He always wanted someone with him. If he went to the shops, or even the off-licence he hated to go by himself. It wasn't that he was frightened in a physical sense; who would be fool enough to take him on? Carole smiled at the thought. No, it was for another reason entirely, but what that reason might be, she had no idea.

Ange was sitting at the kitchen table, and she walked up to her quickly and, squeezing her shoulder affectionately, she said quietly, 'Do you want another cuppa, or a proper drink?'

Carole knew Ange would be more than ready for a tot of whisky, she had already put out the glass and the bottle for her. But this was a game they played on a regular basis. So she waited for her affirmation, and poured the drink she knew was expected of her. Ange grinned and sipped at the fiery liquid happily. It was funny, but Ange was like her own flesh and blood these days. She spent a lot of time here, and she was a great help. She knew that if Ange turned up at her door, it meant Danny Boy was up to his old tricks.

Carole knew that Ange was a godsend to poor Mary and she also knew that Ange couldn't stomach too much of Danny Boy. Which was strange considering he loved her dearly. But she also knew that like anyone involved with him, she needed to get away on a regular basis. Michael was the same, though he would never admit that to anyone, of course. He was far too loyal for that.

As she replenished Ange's glass Carole said lightly, 'Is Danny Boy home yet?'

Ange nodded slightly, worried that because Michael hadn't put in an appearance as yet, she might be putting her foot in it.

Carole knew what was going through the older woman's mind and was annoyed, as if Michael would be doing the dirty on her; he might have his faults but infidelity wasn't one of them, thank God. She knew that as well as she knew her own name. Unlike Mary, who had two daughters and a husband who came home intermittently, she had a charmed life by comparison. Michael was a good provider and a wonderful father. He spent as much time as possible with the kids, and with her. He enjoyed his family, enjoyed being with them. Danny Boy, on the other hand, enjoyed his two girls but still couldn't find it in his heart to forgive Mary for the loss of his first daughter, and all the miscarriages. He gave the girls whatever they wanted when all they really wanted, needed, was a stable home life. At least, that is what she believed. Though Mary had never said anything to her, she knew that things were not right in that house. She also knew that Ange felt the same way, and probably knew a lot more about the situation than she did.

Carole poured another generous tot of whisky for Ange and, grinning, she said archly, 'You are more like me mother than me own mother ever was.'

She meant what she said, but she also knew that hearing the words pleased Ange no end. Since falling out yet again with Annie, she had been very subdued. In fact, she was hard-pushed to speak to Annie herself as it had happened. But, as always, Carole kept her opinions to herself. But it was hard at times, especially as they were all such a big part of her life. She saw more of them than she did her own family. But she knew the value of a quiet tongue, she knew that better than anyone. Once things were said out loud, they could never be taken back. They were out there for ever. But she still felt a great anger and a great urge to, just once, give her honest opinion on the goings-on around her. Instead, she reminded herself that it was none of her business, as her husband had pointed out to her on more than one occasion.

*

Leona and Lainey were refusing to go to bed and, as usual, Mary was on the verge of giving up trying to make them. Then, as she was about to throw in the towel, Danny Boy walked out into the large marble entrance hall of their new home and shouted angrily, 'Bed, the two of you, now.'

Both girls went straight up to their bedrooms without another word. Mary tucked them in, and kissed them goodnight, all the while wondering why Danny Boy was not out and about as usual. He was not even dressed; he had come home earlier and, instead of going back out as usual, he was lounging around in tracksuit bottoms and an old T-shirt. Watching Sky and giving her his orders. These ranged from making him tea, coffee and sandwiches, to pouring him a beer, a brandy, or fetching his cigars. It had been going on since he had come in, and she knew the only reason that he had shouted at the girls was because he was most probably staying in tonight himself and he wanted a bit of peace and quiet. Mary was grateful though, that the girls had gone to bed at last. They gave her so much grief at bedtime. She knew she was her own worst enemy where they were concerned. But, the one time she had shouted at them, really shouted at them to do as they were told, Danny Boy had caught her and beaten her to within an inch of her life in front of them. She'd no authority over them since. They sensed her fear, and they used it against her. But she didn't really blame them, even though it hurt her deeply because, living in this house, you soon learned to use whatever you could to survive. His mother had passed on that little gem of wisdom.

Mary walked quietly back towards the kitchen, but he called out her name and she braced herself for a lecture before walking into the large drawing room where he was sprawled out on the Japanese silk sofa, watching Sky Sports.

She stood before him like an errant child, her nerves taut with the tension in the room. 'What do you want, Dan?' She was smiling gently, her eyes alert for any change in his demeanour. For a warning that he was going to attack her in some way, either physically or verbally.

He watched her for a few moments before saying quietly, 'You shouldn't let them talk to you the way they do.'

Mary shrugged nonchalantly, as if the question didn't require any kind of answer from her.

The way they disregarded her annoyed him, even though he knew he was to blame for it. He felt his wife should assert herself more, though he knew she was incapable of asserting herself in any way, shape or form where him and his children were concerned. He wished at times that she still had a bit of fight in her, still had a bit of passion. But he had knocked that out of her years ago. At times like this he wondered why he was so hateful towards her, wished he could start again with her. Start anew. But that was impossible, no one could go back to change the past. If they could, the world would be a much nicer place, he was sure.

Patting the seat beside him he motioned for her to sit down. She did, as he knew she would. She was like a puppet. A very lovely puppet though, admittedly. She was still stunningly beautiful, and that pleased him in some ways, even as it annoyed him in others. She was like a painted doll with her perfect hair and perfect make-up. Her clothes were, like his, impeccable. She knew how to dress and, more to the point, she also knew how to dress him. He let her choose his apparel because she had an eye for detail. He always looked the part, looked good. He knew she had all the attributes that most powerful men looked for in a partner, but he also knew that he didn't give flying fuck about that. She was his old woman, and that was all he would ever allow her to be in their relationship.

After the baby had died, he had not touched her physically for a long time. She had finally, with the intervention of the medical profession, produced two more daughters, and he knew she worried that he had wanted a son. He didn't disabuse her of that notion, had hinted that he wanted one with each delivery. But, after his father, he was really quite happy to settle for girls in his life. A son, he felt, would only become a rival to him as the years went on, would favour his mother as boys tended to do. No, he liked his girls, they were less complicated and more easily controlled.

Danny then realised that Mary had not said a word, and he felt her discomfort as if it was a living thing. Suddenly, he saw her as others saw her. She had the most fascinating eyes, deep-set and framed by thick dark lashes, they were capable of mesmerising any man she might set out to get for herself. Not that any man in their right mind would even give her a good morning without his express say so.

'I mean it, mare, you should put your foot down with them. Let them know who's boss round here.'

He was attempting to lighten the mood and she knew that. Would have appreciated this effort many years ago, but loved him for trying to be nice to her. Like that was something she should have been grateful for. She smiled gently and said, without thought for the consequences, 'Oh, they know who's boss, Danny Boy, as well as you do, and we know that it ain't me.'

The sadness of her words overwhelmed him for a few seconds and he pulled her into his arms and hugged her tightly. When she was like this he hated that she didn't want him any more, that she was only with him because she was too frightened to leave him. He wanted her love now, needed her to want him still. He kissed her hair, breathing in the sweet smell of her perfume, loving the feel of her body against his. 'Come on, Mary, you know I love you, darlin'.'

He was hugging her tighter now and, as always, it was nothing more than another proof of his ownership over her. She smiled then, and said sadly, 'The worst of it all, Danny, is that I think you really do love me, and that's the problem.'

Michael was listening to the man before him with an expression of such amazement that Arnold started to laugh. Michael looked at his friend and, sighing, he said tightly, 'Listen, Arnie, you can't even joke like this about Danny Boy. He has everyone on his payroll and they tell him everything. And if they tell him what you are insinuating . . .' He left the sentence unfinished.

Arnold was a big lad, and he had his creds; he also had Danny Cadogan's sister in his bed, and given her his children. As far as he was concerned, he had done his bit for humanity. He also had a network of people that he trusted and, when he had jumped on the Cadogan band wagon, they had all come along with him for the ride. Now they had given him some very interesting information and he wanted, in fact needed, to know the truth of it. He trusted

Michael more than he had ever trusted any white man before. They were soulmates in many respects. They had built a good relationship up over the years and they had often ganged up on Danny Boy, without him knowing about it, to talk him out of some of his more foolish acts of violence. So he was not frightened to pass this bit of information on. He knew Michael would need to know the truth of it as much as he did, if not more. After all, he had far more to lose if it all came on top.

The fact that Michael had not said anything for a few moments told Arnold that Michael just might think there was a grain of truth in the accusation. He hoped he was wrong, but he had a bad feeling about it all. This was too outrageous to be a lie. The fact it was so unbelievable was what made it so believable to him.

'Not Danny Boy. Come on, Arnold, who told you all this?'

Arnold sighed heavily. His dreadlocks were longer and thicker than ever and his deep brown eyes were full of intelligence and concern. His whole demeanour was screaming for some kind of affirmation or rejection. Either way, he needed to know the truth.

'David Grey is still his contact, by all accounts and, even after his run in with Danny Boy before, he is still on his payroll, still his go-between, and now he wants shot. He can't do it any more. According to him, Danny has wiped out all his competition by grassing them up, and he has done it so fucking cleverly no one is any the wiser. He makes sure they are well out of his jurisdiction before they even get a hint of capture. He sells them down the river in advance. So he is well out of the frame when it finally goes down. His information guarantees him a fucking blank sheet; he could fucking kill the lot of us, and the Filth would not even dream of accusing him of anything. I mean, think about it, Grey has nothing to *gain* by telling me, has he?'

Michael was listening intently, and the words were penetrating his skull like six-inch nails, but he couldn't let himself believe them. Could not let himself even wonder about them. It was an outrageous accusation. An accusation that could get them killed, especially if the wrong people were to hear about it.

He shook his head with a finality that brooked no argument to the contrary. 'No way, mate, that's fucking bollocks. Grey is a fucking liar, and I don't want to hear any more about this, OK. You know, as well as I do, the Filth are probably trying to get to you. The lying, filthy, slippery bastards that they are. If Danny Boy even suspected you had talked to that cunt, he would out you without a fucking second's thought and he'd be within his rights. You are married to his fucking sister, you have a fucking good earn on his name, and you have the nerve to come in here and say things like that to me?' Arnold felt the cold hand of fear at Michael's words. He had not expected a knock back, that was for sure; he had assumed Michael would have been of the same frame of mind as he was. Now Michael sounded so angry that Arnold wondered at his belief in their so-called friendship. He remembered that Danny Boy and Michael had been friends since they were little kids, and understood then that he would always be an outsider. He had been had over by a Filth, and he couldn't believe he had fallen for it. He had believed it all as verbatim, *still* believed it, if the truth be told. But that was neither here nor there now, he had to try and make amends. He had to convince Michael he was sorry for what he had said, that he saw the error of his ways. That was all he could do to try to limit the damage this outspoken gossiping had caused him. And he had to pray that Michael didn't repeat his accusations to Danny Boy himself. If he did, Annie would find herself a widow and his kids would be fatherless. He had misjudged Michael Miles; he had really believed they were mates, had thought they were close enough for him to talk frankly about his concerns. How fucking wrong could he be? He could be a dead man within hours over this.

'Look, Michael, forget it . . . I was just paranoid, talking fuck-talk.'

Michael waved a hand in front of his face in anger. 'Don't worry, I'll not tell anyone anything about this, and if I was you, I wouldn't either. But you ever accuse Danny Boy of anything like that again, and I will have to take you out meself. Do you get my fucking drift?'

Arnold nodded his huge head, and wished once more that he had kept his big trap shut. When Michael motioned for him to leave the room, to get out of his sight, he left as quickly as he could. He was terrified at what he might have inadvertently caused.

Michael sat in the chair quietly, digesting slowly and carefully what Arnold had just told him. He knew in his heart that it was probably true; he had half-wondered at something like this many times over the years, but he could never allow himself to express the thoughts out loud.

Michael had first suspected Danny Boy of skulduggery concerning Old Bill many years before, when he had accused old Louie Stein of grassing. He had hated himself for the thought, even though the rumour was that Danny Boy's father had served people up on occasion. Nothing had ever been proved about anything though, so he had let it go. But it had returned with a vengeance when Danny had insisted on taking out Frankie Cotton. Frankie was someone who would be missed. Who should have been off-limits. Danny Boy's hatred of him had been without any kind of foundation; it was completely devoid of any logic. Danny Boy saw him as a threat. In more ways than one. He had then removed him with his usual violence, amid rumours of his alleged grassing. Rumours that seemed to be true, seemed to have some foundations.

But Danny Boy had not been worried at all about the consequences of his actions where Cotton was concerned. Michael had felt a niggling doubt at the time, had even tried to talk Danny out of it. But it was already a done deal. He had forced the treacherous thoughts from his mind, telling himself that he was out of order to think those thoughts about his friend. But the real suspicion had been when Danny Boy had managed to get his hands on his own father's signed statements to the police. Not copies, the originals. And, for all his talk of their having an in with the Filth, he knew deep inside that Big Danny Cadogan would have gone to the top with his information. That it had to have been intercepted in some way. The statement had been given, it had been witnessed and signed. No one could retrieve something like that, not once it had gone that far. It would have been taped, it would have been photocopied, no one could have retrieved it without offering something in return.

Either that or Danny Boy Cadogan had been set up somehow.

Not a chance in hell. Big Danny Cadogan had gone to the Filth all right, only he had not realised at the time that his son was already a supergrass in the making.

Grey had been given a hammering, but that had only guaranteed his place as Danny Boy's gofer. Now it seemed to him that Grey could have inadvertently become part of the set-up, and that, like himself, he had not realised it until it was too late. Danny Boy would have offered Grey up on a plate. A bent Filth was not something the Met would really concern themselves with; if they nicked every copper who was on the rob there would be hardly any police presence on the streets at all.

Michael felt sick with apprehension. If what he was thinking was actually true, then where the fuck did that leave him? If this was feasible then Danny Boy had to have served him up as well. He was his fucking partner, the so-called brains of the outfit. Was he next on the list? When Danny Boy felt he had served his purpose, would he be the victim of a capture? Was he living on borrowed time?

He knew Arnold thought it was true, but he was not about to commit himself to anyone, no matter how much he liked them. He had to box-clever with this information. He had to get to the bottom of it, then extricate himself as best he could. But he still could not believe that Danny Boy was capable of grassing. He couldn't get his head round it, couldn't admit that it was a possibility. Michael closed his eyes tightly and felt the familiar pounding in the back of his head heralding the beginning of one of the migraines that had plagued him over the years.

'Thanks, Carole, I appreciate this.' Carole hugged the old woman affectionately. Unlike most of the others, she didn't have a problem with Ange, she really liked her.

'Come on, mate, I'll walk you to your door.' She held onto Ange's arm lightly and walked her up the pathway to her front door. The house was lit up, and she breathed a sigh of relief, normally she had trouble getting the key in the lock because of the darkness.

As they got to the front step the door was opened by Danny Boy. 'Hello, Mum. I was getting worried about you, thought you might be out on the pull.'

Ange smiled happily at her son's friendly words.

He helped her inside and said gaily, 'Stick the kettle on, Muvver.'

Then, smiling at Carole, he said, 'Staying for a cup?'

She shook her head quickly, waving her hands in a gesture of annoyance. 'I better get back, Michael has another migraine. Poor sod, they really knock him for six.'

Danny Boy nodded with mock sympathy. 'The poor little soldier.'

Carole laughed as she walked down the drive towards her car. He waved theatrically at her before shutting the door loudly. Then, going to the kitchen, he sat at the table and lit himself a cigarette. Ange knew he was agitated and, as she made the tea, she watched him surreptitiously. He was smoking in short, sharp puffs, his angry face screwed up in concentration. His obvious annoyance was threatening to spill over and he barked at her, 'What's all this about you looking after the girls while my wife went out? And don't fucking deny it, Mother, Lainey told me. I was in Spain, knocking me fucking pound out to earn a few quid, and my old woman was on the out. And, to add insult to injury, me own mother was babysitting for her.'

He stood up then and Ange shrank back from him, her fear of him overriding her naturally argumentative nature. He had not only bowed his poor wife down, but he had bowed her down as well. She was terrified of him and that knowledge saddened her. She loved him, but she also resented the hold he had on their lives. He moved away from her, and she guessed her fear had made him ashamed. So, pouring the tea, she said, without looking at him, 'She only went to Carole's, they had a chinwag. I was happy enough to watch the girls. What is wrong with that, may I ask?' She sounded like her old self, had the question in her voice, coupled with her complete disregard for whatever answer she might be given. As she stirred his tea, she felt the force of his silence. So, taking her courage in both hands, she looked in his direction and, smiling at her eldest child she said jovially, 'Carole was lonely without your man, and I encouraged Mary to go round there for a few hours. Get out of that house for a while.'

Danny Boy was wrong-footed now and he knew it. That

his mother would take Mary's side over his was a revelation to him.

'Ask young Carole if you don't believe me.'

Danny still didn't say a word to her, just stared at her as if wondering what to do to her.

Ange was fed up with all this and, swallowing her fear, she said quietly, 'You are your father's son, all right. He had the jealousy in him as well.'

Danny Boy sat back in the chair then and said sarcastically, 'Oh, did he? Was that before or after he spunked up all his money on drink and gambling? After, I bet. When he was *drunk*. Let's face it, sober, he fucking hated you, didn't he? I mean, this was the man who threw all our lives away on a game of cards. Who caused me to go out grafting before I had even left school. But, if I am like him, how come my kids ain't fucking starving like we always were? How come you live in this nice house with the bills paid and a fridge full of grub? How come I ain't pissed up all the time, so as I can conveniently forget I have a family? Answer me that, Mother.'

She didn't say a word, and he knew she wouldn't. She couldn't: the truth hurt, as he knew it would. As he had wanted it to.

'And, while we're on the subject, Mum, if he was so jealous, why did you have him back all those times? Even after he had fucking dumped us again and left me with the Murrays and the threat of his fucking gambling debt hanging over my head? My head, not his. *Mine*. He was shacked up with some old sort, it was *me* who had to fucking grow up overnight and scrump you a fucking wage. So, come on, I really want to know the answer to that one, Mum. It's a real melon scratcher as far as I am concerned. So, enlighten me, and then you can answer my original question. Who said you could look after my girls while my wife went out on the piss? Because that is what she would have been doing, and we both know that, don't we?' He was on his dignity now, and his mother wondered at how she had ever thought this man, standing so arrogantly before her, could have been the apple of her eye.

Chapter Twenty-Six

Annie knew that something was wrong, she just wasn't sure what it was. Arnold was like a cat on hot bricks and Michael seemed too quiet somehow. Danny Boy was full of his usual conceitedness, and just seemed to her even more strange than he usually did. For example, he kept asking her if she had ever babysat his girls while poor Mary went out, and if she knew whether their mother had stayed out, had left them overnight. It was like a mission with him, as if the only thing that would stop him asking was when he was told that his questions or, more to the point, his accusations, were true.

She had even sworn on the kids' lives, and he had raised one eyebrow slowly and said quietly, 'Never swear your kids lives away, Annie. Only a fucking whore would do something like that.' He had no interest in the truth, and they both knew that.

She had laughed loudly, in desperation, and said to him angrily, 'But I'm telling you the truth, Danny Boy, why would I lie to you, what the *fuck* would that gain me?'

He had looked at her for long moments, as if she was a lunatic, and then walked off. She wondered, at times, just how anyone allowed him out on his own. He was so obviously a fucking nutter. He was a sadistic, vicious bastard. And she knew that better than anyone; but she actually loved him. For all he was, she loved him, because she knew he would do anything for his family. For her. If it ever came down to that.

Arnold came into the house and she smiled at him happily. He had, somehow or another, grown on her over the years. In fact, she could not imagine her life without him now. They had two handsome little boys, and she knew he worshipped them. Even though the elder one was a bit of a wild card. She could not say for definite who the father was, but he was black enough to satisfy Arnold, and so that was good enough for her. The younger boy, on the other hand, was his father's double, right down to the thick dreadlocked hair that took so long to twist, and the steely blue eyes and thin lips that made him look like a young Damian Marley. He was a looker, and he knew it. But Arnold was not right lately, and that was bothering her. He was very quiet, he seemed distracted. In fact, he showed all the classic signs of someone having an affair. Except he was hardly ever out of her sight these days.

As she poured them both a drink, she said brightly, 'Danny Boy is still convinced poor old Mary is out on the cock. He is so paranoid lately. I just laughed at him and his fucking stupidness, and he got the right ache with me. Really got the arse.' She was roaring again, finding her brother's reactions hilarious. She expected Arnold to laugh as well, agreeing with her, as he usually did, but he didn't this time, and she said seriously, 'Is everything all right with you, Arnold?'

Arnold looked at her, and realised that he did actually love her; as brash and loud as she was, he really cared for her. As he did the boys, but he was nervous now in case he had inadvertently marked his own card with Michael Miles, that there might be a minute chance Michael would report what he had said back to Danny Boy. In his heart, he knew that Michael wouldn't do that to him, but the fear of it happening would always be there. With his accusations he had broken a friendship he had cherished. Accusations that he still believed had an element of truth to them. He now had the added aggravation of having to tell David Grey to take a running jump, and tell him that if he ever approached him again he would be honour-bound to tell Danny Boy what he was saying about him. That should be enough to keep him in line. At least, he hoped it would be anyway. If Danny Boy ever suspected that he had been accused of something that was so heinous in their world, he knew that he would kill him stone-dead. He also had the added fear of

Inspecter David Grey opening his big mouth to someone else, and putting his name in the frame. It was an abortion from start to finish. Why hadn't he just kept his big trap shut, why had he believed that Michael had been *his* mate over Danny Boy's? Those two had been mates since they were kids. He was nothing more than an outsider to them, a complete outsider at that. He might be married to Danny Boy Cadogan's sister, but that was as far as it went. Well, he knew when to retreat, and he knew when to watch his back.

Annie, watching her husband, saw the changing expressions on his handsome face, and wondered once more what the hell could be bothering him. Whatever it was, he was not letting her in on it, that much was for sure. Unlike Arnold, she knew the pitfalls of being involved with her brothers. She knew the danger they presented to the outside world. She also knew that Danny Boy was a dangerous fuck. And, even though he was her brother, she didn't trust him, and she never would.

Mary was lying on the sofa, her back was aching, and she knew she had drunk too much to hide that fact. She would have to plead an illness and, even in her drunken state, she knew she was ill much too often these days, that no one believed her any more. She felt her eyes fill with tears of self pity; Danny had really hurt her again the night before. He had forced her onto the floor in the kitchen, telling her that she was nothing more than a drunken joke, that people were laughing at her. In the end, she had lain there glad of the respite. Enjoying the coolness of the tiles on her skin. It annoyed him that she didn't look as drunk as he knew she was. In fact, she had cooked a dinner for them all and it had been perfection personified. The girls had enjoyed it so much they had asked for seconds. But her back was killing her, and she guessed, rightly, that it was her liver. The palms of her hands were bright-red and itchy, and she knew that was the result of too much alcohol. But it was the only way she could cope with her life, a few drinks took the edge off; she still looked after the girls and, bless their hearts, they were just beginning to understand how hard her life was. As they were getting older, and he couldn't control them so much, they were now getting a taste of his unique outlook on life for themselves. And they were not impressed with it.

She heard his footsteps as he entered the house, their home, and she felt the fear his presence always slammed into her chest. The terrified banging of her heart, the sound so loud in her ears that it drowned out everything else around it. She waited for him to enter the drawing room, waited for his sarcastic comments, his hateful remarks, and she was disappointed.

He was full of good-natured bonhomie, as was sometimes his want. He knelt beside her and kissed her gently on the mouth. He was heart-wrenchingly handsome and, even though she loathed him, she could see how other people, especially women, might perceive him. She knew that he was classed as a decent man by the majority of his contemporaries and she wondered at someone who could fool people so easily. God knew he had fooled her for long enough.

'Bad head again, mare?'

She nodded slightly, wondering if he was going to turn on her in the next twenty seconds.

'Can I get you anything, mate? Aspirin, a cold flannel, how about a large vodka?'

She closed her eyes tightly and waited for the harangue, but it didn't come this time. Instead, he actually did bring her a large vodka, and he placed it carefully on the small glass table by the arm of her sofa. She stared at it in terror. Then, smiling that crooked, gut-churning smile he had, he said gently, 'Go on, drink it. I promise you, I won't say a word. I swear on Leona's life.' He looked so earnest, so caring and understanding.

She shook her head slowly, the ice had caused droplets of water to form on the outside of the glass, and the aroma of the neat vodka was filling her nose. But she didn't touch it. Danny sighed heavily. She was perfect, from her hair to her toenails she was still groomed to within an inch of her life.

'Look, mare, I decided today, that if you want a fucking drink, you can have one. So make the most of it, girl.' He picked the glass up and placed it in her hand. It was cold and slippery and she put her other hand up to steady it, frightened she would drop it. Then, smiling, Danny Boy helped raise it to her mouth. Encouraging her to drink it with soft words of affection. She took a mouthful and savoured the taste of it on her tongue.

'Come on, mare, get that down your Gregory. Then I'll pour you another one.'

She drank it down slowly, without pause. The feel of its icy coldness like an old friend as she drained the glass. Then, looking at Danny Boy she smiled nervously. 'Why are you doing this, Danny?'

She was slurring her words, not so much that it would be noticeable to the average person, but enough for the people close to her to know that she was drunker than usual.

He shrugged nonchalantly. 'I'll go and get you another, shall I?'

As he slipped from the room, she closed her eyes slowly. She was convinced that he was up to something; he was always up to something. She attempted to pull herself to a sitting position, but her arm couldn't connect properly with the leather arm of the sofa so she crashed back down each time. She giggled silently at the knowledge that Danny Boy was not there to witness it. Eventually though, she managed to pull herself up slightly, accomplishing this by digging her heels into the other arm of the sofa, and pushing with all her might.

When Danny finally returned with another glass of neat, iced vodka, she was half sitting up, and more than ready for him. He passed her the glass once more and, sitting beside her on the huge leather sofa, he put his arm around her slim shoulders and said gently, 'Look at your mummy, girls, this is her at her drunken best.'

It was only then that Mary noticed that her two daughters were sitting silently on the sofa opposite her. Then that she knew that they had witnessed her behaviour, her need of a drink.

They were both wide-eyed with bewilderment and when her face finally crumpled and she started to cry, a long, draw-out animal crying, as if she was in physical pain, they were still watching her intently, their beautiful little faces a mixture of fright and deep sorrow at their mother's plight.

Danny was laughing his head off as if this was the best joke in the world. 'Drink up, mare, go for it. I waited at the door to see if you would notice your daughters, or even me for that matter. I mean, let's face it, I ain't exactly little, am I? Most people notice me. But no, not you, true to form, all you could concentrate on was the next drink.'

She was almost hysterical now, the humiliation was so strong that she felt as if she could actually die from the pain she felt inside her. She knew she had snot hanging from her nose and that her make-up was running down her face. But she couldn't stop crying, the noise was getting louder and louder, yet she still couldn't stop it. It was as if, now the flood gates had finally opened, she was crying for all the years she had held the tears back. Had stopped them from falling, had forced them away with sheer willpower.

'Stop it, Mummy, stop, you're scaring me.' Leona's voice was getting higher by the second; her mother's hurt and upset was communicating itself to her two daughters and they were both now visibly upset.

As her two young daughters started to wail with her, frightened by their mother's obvious suffering, Danny Boy just laughed louder and louder. The beautiful house he had bought for them was resounding with the noise of his vicious laughter and his family's despair. It was then that Mary finally knew, once and for all, that this had to stop.

Jonjo was savouring his pint, he loved the first pint of the day; it was like the first fix when he had been on the brown years ago. Only, instead of floating up to cloud nine, he wafted towards the men's toilets. He could piss for England when he got a thirst on, and he had found out quite by accident that he could take his drink. So he had embraced his new pastime with a fervour that had astounded him. For all his drug-taking he had never really liked alcohol, only consuming it to keep him chilled until the next hit. Now though, it made him feel alive, made him aware of his surroundings, and exacerbated the sounds from the music on the jukebox. He loved it. In fact, unbeknownst to him, he was one of the large breed of men and women who should not drink. It made him aggressive, it made him opinionated and, worst of all, it made him reckless.

Sitting in the Blind Beggar he looked around him at the clientele and smiled happily. He was on a good vibe; it was later on, when he had downed ten pints in the belief that he was sober and able to take his drink, that the nastiness would emerge. When someone asked him to go away, or a girl asked him to leave her alone. Or a cab driver would refuse to let him in because he was chundering all over the pavement. That was when he convinced himself that all these people, these strangers, were out to put him on a downer. The misconception that he was happy and everyone else was a miserable bastard would creep into his psyche and he would suddenly decide that the only way to sort it out once and for all was to either glass someone, nut someone, or punch someone, depending on who he decided to fight with on that particular occasion. It was only the fact that he was Danny Boy's brother that had stopped someone from harming him, but he had not sussed that out yet. But for now, he was happy; he was enjoying the first flush of the lager and debating whether to have a whisky chaser.

It was cold out, and he watched as the people around him talked and laughed. He saw them remove their winter coats and settle themselves down for a night's drinking and chatting. He felt the warmth from the heating, coupled with the general camaraderie, and decided he would have one more pint, then go and meet his brother at a little drinking club they frequented in south London. He knew he was already late, but he decided to have another pint anyway.

When Danny Boy and Michael walked in two hours later, he was convinced that they had actually arranged to meet there all along. He tried to explain that to his brother who, he noticed quickly, was not giving him his full attention. That was rather annoying, and he was pleased with himself for not rising to the bait and arguing with him.

Danny Boy was not in a good mood, he could tell, and Michael Miles was in an even worse mood. It occurred to Jonjo that he was very unlucky in many respects. All he wanted was to be happy, but everywhere he went people were determined to be fucking miserable.

*

413

Ange was making herself some cocoa when the back door opened and Danny Boy carried Jonjo inside. He was roaring as usual, and she kept quiet as she listened to Danny putting his brother to bed. The banging and crashing as he tried to get him up the stairs was like someone scratching their nails across a blackboard, setting her teeth on edge. The eventual shouting and hollering of Danny Boy was the last straw.

Ange sat at her kitchen table and, lighting a cigarette, she waited patiently for Danny to come back down. She had automatically made him a cup of cocoa as well, knowing he liked a hot drink in the cold weather.

As he walked into the kitchen, his huge frame making the normally spacious room look small, she pointed at the hot drink and was pleased when he sat down at the table with her. 'Thanks, Mum. This is just what I needed.'

He took a few sips before saying loudly, and with deep annoyance, 'I had to clump him in the end. Fucking real, ain't it? Got him off the skag and he's gone on the piss. He's like the old man, if it ain't one thing with him, then it's another.'

She didn't answer him; she was, as always, subdued in his company these days. He noticed it, but he chose to ignore it. Even he didn't want to admit to himself that his own mother was terrified of him. But he knew that she was and it galled him.

'He needs sorting out, Mum, and I am going to fucking sort him out once and for all.' He laughed at his own words and she smiled on cue.

He placed his mug gently on the table and, looking into his mother's eyes, he said quietly, 'Talk to me will you, Mum?'

She looked so old and so small that it occurred to him she might not be around for as long as he expected. She was so thin now, the weight had dropped off her steadily over the last few years, and she was completely grey now as well. And not even bothering to hide it any more. The wrinkles on her face were deep grooves, and he felt his own age creeping up on him as he looked at her.

'What do you want to talk about, son?' She was talking to him like he was a stranger. As if she was just humouring him. And this was the woman who had birthed him, who had cared for him.

Danny felt a sudden and overwhelming urge to lay his head on her chest and cry, as he had done so many times before, when he had been a kid and someone had hurt him. This woman would always be there to comfort him, to hug him, she had wanted him when he thought no one else in the world did. She had fed him, taught him to walk and talk. She had worked every hour God sent to make sure he was clothed, secure, and he had never once thanked her for that. He had treated her badly, and he wished now that he had not been so judgemental. So harsh in his treatment of her. But, when she had accepted her husband back into her bed after all the upset he had caused, after all he had been forced to do, because of his father's recklessness and selfishness, something inside him had died.

Now though, tonight, he wished he had not been so hard on her, she was after all his mother and she *had* loved him. She had loved her husband more, that was the problem. But he understood her, in a strange way, he knew it wasn't anything personal. Not really, she was just selfish, and her selfishness had destroyed them in the end.

'I'm sorry, Mum, for all the hurt I've put you through, over the old man, over everything really. I am truly sorry.'

He sighed heavily, her sadness was communicating itself to him, and he was sorry for that. He just wanted her to get on with her life. Wanted her to understand how they felt about what his father had done to them. And what he, Danny Boy, had done for them. 'I just wanted to provide for us all, you know. Just for once, Mum, I wanted Jonjo and Annie to not be the scruffy kids in the class. The poor kids whose mum was out cleaning every other fucker's house. I wanted us all to be somebody, just once, to not be Cadogan the drunkard's kids, the gambler's kids. I just wanted us to be like everyone else. Just for once.'

Ange felt a rush of sorrow, that this son of hers, her first-born, had been reduced to thinking like that about his own family. And she knew then that it was her fault he had turned into the man he was. But then she had always suspected that her part in his life had not been exactly what others would regard as helpful. She had used him, used all of them at some point, to get what she had wanted.

Grabbing her son's hand she held it tightly to her chest and, shaking her head in denial, she said brokenly, 'I don't know what we would have done without you, Danny Boy, you kept us going. I know that, son.' Her heart was aching with the love she felt for this child of hers.

He hugged her then, and she enjoyed his embrace for the first time in years. She had glimpsed the young Danny Boy for a few moments; she had seen the child whom she had once adored. The kind lad who had somehow disappeared one day, and who she thought would never again return. She was desperately sorry for this huge, unhappy man because she knew he was broken, and he had been broken so badly that he could never be fixed. Something had snapped inside him all those years ago, and he had become bitter and vengeful overnight. A spiteful and cruel man had emerged, and she knew that was why he was now a *Face*. He had that streak of hate running through him that the real Faces were all in possession of because, without it, they wouldn't be the men they were. But she also knew that in her Danny Boy, unlike most of the Faces around town, that streak of hatred had spilled over into every aspect of his life and ruined any chance of happiness he might have had. He was a ferocious bully who had no qualms about persecuting anyone he felt deserved his attention. Even his poor wife and kids. She was partly responsible for all that, deep inside she knew it, and she swore to herself that she would try and help him and his family as much as she could in the future. It was the least she could do really. Considering.

Michael was walking around the casino, greeting the more salubrious members and giving the newer ones the once-over. It was packed out, and the luxurious leather banquettes were full of good-looking young girls, all in evening dresses, all hoping for a punter with a winning streak. It was funny how the men who gambled seriously liked a beautiful woman beside them, never their wives of course, egging them on. He had decided long ago it was an ego thing, a showing off of their wealth and power to young girls who, they knew, had nothing in comparison. But, personally, he didn't give a shit; he provided the companions, as they were called, in the same way he provided the roulette tables or the poker rooms. It was all the same to him, just profit.

He could smell the peculiar aroma of a casino; expensive after-shave and perfume and, underlying that, the dirty smell of money. Money did stink; he had found that out many years before. It was filthy because it was handled so much, a five-pound note could change hands more often in one day than a junkie's kit. He smiled at the simile. But it was true, the Queen of England could handle it in the morning and, by the evening, it could be nestled in the dirty hand of a horse trader. So money, as much as he loved it, did have a stench to it. He knew that diseases could be passed on through money as well; scabies for one. That fact alone was enough to get *him* using a credit card. As he glanced around the room he saw a dark-haired girl with a slim frame and a wide mouth dipping into a punter's chips every time he turned away. He motioned for one of the waitresses to come over to him, and asked her who the girl was, on the quiet. She had no idea, and that pleased him anyway. Because it meant she didn't work here, so she was either with the man she was fleecing, or she had coaxed herself in with a regular.

He settled by the bar area and watched her for a while. She had bony wrists, and for some reason this made him smile. She had long dark hair and oval-shaped grey eyes. In her navy-blue velvet dress she looked every inch the lady. And she was robbing the punter she was with blind. Kissing him, rubbing up against him, clapping her hands delightedly as he placed his bets; she was a professional all right; half-inching his chips and putting them in her shoulder bag with an ease that said she had done it before.

As Michael watched her work, he saw that she was also working another man, and it was this man who now interested him. He was a good punter, and a high roller. He was also that rarest of gamblers, a good loser. Good losers were few and far between; they were normally people who could more than afford the losses they incurred and just enjoyed the evening's entertainment. They were seriously rich, with no agenda, and they enjoyed beating the bankers.

As the girl started to home in on him, Michael walked over

nonchalantly. The man she had arrived with was not pleased with her change of allegiance, and he was also scrutinising his piles of chips. She had been palming his fifty-pounders, and he was suddenly wondering if he might have been fleeced by her. A loser would blame anyone except themselves. Not that he could prove anything of course. But, smiling in a friendly fashion, Michael suddenly grabbed her firmly by the arm, saying quietly into her ear, 'Excuse me, miss, could I have a quick word?'

She looked him over for long moments before shaking her head slowly. 'No, you can't.'

She had a low, well-modulated voice. And she turned from him as if he had just asked her to flash her tits to all and sundry. He grinned, impressed with her cool demeanour. 'Listen, this is *my* casino, darlin', and if I want to speak to you, I fucking will.' He was getting annoyed by her attitude now and his voice had risen slightly.

She turned back towards him and smiling easily, her perfect teeth making her look like an advert for Colgate, she said haughtily, 'Will this take long?'

He shook his head and she was sensible enough to follow him to the office without further conversation. Once inside, he shut the door firmly and said coldly, 'Give me the money.'

She grinned then, still as cool as a cucumber. 'And what money would that be?'

Michael sighed heavily, blowing out his cheeks noisily before saying loudly. 'Open the fucking bag, lady, before I rip it off your arm and ram it down your throat. You are on a warning as of now. I don't like my punters getting dipped. Now, open the fucking bag before I really get annoyed.'

She smiled again, and he noticed in the harsh glare of the office lights that she wasn't as young as he had first thought. She was at least thirty, but the way she had dipped, she had to have had a lot of experience. It was unusual though for this type of girl to come in here. Their names and their status in the criminal community should have been enough of a deterrent for them. The names Cadogan and Miles could stop the hardest men in their tracks, therefore a fucking pickpocket should have been a doddle.

It was a fucking piss-take. But he swallowed his knob, as always trying to keep the peace. Anyway, she wasn't worth rowing over.

She opened the soft suede bag and he saw it was almost full of chips. She had about a grand's worth in there, maybe more. Not a bad little earner. He removed them quickly.

'If I ever see you in here again, I'll have you forcibly ejected. Do you understand me?'

She nodded, still with the arrogant stance and the sneer that told him she thought this was all amusing to her. She was lovely, it was a shame she had such a lairy attitude. He guessed she was on the game as well because she had that knowing look that told him, and any man in her orbit, that she was definitely up for purchase.

'I think the trouble with this place is that it hasn't got any real protection. I slipped through, and I think you should consider getting some proper doormen. I work for Ali Fahri, he can arrange that for you.'

Michael didn't know whether to laugh at her front, or slap her for her cheek. He opted for the laugh. 'Who the fucking hell is Ali Fahri while he's at home?'

Michael had never heard the name before so he assumed he couldn't be anyone he should be interested in.

'He's your worst nightmare, darling.' She walked from the office then, her dress, from the back, showing the world that she was quite heavy on the hips.

Grinning at her front, Michael poured himself a brandy and put the incident out of his mind. But she had a point, how had she got past the door in the first place? He decided to have a fucking almighty tear-up when they closed, and remind everyone that he paid their wages. He was annoyed, she was a skank, and she should never have got as far as the foyer, let alone into the club itself. But she had a point and that was what was really annoying him.

Danny Boy was still brooding about his brother's latest escapade and he was determined to get him finally sorted. As he pulled up outside the home of Louie Stein he wondered at how his life had shaped up. He sat in the car for a few moments observing Louie's drum. It was a nice old gaff, not palatial, or over-opulent, but a nice enough house all the same. He thought of his own home, which was palatial and opulent, to most of the people he knew anyway, and he decided that he hated the fucking place. As he walked up the path, Louie opened the door and, as he stepped into the warmth of his central heating, he sighed happily. 'You have that heating on too high, but for the first few minutes of coming inside it's fucking handsome, but only when you first come in out of the cold. After that it's fucking terrible.'

Louie laughed as they walked through to the kitchen. On the kitchen table was a bottle of brandy and a plate of sandwiches, Danny was already eating one before he had even sat down. He stuffed it into his mouth, holding it between his teeth, and shrugged off his heavy overcoat.

Louie poured them both a large drink before saying happily, 'You and your stomach! I remember when you were a boy. Always with the food!'

Danny Boy laughed with him. 'I remember you bringing in all sorts of Kosher grub, bleeding handsome that was and all. I used to pop into Blooms for their food every now and then because of it, but it wasn't as good as your wife's.'

Louie smiled happily. 'My father always told me, a good cook is better than a good fuck. And I told *you* that years ago, remember? A fuck you can get anywhere, but a decent meal lasts longer and, in the long run, is much more satisfying.'

They laughed together once more. Danny Boy always enjoyed Louie's company. He could relax with him, this man had known him all his life, at least all his working life anyway. He still kept his ear to the ground and fed him titbits of information he thought Danny Boy might find interesting.

Once or twice a month Danny popped by, and he pretended it was work, but he actually enjoyed seeing the old sod. Louie, he knew, had been fucking good to him, and he would never forget that. As he had got older he had realised just how much Louie had actually done for him. Danny was ashamed now at his youthful arrogance, at how he had taken this man's livelihood without a second's thought, just because he had wanted it. He had given him a fair price, but he knew now that the yard had been what had kept

Louie going. All his talk of selling up had been just that. Talk. Since he had retired, he had got older by the day, had shrunk somehow. Got a lot smaller, and a lot nosier. Danny knew he just wanted to be a part of things still, and he wondered if he would be like that one day in the years to come. He doubted it, he had the strength to keep on top of his game; he had the fucking Smoke tied up. Now Spain was also his, so he had nothing to worry about for the foreseeable future. He was more than capable of seeing off any competition.

'So, what's been happening?'

Louie shrugged, overly casual, which meant he had a juicy little bit of gossip he felt was only worth imparting after he had talked shite for half an hour beforehand. But Danny Boy didn't mind, he knew how to play the game. It was one of his nicer traits, he had always thought. His ability to listen to crap with an interested expression and a devilish smile. He knew Louie was lonely, so he didn't mind indulging him.

'Have you heard about the Williamses, over in Dulwich?'

Danny shook his head in bafflement.

Louie smirked the contented smirk of a schoolboy who has just won all the marbles off his mates. 'They were robbed, and I mean *robbed*. Not the bookies, but the actual offices at the back. You know, where all the real betting goes on, and where they orchestrate the money-laundering operation.'

Danny was scowling now. Whoever had done that dastardly deed had not mentioned it to him, and that meant they owed him a percentage. Though, in fairness, he would not have given it the go-ahead anyway. The Williamses were old mates, they did a lot of deals together and it suddenly occurred to him that they would automatically assume that he was in on it. That was why he had not heard a dicky bird about it. He was supposed to get a drink off anything that occurred in the Smoke. Off everything.

'When was this then?'

Louie caught on then, and said slowly, 'Fuck me, Danny Boy, you should have been consulted. It was a serious fucking wedge, over a quarter of a million gone, and no fucking insurance either. They ain't a bank. It happened yesterday afternoon. Just after the morning rush hour; it was well planned and very well executed. They went in quick, balaclavas and shotguns, and they knew where everything was. It was definitely planned with someone in the know. How else could they have known that they kept emergency money in the back of the fireplace? Even I didn't know that. It had a few loose bricks and they went straight for it by all accounts. Fucking scum, robbing your own. I mean, what the fuck is that all about?'

Danny shook his head in disbelief. 'What a fucking liberty. I better shoot round there and offer me condolences, I hope they don't think I gave the nod for it to go off.'

Louie shrugged and refilled their glasses. 'What you have to do now, Danny Boy, is find out who the culprits are, that's your job ain't it? If you let this one go people will think you're an easy mark.'

Danny nodded but he was troubled. No one in their right mind would go after the Williamses, they were hard fucks, big Irish-Jamaicans with lovely teeth and exceptionally bad tempers. He was annoyed now, in case they thought he might have been in on the deal, but he had heard nothing about it and he would have thought one of the workers might have heard a whisper. Well, whoever it was had better fucking start planning a long holiday. Because, when he got his hands on them, they would be lucky if they ever walked again.

'So, what's the big news then?'

Louie looked into his face and Danny Boy saw the worry etched there.

'Come on, is everything all right with you, mate?'

Louie shook his head and said dramatically, 'The Farhis are out and about again.'

Danny Boy laughed in bewilderment, and asked politely, 'Who the fuck are the Farhis?'

Louie poured them both another drink and said seriously, 'The Farhis, Danny Boy, are most people's worst nightmare.'

Chapter Twenty-Seven

Eli Williams was a big man and even Danny Boy, who was a big lad himself, admitted to that as a fact of life. It was rare for anyone to tower over him and those who did, he did not have a problem with. Danny Boy knew he was too fucking mental to worry about stupid things like that. Anyway, he liked Eli, he always had, and they were of a size. Eli was a kindred spirit in many respects. They had always had a good rapport. It was why they worked so well together, they had been friends since their teens, they had also been partners in a lot of skulduggery that neither of them would want made public.

Eli had a huge head of thick hair, dreadlocked and wild, and he was also very smooth-skinned; he had high cheekbones, which gave him a sculptured look, the Bob Marley guise that he played on for the white girls. He also had the soft chocolate colouring that all the women went mad for, black and white. Eli was an equal opportunity loverman; as long as they were fit, good-looking and of the horizontal persuasion, they were all right with him. He loved his main girl and his kids, but he lived in a world where strange was everywhere, and he was a man who would pursue it with total dedication. He was sex on legs for the majority of the female population and he knew that and, like any man worth his salt, he used it for his own ends.

He was a very conservative dresser though, and he smoked grass constantly, like other people smoked Marlboros. He was permanently stoned, but he could still add up a column of figures in seconds. He was a maths whiz-kid and, in another life, he would have gone to a good grammar school and then an even better university, where he would have been fêted for his mathematical acumen. Like a lot of gifted children, he had been overlooked because of his address and his attitude. He had, therefore, used his natural gift to work out the price of drugs. An eighth, a quarter and, eventually, a kilo. With the bets as well, he was onto a good earn.

Eli could work out anything that involved numbers. He was, as one Old Bill had remarked many years before, one smart fuck. Dreads or no dreads, he was an enigma to them. He should have been looked after, should have been revered for his intelligence, and given the opportunity to nurture it, use it for the common good. Instead, he had gone to the local comprehensive where his fierce intellect had frightened his teachers, who saw mainstream education as the way forward for children who had already been written off. His intelligence made them feel inadequate, so they tried their hardest to suppress it. Until he was left, sitting all alone, and bored out of his brains, waiting for his classmates to finally catch up with him. Which, of course, was never going to happen. So he became another one of the forgotten. One of the comprehensive school's dirty secrets. The really clever kids who never quite made the grade because of their backgrounds and environments. Who eventually used their talents in a criminal capacity, knowing in their hearts they were worth more than a job in a warehouse, but who were also unable to utilise their brainpower for the common good.

Eli was also, as far as Danny Boy was concerned, a really nice bloke, and Danny Boy was offended that he might have believed, even for one second, that *he* could have been involved in the robbery in some way. Though, in reality, he *might* have given it the green light. He knew Eli understood that as well as he did because, in their world, without his say-so, the robbery could not, and should not, have gone ahead. He would never have countenanced something like that. Something that would have gone against his friend's interests. It would have caused bad feeling for everyone involved, and made any kind of peace-offering untenable, as had just been proved.

So, now they both had a grudge against the thieving fuckers, and they both wanted to find them, sooner rather than later. It was unbelievable to them both that someone had the fucking balls to go after them in the first place. Especially knowing that Danny Boy was going to want to know their names, addresses and telephone numbers at some point, if for no other reason than the phenomenal piss-take, a piss-take Danny Boy was taking personally now. Was taking so fucking personally that he had put a fucking price on the fuckers' heads. A price that was guaranteed to get whoever was responsible's own fucking grannies on the blower for a grass up.

Danny had been dismissive at first, then, fucked off with it all, he had felt the urge to express his personal irritation at the circumstances, offering a large reward for any information. He was angry once more at the sheer audacity of the people involved. At their complete and utter disregard for him and his standing in their community. He had what was generally referred to as the right hump about it.

Danny poked his forefinger into Eli's face, saying with suppressed anger, 'Look, Eli, believe this, mate, *someone* will give them up; they fucking won't get away with this for long. Anyone with a few quid in their bin will be suspect now. Think about it; anyone flashing an irregular wedge about, or who is in the possession of any kind of unexplained money, will fucking be interrogated as if they were Irish terrorists having a quiet drink in a Birmingham pub. And, let's face it they are jailed whether they're guilty or not. Guildford Four, Birmingham Six. Ring any fucking bells? So, don't let's get too fucking maudlin, eh? This will be solved quicker than a crossword clue in the *Sun*. So why don't you just fucking relax yourself and stop annoying me.'

Eli shrugged. Then he said, with a passion that Danny Boy could understand, because he would have been the same if he had been in his position, 'Because I want them, Danny Boy. Me little daughter was on me lap, man, she's three years old, and they put the fucking gun in me face. *In me face*. Like I'm nothing. I want them personally like, along with me brothers, who want a bit of them as well. This is about blood. About respect. About not taking the fucking piss.'

Danny nodded in agreement and with exasperation, his voice conveying his own anger at the situation to his friend, 'Even I can see that, Eli, I ain't fucking *stupid*. That's a given, that's fair enough.'

He smiled then, his evil, roguish smile that had helped him on to this road of criminal enterprise. 'But one thing though, Eli, I'd like to be there when you confront them. I want to hear what they have to say for themselves.'

Eli grinned, displaying his perfect teeth for the first time since they had met up. 'You can cheer me on, Danny Boy. Cheer me on.'

Danny nodded silently, whilst racking his brains, trying to work out who the fuck would have the front to do something so utterly cuntish. Whoever they were, they had to be on fucking drugs. Pilled up to the eyebrows. It stood to reason. No one with an IQ above thirty would even attempt something so foolish.

Danny Boy was intrigued, as much as he was annoyed about it all, he still wanted to know who it was. Why they felt they could mug him off with impunity.

'Could you tell if they were black or white?'

Eli shrugged expressively. 'I couldn't tell that, Danny, they had ballys on and gloves. They didn't say one fucking word, just gestured with their guns.'

Danny nodded again, and rethought his earlier scenarios. They had planned it well, whoever they were, they were obviously professionals. They were evidently known about town, otherwise they would not have been so astute, so quiet, and there had not been one fucking word spoken from any of them so they either had voices that were known, or they had accents that could help them cancel out other suspects. That was freaky. There was nothing at all to go on, nothing to even give them a clue of any sort.

But Danny also knew that there were only a few people who would be brave enough to take him on, *let alone* the Williams brothers as well. He was already in the driving seat, had been for a while. He could sit this out. He was willing to do that, just so he could finger the fucker for himself. But he knew that he had to be seen to be as involved in this latest debacle as the Williamses were.

He needed to be the one to sort it out. He wanted to, he just didn't want the added pressure. And all his usual contacts had come up with nothing. Sweet F.A. It was a mystery all right, Agatha Christie would be hard-pushed to make any fucking sense of this latest shite, but he would get to the bottom of it if it was the last thing he did on this earth.

Whoever had thought that robbing the Williams brothers was a viable option had to be in dire need of psychiatric treatment. They had to be nuts. Even he knew that they were nice, respectable men who paid their dues and did their level-best to keep their grudges off of the pavement. Out of the public eye. That was a sensible way of living, especially as so many people in their world felt the urge to take their petty grievances out on to the world stage. He did not see himself in this of course. He saw the others, who had to prove a point in public, as making a foolish move, unless you were the main player like himself. The little fishes, he believed, always had to prove how hard they were, showing off to people who saw their actions as nothing more than a good story, something to talk about in the pub or, if it was a particularly gruesome murder, as something to tell their grandchildren. Their actions were then used though as something to give the *Filth* a handle on them. When all it gave *them* was a fucking reason for the Filth to get warrants out against them, to hassle them *legally*. Therefore all the other people they might be mixing with, or working for, were put under the same spotlight. It was a fucking mug's game; he knew *he* could murder anyone in full view of the general public, and he also knew they wouldn't say a dicky bird. Mind you, one of his minders or any of his lesser minions couldn't get away with something like that. Once they brought that kind of interest down on them all from Old Bill they were on their fucking own.

The Williamses were like him in that respect; they would never shit on their own doorstep. Any violence they might indulge in was done in the comfort and privacy of their own premises, in a decent and acceptable manner. Every now and then a public hammering might be orchestrated, but only when the crime warranted it. When an example might be needed. Even then, it would only be on turf that was classed as safe; in front of people who might talk about it, discuss it, but only to other people in their circle. This was a melon scratcher all right. Whoever had planned this was either on a death wish, or so sure of themselves they didn't think that anyone would dare to question their actions. He was inclined to go with the latter, well, more fool them. The Williams boys were not the type of people to suffer fools gladly, and neither was he, for that matter, and that was who these ponces really needed to be worrying about.

Michael was tired out, and he was also desperately worried about these latest developments. He knew better than anyone how reckless Danny Boy could be when the fancy took him. Danny Boy, he knew, was not about to let anything interfere with his business dealings. By the same token though, *he* was still on the look out for the bastards who had encroached on their personal space. It was such a fucking liberty, there was no way it could be forgotten about.

And, like Danny Boy, he had no intention of letting it go lightly either. This was the time to make an example, and they were both determined to do just that. Unfortunately, no one seemed to have any information about the robbery whatsoever. Which was complete shite, as someone, somewhere, had to have known something. It was too close to home, it had to have been someone with a working knowledge of the Williams' business practices. Danny Boy was taking the whole thing as a personal affront. Saw it as a big fucking conspiracy against him personally. He was paranoid enough as it was, without this lot adding to his trauma. But whatever the truth of it all, they had to get it sorted. For such a big firm to be robbed like that was outrageous enough, but for them to be robbed while under the protection of Danny Boy was absolutely unbelievable.

As he poured out two cups of tea, Michael remarked casually, 'Who do you think it could have been, Danny, I mean, who'd have the front?'

Danny sighed loudly, and then said with complete exasperation and a well-contained fury, 'What you on about, if I had any kind of an inkling, do you really think I'd still be sitting here? I have put out feelers all over the place and there is nothing coming back. Not a fucking whisper. This was either planned by one clever cunt, or by a new firm; people we don't know about. But, whoever they are, when I get my fucking hands on them they are fucking dead.'

'Look, Danny, this don't feel right. It feels like a fucking set-up. Who in the world is going to come up against you?'

It was what Danny Boy needed, and Michael knew that. He was playing up to his ego, as he had many times before when he wanted something done. Danny Boy had to see that this was deathly serious and not a game that involved nothing more than his humungous ego.

'Did it ever occur to you, Danny, that this could be a direct threat to us, to our firm? That whoever this is, obviously thinks they are way out of our jurisdiction. That they can do what they like and we'll swallow.'

Danny Boy didn't answer, he was digesting what he had just heard, and he was not impressed with it all. Eventually, he said quietly, 'So you think we *are* being challenged then? Us personally?'

He was nearly laughing at the idea of it, but Michael also heard a hint of worry in his voice. Because it had finally sunk in, had finally occurred to him that this could be much more serious than they had at first thought. It would never occur to Danny Boy that anyone might have a grudge against them. Danny Boy saw himself as immune to the general public and this was a new concept as far as he was concerned. So Michael had struck while his iron was still relatively hot. He could see Danny Boy's mind ticking over for a few minutes before he said quietly, 'Have you ever heard of the Farhis?'

Michael placed the teas on the desk carefully, the question had thrown him. And, nodding his head slowly, he said, 'Funny you should say that. I had a bird in the casino, and she mentioned that name. Why?'

'Louie tipped me the wink about them, they're a family of berserks. Fucking Turks. Ali, who's the oldest, has just got out of clink. Not here, but in Belgium. He's been away for a while. Now he's back in the Smoke and I think that if we put two and two together . . . According to Louie, he's a fucking right twonk. Thinks he's the dog's knob.'

Michael sipped his tea, pleased that Danny Boy was finally taking this seriously. He felt that the name cropping up twice was more than coincidence. And he said as much. Danny Boy didn't dismiss him, he listened carefully to what he had to say.

'According to Louie, this Ali was a right Face, a raving Turk with an attitude, he reckons he could have made his mark. Unfortunately, or fortunately, depending on what side you're on, he got a capture; he murdered his old woman. She was a working girl, big surprise for a berserk. Typical Turk; he was a fucking pimp, and a dealer, and he got out last month. But he wasn't banged up here, he was banged up in Belgium for years. He got out on an appeal, apparently they had not really done their job properly. Typical fucking Old Bill. His brief argued that, as he was married to her, his fingerprints would have been all over the place anyway. The judge, according to Louie, had been paid a decent wedge to find him not guilty and let him out to aggravate the general population as is his wont. But, before he had his collar felt, he was well on his way to taking over the Smoke. To be honest I didn't really take much notice of any of it, you know what Louie's like. He's a fucking gossip, an old woman at times. But now, I think we might have a culprit. So I think we should pay him a visit. Don't you?'

Michael indicated his agreement as Danny knew he would. 'He's a dead man either way, you know that don't you?'

Michael grinned. 'It had crossed my mind. No matter what happens, we have to take him out anyway, Danny. He is too fucking lairy by half.'

Danny laughed, his handsome face belying his real personality. His smile made him look like a real person, like someone who could actually share a joke with you, or cheer someone up with nothing more than his grin and few choice words. He looked so amiable, so normal, it was uncanny. Michael loved him like a brother, more than a brother in fact; he had no feelings for his real younger brother whatsoever. In fact, he thought he was a tosser, he was honest enough to admit that he didn't even think about him at all most of the time. Danny Boy though, filled his mind up on a daily basis. Other than Carole and his children he was the first thing he thought about when he opened his eyes and was the last thing he thought about as he dropped off to sleep. Now, after everything else, they were about to go to war, with the Turks no less. But even Michael knew that this was a necessary evil, knew that even if they were wrong. A warning would not go amiss anyway, because everyone would hear about it sooner rather than later. This man, Ali Fahri, had come to the wrong place at the wrong time. He had, it seemed, much too high an opinion of himself. He clearly thought that all this was some kind of jolly jape. A forerunner to his taking from them everything they had grafted for. The last thing he needed now was a poxy eejit on his conscience, and he had the feeling that is exactly where this man would end up if he wasn't careful.

'Do you have an address?'

Danny Boy opened his arms wide, his handsome face a picture of abject disbelief. 'Well, what do you fucking think? Louie always gets the Full Monty before he opens his trap. Bless him.'

'Actually, Danny, I think we should deliver him up to the Williamses and let them deal with him, don't you?'

Danny nodded sadly. He had been looking forward to a tear-up. But he was philosophical about it all. They were the wronged party, and it wouldn't hurt to show willing. All they really had to do was show their faces. Whether it was them or it wasn't them, they had to be taken out anyway. Kill two birds with one stone.

Arnold was already at the block of flats in Hackney when he saw the lights of a car come round the corner: he knew it was Michael because the lights were expensive, they were the lights of his Mercedes. In the darkness, as they drove toward him, they looked like devil's eyes. As Michael pulled up he walked to him, and settled himself in the front seat. 'You all right?'

Michael nodded. He still felt uneasy since their conversation. And they both felt the tension between them. 'Yeah, you? You OK?'

Arnold ran his hands through his dreads slowly, a sure sign he was agitated. 'Look, Michael, can we forget I ever said anything?

431

I was out of order, and who would take that liar's word on anything. A Filth with a grudge: not the most compelling argument, eh?' He laughed easily, as did Michael.

'Let it go, will you? It's forgotten about. Now, have you seen Ali or any of his counterparts arrive here in the last half hour?'

Arnold felt a great wave of relief at his words. He had been living in mortal fear of Danny Boy hearing about his accusations; he couldn't sleep with the worry of it. What had he been thinking about when he had said those things? Even if they were true, and he still felt there was a good chance of that, it was not his place to bring it to anyone's attention.

'He's inside, been there all night. He's got a great big fucker with him, I'm assuming he's some kind of minder. Other than that, there's just his bird and a kid.'

Michael nodded. Just then Danny Boy arrived in a black Range Rover: he stepped out of the driver's side and looked, for all the world, like a man on a night out. He was grinning like a stoner and, when Eli Williams and two of his brothers finally emerged from the back of the Range Rover, joints in hand, and machetes hidden inside their coats, Danny Boy started to laugh again.

Arnold knew the Williams brothers well, and they all greeted each other amicably; it was a cold night and their breath was visible as they spoke.

'He's definitely in there, I take it?'

Michael nodded his assent. 'As far as we know, yeah. Unless he's gone on the trot through the back door.'

Eli grinned, he was really looking forward to this. The robbery had been bad enough, but to think it had been perpetrated by a fucking no-neck Turk was unconscionable as far as he was concerned. It was a piss-take, and the sooner he sorted it out, the better for everyone concerned. He wanted his money back.

The lobby of the tower block was dark, not that unusual in this area as the lights were often broken deliberately for the muggers' benefit. As they approached the lifts they were all relaxed. In fact, this night had almost taken on a party atmosphere. Eli and his two brothers, a set of twins called Hector and Dexter, went first. Danny Boy didn't mind, he was only there as an observer anyway, to prove his complete ignorance of any kind of skulduggery. But he wanted to make his mark. Wanted to get his point across about the way things worked in London. How, without his permission, Ali shouldn't even have taken a fucking piss against a wall on his manor without his express say-so, let alone anything else. And by the time this lot had finished with him, he would be lucky if he ended up pissing in a clear plastic bag. That is, if he survived this meeting of course.

As the lift hit the twelfth floor they got out and let out their breaths, all unwilling to breathe in the stench of urine and Florizel disinfectant that was peculiar to lifts in high-rise flats. It amazed Danny Boy that the very people who relied on these lifts to convey them to their abodes were the very people who pissed in them in the first place. Even a fucking dog didn't shit in its own bed, so what did that say about the people who lived here? The teenagers who used these lifts as a fucking urinal should be castrated, and would be, if he had to live here. The stench was disgusting, and that women and their children had to live with it on a daily basis really bothered him. It concerned him because he felt that everyone had the right to breathe fresh air, so he was going to make it his personal crusade to see these lifts became piss-free in the future.

The landing was in darkness; even these lights had been removed or, more to the point, destroyed. Danny Boy wondered at the mentality of people who thought that this way of living was normal, was in some way acceptable. The men here should be making it safe for the local women while, at the same time, ensuring an unfriendly environment for outsiders. Sighing with displeasure, he led the way down to the end of the balcony then, grinning once more, he looked at the three Williams brothers as he kicked the designated door open with a flourish.

No one in the neighbouring flats bothered to come outside to see what was happening, as Danny Boy and the others had already sussed out might be the case. Visits like this were par for the course in these flats, they were sure. As they all bundled inside the door-way, Danny saw the man he assumed was the Turk's bodyguard stepping aside quickly. There was no way he was getting in the middle of this lot, and who could blame him? He was a big lump though, and Danny and the others could only think that he knew a lot more than they did, because he was not indicating that he was scared of them in the slightest. He just walked away from the flat quickly and quietly. Danny shouted out to him loudly and with a smile in his voice, 'Oi, fatboy, the lifts stink of piss, just a word to the wise.' They all laughed at him. Opening the front room door, they saw Fahri standing on the balcony, a look of terror on his face, and a young baby held tightly against his chest.

Danny Boy held up his arms and stopped the Williams brothers in their tracks. They had their machetes out, and were desperate to spill this man's blood.

'Give me the baby, mate.'

Fahri shook his head violently. 'You fucking want me, then you take her as well.'

He was almost gloating, honestly believing that the child he held would stop this lot from wiping the floor with him. Danny stepped back and motioned Eli to take the floor.

'Where's my fucking money, you thieving cunt?' Eli was speaking quietly, but with a seriousness that should have alerted the man he was talking to of his rapidly deteriorating temper. His brothers were already searching the flat, pulling the furniture to pieces, and looking for their money or weapons. They were not disappointed; they dragged the sofa out from against the wall and found a stack of money piled behind it. It was theirs; it still had their personal bands around it, there was thousands there, and it had not been touched. The sofa was really old, scruffy and smelly in a deep-green Dralon, the remainder of its old fringing still running along the bottom, with shiny, greasy arm-rests due to the ingrained dirt all over it. The whole place was filthy, from the worn carpet that was almost bare in places to the black fingermarks around the light switches. This was an old ruse for people who wanted to be on the missing list; the place was a council sub-let. A junkie had obviously been a tenant at some time; there were blood spatters on the walls from amateur druggies taking their first hits, and burn marks that were everywhere from the more experienced junkies who kept their blood in their veins or their syringes, frightened of losing any of it in case they lost the smack as well.

Whoever had been given the original tenancy now resided somewhere else, but was happily using the rent they were paid as a stand-by until their giro arrived. It happened all the time, and was the staple home for a lot of people, especially those who didn't want to be found. On the rougher council estates flats like these were commonplace. They were the norm; they were the reason so many people managed to disappear.

Ali saw the looks of disgust on their faces at the way he was living, his pride kicked in, and he felt the shame at his situation. That he had been found out, that he had a serious capture by people who were not exactly friends of his was bad enough, but to be found in this hovel went against the grain. He was someone, he was better than this, and he knew it. He had money, he had prestige, and he also had an in-built self-destruct button that kept him from realising his full potential. He was also a typical Turk; he saw the girl he was with as nothing more than a bed partner. The child she had delivered him was nothing more than a tool to keep her by his side. He had children all over the place; they were his way of possessing the person for eternity. A child gave him an edge, it was a way of leaving his mark on the women he bedded. Used. He hated that he had been caught out like this, as if this was really him and how he lived, instead of just a hang-out, a hiding place. He felt a deep and abiding shame at his predicament. That these people were looking down on him, instead of respecting him for his past glories was embarrassing; he didn't want to be remembered like this, remembered for living like a fucking animal. In Turkey he lived like a king.

Ali held the child tightly to his breast. She was his bargaining tool, his own personal ransom. His angry and hateful persona was to the fore and he was shouting at the top of his voice, unable to take on board what had happened to him; what was going to happen to him now they had tracked him down.

'Go on, get out of my home, you fucking black bastards . . . I will kill you all . . . You don't fucking scare me . . . I mean it, Danny Boy, you know the fucking score . . . I'll jump and take this fucking baby with me.' He was talking fast, talking bollocks, his open face and his balding head were shiny with the sheen of nervous sweat. He knew his minder had left him out in the open, had stepped away from him and his problems; was saving himself. He knew in his gut he was already a dead man, but he was still willing to try and bargain for his life. He had survived prison, and he had survived solitary. He could survive this.

As they looked at him in disgust, a girl arrived back at the flat. Seeing her front door lying in her hallway, she guessed that there was some kind of upset going on, and her first instinct was to protect her baby. Her child. She ran into the front room, throwing the kebabs she had just purchased on to a small wooden coffee table. She saw the men there and knew immediately that this was a serious situation. She knew that her Ali boy was in deep shit; she had visited him and enjoyed the conjugal visits, had used her pregnancy as a bluff for his getting out of that place. She'd seen them making a good life for themselves and the baby they had created. Now, she saw her dreams dissolving before her eyes. This lot meant business.

The men stared at her, no one was expecting her and they were all wondering what on earth she was doing with this piece of shit, a man old enough to be her father. A man who would use his own child as a bargaining chip. The cold night air had sobered them up, made them realise exactly what they were dealing with. It was a depressing thought. She was a small-boned girl with heavily bleached blond hair, and even heavier make-up, thickly applied to cover the numerous acne scars on her cheeks. Her blusher was so prominent that it made her look like an extra on *Trumpton*. She was very young, and the men were shocked at her arrival. In fact, they were seriously fucked off because they were only interested in him. No one else. They wanted her to take her baby and go. Fuck off out of it. Then, suddenly, she gave a loud and piercing shriek. It went through each of their heads like a butcher's migraine and Danny Boy, who was really getting annoyed now, stormed out on to the balcony and snatching the baby from the man's arms roughly thrust it towards the girl.

'Fuck off. Take your baby and fuck off. He was threatening to throw it off the fucking balcony. If I see your face here again tonight, then I'll do it for him.'

The baby started screaming now, and the girl, who was not a fool, didn't need telling twice. She wanted out of this place and she wanted to leave it in one piece.

Ali Fahri watched as the girl hurriedly left the flat, the kebabs, forgotten about, were still lying on the table in their numerous wrappings. The aroma of the meat was finally escaping into the atmosphere around them, making the room smell almost habitable. The twins were once more tearing the place apart, looking for the rest of the money they had lost, and the weapons that had been used against them. Neither of them wanted any part of Ali Fahri and his imminent demise. They were quite happy to let Eli deal with that part of the evening's entertainment; for all their big talk, they understood now just how precarious life could become if you didn't keep your wits about you. How, overnight, a person's whole world could collapse. That was definitely food for thought.

Ali had been a serious contender in his day, and yet he had been reduced to this, to holding his own child as equity. It was a real eye-opener all right.

Eli walked purposefully towards the man on the small balcony. Ali was tiny in comparison to him, did not look like he could really do any damage to anyone without a gun, or a weapon of some description. Eli felt his own size, felt his superior strength. He saw the fear in his antagonist's eyes and enjoyed it. Embraced it, felt the power that he had over this man, this man who had caused him fucking untold aggravation. Who had the audacity to think Eli was so fucking weak he could be robbed and intimidated and not retaliate. Who was such a cunt he would fucking allow this piece of shite to put a gun in his face while his child was in his arms. A child that he would die for, unlike this cunt in front of him, who would have killed his own flesh and blood to get out of a situation that he had caused in the first place. A situation that he had executed without a moment's thought for what the consequences might be.

As Eli raised the machete above his head he saw Ali put up his arms instinctively, attempting to protect his face, his head; it was this simple action, along with the use of his own child as protection, that made Eli feel even angrier than he did. Ali didn't even have the guts to try and fight him, to try and remove the weapon from his hands. He wasn't going to go down fighting, instead, he was trying to protect himself like a fucking woman would against a man who was obviously her superior in power, strength and, more importantly, intellect. He smashed the machete down with as much brute force as he could muster, and watched with morbid fascination as it severed the man's right hand from his wrist. He watched as the errant limb dropped onto the floor with a dull thud, and the blood started to pump out everywhere. Ali was looking at his severed hand in utter amazement, as if it belonged to someone else, the shock of the attack making him mute. The sight of his own hand on the filthy floor of the balcony was almost unbelievable. Then the pain set in. The awful feeling as his blood was pumped from his body was suddenly all too real. With each beat of his heart he felt it spurting out everywhere, felt the pain as if he was being milked by an invisible hand. People were now watching the drama unfold. Other balconies around them were now lit up, lights were going on all over the place. Ali's final humiliation was now a public spectacle. 'You bastards . . . you fucking black bastards.'

'That's a bit racist ain't it, Ali? What about us, the white bastards?'

Even Eli laughed at that and Ali was in desperate tears at the casualness of the words. 'You are all bastards . . .' His voice was loud, and full of hatred and accusation. He dropped to his knees then, feeling the slippery stickiness of his own blood as it was sucked into the material of his trousers. It was everywhere, all over him, the pumping of his own heart making a deep puddle all around him, causing him to skid heavily onto his elbows as he tried to stand himself up. It was a living nightmare; he was nearly in tears as he saw his own hand lying there in the filth and dirt. And the full force of his predicament hit him when he heard the shouts from the other flats; a chorus of jeers to egg his enemies on to even greater violence and he heard a cacophony of insults from complete strangers who assumed he had to be the one in the wrong. Who were enjoying seeing him laid so low. But Danny Boy and the others were uninterested in the drama they had created. They just wanted it sorted and over with, once and for all. None of them even contemplated that someone might call the police. It simply wasn't going to happen. No one would be that fucking stupid; if these men were willing to do this to the Turk the general consensus was what else were they capable of? Especially to a grass. And the Turk wasn't worth the aggravation anyway. Danny Boy knew that their identities were already being discussed, and this would just be another urban legend, exaggerated and embroidered by all these people who were pleased just to be a part of it. Another tale of his violence to add to *all* the others. The knowledge saddened him in many ways, even as he was pleased about it. The savagery of the attack would keep the Filth at bay. Everyone of them knew that.

'Go on then, Eli, finish him off. We ain't got all fucking night.' Danny was shouting now and his voice, and the urgency in it, communicated itself to Eli, and he brought the machete down onto the man's head with all the force he could muster, splitting his skull open. They watched in fascination as Eli tried unsuccessfully to retrieve it. Tried to pull it back out, but it was stuck there; it was buried deep in Ali's brain.

That's when the man finally started to scream, his voice started babbling out in Turkish, his terrible pain evident to anyone who could hear him, sounding like an animal caught in a man trap. He was trying to get up once more, trying to walk about, as Eli was still trying to remove the offending object from his skull. Eli was slipping all over the place in Ali's blood, it was everywhere, and Ali was still not going back down. He was a strong fucker, there was no doubt about that.

Danny Boy walked over to them and, lifting Ali up from the floor as if he weighed nothing, he wrenched the machete from its new home. Then, he threw Ali over the balcony without a second's thought. He picked up the man's severed hand and threw that off the balcony after him, throwing it as if it was a rugby ball, with all the strength he could muster. Then, passing the bloodied machete back to Eli, he said angrily, 'How long were you going to make that last? For fuck's sake, three of you and one of him, I mean it ain't rocket science is it?' Shaking his head once more, Danny's anger was almost tangible now; his huge muscular body reminding them just how strong he really was. How he was capable of taking them all on without even breaking into a sweat. Then he said casually, his mood changing as always with lightning speed, 'That was fucking terrible really. You got what you came here for though? You got the poke?' The Williams boys nodded gently; the evening's events had left them a little subdued. 'Come on then, back to the yard.'

As they walked out Danny picked up the kebabs and took them with him. At the lift Danny looked at them and said gaily, 'Waste not, want not, eh?'

The twins were still in shock at the night's events, and Eli was not sure just how he felt about Danny Boy's interference in all of this. He felt as if he had been set up somehow, as if he had not really had any control over what had just happened. They had their money back, but it all seemed staged, contrived, somehow. This bloke had not even had a fucking decent minder on his case. When it came down to it he was just a fucking ponce, not worth a wank. What on earth had made him think he could have taken them on in the first place?

As they left the flats they heard the ambulance sirens in the distance. Danny laughed once more and, taking a big bite of his kebab, he said through a mouth full of reconstituted meat and wilting salad, 'Bit fucking late for them, ain't it? Typical fucking national health.' Everyone laughed; suddenly they were glad that it was over.

Chapter Twenty-Eight

Arnold Landers wasn't sleeping and this was affecting his day-to-day living. In fact, he was so tired at times he wondered at how he managed to keep on top of his workload. That Annie had noticed this was also a worry. Danny Boy had eventually welcomed her back into his fold with open arms, even though it had never been really mentioned between them, he'd known that Danny Boy had had the ache with his sister for a long time. He also knew that it was her association with him that had softened Danny Boy towards her; he was always telling him how much he appreciated the way he had taken his sister under his wing. How he saw the way he kept her on the straight and narrow, cared for her, and made her respect herself once more. All these compliments were a heavy burden for Arnold, especially as he didn't feel he warranted them. It also made it impossible for him to ever leave her, not that he wanted to. But the knowledge that anything like that was now completely out of the question did not exactly enhance their relationship. He cared for her but, at the same time, Danny Boy's presence was always there, hovering in the background of their daily lives, reminding him of how precarious his position could be if Annie decided to turn against him.

Becoming a part of the Cadogans had been such a buzz at first, now though, he saw it for what it was, a fucking prison sentence. You could never have another individual thought with people like them, everything you decided was with the Cadogans in the back of your mind. From how they might react to his actions, to how they would perceive his opinions and, worst of all, how they expected him to automatically adopt their points of view, as if anyone who disagreed with them were anarchists, were being deliberately disloyal to the family. He had preferred it when Annie had still hated her brother and wanted to go against him at every opportunity. Now she was basking in his new-found interest in her, in his brotherly concern for her well-being.

Even Jonjo seemed to be socially acceptable these days; he was a useless drunk who was either stoned or coked out of his nut but he had still been given a lot of responsibility in the businesses anyway. Responsibility that *he, Arnold,* was expected to make sure wasn't fucked up in any way. In effect, he was Jonjo's unofficial minder. Basically that meant that he did all the main work, sorted out the employees and made sure that everything ran smoothly. It also meant that he was run off his feet, and yet was still seen as nothing more than the number two, after Jonjo of course, and only given any kind of kudos by Danny Boy in the comfort and privacy of the offices they frequented all over the Smoke. Not an ideal situation for anyone, but it was beginning to wear him down. He was not happy being used like this, and he had to make that point sooner rather than later. If Jonjo had at least a working knowledge of what he was supposed to be doing it wouldn't be too bad, but he was completely in the dark about it. From the nightclubs and the debts right through to the bookies, Jonjo was in complete ignorance about even the most basic workings of anything going on around him. He couldn't even understand that a seven to two bet on a dead cert was just a professional gambler's way of buying money for himself. That they put on seven quid to win two quid back was beyond his comprehension, and he then voiced that opinion to their regular punters, very *loudly,* as he voiced many other opinions that would be best left unsaid.

Jonjo was so fucking backward that he had no chance of ever coming forward. And *he* was carrying him, doing *all* the main work, the real collar, seeing to the day-to-day running of everything. He was the one who was making sure the profits were not tampered with, and that the workforce were doing their jobs properly. He oversaw the bookies, both the legal and the off the books, and made sure the clubs were up for any kind of inspection, from anyone, from the VAT people to the silent investors. He made sure the debts were collected in good time and with the minimum of fuss and the maximum of efficiency. Now, though, it was starting to get him down. He was being royally mugged off and he knew it.

Danny Boy had given him the chance to prove himself, which he had done, and he had then left him to do his level best against all the odds, carrying that ponce of a brother as best he could. Danny Boy had to know that Jonjo was a liability, that he was a fucking ice cream freezer, a silly little geezer with a mistaken belief that he was a major player in the Cadogan organisation. And, even though Jonjo knew that without him in his corner he was fucking finished, that he would be sussed out as a prize cunt within days, he still played the big I am, acted the part of the fucking gangster. He played to an audience who pretended they believed it all because the fact that Danny Boy acted like it was the truth meant they had to as well. Yet they came to Arnold if they needed anything, came to *him* if they wanted anything done.

Just the thought of it was enough to make anyone with half a brain think twice about their position in the world they inhabited. Jonjo was a muppet, and Arnold was not going to carry him any longer. And, to make matters worse, he had also started treating him as if he was a lackey, ordering him about in public and demanding money. It had gone too far, and Arnold knew he had to do something about it sooner rather than later. He had his creds, and they didn't allow for a fucking wank job like Jonjo Cadogan to treat him like the hired help, treat him as if he had no standing in this organisation whatsoever.

Well, today he would find out exactly where he stood. He had brought a lot of good people in with him and they were still loyal; he had the right to withdraw from the Cadogans at any time he chose. He was still nervous though, but he knew that if he didn't do something now, he never would. It would be too late because Jonjo was using his power and his position at every available opportunity. If he let him carry on much longer it would be too late to rectify the situation. He would then stop being so careful, so loyal to his friends. And it was rank stupidity like that was what caused Old Bill to start looking at them a bit too closely, and all the bent Filth in the land couldn't stop the Serious Crime Squad when they set their sights on someone.

Michael was happy. He was pleased with his morning's work. As he drove into the scrapyard he was singing under his breath. Danny was already there, but he wasn't surprised at that, he sometimes thought the man lived there on the quiet. He didn't let that thought take root, the truth of it was not something he wanted to dwell on. As he got out of his air-conditioned car the warmth of the afternoon air hit him like a wall of sweat. It was so hot, the August sun was relentless, and he wondered if the extreme heat in the yard could be caused by the scrap metal around them being baked in the sunlight. He knew that at times the scrap became far too hot to be touched, even with gloves, and they had to hose it down if a punter wanted to purchase it.

Michael went into the office quickly, the stench of the oil and petrol already too much for him to bear. The oil was everywhere, and he knew it was this that could cause the place to go up like a tinderbox. The years of leakage alone was astronomical; the ground soaked with all sorts of flammable materials. It was another reason why they kept the dogs on the prowl, they provided early warnings in more ways than one. An arsonist could easily render this place an inferno in minutes.

Inside the offices, Danny had on three large fans, but they did little more than recycle the stale air that was a constant seeing as the windows didn't open, had all been nailed shut by Louie for security reasons.

'Fucking hot, ain't it? I have drunk the fucking fridge dry!'

Michael grimaced and sat down heavily. 'I have a case of beer in me boot, but it's probably fucking boiling by now.'

Danny laughed, his big, deep booming laugh that always made people forget about his anger and his knack of taking offence on a whim. Something that seemed to be happening more and more lately, and with more and more regularity. 'I'll go and get it, mate, you sit down and have a relax.'

As Michael watched Danny Boy go and fetch the case of beer he was amazed, as he always was, that Danny Boy would even do that for him. He was the only person Danny Boy would have done it for and knowing that made him feel sad. He was under enormous pressure because of his relationship with Danny Boy. People came to him because they knew that he was the only person Danny Boy even remotely respected. He loved the man, even as he wished, at times, that he was on the other side of the world. Danny Boy was once more out of control: this happened periodically, it was as if he needed to get rid of his pent-up anger and frustration. He did this by causing fucking murders with people he felt needed a tug, who he felt needed a physical reminder of his place in the criminal community. That was all bollocks of course. Danny just took umbrage every now and then at someone he saw as a threat, someone he saw as capable of one day taking what he had from him, or someone who was maybe just a bit too good-looking for their own good, or that bit too clever. It didn't matter what the reason was, once he got the thought into his head, no one could convince him otherwise. He would take against someone for the slightest of reasons, or welcome them into the fold for no other reason than they made him laugh.

Danny Boy could go for a drink with his cronies, all open wallet and happy of countenance, and then suddenly someone there was now his biggest enemy, was out to get him. Was now a target for his anger and his frustration. He would then set out to destroy them, and no one would lift a finger to stop him. It was at times like this that Michael really hated this man, even as he was desperately sorry for him. Because he knew that Danny Boy's life had been stunted many years before when his father had left him to cope with the gambling debt and a mother and two siblings who depended on him to make things right. Still did. Well, he had made things right, he had looked after them all and, along the way, he had turned into this vicious, vindictive man who was now about to start a campaign against someone who they both knew deep down didn't deserve any of it.

Michael knew the signs, and he would do his best to provide some damage limitation, but he knew it was a waste of time really.

Danny Boy was on a mission, and no one was going to stop him once he got started. On the bright side though, once he got it out of his system he would calm down again for a while, and life would return to normal, until the next time.

As Danny Boy placed the beers in the fridge, Michael sat back on the old settee and enjoyed the cool air from the fans. He wished he didn't know so much about this dangerous man that he was in partnership with, who he knew he owed so much to; not only his success, but his whole life. He was the actual brains of this outfit, everyone knew that, but Danny Boy was the main man. Without him, no one would bother to give him the time of day. He wasn't really a violent person, not in the way that Danny Boy was, or in the way that most of their contemporaries were. Michael needed a reason to fight, a good reason, but when he had that reason he could hold his own with the best of them. He acted the part when it was necessary but, in truth, he had no real stomach for any of it.

Michael knew though that it was a staple part of their business, that the only reason they were at the top of their game was because they had the reputation for taking out their rivals violently and permanently. Danny Boy Cadogan took no prisoners; if you crossed him in any way, you were obliterated. Simple as that. Well, business rivals were one thing, they were fair game, it was an us-or-them situation. But these terrible grudges that Danny Boy would suddenly amass, for no reason that made any logical kind of sense, would one day prove to be their downfall. He was convinced of that much.

One day Danny Boy Cadogan would come up against his nemesis, would take umbrage against someone who would turn out to be a bigger and better nutter than him. It was the way of the world that they lived in, and Danny Boy's penchant for suddenly taking against someone for no real reason other than he didn't like them was likely to backfire on him with dire consequences. And that meant it would backfire on him as well. So he had a personal stake in all this. But, for the moment, he displayed all the usual signs of a man who was on a mission, and Michael hoped and prayed that whoever had rattled his cage this time round wasn't anyone who would be missed too much and, more importantly, missed by anyone who really mattered.

Mary was still shaking and, no matter how hard she tried, she just couldn't control it this time. Normally she could rein it in, so to speak. She could usually force herself to calm down by sheer willpower. But that was not working for her today. In fact, she had the distinct impression it was actually making her worse. She had already put on her face, as she referred to her morning make-up routine, so she was pleased about that anyway. Once her make-up was in place she could cope with the rest of the day. It was like a mask that she used to hide her real self, to make her into a different person: without the thick make-up and the carefully drawn eyebrows she felt exposed. Felt naked. But the sudden onset of this latest bout of trembling had thrown her. It was so forceful that she couldn't control it at all. Going into the drawing room, she opened the drinks cabinet and poured herself a large vodka. It looked so innocent, the clear liquid in a cut-glass goblet for all the world looking like pure spring water. Yet, as she gulped it down, she felt the burn as the raw alcohol invaded her morning stomach, hitting the bile in her belly, bile that was already trying to make its way upwards, trying to burn her throat out once more.

Mary slipped her hand into her dressing-gown pocket and took out a packet of Rennies; she ate a handful of them quickly, chewing them without thinking, trying to stem the burning. She felt the burning subside and sighed with relief.

Then, pouring herself another large drink, she gulped it down. She felt the shaking subside at last and enjoyed the cloak of calmness that was suddenly surrounding her being. Closing her eyes, Mary burped gently, placing her slim hand with its expensive rings and expensively manicured nails over her mouth in a parody of lady-like manners. She closed her eyes for a few moments, letting the alcohol take effect, waiting for the next stage in her morning routine: the feeling of complete and utter disinterest that seemed to get her through each day. It took longer and longer for it to settle on her lately, but she was patient, and she was never disappointed. When it finally arrived she was so relieved, she celebrated with another drink. She was a functioning alcoholic, she knew this because she had read up on the subject.

Unlike her mother, who had just been a plain old common-or-garden, alcoholic, she was that rarest of breeds. A functioning one. She could cook a dinner, clean a house, do a shop, bath the kids and, if necessary, fuck her husband. She did it all without any kind of feeling or interest. There were other people like her, who could hold down jobs, run businesses, and even operate on other human beings when, all the time, they were as drunk as a fucking skunk. The thought made her want to smile, so she did. She had so little to smile about that when she felt the urge to, she did.

Mary made her way back upstairs. In her bedroom she slipped off her wrap and, looking in the mirror, she saw the bruises on her arms from her husband's last visit. They didn't hurt, which was strange because they looked very sore. It was really hot out and she had to wear long-sleeved tops and trousers.

She sat on the end of her bed, a bed she had made as soon as she had vacated it. It was perfect. She often imagined Danny Boy bouncing a coin on it like the horrible big-mouthed sergeants did in the old war films, making sure that it was tucked in properly and therefore worthy of a man like her husband. Worthy of a man of his calibre. She wanted to smile again but she didn't, she decided he wasn't worth a smile.

Mary sat there, on the edge of her bed, terrified of messing it up, and looked around the lovely room she had planned so carefully. She had imagined, in her sober lunacy, that such a lovely environment might make him be nicer to her. She stood up carefully. Even with the bruises that covered a large part of her and after the births of her children, she still had a good body. It might not be as firm as it had once been, but she was still capable of giving a lot of women a run for their money, and she knew that. It wasn't a big-headed thing, an arrogant belief. It was the truth. She only had to open any newspaper or magazine to see the half-naked bodies of other women, famous women, and compare herself with them. She knew she wasn't lacking as far as that was concerned. Poor Carole was already covered in stretchmarks, and had a belly that wouldn't look out of place on Buddha himself, and her husband, her brother

Michael, still adored her. Actually, so did *her* husband. Danny Boy loved Carole with a vengeance, saw her as the perfect woman. Huge thighs and stretchmarks included. It seemed a jelly belly and fat ankles were now the new requisites needed for keeping your man.

Each birth had seen her go straight back to normal, she'd only had a little bit of sagging on her belly and that had soon disappeared once she had come home. The midwife had been worried about that the last time she had given birth, a stupid young girl with no experience of life whatsoever, who had no concept of the real world that was populated by actual women and children, except for what she had garnered from books. Books she would wager a fortune on had been written by men or, even worse, by one of those ugly women who saw child-bearing as an excuse to stop shaving their body hair, and used their womb as an excuse to make their husbands feel guilty for the rest of their days. And who then felt an urge to tell everyone else how *they* should be feeling. Found the time to write about it with the aid of an Aga and an au pair. Her midwife, the thicko child, as she referred to her in her mind, felt that she was too thin, was too happy and too energetic for a new mum. She had asked her over and over again if she was all right, and Mary had been forced to stifle the urge to smash the girl's head in with the nearest heavy object. But she had been in full make-up and in full control every time the girl had arrived at her home. The last visit had been wonderful; as she had finally left the house, she had slammed the front door loudly behind her then locked it. Had let the silly little bitch know just how fucking irritating she had found her.

Mary was still looking at her naked body when she realised Leona was watching her from the doorway, and she saw the horrified expression on her daughter's face at her wounds. Quickly pulling her dressing gown back on she smiled serenely as her daughter walked to her slowly. Hugging her tightly, Leona said brokenly, 'Oh, Mummy, did you fall over again?'

And Mary knew in those few seconds, in her heart of hearts, that this child knew exactly what had happened to her, probably knew in graphic detail what had occurred, but was already learning the language of lies that was the only way to survive in this household. So she hugged her girl back, there was no feeling inside her any more and she was sorry for that. And she said sweetly, 'Mummy will be OK, darling. I'm just clumsy, that's all. Everyone knows that.'

But the girl's words had destroyed the last vestige of her mother's pride, and nothing would ever really be the same between them again.

Arnold was nervous, but he was still determined to get his point across. He was sitting with Danny Boy and Michael in the back room of a pub they owned in east London. It was a small room and the elderly flock wallpaper on the walls made it seem even smaller that it was. It had a table, four chairs, and a sideboard that had somehow survived the sixties. But it was a good meeting place because few people knew the back room even existed. The pub was on a main road and very busy so it was easy to slip through to the back without being noticed. Danny Boy looked even bigger than usual in these surroundings and, as he poured them a drink, he seemed subdued. Quiet, as if he knew he was going to hear something he didn't really want to.

But Arnold consoled himself with the fact that he had his cred; he wasn't a muppet, he had a good reputation and a decent curriculum vitae. In fact, he could get a job anywhere in the real world, though if he left the employ of Danny Boy he had a feeling that would not be such an easy endeavour. If Danny decided to have him blackballed, he would be finished, and he knew that. But, even knowing that, he was still determined to say his piece. If necessary he would move away, go to another country. But he wasn't fucking rolling over, no way. He couldn't do this any more, he had to make a stand for his own self-respect, for his own peace of mind if nothing else.

As Arnold took the glass of brandy from Danny Boy he could feel the fear that was building up inside his chest. Danny Boy smiled at him in a friendly fashion and he knew that the man did genuinely like him. Michael did as well, he knew that, but when he said his piece he knew it was Danny's reaction that would be the important one; he knew from experience that Michael always waited for Danny's response to anything that went on before he ever gave his opinion on it. An opinion that was always in accordance with Danny Boy's. He also knew though, that Michael would often challenge Danny Boy in private about things he didn't agree with, but never in public. Arnold knew that Michael was the only person in the world that Danny Boy allowed to question his opinions or his actions. He was the lone voice of reason amid the utter chaos that was Danny Boy Cadogan's mind.

And Michael was actually the stronger of the two in many respects because of that. People tended to approach Michael first about new deals, would sound him out before going to Danny Boy. Though he had a feeling that Michael didn't realise that fact or, if he did, he was sensible enough to keep that knowledge very much to himself. Knowing Danny Boy like he did, he suspected it was the latter. Danny Boy could go for months without a psychotic episode and, when that finally happened, anyone could be on the receiving end of his paranoia. Afterwards, he would go back to his usual *friendly*, amiable self, and it would be as if nothing untoward had happened, that his latest ultra-violent outburst had never happened. But his actions would be talked about for months, though his outlandish threats and his seriously disturbing behaviour would be whispered about behind closed doors, in private. This was in case someone mentioned to the man in question that he was being talked about and not in a flattering way. At times his outrageous accusations were so incredible that even his latest victim's worst enemies were not sure they believed them. Danny Cadogan had a rep, and it was not just for his business acumen and his ability to see a good earner. It was also because, after all these years, he was still classed as an unknown quantity, a nutter who had proved that he was seriously unstable on more than one occasion. And while this was what kept him at the top of his game, it was also why he was not trusted one hundred per cent by anyone he dealt with.

Arnold watched as Michael sat back in his seat and, as always, kept a low profile until he heard what everyone had to say. Michael had guessed that there was something personal going down, and he held his drink in both hands, and waited patiently for Arnold to say his piece. Danny Boy was observing Michael, and Arnold got the impression he found his actions almost comical. Turning to the man who was his sister's other half he said gently, 'So, what's the problem, Arnold?'

Danny Boy smiled the disarming smile that made him look so handsome, and so gentle. He was really good-looking, even Arnold had to admit that much. If he didn't know him so well he might have fallen for this best-friend act.

Sighing heavily, Arnold looked into Danny Boy's eyes and, taking a deep gulp of his brandy, he spoke clearly and honestly. 'I ain't happy, Danny Boy, and I feel I have got to say this to you. I know you might not want to hear it and I respect that. But I have to say me piece.'

Danny nodded silently, gesturing for him to carry on talking, his face giving nothing away.

'I love what I do, I love me job, and I do it fucking well. You know that. But it's Jonjo. He treats me like a fucking mug. He takes the money and does nothing, fuck all. He just plays the fucking mafia boy; he's watched one too many Scorsese films. He even walks around with his overcoat around his shoulders. He is costing us a fucking fortune, and he treats me like a gofer. I can't go on working like this and keep any kind of self-respect.' Arnold could hear the whine in his own voice and was angry with himself. But he had to get his point across. He had to say what he felt.

'Is he really walking round with an overcoat around his shoulders?' Danny Boy's voice was low and interested.

Arnold nodded.

'What, in the middle of August? He must be fucking melting. What a cunt, eh, Mike? Only him. Brain of fucking Britain.'

Michael started laughing, and Arnold couldn't help joining him. Danny was shaking his head and chuckling with mirth. He could be funny, he knew that.

'He's a fucking twat, ain't he? I gave him an opening, I knew you would be the one running it all. I mean, *come on*. You have *had* or, should I say, *attempted*, a conversation with Jonjo at least once, I take it. You must have guessed he was just the fall guy. The front man. I mean I love him, he's me brother, but if it ever went pear-shaped I could afford to lose him, but not you. I couldn't afford to lose you. But you're right, Arnold. He needs knocking down a few pegs and I'll see to that personally. From tomorrow, you will be the front man; I know you won't get us in any fucking shit. You're too much of a shrewdie and I am sorry, mate, if you ever felt like you were being treated like a cunt. It was nothing personal. To be honest, I had hoped some of your nous might have rubbed off on me little bro. It's hard when you have to admit publicly that your own brother is about as much use as a fucking chocolate teapot. But there it is, he's his father's son all right, a fucking lazy waster with his eye always on the easiest fucking option.'

Arnold was thrilled at the turn of events, and he wanted to hug this man who had just given him the equivalent of the master key to the Bank of England. He was amazed in one way at how easy it had been, and sorry in another way for Jonjo because he didn't like having to serve him up.

'Thank you, Danny Boy. It was nothing personal to Jonjo, you know that . . .'

Danny grinned. ' 'Course it was fucking personal, but you are right to give me a tug. If you think all this, then the chances are so do other people, and that is not good for business. I will give him an earn, after all he is my little brother, ain't he? But I knew he wasn't making a name for himself, at least not the kind of name I was hoping he would. He is a fucking wanker, but there ain't a lot I can do about that is there? My old mum always said, if brains was gunpowder he couldn't blow his fucking eyebrows off.' They all laughed at the old saying.

Then Michael leaned forward in his chair and finally spoke, 'We'll give him a club to run, that will satisfy his ego without too much thinking involved. I don't think he really thrives well under pressure anyway, Danny Boy.'

Arnold listened to the calm way he expressed his opinion and knew that Michael was on his side in all this. He felt a moment's relief at that knowledge because he knew Michael's approbation would be the icing on the cake as far as Danny Boy was concerned.

'Yeah, a club would be ideal for him; he can walk round it in his fucking overcoat playing the big man. Stick him in a fucking strip club, that should keep him busy for a while. In fact, I will send the fucker on an apprenticeship and tell him if he don't learn the fucking ropes this time he can fuck off and get a job in Ford with all the other losers. He needs a short, sharp shock as the old man used to say. This might be just the thing to bring him to his senses.'

Michael nodded in agreement, and the three men then chatted together amiably for the rest of the night. Arnold was over the moon at how the day had turned out, and felt at last that he was finally making something of his life. He couldn't wait to tell Annie his news, but felt it prudent to wait until Danny Boy gave him the nod to leave. He didn't want to offend him at this stage in the game, especially when Danny Boy was asking him a lot of questions about his plans for the future. Not just for him, but for his little sister as well. The sister who he now loved and adored, and for whom he now wanted nothing but the best. Danny Boy Cadogan changed with the weather and it would augur him well to remember that in the future. As it did anyone who was involved with him in any way, shape or form.

Jonjo was in a private drinking club that Danny Boy had acquired many years before as payment for a debt. A very small debt in comparison to what he had demanded as payment for it. He was coked out of his nut, and acting the part of the hard man, all the time knowing that he would not be expected to actually do anything that even resembled a hard man's usual actions. He just used the power his name held to do whatever he wanted to. He loved the power, loved that he could do what he liked and no one would even dare to challenge him.

Deep inside though, he knew that the very people who he tried so desperately to impress with this behaviour were really laughing at him. They thought he was a fucking muppet, a *clown*. It was this knowledge that made him so mean and so unpredictable. It was this knowledge that made him hate his brother even more than he did himself.

Snorting cocaine and drinking excessively gave him the capacity for self-delusion that was so important to his daily life. But there wasn't enough alcohol or drugs in the world to drown out the truth of his situation and he knew that better than anybody. Better than this crowd of cunts did anyway.

As Jonjo ordered yet another round of drinks, drinks that he would pay for or, more to the point, his brother would pay for, he grinned happily at the people surrounding him. They were all third-class Faces, either on a wage, or used as gofers. None of them had any credence whatsoever, a bit like him.

One of the guys, a young fellow with a good physique and a knack for ferreting out a few quid, was laughing with him. But suddenly, Jonjo didn't like him any more. Suddenly he saw his white, even teeth and heavily lashed blue eyes as being sneaky, saw him as taking the piss out of him. That the boy could take Jonjo out without breaking a sweat was a given, that he would have the sense not to do that given the circumstances and his family connections, was what Jonjo was depending on. The boy's name was Donald Hart, and, when Jonjo turned the full force of his malevolent personality on him, he was more surprised than anyone else at the boy's reaction. 'Are you fucking taking the piss, Donald? I never said you could laugh?'

Donald realised what was going down and he shrugged, tried to keep the peace. He knew that Jonjo was out of bounds in many respects; especially for a smack in the face. But, unlike Jonjo, Donald had too much pride and wasn't going to take his disrespect or, more to the point, let his fucking disillusionment at his own sorry life interfere with his. If Jonjo wanted a row, he decided, he was going to give him one, regardless of the consequences. This was about self-respect now. He didn't have much in life, except his pride and this no-neck was about to remove that from him without a fucking fight.

So Donald shook his head, in denial at the man's words, and said, quietly, 'I don't need your fucking permission to laugh, Jonjo, and, if you want a fucking row then let's have one now, man to man. I'm ready when you are.' Donald put his drink on the bar and stepped away from the throng, flexing his huge shoulders and waiting for the fight to begin.

Jonjo was nonplussed for a few moments; the fact that no one was trying to stop the event, as usually happened in these cases, was evidence of exactly how he was really thought of by these so-called friends of his. Danny had once said, many years before to their father, 'For all your so-called mates, Dad. Drop the R and your friends suddenly become fiends.'

Until now Jonjo had not understood what he had meant; now he did. Like his old man, the people around him were not really his friends, they were *fiends*, people who used him, people who put up with him, and who were now quite happy to watch his destruction by somebody they actually liked, and who they would stand behind, no matter what the score. Danny would hear their side of this story, not his.

Donald was still waiting patiently for him to start the fight he had requested so forcibly and with such a haphazard easiness. He was waiting as if it was a foregone conclusion, as if he was no one of any real consequence; just a tosser who was expected to beg for his life to someone he saw as a complete fucking waster.

Donald had no intention of letting him get away with this. Like Danny Boy Cadogan before him, Donald would rather die than be seen to be a coward, or treated like a cunt in public without any kind of retaliation. He actually wanted this showdown now. He had a point to prove and he would prove it with as much bloodshed as he was capable of. After all, he had nothing to lose now, did he? He might as well be hung for a sheep as a fucking lamb.

'Are you going to fucking get stuck in, Jonjo, only I ain't got all fucking night.'

Jonjo Cadogan had finally met his nemesis. He looked at the men gathered around him, saw the feral looks on their faces, and the pleasure the good hiding he was about to receive would give them and, for the first time ever, he knew he was on his own. He was finally aware of how well Arnold looked after him, at how easy Arnold made his life. And how hard he made Arnold's, by causing an international incident before *EastEnders* had come on the box. He caused ag without a second's thought to what the consequences might be. The consequences never occurred to him, why would they? He was Danny Boy Cadogan's brother and only a lunatic would take him on. Like all cowards, he was wondering how he could talk his way out of this predicament when the first blow landed squarely on his jaw. He went down like a sack of shit, as everyone who had witnessed his humiliation described the scene to anyone who would listen to them. This had been a long time coming, and they had known that far better than he did.

Chapter Twenty-Nine

'So this Donald kicked the shit out of you, is that what you're telling me?'

Jonjo nodded. His head was swollen like a football, at least that was how it felt, anyway.

'You fucking liar, Jonjo. Why lie to me, of all people?'

'I ain't. He fucking jumped me when I weren't expecting it.'

Danny Boy held up his hand as if exhausted, as if he was bored by it. 'I heard he floored you with one punch, after you had offered him out and insulted him first, of course.'

Danny Boy's voice was neutral once more and Jonjo knew that was dangerous. When Danny Boy had an inflection of some sort in his words you were safe. If what he said was without any kind of resonance you were basically fucked. He knew he was fucked. Knew the story had been already relayed over and over to this brother of his. He now knew he was in the wrong, and was expected to put his hand up like a good little boy.

Danny sat on the edge of his bed, the bed their mother had made so carefully, and he smiled into his brother's eyes before grabbing him savagely by the throat. Then he forced Jonjo's head back on to the pillows, pillows that had been so carefully arranged earlier by the woman who had borne them both and, squeezing his throat until he struggled to breathe, he finally released his hold and said quietly, 'You must think I am a cunt. Do you think I am a cunt, Jonjo? Is that it, is that why you fucking shame me in front of my friends and, worse still, my enemies. Even Arnold has had enough of you, and I paid him to watch over you. *Everyone* has had enough of you, Jonjo. *Me* included.'

Jonjo was now shrinking back as far away as he could from his brother and his anger. That the anger was justified just made it worse, because he knew he had no real argument any more. He couldn't even lie his way out of this one as he would normally.

Arnold, he knew, would have ensured that last night's little debacle didn't get that far, he would have nipped it in the bud. Suddenly he wished he had appreciated the man more when he had the fucking chance. Instead, he had treated him like the hired help, like a no one, like a fucking ice cream.

'As of now, you are out, Jonjo. I'm giving you a club to run to save face, mine not yours, and you had better fucking make a good job of it. If you don't, you'll be out in the cold like a fucking polar bear on a big date. I ain't carrying you no more, mate. You had a chance and you blew it. Now, I am giving you another one, so be fucking warned.'

And with that Danny left the room without another word. His anger was still there though, like an electric current that crackled between them. Jonjo knew that he was on his last chance this time, knew he had to try and make some sort of peace with his brother sooner rather than later. He knew that Danny Boy didn't give a shit about him either way, never had. It was a sobering thought, all right. Jonjo heard Danny Boy storm down the stairs and slam the front door with such force that it seemed to rock the very foundations of the building.

'Can we go and see Mummy, now?' Leona's voice brooked no argument and her adamant little attitude made Danny Boy want to laugh. It also made him proud of her, proud that she had that kind of loyalty inside her. She got it from him, he knew he had instilled it in her. He also knew that she was the kind of kid who wouldn't take 'no' for an answer. Danny Boy kissed her gently on the cheek and, when she moved her head away from him, he felt a pain that was so intense it was like a knife twisting in his heart.

'What's wrong, eh? Why are you turning away from me?'

Leona looked at the huge man who was her father, and who she already knew was the terror of everyone around them and, hearing the pain and the angst in his voice, she said with exasperation and a childish honesty, 'You smell of beer and cigars, it's gross. You smell worse than Mummy.' She was breathing heavily, her little chest rising and falling noisily. Her eyes were full of tears, and her voice was caught up in her loneliness.

Leona loved her mother, they both did, and Danny knew that was right, he knew that was how it should be. But it still hurt him.

He had brought them to his latest amour's house, had hoped they might like it here, hoped they might have felt better away from the drunk they had to contend with on a daily basis. He should have known better. It would take more than a few promises and some expensive new toys to get these two to change their allegiance.

'Just stay one night and me and Michelle will make sure you have the best time ever, won't we, Mish?' The girl nodded as she was expected to, her pretty face and her natural kindness to the fore. But the two girls still shook their heads in denial.

'No,' said Leona stubbornly. 'I don't like it here, Daddy. I want to go and see my Mummy. We both do.'

Lainey nodded at her sister's words, too frightened to say anything for herself. This house, with its loud colours and even louder mistress, frightened her. As did the thought of having to stay here all the time. 'Please, Daddy. We want to go home now.'

Danny looked into Lainey's eyes and saw the way she had reacted to her surroundings. He saw how both of his daughters didn't feel relaxed with him or with this new scenario. He was angry at their rejection of him, and they knew this, but he was aware that his anger didn't make them pretend that they felt this was all all right. They loved him enough to be honest with him. He appreciated that; he also knew they were not impressed with this latest set-up of his.

'Don't you like it here, then? You'd rather be with a drunk, is that what you're saying?'

Leona nodded furiously and, raising her eyebrows in deep annoyance, she said unhappily, 'Well, yeah. At least that drunk's our mother. We don't want to live with anyone else, not even you. You can live here if you want. But don't make us live here, Dad. We want our own home and our own mum. Just because you don't want her, doesn't mean that we don't.'

Lainey nodded sadly. As always, she waited for her sister to test the waters of their father's anger. 'Please, Daddy. We want to go home. To our *real* home.' Then she started to cry, the fat tears falling fast and furiously. Her lovely face was screwed-up in pain and her fat cheeks red with her distress. 'I want my mummy, *my* mummy. Not that lady. Please, Daddy . . . take us home.'

Danny nodded then, and took them both out to his car without another word. Settling them into the back seats, he placed the seat belts around them gently. Both girls were quiet now, their beautiful faces strained and their eyes full of fear and worry. Getting into the driving seat Danny didn't start the car up. Instead, he asked them with as much kindness as he could muster, 'You would rather be with your mother than with me, is that it?'

Leona had been sidestepping questions like this since she could remember. She knew how to play the game and she was already adept at being a diplomat. 'No. It's not that and you know it. We just want to go home, we want our mum and our dad. But not that lady, or any other lady. We *have* a mum, and we love her like we love you. We need her, Daddy.'

Danny started the car then and drove them straight back to their mother. He watched them in the rear-view mirror, saw the way they looked at each other in relief, and sighed. The way they held each other's hands impressed him all over again; their loyalty and closeness, not only to each other, but to the woman who had birthed them. And, as much as he wanted to smash their relationship with their mother apart, he just couldn't do it. Not while they needed her, cared so deeply for her, anyway.

They drove back to the house in silence, and as they had both run into their mother's arms and as he saw her hug them both to her tightly, he wondered at the invisible cord that kept a child loving a parent, no matter how bad that parent might be.

Michelle had given him a child, a son, a child he had no real care for. Not in the same way he did these two anyway. Unlike these two girls, the boy engendered no real feelings inside him. None of his outside children did. He had no real love for any of them, or their mothers. Not even the lovely Michelle. It was nothing personal, she was a lovely girl, as lovely girls went. But lovely girls were ten a penny to him in his world. They were the norm; after all, when you hit the big time, ugly birds were not an option. But he knew deep inside that his drunken wife would always get far more of a reaction from him than any of his paramours. And it made him confront a truth he had not ever admitted to until now, though it had always been there in the background of his life. Now, as he saw his two little girls, his *hearts*, both so desperate for her company, for her embrace, he wondered at how she had made them love her almost as much as he loved her. And he did love her, when it suited him to, anyway. Danny drove away with a squealing of tyres and a crunching of gravel that satisfied the anger that was building up inside him once more.

Michael and Arnold were both in the North Pole pub on the North Pole Road, Shepherd's Bush. They were celebrating Arnold's new-found standing, and Michael was ostensibly there to give him some advice about the status he now held in their community. In reality, however, they both knew they were just reiterating the bond that had grown between them, and were making sure that they would not leave each other out of any equation that might benefit either of them in some way in any future activities.

'Donald Hart did you a real favour. Even Danny Boy's had enough of Jonjo now.'

Arnold nodded. His huge head, with its thick dreads, looked far too big for his body. Yet it gave him a look that, even now, was causing more than a few side glances from the females in their vicinity. Michael sat back in his seat and observed this phenomenon; Danny Boy had the same effect on women; they noticed him as soon as he walked in a room. He guessed it was because of Danny's size, but then he wasn't a small man. But Danny Boy carried his size with calculated ease. He also had the added advantage of always looking as if he was on the hunt; he looked at every woman with a twinkle in his eye that told them they were now well in his radar, and that his notice could change their lives. Which it would, only not in the way they anticipated.

Arnold sipped his pint of Guinness and smiled slightly. 'I can't believe this has happened at last. I really thought Danny Boy would let blood out. Would fuck me off.'

Michael shook his head. 'Danny Boy has one thing that keeps him on top, and that is that he never knowingly backs a loser. He put you in place to keep an eye on his little brother and he probably was impressed that you waited so long before you complained about him. Danny Boy is a lot of things, but a fool ain't one of them. What does worry me though is that he is displaying all the signs of a mad half hour. He gets them periodically and, when he does, there is nothing or no one who can talk him round. So, this is a word to the wise. You think you've seen his dark side, well you ain't seen nothing yet.'

Arnold sighed heavily; he was looking around him and wondering at a life that had given him so much and yet asked for so little. He coughed, putting the back of his hand over his mouth in a gentlemanly way. He had half-expected something like this, had known that Michael would want him as an ally, it stood to reason. After his faux pas before, when he had more or less accused Danny Boy of being a grass, he welcomed this new development with not only apprehension, but also happiness. It meant he was finally inside the inner sanctum of the Cadogan organisation. If Michael wanted him on-side, then he had an opportunity to really make his mark in the world. It was an unholy alliance in many ways, they both knew they would be in league together against the one man.

Arnold nodded gently once more. Looking into Michael's eyes he raised his glass in a gesture of acceptance, his whole demeanour telling Michael that he understood him perfectly. That he knew exactly what he was asking of him, wanted from him. And that he was willing to do whatever was necessary to keep their lives sweet.

Everyone knew that Danny Boy sailed close to the wind, that his violence had the desired effect on most people. It was also common knowledge that this same violence, when left unchecked, when it was for no other reason than someone had pissed him off, could also prove to be all of their downfalls.

Up until now, Michael had managed the damage limitation, but it was getting harder and harder to make good with the wronged parties each time something happened. Danny Boy had taken out a Filth, and that would not be forgotten lightly, even by the bent coppers they dealt with on an almost daily basis. It was impossible to have an organisation of their stature without the hidden approval of the government agencies. Everyone needed money these days, and money was something they had in abundance. Since Spain, they were worth more than most multinationals and they lived well, but not too well of course. No need to advertise their success, it was enough that they knew the extent of it without the taxman and such like wanting a large slice as well. They would one day live like kings and enjoy the benefits of their wealth. That was something for the future though, when they were well away from here and well away from harm.

Unfortunately for them, a lot of the Old Bill they bankrolled had the annoying habit of wearing their new-found wealth like a badge of office. It was this that could be the cause of them being investigated by their poorer, less flamboyant, contemporaries. Their ostentatious way of living could cause a lot of trouble for a lot of people and this needed, on occasion, to be pointed out. A Rolex or brand-new Merc didn't go down too well in a police station or its car park. And, unless someone in their family had died and left them a fucking huge legacy, there was no way of explaining their good fortune away. It brought the spotlight down on everyone, and that was not good for business. Why they couldn't just ferret the poke away for a rainy day, he didn't know. It was as if some of the younger men concerned couldn't wait to fucking show off their new acquisitions to their workmates. Workmates who could, and would, put them away for a long time. Not exactly the most intelligent of beings he knew, but they had their uses, otherwise they wouldn't be on the payroll in the first place. He also understood the allure of a few quid, how it could affect somebody who had never before had so much spare cash hanging around. That was human nature, and that was what they relied on to recruit these people. Money, huge amounts of it, was what they reeled them in with, and what so often caused their demise. It burned a hole in their pockets, and that in turn could burn a hole right through their heads if they didn't take the advice to keep a low profile and stop the spending sprees, when offered. It was the downside of sudden wealth, it made people greedy, and he had also noticed how fast they spent their initial payment, and how quickly they came back for more of the same. How they were willing to do more and more for the chance to grab a couple of grand once again. Personally, he liked the gamblers, they never had the money long enough to flash it around and, if they won, they could put their good fortunes down to a horse, a dog or a card game. It was becoming a real problem though, keeping it all in hand.

This was another reason that Michael had asked young Arnold to meet him here; he was about to have a showdown with someone who could be very useful to them in the future but who needed a seriously threatening word of advice in his shell-like, before he fucked it up for everyone. Himself included.

As if on cue, Detective Inspector Jeremy Marsh walked into the pub. He was a tall, thin man with a long face, big yellowing teeth and a fashion sense that defied belief. He looked, for all the world, like a pimp on his day off. From his blow-dried hair to his hire-purchase signet ring, he looked what he was. A complete and utter fucking idiot. He had on a suit that was as expensive as it was noticeable, the more so because it was at least two sizes too large for him. That, Michael assumed, was due to the cocaine habit Jerry boy had acquired in the last six months. He had the glassy-eyed look of the snorter, the man who didn't use it to enhance his daily life, or even keep him awake over and above his designated bedtime. This was a man who used it get out of his box.

Sighing, Michael saw the signs of the paranoid person, all the signs that said this man was beyond any kind of help or friendly advice. He saw someone who was well on the way to saying goodbye to life as he knew it. Plonking himself down on the chair opposite them, Jeremy Marsh smiled widely, his huge mouth stretched to its widest capacity. Not a pretty sight at the best of times, his crazed eyes and coke-sweat made him look even more uninviting to the less drug-inclined of their community. He was wired for sound, of that there was no doubt. He was almost dancing in his chair, the jagged movements overemphasised as he attempted to light a cigarette and order a drink at the same time. The hand holding the lighter was waving towards the crowded pub as he tried, unsuccessfully, to place a cigarette into his mouth.

Leaning forward in his own chair, Michael whispered, 'In case you ain't noticed, this is a pub, so you'll have to walk up to the bar, mate. They ain't got waiter service in here.'

Arnold watched the little scenario with interest as he knew was expected of him. Michael had obviously brought him here to witness this and he was determined not to miss any of it. That this man was off his rocker was apparent, that he was a Filth was a given; he had the look of an Old Bill from the hair down to the thick-soled shoes. He was clearly a friendly one, and obviously here for the bad news.

Michael's body language at this moment was not conducive to a friendly chat and a cheery wave goodbye. He was coiled, ready to spring, and this man was so wired he had not even noticed. Standing up, Arnold said quickly, 'I'll get them in. What do you want?'

Marsh looked up at him as if noticing him for the first time. Which they all knew was the truth of the situation. He was gone.

'A Remy, large.' He had finally lit his cigarette and this pleased him no end. He held it up to Michael's face as if he had just worked out Einstein's theory of relativity on the back of a matchbox.

'Monkey see, Monkey do, eh? We have a few of them in the force nowadays. Good to see you're an equal opportunities employer. Everyone needs cannon fodder, eh?'

As Marsh spoke, he was picking imaginary pieces of lint from his suit jacket, the fingers holding the cigarette were yellowed and burned, and he had the exaggerated movements peculiar to addicts.

'That monkey, as you called him, is Danny Cadogan's brother-in-law, and one of *my* best mates. I don't know what you're fucking snorting, Marsh, but I hope there's a painkiller in there some-where, because you're going to fucking need it with your big mouth.'

Jeremy Marsh was sobering up by the second. His brain had taken on board the fact that he had just insulted his hosts; and it occurred to him that he might not be making the best of impressions. That he had been up all night, and was still on the sniff, was now making him nervous. His coke-induced arrogance was dissolving by the second and being replaced by coke-induced fear. Everything around him was heightened, from the noise of people talking to the colours on the fruit machines. This also pertained to his emotional state. Now, he was shrinking visibly, as the fear took hold.

Arnold came back with the drinks and, placing the large brandy on the table in front of Marsh, he was surprised when the man thanked him humbly. The bravado seemed to have left him, and he looked dejected now, a broken man. He wasn't surprised when Marsh necked his drink in two gulps. Arnold could see a cokehead from sixty paces; he had lived among them all his life. And this was a cokehead of Olympian standards. This was a man on the edge and something had been said since the man had come into the pub, sat down, attempted to light his cigarette and been the recipient of a free drink. Whatever this was, it had the desired effect. He was a shadow of his former self and Michael looked, for all the world, like a man willing to do murder at the drop of the proverbial hat.

As Arnold sat down himself, he was surprised when Michael said to him seriously, 'Bring the monkey out to the car.'

Then he got up and left the pub without a backward glance.

Danny Boy was upset and, as he waited patiently for his guest to arrive at the yard, he pondered this latest mystery that was his life. The girls' reaction had thrown him, especially the baby, Lainey's. It had made him realise that the loyalty he had instilled in them was working against him. That they saw their mother as a viable option over him and all *he* had to offer them was unbelievable.

Yet he knew that, whatever Mary was, and she was a lot of things, a drunkard, slag, fucking pain in the arse, the girls worshipped her. He liked the fact that they didn't want to stay at Michelle's, he could see their point there; she was a fucking accident waiting to happen. Far too emotional for his liking. In reality, she was already dead in the water, an also-ran. She had the saggy belly and stretchmarks that generally heralded his retreat from them and their clutches. He would pay for the kid, he knew what he had to do, but other than that, she was already nothing more than a fading memory.

He liked the girls, always had done. He didn't love them though, except for the first few weeks. Then, once he had them, he lost interest in them. The only one to ever really get him going was Mary Miles, and that was because he knew, deep down, that she hated him. Hated him almost as much as she loved him. She loved him as the father of her children, the same children he had forced from her body with violence and intimidation and the same children he now worshipped and adored. It was strange really, that these two girls of his could engender such deep emotion inside him. Not just because he wanted them to prefer him over their mother which, he admitted, was a big part of his interest in them. But because, all that aside, he saw them as extensions of himself. Little Danny Boys who would one day be grown women, would one day produce children that would have his blood in their veins. Like Methuselah, his house, his bloodline would go on for generation after generation. For maybe nine hundred years. It was a sobering thought.

God knew what he was doing; he knew that when He created a dynasty, it needed strong bloodlines, and he was strong all right but, in many ways, Mary was the stronger of the two. She needed to be to cope with him and everything that came with him. And he was honest enough to admit that, of all the Michelles and other young girls he came into contact with on a daily basis, none of them could hold a candle to her really. She had something they would never have, the strength needed to cope with a man like him. She was still there, drunk as she was, she was still there when he came home and it was this loyalty that kept him from destroying her, even when he felt like it.

Mary was actually a lot more with it than people gave her credit for, and she was a good-looker, a class-dresser and, more to the point, she knew when to keep her nose out of his business. He had seen the way she reacted when one of his paramours was within her vicinity. She didn't even glance in their direction, she acted as if she was too good for them, that she had too much pride to even notice their existence. No wonder the girls had so much heart, they were their mother's daughters, all right. Danny felt a sudden nostalgia come over him, and remembered his Mary when he had plucked her like a flower from the man she had been so unhappy with but who she had been so determined to marry. She had opted for money over love, and who could blame her? The men in his world found love cheap and cheerful; they kicked wives to the kerb without a second's thought, women who had stood by them through thick and thin. It was the nature of these beasts and their women knew that when they took them on. It was why they kept themselves in good nick and were exemplary mothers and home-makers. It was also why it was preferable, for the men they snared, if they had a working knowledge of the legal system. Who wanted a wife who would be silly enough to let the Old Bill in without a fight?

But, even with all that, he knew that Mary had got under his skin more than any other woman in his life to date. No matter what he did to her, or said to her, she kept it to herself. Even her brother, his closest friend, didn't have an inkling about what actually went on behind the large double doors of their home. He treated her like trash, he knew that, yet she still let him into her bed. He had a good one there in many respects, and he knew that better than anyone. Though often it took events like this to remind people of just how lucky they really were.

Danny saw the lights of a car approach the office and stood up expectantly; he could hear the dogs barking as they were rounded up and caged so his visitor could make his way inside without being ripped to pieces.

A gentle tapping on the door brought a smile to his face. He liked good manners, had always appreciated people with the grace and common decency that seemed to be so lacking in most of the population these days. Opening the door with a flourish, he said jovially, and with a laugh in his deep voice, 'Come in, my son. Make yourself at home.' Danny gestured for him to take a seat.

Donald Hart entered the room with obvious trepidation and with his best clothes on his back. This was evident not only by their newness, but by his uneasiness as he sat down. They looked stiff and uncomfortable, and so did young Donald. He had made the effort though, and Danny Boy appreciated that, it showed respect, not only for him, but for the boy in question as well, because it proved that he had respect for himself. Something that Danny Boy knew would always hold him in good stead as far as he was concerned. After all, for all he knew, he was here to get a fucking larruping, a fucking smack for his cheekiness in knocking Jonjo out. He couldn't have made a better impression if he had brought him the head of the Serious Crime Squad on a platter with his dick in his mouth for good measure.

'All right, Donald?'

The young man nodded nervously.

Danny Boy liked the look of him; he had already proved he had heart and, from what he had gathered today, the boy had a good reputation around town. He was reliable and shrewd. He also had a menagerie of siblings to take care of. He had a Jamaican father who had gone on the trot, leaving him with three younger brothers who were all dependent on him for their daily living expenses. And his mother, a very nice woman who still had the looks if not the body, was, by all accounts, very well placed, thanks to this son of hers. She had a small business that she ran from her home that this boy had provided the initial money for; a cleaning operation, employing a lot of women who needed work. He also helped her with everything from their mortgage to their shopping bills. She was also known for her generosity to people down on their luck, or who might be in need of a safe house for a few days. And she was also not averse to having someone bailed out to her address if the need arose. She was an all-rounder who had passed on her values to her eldest child.

Danny Boy was not only impressed, he was humbled by this boy's determination to get on in life. He saw himself in him. Indeed, he saw his brother's humiliation at his hands as fate, because it had brought Donald into his orbit. He would help this boy in any way he could. Like the Bible said, 'Let those among you cast the first stone.'

This boy had sinned, he had smacked his little brother. In their world that was a big sin. A *seriously* big sin. Well, he had no intentions of throwing any stones at him; he was going to reward him instead for his guts. He understood the boy's predicament and he also admired the boy's front in how he had dealt with the situation. So many young men would have backed down, would have thought of him, Danny Boy, and not their own self worth. Well, he was a sinner of renown, and so was this young man and, by the time he had finished with him, he would be a sinner of fucking outrageous proportions.

Let Old Bill cast the first stone, Danny Boy was, as always, ready and able to deal with them. He had something no one else had, and that was a mental facility for knowing who he could trust and who he couldn't. He could trust this kid, and he would shower him with glory because he knew it would come back to him one hundredfold.

Marsh had not spoken for ages and Arnold was getting nervous.

'Give him a poke, will you, make sure he ain't overdosed or something.'

Michael's voice was full of laughter as he said it, he knew that a cokehead could go from having far too much to say for themselves to an introverted nervous wreck in moments.

'He is all right, Michael?'

''Course he is. All that's wrong with him is that he's shitting it. He knows he's out of order and he's contemplating his punishment.' Unlike Arnold, who was really worried about their victim, Michael was playing the game. He was talking for effect.

Michael knew, from experience, the value of a threat over direct action. The thought of something happening was far worse than an actual physical assault; though Marsh would be getting one of those as well, naturally. After all, a threat on its own was pointless unless it was seen through to the bitter end.

Michael agreed with Danny Boy that the laws of the land were not effective because they were never seen through in their entirety. Unless the crime involved money or property, the judicial system saw fit to let people have a pass. To allow burglars and such like to have an easy walk. It was laughable. No wonder there were no boundaries or guidelines for the young people any more. The fact they were young was seen as reason enough to let them get away with anything, including murder. Murders that had no place in the world, murders of complete fucking strangers for a few quid and a rifle in the victim's fridge before they went home to Mummy and Daddy. It was fucking outrageous how these people managed to come out of it all as the wronged party. At least, if they had a grudge, it was with good reason, and the person involved knew the likely outcome of their fucking actions. Rob an old lady, terrify her, grab her little bit of pension, and you got probation; rob a fucking building society and you wouldn't see the light of day for at least twelve years. It was wrong, and even the general public were seeing it from that point of view these days. A creeper, a burglar, was lower than the fucking low in stir. Unless it was a great big house owned by a lord, or suchlike, it was seen as an abomination by the criminal fraternity. The same with muggers and con artists who preyed on the elderly or the infirm. They were bullies who needed to be locked away from society, who, by their very actions, and their complete disregard for the weaker people in their orbit, had forfeited the right to be allowed out to prowl the streets.

And here they were now, with a so-called pillar of society, a Filth who had a gambling habit that was only outweighed by his coke addiction. A man who had been introduced to them by his boss; another fucking waster whose only saving grace was that he agreed with them about the way the law seemed to favour the wankers in their society. This man was responsible for looking after the honest people in society. The people that Michael and his ilk had no interest in robbing at all. In fact, they would be the first ones there if they heard of such an occurrence. Yet it was them who were classed as the blight on society, not this man or the fucking gas-meter bandits who robbed their own. Bent Filth always gave him the hump, especially when they overstepped the mark, when they outgrew their usefulness. As this one had, because of his blatant stupidity, his drunken antics, and his unwavering belief that he was beyond their jurisdiction. Why did Old Bill always believe they were in control, even when they took money each week and, by that very act, they had given up any kind of regard they might been given as a straight Filth? They were lower than fucking second-hand lino; it stood to reason. After all, they were quite happily betraying the people they worked with, as well as the people they were supposed to be protecting.

Michael turned the car onto a dirt road and, as they crept along it in the moonlight, Arnold looked around him with interest. 'Where are we?'

Michael pulled into a small driveway and parked the car under a huge oak tree before answering, 'This is one of Danny Boy's investment properties, it's empty so we can make as much noise as we like.'

He turned in his seat and said to Marsh, 'You can scream the place down and no one will hear you.'

Jeremy was already in mortal fear for his life, as Michael had anticipated. Pulling him from the car he dragged him into the darkness of the garages that lay behind the house. Inside, he put on the light and motioned for Arnold to go to the workbench and wait for him to give him directions. Arnold did as he was asked, but he was feeling nervous; pasting an Old Bill was one thing, taking him out of the ball game was something else entirely. Like Marsh, he was also looking nervously at the tools laid out so neatly on the old wooden bench. From screwdrivers to awls, everything there was more than capable of inflicting serious harm, and both Arnold and Jeremy believed that would be the case.

Michael grinned then. Pulling an old kitchen chair up he sat down heavily before saying quietly, 'You have fucked me off and you know that, don't you?'

Jeremy Marsh nodded his head furiously, his eyes bulging from his head with a mixture of fear and sleep deprivation.

'People are talking about you and your new lifestyle. Horrible *people*, the wrong people, are asking questions about where your money comes from. And that is not something I can allow to happen. You are now what's known as a liability. A fucking albatross hanging around my Gregory Peck. I have had two calls from colleagues of yours warning me that you are bringing attention to yourself. So, what have you got to say in your own defence?'

Jeremy Marsh was so frightened that he was almost struck dumb. He was sweating profusely, it was dripping down from his forehead into his eyes, making them sting. His clothes were stuck to his body and the smell was ripe even in the dusty, oily stench of the garages. He looked like someone from a horror film who had just seen the murderer approach him with a chainsaw. 'Look, Mike, I'm sorry. I can see where you're coming from, and this won't happen again. But you know I can be really useful to you and Danny Boy . . . I have been. Danny and me, we have a rapport. Ask him. Talk to him about it. He'll tell you how much I've helped him get things sorted. Ask him about what I've done for him.'

Michael and Arnold were watching the man with a morbid fascination, he was almost stuttering with fright. Yet both men sensed that he was in possession of knowledge that he felt might get him out of this trouble.

'And what the fuck have you done that's so fucking important, eh?' It was Arnold speaking now and, to push his point home once and for all, he punched Marsh hard in the head. Giving it all his considerable strength he watched in satisfaction as Marsh flinched, drawing his head into his shoulders as the blow landed heavily and noisily on the side of his head. His ear split immediately, the skin holding it in place tearing like rice paper and leaving it hanging there, the blood already soaking into his clothes. He was crying now, silent tears that ran down his face and mingled with the snot from his nose. He was broken and they knew it.

'Come on, then, what makes you so fucking special to Danny Boy, eh?'

Jeremy Marsh knew that he was beaten, knew that he was in far deeper than he had ever imagined. He knew that if he was to come out of this alive he needed something to use as a bargaining tool. All he had was this one thing to help him out of this mess and he couldn't understand why Michael Miles was acting like he was unaware of his usefulness. Was acting like what he did was nothing. Was worth nothing to them.

'Don't you know, Mike? You have to know.'

The question was there, and so was the realisation that maybe Michael Miles really was in the dark about his actual role in the

Cadogan scheme of things. That he suddenly had a bargaining chip, a real one. Pulling himself up to his full height Marsh said loudly and cockily, 'I took over from David Grey. I am Danny Boy's go-between.'

Chapter Thirty

Danny Boy woke up in his own house; he knew that by the smell. It always smelled of perfume and bleach. As he opened his eyes he could feel his wife's slender body tight against him in the huge bed. He had his arms wrapped around her, and he knew that she was only there because she couldn't get away from him. That she was already awake was a foregone conclusion. She never slept when he was beside her, and that thought saddened him this morning. He had loved her the night before, had taken her and enjoyed her in every way possible. Her compliance spurred him on these days. He enjoyed her complete detachment, it made the act so much more exciting. He was like a director, directing her so she did whatever he wanted her to. She said what he wanted her to say, and so acted like she was having the time of her life at his command. Hugging her even tighter to him, he kissed the back of her head gently. 'Make me a cup of Rosie Lee and a bit of Holy Ghost, eh?'

Her husband's voice was so soft, so gentle, that Mary forgot for a little while how dangerous he could be, was grateful for this little kindness he was showing her. Slipping from the bed she pulled on a dressing gown and he sat up as he watched her. Leaning back on the pillows and surveying his surroundings with the practised eye of the bully, he decided to be nice. Decided, today, to overlook her shortcomings. She had been good lately, and he had unloaded another bird in the last few days, causing him to feel the need to be reacquainted with his married life. It was always the same, and Mary knew that. He came home for a while, gave them all the pretence of a home life until he felt the urge to disappear once more for weeks, sometimes months, on end. He'd leave her wondering when he was going to show up for more than a change of clothes and a shower and, more to the point, *how* he would be when he did finally arrive back into the bosom of his family.

Today Mary sighed with relief at his friendliness, at his decision to take it easy on them all. As she was pinning her hair up she could feel him watching her, knew that it was the little things like this that could either set him off on one of his tantrums or, just as easily, reduce him to tears. She never knew what was going to happen, and she felt the nervous tension gripping her belly like a vice. As he watched her pinning up her thick glossy hair the girls came into the room and, seeing him there, propped up against the pillows, a smile on his face, they stopped in their tracks. Then, a split second later, Leona, always the leader, ran into his arms, Lainey following her happily.

'What are you doing here, Daddy?'

Leona's piping little voice and her honest question caused her mother to hunch her shoulders and grit her teeth in terror as she waited for the onslaught. But Danny Boy was on his best behaviour this lovely sunny morning, as was sometimes his wont, and laughing, he said happily, 'I wanted to see me girls, me babes; I've missed you.'

Leona rolled her eyes in mock exasperation, and that just made him laugh even more.

Carole was worried about her husband. He had come in late the night before and, instead of coming to bed as usual, he had sat in their living room alone and in the dark. She had heard him come in; she never really relaxed until she knew he was home anyway. When he had not come up to bed she had got up and looked for him. She wanted to know why he wasn't lying beside her, why he had not even checked on the kids. He always looked in on the kids, and he always came home to her. She wasn't stupid, she knew the life he led, and she knew she was lucky, because Michael wasn't a chancer, didn't need the cachet of a little bird hanging on his every word like Danny Boy. He was happy enough with her and his family. That was why his actions had frightened her, had worried her. He was bothered about something, and she needed to know what that was. Her fear was always that he would get a capture, be nicked by Old Bill. She knew it was a possibility even as she knew that he felt he was far too powerful for that to ever happen to him. But, by the same token, nothing was a definite in their world, and she knew that if the Old Bill wanted them bad enough, they'd get them. If only for no other reason than they were so powerful they might need knocking down a peg or two. Her husband's business was not exactly kosher, and she was as aware as he was of the pitfalls. Unlike him though, she felt there was chance that, for all their might, and all their money, they would never be completely safe from prosecution. It only took one person to start the ball rolling, and that was that. Big sentences brought on big mouths. Michael had said that to her many years before and she had never forgotten it.

So his strange behaviour caused her to wonder what had happened to him in the last twenty-four hours, and why it had made him act so out of character.

She placed a pot of tea on the table and, sitting down opposite her husband, she asked him once more, 'Please, Michael, tell me what's wrong.'

'I can't, mare. I daren't.' He looked at her for long moments, at the heavy dressing gown that didn't hide the roll of fat around her belly. At her open face, the large blue eyes that were now rimmed with black circles from her interrupted sleep. Her hair was all over the place, as always it needed a decent cut, and her hands were trembling with the worry he knew she was feeling. He wished he could confide in her as he always had done, but this was too important to tell anyone about. Even his Carole. If this got out it would be the cause of so much trouble its echo would reverberate for generations. No one would know who the fuck to trust and that would cause a lot of suspicion and a lot of threats both physical and verbal. It was such a dangerous supposition, leaving all the people involved in such a precarious position that everything they were involved in, from the Spanish angle to their everyday businesses, was now in jeopardy.

Michael still wasn't sure he even believed any of it, even though he knew that it was true. He had always known there was something not quite right, that they seemed to lose enemies at opportune moments. That Danny Boy would take his usual umbrage and destroy an enemy, either real or imagined, on a murderous whim, was what had kept his secret from being revealed. That he had been in cahoots with the Filth all this time was such a devastating accusation that no one would accuse him; not anyone in their right mind anyway. For Michael to accuse Danny Boy of being a grass was unthinkable.

But, in his heart of hearts though, he had thought all along that there had been something a little off-kilter; people they had a grievance with disappeared a little too conveniently, he saw that now. They got captures and sent away just in time for them to take over their nefarious businesses. And, indeed, they were seen as life-savers by the men now in their employ, who saw Danny and Michael as their saviours.

That Louie had been the instigator of it didn't surprise him one iota. Danny Boy had tugged him over his alleged grassing it all those years ago. And, knowing him, he had probably seen it an easy way out, an easy option; he had to have known that no one would ever have suspected him.

This was so enormous that Michael didn't know how to deal with it. It affected them all; as Arnold had pointed out, if this became common knowledge, no one was safe from retribution. No one would be trusted any more. It would smash the very foundations of their daily lives.

Danny had never once even given him an inkling that he was not genuine; he had never *once* had real cause to think otherwise. But, somewhere inside his head, he knew that there had been a small element of doubt concerning Danny Boy's ability to literally get away with murder. For all their power, and all their wealth, Michael knew, deep in his gut, that no one could be that fucking lucky.

When Arnold had brought the subject up a while ago, he had not been willing to listen to him, he had brushed it all aside. He had known that if it was ever once said outloud, something would have to be done about it and he didn't want that person to be him.

He loved Danny Boy like a brother, in fact, he loved him more than his own flesh and blood. His own brother was as nothing to him, meant fuck-all in comparison. Which was why this revelation was knocking him for six.

All they had achieved over the years, all their businesses and all their power, had been built on quicksand and, because of Danny Boy's treachery, they could sink without trace at any moment. They weren't safe at all, if Old Bill was in the know, and they *had* to be for Danny Boy's ruse to work, then each and every one of them were in jeopardy. They were in danger of losing not only their lifestyles, but their fucking liberty.

Michael was already working out what monies were accessible, what he had filtered away on his own bat, and what monies were best left alone. It stood to reason that their accounts were probably common knowledge to the Filth; they would be all over them like a cheap suit. He didn't know any of this for a fact, but he knew he had to box-clever for the foreseeable future if he wanted to come out of this lot without a tug, and with any kind of wealth left to him at all. There was only way out of this, as Arnold had pointed out to him late last night, only one way to guarantee they would be safe and secure, and he didn't want to even consider that.

'Drink your tea, Michael.'

He didn't answer her, she knew that he had not even heard her.

Annie was already up and dressed, and she looked good. She knew she looked good. She felt good. The radio was blaring as always, and the house was clean but untidy, as always. The boys were ready for school, and the breakfasts had been consumed with the usual banter and the usual speed. Annie was a cereals woman, and she didn't hide that fact. She believed that as soon as a child could pour their own Sugar Puffs, then that is exactly what they should do. The boys had caught on quickly, and she was left to drink her coffee and smoke her morning cigarettes in relative peace. She was quite happy to cook a dinner but breakfast, she felt, was too early in the day for all that fucking piss-balling around. She was not, as she told her sons at every available opportunity, a morning person. They loved her, and so that was taken on board, digested, and accepted. They were quite happy to see to themselves, and actually preferred it. They could have what they wanted, and their lovely mum provided every kind of breakfast cereal and pop-tart on the market. It worked out well for all of them.

Arnold had been sitting at the breakfast table when they had come down, but no one remarked on it because it was not unusual for him to be just arriving home as they left for school. It was the norm, the boys had never known it any other way.

Arnold looked at his family and listened to their banter, and knew that his wife, his lovely wife, was going to be devastated in the very near future. Because he didn't care what Michael said, something had to be done about this terrible situation, and it had to be done sooner rather than later. The longer it went on, the harder it would be to sort it out. The thing was, how the fuck were they going to resolve this without arousing Danny Boy's suspicion?

Danny Boy would wipe them out without a second's thought if he knew what they had found out; he would destroy them quickly and cleanly, then go about his daily business as if nothing had happened. That was the difference between them, as he had tried to point out to Michael Miles last night. Danny Boy had no real care for anyone or anything; you only had to see how he lived, how he treated his wife and kids.

Michael's loyalty was misplaced, because Danny Boy didn't play by the fucking rules like everyone else. He played the long game, and he played it all by himself. He just gave people the illusion of his allegiance, of his loyalty. In reality, he offered them nothing unless it gained him something in return.

And Danny Boy was married to Michael's sister, and he knew that if Mary had even the remotest inkling of what was going through everyone's mind, she would take Danny Boy's side without even having to think about it. She was like Danny Boy in that respect; she always looked out for number one. At least, that is how she had always come across to him, anyway. With her perfect house, and her perfect clothes, Mary was unreal, and she was also too quiet and far too fucking snooty for his liking. She was her husband's fucking guarantee in respect of Michael Miles; all the time they were related he was beyond suspicion, and he knew that as well as Danny Boy did.

Well, Arnold wasn't going to sit around and wait for that cunt to offer him up to Old Bill when he had lost his usefulness. He would strike first and strike fucking quickly; it was the only way to get this sorted. He might be married to Danny Boy's little sis, but that cut no fucking ice where he was concerned. Danny Boy was a cancer that needed to be removed sooner rather than later.

They had burned their boats last night; the revelation about Grey had been bad enough, but what Marsh had told them had been unbelievable. They had also had the added aggravation of keeping the man under wraps until they knew what they were going to do about it all. It was a mess, a fucking disgrace, the lot of it.

Jonjo was eating his breakfast quietly and conscientiously, his mother was already placing more food on to his plate and he was grateful for that. Grateful for her kindness, for her unspoken loyalty towards him. His fall from grace had been as spectacular as it had been quick, and he knew he had a lot of work before him to repair the damage he had caused with his arrogance and his laziness. The public humiliation was a foregone conclusion; he had made far too many enemies for people not to enjoy his downfall. He accepted that; he was a realist in his own way, and he was also aware that he had not made many friends on account of his bad attitude and his arrogance.

That was the least of his problems, what he needed to do now was inveigle his way back into his brother's good books, and the only way he could do that was to clean his act up. He needed to make a go of the club he had been given, a shithole that was so bad, that just making sure there was toilet paper in the crappers would raise its profile. The strippers were a bit too long in the tooth for his liking, and the décor was reminiscent of the old-style Indian restaurants; all flock wallpaper, purple carpets, chipped paintwork, and ornate coving. A relic left over from its days as a real earner. It stank of fags, spilled lager and lost hope and was peopled with punters who saw a giro as a way of life, and a win on the horses as proof of their innate shrewdness. But Jonjo determined to make something of it; he was already thinking up ideas to bring in a better clientele, and he was also waiting until the time Danny Boy spoke to him once more. He knew a hell of a lot more than any of them realised, and he now knew that knowledge was not necessarily power. In fact, a little knowledge, as a man once said, was a dangerous thing.

'You all right, son?'

Jonjo smiled gently at his mother; she had been so good to him lately and he really wished he had been nicer to her over the years. She had stood by him through thick and thin; she had tried to tell him that he was heading for a fall, and he had ignored her, worse than that, he had abused her verbally. He now saw that she was, in fact, the only real friend he had in the whole wide world. And that knowledge depressed him even as it pleased him. He wished he had utilised his time more wisely, when he had the chance, but it was too late for regrets now. He hated Danny Boy for how he had humiliated him, even as he needed him to earn his daily bread. He had to get his head together, and sort himself out.

Father David Mahoney was, as always, pleased to see Danny Boy Cadogan in the church. He had not been at this parish long, but he knew the story behind this man and he also knew that, for all the talk about him, he was a devout Catholic. He often saw him at the six o'clock Mass, sitting alone, the early morning air clinging to him as he whispered the responses to the Mass quietly almost to himself. He took Holy Communion and always stayed for a while after the Mass, kneeling alone in his pew, praying quietly, his whole body in a gesture of utter obeisance to his Lord. He was an anomaly, his reputation as a hard man was left at the entrance to the church, and he was always very quietly spoken and very respectful, especially when he asked him questions about the Bible, asked his opinion about things that he had read. As he tried to understand the word that was God's law.

Sometimes he would meet another man after Mass, and they would exchange a few words; the man was not a regular church-goer like himself, but they seemed to know each other pretty well. In fact, he often allowed them the use of the sacristy for their intimate chats. Danny Cadogan's donations were so frequent and so generous that Father Mahoney didn't feel he could refuse the man such a small request. Anyway, it was like his use of the phone, it was just something anyone would do for a friend. He didn't feel compromised in any way. Still, he had never mentioned any of this to anyone else.

Now, as Danny sat down on the front pew and looked up at the cross of Christ, he sat beside him and, placing his hands in his lap, he said gently, 'Nice to see you as always, Danny Boy.'

Father Mahoney's Irish lilt was soft and gave his deep voice a velvet quality. His thick dark hair was already speckled with grey and his deep-brown eyes were, as always, filled with a deep sadness. Danny Boy liked him; felt he was exactly what a priest should be. Big, strong and gentle.

'I'm well, Father. Just popped in to say a few prayers. You know me, I love this place, love the peace it brings me.'

The priest nodded and looked around him with pride. 'I know what you mean, Danny, I feel the same meself.'

He looked into Danny Boy's eyes then, and saw the blankness there that he sometimes encountered when he talked to him, and he said sadly, 'Is everything all right with you? I feel you're troubled in some way.'

Danny Boy sat back in his seat and, looking up once more at the huge crucifix above the altar, he answered him with a smile, 'I'm fine, Father. It's not me, it's everybody else.'

They laughed together at his words, then Danny asked quietly, 'Has my friend been in at all this morning?'

'No. No one's been in since the nine o'clock Mass. In fact, I had better get a move on, I'm due to give a Mass at the infant school in twenty minutes. I love the little ones, they are still in awe of the power of their God, they still believe in Him without question.'

Danny grinned, his handsome face softer now, his whole body relaxed and loose. 'God is good, all right, Father. I know that better than anyone. He has always answered my prayers, always kept His eye on me.'

Father Mahoney left him then, pleased that such faith had been rewarded, and wondering what his housekeeper would be serving up for his lunch.

Danny Boy watched him go, and wondered where his ten thirty appointment had got to. He had a lot on today and didn't have the time to hang about.

Michael was already at the yard when he heard Danny Boy's car pull up. It was nearly lunchtime and he had not been expecting him so soon. He put the papers he had been looking at back into the safe and shut it quickly. Already the guilt seemed to be over-whelming him.

As Danny strode through the door he smiled nervously, 'Where you been?'

Danny Boy grinned and said jovially, 'Who are you, the fucking police?'

It was a stock answer and it normally made Michael laugh. Today, though, he didn't find it in the least amusing. Danny stood in front of him, his huge bulk reminding Michael of just how dangerous this man could be as he said seriously, 'Who's rattled your fucking cage, you miserable fucker. You had a row with Carole?'

Michael shrugged, his own bulk seemed to shrink in comparison when he stood beside Danny Boy, even though he knew he was a big man himself. Bigger than average, and he also knew he had a much firmer physique. Danny Boy had run to fat the last few years from his louche lifestyle, from his drinking and his drugging. Yet, he still had the power to intimidate him; it wasn't about size or strength and Michael had always known that. It was about Danny Boy's latent violence. It was about his ability to hurt and maim without any kind of reasoning or care. He was a psychopath, and they both knew that.

'I'm just tired that's all, I didn't get much kip last night.'

Danny was already over his strop and, going to the fridge, he took out two cans of lager. Throwing one to Michael he sat down behind the desk and, opening his own beer, he took a long drink, then burping loudly he said seriously, 'I think Eli is taking us for a pair of cunts.'

Michael opened his own beer and, sitting on the arm of the old sofa, he took a few sips; he was playing for time and they both knew it. Then, eventually, he said quietly on a long, drawn-out sigh. 'Stop it, Danny. Eli is a mate.'

Danny didn't answer him, he was just watching him, staring at him. Michael knew the signs, he had been through this so many times before. Danny Boy would not let up until he had got his way, until Eli was nothing more than a distant memory for everyone concerned, including his family and friends.

Michael had wondered who would be the next recipient of Danny Boy's anger and, of all the people he had thought it might be, Eli Williams had never entered his head once. He didn't know why, because he was a prime candidate. He was young, he was a Face, and he was a rising star in their community. Danny Boy hated to be outshone, hated anyone who he felt might one day pose a threat to him. At least that is what he insinuated anyway. But Eli was not a fucking no-neck, he was someone who wouldn't take this latest development without a fucking fight. He had respect for both Danny Boy and Michael, and he was not afraid to show that respect. He was a diamond geezer, a fucking Brahma. He was a good earner and he had a good rep around town. In fact, Eli was a real mate to both of them, though Danny would conveniently forget that now, of course. He would now argue that he had heard stuff, that was the usual excuse, that he was a grass. Well, Danny Boy would know one better than he would if he came across one. That much had now been established.

Michael sat forward and placed the can of Stella on the desk, then he looked at Danny Boy squarely as he said gravely, 'This ain't going to happen, Danny Boy. Not this time, not to Eli. I mean it.'

Danny Boy didn't bat an eyelid. He just sat there as quiet and as still as a dormouse, a faint smile playing on his thick sensuous lips.

Michael stared back at him, anger building up inside him now; his complete and utter dislike of Danny Boy was threatening to overwhelm him.

Danny laughed softly then. 'I ain't asking your permission, Michael, I was just acquainting you with the facts. Eli is making mugs of us, and if you can't see that then you're as big a cunt as he is.'

Michael shook his head angrily and Danny Boy was suddenly shocked by this vehemence and Michael saw that and was pleased

487

about it. 'No. This is not going to happen, Danny.' Michael pointed a finger towards his friend as he almost yelled, 'You are *not* doing this; Eli is a fucking good bloke and he's proved his loyalty to us on more than one occasion. So, get it out of your head now. It ain't happening.'

Danny Boy was so shocked at Michael's words that he didn't speak for a few minutes and the silence hung between them like a shroud. Then he said, 'What the fucking hell are you on about, Mike? You fucking think I am doing this for a laugh? I have it on good authority that he's been mugging us off behind our backs.'

Michael stood up then and, waving his hands in front of him as if bored by the whole conversation, he shouted, 'And who told you all this then, eh? Give me a name or better still, ring them up, bring them over here and let them tell me what they've heard to me face.' Michael crushed the empty can in his hand noisily, the anger welling up inside him making him pant as if with exertion, 'Don't do this, Danny Boy, I am asking you as a mate. Please don't do this. Don't go against me on this one.'

Never before had he been so adamant about anything. Michael always went along with him eventually, and Danny Boy was not sure how to react to this new situation. He had always been able to talk Michael round, had always been the one to orchestrate and then finish these petty grievances, as he called them to himself. He saw Eli as a real threat now, saw him as a dangerous enemy, especially now that it seemed he had got Michael on his side. That he had Michael, his best friend, batting on his team. They were partners, Michael should be agreeing with him, not taking the side of their enemy, a fucking Drongo who made a good living off them and used them as a stepping stone to a better life.

'I can't believe you're even saying all this, Michael, I can't for the life of me understand why you would defend that cunt over me. Your partner, your best friend.' He was laughing in abject disbelief.

Michael sighed once more, his whole body seemed weighed down with the distress he felt inside of him. 'You do anything to Eli and we're fucking finished, Danny Boy. I mean it.'

Danny sprang from his chair and Michael stood his ground, waited for the blow he was sure was going to come. But Danny

Boy didn't even raise his hand. But he saw Michael's clenched fists and realised that he was willing to fight him over this if necessary; that knowledge astounded him more than anything. Danny Boy ran his hands through his thick, wiry hair, his whole countenance one of complete shock. Never before had they ever had a disagreement like this. Michael would normally try and talk him round, try and cajole him, would try and reason with him. He listened to his friend a lot of the time, and respected what he had to say. But that was about business; this need he felt to get rid of his rival was not something Michael could ever have any control over. In fact, he generally let him get on with it. So this sudden angry outburst had thrown him. He was not expecting it, and he didn't know how to deal with it.

'Michael, you'd better think about what you're saying here because I ain't fucking backing down. Eli and his brothers are taking both of us for a pair of fucking earholes. Now, you think long and hard before you go making any more threats, OK. Because I swear to you that I ain't fucking backing down on this for you or anyone else. They're history, mate.'

Michael looked at his oldest friend; he saw the determination in his eyes and the hatred in his face. Nodding gently he said sadly, 'Then I guess there's nothing else for me to say, is there?'

As he turned to leave, Danny Boy shouted angrily, 'Where the fuck do you think you're going?'

Michael didn't answer him. He walked from the Portakabin and out into the sunshine and looked around him, saw the scrapyard as if for the first time. He suddenly saw the decay everywhere, the dog faeces that littered the ground. Saw the cars that were rusted and deformed from years of lying in the one place and saw the pile of tyres that was growing by the day. Then he saw the pale face of the dogs' owner; knew that he had heard them shouting but knew he didn't know what they were shouting about.

In all the years they had been partners he had never before gone against Danny Boy like that. But then, he knew a lot more than Danny Boy realised, and that was a big part of his stand now. As he climbed into his car he saw Danny Boy watching him from the window, his face a dark scowl and his shoulders hunched up with his anger. For the first time ever, Michael didn't care about Danny Boy Cadogan's feelings. This left him with a huge sense of relief, as if he had just had the weight of the world lifted from his shoulders. He drove home slowly and carefully, his mind once more replaying the events of the last few days. He had to see Arnold and sort out this lot once and for all. They had Marsh in a safe place, but that wouldn't be a safe place for long. Not now he had walked out on Danny Boy. They had to marshal their defences as quickly as possible, because Danny Boy would strike first and ask questions much, much later, especially if he sussed out what was going down. This was make-or-break time; Michael knew there was no going back now.

Danny Boy was unable to take what had just happened on board. As he watched Michael drive out of the yard he felt a terrible sense of foreboding, an awful feeling of loneliness and desolation wash over him. Pouring himself a large brandy he threw it back in two large gulps then, filling the glass once more, he sat back at his desk and pondered the morning's events. Never before had they fallen out like this. Danny knew he had stronged it in the past, had mouthed off to his mate, had forced his opinions on him. But Michael had always swallowed, had always known that he didn't mean the half of it. Michael Miles was the only person he really and truly *cared* about. He loved him. And he knew that his own wife Mary had kept her problems quiet because of the friendship they shared. He knew that if Mary had ever told Michael what happened between them it would have stopped a long time ago, as would their partnership. It was partly her compliance in his angry outbursts that made him dislike her so much at times. She kept her mouth shut so her brother wouldn't have to do anything about it. So her brother wouldn't be in any danger from his friend. The friend who loved him and who loathed her for her weakness. Michael was the only person he genuinely cared about, had ever cared about, for that matter. He depended on him, had always depended on him. And he'd believed that Michael felt the same way as he did. Now though, for Michael to turn on him like that, was as unbelievable as it was unsettling. He didn't know how to deal with this situation. He was rarely thwarted, and Michael's complete disregard for his opinion was something he had never experienced before in his life. Even his mother and father had rarely disagreed with him, what he said invariably went with most of the people he dealt with. He thought that was because they knew he was right. Knew that he was doing what he felt was the best for them all.

Now Michael had turned on him, had given him an ultimatum, and he had meant every word of it and that was what was bothering him so much; Michael was adamant. And he knew Michael when he got a bee in his bonnet about something, he would not back down for anybody, not even for him.

Danny realised that it would be in his best interests to go and see Michael when he had calmed down and agree to his demands. They had too much riding on this for them to fall out over such a silly disagreement. After all, he needed Michael for the day-to-day running of everything; he knew how much he depended on him, needed him on-side.

He smiled then. There were other ways to skin a cat, and Eli was going down whatever anyone might think. He would bide his time and, when this had blown over, he would see Eli out of the frame if it was the last thing he ever did. But until then, he had to get Michael back on board, convince him that he had come round to his way of thinking.

Eli Williams and his brothers were safe for the moment, thanks to Michael and his misguided loyalty. But that didn't mean he wouldn't be going after them in the future. It was Michael he needed to sort out now. Michael, his friend.

Chapter Thirty-One

Mary and Carole were each as surprised as the other at their husbands' falling-out.

'It's just unheard of, ain't it, Mary? I can never remember them being at odds before can you?'

Mary shook her head slowly, the news had completely thrown her.

'Mike just walked in and said, if Danny Boy rings, you haven't seen him?'

Carole nodded again. Her moon-face was as concerned as Mary's. 'He said fuck him, that was his exact words. Fuck him. Then he went into his office and, about five minutes later, he left the house and I ain't seen him since.'

'How did he look as he went out?'

Carole shrugged. 'I've never seen him like it, he was *so* angry. Mary, he scared me, and I have never been scared of him, ever. He's the kindest man I know. What can have happened?'

Mary shook her head, as always she looked perfect. 'Danny loves Michael; sometimes I think he's the only person he really cares about other than the girls. Something has gone wrong, obviously, but what that could be, I have no idea. Danny tells me nothing.'

The two women drank their coffees and Mary laced hers liberally with brandy, she had a feeling if her husband and brother had really fallen out, she would need all the help she could get.

As she lit a cigarette Carole saw the bruises on her friend's forearm and wondered at Michael, at how he could never have noticed his sister's predicament. But then she knew it was beyond his comprehension to think that Danny Boy could hurt his wife; he believed that, for all his violent tempers, and his tantrums, his sister was exempt from her husband's moods because he was her blood. That she was his sister and, as such, Danny Boy would never contemplate hurting her. Then again, he was also blind to her drinking so, maybe, deep down inside himself, he knew, or just guessed at a lot more than he let on. It would all come out in the wash as her old mum used to say whenever a mystery presented itself. And it looked like this particular wash day could be just around the corner. She had a bad feeling about all this, and she didn't know why. All she knew was, that her husband had looked fit to be tied, and that was something she had never seen before.

'Danny, calm yourself, son.'

Danny Boy could feel his mother's fear and it annoyed him. She was his mother, for crying out loud; she was the last person who should feel any worry where he was concerned. That history had shown her different didn't concern him at that time because, as always, he was rewriting the past as he went along. It was a knack he had, he had inherited it from his father, though Ange knew she would never point that out to him.

'Is Jonjo in or not?'

Ange nodded and, pushing at her eldest son roughly, she cried, 'Will you sit down and let me get him? He's in the shower.'

Danny was taken aback at her actions and, as always, his anger left just as quickly as it had arrived and putting his hands up in mock terror, he said, 'All right, Mum, relax! I'll go up to him.'

As he sprinted up the stairs he called out, 'Make a cup of Rosie will you?'

Jonjo was on the landing waiting for him, and Danny Boy grinned at him, deliberately not seeing the livid bruising all over his body from their last encounter.

'All right, Jonjo? I need a few words.'

Jonjo followed him into his bedroom, closing the door behind him. Danny looked around the cluttered room and grinned.

'Fucking hell, all you need are a few Janet Jackson posters on the wall and it could be a fucking teenager's room.'

Danny sat on the bed heavily, the mattress straining under his colossal weight. 'Ain't you got any fucking shame, living with your mum like a little kid?'

Jonjo stood very still and listened very quietly to his brother's harangue. He knew it was pointless answering him in any way as it would just make things worse. He waited until Danny Boy had run out of steam, then he sat down gently on the small stool at the dressing table and said respectfully, 'What can I do for you, Danny Boy?'

Danny was gratified at his brother's whole attitude; this was what he craved, this was what he needed. Unconditional respect, people understanding that he was the man in control, it was what he was good at. What he needed as a salve for all the humiliation he had suffered as a kid, from the scruffy clothes to the home hair-cuts.

Danny loved the way people moved out of his way, how they looked at him with a mixture of curiosity and fear and how their respect was already a given. He even needed it from his own family, in fact he needed it more from them than he did strangers.

'What can *you* do for *me*? Well, that's a fucking funny thing for you to be asking, don't you think? When, like everyone else you wouldn't even be in this poxy little bedroom unless I allowed it.'

Danny Boy wiped a hand across his face slowly, before saying in a gentler voice, 'But you can help me, bruv, so wonders truly will never cease. Have you seen or heard from Marsh at all?'

Jonjo dropped his head on to his chest, he was biting his lip to stop himself from laughing in triumph. Then, sighing gently, he said sincerely, 'Nah. I ain't. But has Michael not said anything to you about him?'

He was gratified at Danny Boy's look of shock and, if he wasn't mistaken, a glimmer of fear was now in his eyes. 'What do you mean? Why would Michael mention him?'

Jonjo stood up then, his whole body stretched out to its fullest. His face, if not exactly arrogant, was certainly devoid of its usual subservience. 'I heard last night that he was on the North Pole

495

Road with Michael and Arnold. I would have assumed they would have mentioned that.'

Danny was digesting this information, and Jonjo looked on with what he felt was well-deserved pleasure at his elder brother's obvious confusion. For once, Danny Boy was not in possession of all the facts, and it gratified Jonjo no end to be the one who finally knew something this big, bullying bastard didn't.

'Who told you that?'

Jonjo shrugged. 'Micky Johns. He was in there scoring, he knew Marsh because he'd had a run-in with him before.'

'And he was definitely with Arnold and Michael?'

Jonjo didn't answer him for a few seconds, enjoying seeing his brother so perplexed. So out of the loop, so baffled by his words and what they might mean to him. Danny Boy though, was not in any mood to wait for answers; he was on him in a flash and, grabbing him round the throat, he literally picked him up off the floor as he bellowed, 'Answer me, you useless cunt! Was he with Michael? *My* Michael?'

Jonjo was nodding now, so furiously he could feel the muscles in his neck straining with the tension. Danny Boy threw him on to the floor as if he weighed nothing; as if he was no more than a small child. An annoying child at that. Stepping over him he left the room, slamming the door behind him.

Jonjo sat up, rubbing his neck where Danny Boy had grabbed him, knowing it was nothing to what he had done to him in the past. Jonjo was laughing though, gently chuckling to himself at his brother's misfortune, when the door sprang open again and Danny Boy was there once more, laying into him with fists and feet. All the time screaming at him, 'Fucking laugh at me, would you? Laugh at me, you fucking lairy little cunt? Funny, am I? Humorous? An object of ridicule? I'll kill ya. You fucking treacherous bastard, I'll fucking kill ya . . .'

Danny was out of control, and the last thing Jonjo remembered was his mother trying to drag Danny Boy off of him, her voice high and blurred with her tears as she took the full force of her son's anger. 'Leave him, stop it, Danny Boy. You'll kill him.' She was lying across her younger son now, her body had already taken a few blows, and Danny Boy looked down at her, knew she would take a hammering if necessary, and attempted to master his phenomenal anger. Tried to calm himself down.

'Get up. Get up, Mum . . .'

She shook her head. 'No. *You* get out of here. I want *you* out of here . . . Out of this house . . .'

Danny laughed at her front then. At her ridiculous demands. 'But it's *my* house, ain't it, Mum?'

Ange looked up at the son she had worshipped and loathed in equal measure over the years and she said loudly, 'Then you can *stick* your house right up your arse. I don't want it any more. If it means I have to dance to your fucking tune for the rest of me days, I'd rather be homeless, Danny Boy . . . I'd rather be on the streets.'

Danny could see the hate for him in her eyes, watched warily as she pulled herself up from the floor with difficulty, needing to use the edge of the bed as leverage. He saw how old she had become overnight and the distress in her face as she said, honestly and humbly, 'I can't do this any more, Danny Boy. You're a fucking maniac, a fucking looney tunes. I did the best I could for all of you, for all me kids. But you, Danny, I lied for you, lied to everyone, the Filth, the school, the priest, and I never cared about any of that until now. But this is the final straw, son. This is the one that broke this donkey's back. I know you better than you know yourself. I know you're a fucking bully, that you even torture that poor woman who married you, and I know you bully everyone in your orbit, me included, because no one has any importance in your life except you. Well, it all stops now. Today.'

Ange was sobbing, her heart was aching with the knowledge that this man who she had loved with all her heart, was never going to change. He would only get worse, and she knew that she couldn't let him do this any more. She couldn't take the fear and the terror of wondering what he was going to do next any more.

She sank down on to the stool, her shoulders trembling with the strength of her sobs, her eyes running with salty tears that mingled with her snot. She covered her face with her hands and moaned in deep pain. The sound was so distressing and so valid, that, for the first time in years, Danny Boy took a mental step back from it.

Danny Boy was watching her; he had never seen her like this before. His mother telling him to go, telling him she didn't want him, had hit him like a blast from a sawn-off shotgun. He put a tentative hand out, tried to touch her shoulder, but she knocked it away with all the force she could muster.

'Get away. Don't you touch me. I know all about you, even poor Michael's had enough of you. Carole told me about your upset . . . Wondered if I knew anything about it. But I tell you something, when I heard, I was pleased he had seen the light where you were concerned. You're like a disease, Danny Boy, a fucking plague, and I can't be a part of it any more. I don't want to be.' She wiped her eyes, and knelt by her younger son, feeling for a pulse.

'You took me fucking money though, didn't ya? Used me when it suited ya . . .'

Ange waved him away from her, shaking her head at his words. 'You crippled your own father and you know what he said to me once? You might have crippled his body. But *you* always have had a crippled mind, and he was right. You're not normal, for all your church-going and your fucking confessions you are tainted and in turn you taint everything and everyone you touch. Now, fuck off out of here, and don't let me clap eyes on you again.'

Danny belted her across the mouth with the back of his hand and watched as the force of it sent her sprawling across the bedroom floor. Her lip split, and already swelling, she lay there for a few seconds, looking at him with tired eyes, 'The hand that strikes a parent will wither and die. Well, you're dead to me now, Danny Boy. Dead as a fucking doornail. So, get out, and leave me in peace.'

Danny left the room then, dazed by her anger, at her words. And he knew that if he stayed, he would hurt her, really hurt her. He knew that the blow he had delivered would haunt him for the rest of his life, but she had asked for it. Had pushed him to the limit. They all had at some point. What a fucking family to be lumbered with; from his father right the way through the card, liars and deceivers all of them. As he left the house, he saw the neighbours all out on their front steps and he held his head up as he walked to his car. The shame of his situation was burning into him like a cancer, and added to his already unstable fury; it stoked a fire that could only be quenched by somebody's death, and he knew exactly who that somebody was going to be.

Arnold and Michael were at a warehouse in Dalston. They were nervous but accepting of what they were going to have to do. It was the lesser of the two evils and they both knew that.

Jeremy Marsh was staring at them sightlessly from underneath the tape they had placed over his eyes the night before. He was very still; he was dead and he stank like a polecat. Both men knew that, though neither of them wanted to mention it just yet. It was a lot to take on board; he had obviously choked on either his own vomit or internal bleeding from the kicking they had given him the night before. Either way, it had saved them a job. All they needed to work out now was where they were going to dump his two-faced, scheming carcass.

As they looked at the dead man, his head almost covered with insulating tape, they knew they had burned their boats. The warehouse was full of clothes and handbags, they were all Jekyll and Hydes, snides. From Prada bags to Gucci shoes. Dior dresses to Wrangler jeans. If it was coveted by the masses, it was in this warehouse. The Jekyll market was worth millions in the right hands, and they distributed to every marketplace and every council-house trader in the land. Somewhere along the line, they collected a piece of that pie, and it was a really massive pie. Now they didn't even know how much of their profits were already common knowledge in the police department. How much was being skimmed off by them, how much Danny Boy might be paying to keep them on his side. To make sure he was still the main man, no matter what, and that was without all the information he was passing on. Passing on to make sure no one could ever oust him. It was sickening, the mere thought of it was untenable. Yet it was a reality and they both knew that.

As they looked down on the inert form of Marsh, Arnold said inquisitively and without any rancour, 'How did the fucker get away with this for so long? I mean, not being funny or anything, but I have to ask you, Michael. Did you never even suss once that he might not be legitimately on the rob? That there might be some kind of fucking con going on?'

Michael sighed and, sitting on a nearby crate, he said honestly, 'I did a couple of times, things didn't always add up. But you knew him, would you have ever have believed he could do something like that? And I honestly believe now, after all this, that if he ever did have a capture, he would not have lasted five minutes in nick, and I think he knew that. Had always known it. Danny Boy could not have stood the day-to-day of prison; the fucking boredom and the sameness. Danny wasn't cut out for the downside of our lifestyle; he would do anything to avoid all that. Nick itself would have destroyed him; the regime, the people, the fucking humiliation of it would have been too much for him.'

Arnold nodded, as if in agreement. 'You sound like you understand why he tucked everyone up. You stand to lose more than anybody if this goes tits up. You were his fucking partner, you know as much, or more than, him about the day-to-day of your businesses.'

'I know that, more than you realise. But, for the same token, all I am saying is that, in a funny way, I understand him, and I know him better than anyone.'

Arnold laughed then. Sarcastically. 'You didn't know him that fucking well, face it, look at where we are now. Look at what he fucking caused with his *worrying* about getting a tug. Didn't mind everyone else getting a fucking tug though, did he?'

Michael held his head in his hands and, almost growling with annoyance, he snapped, 'I never said I agreed with his fucking behaviour, did I? All I said was I *understand* it because I understand *him*, how he thinks, how he feels.'

Arnold was annoyed now, felt that maybe Michael was still capable of taking Danny Boy's side in all this. He pushed his face towards his as he spat at him, 'Yeah, I understand him and all; he *thinks* we're all cunts, and *feels* we're beneath his fucking notice.'

Michael shook his head in annoyance, his eyes were sad at the way Arnold was reacting to his opinions. Opinions he had asked for, requested. He was trying to educate him about the man they were dealing with, and he said as much. Arnold just shrugged, as if anything Michael had to say was beyond his ken. He didn't care about Danny Boy's fucking fears about prison, they all had them. It was part and parcel of the life they had chosen; an occupational hazard. In their line of work though, the sentences were hefty. They weren't about a short sharp shock any more, they were about keeping them off the streets. The government wasn't too worried about the thieves, the burglars and the car-jackers, they were too numerous to mention, let alone fucking bang up. They were in and out in a hearty beat. No, the government wanted the money-makers, the few men who earned a fucking real wedge, and they wanted them away for long periods of time. It was laughable. The fucking scum of society, the muggers, the creepers, the nonces, they were out and about in no time. People like them though, the real Faces, were put away for the duration. Even though by their very acts, by the businesses they were involved in, they actually had no real interaction with the public at all. Not unless it was to sell them something they needed, wanted or desired. It was a fucking disgrace to the nation if anyone ever thought about it properly. No government in the world could exist without a black market; it was the unwritten law, the unspoken truth. How the fuck was the working class expected to have a stake in the world without the likes of them? How the fuck were the Christian Diors and the Tommy Hilfigers supposed to become brand names for the pro-letariat without their products being cloned? It was the same people who bought their snides who then, suddenly, felt the desperate need to possess the real thing. Surely it could only be a good thing for all concerned?

Life was about learning how best to live it, how best to keep on the right side of a jail cell. It was about fucking doing what you had to and watching your back. Now Danny Boy had ruined all that for a fucking lot of people. He had moved the goal posts, and this man who Arnold liked and respected had better not keep on trying to justify his fucking actions, because there was no way he could defend his actions. Not to him, or anyone else involved.

What about the people he had already served up? How many of their contemporaries were doing bird because Danny Boy had decided they were suddenly not worth a wank?

'Don't try and make what Danny Boy's done have some kind of logic behind it, make it seem like it was all right, because it's fucking outrageous. An abomination.'

Michael was pulling his own hair, the pain bringing him back to reality. 'I ain't trying to make fucking excuses for him. All I am saying is, unlike you and everyone else, I know what drove him to do this. I was there when he was demolished mentally by his own fucking father. When he was threatened by the Murrays, and forced to take on the role of provider, breadwinner. All I am trying to say is, as big a wanker as he is, it wasn't because he chose this life. He was forced into it. His father . . .'

Arnold grinned. 'I am assuming this is the same father he had crippled, the same father who topped himself?'

'I know how this sounds, believe me. What I am trying to say is, he was a product of his environment. As we all are in our own little ways.'

Arnold snorted angrily. 'He'll be a fucking product of his environment all right, either in the sea, if we dump the cunt in there, or the earth, if we decide to bury him. Either way, he is fucking already dead as far as I am concerned. How you can try and defend him after what he has done, is beyond my understanding.'

'I do know what you're saying, Arnold, I ain't fucking stupid. But I am trying to make you understand why he is like it. Danny Boy doesn't live by the normal rules . . . Look . . . How about this for an example, eh? I heard he killed a prostitute years ago, when he was really young. He beat her to death. He doesn't know that I know about it, that I knew he'd beaten her to death. I convinced meself for years that it wasn't him, that it was just a coincidence. But I knew it was him, I knew deep down inside me. I also knew that Danny, being Danny, could never live with the hold she had over him. Because he had fucked her. He killed her because of his *own* weakness, not because of hers.'

Arnold was smiling now, and chuckling as if this was the funniest thing he had ever heard in his life. He answered him sarcastically and with complete disrespect, 'And that makes it all right, does it? Shall we have a Kill-the-Brass party for him, like a wedding anniversary, only more morbid? Or, better still, shall we round up a few crump-renters and let him go for it? I mean, who cares about them, eh? Let's declare open season on prostitutes shall we? In fact, it's a shame they caught the Yorkshire Ripper, he could have given him a few pointers. Could have shown him how to use a hammer for the common good.' Arnold was looking at Michael as if he was the equivalent of dog shit. 'That is the most disgusting thing I ever heard. Some poor working girl got the red card because *Danny Boy* was ashamed of cocking her. Can you fucking *hear* yourself, hear what you're saying, Michael? Has it ever occurred to you that you have never felt once that Danny Cadogan's actions might be, in any way, wide of the mark. That he might just be a fucking *nutter*, and a grassing nutter at that. My mother was on the bash at one time, and I *love* her for it; she kept us all. She sacrificed herself for her kids, made sure we were all fed and clothed. And you know what, I am so grateful that a fucking Danny Boy *or* one of his weirdo mates never decided that she was the *culprit* in their shitty, scummy lives. And so therefore didn't feel the urge to batter her brains out to make *them* feel better about themselves.'

He was laughing now, laughing in abject disbelief. 'Thank you, Michael, thank you *so* much for your insight into Danny Boy Cadogan. I am just amazed that Channel 4 ain't doing a documentary on him. How about this for a title, "How a Nutter is Made." '

Arnold shook his head in disbelief, his huge dreads almost alive with his annoyance, with his irritation at his friend's utter stupidity where Danny Cadogan was concerned. 'Look, Michael, Mother Teresa he *ain't*, so you had better decide whether you can go through with the day's events. Because, the way you're talking, I ain't sure I want you on board any more.'

Michael could understand Arnold's anger; knew he was well within his rights. And he also knew he understood on some level about his loyalty to Danny Boy, about how hard this was for him. How hard he found it to believe in his friend's duplicity. All those years he had wondered about him, all the times he had deliberately misunderstood what was going on. Danny Boy had been as aggravating as he had been loving towards him. Danny Boy had angered him and had also brought out the best in him where their

503

friendship was concerned. Consequently, this was the hardest thing he had ever done. Had ever *had* to do. It was going against all he had ever believed in, all he had ever really trusted.

'I ain't defending him, Arnold, I am just trying to give you an insight into how he *thinks*, that's all. I *know* him, I know him better than his wife does and she's me fucking sister. I know him better than his mother, than anyone walking the earth. No one knows him like I do.'

Arnold said sarcastically, and with as much hatred as he could muster, 'Yeah? Well, do me a favour, Michael, don't fucking bother all right? You are fucking out of order, man.'

Arnold was almost beside himself with anger and recrimination; he felt he should have pushed this, pushed the point home when he had first encountered the rumours about Danny Boy while he had the chance. He should have struck while the iron was so hot it was burning a hole through his fucking hand. But he had swallowed, had backed down, and that bothered him now. It bothered him big time. It made him feel like he was a coward, made him feel like he was beneath Danny Boy's notice. Not good enough to question him or question his behaviour. Even though it affected him and all those around him. He poked a finger into Michael's face, the anger inside him erupting, 'Who do *you* think you are? I mean, Danny Boy is a fucking liability to *anyone* and *everyone* he has ever come into contact with. Do you realise that? He is a fucking *grass*, a fucking twenty-four carat *cunt*. So I don't care if he was being shafted up the ring by the chief constable himself, nothing can fucking justify what he's done. Nothing. He did it with malice aforethought and with the mistaken belief that no one would ever find out about his treachery. Well, we did, and he is a dead man. I will make sure of that, even if you won't.'

Michael stopped himself from lamping the young man in front of him. Instead he said, through gritted teeth, 'I know what he did, Arnold, I know it better than anyone. You are preaching to the converted, mate. So don't fucking get clever with me. All I am trying to say is, he has not had the breaks, not like people think he has. You can't even imagine what he had to deal with, mate. I am just trying to make sense of this shit, that's all. I'm trying to find a reason to justify his treachery somehow for my own benefit. You forget that he's been my best friend, my brother, since we were little kids. This ain't easy for me, Arnold. I know it should be, but it ain't.'

Arnold didn't want to hear any of this, had no intention of letting Danny Boy Cadogan walk away from this in one piece. He was not interested in the reasons for Danny Boy Cadogan's double life; he didn't care about that. As far as he was concerned, there was nothing to justify his fucking treacherous behaviour. And Michael Miles should have known that better than anyone.

'So, are you going to wimp out on me then, Michael? Is that what this is about? Are you going to give him a heads-up, after all we've talked about? After all this shit and all this fucking sedition we've had to contend with? Are you thinking of protecting him in some way?'

Michael was really annoyed now at his words and, for the first time ever, Arnold felt threatened by his friend. For the first time he saw the Michael that he had heard about but never actually seen for himself. He seemed to grow in stature suddenly, seemed to swell up with ire. He looked, for once, like the big man he really was; he looked menacing and dangerous. He had shed the niceness that he wore like a cloak, and the innate kindness that made people turn to him instead of Danny Boy when they needed to make a point, or ask for mercy. It occurred to Arnold that someone who could have kept Danny Boy's friendship for all these years had to be stronger than anybody realised. Indeed, had to have a lot more might than he let on to everyone around him.

Stepping angrily towards Arnold, Michael looked almost demonic, his hand was raised in angry denial at what he was being accused of. 'Don't you fucking dare to question me, boy. Don't you even dream that you might have the brains or the sense to question me. I knew this all a long time ago, only I couldn't bring meself to believe any of it, and neither would a lot of people, which is why we've had to box-clever. But, if you insinuate anything like this ever again, I'll fucking rip you in half, you cunt, like a Woolworths' Christmas card.'

Arnold was already stepping away from him, already understood that Michael was not as easy-going as he made out to be. He knew that he was a dangerous fucker when cornered, and he also realised that Danny Boy had understood that a lot better than he did, than anybody did. Michael was the brains and everyone knew that, but now it seemed that he was also the brawn when necessary. Arnold felt this man's complete loyalty to his friend, and his inbuilt honesty, and he knew then, that Michael Miles was capable of far more than he or anyone else had ever thought possible.

The last few days had taught him much, but this was the final lesson; never judge a book by its cover. He realised now that Danny Boy had allied *himself* to Michael Miles, not vice versa, because Danny Boy knew first and foremost that *he*, Michael, was in actual fact the real deal, especially where their work was concerned. He knew that Michael was the one person who could talk round anybody, could garner the respect and admiration that made Danny Boy's personality and his natural viciousness seem even more potent. Danny Boy could never have existed without this man and his innate graciousness. It was Michael's influence that made them such a winning combination, made them so successful. Without Michael Miles, Danny Boy would have been left out on a very precarious limb. It was with stunning clarity that Arnold finally understood that Danny Boy's natural antagonism would never have made such a dent in their world without being tempered by Michael's sensitivity. Without his level-headedness, without his decency. Arnold felt the full force of this knowledge in nanoseconds. The real relationship between the two men was suddenly so obvious that he was amazed that he had never seen it before, and he was miffed at his oversight when it should have been blatantly obvious to anyone with an IQ over twenty-five.

Michael was, in many respects, the stronger of the two. Danny Boy had known that from the off, had understood his own failings and, in fairness to him, he had embraced his friend's strength of character. Hoping it might rub off on him which, of course, had been the case. It was Michael's nous people depended on, and Danny Boy's violence if and when everything fell out of bed. And Arnold knew that Michael was far more aware of this than the people they dealt with on a daily basis.

Arnold could only hope now that Michael would keep his sense of fairness and his determination to do the right thing when this finally went down. They had so much to lose, not least their freedom. But, more importantly, their standing in their community, which was the main reason they earned the serious wedge that they did. No one ever questioned their validity, why would they? This was Danny Boy Cadogan and his sidekick Michael Miles. He basked in the same sunshine as they did. They were believed to be both beyond reproach.

'I am sorry, Michael, I was out of order, mate. But you can't go round trying to justify Danny Boy's fucking mentalness, not now, not after all this.'

Michael knew he was talking the truth, but it didn't make it any easier. Didn't make him feel any better about himself. They both looked down at the corpse of Jeremy Marsh, and the enormity of what they had done hit them once more. A dead Filth was a real bummer in their community, even a bent Filth like this one. Old Bill had a strange loyalty that had nothing to do with the person in question, but more to do with the police force as a whole. They knew that one plod on the take was one too many for the general public to contend with, and they closed ranks faster than a panda car on a Reliant Robin. It was about saving face, was about the shame and degradation of a bent Filth and a bent life being exposed to the general public. It was about keeping the scum on the inside, and keeping the peace where necessary.

'I understand that, Arnold, a damn sight more than you ever will. But never again try and front me up, because I ain't fucking going to swallow next time. And, for all your big fucking trap, and your big fucking talk, if push ever comes to shove I'll kill you.'

Arnold didn't answer him, he just nodded. He knew when he was beaten. He knew that this man had beaten him before any of this trouble had even begun. Unlike him, Michael Miles was already more than acquainted with his usefulness in their world and, unlike him, he was more aware of his capacity for violent retribution than he would ever be. It was a learning curve all right.

Chapter Thirty-Two

Danny Boy was grinning, and he knew that his smile was worth a fortune in the world he had created for himself. His goodwill was the equivalent to money in the bank for anyone he decided to bestow his good humour upon. He was pleased with Louie's reaction to his latest problems, trusted the man's opinion because he had never once put him wrong in all the years they had known each other. He knew he was a bully and, deep down, he knew his bullying was without any kind of reasoning. He bullied because he *enjoyed* it. He loved the power it gave him, believed that it was the fault of the weakest. Believed it was his destiny, that people like him had been created to prey on those weaker than themselves. It was almost biblical. Even the Bible was full of bullying, in fact, it was all based on bullying. The survival of the fittest. From Cain and Abel, right through the card, from Herod to the fucking Romans. Christ himself was only crucified because the Pharisees paid out good wedge to get Him convicted. A bit like the British judicial system; he who had poke walked free. It was the law of the jungle, the survival of the richest. But, unlike Christ, his father had had about as much clout as a tout at Bow Street Court on a Monday morning. You had to make your own luck in this life, you had to take care of yourself, numero uno, number one, and he had managed to do that, against all the odds. Unlike his hero, Christ, he had no intention of taking up the slack for everyone else. As far as he was concerned and, as much as he admired Him, that was a fatal mistake on His part. It was the one part of religion he had trouble

509

with. He understood the logic, after all he wasn't stupid, he just couldn't believe that anyone could be that fucking selfless.

It didn't make sense. He saw the original church of Jesus as a band of men, a gang after a common goal; to take over everything. Now that, he could associate with. However, he couldn't see, for the life of him, how anyone with that much power, healing the sick, raising the dead, could just expire, give up the ghost. Leave that kind of power behind without a second's thought. The fact that He was still being discussed, talked about, even worshipped, two thousand years after the event was a fucking serious heads-up. He never preached sedition, all He ever said was love everyone. And therein lay the reason for Danny Boy's scepticism. He couldn't really believe anyone could not use that kind of power for their own good.

Yet he still believed in Him; in His goodness, and His decency. He knew that He just didn't have that killer instinct, that was, in many ways to His credit he knew; it was also why the Catholic church had to be so fucking snide about a lot of its teachings these days. They knew that good was not enough these days. People wanted more, telly had seen to that. Retribution was the order of the day, and it paid. The belief that Danny was a martyr, however, for the way he took care of Louie, even though he had taken the man's main livelihood from him, had been remarked on by many people. Like his idol, Jesus Christ; there was a similarity between the two of them. He was under the impression though, that he had the *right* idea. He kept in close contact with Louie, looked after him, and made sure he was treated with respect by his peers. That was for Louie's benefit, not his. He knew that would be important to the old man, how he was seen by his peers. Danny Boy understood all that, after all, he wasn't a fucking Philistine. He had no intention of humiliating the poor old fucker. All he wanted was what he saw as his. No more, and no less. His speciousness against Louie Stein, he felt personally, had gone a long way towards the goodwill he now enjoyed from his main competitors. They felt he had done right by him in the end, even though they knew deep down that he hadn't. It was easier to believe that, easier to overlook it all. At least, in public anyway.

510

He knew better than anyone that he had taken Louie's daily bread, and taken it right out of his mouth, with a smile and cheery wave. Louie had not had the guts to give him a tug, had not even felt confident enough to argue his end. He had allowed Danny Boy to take what he believed was rightfully his and that was expected of him, and they had both acted as if it was all perfectly amicable. Perfectly *normal*. But, of course, it wasn't. How could it have been? Danny Boy had taken not only his business, but his pride into the bargain. But fear was a great leveller, and the fear of taking Danny Boy on had ensured Louie's silence. Ensured that he stayed on board and knew his place, keeping his own counsel. Like everyone else in their so-called circle of friends. His father used to shout at his mother, when she caught him on the cock, that she wasn't the only fuck in town, and how true that had turned out to be. In every way.

Louie though, knew his place, talked Danny up at every available opportunity, reminding people of Danny Boy's niche in their world. Danny Boy had insisted on that, had insisted that Louie reminded everyone of his innate kindness, and didn't let on that he felt that his young friend had basically scalped him. As was the case.

Louie also made a point of telling Danny Boy every bit of gossip he heard, and he heard plenty. He had an ear that heard everything; his years of being in the game had guaranteed him a certain cachet in that respect, people talked to him and he had that rare ability of being a really good listener. Louie could sort the wheat from the chaff, or chav, depending on who was being talked about, and that made him indispensable. He knew there had been talk lately that Danny Boy paid him to find out things for him, and he also knew there were not many people willing to admit that outloud, at least not to his face anyway. But it still rankled. Louie was basically a grass now; when he had been grassing to the Filth he had felt within his rights. He had grassed the scum, the fucking granny beaters, the muggers, the creepers, the burglars. At least that is how he had consoled himself.

Now Louie told tales out of school that really burned, made him feel wrong. Tales that made what he was doing detrimental to his own well being. He felt the disloyalty that he had to use to get the information in the first place, he had even paid for it, so great was his need. He wasn't that out of order, passing things he had heard on to Danny Boy. Someone would have done the honours anyway, he knew that.

It was a fact, everyone in the know needed a good chatterbox, someone they could trust, someone to keep them involved with what was going on around them so they didn't have to do the rounds themselves. It kept their feet on the ground as they stepped up the corporate ladder, and kept their fists punching the correct faces. It was no more than good housekeeping, a way to keep one step ahead of your enemies. And Louie, because of his past misdeeds, was the perfect candidate as far as most people were concerned. It kept him on-side. Kept him out of trouble. They knew Danny Boy had taken over from him, and they also wondered whether Louie had really been as agreeable as he had made out at the time. In point of fact, Danny Boy had literally taken all that he had. He had also taken it publicly and with the minimum of fuss. That Danny Boy, as everyone remarked, had this same man to thank for basically everything he had achieved in his life, was unusual to say the least. It was a strange set-up, and though no one would query it outright, a lot of people wondered about Louie's *real* feelings about his removal from the scrapyard and this close friendship that seemed able to endure no matter what happened between them.

Ange felt a strange dragging inside her chest and, as she sat in her son's lovely house, drinking tea and listening to the children play, she wondered if she was feeling the first symptoms of a heart attack. She had a numbness going down her right arm, and she shifted her position slightly to ease it. The house was relatively quiet, and she liked that today. She enjoyed the sound of the kids in the background. They were good girls, kind and gentle. She knew that was Mary's influence, even with the drink overtaking her. And, in reality, who could blame the girl? Anyone would drink if they had to deal with Danny Boy on a daily basis, had to keep him sweet and pander to his wants and his needs. Her own life, like poor Mary's, was fraught with problems and, like her daughter-in-law, these were mainly because her son was a vicious tyrant. His latest victim was his own brother. Danny had no time for anyone, let alone poor Jonjo, who he had always seen as a rival for her affections. Everyone was a rival, as far as he was concerned,

Sometimes, God forgive her, Ange hated Danny Boy for the way he made her feel. She had even wished him dead on more than one occasion. She knew this was a terrible sin and that she should be sorry, but she had a feeling that even He might sympathise with her.

Yet Danny Boy had always been a church-goer, had always been a great believer in the Lord God and, she sometimes wondered uncharitably, if it was because he saw a lot of himself in Him. He had always believed that he was beyond any kind of man-made laws, beyond any kind of retribution. He had always believed that he was better than everyone else. Especially since he had taken out his own father. He thought he was beyond all *laws*, and now he had fallen out with Michael and that worried her because Michael Miles was the only person Danny Boy had ever really cared about.

From the moment her husband had gambled away money that they didn't have, Danny Boy had changed, and she felt responsible for that change deep inside herself. If she had not taken her husband back then so much hatred and violence could have been avoided. Her elder son had never forgiven her for what he saw as her betrayal.

And, now that she was old and alone, terrified of her children and what it seemed they were all capable of when backed into a corner, she understood the damage she had done. She felt the useless tears of old age and disappointment rolling down her withered cheeks and she made no effort to wipe them away. Her Annie, who should have been her rock, her second heart, had no real time for her, and who could blame her? She had never bothered with her or Jonjo. She had never attempted to get close to them in any real way. Now she was paying the price for her fickleness, for her neglect. The pain in her chest was like a tight band, and she tried to ease it by bending forward in her chair. Her face screwed-up with the pain and the disappointment of her life and love. The pain was like a knife being shoved into her heart and she couldn't breathe with the ache of it. Even the lovely surroundings that usually cheered her up, that made her forget her son's real personality, didn't seem to be working their usual magic. Instead she felt the fear of a woman who had outlived her usefulness and had made the mistake of putting all her bets on the one horse.

'Are you all right, Nana?' Lainey looked terrified at her nana's white face and drawn countenance.

Ange shook her head, and said tightly. 'Get your mammy, Lainey, I don't feel well at all.'

The child was alarmed by her nana's tears, and the unnatural brightness in her eyes. She ran up the stairs to get her mother as fast as her little legs would carry her.

'I think you should think long and hard, Danny Boy, keep the Williamses on-side for the time being. I'd front it all out personally until you have uncovered the whereabouts of Marsh, and know for certain what the score is where he's concerned. Fuck them, fuck the lot of them. You and I both know that, without you, Michael Miles means nothing, and he'll be back sniffing round your arsehole like a rent boy sooner rather than later.' Louie waved his hands in front of his face in a gesture of dismissal, his voice angry and loud.

'You're giving all this too much credence; now, Eli will want to know your opinion on it, just remember to get him onside.'

Danny Boy nodded. Louie was a shrewdie, had been in the game for years. Danny was willing to listen to his advice after all, this was the man who had started him off in the game in the first place.

'Michael has really fucked me off though, if it was anyone else, Louie . . .' He left the sentence unfinished, knowing that if he let this get to him too much he would be responsible for the death of his only friend. Only *real* friend. Not that he had completely ruled that scenario out.

Louie smiled sadly, trying to explain his reasoning as succinctly as possible. 'Look, Danny Boy, think about it, this is the first tear-up you've had with Michael in how long? Fuck me, most business partners in our world fall out on a daily basis. I think you need to understand that, after thirty-odd years, a fall-out like yours is fucking mandatory. It's a given at some point, a definite. Michael ain't a mug and, be fair, Danny Boy, you've always ruled the roost where you two are concerned, so it makes sense that at some point he was going to force the issue about something. That's human nature, mate. I'm more amazed that it took him so fucking long. Relax, eh? Let Eli tell you his news and then make your decision afterwards. When you've thought this through.'

Danny listened to what the man had to say, then he answered him with a quiet hatred that was almost tangible.

'But I hate Eli, though; he is a treacherous cunt who wants to side-step me and take what's mine. Mine and Michael's. Though no one else seems to see that. And, even knowing that, for Michael and for the sake of peace and quiet, I am willing to let my feelings slide. I can't be fairer than that, can I?'

Louie shook his head sadly, as if in agreement with what he was hearing. Yet wondering, and not for the first time, exactly what planet Danny Boy Cadogan inhabited, because it certainly wasn't planet Earth. Eli was one of the most trustworthy people in the Smoke; Danny Boy had always found fault with his co-workers at some point, but this time he had taken umbrage against someone who was not only liked and respected, but also revered. Eli was not the man to go up against, he had far too many friends in the right places for that. Not that Danny Boy cared; he had taken against him for some reason and that was basically that. Eli would normally be finished in their world; Danny Boy's active dislike would have been enough to freeze him out.

Except, this time round, Danny Boy had come up against Michael, who had refused to let him get away with his petty grievances. Michael had walked out on Danny Boy over Eli Williams, and Louie knew that would never be forgiven or forgotten. Louie was as terrified of Danny as was everyone else, but it was worse for him because he had given him his first-ever break, and every subsequent break after that. Danny Boy Cadogan had conveniently forgotten all about that though, and he had systematically taken everything that Louie Stein possessed. On top of that, the boy he had once seen as a surrogate son, as his heir, had kept him on-side through nothing more than sheer and unadulterated fear. Louie knew that Danny Boy had no real care for him, didn't even have any regrets at what he had reduced his old friend to.

Danny Boy, as much as Louie cared for him, had proved over and over again, that he had no real concern for anybody in the world other than himself. Louie hated him now, hated the way he was expected to jump when Danny snapped his fingers. And was expected to pretend that Danny Boy's treatment of him was not an issue. Louie was more angry that Danny Boy thought so little of him, and his reputation, that he felt he could use him as a go-between without any gold changing hands, or even his opinion being listened to. He was, in effect, no more than a fucking gofer. That hurt, really hurt. Not that anything like that would ever occur to Danny Boy Cadogan. He was too thick to ever believe that anything he had done might deserve some kind of retribution though, in fairness, as that had never been an issue in the past, Louie understood how Danny Boy might not even care about how he was feeling now. After all, once a week had passed, Danny Boy would feel that the mourning period should be well and truly over and everyone should get back to their daily grind. But Louie hadn't forgotten what had been done to him, and would never forgive the fact that Danny had used him as if he was a fucking Tweenie. As if he was nothing more than a driver or a coffee-maker. Swallowing down this disappointment he said jovially, 'Come on, Danny Boy, let's go and see what Eli has to offer, shall we?'

Danny glanced at his diamond-studded Rolex and nodded, but he wasn't happy about any of it and it showed. He was willing to swallow to get Michael back on track and, once he had achieved that, it was goodbye Vienna as far as he was concerned; Eli and his brothers still rankled. 'One word out of place and the bastard's a memory, and I mean that, Louie. Michael had no reason to strop off about him; he knows better than anyone that I wouldn't have said one word if I didn't have all the relevant facts in my possession.'

Louie nodded gently, unwilling to sink in any deeper where their argument was concerned. Instead, he stood up quickly and said, 'Come on, let's get this show on the road, shall we?'

Danny didn't answer him; he was still wondering how Michael could argue with him and not be the one to apologise first. But he was more than willing to be the big man, to be the one to ask for forgiveness; he knew deep down that Michael would never *really* go against him. At least, he hoped that was the case anyway. They went back far too long and had too much tied up together for any of them to ever take a hike. But Michael's adamant stance had thrown him. The more so because it was so unexpected and so resolute. Also, Danny Boy had no intention of letting him walk away from him, not after all the fucking effort he had put in over the years. Michael might think he had the upper hand, and he might have even let him believe that but, at the end of the day, Michael knew that without him and his reputation as a fucking headcase, they were basically nothing. Alone, Michael Miles was about as scary as a lone skinhead on the Railton Road at two o'clock in the morning. Basically, he was nothing more than a joke. Even if Marsh had opened his big trap, which he seriously doubted, Michael was too entrenched in it all to do anything about it without casting aspersions on himself anyway. He felt that Michael, no matter what might happen, could not really go against him. Danny Boy's natural arrogance had taken over now, and he was once more convinced that no one and nothing could interfere with his daily life.

If necessary, he would put Michael wise; explain the circumstances to him, and encourage him to take an active part in the proceedings from now on.

In fact, this was probably a good thing in many ways; he saw this as something else that Michael could take over and sort out for him. He was suddenly very relieved that the cat was out of the bag at last. Without his backing, without his connections in the police force, they would still be scratching a fucking living like every other mug. He had taken out all their rivals with a few choice words, and a nice few quid.

If he could get Eli on board with this latest venture, Michael would see just how much he wanted to make things right again, how much he was willing to give, *personally*, just to bring them back together once more. Without Michael, he didn't feel he could function properly, didn't feel that he was really a part of anything.

He finally understood that, without Michael by his side, without him doing all the ground work, he *couldn't* operate. He needed him, and that realisation was as terrifying as it was truthful.

As they drove away from Louie's house, Danny Boy felt his spirits lifting, knew that Michael had to be feeling the same way as him. He also knew, in the dark part of his character that, when Michael finally came back into the fold, when he finally understood the error of his ways, Danny was going to show him personally just how foolish he had been because, like Eli Williams and his brothers, Michael Miles would eventually *have* to be wiped off the face of the earth. Danny Boy knew that was a fact, as well as he knew his own name, knew that Michael was a dead man over all this. Knew that he would never be able to let it go. Michael's actions had been tantamount to a mutiny, and that was something he could never allow. If you let one person get a cunt into the conversation, you basically had given them a green light to carry on cunting you until their dying day.

As much as he cared for Michael, and he did care for him, more than he did his own family, he knew deep inside that Michael Miles's days on this earth were now numbered. He knew that he would be honour-bound to take him out at some point, if for no other reason than to prove a point to all those who had mistakenly believed he might be mellowing in his old age. It wouldn't happen immediately, of course, Danny knew he had to get him back on board for appearances' sake, and he also knew that he wasn't ever going to let Michael Miles walk away from him. He wanted to, *wanted* to believe he could forgive him, knew that he needed him desperately. But, ultimately and, in all honesty, once this game was played out, Danny Boy knew that his pride would never let Michael get away with this. He knew that he would never be able to come to terms with what he saw as Michael's betrayal. It was too overdone; he didn't have the personality to let something of this magnitude go, let something so important to him drop. Forgetting about it was not an option, he knew that it would play on his mind until the day Michael died. There was no way Danny could swallow his knob and let this pass.

Michael knew too much, far too much than was good for either of them. At some point, Danny knew, Michael Miles would *have* to pay the price for all this heartache and worry. No matter how much he might need him to run the businesses. No matter how much he wanted to believe his own rhetoric. Once he had a new front man, Michael Miles was fucking history. That meant that his wife, his Mary, Michael's sister, would also be in line for the chop. And that alone was reason enough for him to take out the man he not only needed, but actually loved. And he did love him; Michael was the only person he had ever cared about, really cared about, but then Michael had not tucked him up until now, had he? Michael, he suddenly realised, was now an enemy, was no more to him than an unknown quantity. The more he thought about it, the more plausible it became.

Louie watched him surreptitiously, knowing that Danny Boy had no real intention of seeing any of his promises through to the bitter end. After all, why change the habits of a lifetime? Louie hated him with a vengeance and saw him these days for the bully he was, had always been. When he remembered the young lad that he had mentored, whose father had served him up to his enemies as if he was a Chicken Vindaloo, he felt so miserable and so sad that he could easily cry. When he thought of the young boy he had taken such a shine to, had felt such sorrow for, he didn't see the man he had become, didn't equate that sad and lonely child with this vicious and ignorant individual. He only saw the original Danny Boy with his crooked smile and his grateful demeanour.

Louie knew that Danny Boy Cadogan would use him until the day he died. He knew that Danny saw him as a grass, no more and no less. He also knew that Danny Boy didn't see his own grassing as anything to worry about. In fact, he didn't even think that what he had done over the years to people he had worked with, drank with and socialised with, merited any kind of mention in the grand scheme of things. He just saw it all as a means to an end, and he also believed that the very same people he had served up to the Filth, had actually deserved whatever had befallen them. They were, after all, in his way. Were what he referred to as collateral damage. Danny Boy had a knack of only seeing only what he wanted to see.

Louie Stein wished with all his might that he had been just as blessed and he also wished that a bolt of lightning would destroy Danny Boy Cadogan once and for all so he didn't have to deal with him any more.

Eli was waiting patiently for Danny Boy to arrive and, when the man finally parked his Mercedes and walked towards him with his usual cocky attitude, he felt the urge to really lay into him. Hurt him. But, as always when dealing with Danny Boy, he smiled that wide, white-toothed smile instead. The bright smile that had cost him a small fortune. His dentist had once remarked that he had bought himself a villa on the Costa del Sol and Eli had a sneaking suspicion that he had probably paid for it. But this smile was now a smile that most of his contemporaries could only aspire to; it was perfect, and he knew that better than anyone. He also knew that his new, wide-open smile gave him an edge since the treatment; he found that he smiled more, was far more confident and, for some strange reason, his new railings made him look far more amiable than he actually was. Even his wife had remarked on his new personality, and she knew him better than he knew himself.

Now though, as he saw Danny Boy walking towards him, Eli felt the full force of his dislike; he had been so convinced that Danny Boy was kosher, that Danny Boy was someone to applaud and respect, this news about him had thrown him, had knocked him for six. But, as he saw him striding towards him with his usual cocky gait and his deep-felt conviction that he was the only person in the world who really mattered, Eli knew that he *wanted* to believe the worst about him, that he didn't really care if it was true or not. He hated him, wanted him gone, over with, finished. Smiling back carefully, he led Danny Boy inside the building. And was gratified to see this big man reduced to nothing when he saw Michael Miles and Arnold Landers waiting patiently for his arrival.

That Danny Boy was thrown off-kilter by their presence was obvious, that he felt intimidated by them was also blatantly evident; the way he stopped dead in his tracks was a pointer. He was so fucking sure of himself and his reputation that this scenario had never even occurred to him. It was laughable really.

Eli stood behind him, making sure that he had no escape route, enjoying the feeling of power that this gave him and hating himself for it.

Danny Boy regained his composure quickly; he looked at Arnold and saw immediately, by the man's body language and his composure, that there was nothing he could do to bring him round to his way of thinking. He had already sussed that Eli Williams was playing the part of a bouncer, watching the doorway, making sure he didn't make a run for it at any point. As if *he* would do something like that. But he was caught, he knew that then and there; he was caught bang to fucking rights. His secret was out, and there was no way it could ever be put away again. Even he knew he was in dire straits; knew his actions would be seen as unacceptable.

Danny Boy heard Louie moving from behind him, knew he was making himself scarce and knew then, without a second's thought, that it had to be Louie who had set him up. That he was the reason these people were all looking so pleased with themselves. But it was Michael he wanted to talk to, because Michael was the only person here who could maybe garner him some kind of exit from this building, who could ensure that he walked away from all this. Who was soft enough to forgive him. But, even as he thought about it, he knew that the fact they were here in the first place meant his duplicity was already too well known. Was common knowledge. He was well and truly sussed.

Danny Boy wasn't a fool, he knew he was a dead man. He knew that this day had been a long-time coming, but that it had always been on the cards. If you lived by the sword, it stood to reason that you'd eventually die by the fucker; it wasn't rocket science. He had just not thought his demise would be this soon and so ordinary. He had always pictured himself being shot, seen himself dying nobly, a gaping hole in his head, his chest, in a packed pub or club, with a sneer on his lips. That kind of death he could have swallowed. Could have accepted. It had all the hallmarks of a legend in the making. He could have swallowed something like that, a public execution.

But not this, he was much too young to die; he still had places to go and people to see. He had been sussed right out, and he knew that now, but it still didn't make this any easier. All the people that he had personally despatched over the years; it had never occurred to him that they might have felt like he did now, frightened, accepting of their fate, but, more than anything else, cheated. Until now, it had genuinely never occurred to him that the people he had taken out might still have had dreams and wants; had kids that they might have wanted to see grow up and go out into the world.

That all he had done over the years, all he had achieved, was as nothing, was liable to be snuffed out here, in a filthy warehouse, without any fanfare or any prayers. He hoped his kids, his girls, would never know the truth of this. His wife, he knew, would be relieved, and his siblings would bury him with the correct amount of pomp and ceremony he would require, but without any tears, real tears. After all the drama of his life, he knew then that his death would be a shameful and humiliating experience for all concerned, especially him. He wasn't walking out of here, he knew that much.

As Michael looked into his eyes, Danny saw the deep sadness mirrored that was in his own. He saw the love that Michael had for him, and was gratified that at least he would have that much to take with him. He finally understood the expression beggars and kings because, no matter how much money you might have, or how much prestige you acquired over the years, you would die at some point, and there was nothing anyone could do to stop it. His death was imminent, he knew that because he would have wasted himself long ago if he was in their shoes. He smiled at Michael then, a magnanimous smile, and he opened his arms out wide, as if he understood the situation perfectly which, of course, he did. He felt a chill in the air, could smell the dust and the underlying aroma of cheap leather handbags and even cheaper cotton T-shirts. He looked around him then, saw Eli and Arnold watching him, knew that they were both desperate for his demise. He knew that his death would finally allow them both to rise in the world of criminals, would guarantee them a place beside Michael, running the businesses and sorting the monies. It seemed crazy now, to think that, even after his death, the businesses would still go on regardless, that the world would not stop on its axis because he was gone from it. He wasn't even contemplating a way out of it all; Eli had a machete which he was brandishing happily, Arnold had a long-bladed knife, a fine piece of weaponry from its carved bone handle, its ultra-sharp blade. Everyone was well tooled up, except him.

Michael and Danny looked at each other once more, and Danny Boy said gently, 'We had a good touch, Michael, we made it to the top of the tree. We are Faces, real Faces.'

Michael nodded, understanding his friend's words. 'Yeah, you got what you had always dreamed of, Danny Boy. You're a Face, a well-known and respected Face. *The* Face, in fact.'

Danny said quietly, 'Are you going to do it? You going to take me out?' He was glancing around, instinctively looking for a way out. He saw that Eli's brothers had slipped in behind them and were tooled up and ready to go. He felt strangely gratified that they were mob-handed, that they deemed him so dangerous. It catered to his inflated opinion of himself and what he felt he was capable of. But no one wanted to talk, and he felt the sudden and desperate quiet weighing down on him like a stone. The atmosphere was almost electric; they all felt it, felt the heaviness in the air, saw Danny Boy tense up as if waiting for his chance to let rip. Louie shouted at them then. His nerves were shot and he was sweating profusely, terrified that Danny Boy would either talk his way out of this dilemma or worse, fight his way out of it. He knew he was more than capable of either.

'Kill him, for fuck's sake, just get it over with, will ya! What you waiting for, a fucking film crew?'

Then Louie started coughing, the coughing of old age; it was heavy and wet and the phlegm he spat out was like a piece of rubber. It broke the moment, and Danny Boy went for him like a Rottweiler on Hurlimans. 'You treacherous old bastard.'

As Danny ran across the warehouse floor, he saw Louie trying to dodge him, and he grabbed at him tightly, pulling the man towards him with all the strength he could muster and then throwing him on to the floor. Louie fell down heavily, his bones screaming with the pain of his advanced years. Michael saw Arnold and Eli descend on his old friend. As Eli sliced him across his face with the machete, opening it up like a watermelon, Arnold forced the blade of his knife between Danny Boy's ribs, Stabbing at him repeatedly, forcing it up into his heart. Michael watched in morbid fascination as Arnold brought a machete down over and over again onto Danny Boy's head and shoulders. Opening him up, slicing him up as if he was a piece of meat. The blood was everywhere, seeping out of all his wounds and, even in death, with his life's blood pumping out on to the filthy concrete floor, Danny Boy still looked the part. He still looked like a Face, even though, ironically, he was now without one. It was the sheer size of him, the sheer presence he possessed that caused this illusion. Even in death he had an arrogance that was almost tangible.

Michael was amazed at how Danny had accepted his fate, had not even really tried to fight for his life. Not how he could have anyway. Danny was capable of a real tear-up when the fancy took him. But, looking at him now, a bloody heap on the filthy floor of the warehouse, he knew that Danny would never have been able to live down the shame of being exposed as a grass. Eli ripped open a box of T-shirts and started to wipe his bloody hands on them; the irony was that they had a cannabis leaf on the front with the words, 'Keep Off the Grass' written underneath.

Arnold was staring at Danny Boy's corpse in fascination; it seemed unreal that it had taken so little to destroy him. To finish him off once and for all. Such a huge personality, such a dangerous man, had been wiped off the face of the earth with an ease that reminded them of how effortless death could actually be in the right hands. How quickly death could render even the most fearsome of antagonists harmless.

Michael helped Louie up from the floor. He was obviously in a great deal of pain, but the old man was also elated at the outcome of this day's work. For the first time in years he felt he could really relax. Could finally unwind. He had finally extricated himself from what had been his worst nightmare. The two younger Williams boys had both lit joints, kingers packed full of skunk, the smell already permeating everything around them. The absolute quiet that had descended on them earlier was back once more.

Only this time it was tinged with a feeling of relief for everyone concerned.

Louie hawked in the back of his throat again and spat into what was left of Danny Boy's broken and bloodied face. 'I told you, Danny Boy, what goes round comes round.' Then he started to cry, his shoulders shaking with his guilt and his sorrow at what had taken place. He had loved this man like his own once, and that could never be forgotten. Michael hugged him, and Louie pushed him away roughly. 'He was a cunt! But he was a fucking *Face*. I told him he had no need to take shortcuts, but he wanted it all at once. Like you all do. None of you can wait for anything these days, you want everything immediately. It's why it goes bad, why you end up like this.'

He pointed at Danny Boy then. 'You all want too much too fucking soon. You don't want to earn anything up-front. Wait in line, get your creds. It all has to be *now*. This fucking minute.' He was trying to compose himself, but the waste of a life was just hitting him. His fear was death, and he was an old man. To see so much strength and so much energy snuffed out seemed outrageous.

Eli shook his head sadly. The adrenaline was abating now, and he was feeling relaxed again, hungry.

'Relax, Louie, this had to happen at some point. He was a fucking grass, a fucking two-faced dirty scoundrel. Now, go home, old man, go home and forget all about this.'

Michael was still in shock; Danny had always seemed so indestructible and to see his carcass, bloodied and destroyed, was an enormous event. Yet, at the same time it felt like nothing.

Eli sighed. 'You got the petrol?'

Arnold nodded, then laughed as he said, 'Yeah, 'course I have.' Michael motioned then for Louie to leave and, as he walked out behind him, he said sadly, 'This is the end of an era. Danny Boy Cadogan found dead inside a warehouse full of hookey gear with a bent Filth lying beside him. It'll be a nine-day wonder.' Then, turning back to face them all, he said, 'I'll leave you boys to get the bonfire going. I need a drink and a few hours' kip before the cabaret starts.' No one said a word, just waved nonchalantly, and started what was classed as the clean-up operation.

*

'Are you OK, Ange?' Mary's worried face was hovering over hers, and she wondered how they had got her onto the sofa.

'I feel fine now. I just came over a bit queer, that was all.'

'I've phoned an ambulance, just lie there and take it easy.'

Ange pulled herself up; she could hear the genuine worry in her daughter-in-law's voice and was grateful for that, but she said in panic, '*No!* I don't need an ambulance, I feel fine now. I swear to you, I feel OK.'

She was already in a sitting position, and Mary saw that she was actually looking much better.

'I had a terrible pain in me chest, like a knife, but it was probably just wind. I feel fine now. Please stop the ambulance from coming . . . I feel such a fool.' She was pleading with her daughter-in-law to not make a fuss. But she did feel fine now, as if the weight of the world had been lifted from her shoulders.

'Are you sure you're OK? Why not let them just give you the once-over when they get here, eh? Just to be on the safe side.'

The last thing Mary needed was her husband's mother dropping down dead and him hearing that she had cancelled the ambulance. That would go down like a lead balloon. But, that aside, she liked the old cow; in many ways they were alike, they both lived around the moods of a man they hated while at the same time, they depended on him. The ambulance arrived then, and Mary went to let them in, happy that the decision had been taken out of her hands.

Epilogue

Care-charming Sleep, thou easer of all woes,
Brother to Death . . .

           – John Fletcher 1579–1625
                  Valentinian

Mary and the girls were sitting in the front of the church; they looked lovely, everyone remarked on how good-looking the girls were. Both had the same delicate features as their mother, and the quick, sarcastic wit of their father. They were dressed, as always, like little princesses, and they sat with their heads held high and their backs straight. Mary had a thing about deportment and she looked down on them with pride, a small smile playing on her lips.

'Move up, let Nana sit down.' Ange slipped in beside them, and they grinned as she passed them each a small bag of sweets; she winked at them as if this was all a great conspiracy. Mary pretended not to notice and the girls were thrilled to be part of something so secretive and so exciting. Mary had even allowed Gordon to sit with her family. Now her husband was dead, it seemed pointless to carry on with the grudge. Her wedding day was so long ago, a lifetime gone. Carole and Michael smiled at the little tableau, Carole holding her new son in her arms by the Baptismal font, as Arnold and Annie took their places beside her. The church was packed out, everyone who was anyone had attended and, as the priest began the service, a hush descended quickly. Mary looked around her then, and felt the full force of her new-found freedom. It was as if her life had started all over again when her husband was murdered. She had played the part of the grieving widow to perfection, and now she was emerging from her chrysalis at last, and people were pleased to see her finally getting over her tragic loss.

The police had their opinion about what had happened, and she had hers; Michael and the local Faces had theirs, but no one really gave a shit any more, it was old news. All she knew was that her girls were happy, and so was she. It was like a weight had been lifted from her shoulders and she felt like a teenager again. A seriously rich teenager, who could now do exactly what she liked, when she liked, and with who she liked. Unfortunately, men were not on her agenda, and never would be. She hated them, not all men obviously, only the ones who she saw as a threat. The ones she knew gave her the eye and daydreamed of fucking Danny Boy's widow. They had more chance of getting a blow-job off John the Baptist, though they didn't know that. People said Danny Boy had spoiled her for other men, and she nodded in agreement. He had managed that all right, only not in the way people thought.

She still woke in the night, sweating and trembling as she remembered some of Danny Boy's more outrageous demands. And she remembered how he had nearly drowned her, had helped his own babies vacate her womb, and laughed at her tragic countenance. He saw her love for those poor children as a weakness but was terrified of her having a son, even his own son would have been seen as a threat eventually, she knew that now. But to be able to spend money as she liked, feed the girls what she wanted, use every room in the house, was better than winning the lottery. She had a mobile now as well, something Danny had never let anyone in his orbit possess. He had been convinced that a mobile could be traced, could be used against you. Although in her case, she knew it was because he didn't want her in contact with anyone without his say-so. His birds had all turned up at the funeral; a couple had even brought their kids and she had been really nice to them. People remarked on that still. But she had actually felt sorry for them, because he had left no provision for them or their kids in his will. It was all hers, with her brother Michael as the executor. Well, Michael had given her the fucking lot, and she had not offered one of his whores a fucking bean for their kids. Why should she? They had fucked him knowing she was his wife, had bedded him in the hope that he would find them a better option. She had been unable to do anything about it while he was alive, but dead she could smile and be nice, and inside she could get her revenge absolutely by doing nothing for them. They had been left high and dry, skint and used, well, welcome to what had been her world. Danny Boy had even questioned the grocery bills, had made her explain every penny she had spent to him in graphic detail and this after he had presented her with a piece of jewellery that was worth thousands.

She hated him so much, and it wasn't abating with his demise; if anything, it was growing. She felt the force of her singledom, and she loved it. Loved the fact she could do what the fuck she liked and no one could question it. She was still drunk, but these days it was on happiness; she was drunk on life itself. She still needed a few gulps to take the edge off, but nothing like the amount she had drunk before. The scars were gradually fading, both mental and physical, but the feeling of sheer contentment that enveloped her was gradually settling on to her shoulders and driving the sadness from her mind.

Mary shivered as she looked at the cross of Christ above the altar; she had focused on that at her husband's funeral. She'd had to stop herself from laughing outloud and flinging open the coffin lid, from shouting her happiness and relief at her husband's death from the rooftops. God, she felt, was good. He made the back to bear the burden, well, her burden was wormfood now, and that alone was enough to cheer her up in her darkest moments.

Mary smiled at her girls, glad that they would be able to live their little lives without that bastard ruining every happy moment before they even had the chance to enjoy them. She hoped Danny could see her, see her new life, her new demeanour, and she hoped that he was spitting fire at her blasphemy. She had given his suits to the homeless shelter and she had slung him in the same grave as his father, two wankers stuck together for all eternity. And people thought she had done that because she was a good person, well fuck him, and fuck everyone else. God paid back debts without money, and so could *she*.

Arnold and Annie were standing as godparents. Arnold wondered how their marriage had survived his part in her brother's murder. He thought, at times, that Annie knew what had happened, but he put it down to his own guilt. Not that he regretted any of it, but she was still his wife, and he *had* been rather instrumental in Danny Boy's death. But the truth had never even been hinted at. Danny being found brown bread with a Filth had caused a lot of talk, mainly that he had been taken out by Old Bill. It wouldn't be the first time the Filth had done a spot of house cleaning, they were known to have dispatched more than one Face when the going got a bit too tough. Danny Boy was still a Face, even in death, his name was still synonymous with villainy and corruption. No one even attempted to deny that. He was seen as an unfortunate man who had been removed from this world by a corrupt and disgraced government agency. The word on the street was that Danny Boy had refused to pay off the relevant agencies. No one in the know disagreed with these stories, and they also made a point of not giving them any credence either. They knew that their silence on the matter would ensure that Danny Boy's death would never come back to any of them. It would stay a mystery, and that was what he would have wanted, and what they had all decided would be for the best. In death, Danny Boy still had his little bit of kudos, and that meant that they could bask in his reputation, and take over everything with the minimum of aggro and the maximum of goodwill. They knew that a lot of people had breathed a collective sigh of relief when they had learned of Danny Boy's demise. That was human nature.

That Louie now had his yard back was mentioned only behind closed doors, no one wanted to bring any unwanted attention to themselves these days.

Annie smiled happily at her husband and he smiled back. The priest was asking them to renounce Satan, and Michael looked at Eli with a tiny smile on his face. He knew that Eli was thinking the same as him; Satan, as such, was long gone.

Danny was dead, and Michael missed him, even as he was glad to see the back of him finally. He still missed the closeness they had shared for so long because, as much as Danny Boy could be a bastard, could be a vicious and selfish cunt, he could also be a really good mate. If not to anyone else, then certainly to him. Unlike most people, Danny Boy had really cared for him, and Danny Boy had always looked out for him. Danny had known all along that it was his acumen that had been the main reason they had risen up so far in their world. But he also knew now that it would not have happened so swiftly without his friend's penchant for grassing. That he had never once given any real thought to how they had prospered so quickly Michael did not like to dwell on. Deep inside, he had always known it was too much, too soon. He had known, somewhere deep inside, that it wasn't kosher. And had not wanted to know, if he was really honest. But now Danny was gone, and everyone was gradually coming to terms with it, and they were all working together to limit the damage his death had invoked.

Michael looked at his new son, and thanked God that he could be here today, could see him grow up, could see all his kids grow and mature. He loved Carole, and so had Danny Boy, and Carole still talked about him with genuine affection. She had never been on the receiving end of his ire, had never had to feel the heat of his anger. Yet he knew she was more than aware of what he was capable of. She knew, like he did, that his own sister had lived in mortal fear of him. But, like most people in Danny Boy's orbit, she was grateful for his goodwill. For being allowed to be a part of his life. Danny knew how to do that, how to make people grateful for his attention.

Eli, Michael felt, had been the last straw, that Danny Boy could have wanted to waste him was so outrageous, that he had expected *him* to believe that Eli and all the Williamses were snides was so off the wall that he had been forced to do something about it. Eli was sound, and no one would have swallowed his demise without demanding some kind of explanation, especially his own brothers and his large and loyal workforce. No one would believe that he was after Danny Boy's place in the world, not with any real conviction anyway. Eli was far too clever for that. But Michael knew, as a matter of fact, that Eli was now living on borrowed time. That, unfortunately, was the way of their world. Michael knew that he could not afford to let him get a foothold in any of their businesses; Arnold was of the same opinion. Eli, as much as he liked and admired him, was a dead man walking. Michael was far more like Danny Boy than he had realised, and the knowledge, in a funny way, pleased him. Michael had to protect his assets and, because of

Eli's natural feeling of superiority, he would have to go. It was sound economics. Danny Boy's death had been far too public; after Eli and his brothers were dispatched, Louie would have to go as well. He was far too shrewd to make the same mistakes as Danny Boy. He was happy enough to partner up with Arnold, they spoke the same language and understood their predicament. It was a shame, but that was the way their world worked. Looking at Eli now, seeing his smile and his arrogant stance, Michael knew that it would have to be done sooner rather than later, within the next twenty-four hours. Arnold was right; there was no room for sentiment and, after Danny Boy's untimely demise, it proved that if you left things too long, they could backfire on you. Eli was too strong a personality to let him get any closer than he already was. Michael smiled down at this new son of his. He knew that, for him and his other kids, he would wipe out a hundred Elis or a thousand Danny Boys. Like Danny Boy, they underestimated him, even Arnold who was desperate for him to take him on as partner, and that would also be the main reason why Eli did not believe he would even consider taking him out. Everyone had underestimated him, all his life. Well, more fool them. This was about saving his own life now, and he would save his life at the expense of anyone foolish enough to get in his way. As Michael listened to the priest he wondered once more at a man who had made such an impression in his life, and yet had been removed without any real effort whatsoever. Danny Boy Cadogan had been a learning curve all right. For all of them. London was too small to share, especially with people who knew far too much for their own good.

Ange was holding her granddaughter's little hand in hers. She was happier than she had ever been, and that amazed her. She had lost her husband and her son, and now she realised that, without them hanging around her neck like a pair of fucking albatrosses, she could finally be happy. Really happy. As Ange looked around the church her eyes rested on Jonjo, a useless fuck if ever there was one. He was so weak he made Lily Savage look like George Foreman. She knew she would be looking out for him all his life, he had no loyalty to anyone and, like his father, he also had no real intention of ever going to work. Not real work anyway. She knew he was already back on the brown; it was only a matter of time before he scored a decent batch that would kill the stupid little fucker once and for all. The worst of it was that she felt no real need to try and prevent that happening. It was like pissing in the ocean, it would have no real effect. He was determined to ruin his life, and she was powerless to stop him. She had come to the conclusion, why prolong the agony? She had buried one son, another one wouldn't really make that much difference and, in reality, it would be a relief. She was already dreading the knock on the door that would herald his death, so the sooner it came, the sooner she could get back to her real life. The sooner her younger son might find a modicum of peace.

Annie was also a write-off, like Jonjo, and she took full responsibility for that. Annie was obsessed with Arnold, and God love him he looked after her when most men would have put her out on the pavement. She was a nightmare of jealousy and suspicion. As indeed she had been once, many moons before when sex was still important and the man she had married had taken precedence over everything and everyone in her sad and lonely life. If only these girls realised how fickle life was, how eventually the men that they loved so much, who they had cared for over all others, their kids included, would, without a doubt, eventually wander, both mentally and physically. How humiliating it was when you finally accepted that as a fact. When they saw younger women, saw their contempt for the mother of their children as if it was tattooed on their foreheads. How any man, no matter what they might say to the contrary, would take a twenty year old over a forty year old any day of the week. That was nature, and that was something her Annie was one day going to have to accept. Because men like Arnold would always have a fan club waiting in the wings; it was the way of their world. It was something the more sensible women in their circle accepted and ignored. But Annie wouldn't, she had too high an opinion of herself and her worth. She had never done a day's collar in her life, and she never would. Arnold would always see her all right but, unfortunately, that would never be enough. Like Danny Boy, her other two children saw themselves as a cut above everyone else. She had never really connected with either of her younger children and, as someone had once pointed out, hindsight was a wonderful thing. She could write the script for them now, but they wouldn't listen to her, so it was pointless trying to help them out. She had written them off, as hard as that was to admit.

It was Mary and the girls who were now the reason she got up each day. Mary had been good to her and she didn't deserve it. She had never given her the time of day really. Had never been as kind and as generous as she could have been. Yet, it was only when she was in Mary's home, watching those little girls playing, that she felt any real emotions. Danny Boy was gone, and that was the reason for much rejoicing, even more money coming in for everyone concerned. She knew a lot more than any of them gave her credit for.

Ange looked over at Eli Williams and he winked at her saucily; he was a nice young fella. She had always liked him but, she had never trusted him, and she had told her Danny Boy that; not that he had ever listened to a word she had said. But there was something about him, something she could not explain. It was no more than a feeling. But, since Danny Boy's death, his so-called unexplained death, she had felt it even stronger. At her son's funeral she had felt a great sense of relief and an even greater sense of impending doom. But she knew that anything she felt was of no real interest to the parties concerned.

So she accepted her new place in life, was happy to live the remainder of her time out with the people she loved, and who she knew, loved her.

She had birthed and raised three children, and accepted that she had been the catalyst for each of their downfalls. But she had done the best she could and, whether they liked that or not, it was the truth. You did the best you could, played the hand you were dealt. As she knew to her detriment, hindsight was a wonderful thing. Ange held her rosary gently between her fingers and whispered the Hail Marys with a quiet determination that spoke of her despair, but also of her belief in God. She felt, like most of the family, that Danny Boy's death had somehow given them all a new perspective on life.

For herself, she finally felt at peace. Felt that her son's quest for greatness, his need to be seen as a Face, as someone of note in their world, was what had eventually destroyed him. And, with his death, she had at long last felt able to sleep at night, had finally been able to live her life without fear or favour. As had poor Mary, who she had seen blossom in the last few months from someone who flinched at her own shadow and who had been terrified of even being suspected of holding an opinion of any sort, but who now had a degree of confidence and a real lust for life; neither of which she could have ever enjoyed had her son not met such a violent end. All of this, she now felt, had been a long time coming.

Eli watched the people gathered around with his expensive smile and his natural calm and collected demeanour. He was well liked, and he appreciated that. He knew the value of goodwill and the cost of people's ill temper. He knew that Danny Boy had made the fatal mistake of believing he was too powerful to be thwarted. Well, he had found out the hard way that no one was beyond retribution. Especially people who didn't share their good fortune, who didn't appreciate the people who had placed them in their elevated position in the first place. He understood the value of goodwill, and he also understood that people who worked in their world, who put their liberty on the line every day of their lives, needed to feel appreciated. Needed to earn a good wedge, and be assured that, if they did get a capture, their families would be taken care of. It was one of the only things Danny Boy had got right. He had, in fairness, always looked after his own. Unfortunately, he had often been the reason they had got their collars felt in the first place. He had served up anyone he felt was a threat, or who he felt was not quite his cup of Rosie Lee. In short, he had held everyone in his orbit to ransom. Not that they had realised that, of course. Danny had been far too shrewd for that. Still, eventually his sins had found him out. And Louie had been the one who had introduced him to the grasses' paradise in the first place. He would pay for that in the future. Faces, the Faces they wanted to be, thought they were, had all had their day. They were fucking dinosaurs. It was a new world, and Eli had no intention of waiting around until some little fucker with a Jamaican passport and a Nigerian-funded armoury decided to take him out. Take what he had worked for. There was no *real* underworld anymore, it was a thing of the past. A few well-known families were no match for the new breed of immigrants who saw London, Europe, as a blank canvas, who were hungry and determined to snatch whatever they could, by any means possible.

Faces like Michael, Danny Boy and even him, were just relics that harked back to the olden days when men were men, and their women were glad of it. Those days were gone, and they would never return.

Michael was too entrenched in the old values to ever understand that and, when the time was right, Eli was confident that he would step down, hand over the Smoke, and the Spanish end of their businesses. It was the only way they could keep hold of anything even remotely worth having. He knew from his conversationalists exactly how the street was changing, and changing by the day. He knew from his chatterboxes that a new breed of young black men were making their mark. They were African, they were Asian, they were Caribbean boys; they had one thing in common other than their colour; they were hungry. At the moment they were too busy killing each other, but soon he knew that they would realise that *together* they were much stronger than anyone around them. And, when they did, he would be waiting, and he would utilise them.